STANDING
AT THE
SCRATCH LINE

STANDING
AT THE
SCRATCH LINE

A NOVEL

Guy Johnson

RANDOM HOUSE
New York

To my grandfather,
Bailey Johnson

ACKNOWLEDGMENTS

I am standing on the rotating tip of a pyramid. I am here because I have been lifted onto the shoulders of my friends and family. I would not be here but for their arms, their sweat, their attention, their hearts, and their love. I mention first my family.

To my wife: partner in irreverence, partner in the daily toil, partner in laughter, generator of love, nest creator, ears to my most confidential thoughts, my greatest fears, my sickest jokes; without your smile and your laughter this book may not have come to pass and we know that all the female characters that I create will fall under your judgmental gaze.

To my oldest son, Colin Ashanti Murphy-Johnson: climber at the foot of Kilimanjaro, eyes lifted upward to the heights, having in abundance the strength, stamina, determination, intelligence, and courage to reach the heights, but not truly knowing it. You are now holding your own child in your arms, sheltering it from the weathering sky. We have never been closer in goals and action. It is to your energy that this book is intended to strike. Fatherhood will play a part in everything I intend to write.

To my mother: the Lady with seven-league boots, you who have taught me there is no end to learning, to growing, to reaching higher, to pursuing the right path, and perhaps greater, that all pursuits are lost if there is no love, no investment in others. I continue to emulate you. I continue to say your ideas are mine. I want to be like you: an artist in stride, moving with direction, purpose, and voice.

To Elliott: son of two families, you who have allowed me to win a place in your heart, you who have declared yourself a preteen for nearly three years, your laughter, innocence, and joy continue to open my heart and reacquaint me with the importance of being loving and being human.

To my friends: readers of countless script versions, with all your countless irreconcilable differences, ethnicities, eccentricities, proclivities, and vocations; you are my village. I come to you to be reaffirmed, to see my reflection in your eyes. In my village, I am but one artist among many. Part of my inspiration to write arises from witnessing the struggles and achievements of others in my community. I am in debt to you in all the diffuse ways that humans touch and connect. I mention only the readers, but in no particular order: Janice Jones, Tim Marshall, Paul Schabracq,

Ernie Carpenter, Norman Jayo, Helen Brann, Mike Coward, Dr. Dolly McPherson, Calvin Sharpe, Leland Brown, Carol Langhauser, Al Nellum, Sharon Brown, Mike DuVall, L. Stephen Turer, and Paul Dufeu.

I wish to express my special gratitude to the models and standards of behavior set by Dr. Betty Shabazz and Jessica Mitford—two ladies who were kind enough to accept me as a nephew and lift me with their senses of humor.

Last but not least, Elaine and Bill Petrocelli, who saw the promise in my writing and introduced me to my editor and friend, Manie Barron.

THE SCRATCH LINE

In the early 1900s, when bare-knuckle
fights were still common, a line was
scratched in the dirt or on the pavement
and the two fighters were brought to
stand on opposite sides. At a preordained
signal the fight would begin, then the
line could be crossed. In gambler's
rules, if one of the fighters suffered a
knockdown, there was a break in the
action. The man who delivered the blow
returned to the scratch line and waited.
The fighter who suffered the knockdown had to get up and walk back to the
scratch line if he wanted to continue.
If he did not come to scratch within an
agreed-upon time frame, the fight was
stopped, and the man standing at the
line was declared the winner.

Book I

LEROI

BORDEAUX

TREMAIN

The thick, low-lying fog covered the contours and waterways of the swamp. Only mature trees and shrubs were visible above the milky gray mist. Darkness was beginning to fade in the early morning light, creating the surreal landscape of a nightmare.

Two men propelled a flat-bottomed skiff quietly over the water. There were oars in the boat, but favoring the method practiced by bayou dwellers, both men used long poles. Trees loomed above them through the mist like towering observers as they poled their way down the narrow channels that coursed through a system of small islands. The silence was broken only by the distant bellow of alligators and the soft, incessant buzzing of voracious mosquitoes.

The man in the front took his pole out of the water and listened for sounds ahead. He motioned for his companion to stop poling. Somewhere to the right of the boat, there was an indistinct sound of human voices. High overhead came the long screeches of a pair of cranes calling to each other. The man in the front of the skiff turned and began unwrapping an oilskin bundle, in which there lay two bolt-action rifles, a quiver of arrows, and a homemade longbow. He directed his companion by hand signals to continue poling toward their right.

LeRoi Tremain followed his uncle's directions and quietly poled closer to their quarry. They were heading toward a large channel that fed directly into the gulf. Stealth was of maximum importance. The fog began to dissipate in areas that were close to the open waterways where there was a tidal current. They could not be sure that the mist would afford the same level of protection once they entered the channel.

Uncle Jake motioned for him to stop poling again, and the boat floated quietly forward. Off to their left, somewhere above them, a man coughed. LeRoi put his pole into the water to prevent the boat from continuing out into the channel. If they had continued on, they would have been caught between their quarry and a lookout man. His uncle motioned for him to take the bow and pointed in the direction of the cough. Picking up the bow, LeRoi slid over the side into the dark, brackish water. Jake handed him the quiver and squeezed his arm encouragingly.

LeRoi turned and waded slowly into the opaque vapor. A cold glove of water surrounded him up to his navel. He had to be careful, for he was near the edge of the channel and the waist-high depth dropped away to twelve feet. There could be no splashing. He strung an arrow in his bow and continued forward. He did not know whether he would need the arrow for the man or an alligator, but he intended to be prepared.

The man he was looking for was probably up in one of the trees, which were looming as shadowy presences above him. Twenty feet further into the murkiness, he felt a breeze blowing and the beginnings of the current moving on his right. He was getting too close to the edge of the channel. He changed his direction to angle to his left and waded through a particularly dense patch. When he emerged, a large shadow spun and stood watching him. It was the largest swamp deer he had ever seen. Had he been hunting meat, he would have treasured this moment.

After determining that this intruder had no immediate hostile intention, the deer turned and moved away with a stately dignity. LeRoi needed something to draw the attention of the man in the tree, so he picked up a short, thick piece of branch and threw it hard at the disappearing flank of the deer. The branch hit the deer with a resounding whack and the deer took off at a dead run, splashing its way to safety.

LeRoi heard a surprised "What the hell?" and the chambering of a bullet in a lever-action rifle. As the deer ran away, he saw movement in a tree off to his right. The shadowy outline of a man holding a rifle could be seen about ten feet off the ground. Dropping down into the water until only his head was above its dark surface, LeRoi began his noiseless approach. He figured the man must be standing on some kind of hunting platform. He knew he could hit him from where he was, but he couldn't risk the man calling out. He had to move closer to be certain of a killing shot.

As he moved nearer, he saw that there was a small dinghy moored to the trunk of the tree. In the surreal landscape of gray and white vapor under the trees' overhanging shadowy presences, only the boat had movement as the pull of the current caused it to bump against projecting roots. The man had resumed his stillness and had attempted to hide himself once more. LeRoi could not see the man clearly, but he knew where his chest was because he could see his arm. He was no more than thirty feet away. When he rose out of the water, the bow was already stretched taut with an arrow. The bow had a sweet, bass twang as the arrow was loosed.

LeRoi heard a soft thud and then the clatter of the rifle caroming off the tree into the water. He continued forward cautiously. He had no doubts that the man was hit, but LeRoi couldn't be sure he was dead. He might be waiting with a revolver. He could see the man's foot projecting out beyond the dark outline of the tree. From the way the foot was turned,

LeRoi concluded it was unlikely that the man could see him approaching, but he did not abandon his caution.

The arrow had to be collected. Not only would it serve as evidence against him, but good arrows were nearly impossible to make and were expensive to buy. All his arrows were store-bought and had a distinctive red and yellow shaft, which made it easier for them to be found once they were shot. Standing at the base of the tree, he could still see no movement. The foot was still in the same position, an augury of death.

LeRoi picked up the rifle that was leaning against a root with its stock in the water. He checked the barrel carefully for obstructions, then mounted the rough ladder that led up to the platform. Peering over the rim of the platform, he was surprised at what he saw. His arrow was deeply embedded in the man's rib cage, but that is not what surprised him. It was the badge on the man's chest. LeRoi had been expecting one of the DuMonts or their kin. Instead he found the corpse of a white man who had pale skin, greasy brown hair, and a handlebar mustache. He was obviously a deputy. As LeRoi pulled his arrow free and wiped it off on the body of the deputy, he pondered whether he and his uncle had walked into an ambush. Cupping his hands and blowing into them, he made two quick owl hoots, a signal of alarm.

His signal was answered by six or seven shots. Standing up, LeRoi could see the flash of a gun from another tree platform fifty yards away. As LeRoi shouldered the rifle and took aim, he saw the pinkness of the man's face on the other platform. He squeezed the trigger and saw the man's body jerk backward and fall into the sea of vapor. Several more shots were fired in the distance, but LeRoi couldn't see where they came from.

It was clear the DuMonts had found out about the Tremains' raid and had somehow lured the sheriff's men out to take their side. LeRoi went through the deputy's pockets, checking for valuables. The man had only three dollars, which he took along with the badge. At the base of the tree, he put the rifle and the bow into the small dinghy and paddled out to find how his Uncle Jake had fared. Entering the channel, he let the current carry him. He levered another bullet into the rifle's chamber and set it against the gunwale; he knocked an arrow into his bow. Occasionally, he would row to avoid partially submerged logs and other debris, but for the most part he listened and stared into the fog.

Somewhere ahead of him to his left, a man cried out in pain. LeRoi dug his oar deep into the water to change direction and sent the dinghy slithering across the water. There was another cry, sounding like his Uncle Jake. Up ahead he saw movement around the dim outline of an island. He let the dinghy come to rest in a small thicket of bushes forty feet distant from the island. There were sounds of heated conversation.

"Get this cargo back aboard the *Sea Horse* while I find out how this nigger knew about our meeting." It was a voice of authority.

Another voice responded, "Aye, aye, sir."

A man cried out again. It was a long wail of agony and this time LeRoi knew it was his uncle.

The gruff voice spoke again. "Tell me, nigger, how did you know that we was going to be meeting here? It ain't gon' get no easier for you. You might as well talk now and save yourself a lot of pain."

The other voice called out, "Billy! Billy, bring the boat in. We need to load up!"

LeRoi heard the sound of an engine start and saw a small twenty-five-foot cargo boat chug into view. It was the type of boat that small-time traders used to sell their wares along the distant reaches of the bayou. The *Sea Horse* passed within fifteen feet of LeRoi on its way to the island. Billy was visible as he steered the boat to its makeshift mooring. LeRoi drew back his bow and let the arrow fly.

The force of the arrow penetrating into his shoulder knocked Billy into the water with a splash. There was no other sound except the engine of the *Sea Horse*. The boat continued chugging toward the island.

"Billy! Billy! Back off the steam! You're going to run aground!" The *Sea Horse* continued on its course. "Billy! Billy! Are you daft, man?"

"What's going on over there?" the authoritative voice demanded.

"I don't know, sir! He's got way too much speed!"

LeRoi pushed off from the thicket and followed the *Sea Horse*, using the boat to shield his approach. Before the boat crashed into the island, he heard his uncle call out defiantly in a voice racked with pain, "Just kill me, cracker! I ain't telling you shit!"

The *Sea Horse* plowed into the foliage growing at the water's edge. LeRoi saw a man clamber aboard and pull the levers to stop the engine. Before the man could turn around, an arrow struck into the woodwork above his head. The man swiveled and jumped over the side of the boat into the water. As he splashed away he shouted out, "There's more of 'em, sir! There's more of 'em!"

"Jimmy Lee? Jimmy Lee?" the voice called out. "Are you alright, man?"

"I ain't hit, but there's more of 'em! I'm gettin' out of here!"

"You better come back here, Jimmy Lee!"

LeRoi cursed himself silently for missing the man in the boat, but the movement of the dinghy had made his shot go wide. He paddled alongside the *Sea Horse* and climbed in. LeRoi took another arrow from his quiver and waited. He heard a man walk through the underbrush to the prow of the boat. LeRoi waited until he started to walk around to the side before he stood up. As soon as he reached a standing position, LeRoi saw the man swing a double-barreled shotgun in his direction. He ducked as both barrels discharged just above his head, shattering the glass windshield and splintering the wood of the navigation cabin. LeRoi stood up again, hoping to catch the man loading more shells into his shotgun, only to find him running away through the trees. Aiming carefully, he caught the fleeing figure in the thigh. The man went down but got up limping. He could be heard splashing into the water on the other side of the island. LeRoi got out of the boat cautiously and scouted the island to ensure that there were no more enemies about. He could still hear the injured man making his way noisily through the water to safety.

Uncle Jake was lying next to a smoldering fire. He was bleeding from a bullet wound to his stomach, blood oozing out with every intake of breath, covering his shirt and pants with its dark maroon stain. There were burn marks on his uncle's face and neck. LeRoi knelt and lifted up his uncle's head.

Jake opened his eyes slowly. "I'm gut-shot, boy. I'm gut-shot. I ain't gon' be making it home with you this time."

LeRoi said nothing. His uncle was growing steadily weaker as he watched. He felt a vast void within himself.

"You got to get out of here!" his uncle whispered. "We done walked in on some gun-running business. We done killed some pirates too. They'll be coming back here as soon as they find out what happened."

"I think I killed a couple of sheriff deputies too," LeRoi mumbled, unable to take his eyes off the blood pumping out of his uncle's wound.

"Damn! Big stars fallin'; won't be long before day," his uncle gasped. "Help me to the boat, boy. I want to be buried with my people."

As LeRoi carefully lifted his uncle in his arms he said, "Looks like those DuMonts tricked us into an ambush."

"That may be true, but two of 'em paid for this trickery. They's lying on the other side of the island. I shot them first."

In the distance they heard a man bellowing, "Ahoy! Ahoy Barracuda! Ahoy! We've been attacked! Ahoy Barracuda!"

LeRoi carried his uncle to the *Sea Horse*. If there was any chance of his survival, he had to be gotten home quickly and only the *Sea Horse* could do it.

"Don't leave them guns and ammunition," his uncle advised as LeRoi laid him down in the *Sea Horse*. Sweat was streaming down Jake's face. "We gon' need all the guns and ammo we can get if the pirates find out we was the ones who broke up this deal."

LeRoi made sure he could push the *Sea Horse* back into the water before he started loading the boxes of rifles and ammunition. The boxes containing the rifles weighed so much that he had to drag them to the boat, lift them against the gunwale, and slide them over the side. He loaded all the ammunition before he heard the sound of another steam engine chugging in the distance. Out of ten boxes of rifles and ammunition, he left three. He pushed off and clambered aboard the *Sea Horse*.

LeRoi was numb. He didn't want his uncle to die. He focused his attention on getting the steam engine started. He pitched six logs into the fire to raise the boiler's heat and waited for a head of steam. The engine stalled several times before it engaged with a slow mechanical clatter. LeRoi backed the boat out into the channel and turned the boat upriver. After fifteen minutes of steaming in midchannel, he passed the dark shape of a massive mangrove tree and turned into a small slough.

As soon as he rounded the first turn in the slough, three hundred yards from its entrance, he released the pressure in the boiler and cut the engine. Then he went to check on his uncle. Jake was unconscious and breathing shallow breaths. LeRoi attempted to make him as comfortable as possible and put a bundle of clothing under his head. He picked up a long stout pole, which all bayou boats carried, and began poling the *Sea Horse* slowly along. He didn't want the noise of the steam engine to give away his position. He knew that within half a mile a larger waterway intersected and he would be able to start the steam engine again. Soon the trees overhanging the water created a dense canopy that cut the light and gave the impression of a long, winding tunnel. The fog grew progressively thinner as LeRoi pushed the *Sea Horse* further along the slough.

It was hard work, but LeRoi poled the boat steadily, changing sides to keep the craft in the center of the slough. He refused to quit. He felt that if he could just get his uncle home alive, perhaps there was a chance. There were other things to think about. He and his Uncle Jake had created a problem for the family because white men had been killed. If it had been only DuMonts that had been killed, there would have been no problem. No one would have even investigated their death. It was different when colored men killed whites, particularly sheriff's men.

LeRoi did not waste a moment of sorrow for the men he killed. It was not a moral question for him; it was what he had been raised to do. His family had been feuding with the DuMonts for generations. Before he was ten years old, LeRoi had seen his father and two older brothers killed during a DuMont raid on the Tremains' corn liquor still. It was a memory that remained close to the surface. He would have been killed as well if he had not hidden in the surrounding underbrush. From that day on, he couldn't wait to go out and spill DuMont blood. As far as he was concerned, death was a natural consequence for those who were not careful or alert. His only concern about killing whites was the heat that it might bring down on his family.

LeRoi, large and unusually muscular for his age, took part in his first raid against the DuMonts when he was fourteen years old. During that raid he became what his uncle called "blooded" because he killed his first man. On his next raid, he was blooded again, but he was given greater respect for pulling an injured cousin to safety while under fire. The *Sea Horse*, rifles, and ammunition represented the booty from his fifth raid on the DuMonts and he was not yet eighteen years old.

LeRoi stopped poling and checked on his uncle, only to find that Jake was dead. He had passed away without returning to consciousness. The blood from his wound had stopped pulsing out of his body and was congealing on the deck. Jake's face had the look of serenity. If it wasn't for the coldness of his skin and the lack of respiratory movement, he could have been mistaken for being asleep. But he was not asleep, he was dead, and no amount of praying would bring him back.

Uncle Jake had taken him under his wing and had served as a surrogate father after LeRoi's own father had been killed. LeRoi felt as if his heart had been ripped out of his chest. He dropped to his knees, fighting back tears, and cupped his face in his hands. It seemed that nearly everyone that he cared for was being snatched from him. It seemed like a punishment to him.

The *Sea Horse* scraped bottom and jerked to a halt. LeRoi slipped listlessly into the water, which was barely four feet deep, and checked for the obstruction. A log had been laid across the creek and embedded into the bank on both sides, one of the logs his family had planted to prevent large boats from using the slough. By rocking the *Sea Horse* up and down, he was able to jockey the boat over the log with only a few serious scrapes.

LeRoi had no words for the sadness he felt as he got back into the boat. He had only formless emotions, which brought the taste of bile into his mouth. He picked up the pole, took a deep breath, and stuck it back into the water; shoving hard, he propelled the *Sea Horse* on down the slough. He could not have said that he loved his uncle, for he had never used that word in relationship to himself, but he felt the agony of loss. And as with all such negative feelings for which he had no words, LeRoi had to distill them into something purer—like anger or hatred—in order to understand them. He burned with a hatred that was beyond his years. He now had a greater debt to repay the DuMonts, one he would never forget.

He remembered a story one of his Sunday-school teachers had told. It was about how when each person is born, he starts off as a blank page, and with the passing of each day, more of his life is written on the page. People died when there was no more room on the page to write. He had felt then, and he felt now, if he had ever started off as a blank page, it was no longer true. He felt like his page was already filling up with little mean words about loneliness, pain, and disappointment. There didn't appear to be room on his page for words about happiness or joy.

S ATURDAY, M ARCH 1 8, 1 9 1 6

The funeral for Jake Tremain was held the weekend following his death. He was laid to rest in the family graveyard, which was located on a small hill behind the main house, the highest ground on the Tremain farm. The event was not attended by anyone outside immediate family and friends, but there were still almost seventy-five people. All the blood relatives were there, including LeRoi's crippled great uncle, who was the unchallenged head of the family.

The mood was particularly somber because Jake Tremain was popular, but there was also something else in the air, something undefinable. LeRoi felt it in the stares he received and in the way people stopped talking when he walked past. Everyone knew that white men had been killed and there was concern and worry etched on the faces of the women. The men acknowledged him with curt nods and somber looks. No one came to stand next to him. As the preacher said the last words over the coffin, LeRoi stood off to the side by himself.

After the service, food was served. LeRoi was just finishing a plate of fried catfish and corn pone when one of his younger cousins came up to him and told him that his great-uncle wanted to see him back at the barn. A chill went through him, for the barn was the traditional place of family celebrations or family meetings whenever something terrible had happened. No one had to tell him this was not a time of celebration.

It was a large wooden structure that contained a hayloft and had a fence dividing the ground floor. On one side of the fence sick animals were kept, and the other side was used primarily for storage of farm staples like grain and feed. When LeRoi walked in, he saw that all the adult men of the Tremain family were standing around his great-uncle, Henry Tremain, who was sitting on a milking stool. All conversation stopped as he walked up to Papa Henry, as the old man was called. LeRoi looked around at the solemn faces and saw few smiles. His skill with weapons had earned him grudging respect, but his youthful arrogance was not appreciated.

"You call me, Papa Henry?" he asked, trying to control the beating of his heart.

His grandfather had light, reddish brown skin and gray, wavy hair; his eyes were dark, and glinted like coals—the combined evidence of his African and Choctaw ancestry. "We got us a problem, son," the old man spoke slowly. "The sheriff knows you was in on the killin' of them deputies. Those DuMont dogs went yappin' to him as soon as they heard about your arrows. Now, the sheriff wants to come on our land lookin' for you. He gon' try to come with a big posse and we can't have that."

"What can we do about it, Papa Henry?" LeRoi asked. His face appeared unconcerned, but fear was knotting his stomach.

"Well, we been talkin' and talkin' and the best way, I think," Papa Henry paused before continuing, "is for you to leave the area for a while."

"What's a while, Papa?" LeRoi had only been to New Orleans a few times. Other than that, he had never left the rolling hills and swampland that surrounded his family's farm.

"A couple years at least, maybe more. We got to let this whole thing die down a little taste, before I can tell you when you can come back."

LeRoi stared down at the hard-packed earthen floor of the barn and shook his head. He had grown up within a network of aunts, uncles, and cousins. He had never been alone. "It ain't fair that I got to leave. I only did what Uncle Jake told me to. You hid LeMar for almost two years and he killed some white folk. How come you can't do that for me? How come I got to go?"

"First thing is LeMar didn't kill no deputies, and second thing is, he didn't take nothin' from the pirates. He just killed some swamp trash. You done killed both John Law and some pirates. We gon' be pretty hard-pressed between the two: the badge on one side and them seafaring thieves on the other."

"What happens to my daddy's farm? Mama can't work it without me."

"That's one of the prime lots. Maybe it's time to give Clara and Benjamin a chance at farmin' it. I think your mama needs to move into the main house where she can be safe."

"Nobody is takin' my daddy's farm! It's mine by rights. Every year me and Mama worked hard gettin' the crops in. Ain't nobody come out to help us except Uncle Jake."

There was an angry murmur from the men standing around Papa Henry. They were incensed that LeRoi would dare challenge the head of the family's decision.

The old man waved everyone to silence. "Ain't nobody in this family own any land but me. I say who lives where and for how long. Now, as long as you my blood, you got a home and some land. It may not be the parcel your daddy worked, but it will feed your family when you get one in the future. Hear me, boy, ain't nobody gon' steal nothin' from you. Jes' do what I'm askin' you to do."

LeRoi realized that it was no good arguing. It would just set everyone against him. "What you want me to do, Papa?"

"There is a freight train carrying colored soldiers passing north of here around four-thirty in the morning. It'll be stopping to take on water by Dead Man's Slough. You can board the caboose, 'cause Bodeen Walker, your mother's cousin, is the head porter. He'll help hide you until you're out of Louisiana. From there you on your own."

LeRoi shook his head. "That's it? I don't get no money or nothin'? All you care about is that I'm gone? What about the *Sea Horse* and them guns?"

" 'Course we'll give you some travelin' money," Papa Henry replied. "We thought maybe you would decide to join the army, then your board and lodgin' would be taken care of for a couple years. Ain't no doubt you old enough."

"I'll go, Papa," LeRoi said sadly. The tension in the room disappeared. Some of the men began to talk among themselves, but LeRoi's next words caused the room to fall silent. "I'll go now, but when I come back, I takin' over my daddy's farm. I don't care who's livin' there. I swear on the blood of my father, I'll kill the man that stands in my way." LeRoi turned to leave the barn, but a voice made him turn back.

"Damn shame you didn't have brains enough to collect all of your arrows before you ran away."

LeRoi turned to face the speaker. He wasn't a Tremain. He was Benjamin Willets and he was married to LeRoi's Aunt Clara. "Why you talkin'? You ain't a Tremain!"

The man had been whittling a piece of wood with a hunting knife and he pointed the knife at LeRoi.

"You ain't got enough respect for your elders! If'en you don't watch your mouth, somebody gon' have to teach you respect," he said.

LeRoi pulled out his bowie from its sheath. "Why don't you come on and teach me some respect?" LeRoi asked. The men around him began edging away from Benjamin. Everyone knew of LeRoi's ability to throw a knife with either hand.

"Ain't no reason for us to start fightin' among ourselves, is there?" Papa Henry asked angrily. "In a few days we gon' have more enemies 'round than we can shake a stick at. We gon' need every man we got." The old man's words silenced the grumbling around him. He turned his dark eyes on LeRoi. "We'll give you travelin' money, boy, and we gon' see to yo' mother. She ain't gon' want for nothin'."

LeRoi nodded his head grudgingly and controlled his anger, but in his heart he felt that his family was giving him a raw deal. He was being forced to leave everything he knew. He felt abandoned. The protective shell and numerical strength was being stripped away. Now he would have to face the world alone. He knew that if his father or Uncle Jake were still alive, there would be a different solution to this problem.

"Just remember," LeRoi advised the assembly through gritted teeth. "If I have to come through hellfire, I'll be back!" Without another word, he left the barn.

Sunday, March 19, 1916

The sky was dark and the stars were twinkling when the *Arkansas Shuttle* gathered steam and pulled away from Dead Man's Slough. In the early morning darkness, the smoke billowing out of the train's smokestack looked blue, and the light above the engine's cowcatcher made the tracks in front glisten like parallel ribbons of silver in the distance.

LeRoi sat on Captain Sam Mack's favorite mare atop Beaumont Ridge, watching the train follow the contours of the rolling hills. The mare was extremely high-strung and the train's whistle made her boggle and rear up. Easily maintaining his seat, LeRoi soothed her with caresses and calm words.

Early the previous evening he had slipped into the forests surrounding the Tremain farm and made his way to Nellum's Crossing. Since he thought his family had forsaken him, LeRoi's pride would not allow him to accept anything from them. He went fifteen miles on foot to the only man he knew would help. He went to Captain Sam Mack. Since their youth, LeRoi's father and Sam Mack had a bond that was stronger than blood and it defied the custom and mores of the time. It did not matter that Mack was white. He had been present at LeRoi's birth, as LeRoi's father had been present at the births of Mack's two sons. To LeRoi, they were family. Although he arrived at the house long past dinner, he was fed a good meal, given fifty dollars' traveling money, and sent off with the mare and a hug from Mack's wife.

Beaumont Ridge was a huge fold in the earth that curved around for about fifteen miles and ended just after Shannon Junction. With a light kick, he urged the mare into a cantering gallop and rode along the slope of the ridge. It was his intent to get on board the train after it had passed the junction. His Uncle Jake had told him that if he ever had to escape the law by train, he shouldn't board it until it had left the parish; that way he was beyond the jurisdiction of local law enforcement.

The junction consisted of a flat open area with several large storage sheds, a small train depot, and a large dock that jutted into a wide man-made canal. It had been built for transferring shipments of cargo from trains to riverboats and barges. Normally, the depot was attended by a freight master and a couple of colored stevedores. This morning was different. There were about twenty armed white horsemen milling around the depot. Even from this distance, he could see shiny reflections on their chests. It was not difficult for him to conclude that these men were deputies and that the badges were the source of the reflections.

By the time LeRoi rode his mare through the trees and underbrush along the ridge to a spot overlooking Shannon Junction, the train was already there. Streaks of dawn were beginning to lighten the sky. Guiding the mare into a stand of small trees, he watched. The posse made everyone who had been a passenger in the caboose stand out on the platform. From where he sat, LeRoi could see there were three colored men who were receiving some rough handling from members of the posse. One of the colored men was being beaten with riding crops. He was lying on the ground in a fetal position while his tormentors stood around him in a circle, swinging their heavy crops at his head and shoulders. Suddenly, colored soldiers with rifles began pouring out of the train. Soon the horsemen were surrounded by a sea of black and brown faces in green khaki.

LeRoi saw a large brown-skinned man lift his arm and all the colored soldiers lifted their rifles and pointed them at the posse, whose leader walked to his horse and mounted. His deputies followed suit. They then rode single file through the throng of colored soldiers.

LeRoi nodded his head in approval. Maybe being a soldier wasn't such a bad idea after all. It looked like men in the army stuck together and helped one another. His heart was heavy. He was about to leave everything he knew and cared about for the unknown. As he rode on to Sycamore Bridge, where he planned to board the train, he made up his mind to enlist.

He recalled how his mother had tried to get him to go to church before he left, mouthing words about hell and damnation. Her eyes filled with tears as she told him to memorize the Ten Commandments. She was a weak and broken-spirited woman who had no effect on him. It was strange, he felt almost no love for her, and saying good-bye to her was nearly painless.

The most intense emotion he felt was the desire for the warmth and security that a strong family could provide. LeRoi had a clan mentality. All his life he had lived in an environment of strong blood ties. He was a product of the interweaving web of an extended family. He had no concept of national patriotism or regional allegiance. The only loyalty he had ever known was to his family. He swore to himself that one day he would be the head of his own family. It would be a new branch of the Tremains and it would dominate all the others. This thought was to be a driving force in his life, powered by a deep reservoir of indignation and pain.

THURSDAY, DECEMBER 27, 1917

The snow fell in big, soft clumps, blanketing the landscape. LeRoi looked out of the bunker, down the hill to where the main military encampment sprawled in a small valley. The pristine cover of white made the orderly row of canvas tents look almost inviting. But LeRoi knew that under the virgin white snow was mud deep enough to stall a tank. The officer who had directed that the camp be built in the valley hadn't thought about drainage, and now it had been snowing steadily for nearly two days. When the snow melted the camp was going to be in the middle of a river. Beyond the valley in which the camp lay was a row of jutting snowcapped mountains, a high crystalline mass rising to Mont Blanc.

LeRoi ducked back through the tarp into the darkness of the bunker and confronted the strong smell of men living in close quarters under the lights of kerosene lamps.

"What's it look like out there, LT?" Big Ed asked from his cot.

"More Eskimo weather," LeRoi answered tersely. He sat down and lighted another small kerosene lamp and began cleaning his guns.

"That's right, you don't like snow," Big Ed continued. "Great Googa mooga, man, you'd hate Nebraska. It snows from October through March every year. I remember a time—"

"Big Ed, when is the last time you cleaned your guns?" LeRoi interrupted. He was in no mood for chitchat.

Big Ed Harrison sat up with a questioning look on his face. "Damn if I know. Why?"

"These crackers might send us out anytime. In this kind of weather, guns freeze up. You got to keep them oiled."

"I guess you're right, LT," Big Ed said easily. He got up off his cot and stoop-walked over to his gun. He was a massive, hulking, brown-skinned man, almost six foot six inches tall and nearly three hundred pounds, almost all muscle. A big Nebraska farm boy, he had a friendly, easy disposition. His ready smile was contagious, even though it exposed a wide gap between his two front teeth.

"You think they'd send us out again? We just came back from three days on patrol. Last night was the first night we slept in the bunker in more'n two weeks. We been sent damn near everywhere. Our squad's taken some big hits. We got three men dead and one injured. They got to know we needs rest."

LeRoi pulled the bolt of his Springfield .30-06 free from its tracks. He set the bolt on a cloth that he had laid out for the purpose, examined the rifle's cartridge-feeding mechanism. "We arrived here in August with two full battalions of the Three hundred Fifty-first Regiment. What we got left: two platoons that ain't even half-strength? These people is using us like bait. Ain't no white units suffering them kind of losses. They throwing our lives away. They don't care what happens to us. They'll send us out to soften up some other target."

"If you feels that bad, why do you keep on?" Big Ed asked sincerely. He was twenty-two, and yet in his understanding of the world, he was younger than nineteen-year-old LeRoi. Big Ed continued speaking. "I tell you the only reason I keep on day after day, is thinkin' about seein' home again. Sometimes I just think about how rich and dark the dirt is back home and sometimes how you can just drive for miles and not see nothing but the green and gold of corn. We ain't got much of a farm, but I was starting to make a difference. We had a real good crop the last two years."

"So, you want to be a farmer, huh?"

"It's what I dream about: standing behind a plow in the afternoon sun, drinking a cold glass of water, sweat drippin' off'en me, and the rich smell of tilled earth. If I didn't have that, I'd go crazy. I don't mind fightin' for my country but seein' all these people die is gettin' to me. Every time I close my eyes, I dream about home."

"I don't dream much," LeRoi admitted. "Especially about home. As far as fightin' for my country, I could give a shit! This war ain't done nothin' to make me patriotic. All I really care about is getting back home and settlin' some debts. I owe some folks a seein' to and I damn sho' gon' see that they get it!"

"Why don't you knock some officer down and a get stuck in the cala-boose? They probably wouldn't let you out 'til the war was over."

"What?" LeRoi barked while pushing a cleaning rod with a bit of cloth through the barrel. He gave his companion a questioning look. "And let these crackers hang me for hitting an officer during military operations? I rather be bit in the ass by a snaggletooth mule and sent to Mississippi to live! I ain't lettin' these crackers get anythin' on me. If I go down, I wants to go down shootin'."

There was movement at the doorway as two men pushed through the tarp and entered. LeRoi had his Colt .45 pistol drawn when the men cleared the canvas.

The smaller man, "Professor" Darwin Morris, saw LeRoi's gun and said, "I brought you your food, don't worry." He was a dark-skinned, wiry man who wore round, wire-rimmed glasses. A college graduate, he was at twenty-six one of the oldest men in the squad. "Of course, once you taste it, you might want to pull your gun again." Professor was from Brooklyn and had a decidedly New York accent.

The other man, Slick Walters, who entered with Professor, spoke. "The food ain't that bad. We definitely got meat in our stew this time, but it cost me a carton of cigs." Slick was also from New York, but he hailed from Harlem, which was the other side of the world from Brooklyn. He handed Big Ed a metal mess plate with stew in it. "We gon' have to slip out to the town and pick up some stores." Slick was the wheeler-dealer and black-market specialist in the group. He stored his black-market goods in a German-occupied town five miles on the other side of the front lines. All the members of the squad had benefited from Slick's black-market trade, so when sorties were necessary to restock, he had the company of two or three squad members.

"Before we plan anything," LeRoi recommended, "we should check with Sarge. We may get sent out again."

Slick grimaced. "Not again! We just came back! How am I supposed to do business if I ain't got no time in camp? These mothers must just want to kill us off! I swear before God, they just want to kill us off!" Slick was a chocolate-colored man who never smiled. Instead, he sneered.

"We have to prove our patriotism over and over again," Professor said quietly, looking up from his diary, in which he had been writing. "You have to remember what W. E. B. DuBois wrote in *The Crisis*—"

"Who gives a damn about him?" Slick declared angrily. "He's just an-other high yellow nigger who had the money to buy his way out of the service!"

LeRoi, who had been eating his lukewarm stew, picked up his rifle and slammed the bolt home, then asked, "High yellow what?"

There was a moment of silence before Slick stammered out an apology. "I didn't mean nothing against you, you know that, LT. I just meant, if the man ain't here risking his life with us, he ain't got shit to say!"

All the men in the Second Battalion of the 351st Negro Regiment had been stationed briefly at Fort Dodge, outside Des Moines, Iowa, before being transferred to fight in Alsace-Lorraine. Off the base, LeRoi had proven many times that he had the capacity to spill blood, and the fact that none of his enemies was alive or physically well enough to make the trip over to Europe was not lost on the other men in the battalion.

The conversation was interrupted by a sharp knock on the log above the entrance. All the men picked up and cocked their weapons. "Who goes there?" LeRoi called out.

"Sergeant Williams and Platoon Lieutenant McHenry," a voice answered back in clipped tones.

"Damn," Slick growled disgustedly. "It's that boot-licking sergeant and his master."

The canvas split and two men entered. The bunker's occupants stood up in accordance with military discipline.

"At ease, men," the lieutenant said as he waited for his eyes to adjust to the dim light of the lantern. He was young, not much older than LeRoi. Of medium height, he was on the plump side of stocky. "It's as cold as a well digger's ass in Nome, Alaska," he said jokingly, but no one laughed. His face was pink from the cold and he rubbed his pale hands together vigorously.

The sergeant spoke. "The lieutenant wants to tell you boys about your next assignment. So listen up!" The sergeant was a dark brown–skinned man who was in his late thirties, and he had been in the service for nearly twenty years before the war started. He was military spit and polish down to the bone. Even after four months on the front lines, his uniform looked like recent issue and his boots were shiny.

"I've just come from HQ and I have our orders," the lieutenant said as he pulled a map from the chest pocket of his jacket and unfolded it on LeRoi's cot. "We're going to merge the two remaining platoons of the Three hundred Fifty-first into one, consisting of four squads. We'll be renamed the First Platoon of the Three hundred Fifty-first Regiment. I know you men have taken some devastating losses in personnel and that you've been on the front line continuously since you arrived. I spoke with Lieutenant Colonel Olsen and he assured me that after this mission you boys would get a well-deserved rest. He gave me his word."

Slick mimicked softly in a high voice, "He gave me his word."

Sergeant Williams instantly turned on Slick. "Watch your mouth,

Walters. You're in the presence of an officer!" He gave Slick a threatening stare.

McHenry continued. "We're starting a big offensive tomorrow night and several infantry battalions are going to join in the attack. We know the Germans are pulling out of Saint Die to reinforce their position at Ribeauville. In order to do that they must go through this pass at Kastledorf Bridge." McHenry pointed to a spot on the map. "Since we can't possibly mobilize all our troops in time to stop them, it's been decided that if we can send a small group in tonight, maybe we can blow the bridge up if the Germans haven't gotten through yet, or if they moved the bulk of their troops and equipment, maybe we can stop them from blowing the bridge up."

LeRoi looked at the map and asked, "Don't all these squiggly lines mean mountains?"

"Why yes, Kastledorf is only fifteen miles from here—"

Slick's sarcasm was barely disguised. "I knows you and the sarge done thought about this, but how you gon' get forty men fifteen miles deep into Kraut territory by tonight? 'Cause it may be fifteen miles as the crow flies, but it's a good twenty-five if you traveling by road. If you don't follow the road it's gon' be even more."

The sergeant turned to Slick. "The lieutenant doesn't have to answer to a private! Now, I warned you—"

"That's alright, Sergeant. I'll handle this," McHenry said evenly. "Listen, Walters, I didn't want this assignment to a colored unit, but that's what the army gave me. So I took it and I didn't look back. After nearly four months on the front lines with the Second Battalion of the Three hundred Fifty-first Regiment, I see that you colored men are as good as soldiers as any unit of white men. The only reason I don't court-martial you for insubordination right now is that I know you men haven't had a decent rest in weeks. But if you ever approach me again in such a disrespectful manner, I'll have you up on charges so fast, it'll make your head spin. Do I make myself clear?"

Slick grimaced and nodded his head reluctantly.

"Do I make myself clear?" McHenry demanded.

"Yes, sir."

After Slick had been faced down, all the men in the bunker listened quietly as the lieutenant outlined the plan and spelled out the deadline for being travel-ready. McHenry left as soon as he finished his briefing. The sergeant remained behind, leaning against one of the bunker's log supports. The four men began sorting through their duffel bags for clothing and equipment. There were no words spoken; there was only the sound of equipment being checked. Each man was aware that the sergeant hadn't left, and since it wasn't his practice to visit, they all knew he had something further to say.

The tension steadily built until Slick finally turned to the sergeant and said, "Alright, what you got to say? You sitting here like a big dog. Let's hear your bark!"

The sergeant turned and faced Slick. "You're a nasty piece of work. You're the type of Negro who makes it hard for colored men to succeed in the military. You don't know nothing about honor, hard work, or loyalty to your country. You're everything bad that they say about colored people, always trying to con somebody or trick people into doing your work.

"I saw you taking jewelry off of dead people's fingers, then going through their pockets to take their possessions. I can look the other way when it's guns and ammo, but I won't stand for stealing from the dead for personal gain. Ain't nothing that can discredit a unit faster than a reputation of stealing from the dead. If I see you doing it again, I'll shoot you on the spot myself. You got that?"

Slick pulled a switchblade from his pocket and opened it with a flick of his wrist. "Come on, sucker, I got somethin' for you," he taunted.

The sergeant laughed. "You think I'm afraid of that? Hell, I'll ram that little blade so far up your ass that you'll have a metal tongue. Now, if you had spent the year at Fort Dodge working with me every day on your hand-to-hand technique like Tremain here did, I might be afraid of you. But you goldbricked on that too. So, it's time for a final lesson."

Professor stood up and got in between Slick and the sergeant. "We're surrounded by enemies. Shouldn't we try harder to stick together? This isn't the kind of note we'd like to start this mission on, is it?"

Big Ed stood up. "The Professor's right. Colored people ought to stick together. We gon' need everyone we got, if we gon' come back from this one."

LeRoi watched the scene unfold in front of him and didn't feel any need to intervene.

Since there were two men between him and his intended quarry, Sergeant Williams stepped back. "Any time you want to bring that little pig sticker and challenge me, Walters, I'll be ready." He looked around and saw that LeRoi was just sitting and watching. "You think an old man like me stands a chance against a young buck like Walters?"

"I think you'll kill him," answered LeRoi in a matter-of-fact tone. "But that ain't what worries me. I want to know how we gon' get back from this mission, that's what worries me. We don't know the country around this bridge. We ain't got no planned route of escape. It looks to me like we bein' sacrificed again. What do you think, Sarge?"

"I think that we follow orders and put ourselves in the hands of the Lord."

Slick sucked his teeth and shook his head disgustedly. The other men were silent.

"Of course, the good Lord helps those who help themselves," Sergeant Williams continued. "So, I think that we'll send a couple of our best shots high above the bridge to cover our retreat and to check out possible escape routes."

"How is that going to help us if we run into that German artillery division?" Professor asked. "We're going to need more fire power than the small arms we were issued."

"A couple of howitzers could blast us to hell!" Slick interjected.

"Is this a suicide mission, Sarge?" Big Ed asked. "Is they sacrificing us?"

The sergeant thought for a moment before he answered. "All I know is if you fight bravely and carry out your orders, you gon' make things better for the colored men who come after you. If it's your time to die, it's your time. Ain't nothing can change that, but if you fight bravely, it'll get recognized."

Slick questioned Big Ed. "You didn't expect him to say nothing else, did you?"

The sergeant pointed to Slick. "One more word and I'll do you now!"

"Can you get us some small artillery, like those forty millimeter cannons we saw on the outskirts of that little town we passed through to get here?" Professor asked.

"All the weaponry we gon' get through channels is what was already issued," Williams answered. "But I know you boys confiscated some German mortars and a big Vickers machine gun in one of our last raids. You must have them stored someplace. If you still got possession, we need them now."

"If we had the guns you's talking about, how would we move them through mountainous country, twenty-five miles beyond the German lines?" LeRoi asked in a tone that indicated casual interest. He knew that the sergeant was aware that his squad had begun to pilfer enemy equipment and ammunition, storing it on the German side of the lines.

"We're going to catch a train and let it carry us within four miles of our target. We'll have a quick hike through a pass in the mountains and then down to the bridge. But if we're going to get out of this with our lives, we're going to need everything you men have, uh, collected, especially that Vickers."

"Carrying the Vickers and all the ammunition is hard enough on flat ground," LeRoi advised. "And you damn sure can't be no mountain goat with it."

Professor added, "The Vickers weighs over one hundred seventy-five pounds and you can shoot three hundred pounds of ammunition in twenty minutes. We'd have to carry that gun, plus over a thousand pounds of ammunition, and then we'd still have to fire the gun sparingly."

"Talk that 'white talk,' Professor! Talk it!" Big Ed said with a big smile, clapping his hands together for emphasis. "Tell him why it's a bad idea. I knows where this is goin'. If we takes it, I'll be the one who carries that old, bulky sucker. Four miles is the lifetime of a cow with that thing on your shoulder. The Krauts put it on a cart to move it."

"How long does a cow live anyway?" asked Slick.

Sergeant Williams said, "We've got forty men. Every man can take a share of the weight. We may have to disassemble the Vickers in order to take it with us—"

"You mean take it apart, sir?" Big Ed interrupted.

The sergeant nodded affirmatively and waited for Big Ed's response.

"Well, I'm the handiest guy with a wrench in this group and if I had all day, I could easy figure this gun out. But I still wouldn't want to try to put it back together again in the dark by flashlight."

"If you men want to increase your chances of living, you'll find a way to bring that damned machine gun and some mortars! I can't order you 'cause technically I don't know that you got this stuff, but if you expect to survive after we hit the bridge, it will be because we have covering fire from that big gun." The sergeant stood up and walked over to the hanging canvas that served as a doorway. Before he walked out he turned and said, "In case you decide to get the gun, we'll rendezvous on the other side of the lines, five miles east of Saint-Germain on the ridge above the railroad tracks at oh-four-thirty sharp. It's below the ruins of an old chalet."

Sergeant Williams paused and looked at the men and saw their resentful faces. He was silent for a moment before he continued speaking. "I know you men have been keeping and using enemy equipment to make up for shortages in supplies. It's a violation of the code but as long as it wasn't done in my face, I did my best to look the other way. I know that the Negro troops are at the bottom of the totem pole when it comes to getting supplies and leave time, and the first to be called upon when there's a dangerous mission or latrine duty. It ain't no secret, we don't get first crack at the ammunition and we don't get issued the newest weapons. But it seems to me that you boys found the answer to that problem. I noticed that all four of you carry the German rapid-fire gun in addition to your army-issue Springfields. I have to say, I admire your ingenuity. Use that ingenuity to bring that Vickers." Turning on his heel, he left the bunker.

Slick was the first to speak. "I swear I'm gon' kill that motherfucker! He been ridin' me ever since Fort Dodge. He's just a Tom for Mr. Charlie! I can't stand him!"

"It sounds to me like the sarge thinks that this time it may be our butts," Professor said, putting away his diary. "I mean, it sounds like even he thinks it's a suicide mission."

"Who gives a shit what he thinks?" Slick declared angrily.

"I do," answered LeRoi. "I think we better get out of here as soon as possible, get over to where we stashed the gun, and figure out how to take it apart."

"I'm with you," Professor agreed.

"Wait a minute! Wait a minute!" Slick interjected. "You just gon' bring the gun like he asked? Whatchoo thinking? I got that stuff sold. It's like money in the bank."

"I'm more interested in living than having money," LeRoi answered.

"Me too," Professor added.

"Now, it took all of us to get the gun and the ammo stored. How you plan to move it with just the two of you?" Slick asked with a smug look.

"Is it just the two of us?" LeRoi asked, looking at Big Ed.

"Nope," Big Ed said. "I'm going with you, LT."

"Whoa! Wait a minute, Big Ed. You and me supposed to be tight. If I don't go, you don't go. What's going on here?"

"You been outvoted, Slick," LeRoi interjected with a slight edge on his voice. "Make up your mind whether you coming with us or not, 'cause we got to get out of here now."

Slick said nothing. He merely stood watching as his three companions continued packing their equipment and readying their kits for light travel. As guns were being checked, Slick blurted out, "I got an idea. How about if we go ahead and leave camp as if we're going to pick up the Vickers, but we get delayed by a German patrol and never show up? We miss the suicide mission. Ain't that an idea?"

"I mean to be on that ridge at four-thirty sharp," answered LeRoi. "With or without the gun. I ain't got no family now but my squad and my platoon and I ain't ever gon' let down family who's depending on me! I know what it feels like! So believe me, if I don't bring the Vickers with me, there'll be a damn good reason and it won't be something I made up." He stood up. "You ready to hit it?" he asked Big Ed and Professor.

"Alright! Alright, I'm coming," Slick said reluctantly. "I don't see how come you all so patriotic all of a sudden." He began packing his equipment.

"This isn't patriotism, man," Professor answered. "This is standing with one's own people. If we figure out a way to bring that gun, we're going to save colored men's lives. Nobody else is worrying about it, so I think it's up to us."

"Shit, we don't even know half these niggers!"

"It don't matter," LeRoi said. "They're our people. They got our color skin or something close to it. We know a little about what they been through, 'cause we been through it. They are family! The only family we got is the colored soldiers fightin' next to us."

"What family?" Slick scoffed. "You been niggers together?

LeRoi pulled a knife from his boot and threw it with his left hand in one motion. The knife stuck in a log beam and quivered about four inches from Slick's face. "Don't forget who you talkin' to," LeRoi advised. "I've told you before that I don't like the word *nigger!*" Slick edged away from the knife as LeRoi came over to collect it.

"Let's pull out," LeRoi said, lifting his pack on his back and picking up his guns.

The men left the bunker and headed uphill, straight for the trees. The snow continued to fall. Beyond the valley, the distant mountains' jagged outlines dominated the landscape with dark uneven shapes and snow-capped peaks. There was no breeze, but there was a slight chill in the air. They trudged single file in silence, hearing only the crunching sounds of their boots. There was ten feet or more between each man. The trees of the forest closed in around them like silent mourners at a funeral. They were headed for an old riverbed that was covered by brush and scrub trees. The riverbed was a deep, long-running scar down the face of the hillside, yet it could not be seen for any distance due to the density of the surrounding trees. The men descended into it and followed the defile down the hill toward the German lines.

At the bottom of the hill two hundred yards of snow-covered barbed wire extended in circular rolls across an uneven, bombed-out meadow to the first line of the German trenches. Halfway down the hill, the riverbed was joined by another creek. The men had to be careful because the footing was extremely slippery. There were two or three inches of water now flowing at the bottom of the bed underneath the snow and the men sought to stay out of it if they could.

LeRoi was in the lead and signaled a halt. He began pulling away several large pieces of brush on the uphill side of the riverbed and exposed a culvert that was four and a half feet in diameter. After taking a careful look at the surrounding landscape with his German binoculars, he quickly entered the darkness of the culvert on his hands and knees. He was followed one by one by his companions. The last man had the responsibility of pulling the covering brush back in place.

The culvert was part of an old reservoir drainage system that had been bombarded into disrepair. There were several places along its length where the walls had been totally ruptured by bombs through which the snow-covered hillsides could be seen. For the most part, the interior of the culvert was dark and was only occasionally illuminated by LeRoi's flashlight. The length of the culvert extended from where LeRoi and his companions had entered it to Saint Die Reservoir, high above the town that was its namesake.

The men did not leave the culvert until they had traveled nearly a mile within it. When they did exit, they were surrounded once more by a dense evergreen forest. From their previous forays in the area, they knew that there was a small German patrol station above them, guarding the road that entered Saint Die from Luneville. Below them were the lights of the German trench lines spread out like an endless maze. Their objective was a partially destroyed small town named Côte d'Saar, two miles on the other side of Saint Die. The trail was rocky and steep and the men made poor time because stealth was important. They knew that the Germans patrolled the area frequently. Much time was lost while the men sat quietly and surveyed their surroundings prior to moving.

Côte d'Saar was an old fort city that presided over a particularly calm stretch of the Saar River, which meandered slowly through a broad valley. After repeated air strikes by both German forces and the Allies, most of the town had been abandoned, its buildings in ruins. There was still a group of residents who had refused to leave their homes, but they generally hid from soldiers and were rarely seen. The onset of winter and the lack of food had forced even these hardy mountain people to take shelter in Saint Die.

There were no lights, nor was there any discernible movement. Nonetheless, LeRoi spent half an hour watching the town and the surrounding area before he signaled that it was alright to move forward. Their destination was a roofless stone warehouse set on a small hill on the edge of town. Once the men were inside the building, they had Professor serve as a lookout and they checked the structure for booby traps. After assuring themselves that all was safe, LeRoi, Slick, and Big Ed turned their attention to moving a large metal plate along a section of wall. Once the plate had been moved, it exposed a staircase leading down into the depths of the building. LeRoi and Big Ed descended into the darkness with their guns at the ready, but they were only met with the scurrying sound of rodents. Big Ed came back up the stairs with a large tarp, which he hung over the entrance leading to the stairs.

Once the tarp was up, Slick lit an oil lantern and hooked it to an overhead beam. The basement was filled with all sorts of supplies, gear, weapons, and ammunition. It looked like an armory. Once the men had decided to keep their own storehouse, they had been very industrious. The Vickers was perched on its tripod in the far corner. It was just after midnight when they started working on the big machine gun and nearly two in the morning when they had it disassembled and packed into three bundles. It was clear to everyone that the four of them could not possibly carry the gun and ammunition. It was decided that the gun would be brought along and then ammunition would have to be stolen from somewhere near Kastledorf.

A hissed warning from Professor had the men dousing their lights and scrambling up the staircase in darkness. As they joined Professor, he pointed out a lone German military vehicle with its lights on, parked in the town square. It was a small troop carrier capable of holding eight to ten men. There were six soldiers standing around the vehicle talking.

"There's our transportation," whispered Professor. "We'll even be able to carry some ammunition, won't we?"

"How many soldiers you seen?" asked LeRoi, forming a plan in his mind.

"Just those men in front of that truck."

"Whoa, you ain't thinking what I think you's thinking, is you?" Slick questioned LeRoi.

"Yeah, we gon' get that truck." LeRoi turned and looked at Slick. "You got a problem with that?"

"We taking racehorse chances here, for what? It's gon' be the same when we get home: a nigger is still a nigger. Ain't nothin' gon' change. Uncle Sam ain't my uncle, he's just Mr. Charlie to me."

LeRoi poked Slick in the chest. "The Three hundred Fifty-first is family! I don't give two shits about Uncle Sam or patriotism, but I'll kill and die for family! You in or not?"

Slick sighed. "I'm gon' help. You's the boss."

LeRoi quickly outlined a plan and sent Big Ed and Slick off in different directions. He figured that he and his companions had the advantage because they knew the town very well. He had Professor climb the only church tower still standing and prepare for covering fire in case things went wrong. He slipped out of the building and headed toward the vehicle. His plan was quite simple. Slick would create noisy diversion, which would force the soldiers to investigate. The soldiers would be picked off one by one. It was his intention to get as close to the vehicle as possible before firing his weapon. He preferred to kill quietly, with his knife if possible.

As LeRoi picked his way through the debris and destruction of the demolished town, he was surprised at how things could be so different yet remain the same. Here he was a colored man from Louisiana, stalking white men in a little town in France. And yet it had a sameness about it, like when he was out on a raid against the DuMonts. If someone was to have told him a year and a half ago that he would be trained to kill and then ordered to go out and kill white men, he would have called the remark insane. But here he was. An alley between two roofless stone houses loomed ahead of him. LeRoi had to be careful moving about in the snow. It had been snowing for several hours without a break and the snow was now building into small drifts, making footing among the rubble very slippery. He slid the safety off his Bergmann and crouched down as he slowly continued forward.

LeRoi had changed substantially since his induction into the army. His four and a half months on the front lines had had the biggest effect on him. Not only had he been trained to fight and kill efficiently, but he discovered that he liked it. There was a level of excitement in playing in the game of death that was thrilling to him. For the first time in his life, he woke up each morning with a sense of purpose. He had never told his bunk mates, but he preferred to be out on squad patrol, not because he liked to risk his life, but because he was in control and there was no one to order him about. He was left to his own ingenuity to kill the enemy any way possible, but sometimes he wished they were American whites.

The end of the alley led to a corner of the town square. From the edge of the building to his left he could see through the falling snow that the same six men were still standing in front of the truck, smoking and talking. LeRoi could even hear an occasional laugh. They did not appear to be concerned with the need for alertness. He settled himself and waited for Slick's diversion. He felt fortunate that the truck's lights were facing away from him and that the truck was close enough for him to cover the distance in ten good strides. He unslung his Springfield and leaned it against the building, then pulled his two throwing knives from his boots and stuck them in his belt. He strapped two heavy, studded leather bands on his wrists. Experience had taught him that his defense was vastly improved in hand-to-hand combat when he could use his lower forearm to both attack and block. The Bergmann was checked and then slung so that the gun hung in the small of his back. He pulled his .45 government-issue automatic pistol and tested the slide. He liked to feel the gun's weight in his hand. He was ready. Leaning back against the wall, he took deep breaths, trying to relax. The only sounds he heard were the harsh consonants of German in the town square as the men talked and the snow continued to fall.

The Germans did not feel the need for caution because they were part of an augmented canine unit. They were in fact waiting for the return of four men and two dogs, who had been dropped at the edge of town to search the ruins for the local residents, known to fire upon German military units. Côte d'Saar was the last stop on their patrol route before returning to the garrison. No evidence of any resistance had ever been discovered in the region, so the soldiers had begun to take patrols lightly. When the loud metallic clattering began, emanating from the opposite side of town from which they had entered, the soldiers were momentarily confused. The headlights of the truck were turned off. After a few minutes of argument, four soldiers were sent out to investigate. Neither of the two remaining Germans saw LeRoi sprint across the square to the far side of the vehicle.

The sound of the four soldiers leaving the square had covered his approach, but once LeRoi reached the side of the truck all was quiet. After several seconds he could hear the two Germans whispering to each other. He was edging around the rear of the truck when he heard the door open and the sound of footsteps coming his way. Pulling a knife from his belt, he prepared to spring. The German soldier rounded the corner and didn't get a chance to raise his arm or even speak. With one savage cut, LeRoi slit the man's throat, then moved out of the way to let the body fall. There was a brief gurgling sound as the man writhed frantically in the reddening snow and died.

"Karl? Karl?" the other soldier called out.

The sound of gunfire rang out from the direction that the four soldiers had taken. LeRoi heard a rifle being cocked in the truck.

"Karl? Karl?" The soldier was now whispering from inside the truck.

LeRoi had ducked around the side and was grateful that the left rearview mirror was frosted over. Squatting by the driver's door, he flung it open. Simultaneously, a rifle was discharged and a bullet whistled over his head. LeRoi reached up and fired his pistol several times into the truck and heard the man inside grunt and fall out the passenger-side door.

LeRoi started around the truck to make sure the other man was dead when he heard a shot ring out from the church tower. He did not get a chance to turn around before the dog hit him. The big German shepherd had sunk its teeth into the wristband of his gun arm. The weight of the dog's lunge hurled him to the ground. The force of the animal's attack caused him to drop his pistol and his Bergmann was underneath his body. LeRoi pulled his knife from his belt and stabbed the dog several times, but the animal kept attacking, aiming for a grip on his throat. Finally, LeRoi was able to sink his knife deep into the animal's chest and push it off of him.

Shots rang out from the far corner of the square and bullets ricocheted off the cobblestones and whizzed above him. He rolled over and pulled the Bergmann free and fired a burst in return. Scrambling to his feet, he took refuge behind the truck. The shots were coming from the shelter of a stone staircase in the corner of the square. Keeping the truck between him and the source of the gunfire, LeRoi circled the vehicle. He wanted to get clear of the truck because he knew it could easily be blown sky high. He saw the German soldier he shot, lying on his back in the snow, struggling to turn over. The man was bleeding from several different wounds. LeRoi stooped down quickly and removed the man's Luger from his holster and shot him. The dead man also had four hand grenades strapped to his belt. They were called "potato mashers" by the American troops because of their unique shape, but they worked extremely well, better in fact than army issue. LeRoi removed them, pulling the pins out of two and heaved them toward the staircase. He took off running before the grenades detonated.

LeRoi reached the alleyway just after the explosions occurred. From the safety of the alley, he watched as the whole building collapsed forward onto the staircase. There were screams as men were crushed by the falling structure. In a few minutes all was still again. LeRoi walked out into the square, keeping an eye on the rubble at the far end. He saw Big Ed limping forward from a side street. His pants were torn and there was blood trickling from an open wound on his thigh. From the far side of the square, Slick could be seen clambering over the rubble. He waved his Bergmann over his head. LeRoi turned and signaled to the church tower with his flashlight, telling the Professor to stay alert.

Inside the truck, the keys were still in the ignition. LeRoi pushed the igniter button, and the engine sputtered, then began to purr. He backed up to where Big Ed was waiting.

"Goddamned dog attacked me! It caught me by surprise," Big Ed explained as he clambered in the back of the truck. "I had to beat it off with the butt of my rifle. Goddamned thing came flying out of the falling snow like some kind of ghost! Still, I got three of them boys!"

"You need a tourniquet?" LeRoi asked.

"Naw, it ain't spurtin'! I can wait till we get out of here," Big Ed said as he made himself comfortable between the benches. "All the noise we made, this whole town will be crawling with Germans in no time! We best pick up and get out! I never liked this town no way. Can't grow nothing here, the soil's too rocky."

"Where's your buddy?" LeRoi inquired as he swung the truck around and drove over to where he had last seen Slick. He slid down the window, then called out, "Slick! Slick! We got to head out, man! You better get your ass over here or you gon' get left!"

Slick appeared, scrambling over the rubble of the fallen building. He beckoned to the truck, indicating he wanted them to follow him. He turned to go back the way he had come when LeRoi shouted, "We gon' leave your grave-robbin' ass!"

Slick turned and shouted back, "I found a box of gold! A real box of gold! It's too heavy for one man to carry. I can use some help!"

"Leave it!" LeRoi ordered. "We need to get out of here! We gon' have Germans down on our necks any minute!"

"This is a real box of gold! It's right here! All we got to do is lift up and carry it away! We can't walk away from this! Our money problems will be over!"

LeRoi left the truck idling with the brake on and scrambled up the mountain of debris. "If you're lying, yo' ass is mine!"

Slick led him to the back side of the destroyed building and there in the snow where Slick had dragged it was a squat metal box. "Open it," Slick urged. LeRoi flipped back the lid and saw that the box was filled with coins and jewelry made of gold. Slick was excited. "There's two more boxes like this! This buildin' was some kind of bank! There's a big crack in the vault showin' paper money and everythin'. With a little diggin' we gon' be rich!"

"Sorry, Slick, this is all we got time for." LeRoi closed the box. "I wants that gun mor'n I wants gold! I's ready to carry this one, but no mo'!"

Slick was aghast. The prospect of unlimited wealth was being turned down. "Nigger, you must be stupid! We got a treasure for the takin' and you gon' leave it for some damn gun? Nigger, please!"

LeRoi growled, "Pick up the box! We'll take this one back to the truck!"

Slick saw something in LeRoi's eyes that made him swallow any more words of contempt. He bent down and grasped the handle and lifted it in unison with LeRoi. The two men struggled and staggered with the weight of the box, but finally wrestled it back to the truck. Big Ed slid over so that they could push the box onto the truck bed.

"We best get on and pick up that Vickers," Big Ed suggested. "Them Germans got to come and investigate!"

Slick looked back toward the building's ruins and then into LeRoi's eyes. He decided on the wiser course and got into the back with Big Ed. LeRoi jumped in the cab and drove the truck without lights back to their storage site.

Professor met them at the door. "I saw lights coming this way down the road from Saint Die. Looks like a couple of squads coming right for us."

"Let's get the gun loaded," LeRoi urged.

"Damn! What about my supplies, my cigarettes, my uniforms?" Slick groused.

"We's only taking ammunition and mortars. Everything else got to stay! We ain't dyin' over no cigarettes and uniforms!" LeRoi barked as he headed down to the basement to get the Vickers.

With Big Ed keeping lookout, it took them twenty minutes to load the ammunition and the guns onto the truck. LeRoi was directing as he worked. Professor and Slick were sweating from exertion when the last box was loaded. Big Ed gave a warning whistle, indicating that the German trucks were within a mile of the town. LeRoi disappeared in the darkened building one last time. He emerged after a couple of minutes, climbed into the cab, and gunned the truck's engines as he sped out onto the darkened highway.

The two-lane road was a tortuous, twisting ribbon that followed the contours of the mountainside as it slowly climbed above the placid Saar. In the dark, with no lights, it was sometimes difficult to determine where the road actually lay beneath the snow. LeRoi did not let up on his speed and he barely kept the skidding, careening vehicle on track. Several times the truck actually scraped against the railings built to prevent vehicles from hurtling down the steep mountainside. The road dropped and curved into a pass between two peaks that turned into a straightaway with a half-mile visibility. LeRoi could see the lights of a small roadblock in the distance. He did not decrease his speed, but kept barreling down the highway with the accelerator pushed to the floor.

As the truck neared the roadblock, they saw lights being waved back and forth by the men staffing the checkpoint, but LeRoi ignored the signal and veered partially off the road in order to knock down the shelter upon which the telephone line was connected. There were shouts and curses as the German soldiers leapt out of the way. One fired two shots at point-blank range. None of the occupants was hit but two windows were shattered and flying glass was everywhere. The truck slammed into the post that served as support for the wooden pole that swung down and blocked passage. The post snapped and flew off to the right, and then the truck hit the wooden shelter and splintered the whole front of it. As it collapsed, the truck continued down the highway. More shots were fired by the Germans, but the bullets went astray.

The ride was rough and bumpy as the truck sped around a sharp curve that led out of the pass and down along the side of the mountain. By now, the snow had stopped falling and the sky appeared to be lighter. For the first time, they could see, high above them, the glow from the lights of

Saint Die in the surrounding darkness. Each time the truck hit a bump in
the road, everything in it was momentarily airborne. Professor, who was
occupying the front passenger seat, had one foot braced against the dashboard. He looked across at LeRoi and saw him smiling. "What are you
smiling about?" he asked as he cleaned his glasses. "We nearly got our asses
shot off back there! And I can't figure out how you're planning to get to
the ridge."

"You remember that old logging road that was a couple of valleys
south of Saint Die? If I can find it, it's got to end up somewhere near
Saint-Germain. How you doing back there, Big Ed?" LeRoi called over
his shoulder.

"He'll make it," Slick answered. "It ain't deep, but it's a long gash. He
can't talk right now 'cause he's biting down on leather. I poured some
schnapps on it and gon' pour some more as soon you stop bumpin' around."

"You gon' have to wait a minute. I want to get off this roadway first,"
LeRoi answered. He drove on for several more miles, then took the first
large dirt road leading off into the trees. The road curved around the
mountain and began to climb sharply. LeRoi followed it until it forked.
He killed the engine and said, "We got to scout from here on. I don't want
to drive into no German patrols. The ridge can't be but three, four miles
from here."

"I'll stay here with Big Ed, if you don't mind," Slick offered.

LeRoi got out of the truck and walked around to the back. He pulled
the canvas back and saw that the metal box was open. "You want to bury
the gold now and split it between the four of us? Or do you want to wait
and share it with the whole platoon?"

Slick sputtered, "How you get four? They's only three people in on
this."

"What about Professor, or don't he count?"

"What gold?" Professor asked.

"Don't get greedy, Slick," Big Ed advised. "There's plenty for all of us.
You can't leave Professor out. He's one of us."

"What gold?" Professor asked again.

"Show him, Slick," LeRoi said.

Reluctantly, Slick opened the box and Professor climbed in the back to
view its contents.

"My God!" Professor exclaimed. "This is a fortune! And because
they're coins and jewelry, it's probably worth more than just the gold. I
can't even remember the last time a country minted its coins in gold. This
is an heirloom!"

"I say we bury it now and get on with our mission," LeRoi said.

"Nigger, I found it," Slick declared. "I should be the one who says what happens to it. You the one that walked away from two more boxes just like this!"

"Get out of the truck, Slick. I wants a word with you."

There was a moment of silence. "Why I got to get out of the truck?"

LeRoi growled. "Get out of the truck!"

Professor looked at LeRoi. "What's going on, LT?"

"Stay out of it, Professor!" LeRoi warned. "This is between me and Slick!"

"What I do to you, man?" Slick questioned, making no move to get out of the truck.

"I've told you befo' not to call me nigger! I hates that word! Whenever I hears it, don't matter who's sayin' it, I see white skin and white thinkin'! The white man got you callin' yo'self what he calls you when he don't want to be polite! That ain't me. I ain't never gon' be a nigger! If you don't know me well enough to call me by my first name, call me Mister! Now figure out what you want done with the gold. Professor and me are going to scout for a road leading up to the ridge."

"That's fine with me," Slick answered, unable to keep the smile off his face. "Me and Big Ed will take charge of it."

"Let's go, Professor," LeRoi said as he started uphill into the forest. He knew that Slick was not a woodsman. If he hid something the size of the gold's metal box, its location would be obvious to a practiced observer. Professor picked up his gun and pack and trudged after him.

They were in a heavily wooded area. As they passed through a clearing, a loud explosion echoed through the mountain gorges and a bright flash shimmered and turned into flames along the highway from Saint Die.

"What the hell is that?" Professor whispered, dropping to his knees as a precautionary measure.

"Côte d'Saar," answered LeRoi, kneeling beside his companion. "It's a little welcoming present that I left for our German friends. I was gon' be sure that they couldn't use none of Slick's armory."

Staring across the canyon at the distant flames, which were reflected on the wide, black surface of the meandering Saar, Professor nodded his head. "Looks like you did a pretty good job."

"Yep," LeRoi answered as he rose and continued uphill. They kept the winding road to their left as they climbed. The hill they were climbing was but a low branching arm of a curling spine of mountains that reached white fingers into the night sky. Even as LeRoi and Professor breasted the shoulder of the hill, they were still beneath the tree line. Their progress was slowed because the forest was not always able to provide cover. There were great stands where unregulated logging had left acres of snow-covered tree stumps. They skirted these open areas and stayed within the cover of the trees, but each time they would take the precaution to kneel in the underbrush and search their surroundings for movement.

During one such stop, after they had assured themselves that they were alone, Professor turned to LeRoi and said, "Why don't we take a break here? We must have climbed a couple thousand feet."

LeRoi nodded and moved deeper under the snow-laden branches of a big pine.

Professor followed suit and shortly they were both seated on their packs with their backs to the tree's trunk. Professor rubbed some pine needles between his fingers and then smelled the essence. "For a moment back there at the truck I thought you might attack Slick."

"It was close," LeRoi admitted.

Professor was surprised. "You would have fought him over a word? Slick's been with us since Fort Dodge."

"*Nigger* ain't just a word! It's a way of thinkin'. They want you to think that the colored man is weak and lazy, and ain't got no determination! It ain't so and I ain't gon' play the part. I wants respect and I don't mind fightin' to keep it! I don't plan on livin' my life in them little cramped billets America has set aside for colored men! Despite all its prejudice the army taught me one good thing—how to fight—and I plan on usin' everythin' I learned when I get home!"

"That's the problem all around: man is much better at killing than he is at understanding, better at killing than at living. History is written in the blood of those made invisible by the victors. As if killing was the measure of man." Professor shook his head in disgust. He looked at his friend's calm, undisturbed expression and realized that his words had blown past LeRoi like bits of debris carried on a strong wind, seen but not remembered, just patterns of light and shadow. "Aren't you afraid of dying?" he asked.

LeRoi responded slowly, but kept his eyes probing the shadows of the surrounding forest. "I ain't worried about it. Anyways, I figure I got some time befo' my page gets filled in."

"What do you mean, 'Before your page gets filled in'?"

"Oh, just somethin' a schoolteacher once told me. Don't remember her exact words, but she said somethin' like all of us starts life with a blank page and you die when yo' page is filled up. Way she got it figured, everythin' you do and everythin' that happens to you is writ on that page." LeRoi checked his watch. "Let's move it."

They hoisted their packs and backtracked around the outskirts of the logged clearing and followed a streambed down through a small valley. As they were climbing out of the valley, a break in the trees revealed the glint of railroad tracks winding through a distant pass below them. They knew that their destination was close. As they crested another ridge, they saw dark shapes moving in the darkness of the trees above the railroad tracks. A line of men emerged and marched single file down the slope toward the tracks.

Professor slumped down into the snow. "Holy shit! Are those Germans?"

LeRoi, with his binoculars focused on the distant men, smiled. "No. That's the Three hundred Fifty-first! I can tell by the walk. Look." He handed the binoculars to Professor. "Tell me if that ain't Fat George Cunningham from the Second Platoon waddling his big ass down the hill?"

FRIDAY, DECEMBER 28, 1917

It was 0700 before LeRoi's team got the big Vickers set up to guard the pass from Kastledorf to Ribeauville. The temperature had dropped twenty degrees since the snow had stopped falling, which made assembling the big gun all the more difficult. If bare skin touched the larger metallic pieces, it immediately adhered to the frozen steel. Even the lubricant was gunky and resistant. LeRoi and Big Ed toiled in GI-issue woolen mittens, which limited their dexterity with the numerous screws and bolts, but the men's persistence was eventually rewarded. The machine gun sat on a platform made of ammunition boxes in a recess that was dug out of a frozen earthen ridge of the mountain by pick and shovel. The recess was set among the trees and was not visible from the road below. The gun's firing lanes covered the entrance to the near side of the bridge as well as the highway and adjacent checkpoint structure on the far-western span of Kastledorf Bridge.

The sky was cloudless and blue, and a chill breeze eddied in and through the mountain gorges. Big Ed pushed himself to his feet. The dog bite was beginning to throb again. The medic had stanched the flow of blood and taped him up. Now he had to move around to avoid the paralyzing stiffness that resulted from prolonged sitting in cold weather. He had a makeshift crutch that allowed him to hobble slowly back and forth.

"Remember what the medic said," advised Professor, who was squatting down, writing in his diary. "You don't want to walk around too much and start the blood to flowing again."

"Gotta move, Professor," Big Ed explained. "I sit too long, the pain just comes roaring up my leg. Man, I wish that white platoon that's 'sposed to join us would get here. I know their medic's got something for pain."

Professor turned a surprised face toward Big Ed. "What? They're actually sending some white boys to fight alongside of us? This doesn't sound like the American army I know."

"Yes siree. That's straight from the sergeant. You can write that in your book."

LeRoi emerged from a stand of trees above the recess. "What are you doin' walkin' around?" he asked Big Ed.

"My leg was freezin' up on me. I had to get up and move," Big Ed answered. "Tell Professor, ain't it true that Sarge said a white platoon was being sent here?"

"Yes, Sarge said they was coming in support," LeRoi agreed. "But don't get it twisted. The way he said it, didn't sound like they was gon' fight side by side with us."

"Same old stuff," Professor commented with resignation as he closed his diary. He took off his glasses and wiped his forehead. "They'll wait until the Germans have shot us up before they expend a bullet."

LeRoi stated with cold emphasis, "I don't intend to die behind no 'Okie Doke.' I told you, Professor, I's plannin' on seein' New Orleans again. And if I do go down, I plans to go down shootin', takin' peckerwoods with me. German or American, they all the same to me."

Sergeant Williams strode out of the trees. "Tremain, your voice carries. You're a good soldier. It would be a shame to have your military record tarnished because of your mouth." He leaned his rifle against a nearby tree and saluted.

The men stood and saluted. Even Big Ed clambered to his feet. The sergeant took off his helmet and knelt down. "As you were, men." Characteristically, he looked neat. "We got a problem. We got a couple of German squads coming up the railroad track by handcar. A scout flashed us a warning with a signal lamp. We're talking around twenty men. We're going have to deal with them before they get dug in. They're sitting on our exit route."

"You're not thinking about us leaving by handcar, are you?" Professor asked.

"What's a handcar?" Big Ed asked.

"One of them flatbed, hand-cranked things you see around railroad construction," LeRoi answered. "It ain't got no engine so you got to pump the crank up and down."

"No, we're going to meet up with some of the locals who are fighting the Germans. They're going to help us to escape. They know the best way through the mountains back to our lines."

"The locals?" Professor questioned. "Sarge, I heard they were wiped out in this area."

"These people are pretty well organized into a citizen's militia. They call themselves the Lions of the Mountains and they're mobilizing to blow up Kastledorf Bridge. Lieutenant McHenry is meeting with their leaders right now. They don't want the Germans to reinforce their position at Ribeauville any more than we do.

"LT, you and Professor are going to intercept the handcars by the outbuildings that are by that little train depot we passed on the backside of the mountain. The lieutenant, Slick, the rest of your squad along with the local people will attack from the opposite side. Check with the lieutenant. Some of these local militia have some new kind of thing that screws onto the barrel of a pistol and muffles its discharge. They got them off some storm troopers who were caught behind our lines. They may loan you a couple of these modified pistols. I don't know how we can manage it, but I'd like to take out these squads with as little noise as possible. If we don't have to alert those men down there," the sergeant nodded his head in the direction of a small checkpoint shelter that was constructed at the western entrance of the bridge, "it'll be to our benefit."

There was a telephone line originating from the checkpoint shelter that was tacked across the underside of the bridge's solid rock and mortar structure. There was a military transport truck parked off the road next to the shelter and another on the other side of the bridge. There were approximately thirty German soldiers guarding the bridge, many of whom possessed binoculars and were busy studying the terrain both below and around the bridge.

"Where's Second Squad?" Professor asked. "Are they down there where the Germans are looking?"

"Below the bridge. They got the assignment to blow it up," the sergeant answered quietly. "If all has gone well, they've laid the detonators by now and are safely hidden somewhere on the other side of the gorge."

"You can't cross that river anywhere down near here. It's deep and the water's rushing too fast," LeRoi observed. "If they ain't come up to the road, they probably still down below the bridge somewhere."

"Then it's on us to save their asses!" the sergeant asserted. "Let's get this first assignment out of the way. Big Ed, you position the machine gun on that shelter. If you hear shots fired, the first thing that I want you to do is take out that telephone line."

"Who gon' work the mortars?" Big Ed asked.

"Don't worry about the mortars. We won't fire them until the squads are clear or the bridge has been blown. I'll send someone to check and make sure the outbuildings are empty."

Professor and LeRoi reported to the lieutenant in a stand of trees where he was meeting with the headman of the local civilian brigade. The meeting place was about a half mile from where Big Ed had set up the Vickers, about five hundred feet from the train depot.

"Yes, Tremain and Morris," McHenry said as he hurriedly returned their salute, "we have a job for a couple of sharpshooters. I've been telling André that you are two of the best shots in the whole division."

A short, squat man stepped forward and held his hand out to LeRoi. LeRoi was momentarily hesitant. Other than Captain Mack and his family, he had not met many whites who extended the true hand of friendship. And the army's code of conduct, of course, made it official that Negro servicemen were inferior. He stared into the man's blue green eyes, looking for evidence of patronization. Finding none, he shook his hand.

"He say you very good shot." André nodded his head, a smile crinkling his eyes. "Maybe you hit something so we see?" He handed Professor and LeRoi Lugers with metallic cylinders attached to the end of the barrels.

Professor shook his head. "I'm better with a rifle."

LeRoi took the second Luger and fired one bullet from each gun into the trunk of a tree twenty yards distant. The guns' discharges sounded like muffled thuds. The sound of the bullets hitting the tree made more noise than the actual firing of the guns. LeRoi noticed that the gun in his left hand fired low while the one in his right seemed true. He switched hands and pointed to a row of pine cones on a lower branch of the tree that had been his original target. He fired the guns in steady succession, hitting pine cones with each shot. He quit when all the pine cones had been shot off the branch.

"*Formidable!*" declared André. "But can you kill Germans with such accuracy?"

Now it was LeRoi's turn to smile. "Anytime."

Professor was situated above the depot on the ridge leading up to the Vickers machine gun. It allowed him a clear view of the railroad tracks and the depot. LeRoi hid among the outbuildings. He had on a German greatcoat and a German helmet. The Lugers were in his hands and extra magazines were in his pockets. He took several deep breaths as the sound of clanking drew nearer on the tracks. The first team of soldiers on a handcar came into view. There were eight men on the first car, four of whom were industriously involved in cranking the car along. The remaining four were watching the countryside with their guns at the ready. One man carried a Lewis machine gun in the crook of his arm. LeRoi resolved to kill him first.

There was no wind. There was no sound of birds. There was only the distant metal clatter of the handcar drawing nearer in the surrounding silence. LeRoi did not stop to consider that he was about to take more human lives. He had adapted to the rules of war. An enemy soldier's life or death was nothing to him. The Germans were merely things to be killed. If he mourned at all, it was for the colored dead, men with whom he had shared coffee and jokes over small fires, men whose personalities and conversations were now lost in unrecorded history. LeRoi saw his breath as he exhaled and thought that at least there would be no lingering smell of death.

The handcar cranked up to the depot. The four soldiers who had supplied the power took seats and rested while three of their companions leaped down to check out the depot. The man with the Lewis stayed on the handcar and watched warily. LeRoi waited until his back was turned and started walking toward the handcar. He wanted to get close enough to get a sure shot. When he was within twenty paces, one of the resting Germans saw him and shouted halt.

LeRoi answered with guns blazing. The man who shouted and the man with the Lewis were dead before they hit the ground. Two other men were killed by fire from the other side of the tracks. The fifth soldier was seriously injured and fell off the handcar. Only the man's shout had been heard; the soft thudding sounds of the silencers were lost in the general activity. Of the three soldiers who had entered the depot, two were killed as they exited and the third threw down his gun in surrender and was taken prisoner.

The dead were dragged away and the ambushers returned to their hiding places, awaiting the next arrivals. LeRoi was the first to the Lewis machine gun. He picked it up and carried it, plus a forty-pound box of ammunition, behind some trees at the edge of the clearing. The Lewis weighed forty-five pounds and, as a much smaller weapon than the Vickers, was more suited to the type of missions to which LeRoi's squad was assigned. He wanted to make sure his squad got to use it.

The second handcar was more difficult to attack. The soldiers did not come in all the way, but stopped some distance from the depot and hailed the soldiers who had preceded them. When there was no answer, the soldiers started to crank in the opposite direction, but LeRoi opened fire on them from behind the last outbuilding. Three soldiers fell off the handcar. His opening fusillade made the crankers drop the crank and grab their weapons. Their return fire splintered the wood above his head. LeRoi ran around to the other side of the building and emptied his guns at the figures on the handcar. He threw himself backward down in the snow behind the building to avoid giving the Germans a target. He popped new magazines into his Lugers and got to his feet cautiously. A salvo of pistol fire from the opposite side of the tracks caught the Germans in a cross fire of whizzing bullets.

The skirmish was over before the Germans could fire again. No one was left alive on the handcar. The riders on the last handcar had appeared in time to see their comrades fall. Their crankers were working energetically to return from whence they came. Shots began to ring out along the track as snipers began to take their toll on the German soldiers who struggled to pump the handcar along.

The steady drumming of the Vickers echoed over the ridge. Big Ed was following orders. On the ridge behind him, LeRoi heard Professor's Springfield fire at a measured pace. Across the tracks he heard the lieutenant shout, "Cease Fire! Cease Fire!"

A couple of the German soldiers, lying near the tracks, were struggling to sit up. One actually pushed himself erect to a sitting position. LeRoi aimed one of his Lugers at the man's head, but the voice of the lieutenant stopped him.

"Hold it there, Tremain! I ordered cease fire!" The lieutenant and a Negro soldier named Ike Evans were crossing the tracks, walking toward the injured Germans. "We are not savages, Tremain! Just because we're at war doesn't mean we have to act like we're from the jungle!" With a wave of his hand, McHenry sent Evans to check on the Germans. "If I have to speak to you about this again, I'll have you up on charges. Do I make myself clear?"

"Yes, sir," LeRoi responded, thinking that he'd rather shoot the lieutenant than the Germans.

Two shots rang out and Evans fell over backward and hit the snow with a grunt. The seated German had a smoking Luger in his hand, pointing directly at the lieutenant, who was twenty feet away. The German laughed and blood dripped out of his mouth. He coughed and raised the gun. McHenry stood transfixed, like a hare caught in the gaze of a snake.

The German hesitated and did not pull the trigger, perhaps savoring the power of the moment. His delay saved McHenry's life. LeRoi had been waiting for the German to shoot the lieutenant. When he didn't, LeRoi got impatient and shot the German in the head. He also shot the other

German, who was still moving, and then slowly swung the barrel in McHenry's direction. He was seething. Evans had been in his induction group.

"Good shooting, Tremain," Sergeant Williams said, slapping LeRoi on the back as he came running out of the trees. Williams kept running until he reached the spot where Evans was lying. Williams stooped quickly, checking for vital signs, but there were none. André, following the sergeant, trotted past LeRoi, and said, "C'est bon. Très bien!"

Slick came walking down the tracks from the depot. He was talking loudly. "Some shootin'. I saw you from the top of the depot. Boy, you was smokin'! I wonder if there is some kind of medal in all that? They probably don't give medals to colored folks, huh?" Slick's voice was loud and his tone was taunting. He had seen LeRoi save McHenry's life. Now he was testing how far he could stretch the lieutenant's gratitude. Slick walked up to LeRoi with the upturned palm of his hand stuck out to be slapped, as if he and LeRoi shared some private joke.

LeRoi looked from Slick's face to his hand, then back again. "You always stirring shit, ain't ya? You always try to drag in somebody else too. Let me tell it to you straight." LeRoi popped the magazines out of his Lugers and checked the rounds as he spoke. "I stir my own shit and I choose whether I'm gon' jump in it or not. I don't need no extra."

"You awful high and mighty," Slick sputtered. "I saw you was ready to kill Mr. Charlie. You ain't fooled no one but maybe the fool himself. How come you just got to ignore my hand? Just pretend like you didn't see it? That ain't right!"

"You's the one pretendin'," LeRoi answered. "You was signifyin' at the lieutenant the whole time you was talkin'. You wasn't talkin' to me. That's yo' shit. Then you want to pretend that I was part of it. Like drag me in without me havin' no say at all? You the one that's wrong. I cut you slack 'cause you's a bunk mate, but you usin' up my patience!"

"Ah, man, you always take things the wrong way. We supposed to be tight! You's way too sensitive!"

LeRoi stood up and went over to where he set the Lewis down and checked out the gun for damage. He was still checking the action of its breechblock when Williams walked over to him.

"I just want you to know, Tremain, that I saw you from the trees and I saw you struggling with temptation. It's the temptation that every colored man who has worn a uniform for his country has felt at some time during his military service. I'm glad you fought the temptation and won. You'll find it doesn't make much difference anyway. They just send a new fool and he ends up being worse than the man who preceded him. You do better if you can reach an understanding, because there are all sorts of fools in the service. Prejudice is the army's middle name."

"Seem to be the first name and last name too," LeRoi commented dryly.

"LT, I been part of this man's army for over twenty years. I rode with the Rough Riders in Puerto Rico. We were still called 'buffalo soldiers' then. There's been many a time that I had my sights on a white officer and a couple times I had to go ahead and pull the trigger, but I never did it in a way that would bring dishonor on the reputation of the Negro fighting man. Too many colored men have died maintaining the honor of their uniform for us to lose all that because of one hothead."

LeRoi looked up at the sergeant with surprise. He was speechless. He never expected to hear 'Old-Follow-the-Rules-to-the-Letter' Williams say that he had ever thought about killing a white officer, much less admitting he had killed a couple. He felt a new respect for the sergeant.

"There's something else, son," Williams continued. "Prejudice is like gravity. You can't waste time thinkin' about it. You just have to keep on pushin' against it. You just worry about bein' a man and you'll do yo' part in the struggle."

"Don't you just want to explode sometimes?" LeRoi asked. "Don't you want to say to hell with the rules?"

Williams shook his head. "No, I'm doin' my part. The toughest thing about bein' a man is not explodin'! You see, because of soldiers like me, with blood and guts and spit and polish, one day there'll be a Negro general in the army; maybe even in yo' lifetime."

"You got 'Frontline Fever' if you believe that!" LeRoi scoffed.

"If I didn't have that as my dream, I would explode! There'd be nothin' to sacrifice for!"

"I feel like explodin' all the time!" LeRoi admitted. He held up his thumb and index finger. "Sometimes I'm this close!"

"A man has got to find himself a star and head for it," Williams asserted. "It's got to guide him through the trials! Killin' comes easily to you. You got to watch yourself. You don't want to lose your soul!"

"Sometimes I wonders if I got a soul," LeRoi mused.

"It takes a bit of livin' to find it," Williams acknowledged. "You gon' be alright. You one of the men that I count on to do right. You got the weight of many lives on your shoulders. I need you to be strong. Don't disappoint me!"

"You don't have to worry, Sarge. I ain't gon' do nothin' that's gon' bring dishonor on the Three hundred Fifty-first."

"Good, here's your first test," said Williams. "You're going to need all the restraint you have because Red McGraw and his rednecks are coming up here. André's people saw them coming up from the river. We're all going to need a lot of discipline. We can't let them draw us into any fights."

LeRoi shook his head disbelievingly. All the colored soldiers had heard about McGraw and how he and his squad had lynched two colored soldiers because they had been seen with French white women. It was common knowledge that the army had conducted no investigation into the two deaths and McGraw's squad had gone unpunished.

"How come they sending McGraw out here?" LeRoi asked. "Don't they know his feelings about colored people?"

"God as my witness, I don't know," Williams answered, shaking his head sadly.

The sound of a woman's shrieks rent the air. The screams came from the depot. The sergeant started running immediately toward the building. McHenry also trotted toward the origin of the sound. The door of the depot crashed open and Slick emerged, dragging a German woman by the arm. She was in military uniform and was fighting to escape his grip. She swung around and tried to scratch out his eyes. Slick backhanded the woman across the face and she fell in a heap at his feet.

"I caught her on the telephone!" Slick shouted in explanation. "She was calling German headquarters!"

From the other side of the tracks a voice called out, "What are you doing, nigger?" Red McGraw's squad emerged from the cover of the forest and took up positions around the depot platform.

Slick was momentarily at a loss for words when he saw the angry white faces surrounding him. "I uh, uh, found her on the tele—"

"You hit her, didn't you, nigger?" An angry voice interrupted Slick's explanation.

"Looks like we got to teach him a lesson, Sarge," another voice called out.

"Wait," Sergeant Williams shouted. "She's a hostile! She was telling German headquarters about—"

Shots were fired. Slick had tried to pull his Bergmann free of his jacket and his movement was seen. The first bullets hit him in the shoulder and chest and knocked him back into the depot. The rest of the fusillade hit the German woman as she tried to rise and escape. The force of the lead hitting her body drove her slumping back against the wall. She quivered a moment and lay still.

"Stop! Goddamn it!" shouted Sergeant Williams again as he tried to intercede.

"He's behind you, Tony!" one of McGraw's men yelled and fired at Williams. The bullets passed over Williams's head as he dove for the snow.

The man who had shot at Sergeant Williams was killed when a bullet tore through his throat. The crack of Professor's Springfield sounded regularly as he strafed McGraw's men. They all ran for cover. Another man was killed before he could hide behind a handcar.

McHenry shouted, "Cease fire! Cease fire! These are friendlies!"

"We got two dead soldiers here! Get back where you belong, nigger lover!" a voice growled at him from behind a handcar.

Sergeant Williams rolled to his feet and sprinted for cover, but he was cut down by a hail of bullets from McGraw's men.

The lieutenant shouted again, "We're all Americans here! Cease fire! Cease fire! We're killing our own!"

A voice answered, "If you want the shooting to stop, send the niggers out!"

LeRoi had been working his way behind McGraw's squad. They were lying behind the handcars and firing between the wheels. As he passed behind the buildings and slipped into the trees, he saw several of the weathered faces of the local militia. He swung the Lewis in their direction, but they merely shook their heads, indicating that it was not their fight. He continued on until he was directly behind McGraw's men.

Someone shouted, "Send the niggers out and it'll be over!"

LeRoi opened fire with the Lewis and felt the powerful recoil of the gun as he expended the forty-seven-round magazine on the exposed backs of the men. As the rhythm of the recoil shuddered through him, he saw the countless faces and bodies of colored soldiers who had died in the trenches beside him. Anger and hatred welled up within him and overwhelmed any concern for his own physical safety. He was finally killing the true enemy and he didn't care if he died in the act. He dropped the empty Lewis and drew both his Colt pistols. The fusillade of bullets from the Lewis had killed nearly every man in McGraw's squad. A cold fury drove LeRoi onward as he moved carefully through the bodies, killing those who were not dead, until he reached McGraw himself.

Sergeant McGraw's right arm was shattered and hung useless at his side. With his left hand he pushed away his M1917 automatic rifle and managed a smile. "I guess you won this round, nigger. But when I get back, they're going to hang your black ass!"

"What makes you think you gon' get back?" LeRoi asked as he picked up a coil of rope from the handcar.

McGraw pushed his red hair out of his eyes. "I'm a sergeant in the U.S. Army. You ain't going to shoot me while I'm unarmed!"

"What makes you think I'm gon' shoot you?" LeRoi asked as he quickly made a noose on one end of the rope.

Sergeant McGraw made a grab at the rifle he had pushed away, but LeRoi savagely kicked his shattered arm. McGraw screamed in agony, nearly passing out from the pain.

There was a metal lamppost with a horizontal arm that held the lamp. LeRoi walked over and threw the noose around the horizontal arm. He went back and pulled McGraw roughly to his feet. He wrestled and shoved McGraw to the lamppost.

When LeRoi slipped the noose around his neck, McGraw began to scream for help. LeRoi head-butted him across the bridge of his nose and his screams stopped midsyllable. McGraw fell backward into the snow. LeRoi grabbed the rope tightly and began to walk away from McGraw's supine form. With each step, he pulled the sergeant further erect. He didn't have sufficient traction in the wet snow to pull McGraw all the way off the ground, so LeRoi crossed the tracks and positioned himself on the other side of a handcar. He braced one foot against a wheel and hauled the thrashing body of McGraw aloft.

"Let go of that rope! Or I swear to God that I'll shoot!"

LeRoi twisted his torso with an effort and saw that it was Lieutenant McHenry, pointing a pistol at him. He let go of the rope and McGraw fell against the lamppost with a thud. LeRoi turned slowly toward McHenry. He had a smirk on his face as he watched the pale, trembling face of the lieutenant.

"I saved your life and you just gon' shoot me? I ain't got no right to defend myself? Yet, you stood by when they was killin' us, didn't you? It was alright when it's peckerwoods killin' coloreds, but don't let coloreds pick up a gun and fight back! I got yo' number! Ain't no use in wastin' time." LeRoi threw open his jacket and exposed his pistols. "I'm ready to die right now and I'm gon' take you with me!"

"I order you to drop your weapons! One false move and I'll shoot," McHenry answered, unable to stop his trembling. "All I want to do is stop the killing."

"Sergeant Williams is dead!" Professor shouted as he stood over the body of the fallen sergeant. He aimed his rifle at the lieutenant. "You stood by and watched them kill him! They are murderers and deserve to die! When you pull that trigger, it'll be the last thing you do!"

"Morris, what are you doing?" exclaimed McHenry. "Put down that gun!"

"If he don't shoot you, we will." Three Negro soldiers crossed the tracks with their rifles trained on the lieutenant. The soldier who had spoken first continued. "We ain't letting no more colored soldiers get killed! We done watched enough of our own get it. Now we full up with it!"

"Tell him, Smitty," one of his companions urged.

The lieutenant let his gun hand fall to his side and turned. "This is mutiny under fire! You will all be court-martialed."

"But you'll be dead!" Professor countered.

McHenry looked around at the brown faces surrounding him and holstered his gun. "Okay, what now?" His voice was filled with bravado, but everyone could see he was still trembling. No one moved as the soldiers waited to see if one among them would kill the lieutenant.

Several of the militia, with their headman in the lead, crossed the tracks and walked around looking at the bodies of the soldiers. The Negro soldiers were growing more nervous by the minute; they didn't know whether to open fire on the locals or not.

"They killed by Germans," André said with a sweep of his hand, indicating the bodies of McGraw's squad. He was standing on the depot platform. "How you say, it was terrible fight. Many die, but we gain victory. Yes?" He rapidly translated his statement into French for his men who were gathering in front of the depot.

There was a rousing cheer from André's men and he nodded to the lieutenant. "This is what we will report. I tell you that we too have had problems with this McGraw. He and some of his men raped the wife of one of my fighters. Because we did not know which ones did it, nothing was done. We have not forgotten. So, for this we will say it was Germans. You agree or no?"

McHenry looked around at his subordinates and saw by their eyes that they were still ready to kill him. He swallowed and said hoarsely, "I just wanted to stop the shooting." His eyes darted from brown face to brown face. Like a fish caught in a tidal pool, he had nowhere to go. He cleared his throat and said, "You men don't have to worry about anything. My report will be consistent with his." McHenry walked slowly through the circle of Negro soldiers.

"You checked on Slick?" LeRoi asked Professor, who had walked up to stand beside him.

"No. Everything happened so fast, I just barely got to the sarge." Professor took off his glasses and began cleaning them absentmindedly. "I've seen so much death since we've been over here. There must be twenty, thirty bodies around here right now. I'm getting sick to my stomach of it!"

"Better to be standing and sick to your stomach than dead," LeRoi said, mounting the stairs to the depot. He waved Professor to join him.

"You don't understand, LT. I'm not like you," Professor responded. "I'm not a violent man. I only joined the army because I thought it was the right thing to do. I'm not so sure now."

"This war ain't gon' change shit," LeRoi said. "The rich'll still be rich and the poor'll still be poor. And if you're white, you're alright and, if you're black, get back! That ain't gon' change."

"I listened to DuBois and it sounded like he was on to something with his 'Fight the war now and put the struggle on hold.' It still seems like the right thing, but I really didn't think I would be fighting other Americans no matter what their beliefs. I could never write about this. No one would believe it."

"Believe this: sometimes I don't know which way to point my rifle. They all the same to me. I was lookin' at their bodies," LeRoi indicated McGraw's squad with a wave of his hand. "The only difference is their uniforms. They look like Germans. Shit, they is Germans!"

They entered the depot and saw André tending to Slick on the floor. By the color of his face and the glassy look in his eyes, they could tell he was dying. Professor laid his rifle down and knelt beside Slick. André continued to work on Slick's other side, trying to stanch the flow of blood.

"I guess McGraw's boys must be dead, if you and LT is walkin' in here, Professor," Slick whispered.

"Yes, they're dead, but we paid for it dearly," Professor answered. "Sarge is dead and you're hit pretty bad."

"At least I won't have to kill him now," Slick tried to laugh but gurgled instead. He raised his hand to LeRoi. "We still bunk mates, we still friends, ain't we, LT?"

LeRoi grasped Slick's hand and said, "Until the end of time, Bubba. Until the end of time."

"I need you to promise me—" A spasm racked Slick's body. His voice was noticeably weaker when he continued speaking. "I need you to promise me that you'll go to Harlem and buy a round of drinks on me at Daddy Sweets' International Tavern on Lennox Avenue. Let my people know I died fighting crackers."

"We'll say 'Slick Walters sent us,' " Professor said, holding on to Slick's other hand.

"Better say, 'Eddie Walters,' " Slick advised. "Slick is a handle I got since I joined the army. And find my sister and give her my share and see—" He coughed to clear his throat. He looked from LeRoi to Professor and back. There was fear in his eyes. "I'm gon' die, but I don't want to die a nigger! I ain't no nigger! I ain't no nigger, is I?"

"When you started to fight back, you stopped bein' a nigger!" LeRoi assured him. "McGraw and his squad ain't gon' be botherin' nobody else. You and Sergeant Williams is part of the struggle and we gon' remember you that way!"

Slick whispered, " 'Til the end of time. 'Til—" His voice faltered and stopped.

Professor stood up and grabbed his rifle. He pushed past LeRoi saying, "I'm going to be sick."

LeRoi looked down at Slick's lifeless body and shook his head. The sergeant was dead. Evans was dead. LeRoi was too overwhelmed for sadness. The line between life and death seemed to be growing thinner as each day passed. One moment a man was alive, the next moment he was dead. When LeRoi stood up he wondered whether he too was also destined to die on foreign soil in some nameless valley—whether he, like Slick, would be left unburied to rot and draw flies. LeRoi suppressed the question. He was planning on living at least as far as New Orleans.

André closed Slick's eyes and stood up. "The bridge. We go now to the bridge, yes?"

"No, first I finish with McGraw."

"*Il est mort.* He is dead. He hit head on lamppost when he fall, much blood. It is finished. We go bridge now, yes?"

"Yes." LeRoi nodded.

"Your name?" André asked as they walked out of the depot.

"LeRoi Tremain."

"How you spell?"

LeRoi had to spell it out several times before André understood.

"Ah, *Le Roi*," André said, giving it the French pronunciation. "*C'est vrai. Vous êtes le Roi du Mort.* You are the King of Death."

"I like that, 'The King.' That shows," he said with a wink at Professor, "I'm livin' as a man!"

WEDNESDAY, MARCH 13, 1918

The plaintive blues notes of a guitar resonated in spite of a steady, frigid breeze that came from the north and rushed through the city of canvas tents. It was six-thirty in the evening. The glow of twilight was still in the night sky. There were smells that not even the cold could suppress: cooked meat and human waste, depending upon which way the wind blew. It promised to be another cold night because the sky was cloudless. The stars had not yet emerged in their brilliance and the moon was low on the horizon. The temperature had been in the thirties for nearly two weeks. Not cold enough to kill, but enough to stiffen joints and make sleeping occasionally difficult.

Big Ed was sitting in his tent in a broken-down camp chair, talking to Professor and Sergeant King Tremain. His two visitors were sitting on the two cots cramped together because the remainder of the space in the tent was taken up with cases of musical equipment. "When did you guys get in?"

Professor answered, "King and I got in from the front a couple of days ago. We would've come to visit sooner. But we've been busy with picking up new uniforms and getting our transfer papers."

Big Ed set down his tin and turned to King. "I want to ask you a question and it's sort of what you call, uh, awkward, uh, LT. I hear just about everybody callin' you 'King' now. I know you don't like bein' called out of your name, but I knew you as LT. I sort got used to . . . uh—"

"You can call me LT, Big Ed. You one of my Ace Boons. I know where yo' heart is."

Big Ed smiled and said, "I know how you got made sergeant, but I don't rightly remember anybody calling you King before I got transferred, unless it was those mountain fighters by Kastledorf Bridge," Big Ed said.

"It don't matter. I just like it better than LeRoi. For some reason I ain't never liked the name LeRoi," King answered.

Professor explained, "You're right, Big Ed; it all started back at the bridge after LT chased Lieutenant McHenry, God rest his soul, into that minefield. Then Smitty and some of the boys began calling him King because the 'Lion' fighters were calling him the King of Death. Soon everyone was calling him King."

"I guess that slipped my mind. I was transferred down here in January and by mid-February stories were drifting in 'bout Sergeant King Tremain and his suicide squad."

"We came here to talk about something else," Professor reminded his two companions. "Big Ed, we've got to get back. We've been assigned latrine duty tonight on Duck Mountain. So I want to make sure you fellows know what's happening before we start gabbing and losing track of time. I just got a letter from my mother saying that the three heavy trunks that we shipped have arrived safely. My father is looking into having a few of the coins appraised for authenticity and value. He won't make any deals or do anything without our approval. My father thinks that our money worries are over because even if we just sold the gold for its weight, we'd have nearly eight thousand dollars a piece."

"Eight thousand dollars!" Big Ed exclaimed. "We's rich! It only take seven hundred to pay off my father's whole mortgage! We's rich, man!"

"Slick's got an equal share?" King asked.

"Of course, just like you said," Professor answered.

"Good, then it's alright with me," King said. "I just want the man to get his dying wish."

"Eight thousand dollars, that'll buy a mess of livestock," Big Ed clapped his hands.

"A real good brownstone in Brooklyn costs about five, six hundred dollars. With this money, I'll own my own home and go back to law school," Professor said.

Big Ed teased King. "You keep winning at cards and dice the way you did the last time you were in camp and you'll be takin' that much money home with you, Sarge. The way I hears it, you was out there shearing the sheep of all their wool."

"A man shouldn't come to the table to play at games of chance unless he's prepared to lose," King said with a slight smile.

"Way I hears it," Big Ed said with laugh, "you takes all the chance out of it and worse, you make the cheaters pay."

"Oh!" Professor had an incredulous look as he said, "I heard something about King taking a strong magnet to a dice game and after some GI made his third seven in a row, he pulled out a magnet and sucked the man's dice off the blanket."

"Then hit the man upside his head with the butt of a pistol," Big Ed added. "I was there. It was somethin' else. You should write that down in your book, Professor. You gon' have a helluva story."

"I'll write it in my diary, but nobody will believe that I just recorded events. Nobody wants to believe the terrible insanity, stupidity, and bigotry of this war. I didn't want to believe it myself until it was pushed in my face," Professor said. "If I published my diary, it would have to be as fiction and the problem with fiction is that it has to be believable. What we've seen and done isn't believable."

There was a moment of silence, interrupted by a loud tapping on the tent pole outside.

"Who is it?" called out Big Ed.

"Captain Grey," a voice answered.

"Come on in, Cap'n," Big Ed said, as they all scrambled to their feet.

Captain Weldon Grey ducked under the canvas flap and returned the salute of the tent's occupants. Big Ed tried to offer him his chair, but the captain waved him off and took a seat on the cot beside Professor.

"You don't have much room in here," the captain commented as he looked around.

"Them cases ain't mine," Big Ed explained. "I got a sergeant from the Three hundred Sixty-ninth bunkin' with me. He's some kind of musician and he's got guys comin' at all hours of the night. Some nights I can't get no rest."

"You ought to talk with 'em, make 'em understand," Grey directed. He nodded to both Professor and King and said, "I'm glad to see you men here. I need to talk with both of you." Weldon Grey of the Bostonian Greys traced his ancestry directly to Crispus Attucks. His family boasted that it had sons fighting in every major American war starting with the American Revolution, so it was only natural that Weldon, a college graduate, should be admitted to officer training school for Negro soldiers at Fort Dodge, outside of Des Moines. He was among the more popular of the colored officers because he was known to stand up for his men.

"You need to speak to us, Captain?" Professor questioned. It wasn't often that an officer at the rank of captain took the time to talk to enlisted men other than to discharge commands.

"Yes, Morris, I've got some regimental news and some camp news that will interest both of you, but first I need to cover some things with Corporal Harrison, our mechanical wizard." Captain Grey turned to face Big Ed. "Did you get those brake parts I requested?"

"Yes, sir! But Sergeant O'Shaughnessy had them installed on Captain Davidson's trucks." Captain Davidson was a white officer who commanded an infantry transport division similar to Captain Grey's, except that Captain Davidson and his men were all white.

"Was my name and rank on the transport order?" Grey asked.

"Yes, sir. It was made out to your division, with your army posting." Big Ed answered.

"It's my job to keep twenty-five trucks and five jeeps oiled and running. Since there's an official record, I'll have to report this to my commanding officer."

"There's another way," Big Ed suggested. "Captain Kocian has a shipment of brake parts sitting on the other side the truck depot."

"What are you proposing, Harrison?"

"Well, me and a couple of grease monkeys could probably do three trucks a night until they catch us. They checks storage 'bout every two weeks. We might could get as many as fifteen trucks done, maybe more."

"Damn good idea! Get started on that ASAP! Requisition any assistance you need from my lieutenant. If I have to steal to keep running, I'll do it. Meanwhile, I'll take O'Shaughnessy's decisions up with Command."

Captain Grey turned to Professor and King and smiled. He was a handsome man with a pronounced widow's peak, a broad, flat nose, and a flashing smile. "It's pretty clear, the Three hundred Fifty-first Infantry Battalion is no more. I think there's only about seven or eight men, including you two, who are left from that battalion. It will become a ghost battalion. The losses that the Three hundred Fifty-first suffered are so great compared to the losses of the white battalions that were on the front lines at the same time, that the only logical conclusion is that you men were used as cannon fodder. Since the army won't admit that, the whole battalion will disappear from the record books."

"How does that affect us, sir?" Professor asked.

"You and the remnants of your squad have been transferred to the Three hundred Sixty-ninth Regiment effective immediately. They're short one sergeant and lieutenant and they need to fill out a couple of squads. You'll maintain your stripes, Sergeant Tremain. They know you men have been tested in action. They're going to move out early Sunday morning. They've been attached to the French army, which is situated for the big push toward the Marne. You have a choice: you can be reassigned to the Red Ball Express and work in my division or you can be assigned the Three hundred Sixty-ninth Regiment and participate in the big offensive this fall."

"I want to go with the Three hundred Sixty-ninth," King said without hesitation. "I already picked up my uniform." King displayed the regimental emblem of the coiled white rattler on his shoulder.

"The cap'n's givin' you a chance to get off the front line, man!" Big Ed could not believe his ears. "We could be together. No more dodgin' bullets all the time." Big Ed looked from King to Professor.

Professor returned his look for a moment, then turned to Grey and said, "Thank you for the opportunity, Captain, but I too have already picked up my uniform. I want to go with the Three hundred Sixty-ninth. Please don't take it as a reflection of our esteem for you."

The captain shook his head in disbelief. "You men baffle me. You've been in the frontline trenches since you got here. From what I've heard, you've done a lot of suicide missions and have done more of your share of putting your life on the line than most. No one would dispute your courage or your patriotism if you chose to serve the remainder of this war behind the lines. The Red Ball Express has its esprit de corps. We do an important job. Without us, the war cannot be won. You'd be doing honorable work. You have until this Friday to change your minds. I hope you men will give my offer careful consideration."

Grey coughed and continued. "I've heard that there is gambling going on and that soldiers under my command are participating in it. The High Command might have overlooked this had it not been coupled with violence." At this point Grey gave King a hard look before continuing. "I know I don't have to quote you men the army article that prohibits gambling, but let me tell you this. HQ has put out a bulletin on this matter and they intend to come down hard on anybody they catch, particularly if they happen to be Negro soldiers. Do I need to speak any clearer?"

"They don't say nothin' about the bare-knuckle bouts?" King asked. "A couple men been beat damn near to death and lot of bettin' and gamblin' goes on during the fights."

"I think their major concern is high-stakes card games where white players are often left penniless and owing Negro soldiers their army pay for the rest of the year," Grey answered. "HQ probably recognizes that you can't stop everything and as long as the fights are kept out of their view, they'll continue to look the other way."

Captain Grey stood up. "Alright men, remain as you were. Corporal Harrison, get your team together for tonight. I'll have three trucks ready for you to start on by midnight. And Sergeant Tremain, heed my warning. You're a good soldier and a leader among the men. I'd hate to see you get court-martialed for gambling!" Captain Grey saluted and left the tent.

Big Ed waited until the captain left and sputtered, "I don't know what's wrong with you guys. He offered you positions behind the lines. You got a real good chance making it through the war alive."

"Working as a porter and stevedore?" Professor asked. "I've taken too much humiliation to become a soldier to give it up. As long as the army wants me in a menial job, I prefer to carry a gun!"

"Menial, that's just a word!" Big Ed said. "All that matters is that you live through the war. Now that I'm working as a mechanic in motorized transport, I ain't had to lift a gun in months."

"You's called a porter. They didn't make you no mechanic, you just work as a mechanic. If they made you a mechanic, the white boys would shit a brick," King observed. "They treat you like shit and they know you know ten times more than they do about truck repair, but they still treat you like shit!"

"If I'm alive and healthy at the end of the war, bein' treated like shit will be worth it," Big Ed answered. "I got me some farm work in my future. I'm looking forward to feeling that dark Nebraska soil between my fingers."

"Ain't nothin' I want that is worth takin' shit for," King said.

"That's 'cause you don't really want nothin'. If you wanted somethin', you'd sacrifice your pride," Big Ed said.

"You got it wrong," King answered. "I do want somethin', but there ain't nothin' I want more than bein' my own man." King stood up and made his way out of the tent. Big Ed and Professor followed him out. "Ask Professor why he chose to go back to the front. He say he ain't a man of violence."

It was brisk and cold. The brightness of the stars were dimmed some-what by the bright perimeter lights around the encampment. The three men stood in front of several long rows of tents, many of which were lit by the glow of kerosene lamps, and heard the sounds of men laughing and talking as well as the clanking of engines and machinery.

Rubbing his hands for warmth, Big Ed asked Professor, "Why did you choose to go back to the front? It sure don't seem smart."

"Because I'm fed up with all this prejudice and I can't seem to escape it as long as I'm around American whites! This bullshit with the brakes is just another part of an unrelenting saga of whites needing to keep us down in the midst of fighting a war. You'd think that they would want to concentrate on their enemies."

Professor waved his hand beyond the camp, indicating the German lines. "The war is much clearer to me when I'm out there, especially if I'm going to be fighting alongside the French. The enemy is clearer. The enemy is always the Germans.

"I came here to fight for my country and show that my people are worthy of being treated as first-class citizens. Yet I see for every victory we win, it's being discounted or attributed to someone else. It's driving me crazy. For all the blood that has been spilt, not a damn thing has been proven. The Three hundred Fifty-first will be wiped off the record books as if it never existed! All those colored men who died will never get credit for their courage and sacrifice!"

"That's the problem with all them rules and morals and shit you got, Professor; the world don't care 'bout that," King said, bending down to touch his toes. The cot had made him slightly stiff. "The world don't care about that. It gon' do what it has always done. The strong take all and the hell with the meek. You tryin' to hold on to them rules while the world's going crazy is like a mouse tryin' to cross a meadow durin' a cattle stampede. The whole world's shakin' around you. It don't matter how fast you run or how good you do whatever you doin', if you don't find a hole soon, and a deep one, it's your butt."

"Ain't you got no rules, LT?" Big Ed asked.

"I just got two rules: be courageous and don't take no shit!"

SATURDAY, MARCH 16, 1918

Sergeant Bull Robinson was one of the top knuckle fighters in camp. Not as tall as King, he had tremendously long, powerful arms and fists as big as hams. He was a bully with a vicious streak. When King and Professor stumbled into Bull pummeling a soldier from the 369th behind the mess hall, they put an end to the fight and Bull's bad intentions. After a minor scuffle, it was decided that King and Bull would fight over the scratch line in the warehouse behind the armory on Saturday.

The word of the fight spread through the camp. Most everyone had seen Bull Robinson in action, but only a few had witnessed King. The cardplayers and gamblers had seen King dispatch a few poor losers, but none of those were on par with Bull. Still the cold-blooded efficiency of King's actions prior to the MPs' arrival was often brought up in discussion. There were those who thought it was only Bull's agility that saved him from getting his throat cut and had King followed up on his advantage, there might not be a need for another fight.

Beyond the dispute of which man would win, it was King's words that captured everyone's interest. "I didn't come to play. I came to kill." The Negro barbers even turned it into a joke while they were cutting hair. One would say in a high voice, "You got a knife!" His companion would respond in a low voice, "So what? I told you, I didn't come to play."

The soldiers of the 369th had no knowledge of King other than that he was battle-tested, but many knew Willis Broadwater, the man who had been beaten by Bull Robinson before King and Professor interceded. Willis was one of the premier drummers in the regimental band and good friends with Sergeant Jim Europe, the regimental bandleader who shared the tent with Big Ed. Tempers were running hot; there were many voices raised in support of vengeance. All the next day, there were rumblings that the 369th would march on the Sixth Infantry Transport Division, but cooler heads prevailed. It was decided that any vengeance be planned after the impending fight, if it was necessary. Sergeant Europe held several meetings in Big Ed's tent with other regimental sergeants from the 369th and they decided to make sure that the fight would be well attended by their soldiers.

At three o'clock on the day of the fight, Big Ed showed up at King and Professor's tent with a newly oiled and cleaned Lewis machine gun wrapped up in a blanket. "Just in case," was all he said.

The warehouse where the fight was designated to take place was a large, high-ceilinged room made out of corrugated tin and was set on a cement foundation. Seats were arranged by stacking crates in rising steps against the four walls. The ring was a rectangle of bare, unpolished cement. The fight was scheduled to start at six. At five o'clock King walked in with Big Ed and the remaining four members of his squad. The place was jam-packed with soldiers. There were at least four hundred soldiers seated, shoulder to shoulder, on the crates around the fighting area. A silence fell over the crowd as King entered. It was the silence of anticipation as all heads turned and watched. It was eerie because an unsupervised group of enlisted men are always roisterous and noisy and yet in the whole vast, echoing tin box, there was only the sound of King and his friends walking to the far edge of the ring where there a table and three chairs were set up. It was several seconds before conversation began anew. Professor surreptitiously directed squad members to various positions throughout the warehouse. Big Ed took up position at the table as one of King's seconds.

At five-thirty Bull Robinson appeared with his entourage. There was no cheering or noise for his arrival either. In the silence there was an expectation that was electric. The psyche of four hundred men licked its collective lips. There was muted discussion among Bull's party and a person was chosen to approach the scratch line, which had been drawn bisecting the fighting area. Professor went to meet Bull's emissary. Another brief discussion ensued and Professor walked back to the table to talk with King and Big Ed.

"What do they want?" Big Ed asked.

"They want us to announce that there are no rules, no rounds will be called, that the scratch line will only be used at the beginning of the fight, and that we have requested 'to the death.' "

"Fine with me," agreed King.

As Professor approached the scratch line, Bull's second called out, "This is hand-to-hand, kicking permitted. No weapons allowed. Each fighter will step to the scratch line and let himself be checked by his opponent's second."

Professor called in the same manner, "There are no rules. If a man is down the fight continues. No rounds will be called. To the death, unless stopped by seconds. A towel thrown into the ring will serve as surrender."

King stepped to the line bare-chested; all he had taken off was his shirt. He had filled out considerably since joining the army and he now possessed the muscular bulk to go with his six-foot-two-inch height. He didn't wear special clothes. He wore his regular army fatigues and GI boots. King had a slight smile on his face as he was patted down. Bull Robinson, on the other hand, was the height of fashion. He wore a red silk robe and had real boxing shoes on his feet. When he doffed his robe, underneath he wore red-and-black fighting tights. The sweat was pouring off of the dark brown skin of his face. He had been warming up before he came into the warehouse. Bull raised arms to the crowd and then shadowboxed until he was directly opposite King. Bull pointed at King and shouted, "I'm gon' get you! I'm gon' get you!" while Professor patted him down.

"Seconds out" was called and the fight began. It started with a feeling-out session. The two men circled each other. Bull took several arcing swings, but King easily eluded them. King was taller than his opponent by a good four inches, but there was no reach advantage due to Bull's long arms. King stepped in as a feint and Bull responded with an awkward kick that was telegraphed before it arrived.

King saw something shiny on the tip of Bull's shoe as it missed him. Bull had nails sewn into his shoes. It made King laugh out loud. It was humorous, as if the nails would make the difference. King was confident in himself. He wanted to get close to the man, feel his flesh in his hands. He didn't want to waste energy with punches unless he could cripple or hurt. He was searching for openings and patterns between Bull's hands, seeking a spot to repeatedly attack. King sidestepped a clubbing overhand right and lunged, striking to put out an eye with one of his outstretched fingers. Bull ducked his head at the last moment and spun away. King laughed again.

There was a slight cut just below Bull's eyebrow and a trickle of blood ran down his face. Bull beat his chest with his fists and yelled, "Come on! Let's fight!" He started forward, swinging forcefully, hoping to connect. King dodged his first few swings easily. He blocked another overhand right, but Bull saw King's right shoulder move backward as if to throw a punch and swung his own left hook swiftly before King could react. It landed almost flush on the side of King's head and Bull saw him stagger. Unable to contain himself, Bull attacked with both hands swinging, but was only able to land glancing blows on King's shoulders and arms. Bull drew back his fist, ready to put all his force into the next punch, when King lowered his head and charged into his chest. The force of the charge hit Bull in his sternum, lifting him off his feet and knocking him backward to land heavily on the cement. He rolled to his feet but he was hurting. The cement had delivered its own strike.

King laughed again. This time it was from deep within him. He had felt the numbing force of Bull's attack, but he had also seen a weakness, one that would lead quickly to death. He moved in on Bull, trying to lure him into throwing the clubbing overhand right. King had seen that Bull was almost off balance when he finished throwing that punch. He was vulnerable from an attack from his right. Bull was wary now and he refused to be drawn into an attack. King shifted from side to side trying to press his opponent, but Bull backed away.

Finally, King walked back to the center of the scratch line and said loudly, "If you want to fight, come to the scratch line. Otherwise take your cowardly ass home!"

Bull was incensed. "Let's fight, sucker!" Bull came forward swinging, thinking that King was now planning to fight his fight. He did not live long enough to discover his mistake. As soon as Bull threw his overhand right, King lunged under it and attacked from the side, grabbing Bull's throat in a vicelike grip with his right hand. Bull, attempting to escape the hold on his neck, moved backward, thrashing his arms. King was ready and leg-swept him, causing him to fall backward toward the cement. Pulling Bull's head back with his left hand, King forced Bull's head and shoulders to fall across his knee, breaking Bull's neck with a loud snap in the process. Bull's body jerked spastically, but he was dead in seconds.

King pushed the lifeless body off of him, stood up, then went to stand at the scratch line. After several seconds, he returned to the table and put on his shirt. He had barely broken a sweat. There was silence again. This time it was a stunned and shocked silence.

A voice called out, "That weren't no boxin'! That weren't no fair fight!" It was one of Bull's seconds. His entourage had moved out to surround the body. Another man in the group pointed at King and shouted, "He's a murderer! We should arrest his ass!"

King picked up the bundle of blankets in which the Lewis was wrapped and placed it on the table. He unwrapped the gun casually without the slightest hint of urgency. When he picked it up and swung it in the direction of Bull's people, a deeper silence fell upon the crowd. Everyone waited for what the next few seconds would bring.

"You was sayin'?" King prompted the man who had accused him. The man shook his head in fear and attempted to back behind the others in his group, but they all backed up with him. They continued until Bull's body once more lay in front of them. Then they stopped.

A Southern voice high up on the crates, belonging to a soldier of the 369th, yelled out, "I came to kill! I came to kill!" Suddenly the chant was taken up by soldiers all around the warehouse until it was hundreds of voices strong. "I came to kill! I came to kill!" The soldiers began to stamp their feet in time to the chant. "I came to kill! I came to kill!" The soldiers were like long-caged animals that had been released. The chant grew louder. No doubt some of the energy derived from the fact that most Negro soldiers were restricted to support functions and only a very small percent saw action as gun-carrying warriors. The irony of the chant was not lost on the men; it was a declaration against the servile brand that had been placed upon them and they took it to their bosom.

Big green military transport trucks rumbled back and forth continuously in the bright morning light, carrying soldiers of "Little Harlem" to the site of the victory parade in downtown Manhattan. Platoons of colored soldiers were marching to their embarkation points to stand at parade rest until their transportation arrived. Little Harlem was the common name used for the segregated area of the army base in which the colored soldiers of the 369th Battalion were bivouacked. The name was particularly appropriate because the vast majority of soldiers in the 369th were from the New York National Guard and most of them were citizens of New York City.

There was a shortage of Quonset huts at Groton army base due to the numbers of soldiers of all races demobilizing at the center; therefore, there were never enough for colored soldiers. Once again they were billeted in tents. It was cold, but for some strange reason it wasn't as cold as France or Germany. They were on home soil. The colored soldiers didn't spend much time complaining because ample leave was given and most didn't have to spend a lot of time on the base. After all, New York City was only a two-and-a-half-hour ride by bus. For the most part, the men were impatient to be demobilized and to return to their civilian lives. This day, however, was different. It was the day the City of New York was going to recognize its own and allow the 369th to march through Manhattan into Harlem.

There were three soldiers sitting on a bench beside a large stack of musical equipment cases in front of neat rows upon rows of canvas tents. They were musicians. One was maintaining a complex tapping rhythm with a pair of drumsticks on a wooden bench. His two companions were humming out a ragtime melody through their brass mouthpieces. The trucks continued to roll past with engines growling and the shriek of brakes. The air was also full of the sounds of sergeants barking out step orders to marching platoons of soldiers whose leather boot steps gave meter to the surrounding chaos. The three soldiers continued with their tune. Each man appeared to take his contribution quite seriously. One of the men with a brass mouthpiece found a particularly hip-gyrating melodic air that he repeated until the other musician played a countertempo harmony beneath it. The drummer acknowledged the creativeness of his companions with a percussive combination that changed the emphasis of the beat. The musicians interwove their individual strands of music together into a simple, textured braid that evoked the mood and temper of Harlem on a Saturday night.

They might have continued playing for some time had they not been interrupted. A dark-skinned man, wearing the uniform of the 369th and carrying a snare drum, interrupted them rudely.

"Have you niggers seen Jim?"

"You talkin' about Lieutenant Europe?" the drummer asked without warmth.

"Yeah, I'm talkin' about him. Ain't you got ears, nigger? Who the hell else would I be askin' for?"

"Jimmy Dobson, Jim Walker," the drummer answered, not allowing himself to be provoked.

"Then there's James Hewlit, Jim Witherspoon, Jim Doggett," volunteered the taller of the men playing the brass mouthpiece.

"He ain't here yet, Tyrone," the third man said. There was a look of concern in his eyes. "We're waitin' for him."

"You see that shit," Tyrone exclaimed. "Only my brother, Maurice, talks straight. That's why I ain't got no time for you suckers!"

"It's mutual," the taller man answered and began to blow a melody in his mouthpiece. The drummer picked up his cue and began to beat out a counterrhythm.

Tyrone didn't take the hint. He stood fast and asked his brother, "Mo, did you talk to him about me? I got me a fine little sister ready to come to our first gig. I just got to know when it is."

"I ain't had a chance to talk with him," Maurice explained. "He been staying off base on leave. I'll ask him about it today when I see him. If'en I was you, I wouldn't put too much hope in it though, since he already done said no."

"I ain't askin' to be in the travelin' band," Tyrone protested. "I just wants to be one of the house drummers when he open his club. Sometimes he got as many as two, three drummers in the house band. I'm as good as any one of them."

"Hey, Thigpin! Your bus is boardin'. If you're going to the parade, you better get on now!" A sergeant was walking toward the group. "You hear me, Tyrone?" the sergeant demanded.

"Yeah, yeah, I hear you," Tyrone answered in a disgruntled tone. "You remember to ask him, Mo!" Tyrone said as he turned and trotted away.

"I will, Ty," Maurice called after his brother.

Maurice's two companions stopped their duet as soon as Tyrone departed and watched him climb aboard his bus.

"Mo, why don't you tell your brother the truth, man? Why don't you tell him he can't play?" the other mouthpiece man asked.

"That's my kid brother, Slim. How am I gon' tell him that? That's a hard punch in the stomach and I don't have the heart to do it. I can't do it."

"Slim is right, ol' son," the drummer said. "Best you do it, then you can kinda' go gentle and slow with it. If you leaves it to somebody else, they gon' land on him with both feets."

Slim nodded his head in agreement and said, by way of confirmation, "He got the same chops now that he had when we first heard him. He ain't woodshedded or done nothin' to improve hisself!"

"I just can't do it. He's the reason I'm in the band."

"There's Lieutenant Europe," the drummer said, pointing across the parade grounds at a shiny new car stopping in front of Colonel Hayward's office.

"What kind of car is that?" Slim asked as he saw four men get out of the vehicle.

"Damned if I know," Maurice answered as he too watched as Jim Europe entered Hayward's office alone, leaving his three companions to wait on the porch. "Seems to me everybody got a car now. When I left for the service, there was only a couple of car companies, now there's seven or eight, maybe more."

"Who is that young-looking sergeant standing on the porch with Sissle?" Slim asked.

"You don't know King Tremain?" Maurice asked with surprise. "Sergeant King Tremain?"

"The 'I came to kill' Tremain? I thought that was just a made-up story. I didn't know he was real," Slim answered.

"It's a story alright," confirmed Maurice. He pointed to the drummer. "But ain't nothin' made up. Willis was there!"

"I fought on the line with him and I'll tell you, he's a killing machine," Maurice said. "When you were in his platoon, you didn't have to worry about getting stupid orders more than once. Lieutenants and captains disappeared by the handful. And if the truth be told, he should have been awarded two or three Croix de Guerre medals. He even went back across the lines for Lieutenant Cameron and carried his ass to safety. He is one crazy Negro." Maurice laughed humorlessly and continued speaking. "He and members of his squad used to sneak across German lines, without orders, just to kill German soldiers for their guns and equipment. I tell you, I was only too happy to hear from my brother and learn that the regimental band needed a trumpet player. I transferred immediately. That King Tremain is scary!"

A company of colored soldiers marched past, led by a white lieutenant. The three men waited until the sound of marching feet diminished before continuing their conversation. There was a squeal of brakes as a troop carrier screeched to a stop when the company marched in front of it.

"Maurice, you hit it, ol' son," Willis agreed, continuing the discussion. "He ain't no regular human. He ain't twenty-one yet, but you could go a long way before you found somebody as cold-blooded as him."

"What's Lieutenant Europe doin' hangin' around with a guy like that for?" Slim asked.

"He and that short man that's with him gon' be backers in Jim's new club," answered Willis.

"So that's why he was askin' if I want to stay in New York," Slim exclaimed. "I thought he was goin' to do some kinda travelin' revue. I didn't know he was openin' a new club."

"What do you think Tyrone was goin' on about?" asked Willis.

"Let's take that tune from the top," Maurice suggested, blowing the first few bars through his mouthpiece.

When King Tremain got out of the transport truck on Thirty-fourth Street in downtown Manhattan, he was awed again by the size of the buildings. He had spent two weeks in the city, but the sensation that the sky seemed farther away had not abated. He shouted orders to his platoon to assemble in the tight marching formation utilized by the French army. He quick-marched his unit into position. The sound of his platoon's precision marching filled him with a sense of power. He liked to hear forty soldiers' boots hit the pavement simultaneously so that each step taken was taken as if by one man.

After a half hour of standing in formation, the regimental band began to play the "Battle Hymn of the Republic." The whole regiment of thirteen hundred men began to quick-march up Thirty-fourth Street in tight formations. Every man was in step as the sea of olive and brown swept like a wave. It was a sight that had never been seen in the United States. The 369th Infantry Colored Regiment home from war, battered and bruised, but triumphant. Denied the chance to participate in the victory parades in Paris by the American War Department, who didn't want Negro soldiers receiving accolades, the 369th was given a warrior's welcome by New York City.

Everywhere he looked, King saw smiling faces, and for a brief moment he wondered if things would actually be different. People clogged the sidewalks, waving and shouting. Pieces of paper fell from the sky like oversized snowflakes. It was only the sound of leather boots striking pavement that

kept him from being distracted in the pandemonium of a ticker tape parade. He felt an immense pride as well as gratitude that at least this war effort by colored Americans was getting recognized.

The band switched to a rapid-paced marching tune and the 369th trotted onto Fifth Avenue, heading uptown. The onlookers realized that the
units parading before them were not ornamental military showpieces but
hardened fighting men whose dented helmets and rusted bayonets had
been earned in battle. These were real soldiers who had fought for over six
months in the trenches in northern France. Their victory was not without
price. They had left eight hundred men dead on foreign soil.

The 369th broke into a trot four blocks before the reviewing stand and
shouted "Hell Fighters! Hell Fighters!" in cadence to every twelfth step.
The people along the route of the parade marveled at the precision of
thirteen hundred men, but when the troops broke into a trot and began to
shout in cadence, the crowd became frenetic. The echoing voices of thirteen hundred men ricocheting in the cement canyons turned into a flash
flood of sound.

King Tremain, marching five steps in front of his platoon, stared at the
faces on the reviewing stand and noted that there was not one colored
face among them. It was not enough to dampen the exhilaration he felt in
his heart, but he realized that the war would not make a difference in the
lives of colored folk. King was beginning to perspire in his heavy wool uniform, but he ignored it, focusing instead on watching women out of the
corner of his eye. There were many beautiful black and brown women all
along the parade route. King felt the compelling need for some genuine
female companionship and affection, rather than the purchased professional sexual attention he had had in the past. It was the only worry on his
mind.

The band started another military marching tune and King called out
the requisite change in step. The regiment held its tight formations as it
marched past blocks and blocks of waving onlookers. All the music played
by the band were classic military marches until the 369th entered Harlem.
At 125th Street, the band began to play "Here Comes My Daddy" and the
huge black presence that was Harlem threw back its head and laughed to
the heavens, exposing flashing white teeth, then reached out its massive
arms to welcome its fighters home. From every lamppost and building flew
pennants and banners bearing the insignia of the white rattler. From the
windows to the rooftops, there were colored people cheering the returning fathers and sons and nephews. Women ran out into the street to
march arm in arm with the soldiers.

The tight formation of the units spread out as bystanders flocked into the street to join in the historic victory march. It was a time when a victory for any colored man was a victory for all. The people of Harlem felt they had a right to march with the 369th. Had they not fought the same battle on the home front? They too suffered losses, not only sons lost in the war, but in the daily indignities and constant bigotry of everyday life. So, in the year of race riots, lynchings, and Klan resurgence, Harlem dearly needed the victory that the 369th brought home, and it needed to see its young black men come marching home with heads held high.

By the time he reached the reviewing stands at 130th Street, King had a woman on each arm and appeared to have no trouble in talking to either of them.

TUESDAY, FEBRUARY 25, 1919

The corner office was large and elegantly furnished with lush leather chairs and polished tables. Two walls of the office were taken up by floor-to-ceiling windows that looked down on the traffic of Fifth Avenue fifteen floors below. King had never been in a building so high above the ground, and he felt uneasy as he walked over to the window and looked out over the cityscape. He recognized that he was in the presence of wealth and it made him feel distrustful of the person in whose office he was waiting.

King turned to Professor and Big Ed. "You sure we can trust this man?"

"He's treated me fairly," Professor answered. "Also, Ira Goldbaum served as a lieutenant in the Three hundred Sixty-ninth and all the colored soldiers who served under him have good things to say about him."

"Yeah, I remember the name. But we talkin' about money now, and money brings out greed in a man," King rejoined.

"We've got to trust someone," Professor advised. "We don't have the contacts to deal with the gold coins or the jewelry. If you want to wait a couple of years, we might be able to work out a currency exchange, but even then we should be represented by an attorney. Goldbaum is teaching law at Columbia and he is helping me reenroll in college. I knew him before I enlisted. He was one of my law professors and he'll probably be one of my law professors again. I think he's our best bet."

"I didn't risk my life to go back to Côte d'Saar for those other two boxes of gold to throw it all away now," King replied.

Further conversation was inhibited by the entrance of a tall, thin, blond-haired white man who had a large beak of a nose and penetrating blue eyes. The man walked with a cane and his limp was pronounced. His right leg was stiff at the knee. King turned to face the man and recognized him. King had saved his life one late afternoon in northern France. He had found the man with a shattered leg, lying at the bottom of a trench into which mustard gas was seeping, and had pulled him out. King reached out and shook the hand that was offered him.

The man, as if reading his mind, said, "I'm Ira Goldbaum. You saved my life, remember?"

"Sho'," answered King with a slight smile. He remembered the incident, but it was not a special event for him. He had acted on impulse. If the truth be told, he had almost left the man to die, except that he remembered some Negro soldiers saying good things about him. He looked at Goldbaum with greater interest. He was dressed in expensive clothes, wearing a gold watch, and his hands were manicured. The man looked as if he was doing quite well financially.

After the introductions were complete, Ira sat on the edge of his desk. "Exactly how can I help you men?"

"You ain't prosecutin' or defendin' criminals?" King asked.

"No, I work in corporate law."

"What's that?" Big Ed asked.

"I set up corporations for people with money. I set up businesses as tax shelters. I've set up investment companies. Why are you interested?"

"I just wanted to know what corporate law is," Big Ed answered.

Ira laughed. "I generally say, 'My job is to help people hide money legally,' but I provide the full range of legal services for my clients."

King's attention was piqued when Ira mentioned "hiding money legally." He had never given much consideration as to what he should do with money. King kept the money he had won gambling along with what he received from demobilization hidden in the wall of his flat. He studied Goldbaum and hoped that Professor's trust wasn't misplaced.

Professor got up from his chair and went over to the desk, placing a large golden coin on the polished surface. "We have a trunk load of these."

Ira examined the coin carefully. "Is this authentic?"

"We have gotten some offers that seem to confirm their authenticity," Professor answered. "We found them along with quite a bit of jewelry in northern France and shipped them home."

"It's a good thing you didn't divulge to the French authorities that you were in possession of these. They would have demanded that the coins be turned over immediately to the government. In fact, if I bring these to the attention of people who know about this sort of thing, there may still be some question as to how you got them."

"We've come to you to have you find us the best deal possible and to protect us from treachery," Professor spoke slowly, giving particular emphasis to the last word.

"We knows all about treachery," King added as he walked over to one of the large windows and looked down at the streets below. "And we know how to repay it."

Ira smiled. "Gentlemen, if you're asking my firm to represent you, you need not worry about treachery. I have built my reputation on honesty and fairness and I expect to continue with that code of ethics. Furthermore," he turned to face King, "I have not forgotten that you saved my life and that I am indebted to you. I repay all my debts honorably."

There was a moment of silence as King looked at his two friends. Big Ed nodded his head, indicating it was alright with him. Professor nodded his approval as well. King looked down on the traffic below. It was a long way down. He was reminded again of how fleeting life was. His thoughts touched on the realization that the pleasure of breath that Ira drew today was the result of idle conversation between colored soldiers around a campfire in the frozen mountains of northern France.

King turned to Ira. "Let's do business."

FRIDAY, MARCH 28, 1919

The lights went down and five brown-skinned women, with their hair hot-combed, tap-danced into the circle of spotlights in the Rockland Palace Revue. The rhythms tapped out by their feet were accompanied by a lone clarinet and a drummer playing a high hat. The audience sat around the circular dance floor in an intimate semidarkness that was only partially lightened by the candles on their tables.

The dancers twirled and spun through their dance steps as their truncated costumes of sequins and nets shimmered under the spots. Near the end of the act, each woman was given an opportunity to display her most difficult tap combination. As the different dancers took their turn, different instruments would join in syncopation with the tap rhythm. The first was accompanied by a stand-up bass, the second by a cornet, the next by

banjo, the fourth by saxophone, and the last by piano. The women dancing with the banjo and the piano accompanists received the loudest applause.

As the lights went up and the dancers trooped back to their dressing
rooms, Big Ed was enthusiastic. He stood up and applauded loudly. "Did
you see that big-leg girl? Man, that honey was lookin' good! Lord! Lord!"

"Sit down, Big Ed, there's more to come," Jim Europe said with a laugh.
"You act like you just got out of the army a couple a weeks ago."

"I did just get out!" Big Ed said. "I got demobbed same time as you
boys." His consternation caused a chuckle around the table.

"I think he's talking about that lean and hungry look you got on your
face, Big Ed," Noble Sissle said. "You look like you could've eaten that girl
alive."

"Shoot, just let me get under her hood and check out those pistons and
I'll be goin' like sixty," Big Ed confirmed.

King smiled and said, "Hold on, Big Ed. I think the boys are tryin' to
pull your coat. Because if you look that hungry, you gon' end up payin' for
it."

"I want to meet that girl, Jim! Can you set it up?" Big Ed persisted.

"Why don't I invite her and her friends to come to our opening-day
picnic next week?"

"You'd do that for me?" Big Ed was effusive.

"Damn, you'd think you'd given the girl to him," Noble chuckled.

"Listen, boys, I have to get backstage and get dressed for the full orchestra's appearance." Jim stood up. "I think you can rest easy with your
investment, gentlemen. It looks like we're going to make a lot of money
in this club."

"You boys is lucky that you got this deal to come together so quick,"
Noble commented, shaking his head. "If the Rockland Palace hadn't been
sitting vacant for six months, you wouldn't have been able to swing it."

"We's lucky we got our money situation straightened out so fast," Big
Ed explained. "That's what made all this possible."

"Yeah, you fellows must have found a gold mine in France," Noble
nodded. "You just got to make sure that somebody else don't end up ben-
efitting from your investment."

"Mr. Europe!" a young waiter hurried over to the table. "Mr. Europe,
some white mens is trying to force their way backstage. They said that you
wouldn't mind, but Vince sent me over to check with you." The waiter
was wearing the red waistcoat and black pants that was the club uniform.

"Tell Vince he was right to check with me," Jim said. "Direct these
men back to my office. I'll meet them there."

"Up jumped the devil!" Noble declared with a frown of disgust.

"Well, here's our first hurdle with the mob," Jim said with resignation. "You want to come back and help protect your investment?" he asked King.

"The mob you been tellin' me about?"

"The very same!" Noble answered. "An Italian underground organization that runs the protection rackets and controls all the big gambling money. They make you pay protection money in order to stay in business. Otherwise, they destroy your business. I warned you guys about this. It's why I didn't want to come in on this deal. I'm through with fighting. I don't want to ever pick up a gun again."

"It shouldn't get to that. We can afford to pay five percent off the top, but not more," Jim answered. "I just hope they aren't greedier than that."

"Let's go back and see," King suggested. There was so much about New York that he didn't understand. The strangeness and newness of the city with its millions of people sometimes threatened to overwhelm him. But strong-arm techniques were the same the world over. This was something he understood.

"You need me?" Big Ed asked, starting to rise.

"No, sit tight," King advised. "I'll be back before the show starts."

On the way to the office Jim explained his strategy. "This is the price of doing business in New York. I figured they'd come sooner or later. If we can hold them to five percent off the top, we got no problem. Let me do the talking. I've met most of these guys before. I had to pay when I ran the Clef Club too."

"Why pay them at all?" King asked.

"Because it's cheaper than going to war and I don't want to have to look over my shoulder for the rest of my life."

"Why not make them look over their shoulders?" King continued.

"I'm not a soldier now and really I never was. I'm a bandleader, a composer, and a musician. I'm not ready to do any more fighting. It's hard enough trying to arrange tunes and keep the orchestra together. I feel the same way Noble does except that this is part of my dream." Jim waved his hand around, indicating the club's red and black decor.

"You can't let people walk on you, no matter what," King asserted with a certain grimness.

"Just let me do the talking," Jim said.

"You got it," King answered, and followed with an enigmatic smile.

Vince Gilroy was standing by the curtains leading backstage with a cigarette hanging out of his mouth. He was tall, lanky, and dark skinned and had a flattened nose. The scars on his face were proof that he did not always live among the most polite company, but he was the best stage manager north of the Potomac.

"I took Minetti and his boys back to your office," Vincent said, flicking his ashes in the direction of an ashtray. "They didn't look happy to me. I think they mean to rough you up. You want me to get some help?"

"He won't need it," King answered, another smile on his face.

"Well, he's got another problem," Vince retorted, blowing a smoke ring. "Tyrone Thigpin is back there making a scene about how he should be in the house band. And he's demanding to see 'that puffed-up Europe.' "

"Buy him a drink, Vince, and tell him I'll talk with him later," Jim suggested.

"I think he's had enough fire water for this whole week."

King followed Jim through the curtains and entered a large hallway. Almost immediately they were accosted by a shouting voice. "So, you finally decided to show up at work! You done graced us with your presence!"

"Quiet! Goddamn it!" Vince hissed. "There's people with families who need the money they make here! We got a show to put on!"

Tyrone came tipping across the hallway with a sheepish smile and his finger held up to his lips as if he was telling everyone to be quiet. It was obvious from his gait that he had drunk a considerable amount of some alcoholic beverage. Although Jim attempted to brush past him, Tyrone blocked his way.

"I told everybody when you got here, we was gon' straighten this out 'cause we go back a long ways. We was overseas together. Ain't that right?" Tyrone tried to put his arm around Jim's shoulders as if indeed they were friends.

Jim pushed him away. "You're drunk and I'm busy. Why don't we talk about this later, just the two of us?" Jim made an effort to pass, but Tyrone blocked his way again.

Tyrone's expression changed from a smile to a snarl. "Ain't no reason for you to disrespect me, nigger! Don't act so high and mighty!"

"You're drunk, Tyrone. Let's talk when you're sober," Jim advised him, pushing past him even more forcefully.

A troop of six women dancers, dressed in outfits that exposed a lot of midriff and leg, exited the stage into the hallway. They were laughing and talking among themselves on their way to their dressing rooms when Tyrone grabbed Jim by the arm and swung him around roughly.

"I ain't got no need to meet with you alone! Tell these people I's your new house drummer! Tell 'em! I wants everybody to know!"

Jim gritted his teeth and muttered. "You don't work here now and you never will! I've tried to be polite, but you're a fool!"

Tyrone raised his voice. "All this is 'cause you don't like me, huh?"

Jim swung around and faced his adversary. "You're right, I don't like you, but I don't hire you because you can't play! You may think your snare drumming makes you a drummer, but to a musician, you're just a snare drummer in search of a parade! You got no foot and the only framework you can lay down is in four/four time and what you lay down is weak and repetitive! You have the picture now?" Jim turned and walked away.

The women who had been standing around watching the interchange began to ooh and ahh. One said, "That was too crisp!"

"Crisp as toast!" said another, giggling behind her hands. "In search of a parade, Lord help me. Did Europe hit the nail on the head?" she asked, turning to a friend for confirmation.

"To the paradiddle, honey," the woman said, shaking her head at Tyrone. "To the paradiddle." It was clear that Tyrone had made no friends in the chorus line.

"The poor boy was so badly burnt," ventured the woman who had spoken first, "it look like the heat shrunk up his naps!" she said, referring to the sweaty condition of Tyrone's greasy, unkempt hair. The women all laughed and walked away, looking back at Tyrone as they went.

Tyrone started after the women and there was an angry look on his face. King stepped into his path and said, "No more talkin'. It's about time for you to leave or make your move." If it had been his call, he would have ended the Tyrone disturbance within ten seconds of learning of it. Everything that he'd seen of Tyrone was repulsive. Now, it was just him and Tyrone.

Tyrone stared up at King in confusion. Then his face set in an angry frown. He put his hand into the pocket where he kept his switchblade. "What'd you mean, make my move?"

As he edged closer to Tyrone, King whispered, "All you done is talk! It's time to take it to the mat!" King smiled and felt the ache of anticipation. He wanted Tyrone to pull his knife. "Don't tell me you're a chicken-shit and a coward," he goaded, keeping his voice low. King was on his toes, prepared for anything.

"I ain't got no truck with you," Tyrone said, pulling his hand out of his pocket and putting it behind his back.

King had seen the hidden knife gambit many times. "Have you got the blade opened yet?" King asked. He was now within striking distance. "This is yo' last chance to go out that door walkin'!"

The look in King's eyes and the tone in his voice made Tyrone drop his knife and kick it away. "I ain't fightin'. I jus' gon' walk out of here." He stepped back. He began to tremble. There was something about King's quiet ferocity that struck fear into him and made him think that perhaps the rumors were true.

King exposed his bowie, which he had palmed and kept concealed in the sleeve of his jacket, then shoved it back into its waist sheath. "Get out!" he ordered.

Tyrone did not even bother to pick up his knife. He was sick realizing how close he had come to being killed. He walked out into the street without a backward glance.

King was mildly disappointed. He sorely missed the excitement of conflict. He exhaled slowly. There had been a certain monotony to the passing days that had certainly not existed during the war. The rules of war had been rescinded; they had been folded and put away with the uniforms. He was now supposed to lay down his weapons and set aside his taste for excitement.

King walked over to the door of Jim's office and tried to calm himself. He took a couple of deep breaths and walked in the door without knocking.

Immediately, a smallish, swarthy white man tried to push him roughly out the door. "We got enough niggers in here."

Reacting without thinking, King knocked the man's hands aside and grabbed his throat, squeezing with intent to cripple or kill. It was only the movement of a large white man that saved the little man's life. King did not have time to fully crush his windpipe before he turned to deal with another adversary. He threw the little man backward onto the floor, where he lay choking, gasping, and struggling for air. King saw the big man go for his gun and opened his jacket, exposing his own pistols. "Go ahead," he taunted as he kept walking toward the big man.

While King closed the space between them, the big man hesitated. When he drew back to punch the approaching King, it was too late. King flung himself on the man, snapping his head forward at the last minute and head-butting the man over his nose and mouth. The man stumbled backward from the force of the attack. King pursued, striking swiftly with the heel of his palm at the base of the man's nose. He missed the killing blow, but had nonetheless knocked his opponent headlong into the desk. The man's head cracked against the solid mahogany and he lay silent on the floor.

The exhilaration King felt from this brief physical exertion made him throw back his head and laugh. It was the terrible laugh of a spirit freed by violence. He felt truly alive. It was almost like patrol. He pulled out a pistol and screwed a silencer onto the barrel, glanced over at Jim Europe, who looked as if he had been roughed up a bit, and said with a smile, "Let's hear about the deal these fine gentlemen is offering."

There was a tough-looking white man with greased-back hair and bushy eyebrows sitting behind Jim's desk. He wore an expensive, dark, pinstriped double-breasted suit and had his two-toned shoes up on the desk. He had watched King's entrance and subsequent destruction of his men in silence. Slowly he reached into his pocket, pulled out a pack of cigarettes, lit one, and offered the pack to King.

"No, thanks," King said with a friendly smile. He went over and examined the little man who appeared to be breathing almost regularly. He lifted his foot and stomped down hard on the man's head. "I ain't never liked the word *nigger*," King explained to the man in the pinstriped suit. "But I do likes a cigar." He walked over and studied the big man's prone figure and determined that he was unconscious. King took out a cellophane-wrapped cigar from his jacket. He went and sat on the desk next to where the white man had put his feet.

"You want a job?" the man asked.

King laughed. "I couldn't work for you."

"Why not? Ask anybody. I pay well."

"The money ain' the problem," King answered with a chuckle. "I just don't think you want to call me what I want to be called."

With a casual movement, the man flicked his ashes on the floor. "And what might that be?"

"I want to be called Mister, like Mr. Tremain. Ain't that big a request, really. Anyways, I got me a job. I'm part owner of this establishment. And I can tell by your two friends that we might not get along real good. Now, how about tellin' me about yo' offer?" King put the pistol down on the desk.

"You must be a new nigger in town and don't know who I am and who I represent."

King took a wooden match out of his coat and quickly scratched it against the man's cheek. The match flared into flame. "Who is you and who you represent?" he asked.

The man touched his cheek and anger briefly flared in his eyes. Then he too smiled. His eyes wandered to the desk where King had laid the pistol.

"Go ahead and reach for it," King urged as he puffed on the cigar.

The man turned to Jim, who had been standing against the wall. "Is this the partner who you said wouldn't go for more than five percent off the top?"

"He's one of them," Jim said, trying to straighten his torn shirt. His lip was also bleeding.

"I accept. The Minetti Family will accept five percent for six months. I have the authority to make this deal. I am Tino Minetti. But understand me, you're niggers and that's what I'll call you! I'll take the first payment now, niggers!" Minetti stood up.

King hit him before he was fully erect. "I did tell you I didn't like the word *nigger*. I ain't ever been a nigger and I ain't ever gon' be what a white man calls me, unless it's Mister!"

"What are you doing?" shouted Jim. "He was going to accept our deal. Are you crazy?"

King came over and grabbed Jim by the collar. "Are *you* crazy? You think they gon' let you be an exception. You better take a look around at yo' world. These boys would be the first to come back and blow yo' ass away." He let go of Jim. "They keep their power by intimidatin' and killin'. If I can find out somethin' about who sent 'em and their operation, it's possible we might be able to shake 'em up and make 'em forget all about us."

"What's going to happen to these men?"

"They ain't ever goin' home, but you don't worry about that. Just go get Big Ed and have him bring the truck around to the back. Get on with the show."

"This is what I wanted to avoid," Jim said, shaking his head.

"Noble was right," King said. "It's like death and taxes. Can't really get away from the rough stuff, if you open a business like this." He watched Jim leave the office without speaking. When the door closed, King smiled broadly. He hadn't planned on staying in the city long, but perhaps he would like New York after all. King picked up a pad and began writing down the names of the men he wanted to contact, as well as his potential facility and transportation needs. He would be able to put his military training to use and he had a pool of trained men to choose from. This was something he understood. This was war.

SATURDAY, APRIL 5, 1919

The day of the picnic was absolutely clear, but since there was a chance of rain, the picnic had been relocated to Jim Europe's aunt's house in Brooklyn, since she could accommodate more guests inside if that was necessary. Jim's adopted aunt, Mrs. Iona Washington, had a large backyard with four long wooden tables. She was a thin, brown-skinned woman in her early fifties who wore her salt-and-pepper hair tied in a neat bun on top of her head. Since she had no children of her own, her adopted nephew Jim was the light of her life. She had eagerly organized the early arrivals into squads and assigned them various chores. The women were inside cutting up fruit and assisting with the hot foods while the men were in the yard splitting wood for the grill and chopping ice blocks.

Big Ed was splitting three-foot lengths of oak, King selectively placed additional wood in the grill's firebox, and Professor sat at a table adjacent to the grill turning pieces of meat marinading in a gigantic bowl. The three men worked without speaking, each focusing on his particular assignment, working in the quietude engendered by familiarity. This sweet intangible sense of harmony was disrupted when Jim Europe joined their group.

He was obviously upset, pacing back and forth several times before he ventured a word. "I can't stand it! I really need to know what happened to those men last week!"

"What men?" asked Professor.

"I don't have time to explain it," Jim said impatiently. He stared at King. "Did you let them go?"

"I dropped them off at a friend's for safe keeping," King said with a smile. "Don't worry. They won't be traced back to the Palace."

"What do you mean, don't worry?" Jim demanded. "These guys are killers. They have an army!"

"So do we," King answered. "Why don't you let me take care of this side of the business? You book the acts. I'll provide security."

Jim couldn't let it go. "This is New York! People don't just disappear. This isn't wartime France! These guys have bought off the cops. If we don't do business with them, the cops'll close us down."

"They ain't the only ones who can pay off the cops," King answered. He turned to Professor. "Bring over them ribs. I'm ready to put some wet hickory chips on the fire now."

"How long do we have until they find the bodies?" Jim asked.

"Leave it, Jim," King said quietly. "They ain't gon' find no bodies, least ways not the way you mean. Don't ask no more questions unless you ready to participate as a soldier."

"What do I tell the next collector that the Minettis send?" Jim asked. "I don't want to seem like I'm not thankful for your partnership, but you've started a war! These men have the power to break careers, destroy businesses, and end lives! This is something that we should have a serious talk about before anything else is done!"

"If someone comes to collect, pay 'em ten percent off the top!" King replied.

"What about Tino and his men? They were seen at the club! People talk! Suppose . . . ?" Jim was momentarily dumbfounded by his inability to reach King.

"Who's gon' talk?" King challenged. "Ain't nobody seen nothin'. All we have to say is that they came by and told us the conditions to stay open and we paid 'em! We gave them ten percent off the top!" King opened the grill and smoke billowed out.

Jim looked King in the eye and spoke quietly. "I got to live here. I've got people here. I'm vulnerable. Your people are a long way from here. You can operate like a lone wolf. I can't."

"If you don't crack, nothin' else will," King advised.

Jim sighed and walked away.

"What's going on?" Professor asked. "You taking on the mob and you haven't even been in New York three months?"

"They was set to put the squeeze on us and it looked to me like they wanted to hurt somebody or make an example of them. I knew it wasn't gon' be me and I didn't feel like lettin' it happen to my partner neither. Plus, I've always found that if somebody wants to hurt you, the best thing to do is get rid of them permanently."

"You did that?" Professor asked.

"Well," King responded, "by Wednesday they were permanently gone."

"You're messing with some big-time people now," Professor said with a note of concern in his voice. "Are you sure you've covered any possible trace to you or Jim? They'd kill his whole family if they found out."

"Is they bigger than the German army?" King said as he swung around to face Professor. "You know I ain't ever led no squad into somethin' they didn't know about first. You know I ain't never left a squad member on the battlefield if he was alive. I ain't reckless about the lives under my command. I know Jim has weak spots. I'm on top of it."

"Why didn't you kill them immediately?" Professor asked. It wasn't like King to let enemies live for a week if it was within his power to kill them right away.

King looked around to see if there were other people close by. He leaned toward Professor. "What's your interest? You gon' join in?"

"I just wanted to hear how well you had things thought out," Professor explained. "And no, I don't plan on joining you. I want my life to follow a different path."

"He got it planned to the tee," Big Ed said, referring to King. "Ain't no way they gon' know it's us. We got us a plan and there's money in it too.

Your share would probably be enough for you to start that school you always talkin' about, wouldn't it, King?"

"Probably, but he ain't interested in stealin' from the white man. He want to take it legit and legal," King smiled, flashing white teeth.

"Enough for the school?" Professor questioned. "Full cost, we're talking almost forty thousand dollars. Is that the total take or is that each?"

"Oh, we's talkin' each and we may get more'n that," Big Ed laughed. "We expecting to take—"

"That's enough," King interrupted. He looked at Professor. "You in?"

"Even if there wasn't money involved, I knew you'd try to bamboozle me into joining," Professor shook his head. "Yes, I'm in. What do you have?"

"We gon' wait a couple of weeks and hit the main Minetti collection house over on East Sixth Street. They just moved there two weeks ago. We got the layout, the passwords, everythin'," King said. "It'll be like chasin' McHenry into that minefield. We got the upper hand."

Professor was awestruck. "Are you crazy? They'll search for years to find the people who would dare to steal from them. Then they'll kill everybody. This is madness!"

"They won't ever know it's us," King answered. "They got a big territory fight goin' with Gus Milano. On Wednesday we hit Milano's favorite restaurant and killed about four of his boys. We left a couple of Minetti's boys in a car across the street with a machine gun."

"Suppose they question them?" Professor asked.

"They ain't gon' question them," King asserted, " 'cause we blew up the car before we left."

Professor was amazed. "How did you get to know all this information so quickly? You just took these guys last weekend."

"Remember Cap Strickland?" Big Ed asked. "That sergeant in C Company?"

"The one who liked to torture German prisoners under the pretense of interrogating them?" Professor asked. "Sure, how could I forget one of the most deranged people I've ever met?"

King said, "We took Minetti and his boys over there. Cap's family got a caterin' warehouse in Brooklyn. Cap was only too happy to try out his stuff. Two of the guys was soft and they broke in minutes. The third one didn't say nothin' 'til we worked on 'em a bit. Anyways, by Sunday night, we knew what we needed to know."

"When do you hit Minetti's?"

"Next week or two. We wants to wait until Milano has figured out that it was Minetti who did his boys. We want the two families to be fightin' when we hit," King answered as he lifted the grill's cover.

"You haven't told Jim any of this? That doesn't seem right, if he's a partner."

"He ain't got the stomach for it," King answered, lighting up a cheroot. "I don't expect him to be too pleased with me anytime soon. He wanted to lay down and let these fools walk over him. Since I didn't go for that, we ain't seein' eye to eye."

"Jim's bought us all tickets to go to the opening of the 'Maid of Harlem' tonight. Are you still going or are you planning to skip that?"

King smiled. "That depends on Jim."

Professor shook his head. He had an intuition that King's penchant for violence would lead him into trouble sooner or later, but it was still a surprise that it had happened so soon. "How many people know about your plan to hit the Minettis' collection house?"

"Three: you, Big Ed, and me. Everything's on a need-to-know basis."

Big Ed said, "King got it planned like it was a military mission."

"How many people on your team?" Professor asked.

"Eight, includin' you. Except for Cap, everybody's from our squad." King dropped his voice because a group of about fifteen people came out of the house and were milling around. "We'll go over the plan at Smitty's house some time next week."

King went over and sat on a bench under the kitchen window. Although his thoughts often returned to New Orleans, King knew he had not tasted all of New York's delights. Even if there was no military action against the Minettis, he would have stayed for the lights of the city. Its flashing neon colors intrigued him. Sometimes he would go to Times Square at night and stand in the shadows, marveling at the miracles of electricity. He also loved the big-city pace and sophistication. But the principal factors keeping him in New York were his reluctance to break up his close relationships with his army comrades and the fact that he loved the new music being played by Europe's band.

Living outside of New Orleans, King had heard plenty of the ragtime music being played by local musicians. Nonetheless, he had never heard jazz played before he heard Europe's sixty-seven-piece marching band lead the 369th to join the French Seventh Army in a small town south of the Marne. As the regiment reassembled in rank upon rank before an impromptu reviewing stand in a meadow outside of town, the band broke into some hip, swinging music with wah-wah trumpets. King had never heard such music before, but he recognized it instantly and took it for his own. The music seemed to embody the spirit of the whole regiment. There was a proud smile on every colored soldier's face. It was a memory that King carried with him throughout the rest of the war.

Over his head, King heard the sounds of women's voices. There appeared to be three different women standing at the window. Their exchanges fluttered down to him without loss of clarity. They were discussing the available men at the party, along with what facts they knew about them.

"See that short, dark one with the glasses?" said one woman with a husky voice. "He's one of Jim's partner's in the Rockland. So you know he's got money."

"How you find this stuff out, Mamie? He don't look like nothing particular. How did he get hooked up with Jimmy Reese?" asked a high-pitched voice. "He don't look show biz."

Mamie responded, "They were in the army together. All three of his partners. The one with the glasses and—See that big fellow sitting across the table from him? He's another partner, but wait, baby, until you see the third one. He's the doll. He ain't but twenty and is good-looking as can be."

"I heard about him. He's the dangerous one," the third voice joined in. "He was in a suicide squad behind the lines. I've seen him. He's good-looking alright, but there's something cold in his eyes. They say he'd as soon kill you as shake hands with you."

The high-pitched voice responded with emphasis, "But Leah, he has money, so you'll die rich!" Her remark brought laughter from her two friends.

"Alice sounds like she's changed her requirements from looks to money," the third voice said with a chuckle.

Mamie dropped her voice conspiratorially. "How bad can a twenty-year-old be, especially if he has lots of money?" The women began laughing again.

The third voice said, "He's too young."

"For who?" exclaimed Mamie. "I'm so tired of old, burned-out entertainers and agents that some young, virile buck may be just what I need."

"What? Are you thinking about that palm reader's predictions, Mamie? Or, are you just using that as an excuse to lay some of that thigh on him?"

"If he's the one the palm reader was talking about, I'll lay it on him until he hollers, Leah. Until the boy absolutely hollers. He hasn't ever had what I'm going to put on him. Hell, they don't even have a name for it! You know at twenty, he's still as hard as a rock and I'm going to hang on it like I was a coat. One hundred and thirty pounds of wildcat will wear his young ass out!"

"You're crazy, Mamie!" Alice exclaimed.

Leah teased, "You better make that one hundred and fifty pounds, Mamie. It's been a while since you danced in the chorus line."

"But when I do dance, I always get applause," Mamie asserted. The clinking of glassware and the sound of porcelain being scraped interrupted the conversation briefly.

"I think I'd like to see what that big man's all about," Leah said contemplatively. "What do you know about him?"

"Oh, I hear Aunt Iona calling me," Alice complained. "Let me go see what she wants. You two can divide up the men between you."

"I'll save you a seat at the table when we eat," Mamie offered. A minute or two of silence passed. Then Mamie said affectionately, "Poor Alice! She always seems to have problems finding good men. She lets her heart go in the presence of fools!!"

"Enough of her history," Leah interjected. "Now, how about telling me about that big chunk of a man."

"I don't know much about him other than he was in the army with Jim," Mamie answered. "I do know he's only twenty-two or twenty-three years old. I wonder how did all these young guys get so much money?"

"He's only three years younger than I am," Leah said. "That's nothing."

Mamie countered, "Leah, please. I was with you when you celebrated your twenty-sixth last year. And I think that was the second time we celebrated it."

There was no further conversation from the window. King smiled. He liked Mamie. Since he had arrived in New York, King had found himself going to prostitutes. The truth was that he did not understand the fast-moving New York women. He couldn't figure out their motives or their actions. There were beautiful women around him all the time, some offering open invitations, yet he could not relinquish his guard. There was an instinctual fear of letting someone he did not understand within his defenses. When he paid for sex there was no personal investment, but all he got in return was purchased time. Inside him, there was a hunger for something more.

When Miss Mamie Walcott was asked to sing the "Star Spangled Banner" for the brave boys of the 369th, King took note.

A shapely, chocolate-skinned woman wearing a conservative, calf-length dress came up and stood beside the table. She began singing without preliminaries, starting off in a soft contralto, weaving her voice into the melody. She caught her audience by hitting some husky low notes. Then bar by bar she reeled them in, like a fisherman with a net. King was mesmerized like everyone else as she closed her eyes and threw back her head. Her next notes seem to hit the sky. King felt swept away, as if he were fifty feet off the ground, looking down upon his surroundings. Mamie ended the anthem by hitting the low notes once more. There was loud applause from everyone.

King had never heard the anthem sung so movingly. Mamie curtsied elegantly and then walked directly past him. He was still applauding when their eyes met. He smiled and nodded his head in acknowledgment of her effort. She nodded in return and headed for her friends.

"She's got a voice, doesn't she?" Jim asked as he ambled over to stand beside King.

"Like a bird," King agreed. "I ain't never heard nothin' like it."

Jim looked around at the surrounding people, some of whom were now eating from plates heaped with food. "There's about five or six people here right now that know music better than Mamie Walcott, have more powerful voices, and have more talent in translating it than she does. Hell, damn near everybody here can sing. My Aunt Iona used to hit two octaves when she was in the choir. There's talent bursting out at the seams and most of it will go unrecognized. It's a daily tragedy. Talent is like a ladder, it'll either take you up to God or down to Hell. It depends on how you use it."

King thought Jim's words over before he spoke. "Why, if there are people willin' to pay, will they go unrecognized? There's a thousand places that have music in New York."

"Most of those places don't pay a living wage. You can scrimp along on the edge of the entertainment world for years without ever making enough to pay two months' rent in advance. That's why my . . . er, our club is so important. I pay top wages to everyone. All I ask is that they be very good at what they do. Because the Rockland Palace has prestige, artists who work in it have the opportunity to be seen and make a name for themselves. I want the Rockland to be the birthplace of stars. The other thing that makes the Rockland important is that in all of New York, there are not many top-of-the-line cabarets that let our people in as part of the audience. Mostly, we provide the entertainment, serve, and clean up. The Rockland Palace is different. We welcome ladies and gentlemen of color. We give them the chance to see the best colored musicians, singers, and dancers that New York has to offer."

Mamie Walcott walked over with two heavily laden plates. "You boys interested in eating?" she asked with a smile.

"Yes, ma'am," King responded, taking a plate from her. "I appreciates yo' kindness."

Mamie nodded to him and turned to face Jim.

"Thanks, Mamie," Jim said with a smile. "Have you met Sergeant King Tremain? He was in my company when we were fighting for the Red Hand in France. He was complimenting your performance."

"Glad to meet you, Sergeant Tremain," Mamie said, offering her hand.

"It's my pleasure, ma'am," King answered, taking her hand. "But just plain King Tremain will do. The uniform is gone, the man remains."

"I see," Mamie said, arching her eyebrows. She slipped her hand out of his and then turned into the milling traffic, heading for the tables where the food was set out.

"I need to sit down to eat." Jim gestured to two spaces at the end of one of the tables. "If you don't mind, I'd like to continue our conversation."

King nodded. He knew that Jim wanted to talk about the situation with the Minettis. It was clear Jim didn't want an out-and-out war, that he would rather pay. It wasn't a question of courage. Jim had proven his mettle in the frontline trenches, under the constant bombardment of German cannon. The real problem was that King was not prepared to be slapped around or bullied and he knew of only one way to protect his dignity and his investment. He didn't see any place to compromise and he realized that serious disagreements of this nature ended partnerships and occasionally friendships. King carried his plate toward the table. With each step his appetite diminished.

Although he knew a lot of people, King Tremain had very few friends. Jim Europe was both a friend and a mentor. King had no wish to force what he felt was inevitable and lose Jim's friendship. Jim could concede security to him or buy him out. There wasn't much else. King realized that they were approaching the matter from very different angles. To King it was a business matter, but to Jim it was a dream, a cause, a mission. King had learned through watching men die that if you wanted to live, passion didn't matter. You had to take precautions.

"King," Jim said in a low voice, "I need to know what you're doing with the Minettis. I think I'm entitled to know what's going on. I've got my heart and soul tied up in the Palace. I don't want it lost over misunderstandings of what is important."

"What's important, Jim?"

"Remembering what we're about. My grandfather used to say the way you tell who's most intelligent is find the man who remembers what he is about longer than the others. So, what are we about here? Are we interested in carving a piece of territory out of the Minetti holdings or are we interested in providing a quality stage for colored performers and audiences? I'm interested in the latter. I've had my stint of warfare and I didn't like it. My creative spirit just shriveled up and died. That's why I was happy to transfer back to the band assignment after I was injured. I didn't want to go back on the front line again. It killed something inside of me. Whatever it is, now it's alive again and I don't ever want to take a chance of killing it again. It might not come back."

Jim stopped to wave at some new arrivals before he continued. "Have you been listening to my recent arrangements? I'm into something new. This music is part of the new jazz trend. Even LaRoca is copying my stuff. I am really cooking right now; the creative juices are flowing. I feel like this music is going to be heard all over the world."

"What's your point, Jim?" King asked.

"No amount of money is worth losing this spirit I feel. I mean, I hear the angels singing and I've been putting it on paper. I've got me a connection to God that I can't risk breaking. I don't have time to fight the Minettis! All I want to do is orchestrate my music and book shows at the Palace. The money isn't important!"

"I said you could pay the next Minetti man that comes to collect," King answered. "But now we're in the middle of a fast-running stream. Ain't no way to change directions now."

"You sure there's no chance they'll hit the Palace?"

"If they do, it'll be the Milanos and only because they think you're in Minetti's pocket. But I don't think the Milanos will have time for that."

"How do you know so much?"

"If you're interested in soldierin', I'll tell you. If you just want to do your music, let me handle the security side of things."

"You know they'll kill everyone in my family if they find out?" Jim asked, looking straight into King's eyes. "My aunt, my uncle, everybody they can find."

"Ain't gon' happen," King responded. "I'm keepin' an eye on every turn. There ain't nothin' to lead them to us."

"Isn't there any way to stop what's going on and just pay the money?"

"No. Anyway, they wouldn't have stopped at a payoff," King explained. "The men we picked up told us all about their plans. They wanted a big percentage of the business and they would've pushed you until they got it! You was gon' get yo' butt whipped a lot! And in the end they was gon' take it over!"

Jim gave King an incredulous look. "They never took over the Clef!"

"They liked the Rockland, Jim. They wanted it," King confirmed. "I heard the man say it myself."

"I have no choice but to trust you, King. I sure hope you've got this as well thought out as you think." Jim stood up and put his hand on King's shoulder. "I'm trusting the lives of my family in your care." He picked up his plate and walked away, leaving King with his thoughts until Big Ed sat down across from him.

"Smitty's here," Big Ed said quietly, "and he's got some real news."

"That's right!" Smitty agreed as he sat down. "Solomon McGee's been watchin' the Minetti collection house like you ordered and he saw the Milanos hit it around noon today. They blew off the front door with dynamite and just fired their machine guns into the smokin' building."

"Damn! That means we ain't gon' be able to take them for a while," King said with exasperation. "Did Cap find out from that man we dropped off where the Milanos' collection house is yet?"

"No," answered Smitty, "but we know the route the Minettis'll take to collect their money from their different businesses. Since they can't use their collection house, they're using a van to make the cash pickups."

"I think we'll lay low for a while," King said. "We don't want to give either of them reason to think that maybe they had some help at killing each other. Cancel the meeting at your house, Smitty. We'll get together next week at Cap's. Let's just go and enjoy the show tonight at the Lincoln."

Smitty smiled. "That sounds good to me. If you don't mind, I'm gon' go over and play some bones."

"Go ahead," King said with a nod of his head. Smitty smiled again. His white teeth flashed against the dark brown contrast of his skin. King smiled in return and for a brief moment thought back to the day Slick was killed. He remembered how sunken Smitty's eyes were on that day.

"You alright?" Big Ed questioned.

"Yeah, I'm just thinkin'," King said.

"I see that big-leg girl, that dancer from the Palace. I'm gon' go and talk to her," Big Ed said, standing up. "I'll catch you later."

For nearly twenty minutes King watched the ebb and flow of the numerous shades of brown faces eating, laughing, and talking around him. He wished he could join them, but the luster of the afternoon had gone. Had he come by himself, he would have left, but he and Big Ed had come together. He felt the weight of Jim's trust on his shoulders and knew that he would have to use all of his skills to keep Jim's family from being in danger.

Aunt Iona came over to the table where King was sitting and said, "Young man, I need to clean off this table because the music is about to start. Do you mind moving?"

King rose. "No, ma'am, it ain't no problem." King left the house and went to find Big Ed and say good-bye to Jim Europe. He found Big Ed standing by the gate with Professor, Smitty, and Jim Europe. They were in intense discussion.

When King approached, Jim turned to him. "I'm not happy with this! I'm not saying that you're not right about Minetti, but I tell you this, I don't want any gunplay at the Rockland or around me! The minute that happens, our partnership is finished. My life is the music and I won't let anyone taint that! I don't want the gloom of war around me! I've got a booking in Boston for the orchestra coming up in a couple of weeks. We're booked there for a month."

"I plan on bein' at the Palace regular like," King advised Jim.

"Of course," Jim answered. Jim offered his hand to King. "I know you're probably saving my life, but I'm not happy with this. This isn't what I dreamed. I'm going in to help my aunt clean up. I guess I'll see you gentlemen later at the Lincoln." He shook hands all around, then hurried away toward the house.

"Whatchoo think?" Big Ed asked amiably as he glanced at King.

"Still figurin'," King replied, watching Jim enter the house.

"Any likelihood they'll trace Minetti's men to the Rockland?" Professor asked.

"Nope, Smitty reported that the Milanos and the Minettis got an all-out war goin'," King answered without enthusiasm. "They ain't studyin' us. They gon' be on guard against the Milanos. So we gon' just have to wait until things cool off. Everybody'll be contacted when we ready to go."

"If that's the case, I've got studying to do," said Professor. "I've got several tests coming up next week. Smitty, can you drop me by my house? It's close by."

"Be happy to give you a ride, Professor," Smitty said with a slight smile, which gave his dark brown face a melancholy look.

"I'm ready to go, too," King said. "What about you, Big Ed?"

"Well, that big-leg girl name Leah want to drive me over to see her apartment before her show tonight. I just wanted to be friendly so I told her I'd go along with her."

"Have a good time," King said as Big Ed headed toward the house. He turned and said his good-byes to Professor and Smitty.

King watched his friends walk away. He went around the front to where he had parked his own car and took a deep breath. He leaned against a fender and lit a small cigar. The sky was full of clouds, which were propelled across its expanse, changing into different shapes as the wind coursed through them. A sudden opening in the clouds allowed a shaft of sunlight to shoot through to the darkened earth below, lancing across the dim contours of the landscape like a spotlight. For a moment the opening in the clouds appeared to be shaped like a gigantic eye and the beam moved quickly across the valleys and lowlands toward the hills from which King was watching. The shaft of light moved as if directed, as if the eye of God had materialized out of the gaseous mass and was now searching for something.

King made no sudden moves, nor did he feel any specific fear. He was a fatalist. He agreed with Sergeant Williams: if it was his time, it was his time. There was no avoiding the hand of fate. The beam faded just before it touched his car. He smiled because it had not touched his car and therefore could not be a symbol or an omen. King placed faith in neither God nor demon, neither heaven nor hell, and yet he was slightly superstitious. His experiences in the war had taught him that luck played as important a role as wariness and intelligence in the pursuit of survival. It was his feeling that luck could be enhanced by careful observation of the omens and symbols. But he was not a slave to "sign." If the path he chose went against it, so be it: one could not always travel with luck or fate as companions. Sometimes they were strangers to be met as enemies. He took a final puff of his cigar and threw it into the gutter, where it sizzled briefly in the dampness. The winds swirled around him.

A light brown sedan honked as it went by. King saw the hunched-over form of Big Ed in the passenger's seat as the car headed down the hill. The front door slammed and King heard the sound of a woman's high heels hurrying down the stairs.

King wondered whether he was missing some crucial fact because he had decided on a course of action that everyone thought was insane. Yet it all seemed very logical to him. Every organization's operations were vulnerable to attack by those willing to use secrecy and discipline. It was the first rule of military training. Crime organizations were no different than any other. But he understood and sympathized with Europe's reluctance to get into an armed conflict. After they hit Minetti's collection house, he planned to donate his percentage of the Palace to Europe. Then there would be nothing to keep him in New York. Once he had insured the ongoing viability of his investments with Goldbaum, he and Big Ed could go on down to New Orleans. But these thoughts vanished when he saw Mamie Walcott come out of the house.

He tipped his hat to her. "Can I offer you a ride?"

"Well, Mr. Tremain, I would like a lift home. I've got to be at the theater in three hours, but my apartment may be out of your way."

"I'd be happy to oblige." King opened the car door for her and helped her enter, then went around and got in. He started the car and nosed it into traffic. "Where to?" he asked.

Mamie had a little walk-up apartment on the Lower East Side and as King negotiated his way out of Brooklyn across the bridge to Manhattan, following her directions, the conversation between them was easy and frank. Mamie had a low husky laugh, which bubbled to the surface regularly. King learned that she was originally from Mississippi and had come up north in her late teens to live with her Aunt Iona because her father had been seriously injured in a farming accident and her mother was totally engaged in trying to nurse him back to health. As soon as she arrived, Mamie was an instant New Yorker. She found a number of venues for her singing that were not available to her in Mississippi. She sang blues and ballads in a string of small bars until she met Jim Europe. He had helped to get her career started. Now it was only a question of time until she got her chance at the "big time."

King stopped the car in front of her apartment and placed his hand on her leg before she opened the car door. "I'd like to see you again," he said quietly.

Mamie stared down at his hand, which remained on her leg, then looked him in the eye. "You're bold. You don't even know me."

"I overheard yo' conversation with Leah and Alice when you was in the kitchen. I thought maybe we could work out an arrangement," King ventured, a smile flashing across his face. "I know you want to own your own club some day. Maybe I could help you along with that. Anyways, I always wanted to meet a woman that could make me holler and who could do things there ain't names for."

Mamie laughed. "You heard that, huh?" King nodded, smiling broadly. Mamie laughed again and said, "You're still bold. You just put your hand on my leg without so much as a 'by-your-leave.'" Mamie pushed his hand away. "What's this arrangement you're talking about? You aren't trying to buy me, are you?" she asked with an innocent smile.

King sensed that she was having a good time—at least she made no effort to get out of the car right away—but he had no idea whether she was serious or if she was toying with him. He had no words for his confusion, and it was this lack of understanding that drove him to pay for sex rather than try to establish a relationship. He explained, "I'm new to New York. I don't know the ways of the people here. I need somebody to pull my coat, like you's doin' for Alice. I got money. I can show a woman a good time, but I ain't seen nothin' but fast-talkin' women who think they slick. I'm looking for somethin' steady. I ain't ready to settle down, but I likes the idea of the right woman on my arm. I heard what you had to say in the kitchen and I liked it. You seem down to earth. I like that. I hear you want to start yo' own club. I think I can help."

"But I got to be seeing you first, is that right?" Mamie asked with raised eyebrows.

"Yeah, I thought we could go places together—"

"Does seeing me mean bedding me?"

"You ain't got to do nothin' you don't want to do," King asserted. "I don't know much about New York women or how to treat them, so if I offended you, I'm sorry," King admitted. "I was hopin' I could learn some of that off of you."

Mamie softened. "You're a good-looking man. I wouldn't mind being seen with you, but you've got to do something about your clothes, honey!"

King looked down at his suit, which was one of the two that he had made for him by a Chinese tailor after he arrived from France. "What's wrong with my clothes?" he asked. He looked down again. His suit was cut in the current fashion.

"They're dirty and you're dirty," Mamie said crisply. "A woman wants to be romanced. She wants a man who bathes every day and wears a clean shirt each time he sees her. You need to take that suit to a laundry to be cleaned. Before I left Mississippi I smelled all the body odor I needed to smell for my whole life. We got indoor plumbing and piped-in hot water in New York City. There ain't no excuse for letting body odor build up."

"I only wears my shirts two or three days. Didn't know I was creatin' a problem," King said and it was true. Sometimes along the frontline trenches in France, the men went without showers for weeks at a time. King realized immediately that he should have seen that different cleanliness standards had to be applied once he returned to the States. He was embarrassed.

It was dark by the time King parked his car and walked up to the flat he and Big Ed shared. It was on the top floor of a four-story walk-up and looked out upon a grassy area that had a rough baseball diamond. King went out on the roof and saw brief glimpses of the stars as the dark gray clouds continued their roiling motion across the night sky. He lit another small cigar and basked in the thoughts of Mamie. He had agreed to pick her up and take her to the theater at seven that evening. He felt a tremor of excitement pass through him. What he liked most about Mamie was that she was easy to talk to, that she listened and then offered intelligent responses. Most of what he knew of women was learned while in the army, and there were not many opportunities for colored soldiers to meet women who weren't selling themselves. Mamie was his first real woman.

The wind gusted briefly. Above him, through a wide opening in the clouds, King saw the Big Dipper and the path of the Milky Way. The pale shape of a half-moon glimmered behind the clouds before all was again hidden behind an onrushing wall of cumulus. For King, life was changing like the sky; it was marching along with its usual pressures and demands. He was being forced to adapt to a different mode. He had grown used to the demands of the army. In uniform, one always knew what was required. Now he had to learn the rules of New York City streets. He went downstairs to run himself a bath.

Later that night King drove Mamie home from the theater. The waning moon and the stars had the sky to themselves. The clouds were gone. The brightness of the night sky was defused by the electric brilliance of the city. King commented on it as he stopped to let a horse-drawn wagon pass. "Seems like there ain't no night sky in New York. That's one thing I sure do miss."

"Is the sky bright where you come from?" Mamie asked, staring at King in the changing shadows of the car's interior. Despite her better judgment, she was attracted to his youthful and masculine handsomeness. She thought of the palm reader's words and wondered what she was getting into by allowing King to approach her. In the theater community there were many handsome and pretty people but not many masculine ones. Yet his looks were only a small part of her attraction to him. There was something mysterious about him that excited her.

King brought the car to a stop for an electric stop signal and answered her. "Yeah, but it's different. It seems closer, like you can reach up and touch it. And when the clouds cover up the sky, it's like yo' legs under yo' dress: all you have to do is reach out and push the material away." King reached down and pulled her dress and coat back and exposed her stockinged legs. He would have pushed her dress higher but she put a restraining hand on his.

"Looking for something?" she asked, but she did not remove his hand from her leg.

"I'm always lookin' for somethin' good," he answered with another smile. The signal changed and King took his hand away to shift gears. King returned to his original topic and said, "I guess the stars is bright anywhere there ain't no big city, but it ain't close like it is down in the bayous. Them stars was plenty bright in northern France, but they was a million miles away and you knew it. You never thought about reaching up and touching them. In the bayous the stars and moon is just over your head and you knows they is alive 'cause they is twinklin' and you can feel their strength." He turned and gave her a smile that flashed his even, white teeth.

Mamie returned his smile and pulled her coat and dress back over her knees. "You're from Louisiana? Where they have alligators?" she asked.

"Yep, I'm from 'gator country, where the bugs weigh a pound each and the lizards and snakes speak Cajun, and other varmints roam freely. My people have a farm just outside of New Orleans."

"I come from a really small, small town in Mississippi called Three River Junction," Mamie said. "I was happy to escape it. I never wanted to return after I saw the city's lights and opportunities. Do you ever miss your home?"

"I think about it but I don't miss it. I know I've got to go back and finish some important business, but there ain't no rush. It'll keep until I get there." King turned the car down a narrow street and pulled to the curb in front of an old brownstone. He turned to Mamie and once again put his hand underneath both her coat and her dress and let it rest on the stockinged smoothness of her knee.

Mamie did not flinch or move. She did not try to remove his hand and merely watched him in the darkness. "Is this part of our arrangement?" she asked.

King kept his hand on her leg while he looked at her and said, "Ain't nothin' happenin' unless you wants it."

"Suppose I haven't made up my mind yet?"

"When do you think you gon' make up yo' mind?" His hand gently pulled her legs open and caressed the soft skin above her stockings.

"Why don't we go inside and talk things over?" Despite her doubts, Mamie realized that she had already committed herself in his direction, not by any specific action but in her mind. She was in a rut with her career and her life. There appeared to be nothing on the horizon other than King, which had the possibility of changing her circumstances. She did not feel that she was taking advantage of him. He would get his money's worth. After all, they had an arrangement.

"That sounds alright with me," King responded as he put his free hand behind her neck and kissed her. He pressed his mouth against her pliant lips and felt her tremble before she pushed him away.

"I want to get inside," Mamie protested.

"So do I," King responded with one of his rare attempts at humor.

As Mamie was fishing for her key to the front door, she asked King, "Do you believe in destiny, that things can be preordained?"

"Is you talkin' about somebody seein' the future, or is you talkin' about everythin' that's gon' happen tomorrow is already set?"

Mamie opened the door and they started up a narrow staircase. "I'm talking about a bit of both. Two months ago, a palm reader told me about you. She said that a younger man was going to come into my life and change it. Are you the one?"

"I sho' can't answer that, but what I can say is most people who predicts the future is shammin'. I got two aunts who makes their living doin' it and they can't find their own butts without help. They say things could be true for anybody."

"This palm reader doesn't just read palms, she reads sign and omens. You tell her what has happened to you and she explains it. Like, do you remember before you drove me home today there was a break in the clouds and a shaft of sunlight came through like a holy spotlight?"

"You saw that too, huh?"

"How it almost came up and touched you? Yes, I saw it. She said there would be a sign."

"Then you saw Leah and Big Ed drive away before you came out of the house."

"Is that a question?" Mamie asked as they stopped in front of her apartment and she unlocked the door.

"Naw, it ain't," King said after they had stepped into the apartment and closed the door. He spun her around and pressed her shoulders back against the wall. "But I do got a question," he said as he opened her coat and let his hands softly caress her breasts. He stepped closer to her until their bodies were touching. "What if I am the one?" he asked as his lips brushed hers.

She stared at him with a little smile. "Then you'll get it all, until you holler." She opened her mouth and kissed him in return, pressing her pelvis against him.

As they made their way into the sitting room, King thought that maybe it wasn't a bad omen that the shaft of sunlight didn't touch him.

MONDAY, APRIL 14, 1919

Don Vitorio Minetti ran his fingers through his gray hair and sighed tiredly. Everything was so damned complicated. It appeared that every decision within his family empire had to come before him for approval. He stood up and moved his slight frame toward the window. He was in his late fifties and dying from a consumptive cough. As if the routine chores were not enough, his younger brother's son had attacked a lieutenant of the Milano Family and killed several of their soldiers. Consequently, the Milanos had struck back, killing three of Minetti's men. He was on the precipice of a full-scale war. But Vitorio was ready for it. He had been watching how the Milanos had been pushing the lines of their territory. So he had begun stockpiling weapons and making plans. He stared out the window at his carefully planted garden. It and its ornate fountain brought him no pleasure. A war, even if it was won, was always costly.

Vitorio returned to his desk and shuffled through some papers. Trouble came not single-handed, but in battalions, he thought as he picked up his revenue sheet. He had problems collecting in Harlem. No payment had been received from the newly opened Rockland Palace. On top of that, Vitorio was in the midst of negotiations with the Guistis because his hardheaded eldest son had beaten his own wife, Maria Guisti Minetti, with a belt buckle, and she had returned to her family with bruises and scars. It was too much. Now he had his cousin waiting in his anteroom to see him about her daughter, who had been impregnated by a goddamned Irishman. But the most pressing thing on his mind was that the payment was late.

He couldn't allow late payments. Rest easy on the whip and niggers got lazy. He had to put some pressure on the owners of the Rockland Palace. He didn't know whether his nephew, Tino, had actually gone to the Rockland before he had attacked the Milanos. Nonetheless, his reputation was at stake. The Palace was one of the three major clubs in Harlem that was not paying protection. The other two were owned by powerful white men. He couldn't allow niggers to resist paying protection without spilling some of their blood.

The door opened and one of his lieutenants entered the room. Vitorio was pouring himself a glass of grappa from a crystal decanter. "What is it, Marco?" he asked, swishing the wine around in his glass.

"It's about your nephew, Tino."

"Finally you have come up with something! Was there any evidence of money in the wreckage?"

"No, and I had Sergeant Murphy sift through it. You know, Don Vito, Tino was hotheaded but I don't think he would have attacked the Milanos like this and sacrifice his own life."

Vitorio looked at Marco contemplatively. "Who do you think might have benefited from such an act?"

"I don't know yet. Maybe one of the other families. It was definitely a cold-blooded and professional hit."

Vitorio set down his glass, as his body was racked by coughs. "You don't think the Milanos could be behind this?" gasped Vitorio. "Tino was a major lieutenant in our organization."

"No, it doesn't seem like their work. Why would they sacrifice Carlo Petino and two of his best soldiers? Tino isn't worth that! No offense, sir." Marco bowed his head respectfully.

"Find out what you can! Question everybody! Hurt some people! I don't care if we kill the innocent. And I want you to take some men and kill a couple of the owners of the Rockland too! The world isn't going to be any worse off with a few less niggers. I want to send a message to these people!"

"Okay, sir. Is there anything else?"

"Yes, Marco, be careful that my brother, Antonio, doesn't hear you saying such things about his son! He is already jealous of the trust I place in you. Your candor will get you in trouble one day." Vitorio sipped his grappa, then said, "Send some nice flowers to my brother's family and make arrangements. Tino's death deserves a first-class funeral! Thank God, someone else killed the little shit before I had to."

MONDAY, APRIL 21, 1919

Tyrone Thigpin shivered in the front passenger seat of the Packard as a stinging rain pelted him through the half-open window. He was watching the people entering the Biloxi Roadhouse Café. Next to him on the driver's side, an Italian named Lefty smoked a lumpy, hand-rolled cigarette. Behind him sat two other Italians armed with machine guns. He didn't know their names or even what they looked like because their overcoat collars were turned up and their hats were pulled down. When he had first gotten into the car earlier that evening, he had tried to look at the men in the backseat, but all he saw was the glinting reflection of weasel-like eyes in the vehicle's semidarkness.

Tyrone wondered if the Italians planned to kill him. He wiped the water off his face and stared at three colored men who stood under the restaurant's canopied entrance talking. He could not see their faces for the only light came from the tubes of blue and red neon that ringed the entrance. Nonetheless, he could tell by posture and size that King was not among them. The Italians were waiting to kill King. His soul purpose for being in the car was to point King out.   sole

Tyrone had heard from his brother that King was seeing Mamie Walcott and that the "Maid of Harlem" cast was having a party at the Biloxi for one of the dancers who was leaving the show. Tyrone had put two and two together and had figured that King would attend with Mamie. He sure hoped that his guess was right. They had been sitting in the car across the street from the restaurant for more than an hour. It was nearly ten o'clock. Sitting in the darkness intermittently illuminated by passing cars, listening to the breathing of men who did not care whether he lived or died, was frightening to Tyrone. He wished he was somewhere other than the damp, cramped darkness of the Packard.

When Marco Volante had first placed five hundred dollars in his hand and said there was five hundred more when the job was done, Tyrone didn't think it was going to be at all difficult setting up King for a hit. He received the money from Volante with the understanding that all he had to do was point out King and that would be it. He soon found out he had it all wrong. They wanted him present at the time of the hit. He had argued to no avail and soon was sporting a huge black eye for his resistance. Tyrone did not like his new friends and decided to volunteer nothing additional.

He was beginning to wonder whether or not it had been a godsend that he had been waiting in the alley when King Tremain and his friend brought out a semiconscious Tino Minetti and placed him in a truck. He also saw Tremain and his friend carry out two lumpy bundles of carpet. Right away Tyrone knew he had some valuable information. He had recognized Tino Minetti when he and his men had first gone into Europe's office.

Tyrone stared out into the rain. He tried hard to stop his teeth from chattering. This was the second attempt at getting King and he could see that their patience was wearing thin. An unshaven, dark brown face suddenly appeared at the window. The eyes looked half-glazed and disoriented. "You got money for soup?" the beggar demanded.

Tyrone nearly leaped out of his skin from fright. "Go away! Go away!" he sputtered, drawing away from the window.

"All I needs is a nickel," the man whined as rainwater dripped down his face, falling in rivulets from the straggly ends of his beard. "Just give me five cent, please! I done fallen on hard times!" The smell of cheap whisky escorted the sound of his words.

"He's blocking my view of the door, Ferdie," Lefty said in a low tone.

The man behind Tyrone rolled down his window and growled. "Beat it, nigger, if you know what's good for you!"

The beggar drew back at the sight of the white man in the rear seat. His eyes shifted past Tyrone to Lefty and then back to Ferdie. "Okay, white mens, okay. Anything you say. I's outa here pronto!" Before he turned away he had a good long look at Tyrone. Then he stumbled into the sluicing rain.

Tyrone sank down in the seat; he was made. He had seen the old drunk many times before and the man had had a good look at him as well. If anything should happen to King tonight, it would take no brains to connect Tyrone and his companions to the crime. Tyrone wasn't hot, but he began to sweat. The news of his involvement would be on the streets before morning. What would his life be like if it was known that he had assisted the mob with a hit?

• • •

When King assisted Mamie out of his car, holding an umbrella over her head, he did not see Tyrone get out of a black sedan and follow him into the restaurant. The rain was still falling steadily. King's only thought was to get Mamie inside before her beautiful linen dress was ruined. He grabbed her arm and escorted her into the restaurant and then returned to move his car.

As he walked out into the rain, three shiny black sedans pulled up. White people dressed in evening clothes began to get out of the vehicles. They were obviously a group from the Upper East Side who were intent on enjoying every nook and cranny that the dark brown arms of Harlem had to offer. They had stopped at a number of other places before the Biloxi. Several of the couples were already drunk and were talking loudly, as if all the colored people around them didn't exist. King did not waste a glance on them, but got into his car and drove around the corner into the alley by the restaurant's back entrance.

Although King would have spurned the thought, he owed his life to the loud-talking whites; but for them, Lefty and his men would have opened fire. Lefty had no hesitation in killing four or five innocent colored men and women, but it was different with whites. Lefty knew that if some socialite's daughter or businessman's son was killed there would be a very thorough investigation. He cautioned his men to wait. It was his intent to follow King's car down the alley, but one of the sedans blocked the entrance to the alley while its driver had a shouting exchange with someone on the sidewalk. Lefty pounded his horn and cursed. When the sedan moved out of the way, Lefty accelerated into the alley, then decided to slow down to a reasonable pace. He saw King through the obscuring rain get out of his car and enter the back door of the restaurant.

King stopped under a makeshift awning to drain the water off his hat and coat. There was a line of three or four people waiting for handouts from the kitchen. He heard an old grizzled drunk say, "See! See, that's the car with the white mens waitin' in it." The old man pointed down the alley. "They told me to get away! Now, they comin' this way and it ain't good luck that's bringing 'em."

King saw the vehicle slowly driving toward the restaurant's back door and decided that it was not in his best interest to stand in such a vulnerable spot. He opened the door and stepped inside. He closed the door behind him and entered a short hallway that opened onto a large, well-lighted kitchen. There was a bathroom off the hallway, which King stepped into. He left the door open a crack and waited to see if someone would attempt to follow him into the restaurant. After waiting several minutes, King returned to the back door and opened it. The car was gone. The people were still waiting under the canopy for handouts. A few of them had looked at him hopefully when he opened the door.

A hand fell on his shoulder. "What are you doin' back here, boy?"

From the gravelly voice, King knew that Butterball Brown was behind him. The door swung shut when he turned to face the Biloxi's owner. Butterball's plump face dimpled and smiled. "Mamie's waiting out there for your young ass! If that was my woman, I'd stick to her like white on rice. I'd put her on the back burner and cook her slow like she was a cream sauce." Butterball rotated his sizable girth as he said this and ended it with a pelvic thrust.

King laughed lightly. Butterball was one of the few people King had met in New York with whom he felt absolutely comfortable. Butterball was a personality. He was obsessed with cooking and women, in that order. Everything he said related to either food or sex and generally both. Butterball Brown was the reason people flocked to the Biloxi. He was a top chef. His specialty was fowl. From squab to geese, he cooked them all. His Duck with Oranges was known to be the best on the eastern seaboard. He was a rotund man with a broad smile and golden-brown skin. With his dimpled cheeks and laughing eyes, sometimes he looked like a gigantic elf in his chef's cap, but the image was deceptive. There was strength and dedication underneath his jovial exterior. As more than one adversary had discovered, Butterball Brown could be a formidable foe.

King returned his attention to the men waiting in the rain. "I think I got a problem: there's somebody waitin' in a car outside. I heard one of yo' 'late diners' say that there was white men waitin' in that car." "Late diners" is how Butterball referred to the people who assembled in the alley for handouts at the close of business.

Butterball opened the door. "Which one?" he growled, indicating the men waiting under the canopy. King gestured to one of the men. Butterball called out, "Joe Deavers! Come here, man!"

A scraggly, unkempt man shuffled over to the door and stood swaying before them.

"You know something about a car with white men sitting in it?"

"They down the alley, still waitin'," Joe said, turning to peer in the direction of the car. "They had a colored man with them, but he and one of the white mens went into the Biloxi."

"Thanks, Joe. I'll give you an extra serving for that," Butterball said and closed the door. "Something's cooking," he said as he turned to face King. "I guess we have to make sure that it's not your goose." Butterball chuckled, and it sounded like large bolts being rattled in a clay pot.

King smiled as well. "How many ways are there out of here?" He wasn't worried. Actually, he felt excitement, but it was always a good idea to know the exits.

"There are more ways out of here, boy, than holes in a sieve. If you wanted to, you could go down to the basement and you could go around the stairs, straight toward the front, and you'd find a door that opens into the sewer. All you have to do is climb down the ladder and you can follow the sewer wherever you want to go."

"The sewer?" King questioned, with a frown on his face. "Under the street?" New York was bad enough with all its tall buildings blocking out the sky, but King could not imagine willingly going into a subterranean tunnel in a city with rats the size of cats. He had seen them running in packs for the curbside drains when he'd driven his car along deserted streets in the early morning. King didn't particularly mind rats; it was the thought of dealing with hundreds of them in a dark, confined space that didn't appeal to him.

"I've used it plenty of times myself," Butterball insisted. "I had this Second Cook once who wanted to marinade me in hot chicken broth. It was a love affair made in hell but damn! She was a master at chopping and mincing. The blade would whir—"

"Is you really suggestin' that Mamie and me use the sewer?" King cut in.

"Oh, Mamie," Butterball acknowledged. "You could still go down to the basement and across to the next building. I share a coal delivery room with them. It's not far, but it's a different exit."

"No thanks. I think I'll join Mamie and leave those men to stew in the rain awhile."

"Don't wait too late. You might have to use the sewers," Butterball cautioned.

King followed Butterball through the bustling activity of the kitchen, which despite the lateness of the hour still had two cooks preparing food while other staff had commenced the cleanup operations. Butterball stopped at the swinging doors that led into the dining rooms. He had a policy of not leaving the kitchen until the stoves were turned off. King went through the doors into the dining area and made his way to the table where Mamie was sitting. From what Old Joe Deavers had said, King knew that the ambushers had a spotter in the restaurant. King let his eyes wander over the customers. He was looking for a single man.

The restaurant as usual was full and the bar was doing a lively business. King saw that a band had set up in an alcove off the main dining area and tables had been cleared away to provide space for the cast to toast their departing friend with a gift of their art. Big Ed waved to him from across the room. King waved back and sat down.

Mamie was a little upset that King took so long to get to the table, but she soon got past it once drinks were ordered and the conversation was flowing between them.

"So who's going to sing next?" King asked after Mamie had informed him of the singers he had missed. He saw no reason to worry her about the white men in the car.

"Reola Mumford," Mamie answered. "She's that little, dark brown–skinned woman in the yellow dress. Wait until you hear her."

The little woman stepped up and took the microphone. She nodded to the drummer and kept nodding as she swiveled to face the audience. She opened her mouth and a high piercing note issued. She worked her way down the scale following melodic harmonies. She was forming syllables, but King did not understand the words she was singing. The only thing that separated her effort from babbling was that every note was bell-like and clarion-clear. He had never heard an operatic solo before, but the music stirred him. The song was a beautiful, slow ballad that allowed the artist the space to sculpt the music in her own special image. The piano joined in playing the chords of the melody. The woman closed her eyes and let her ear guide her through the strange, wistful music. It was a sad and haunting melody and by the time she finished, there were a number of faces in her audience that glistened with tears.

King applauded loudly along with the rest of the audience when she finished singing. "What language was that?" King asked as the applause died down.

"She was singing in Italian. She sang at La Scala in Rome," Mamie said admiringly. "It's sad that despite such great talent, she can't get a job singing with an American opera company."

"She got to get past it if she wants to sing. Maybe, she's got to go back to Europe. There was a sergeant in the army who used to say, 'Prejudice is like gravity; you got to keep pushin' against it without spending too much time thinking about it.' He used to tell us that all the time to help us forget how the army was treatin' us. I hated hearin' it then, but I got to say that in the long term, I think he was right. You can spend too much time thinkin' about things and they just get bigger than they is. You just got to keep on pushin' everyday against the things that cages you in!"

Mamie smiled at King but she did not speak. Everything was so clear-cut for him, white and black, and well defined. Part of it she realized was his youth, yet there was more to it than that, for he was a strange combination of things. He was a man, the war had made him old before his time, and yet he was still a child in so many ways, a dangerous child, but a child nonetheless. Perhaps only a woman could have seen the child in him as she did, for she saw both his innocence and his wide-eyed fascination. She saw it in his numerous questions and in his hesitant efforts to reach out to her, not physically but in conversation, after the animal urges had been sated. He was so different than anyone she had ever known. His raw, un-restrained animal vitality seemed to embody a lust for living that was only equaled by his willingness to face death.

The band started to play dance music and people began to table-hop, moving from group to group, greeting friends and telling stories. Mamie wanted to go over and say hello to the dancer who was leaving to join an-other show and she wanted King to escort her. The next hour was a blur to King; the people he was introduced to, the hands he shook, the faces he talked to were just snapshots to be thrown in a drawer, never to be seen again. His mind did not even stop to catalog them. He was preoccupied with finding the spotter. During their table-hopping he and Mamie stopped at Big Ed's table and King had a chance to study the rest of the pa-trons while his friends talked.

The Biloxi Roadhouse Café was crowded, as it usually was on a Mon-day night. Most cabarets and clubs were closed on that day, so the Biloxi enjoyed the benefits of decreased competition and over the years became the place to be on a Monday night. A substantial percentage of the clien-tele were performers of one type or another. Musicians often came with their instruments and singers came ready to sing because the Monday night jam session was an institution held in high repute. A lot of out-of-work singers and musicians joined the jam session to showcase their tal-ent. As a result, there were numerous single people in the restaurant and bar. King was looking for a needle in a haystack and he knew it. It would take a miracle or a mistake by the spotter for King to identify the man.

King excused himself from the table and tapped Big Ed on the shoul-der, indicating that he should follow. Big Ed rose without question and walked over to the bar with King. They ordered drinks and then King in-formed him of the situation. Big Ed listened without interruption, nod-ding his head as King discussed the various scenarios that might have led the men to him. King was concerned someone in the Minetti organi-zation had tracked him down as a result of the disappearance of Tino Minetti.

The Biloxi was one of the few classy establishments where the social in-termingling of colored people and whites was not a strained, self-conscious act. It was not uncommon for there to be more white customers than col-ored and there were always more than a few tables occupied by interracial couples. Thus, it was not a surprise when King saw Ira Goldbaum.

"Hello, King," Ira said in a warm and friendly tone. "Looks like the Biloxi's really doing well tonight. I haven't seen it this crowded on a Mon-day night in some time."

King nodded in agreement.

"I've been seeing a lot of one of your squad members," Ira volunteered. "He's in two of the law classes that I teach at Columbia University."

"You talkin' about Professor?" Big Ed asked with a big smile. Big Ed looked at King. "He's talkin' about Professor! Ain't that somethin'?"

"If you mean Darwin Morris, you're right," Ira said with a smile. "Even before the war he was one of my best students and he's now law-clerking in my legal firm. He shows a lot of promise."

"So now you one of Professor's professors," Big Ed said in awed tone.

King turned so that he could look over Ira's left shoulder and saw Tyrone Thigpin staring at him. When their eyes locked, Tyrone nodded guiltily and looked away.

"He's a good man," Ira said, referring to Professor. "I am not only his teacher but his friend."

"What are you doin' here, Lieutenant?" King asked. He used Ira's military title because he wasn't comfortable calling whites by their first names; that seemed to indicate a level of familiarity he didn't feel. Nor was he going to call anyone by their last name when they addressed him by his first name.

Ira had none of these concerns. He was effusive in his response. "I love this place: the music and the food! My wife and I come here often to eat. Sometimes I come by myself for the jam sessions. Ever since Jim Europe introduced me to it, I've loved this jazz music. In my law business, I recently set up the corporation papers for a phonograph record company. Part of my fee will include copies of any of the jazz records they produce."

"Look, Lieutenant, I wants to talk some with you about corporate law, but right now I got some business to tend to," King explained. He wanted to find Tyrone and have a private discussion with him.

"Of course, I just wanted to come over and ask if my wife and I could ask you over for dinner sometime. I wanted to thank you personally for saving my life and I wanted you to know that my gratitude ran deeper than mere words allow."

"Sho', we can do that," King agreed, thinking that the event would never come to fruition.

Big Ed and he scoured the Biloxi but could not find a sign of Tyrone anywhere. King sensed that he needed to make a move. He needed to do something unexpected. Otherwise he would be reacting to the plans of others. King and Big Ed stood inside the kitchen doors staring out on the dining room.

"I need you to make sure Mamie doesn't get hurt," King confided in Big Ed. "I'm going to try to take care of this right now. I think I'm going to pay these boys a surprise visit. I ain't plannin' on leavin' by no sewer."

"You gon' need cover?" Big Ed asked.

"No, you just take care of Leah and Mamie; that's yo' job. I'll tend to these others. Keep an eye out for Tyrone. He might have one of them white boys with him," King advised Big Ed as he headed for the kitchen. King had no particular plan when he went through the kitchen doors, but his instinct told him he had to make his move immediately. It was nearly midnight.

King was standing in the back hallway by the doorway into the kitchen talking with Butterball when three young colored men came running through the back door. They were soaking wet from the rain and mincing oaths. "Damn, it's like someone turned on the tap!" exclaimed the tallest of the three. He looked down at his feet and said, "Ah, man, these was my good shoes too!"

"Them's yo' only shoes," corrected the shortest of the three.

"Get you a rain sheet, man," urged the third companion, who was stocky and heavyset. He opened the tarp in which he had wrapped himself and showed how dry his clothes were.

"That wouldn't do nothing for my feets," the tall man scoffed.

"Then come barefeet," asserted the short man with an infectious laugh. "Because you sure is gon' be barefootin' when them sad-ass shoes you got falls apart next week." Both he and the heavyset man guffawed.

"You on my last nerve, J.J." warned the tall man.

"Oh, God!" J.J. exclaimed, looking around on the floor, "I left the cleanser in the car!"

"See! See!" declared the tall man. "God don't like ugly."

The interchange between the men gave King an idea. He whispered in Butterball's ear and Butterball nodded in agreement.

"Where'd you park, J.J.?" Butterball asked.

"I parked in the alley, Mr. Brown, where I usually park. Did I do wrong?" The little man's tone conveyed respect and honest concern. Like most of the employees on Butterball Brown's staff, J.J. was very appreciative of the chance to work at the Biloxi and he did not want to do anything to jeopardize his job.

"No, it's fine, J.J.," Butterball smiled. "Did you park behind any other cars?"

"Yeah, we parked behind a big black Packard."

Butterball gave no indication of the value of J.J.'s answer. "Well, we're not going to close for another couple of hours. Why don't you boys grab a bite to eat, then begin your work. Maybe by the time you finish eating, the rain will have stopped and you will be able to get the cleanser without getting wet."

There was an immediate chorus of gratitude from the men. "Sho' 'nough, Mr. Brown. If that's alright with you, we'd like to sit down to some vittles."

"Thank you kindly, Mr. Brown. The place'll be sparklin' clean tomorrow mornin'."

"Yes, sir! Thank you, sir."

When the men passed him in the hall, King asked the heavyset man if he could borrow his rain sheet. The man gave King the once-over, but when he saw Butterball nod his approval, he relented and handed over the tarp. When the men had disappeared into the kitchen, King quickly doffed his shirt and jacket, then strapped on his holsters and put the tarp over his bare shoulders. Butterball took King's clothes and indicated that they would be in his office.

King pulled the silencers from their sheaths and screwed them onto the barrels of his .45s. He pulled the tarp over his head and stepped out the door. The first thing he encountered was the sound of the rain falling on the canopy. It fell with a loud, continuous drumming sound akin to the long drumroll that precedes a firing squad. King smiled; it was appropriate.

King patiently made his way through the throng of silent waiters, then wrapped the tarp more firmly about himself and ran out into the rain toward the black Packard. The rain fell in obscuring sheets of water, and with the darkness of the alley it was ideal for him. The rain pounded down on the tarp he was wearing with a hypnotic monotony. As he passed the Packard, he noticed that there was one window barely halfway open. The other windows were closed and misted over. He went to the rear of the car parked behind the Packard and used a knife to pry open its trunk. Cold rainwater ran down his hands onto the blade as he popped the lock. He raised the trunk and closed it with a slam. Since the only light in the alley came from the bulb over the Biloxi's back door, he knew he was hidden in darkness, but he wanted to provide sounds that would indicate the normalcy of returning for a forgotten item.

Looking over the top of the car he had broken into, King saw the glow of a cigarette in the backseat of the Packard. He pulled his Colt pistols from their holsters and trotted back toward the Biloxi, but when he was abreast of the Packard, King turned and fired both pistols through the windows into the car. The windows shattered immediately, spraying glass everywhere. The soft cough of the pistols made less noise than the disintegration of the glass.

King kept firing until he had emptied both magazines. Then he quickly loaded two more into the pistols. He looked into the car; there was only one body in the backseat. King checked for a pulse; the man was dead. He glanced up and down the alley but everything beyond thirty feet was obscured by rain. He was certain that the sound had not carried far. He quickly entered the Packard, found the key in the ignition, and started the car. He drove the vehicle around the corner and left it one street over from the entrance of the restaurant.

With the tarp wrapped around him, King trotted toward the Biloxi in the pouring rain. Water was flowing in the gutters and flooding across the alley. He splashed through puddles as he watched for signs of the men from the black Packard. King was particularly alert when he neared the Biloxi, but he saw nothing but the torrent of rain falling from the darkness of the sky. He moved cautiously through the people who were waiting for food before he entered the restaurant. They moved aside for him as if they recognized that he did not belong.

King changed back into his clothes in Butterball's office. His pants were soaking wet from the knees down and his leather shoes were squeaking with water. Fortunately, his pants were a dark blue wool and the dampness was barely noticeable. He dried off his guns and ensured that the carriages and chamber feed mechanisms were working smoothly. He returned the pistols to their holsters, adjusted his jacket, and then checked his image in the wall mirror. A youthful, clean-shaven, light brown–skinned face stared back at him. His hair was cut military short, close to the scalp. His suit was well tailored and made of good material. Overall he was pleased with his image.

King entered the kitchen wondering how many men were with Tyrone. The bright lights, the clash of pans, and the rushing staff dressed in white tunics were a little unnerving to King because he was wary of noise and fast movement. He continued through the swinging doors, entered the main dining room, and saw that many of the diners had gathered around the alcove where the musicians were playing. As he was making his way over to the table where he and Mamie had sat, Ira Goldbaum intercepted him.

"Have you seen my wife?" Ira asked in a hoarse, agitated voice.

"I ain't seen her, but I ain't been lookin' either. I'll keep an eye out for her, if you need."

"Do that! Do that! I just saw a man with a machine gun under his coat! I've got to get her and get out of here! This looks like a mob hit! I didn't think they'd be so bold!"

"You think they's after you?" King asked with surprise.

Ira looked King in the eye. "They've got no reason to love me. They'd be happy to see me killed in a spray of bullets, even if I'm not the principal target." He glanced anxiously around the dining room, then muttered, "I've got no time for more explaining. I've got to find my wife."

"Just tell me what the guy with the machine gun looked like and where you last saw him and maybe I can distract him for you," King said as if he was only trying to be helpful.

Ira answered hurriedly, while glancing around the room. "By the men's room, wearing a long brown coat and a black fedora. He's a short man who walks with a swagger."

King turned and walked rapidly toward the men's room. The rest rooms were located adjacent to the cloakroom along the right side of the restaurant as one entered through the front door. There was a steady traffic of both men and women in and around the rest rooms. King saw the little man standing against the maroon satin curtains that lined the walls, his pale white face pinched up in a sneer. He stared challengingly at everyone who passed. His right hand was plunged deep in the pocket of his long brown coat, which was buttoned only with one button, obviously for swinging the machine gun into firing position. The man shifted his weight from foot to foot. He was anxious. He looked like a man who had something to prove.

King checked the length of the restaurant, searching for the man's accomplices. Just beyond the men's room was a shoe shine stand with three chairs run by old Slap Thomas. The two outside chairs were occupied, one by a white man upon whom Slap was working and the other by a man whose head and torso were hidden by an upheld newspaper, but his brown-skinned hands and two-toned brown shoes were visible. The newspaper was suspicious. Tyrone was nowhere to be seen. There was no time to investigate; the man with the machine gun was on the move.

King watched the man walk through a recessed door and enter a hallway that led to another door that opened out onto a covered patio. King knew that the covered patio had an exit onto the alley behind the restaurant. He looked back at the shoe shine stand and the colored man with the paper and the two-toned shoes was gone. King smiled; he figured the man was somewhere behind him. King reasoned that he couldn't afford a gunfight in a public place. Not only would it draw police attention, but it would give the mob a clearer picture of the person with whom they were dealing.

He figured that the short man had probably gone to check with his companion in the car and when he discovered that the car was no longer where it should be, he would come running back. If King could surprise him as he came out of the hallway, he would catch him distracted, perhaps a tad slower on the reflexes. A moment's hesitation was all that King needed. The problem now was how to shake the spotter.

The issue was still unresolved when King saw a group of white women on their way to the women's room. He noticed how free and easy the chatter passed among them. He also noticed that a couple of them, particularly a heavyset woman, were weaving drunkenly as they walked. King had moved to stand next to the door of the hallway. The women entered the rest room and left King chuckling cynically at the twists of life that allowed white women to feel comfortable enough to be drunk on the colored side of the tracks while colored people had to be on guard no matter which side they were on.

King walked into the recessed hallway leading to the patio and looked for a place to hide. The shiny maroon curtains that hung along the wall from ceiling to floor between the rest rooms and the door to the patio hid a storeroom, which also had a recessed doorway. If he stepped behind the curtains while in the hallway leading to the patio, he wouldn't be seen. He could make his way to the storeroom and wait for his pursuers to make a move. King slipped behind the curtains. There was about one and a half to two feet between the wall and the curtains, which, for all their seeming richness, were fairly sheer. He could see the shapes of people outlined against the lights as they passed.

As he was making his way to the storeroom behind the curtains, the body of a big white woman stumbled into the sheer satin and fell heavily against the wall. She was sliding toward the floor when another woman came to her assistance.

"Doris, are you alright?" asked a female voice with a heavy Bronx accent.

"Men are pigs!" Doris rejoined angrily as she continued her slide to the floor, threatening to pull all the curtains from their fastenings.

"Doris, get yourself together!" the woman said, pulling her friend to her feet. "You think you's got problems. At least Melvin comes home with the paycheck. My husband's such a fool, he gambles away half he earns before I see it!"

"They're all pigs, Sheila! They're all pigs!" Doris said as she staggered into the curtains again. She belched loudly and growled, "Goddamn drapes! Oh, I just want to tear his balls off!" The woman's voice was loud, with the same brash accent as her friend.

King could see both women quite clearly silhouetted against the lights. There was only four feet separating him from the entrance to the storeroom, but he was hesitant to traverse the distance with the heavyset white woman swaying unstably so close to the curtains. He was in a vulnerable position and he knew it. While deciding to chance easing behind the women, King saw the silhouette of the little man with the machine gun come through the door from the patio. He walked up to the mouth of the recessed doorway and stood, peering around. He was standing about three feet from King.

King stood perfectly still and regulated his breathing. It would be easy to kill the little man silently, but he would only kill in the restaurant if he had no other choice.

Another man joined the little man at the mouth of the doorway and hissed, "Did you see him?"

"Who?" the little man responded in a high squeaky voice.

"The nigger! The hit! He just walked out of here not three minutes ago! You must have walked right past him."

"I din't see nobody, Lefty. But there's something funny going on, I can tell you that! I went out—"

Lefty interrupted. "What the hell're you telling me? You didn't see nobody! I told you I saw him go through this door! Don't bullshit me!"

The little man would not be bullied. He turned and faced Lefty. His voice took on a serious tone. "I told ya, I din't see nobody. And I'm tellin' you agin, I din't see nobody!"

The little man was now standing next to the curtains but had his back to King. From his left, King saw the heavyset woman make a sudden corrective movement, then sway back on her heels and totter backward out of control as if she were headed downhill. Her trajectory was leading toward a simultaneous collision with the little man and the curtains. King prepared himself to take advantage of the confusion that would be created. At one point in her stumbling backward, Doris reached out for the curtains for support, but King snatched them out of her grasp. He had no desire to see her rip them from their moorings. Without benefit of something to counter her inertia, Doris fell heavily against the little man, knocking his black fedora to the ground.

The little man spun to face his attacker, ready to pull his machine gun from hiding, and saw that it was a woman. "What the hell are you doing?" he demanded with an angry scowl.

"Looking for the women's lounge," Doris answered, slurring her words and holding her stomach. "I'm feeling sick." She swayed dangerously off balance before she regained control of her equilibrium. She looked down and saw that she had dropped a piece of jewelry. "Oh, my mother's pin."

The little man picked up his hat and turned his back on her disdainfully. "Damned drunks!"

Doris bent over to pick up her pin but she was so unstable that she had to make several attempts. Finally, she stooped to grasp it but, as she did so, her buttocks were pressing deep into the curtains. On impulse, King pinched the woman's behind very hard. The woman leaped straight up in the air and shrieked. Given her condition, it was an athletic move that one wouldn't have thought her capable of making. What was even more miraculous was that she only staggered a little bit when she landed. She was still swaying unevenly when she turned on the little man and pointed a finger at him. "Ya' little wart! Ya' low-down bum, trying to strong-arm a feel from me, a married woman! Who do you think you're messin' with? I'll break your jaw, you little pig!"

The little man turned to face the woman again. "Shut yer yap, woman! I din't do nothin'! But I'm gettin' real tired of your drunken squawkin'!"

"You tired, are you? You ain't seen tired!" Doris declared, shifting her weight noticeably—she was too unstable to stand still. She continued, raising her voice. "I'm the one that's tired. I got a two-timin' husband who's got the gall to have his girlfriend sit at my table! My feet are killin' me and I got one ragin' headache! So, give me any more lip and I'll knock your scrawny little ass into next week!"

"Ahhhh, ya' couldn't knock the ash off the end of my cigarette!" The little man dismissed her with a wave of his hand and straightened the brim of his hat with a swaggering gesture. It was like waving a red flag at a bull.

Doris was a woman of robust stature with massive breasts and powerful shoulders. She charged the little man like a tank, running right at him. Unfortunately, her alcohol consumption affected her aim. She missed the little man, who dodged her easily, and ran directly into Lefty, who was blindsided because he was studying the crowd for King. Their heads cracked together. The impact knocked Lefty off his feet and sent him skidding across the floor on his back. Doris staggered around holding her forehead with both hands, but surprisingly she maintained her balance. She wailed as she struggled to stay erect, "Oh, God, my head! My head!"

King watched as Lefty struggled to his feet and saw the look of rabid anger on his face. Lefty started toward Doris with his fists balled up, but his companion intercepted him.

The little man grabbed Lefty's arm. "Forget her. We got business to tend to."

Lefty shrugged off the little man's hand and said, "It'll keep for a minute. Mostly, I just want to knock this old bitch out!"

The little man backed out of the way and stood against the curtain. "Have it your way."

Doris saw Lefty coming toward her. She saw the look in his eyes and suddenly he personified all the cruel, senseless men who had populated her life. She was unafraid; in fact, she was ready to do battle. She tottered forward to meet him.

The little man was standing with his back to the curtains. It was too inviting a target; King could not resist. King hit him on his head with the butt of his pistol and the little man fell like a sack of potatoes.

The collapse of his companion brought Lefty back to the purpose of his mission. He stared around wildly, seeking the cause of the little man's fall. He turned into the flailing arms of the oncoming Doris, who promptly whacked him across the face with a loud slap. In trying to avoid the rest of Doris's attack, Lefty fell backward over the little man's fallen body. He rose to his feet, cursing. "Goddamn it! You old bat, you asked for it now!" Lefty started for Doris, but he was once more intercepted, this time by the waiter who was now carrying a heavily stacked tray of used glasses. He cautioned, "Now, suh, I knows you ain't thinkin' 'bout hittin' no lady, is you?"

Lefty shoved the waiter out of his way roughly, knocking the tray full of glasses from his hands. The glasses crashed to the floor, leaving the waiter holding an empty tray, which he promptly used as a weapon, banging Lefty solidly on the back of his head. Lefty turned angrily to face the waiter. Doris, who had been staring about drunkenly looking for her enemies, now collapsed with a loud belch into the curtains, falling into the recessed doorway of the storeroom. The curtains, unable to bear her weight, were pulled from their moorings, exposing King.

Lefty turned, saw King standing not five feet away with a pistol in his hand, and was momentarily immobilized. Sheila's loud, brash voice cut through the tableau. She had returned with reinforcements. "There's one of the bastards that attacked poor Doris!" she screamed, pointing at Lefty. Lefty saw the forces arrayed against him and turned and ran out the door leading to the patio. He was followed by five or six angry white men.

King holstered his weapon unobtrusively and stepped over the little man's body. He was standing on the periphery when Butterball Brown appeared with a large meat cleaver and demanded, "What's going on here?" King walked over to him, briefly explained the situation, and advised him about the machine gun and the small man still lying under the curtains. Butterball agreed to take the little man and put him, tied and gagged, in the storeroom in the back.

There was a chorus of voices around Doris's unconscious body, with Sheila's being the loudest. People were attempting to remove Doris from the entangled curtains, where she lay with only her feet exposed.

Big Ed came up to King. Leah and Mamie were with him. "We better get out of here before that guy calls for backup," said Big Ed.

"Are you alright?" Mamie inquired, running her hands affectionately over King's shoulders. King answered with a nod and then ushered his friends through the kitchen to the back door. On their way to the kitchen they encountered Ira and his wife, who were also intending to use the Biloxi's back door as an emergency exit.

"We heard the commotion and decided that the back door was the best way out," Ira said with his arm around his wife's shoulders.

"I don't know about that," King warned. "One of them got chased out into the alley."

"Let me go first and take a look," Big Ed offered. "He doesn't know me."

"Do you know him? What he looks like?" King asked doubtfully. Big Ed shook his head. "Then I'll go first." King pushed open the door and stepped outside. The rain had stopped and all the late diners were gone. The light over the back door cast elongated shadows everywhere that King looked. He dropped into a crouch and slipped behind one of the large garbage cans that was in the shadows against the wall.

Without waiting for King's all clear, Ira and Big Ed came out of the building and stood out in the middle of the alley. Ira waved in the direction of the Biloxi for the women to come out. There was no movement in the alley other than that of Ira and Big Ed. King got to his feet and walked over to join them. As the women walked out the back door, a man stood up from behind a car that was parked down the alley and began firing his weapon in the direction of the three men.

"Watch out!" shouted Ira as he pushed King aside. The first bullet hit Ira in the shoulder with a sickening thud and spun him around. The second bullet creased King's ear as he fell to the wet pavement. The third bullet ricocheted off the building over King's head. King began returning the fire while still on the ground. One of his shots knocked the man backward out of sight.

King crawled over to check on Ira, who was gasping with pain. Ira was holding his left shoulder while blood pulsed between his fingers. When King saw that the wound was not in a vital spot, he patted Ira's shoulder and took off in a crouching run toward the car that was shielding their attacker. The man had started running toward the end of the alley, hoping to make it to the corner. King stood and fired off a quick shot. The man's body jerked as he stumbled and fell. He staggered to his feet again and continued running for the corner. He was almost there when King's next shot knocked him off his feet again.

"Call a doctor, please!" screamed Ira's wife as she rushed to her husband's side. Big Ed picked himself off the pavement, went over to Ira, and applied pressure to the wound to limit the loss of blood. Leah ran back inside the Biloxi to call an ambulance. King trotted toward the end of the alley, expecting to find his assailant lying in the street. The man was gone. There was a trail of blood leading toward to the corner. King approached the corner cautiously and when he reached it, he saw a taxi accelerating away from the curb.

Mamie Walcott picked up the tray of drinks and carried it into her living room. King and Big Ed and a couple of their army buddies were meeting to decide what action to take as a response to the attempted hit earlier that week. The conversation between the men was quiet, but there was an underlying tension that permeated the room. She set the drinks down and let her hand slide caressingly across King's shoulders, then left the room, for the men had stopped talking as soon as she entered. It made her feel like a stranger in her own apartment.

She lit a cigarette and sat down in the kitchen. She let the smoke out slowly, savoring its taste. King had spent the last week with her and they were beginning to learn about each other. In time it was the blink of an eye, but it felt old and comfortable, like a pair of shoes that had molded to the wearer's feet. It wasn't just the sex, although he had awakened in her an animal energy that she had thought was long ago exhausted. She liked the fact that he never forced things, but always allowed her to move at her own speed. She knew by the feel of his hands that he had been with other women. There was a confidence and electricity in his touch that caused her skin to tingle and the memory of the way their bodies moved together made her anxious with anticipation when she knew that she would see him soon. There was a maleness about him that seemed almost prehistoric and it appeared to fit seamlessly with her womanness in a manner that she had never before experienced. He had slipped beneath her armor and touched her in tender places. It didn't make sense. He was too young to stir her heart.

She could still see King talking earnestly with his companions at the opposite end of the hall that separated the two rooms. The bullets that whizzed over her head on Monday night had reminded her of how fragile life actually was, a slender thread so easily pulled beyond its tensile strength. She had seen many shootings in Harlem, and instead of frightening her, it made her feel safer with King. She smiled to think, she had almost walked away from the opportunity to know him and now she was greedy for the hours they spent together.

King walked down the hallway toward the kitchen. "Did we drink all that brandy I bought?" he asked her with a slight smile.

"No, honey," she said, standing up and going over to the pantry. "We have two bottles left." She handed him a fifth of brandy. He had followed her and was standing right next to her as she turned to face him. She felt his warm hand slide slowly down her back to her buttocks and felt him slowly squeeze her buttocks. It didn't surprise her that she was already wet and that her body fairly tingled with his touch. He set the brandy on the table and lifted her chin and kissed her lips.

"Ain't no woman got a behind like a colored woman!" he proclaimed softly as he picked up the brandy and headed back into the living room.

FRIDAY, APRIL 25, 1919

The smell of burning tar was everywhere. King, Smitty, and Professor were working in their coveralls, pouring and spreading the hot black mixture on the roof of a tenement in the heart of Little Italy. The weather was clear for the first time in weeks. The morning sun rose like a golden orb in the cloudless blue sky.

King wiped the sweat from his forehead and checked the tar bucket. It was empty. He fastened a rope to the bucket and swung it over the side of the building and lowered it to Big Ed on the street below, who was heating the tar mixture in a large cauldron on the back of a truck. When the bucket was filled, King pulled it hand-over-hand back to the roof.

The three men had been working on the roof for nearly two days, but this morning, if all went well, would be the last. It was eleven-thirty and they were only waiting until noon. The smell of tar was beginning to nauseate King, but he did not slacken in his work. He bent to it as if he was a professional. Smitty was the supervisor because he was the only one with experience working with tar. Every once in a while one of the men would stop, as if to give his back a break and look around. Although they would look up and down the street, only one building was of concern to them; that was the building with the roof garden restaurant across the street near the end of the block.

At eleven-forty-five a white man in a black suit and a black fedora came out on the roof garden and looked around. If he saw the three colored men working on the roof down the block, he gave no indication, but he did signal to someone across the street from the restaurant. His signal was not missed by the men spreading tar on the roof.

"You see who he was wavin' at?" King asked Smitty while continuing to spread the tar.

"Yeah," Smitty answered as he was lowering the bucket for another load. "He's on a roof on this side of the street down the block."

"Does it look like they're on to us?" Professor asked, leaning on the handle of his spreader.

"Nope, just routine security. They ain't studyin' us."

"Good," King declared. "Let's make this last bucket last until lunch." The three men worked industriously for the next fifteen minutes.

"Damn!" Professor exclaimed. "The owner of this building is getting a hell of a deal at our expense." He wiped the sweat from his forehead and took off his glasses. "I'm working so hard my glasses are getting steamed up!"

"Don't worry about doin' more. He's there now," Smitty said as he lowered the bucket to Big Ed below. Smitty made an eating motion to Big Ed, who then tied the rope to a bundle with a long narrow loaf of Italian bread sticking out of it and sent it up. Big Ed began clearing the tar truck for travel. It was important that he be gone by the time the shooting began.

In the corner of the roof facing the rooftop garden they had constructed a canvas shelter where they had made a show of taking their food. However, today they set up two guns on tripods under the canvas. One was a repeating automatic rifle and the other was a long-barreled sniping rifle. Both were equipped with scopes and silencers.

King and Professor ducked under the canvas while Smitty bundled up the rest of their equipment and lowered it to Big Ed below. Professor cleaned his glasses and shouldered the sniper rifle. King checked the magazines for the repeater and smiled briefly. They were waiting for the all clear from Smitty.

Professor stared at King under the shade of the canvas and asked, "Are you sure this will divert them from our trail? Or are we doing this to satisfy your blood lust?"

"It'll be just like a pack of wild dogs when you kill their leader. They don't do no huntin' until a new leader has fought his way to the top spot."

"I hope you're right and we're not just loosing the hounds of hell upon ourselves and our friends," Professor said, looking through the scope on his rifle.

"Ain't you learned yet? We're the hounds from hell and we bring death with us!"

"I think that's true for you, but I don't consider myself part of that. This is my last mission. I intend to put away my weapons and return to the world of books and law. I get no pleasure from spilling blood and, to tell the truth, I'm getting sick of it. I want to return to the world of picket fences where milk is delivered in the morning and children's laughter is not far away."

"You one of the best shots with a rifle there is. It'll be a pity to lose you, but you got to travel by the light you see."

Smitty ducked under the canvas. "All clear! Big Ed just drove away."

"You got a clear shot of Ol' Man Minetti yet?" King asked, sighting his weapon on one of the sentries on the roof garden.

"I will in a moment. Someone just joined him at the table and they're blocking my view."

"Count down from three when you's ready to fire," King directed. "Smitty, why don't you go down into the back alley and start the car 'cause we gon' hit the streets runnin'."

"You got it," Smitty answered, and he crawled out from under the canvas.

"Three, two, one: fire!" Professor counted down and squeezed off two shots in sharp succession. King opened fired at the same time, spraying bullets along the walkway of the roof garden. Then he turned his gun toward the lookout on the roof down the block from them and shot the man through his binoculars.

"It's a hit," Professor said without enthusiasm. He paused as if momentarily lost in thought. "I killed another man today for no other reason than the pursuit of money." He said the words almost dreamily.

"Have you lost your mind?" King demanded. "You ain't got time for that shit now! Pick up yo' shell casings!" he ordered as he scrambled to pick up the brass ejected from his weapon. "We don't want to leave no evidence of military issue. We got to double-time it!"

After collecting the casings, they wrapped their weapons in canvas and scurried across the roof to the door leading to an interior stairway. In minutes they were outside and scrambling into a rusted older car that had been stolen for the occasion. Smitty drove away along a predetermined route complying with the speed limits.

The scene back on the roof garden was pandemonium. Vitorio Minetti was dead, along with several of his trusted lieutenants who were dining with him. Through some strange freak of circumstance, only Marco Volante was alive and unscratched.

"Goddamn it! I say we hit them with everything we got!" Antonio Minetti shouted, banging his fist on the table. "My brother, Vito, wasn't dead ten hours before those slimy Milanos sent that phoney peace offering. They started a war and now they want to make up! I say kill them all!" He adjusted the patch over his left eye, the result of a past feud with the Milanos. He looked around at the six men who were seated at the table.

"There isn't much chance of peace now that you killed the peace messenger who was Milano's youngest son," Marco Volante said without warmth. He had never liked Vitorio's younger brother, "Tony the Tiger," a name earned by his hot temper and his tendency to impetuous violence.

"I just want to know how come you're still alive when everyone else on that roof was killed! That's what I want to know!" Antonio demanded. His face was reddening with rage. He was a short, square block of a man with a jutting jaw that seemed to distend even farther when he was angry. "How do we know you didn't set up this hit, huh?"

"It was pure luck that I'm still here," Marco explained evenly. "The shots came from more than two hundred yards away. If I had planned this, I wouldn't have been on the roof at the time."

Don Fredo Pascarella interjected. "We play into the Milanos' hands if we begin to fight among ourselves." Don Pascarella was an older man with silver-gray hair who had earned respect for his years of wise counsel. There was a collective nod from around the table as others agreed with him.

"I investigated the building where the shots came from," Marco stated. "And I don't think the Milanos were behind this attack."

There was a chorus of disbelief from most of the men, with the exception of Don Pascarella. "Who do you think did it?"

"I don't know exactly. I'm still working on it, but I checked with the owner of the building, Ernie Buscaglia, and he told me that there were some blacks tarring his roof that day—"

Antonio shouted, "Oh my God! Don't tell me you think some niggers did this? Do you believe we're as stupid as you?"

"Jungle bunnies don't have any reason to get involved with our war and they ain't got no courage for fighting," agreed Sal Guisti.

"What makes you think it wasn't the Milanos?" Don Pascarella asked Marco.

"Because Buscaglia told me that these blacks were working for a Polack roofing company named Kowalski's. I checked and there ain't no roofing firm named Kowalski's. Plus, Tino and the two soldiers were sent to set up collection payments from a new club in Harlem. They weren't sent out to hit the Milanos. I think—"

"You think! You think!" Antonio shouted derisively. "So some Polacks run a fly-by-night roofing company and my son Tino, God rest his soul, saw an opportunity to hit the Milanos and took it! I'm beginning to believe you're trying to protect the Milanos from the force of our vengeance."

"I think you're right, Tony," Sal agreed, but he always agreed with everything that Antonio said.

"Listen to what I have to say before you jump to conclusions. Lefty Marchetti died in Saint John's Hospital last Tuesday. He had been sent—"

"Who is Lefty Marchetti?" demanded Antonio.

"He was one of Don Fredo's godsons," Marco answered. "He had been sent out to put a hit on the nigger owners of the Rockland Palace because we think they are behind the killing of Tino."

"This is bullshit! Niggers wouldn't dare attack my son! They haven't got the balls!" Antonio interjected. "He could beat up five niggers without pulling out a weapon!"

"Please let him finish," Don Pascarella advised.

"Lefty went out with two men after a black guy named Tremain. Lefty was shot three times and the two other men ended up in a car the next day that crashed into one of the Milanos' gambling clubs. Before he died, he told me that they had never been anywhere near the Milanos."

"Are we going to believe this coward? If the niggers were this smart, we wouldn't be able to run Harlem the way we do! I tell you he's working for the other side!" Antonio pointed his finger at Marco.

"I'm no coward and I have no love for the Milanos," Marco defended himself. "A war with the Milanos will be costly and many people on both sides will die. Why move forward with such a decision until we're absolutely sure that the Milanos are the ones that started this!"

"We don't have time for this bullshit!" declared Antonio, adjusting his eye patch. "We have everyone here. I say we vote on who'll now lead the family!" The succession of the title was not hereditary. Nor was an election normally held. However, Don Vito had decreed at the outset of the war with the Milanos that if he should be killed, there should be no conflict within the family for leadership. It should be settled by a vote of his lieutenants and Don Fredo, who had ten years before been allowed to break off and start his own family.

There were assents all around the table. Small pieces of paper were passed out and each man wrote in a name. It was a formality. Everyone knew that Antonio had enough votes to take the position as Don. He had started lobbying quietly for position as soon as Don Vito had spoken. Oscar Bonaviti read the results. There were six votes for Antonio and one for Don Pascarella, which meant that someone had voted for the Minetti family to merge with the Pascarellas.

Don Antonio stood up and pointed to Marco Volante. "Get out! I don't trust you and you won't be part of my inner council!"

"You're wrong, but I guess in the land of the blind, the one-eyed man is king!"

Don Antonio started around the table, his face purple with rage. "I'll kill you myself, you impudent dog! You'll never insult a Minetti again!"

Don Fredo Pascarella stood up, his silver hair shining in the light. "Don't let your temper rule your thinking, Don Antonio. Remember, you are now the leader of the family! You do nothing with your own hands that would endanger the leadership of your family! You think and rethink every decision to ensure the welfare of your family! These things you know. You must now apply them."

Don Fredo ruled one of the larger branches of the sprawling interrelated Minetti family, and though he did not wield the power of Don Vitorio, he was a man to be respected and feared. Even Don Antonio, with his new authority, knew that he did not want to come into conflict with Don Fredo during the first days of his reign.

Don Antonio was stopped in midstride. He realized he was on the brink of losing face. "Take this fool out of my sight before . . . before I have to do something he'll regret!"

"I think I can find him a position with my cousin in Chicago," Don Fredo said smoothly. "I can understand your distrust, Don Antonio, and certainly he should not be part of your council. If his father had not been a long and loyal soldier for me, I would not now make this effort, but I owe the memory of his father at least this."

As Don Fredo and Marco Volante were gathering their coats to depart, they heard Don Antonio give his first orders. "I want the owner of that building dead by tonight! We're going to hit the Milanos with everything we have. We'll write the name of Minetti in their blood!"

Later, in the car with Marco, Don Fredo said, "You did two extremely foolish things today, Marco. First, it was stupid of you to insult Don Antonio. He will remember it and, when time permits, attempt to exact his vengeance. I thought you had been trained better than to make unnecessary enemies."

"Pardon me, Don Fredo, but he has always disliked me. He is not a new enemy."

"But now you have given him an excuse to seek you out." Don Fredo patted Marco's leg. "You must never give a man who has been accorded the position of Don a reason to look in your direction in anger."

"Thank you, Don Fredo. I will not make that mistake again," Marco said humbly. "You said I had done two stupid things, Don Fredo. What was the other?"

"Voting for me of course," answered the Don gruffly.

"But I voted for you because I thought you would be the best leader for the family. Don Antonio will just lead us blindly into a war. I thought that others would vote along with me."

"Then you didn't do your homework. Everyone knew that Antonio had the votes, so they voted for the man who would win. They did not expose themselves or their loyalties, nor will they be regarded with suspicion. I could have taken the vote if I had been foolish, but I knew that Antonio would attempt to fight if he was not elected. I could not afford to fight both the Milanos and Antonio, so I conceded without argument."

Marco was unable to contain himself. "But this war with the Milanos was started by blacks. We need not lose more lives—"

"I know that!" Don Fredo said sharply. "What you do not realize is that this war is good for us. First, we are stronger than they are. Don Vitorio had been preparing for a long time for this war. We are ready. The second reason is that there may be many casualties. In war there are many opportunities to reward brashness with its due."

"I hope that I will be around to see it," Marco said with a smile.

"You will not, if you value your life," Don Fredo advised. "You will go to my cousin's in Chicago after you have taken care of these blacks. I will give you whatever you need, but I want it done quietly. I have no wish to explain to the new Don what we're doing. So, no blown-up buildings, no firebombed cars. Only bodies. Bodies are always being found in Harlem. You have ten days, no more."

MONDAY, APRIL 28, 1919

King was at Mamie's apartment when Smitty brought him the news that Professor had been shot outside the Rockland Palace. King and Mamie were just about to sit down to eat her home-cooked smothered chicken with gravy and biscuits. It was going to be a quiet evening for both of them. The mood was romantic: there was a Bessie Smith record playing on the phonograph and lighted candles on the tables. The ambience was disrupted by an insistent knocking at the front door. Mamie stood still by the table, a frightened look on her face, her body trembling. King moved swiftly and silently, collecting his pistols and checking his double-barreled shotgun. He blew out the candles, turned the light off in the kitchen, and then stood next to the window, peering down at the street below. There was no evidence of unusual activity.

The knocking continued. The apartment was in darkness except for the pale light that glimmered through the lace curtains. King picked up his shotgun and crept over to stand beside the door. He beckoned to Mamie to speak.

"Who is it?" Mamie squeaked, her throat so tight she almost couldn't speak.

"It's me, Smitty! I got to talk to King!"

"You by yo'self, Smitty?" King asked through the crack of the door.

"Yeah, man! I knows I's interruptin' but, man, somethin' bad's happened!"

King cocked both barrels of his shotgun and opened the door.

A flood of light from a bulb in the hallway washed away the darkness of the apartment. As Smitty rushed in King stepped out and checked the hallway and the stairs, then returned to the apartment. As he closed the door, he spun on Smitty. "What the hell do you think you's doin' bangin' on my do' like that?" he growled, staring at Smitty's eyes.

"Professor been shot!" Smitty blurted out. "We was at that charity thing that Professor helped organize at the Palace for his church. When we came out, some white mens was waitin' for us in a car in front of the Palace! They used machine guns! We'd all be dead if Cap hadn't thrown a hand grenade on 'em!"

"Where's Professor now, and how bad is he?" King demanded while putting away his shotgun. He pulled the pistols from his belt and donned his holster and jacket.

"At the colored hospital, Saint John's of Zion. They got that good colored doctor, you know that old one—I can't remember his name. Anyway, they say Professor's got a chance, but he been gut-shot. So, I don't know. And Professor's actin' crazy too; he won't even let them give him no morphine."

"Long as he's alive, he's got a chance!" King asserted. "I'm goin' there right now!"

"But what are we gon' do? They know who we is!"

"Anybody else hurt at the Rockland?" King asked, ignoring Smitty's question.

"Yeah, they shot some big-time society white people! I think they got more'n a couple of colored folks too! I know Wilkie, the doorman, got hit in the leg!"

"How you know it was you they was after?" King asked as he pulled all the shades on the windows.

"They was lookin' directly at us! They shot them other people 'cause they was behind us when we ducked. We was lucky! I just got nicked here an' here." Smitty indicated the side of his rib cage and his outer arm. "Cap came up on the car from the street side and shot the driver and then dropped the hand grenade in there sweet as pie."

"Then the people makin' the hit is all dead?" King asked, lighting a cheroot. He quickly went through a methodical check of his guns.

"Yeah, they was blowed up!"

"Then ain't nobody told nobody exactly who was hit. We got time to hit them back! Twice over!" He turned and walked toward the bedroom. "Mamie, I want you and Leah to take a couple of suites at the Theresa Hotel and wait there for me and Big Ed."

Mamie opened the door. "Where are you going?"

"I'm gon' go see Professor and then meet with the boys. Don't worry. Everything is gon' be alright!"

"Please don't treat me like a fool," Mamie said without rancor. "Tell me why I have to stay at the Theresa. Who should I be afraid of?"

"The Minetti family may have identified us. If that's so, it's only a question of time 'til they find this place. Now, I got to go!"

On the way down the staircase King directed Smitty to contact the whole team for a meeting at midnight at the warehouse that had been rented at the edge of Harlem. He also told him to have Big Ed meet him at the hospital. Smitty nodded quietly and drove off.

When King entered the hospital he did so through the delivery entrance. Although the drive to the hospital was uneventful, he saw no reason not to take precautions. He inquired as to Professor's location at the registration desk. He was given a ward number by a crisp young dark brown–skinned woman dressed in a heavily starched white uniform. She gave him directions quickly and efficiently then returned to her filing. He made his way to the third floor ward and entered a huge room with beds in rows along the walls as well as in the center of the ward. King walked down the aisles between the beds, looking both left and right for the shine of Professor's glasses. Near the back of the ward, there was a row of beds screened off from the rest by curtains. King saw a couple of nurses and a doctor standing outside one particular curtained-off bed and went to speak to them.

King waited for a break in the conversation and then politely asked, "Pardon me. I'm lookin' fo' my friend, Darwin Morris. I was told he was on this ward."

"He's over there," a nurse answered. She gestured to one of the en-closed beds. King nodded his thanks and walked over to the enclosure.

Professor's face seemed ashy pale when King entered the curtained area around his bed. He did not have on his glasses and his eyes looked unfo-cused. A low-wattage bulb hanging high overhead cast dim light on the bloodstained bandages and bedding around Professor. Everything looked dirty and unwashed. King gritted his teeth and tried not to show his anger. As sweat beaded on Professor's forehead and trickled down his cheeks, he smiled at King weakly and struggled to mask the pain.

King stepped outside the curtains and saw the nurses in an argument with the doctor and a security guard. King walked swiftly over to them. The conversation stopped when he neared. King strode up to the doctor. "Get my friend in a private room and make sure he gets first-class atten-tion, startin' now! Money ain't no obstacle! I'll pay whatever is neces-sary!" He took out a money clip with a thick wad of bills and held it up for the medical staff to see.

"We have procedures here," the doctor answered tiredly. "Just because some country hick comes in waving money, we don't go run—"

King slapped the doctor and knocked him backward. "You supposed to be here savin' lives, Goddamn it! And you best put yo' foot forward now! My friend is dyin' while talkin' is goin' on! He needs medical attention now!" King looked beyond the doctor to the security guard. The guard was a big man, taller than King and stocky, but he showed no interest in taking the doctor's side. King opened his jacket and exposed his pistols. He looked at the guard. "What are you gon' do?"

"Nothin', Mr. Tremain. I's just tryin' to do my job. I ain't lookin' fo' no trouble."

"You know me?" King demanded, a little surprised.

"Yes, suh. Least ways, I seen you at the Rockland Palace. I knows you is one of the owners of the Rockland Palace. Yes, suh, I heard of you."

"Things is about to get hot!" King advised. He turned to the medical staff. "I need to see some action!" King pulled a bowie knife from a sheath at the small of his back. The nurses gasped when they saw the glint of the blade. The doctor flinched as King put the knife against his neck. "I'm prepared to kill and die for what I want. Are you?" King asked him. The doctor shook his head worriedly.

King looked at the doctor and smiled. "You got one way to save yo'self! Get my friend some medical attention now!" King pressed the blade against the doctor's neck to punctuate his words and then sheathed the blade.

"One last thing," King said, continuing to stare at the nurses. "If my friend dies, I might think you people didn't do yo' best. I don't think you all would like them consequences at all." King turned without further word and returned to Professor's bedside.

Professor lay on his back, propped up with pillows. He looked up into King's eyes and there was a slight smile upon his trembling lips. "Was that you causing all the commotion out there?"

"I was just gettin' some things straight with the folks who work here."

"You asked me on Buscaglia's roof if I was crazy. Do you remember that?" Professor asked weakly. King nodded. Professor continued wheezingly, "You're the one that's lost your mind! You can't start fights in a hospital!" He started coughing. The reflex racked his body. Blood oozed out slowly beneath bandages.

"You got to save yo' energy," King advised, moving to his side.

"For what?" Professor asked sarcastically. "I'm not going to need it where I'm going."

"Whatchoo sayin', man?" demanded King. "That ain't right! Where's yo grit? You gon' fight this with all you got, ain't you?"

"Gut-shot, that's what I am. How many men have we seen walk away from such a wound. Hell, they tried to sew me back together, but it's beyond them. Man has no power over the miracle that God has wrought."

"They gon' move you to a private room and make sure you get first-class attention," King said encouragingly. "But yo' spirit is the most important! You got to believe you can."

Professor let his eyes drift to the ceiling and stared for a moment at the bulb glowing overhead. It was a light that would preside over his death without giving any real illumination. "I'm ready, heaven or hell," he said softly.

"I don't understand you, Professor. This ain't like you. What made you so ready for death?"

"You remember that conversation we had in the mountains above Côte d'Saar when you told me that story about everybody starting off with a blank page? Well, my page seems to be filled up. It's funny, I thought I had a lot more blank space."

"Pick up the pen yo'self! There's always some space to write more if you got the spirit!" King asserted.

"Ever since I realized that I lived while others died, I knew I was destined to die by violence. Then after killing so many people, some who had nothing to do with the preservation of God and country or any other principle or redeeming trait, I figured that maybe I earned this way to die."

"Nobody earns a way to die," King corrected. "I seen plenty good people die young while bad ones live on and on. 'What goes around comes around' don't happen exactly. There's always a way, a chance, some way to air. You got to find that way before you drown in yo' own doubt."

"I'm worried about you. I'm not worried about me," Professor wheezed. "Whatever my destiny, I can't change it by worrying. You, on the other hand, are going to live. Perhaps my passing will help you learn the lesson that you must drop this war-against-the-world attitude that you carry around with you, or eventually you will be overwhelmed by sheer numbers. Eventually, if you keep on this path, your ending will not be as pleasant as mine."

"You's gettin' all dramatic, Professor," King said with a tone of dismissal. "I didn't start any of the stuff that's happened. I'm just standin' at the scratch line, that's all."

"If you continue on, names will be scratched off the list of the living, but some of them will be your friends and they'll die like me."

"You sayin' that I'm the cause you's lyin' here?" King asked. "You's a man. You could of walked away anytime you wanted."

Professor shook his head with an effort. "There's no doubt, I am responsible for my decisions. As I said earlier, I earned this bed and this way out. I'm not blaming you. What I'm saying is that if you continue to live this kind of life, your friends will probably be involved in it as well. Over time, someone has to catch the bullets. There's bound to be at least one good shot on the other side. People you care about will be falling all around you. Pretty soon there won't be anybody around who's known you for a long time. Think about Big Ed. He'll follow you anywhere. Do you want to see him lying here like this?"

"Professor, I ain't messed with no one who didn't mess with me first. If people want to travel along with me, well, there's some dangers. Sometimes that's the cost. It's part of life. I expect men to make their own decisions. I don't know no other way to live."

"That may be the most painful truth you've ever spoken," Professor gasped. "You're prisoner of your own ignorance, as each of us is before God."

"You insultin' me, Professor?"

"No, I'm not. You must receive love and nurturing in childhood in order to respect and nurture human life."

"I was taught to hunt and shoot when I was a kid and that's about it."

"There are other ways to live, but since you don't know them, you can't try them." Professor paused to get his breath.

"Let me get that doctor," King stood up.

"No, I want to finish first," Professor protested. "You are a natural born leader. With some education, you could help organize our people. You could be somebody other than just a dangerous man. You could be loved and respected, the highest award that humans can give." Professor started to cough and gag.

King stepped out of the curtains and called for the doctor. The nurses came running and an elderly dark brown–skinned man with salt-and-pepper hair limped rapidly to the bedside. The man began checking over Professor quickly and thoroughly. "Let's move him back to surgery," the old man told the nurses. They began to get Professor ready for surgery. The man turned and faced King. "I'm Dr. Wilson. We're going to have to go back in. He seems to have a lot of internal hemorrhaging. We'll do the best we can for him." The doctor turned away and began giving directions to the nurses. At one point he asked, "Why hasn't this man been sedated? All his moving around probably caused the hemorrhaging."

"Because I didn't want my last hours all drugged up and distorted," Professor hissed, barely able to speak. He rolled his head toward King, his eyes glazed with pain. When he spoke, each word was fainter and weaker than the one that preceded it. "Good-bye, my friend. I guess I've dropped the pen. There'll be no more writing on my page—" His body was racked by coughing once more. His bed was rapidly rolled away to the operating room.

King watched as the bed disappeared through some double doors at the back of the ward. He wanted to scream or hit something hard with his fist, but he just stood staring at the light green double doors through which Professor had passed.

Big Ed arrived after Professor had been pronounced dead. King was sitting listlessly in the hallway, lost in thought, when Big Ed sat down by his side. "He's gone" was all that King could say.

Big Ed put his face in his hands and started weeping. There was no sound. Tears streamed silently through his fingers and down his arms. He and King sat quietly in the hall, mourning Professor's passage as occasional hospital personnel passed. "This one hurts," Big Ed said, his voice partly muffled by his hands. "All the people we saw get it, this one hurts the most. It don't seem right. It don't seem fair. Professor was the one who shouldn't have died this way. He was always talkin' about how we shouldn't think of human life as cheap.

"If God is up there, what must he be thinkin'?" Big Ed asked plaintively. "We ain't gon' never have another friend like Professor: full of book learnin', but never ridin' high and mighty, just shoulder to shoulder and down-to-earth as can be. Man, I loved that boy, big words and everything. He was like a brother to me. I just feels like I got hit right smack in my stomach. It's hard to breathe."

King stood up and started walking down the hall.

Big Ed got to his feet questioningly. "Where you goin'?" he called after King.

"I'm gon' spill some blood for this," King answered without inflection.

Big Ed hurried after him. "I wants to come too. I figures we owe them somethin' big and I wants to be there to pay it!"

WEDNESDAY, APRIL 30, 1919

King perused several different daily papers while drinking his coffee in the restaurant of the Theresa Hotel, trying not to let his thoughts dwell on Professor's death. But seeing no mention of the colored people who had been killed or hurt in the attack at the Rockland Palace drew his thoughts back to Professor like iron filings to a magnet. There had been no comment the day before of colored casualties when the story first hit the headlines. It seemed particularly disrespectful to have Professor die without public notice.

Big Ed hailed King from the door of the lobby and walked over to join him. "All's set for Saturday morning," Big Ed said quietly. "Where you at? You look like you's letting yo' thinkin' drift like a lazy bird on the wind."

"I was just thinkin' about how Professor spent all that time in boot camp teaching us to read. I was rememberin' how strict he was. How he used to say if'en we didn't read every day, we wouldn't never learn."

Big Ed shook his head. "Yeah and, if whites can learn it, it should be easy for us, considerin' how smart Negroes had to be to survive under slavery."

"Professor was somethin' else!"

"I didn't even know what the word *thrive* meant until I met him." Big Ed smiled. "Do you remember when we went up to Slick's bar and bought a round for the house? And that drunk fool wanted to start a fight sayin' Slick was a coward and a sneak. And how Professor started talkin' about Slick dyin' bravely for his country and that his death needed respect. Eventually, he won over everybody."

"Sho' did." King chuckled. He glanced down at his pocket watch and asked, "What time did you say Smitty was gettin' here?"

"Around ten this morning. He ain't late yet. Oh, by the way, you seen the papers?"

"Yeah, looks like the Rockland Palace shooting is drawing all sorts of attention. And them Italians shouldn't have shot the district attorney's brother!"

Big Ed nodded his head in agreement. "The papers is sayin' the Mafia did a hit on him to try and scare his brother into droppin' his anticrime program. They even got senators from Washington, D.C., callin' the mayor about 'organized crime.' "

King smiled evilly. "Bet them Italians ain't seen this much light since they got off the ship! This'll put a cramp in their operations, but we got to be careful that all this light doesn't cause them to sit down at a table to iron things out. They gon' want to appear respectable."

"They ain't nothin' but thugs! Maybe, next time, we let 'em know the Three hundred Sixty-ninth is home!"

"No, it ain't smart for us to come out in the open," King advised. "We gon' do best if we runs under the enemy's colors. Let the papers say whatever they want. If we gets the hits we's workin' on, it don't matter who they give credit to."

"It seems to me got to make these thugs know they can't send their soldiers into Harlem."

"Long as we can hit two or three of their collections houses, we can cripple 'em. They'll spend two, three years fightin' it out. We won't even be on their mind."

"That'll give us more than enough to get Professor's school off the ground. I'm thinkin' about puttin' some of my own money in now."

"Don't count yo' eggs before they hatch," King cautioned. "We gots to concentrate on hittin' everythin' on stroke Saturday. If we hits on stroke, then the next thing is for everybody to lay dead a couple of years 'til things cool down. After that, people can celebrate all they want."

"A couple of years? That's a long time to sit on money. Hell, everythin's goin' so smooth right now, they must think they got us! You know we wouldn't have caught Tyrone just walkin' around if he didn't think they had us!"

"You can't depend on that, 'cause you know Tyrone was a fool. If they is as well organized as people say, we gon' have to sit on the money for a long piece. We don't want to give no sign of big money. They's waitin' to see what gon' shake out from the shootin'. They might just have set Tyrone up to throw us off. Ain't nothin' to be happy about except he's dead and he died a fool's death with no honor and no dignity." King sucked his teeth dismissively. "The dog told everythin' he knew with hardly any prodding. He was a big disappointment."

"You kept him alive a long time anyway. I just don't see how you can do that kind of thing." Big Ed shook his head.

"He died in pain because he had a hand in them killin' Professor!" King declared. "I'd kept him alive longer if I could! Anyway, his information led to the whole setup at Lefty's apartment on Saturday."

"You knows I'm talkin' about torturin'!" Big Ed hissed. "You knows you tortured that man long after he told you everythin' he knew. You don't want to be like Cap!"

"The biggest difference between me and Cap is that he likes it and I do it 'cause I have to or for revenge. We didn't have no time to find out what we know now another way! I ain't got no love to hear people scream, but if I need to know somethin' I'm gon' find it out. We ain't talkin' about no innocent citizens here now! Let me tell you, ain't no mercy for the enemy. They got every advantage on us. They gots the police and the politicians! We got to be smart and ruthless just to break even 'cause we ain't gon' win. I only plans to fight people one time. After that there should be less of them 'cause I ain't fightin' to play!"

"It just don't seem right to me. Even enemies, it just don't seem right to me."

"Ain't nobody gon' ask you to do somethin' you don't want to do neither," King asserted. "I ain't sayin' it's right. I'm just sayin' I'm gon' do what's necessary." King saw Smitty walk into the hotel and waved him over. "Here's Smitty. Let's find out if torturin' done brought us some new information."

After greeting both King and Big Ed, Smitty sat down in one of the adjoining easy chairs. "I got big news! It's confirmed! Tyrone was right: the Minettis have planned a big meetin' in Lefty's apartment on Saturday, May ninth. They gon' have the new Don, Tony the Tiger, there meetin' with Pascarella."

"You sho about this?" King asked suspiciously. "It don't seem right that Tyrone would overhear information like this. You sho it ain't a trap?"

"We picked up one of their boys and ran him through Cap's place. The fella was actually spyin' for the Cuomo Family, which is one of the Minettis' allies. He told us that the Minettis are planning to hit all of the Milanos' supporters on the same day as Pascarella and Tony the Tiger are meetin'. He even had info on where the Minettis' gangsters will be. So now we know where everybody's gon' be. We could just let the Minettis wipe out the Milanos and then do them ourselves. Damn, we could make them afraid to come into Harlem."

"We don't want that," King corrected. "You's forgettin' that all these people is white. If we was to come out in the open, the Mafia and the police would get together and come after us. They ain't gon' allow no independent colored action to stare in the face of white society." King smiled. The army had taught him a great deal about strategy and the value of stealth. He leaned forward and dropped his voice. "What we need is two more sharpshooters. There may be a couple in the men we assembled."

His two companions leaned forward to hear more clearly the plan that King was revealing. Anyone looking on would have seen three colored men talking intimately in the lobby of the Theresa Hotel, a most unusual place to plan the assassinations of the heads of two different crime families.

SATURDAY, MAY 3, 1919

The black limousine rolled quietly through Manhattan's early afternoon traffic. With the windows rolled up, all the street sounds were muffled. Marco Volante stared out at the passing cars and meandering pedestrians and wondered if this was going to be the last day he would see such sights. He stared at the back of Turo's head as the big man guided the car through a busy intersection and wondered whether he would be the man assigned. It was a windless, gray, overcast day with no hint of either sun or rain. It was an insignificant day on which to die.

By the time the car entered the Bronx, Marco had developed an explanation that had the potential of saving his life. His heart was somewhat lighter when they pulled up in front of Don Pascarella's building. The door was opened for the Don and he slid in next to Marco without a nod. The Don's bodyguard, Ricky Osso, got into the front passenger seat. The car eased into the traffic and continued on to the meeting place.

After they had been driving for several minutes, the Don favored Marco with an angry glance. "My hands are tied. You fucked up royally! I told you no explosions, no car bombs! All I wanted was colored bodies. And what do I get? A car bomb and a massacre! Two white women were shot along with the district attorney's brother! We have more heat on us now than we've ever experienced before. All the families are clamoring against us for this stupidity! You may have done what the Milanos have tried and failed to do, and that is to isolate us from the rest of the families!

"Now, Don Minetti has called a meeting and you're the main topic. He wants to know what we've been doing in Harlem that we didn't clear through him and he's got a right to know. After all, in wartime, everything must be approved by the head of the family." Don Pascarella paused and gave Marco a long, silent look before continuing. "He may want your life for this and I'll have no choice. I may even be forced to have one of my men do it. Your father, God rest his soul, must be turning over in his grave."

After several minutes, Marco asked, "Don Pascarella, may I speak?"

The Don nodded his head and said, "As if it could make a difference."

"The men I sent into Harlem didn't have any explosives. Someone threw a hand grenade into their car," Marco declared, trying to keep the fear out of his voice. "Those niggers must have done it. We didn't know that they would be so well armed."

"That still doesn't explain why the DA's brother and two white women were shot," the Don rasped out impatiently.

Marco looked down at his hands. "I can't explain that. All I know is that I used the people that you suggested and gave them orders as clearly as I could."

"If you live beyond today, maybe next time you'll be present on the scene to direct your people. The repercussions were too great for you to leave this in a lowly soldier's hands. I had expected that you would over-see things yourself."

There was no more discussion until they arrived at the meeting place. The limousine had pulled into an alley behind a row of large tenements. Turo gave Marco a grim smile as he opened the door for him and directed him toward a three-story brick building near the end of the row of build-ings. Marco was surprised that the Dons had decided to use Lefty's old apartment building as the site for their meeting. Once inside the back door he was frisked under the depressing light of a low-wattage bulb by Don Minetti's driver. Don Pascarella walked up the darkened stairs with-out pausing. No one dared to check if he was carrying weapons. Marco was followed up the dimly lit stairs by Don Minetti's driver, who was a solid chunk of a man with a swarthy complexion. Marco knew that this man specialized in the garrote and it made him extremely uncomfortable walking in front of him. He listened to the man's steps behind him in the shadows all the way up to the second floor.

They entered a small apartment that had been cleared of furniture. All that was left was a table with two chairs and these were located in the liv-ing room, which was the largest room in the apartment. The only light came from three large bay windows that had sheer curtains hanging in front. Although Marco recognized they were using Lefty's old apartment, what captured his attention was that there were only two chairs. This was a statement by Tony the Tiger. It did not look like he, Marco Volante, would leave this apartment alive.

Don Pascarella sat down at the table and asked for a glass of water. He no longer looked at Marco. The water was brought in immediately by Turo, Don Pascarella's own driver.

After fifteen minutes of silent waiting, Don Minetti's voice was heard as he ascended the stairs. Don Minetti had disrespected Don Pascarella by keeping him waiting. It was an unnecessary aggravation that showed the pettiness of Antonio Minetti.

Don Minetti entered the room. "Don Fredo, I was delayed. I had to tighten a few loose ends." He made the gesture of using the garrote. "Bring me some Strega to drink," he ordered as he sat down across from Pascarella. This too was an insult to Pascarella, for Minetti as the host of the meeting should have had his men offer Pascarella refreshments while he was waiting, as is due a man of respect.

Marco was standing by the windows watching. Minetti didn't even glance in his direction. The tension in the room had steadily grown. Minetti's driver walked into the room carrying a tray with a bottle of yellow liquid and two glasses. The sound of his leather shoes moving across the floor was the only noise in the apartment. Marco watched as the driver poured each Don a glass of the liquid and set the bottle on the table.

After his driver had moved a respectable distance away, Minetti leaned forward. "What is this business you're doing in Harlem?" He had the air of a man talking to his servant. There was no doubt, Tony the Tiger lacked his dead brother's warmth and charm.

Pascarella answered as if he did not notice Minetti's tone. "Your brother asked me to follow through and make an example of the owners of this Rockland Palace. They are the only place on the West Side that doesn't pay its protection. He wanted to leave a message for the rest of Harlem. This was the request that we attempted to fulfill. It was supposed to be a quiet job, but we ran into better-armed adversaries than we planned."

"What is this shit?" demanded Minetti. "You got the whole of the eastern seaboard on our asses and you're talking teachin' niggers a lesson? I don't have time for this bullshit! Tell it to me straight!" Minetti's tone was clearly uncalled for, considering Pascarella's rank. Everyone waited to see how Pascarella would handle this latest insult.

Don Pascarella smiled and waved his hand to his men, signaling them to hold their anger. "No need to speak so harshly, Don Minetti. We need each other. You must remember that we are at war and neither can win without the other's help. In this time of turmoil we both need someone we can trust, on whom we can turn our backs. But a partnership must also be based upon respect. We both need to keep in mind that without respect there is chaos." There were nods around the room, even from Minetti's men, in response to the wisdom of Pascarella's words. Minetti had over-stepped the line and he had been properly and respectfully warned. As important to the soldiers staring across the room at each other was that Don Pascarella had left the door open for Family unity by his mention of part-nership. All attention turned to Minetti, waiting for his reaction. It was like a verbal chess match.

There was a moment's silence as Minetti composed himself. "You're right! I let my anger speak." There was an unobtrusive relaxing of tension, but when Minetti continued, his tone was only partially moderated. "I guess I'm mad because most of my operations have been shut down be-cause of this wildcat hit at some nigger-show hangout. I just want to know who set up the hit on the DA's brother!"

"He wasn't the target," Pascarella answered in clipped tones. "The col-ored owners were the targets. At first, they returned fire. When they were hit, they went down like papier-mâché, exposing the people behind them. We didn't know that these people would be in attendance. They were hit as spillover."

Minetti started to say something, but visibly held himself back. He asked in a hoarse voice, "Who planned this job?"

Marco stepped forward. "I did, Don Minetti. It was a tactical mistake. I didn't know that they would be so well prepared. Don Pascarella told me what he wanted. I failed to follow his directions."

"If it ain't the cocky little rooster," Minetti sneered, staring at Marco. "I knew you were mixed up in this. If you had been working directly for the Milanos, you couldn't have done us more harm. I still think you're working for them!" Minetti turned and addressed his men. "Hell, he don't even follow orders. He was told to do a quiet little job and he had his men loaded for bear. I heard they blew themselves up before they insured the hit was dead!"

"That's not true!" Marco protested.

Minetti sat up straight. "Are you calling me a liar?"

"No, Don Minetti, I'm not disrespecting you in any way," Marco an-swered carefully. "I just wanted you to know that I checked their weapons before they left and they had no explosives."

Minetti demanded, "Then how'd their car blow up?"

"The colored targets had hand grenades. They must've—"

"Are you shitting me?" Minetti interjected. "Niggers again? You must have balls the size of a mouse if you're having this much trouble with niggers! I don't know what to do with a guy who fucks up and has no balls. What do you do with him?" Minetti looked around the room at the men from both sides, asking for their judgment.

"These men had hand grenades, Don Minetti. Our people don't have hand grenades!"

Minetti turned to his driver. "Hey, Vince, give me one of your surprises!" Vince came forward and pulled a hand grenade from his pocket and placed it on the table. Minetti barked an order to Marco. "Pick it up!" Marco picked up the grenade and felt its weight in his hands. "Is that what you're talking about?" Minetti demanded. Marco nodded silently. Minetti continued with an evil smile. "I bought five boxes of these about three months ago when all that army surplus was being sold on the black market. I've just been waiting for the right time to use them. I bet the Milanos bought some too." Marco was speechless. Minetti asked again, "What do you do with a punk who fucks up and has no balls?"

Marco saw his world cave in. The question's answer was his death verdict. There was nowhere for him to turn. He saw Vince take a long, narrow piece of cord out of his pocket. Marco realized that begging would not save his life, nor did he have a chance of reaching Minetti before he was intercepted. He spat in Minetti's direction. "You're a fool. A good Don would have known that I have been loyal—" The words he was about to hurl at Minetti were interrupted by a tremendous explosion and a searing pain in his left shoulder as he was thrown forward. He started to get up and felt more than heard a dull, slapping sound against his earlobe. The pain shot across his consciousness as blood spattered on his hands. Through the red haze he saw a red hole appear in Minetti's chest as the man's torso jerked backward. Marco fell facedown on the floor as a hail of bullets tore through the apartment, killing everyone in their path. The bullets continued to splinter through the walls for fifteen seconds, but it seemed like hours.

When the firing stopped, Marco staggered to his feet, unable to use his left arm. Blood was running down the front of his jacket. He stumbled over to the table and saw that Pascarella was also wounded in the chest. He was checking the extent of Pascarella's injuries when he heard a snapping sound. Marco looked up and saw that Vince was leaning against the door, snapping the garrote taut in his hands. Marco saw that Vince had been shot in the thigh and could not stand without the support of the door. He did not need to be told that Vince intended to kill him. He could outmaneuver Vince, but he could not wrestle with him. Vince had the use of both of his hands.

Vince hopped toward the table in an attempt to block the path to the exit. Marco watched, silently cursing the injury that caused his left arm to be useless to him. Marco had one chance and that was to get to the bathroom. He remembered that Lefty kept an additional gun behind the water tank over the toilet. Vince smiled at him and snapped the cord taut a couple of times. Marco waited. Vince stood at the opposite end of the table and pushed it toward his victim. He knew that if he could get his hands on Marco, it would be over in minutes.

Marco surprised Vince by shoving the table hard, using his legs to drive the table into Vince's injured thigh. Vince fell to the floor with a grunt of pain. Marco rushed around the table, heading for the bathroom, but Vince with a superhuman effort lunged across the floor, tripping him. Marco stumbled headlong into the hallway leading to the bathroom and fell into a heap. As he struggled to his feet he heard a sound like something being dragged across the floor. Just before he shut and locked the bathroom door behind him, he saw Vince pulling himself into the approaching hallway. Marco immediately climbed upon the toilet seat and began thrusting his hand behind the tank, searching for the gun. Behind him, he heard Vince slamming his body against the bathroom door. Marco stared over his shoulder and saw that the door would not withstand much more. It quivered each time Vince threw himself against it. He redoubled his efforts, seeking the gun. Finally, he discovered an object, on the left side of the tank, that was awkward for him to reach with his right hand. He got a grip on it and pulled it free. It was a small-caliber revolver wrapped in tape. He fought to remove the tape from the trigger using his one good hand and his mouth, trying to bite through the tape.

Vince threw his shoulder against the door with all the force he could muster and it trembled and gave way. He fell into the bathroom and landed by the tub. The pain from the fall made his vision go dim but he did not lose consciousness. He saw Marco standing on the toilet seat chewing on something. He laughed. It would not be said that Vincent Gatti did not finish an assignment. He snapped the cord a couple of times as he pulled himself erect. He stared at his intended victim and discovered that Marco was pointing the barrel of a small gun at him. He saw the weapon discharge and threw back his head to laugh at the idea that a woman's gun would be effective against him. His laugh was stopped by blackness and there were no further thoughts.

In the living room Marco knelt down beside Pascarella. The Don was fading. "I'll get help," Marco volunteered. "We'll have a doctor up here in no time."

"No! You get your ass out of here!" Pascarella hissed. His eyes opened but flickered and blinked with pain. "There's a ticket waiting for you at

Grand Central Station. Get to Chicago. My cousin's expecting you. If I live, I'll call you when things quiet down. Otherwise, stay in Chicago. Go now! I owe this to your father who saved my life many times! Go!" The Don closed his eyes and breathed shallow breaths. He opened his eyes and looked directly at Marco. "I know this wasn't you. I know it was that black soldier, like you've been saying all along." The words hissed out of Pascarella's mouth liked air leaking from a tire. "I should have foreseen this turn of events. We should have expected that the war would have trained the blacks to kill with strategy." Pascarella groaned; his face was sweaty and pale. "Go! Go!" he whispered as he passed out.

Marco pressed Pascarella's shoulder with affection and stood up. He pulled an unstained jacket off of Ricky Osso. It was too big, but it was better than a bloodstained one that fit. At the door of the apartment he heard men coming up the steps. Marco hurried up to the third floor. There was a doorway at the end of the hallway on the third floor that connected with the adjoining building. Lefty had once shown him this exit when the police were searching for them. Marco slipped through the door and entered another hallway. He descended the stairs, taking his time, trying not to hurry. He knew only one thing and that was that he would not rest until he was sure that King Tremain and his buddies were dead, no matter if it took a lifetime. Marco was the only surviving person who knew of King's involvement in the early mafioso wars.

TUESDAY, MAY 6, 1919

Ira Goldbaum stood looking out of one of the huge windows of his office thinking of death. The morning sky was a crisp blue and there were only a few sluggish clouds gradually passing overhead. The haze that had been lying on the city like a veil of cobwebs was gone, blown away by a midnight wind. Death was on his mind. He had received a call early in the morning telling him that Jim Europe had been killed in Boston the day before.

The recurring pain in his shoulder and back distracted him. He adjusted his left arm in his sling. It seemed impossible to find a comfortable position for it. The pain never seemed far away and the sling, although it permitted him to move around more easily, had become an object of annoyance as well. But he couldn't complain too much. He knew that he had been extremely fortunate that the bullet had missed his vital organs and just chipped off a piece of rib.

Ira took a slow, deep breath and turned his gaze back upon the beauty of his view. He was happy to be alive and back at work. For a while there when he was recuperating in the hospital, he had a sense of déjà vu, like he was back in the hospital in France and feeling once more the fear that he would die of an infection. The change in country and time made no difference. He had the same sense of foreboding when he first awoke in his hospital bed after the surgery to remove the bullet and it remained with him like a shadow. Even the daily visits by his wife and parents hadn't gotten rid of the feeling. Then, just as he was venturing on brief journeys from his hospital bed, he heard that Darwin Morris had been shot. It had been a staggering blow to him.

There was a brief knock at the door and a shapely woman in her mid-thirties entered, bringing in a tray with a coffee decanter and cup. Under her arm she had a newspaper. She set the tray and the paper on his desk. "It's hard finding that colored newspaper around here. If you think you'll need it regularly, I can have one of our custodians pick it up on his way to work. Shouldn't you be resting your arm?" There was a slight trace of censure in her voice, but she gave him a smile that was quite charming.

Ira returned her smile. "Thank you, I should be resting it more. Why don't you have one of the custodians pick up the paper for me? I'd like to keep in touch with how Harlem is accepting the promotional campaigns of our client's record companies." Ira picked up the paper and said, "Thanks for the paper and the coffee, Mary." He returned to the chair behind his desk and saw that Mary had not left and was waiting for something. "Yes?" he asked.

"I thought maybe you were looking for some mention of our law clerk Darwin in there and I just wanted to tell you that it isn't in this edition. Moses Posey, one of the custodians, saw a big write-up about him and his friends in Sunday's *Amsterdam Sentinel*. That little man. You'd never know from the looks of him that he ever fought in a war overseas in a suicide squad. He seemed so quiet. And I certainly didn't know he was part owner of the Rockland Palace. That's one of the nicest clubs in Harlem."

"There was more to him than meets the eye," Ira answered as he turned and faced the window. He felt a great weight on his heart. Ira had immediately recognized that Darwin was someone worthy of investment when he first met him. Prior to the war Ira had seen him struggle against racist policies to enroll in Columbia's law school. He had reached out to Darwin then and was rewarded with a new and interesting friendship. Until he met Darwin, Ira had lived primarily in a Jewish community and had never known people of color in anything but servile roles. His experiences with Darwin made him volunteer, against his family's protests, for an officer's slot with the 369th. Despite his injuries at the front, he never regretted his decision. Not only had he struck a blow against his father's oppressors, he felt that his life had been opened to a whole new world. He had become an aficionado of the new jazz music and often went to shows in Harlem.

He opened the *Amsterdam Sentinel* and there it was on the second page. Jim Europe had been killed in a Boston theater. The article indicated that he had been stabbed to death by another colored musician. The assailant was killed in a scuffle following Europe's murder. Ira let the paper fall from his hands. He stared out the window feeling totally depressed.

While recuperating from his wound, Ira had read all the newspapers and they were full of articles concerning the war between rival underworld families. There was no mention of Negroes being involved in any way. Nor did it mention them as victims. The attempt at the Rockland Palace would have been but a footnote in the episodic killings to the readers of the major newspapers if the district attorney's brother hadn't been among the injured.

Two weeks passed with only a few minor incidents. The papers began to do in-depth analyses on every report that was related to the underworld wars. Then holy hell broke out: Tony the Tiger and all his bodyguards were assassinated in a machine-gun attack. Pascarella, another underworld figure, was also killed in the same attack. Across town, Cuomo and Gus Milano were also killed on the same day. A number of lesser-known underworld lieutenants and enforcers experienced untimely deaths within days of Gus Milano's passing. There appeared to be one perspective only coming from the big dailies. One reporter coined it the "Battle of Blood" between the various families of organized crime. Several major papers, under the umbrella of objective reporting, put forth the contention that the attempt at the Rockland was the direct result of the district attorney's crime-fighting program, that it was essentially a scare tactic by underworld figures to control the course of ongoing investigations. Various editors harangued their readership with stories about the arrogance of "Organized Crime." The brouhaha that was generated brought the attention of the state legislators, who further declaimed that "the underworld must be stopped from growing at all costs."

The coffee was hot and strong. Ira took several swallows as he allowed his mind to mull over Morris and Europe's deaths. It was strange that two men who had survived in excess of six months straight in the frontline trenches in wartime could be killed within weeks of each other during peacetime in the United States. And the strangest piece in the puzzle was King Tremain. Ira's wife had relayed to him how King had pulled a pistol out of nowhere after Ira had been shot and hit their assailant twice as he ran into the shadows. She described the marksmanship as a miracle but it sounded to Ira more like King was prepared for an attack rather than it being an example of spectacular marksmanship.

There was a tap on the door and Mary stuck her head in the room and said that his eleven o'clock delivery had arrived downstairs, but the doorman was reluctant to let the deliverymen come up because they had a steamer trunk on a dolly. Ira knew immediately that it was King. He told Mary to have them sent to his office. As he waited, he remembered Darwin coming to work one afternoon several weeks before and how distracted he seemed, unable to complete the simplest assignment without falling into a daydream. When Ira had questioned him about his state of mind, Darwin would only say that his concept of justice and law were off balance. No matter how Ira pressed him, Darwin would say no more. Finally, Ira let him go home early. Ira remembered the incident because Darwin had smelled of roofing pitch. The very next morning Ira had read that Vitorio Minetti had been shot and killed on the preceding day as he ate lunch at a roof-garden restaurant.

There was a tap at the door and King Tremain and Big Ed Harrison came into the office wearing custodian coveralls. Harrison was lugging a large, battered steamer trunk on a dolly. Harrison slid the trunk off the dolly in front of Ira's desk and then sat in one of the leather chairs. Ira saw Mary standing in the doorway waiting. "Thank you, Mary." She looked questioningly at him for a moment and then closed the door. Ira turned and saw King staring at him. King was a tall light-skinned man with a muscular build and a menacing look. His hard brown eyes glinted like dark pieces of obsidian. Ira had noticed there was rarely warmth in his expression.

"Have you seen the paper?" Ira asked, indicating the *Amsterdam Sentinel*. His shoulder throbbed painfully. He sat down and rested the weight of the sling on the arm of the chair.

"We heard about Jim last night," King answered tonelessly.

"Do you think the Minettis were responsible for his death?"

"Don't matter what we think. Jim's dead. Ain't nothin' gon' change that. Don't matter who we kill, Jim is gone."

Ira was noticeably taken aback by King's last sentence but he recovered quickly. "It's a terrible loss," Ira offered. "He was a good man and a great musician. His music certainly changed my life."

"The world done lost a genius yesterday and ain't but a few people know. It's a shame," Big Ed added with an air of sadness. It appeared that no one in the room had anything else to say on the subject.

To get the conversation going again, Ira said, "I wanted to thank you both for sending flowers and coming to visit me while I was in the hospital. I really appreciated it."

"Weren't nothin'," King answered politely. "After all, you took a bullet that could've hit anybody. We just wanted to show our thanks. You don't find white people like you too many places. Professor always spoke high of you."

"There's a death that hit close to home." Ira sighed. "I'd like to know who caused his death!"

A tight-lipped smile crossed King's face. "The people who had a hand in killin' Professor paid with their lives and some of them died in pain."

Once again there was silence in the room. Ira had no doubt that King spoke the truth and that King knew it was the truth from firsthand knowledge. The implications of that line of thought were abundantly clear. Ira decided to veer the conversation in a safer direction.

"At Darwin's funeral you said that you wanted to see me on a business matter," Ira said in his most professional voice, shuffling through items in his desk drawer, looking for a pen. "I assume this trunk has something to do with the subject of your business?"

"All in good time, Lieutenant," King said. "I want to ask you some questions first. You said once that you hide money legally, you know, create corporations and such?"

"Yes?"

"We want you to set up a couple of them corporations for us. We want to do everythin' real legal. We got some money and we want to invest it in land."

The law was firmer ground for Ira and he felt comfortable answering. "Well, you need an awful lot of money to make it worth your while to incorporate—"

"How much?" interrupted King.

"That depends upon your tax liabilities and what steps you want to take to reduce them."

"I don't know nothin' about no tax liabilities," King stated. "What's that all about?"

"It's not that simple to explain, but basically you pay Uncle Sam a percentage of the money you earn annually and that percentage depends upon the amount of money you earn and the type of tax shelters you employ. This is a pretty complex subject and can take years to understand, so your best bet is to hire an expert to take a look at your income and your expenses to determine your tax liability. I don't think you men really need a lawyer to set up a corporation. You need an accountant. I can have my office refer one."

"How'd you make the decision we don't need no lawyer?" King asked, lighting a cheroot.

"I assumed that you're talking about the money you're making from Rockland Palace?"

"No, we're talkin' about some other money," King answered, blowing smoke rings.

"How much are you talking about?"

"Tell him, Big Ed."

Big Ed pulled a slip of paper from his pocket and read, "One hundred thirty-five thousand four hundred eighty-six dollars."

There was a long silence in the office. Then Ira said, "I guess that I don't have to ask where this money came from, do I? Is that it in the trunk?"

"The answer to the second question is yes, but the answer to the first depends on whether you asks all yo' clients where they money comes from," King said warily.

"Most of my clients have an audit trail for their money, meaning that they earned it legally. So I don't have to create layers of false businesses."

"I don't know what all that means, but can you make the money legal?" King asked. "Can you do it and account for the money to us? We'll pay you the going rate. We don't expect nothin' free, but we ain't givin' nothin' away neither. What's yo' answer?"

"You have one hundred thirty-five thousand dollars in cash?"

"That's right! Open up the trunk and show him the money, Big Ed."

Big Ed rose and went to the trunk. He pulled out a set of keys and unlocked three different locks before he swung the top open. There lying in piles lay packets of bills. Ira pulled himself to his feet and walked around to look at the money. Closer inspection revealed that there were packets of one-dollar bills, fives, tens, twenties, fifties, and hundreds.

"How hot is it?" Ira asked. "Will I have to move my wife and family?" He attempted to inject humor into the conversation, but there was too much truth in his question for it to be funny.

"They still fightin' each other. That ain't gon' get cleared up for a piece. Plus, we left them some things to keep things stirred up so that they ain't gon' quit for a while. We expect once they sit down at a table together they gon' figure out some of what has happened, but we plans to be long gone by then. We got a place to store the money, but we thought maybe we could make some money while we're storin' it."

"This is the most cash money I've ever seen," Ira said, slightly awed.

"Can you do it or not? That's what we want to know." King demanded.

"I can do it, but it's very time-consuming. But before I spend any time on this, I need to be absolutely certain that this money can't possibly be traced to me or my firm."

"How come you think we come in these overalls?" questioned King. "Ain't nobody followed us and in this building we's just deliverymen. Ain't nobody know nothin' about what we doin' here. I made extra sure we wasn't followed. There ain't no hook to you exceptin' through us two. Ain't nobody in on this but us. This here is our money! We splittin' it three ways, countin' Professor's share. Now, you want to do business or, what?"

"I'll assist you in any legal way that I can, as long as my family and business are secure. Other than that, I'm always interested in anything lucrative, but I'll take particular interest in this because the Minettis were involved in Darwin's death. So as long as there's no possibility it can get traced to me or my firm, I'm in."

"Let's be for real. If it get traced to you, you ain't gon' have no choice about whether you's in or not. You gon' have to figure out what you gon' do when that time comes. But I don't think you got nothin' to worry about. We ain't told nobody about our connection with you and we played close to the chest about where our money come from. I just think everything depends on how you fence the cash." King walked around to the front of the desk and dropped into an overstuffed chair adjacent to the steamer trunk. He gave Ira a long, measured look. "I don't care how you do it as long as you can account for the money. I don't expect none of that money to disappear on its own neither. Other than a few of the men in the Three hundred Sixty-ninth, I ain't found many I could trust and I ain't never trusted but one white man before. So I want you to know I made arrangements that if anythin' happens to me or Big Ed, like we get arrested, or for some strange reason our money disappears, you got real problems."

Ira was indignant. "I've based my career on my word and I've lived up to it. I don't do business founded on threats and misunderstandings. I don't need your business if you don't trust me."

"It ain't that," Big Ed answered. "You got to understand we been at war. King just want to get to the details quick. We got plenty reason to trust you, but we also know there's plenty temptations that can make it fail too. This ain't no time for us to drop our guard."

"We also got some other business too," King added. "We want to set up a corporation for the Rockland Palace and we got a manager already picked. I want it set up so that if she can run it for five years without losin' money, she can have my share in the place. Then we needs another corporation set up so we can buy a couple of warehouses with security in a good area somewheres out of town and store some crates in them."

"What's in the crates?" Ira asked.

"If you need to know, I'll tell you. If it's just curiosity, that's another thing."

"I need to know because it will determine the type of precautions that I need to take in setting up the corporation."

"It's army munitions, equipment, and weapons that we bought on the black market."

"Two warehouses full?" Ira asked with surprise.

"Not yet, but we expectin' some more deliveries. One warehouse is for storage, the other's for deliveries. We figures you got to set up a phoney storefront business to pay for the deliveries, so it don't get traced through to your business. You can use that same storefront to pay for our two security squads too. We already got our men picked out. They'll check out the deliveries to make sure everythin's on the up and up."

"What if the deliveries are not on the up and up?"

King smiled. "The people we're dealin' with know that if I'm cheated, they'll pay with their lives."

"And if they make themselves hard to find?" Ira mused.

"I'll find them. I know their relatives and their friends."

"Are you taking lessons from the mob?" Ira asked, shaking his head.

"They taught me some hard lessons. They was real good teachers."

"I don't want to know anymore about your business relationships or your activities. I'll represent you better if all I'm doing is investing your money and setting up businesses. What's your time schedule for wanting all this accomplished? There's a lot of work to be done before all these corporations get set up."

"Let's talk about yo' fee first. We gon' need to know what you think is fair from fencin' the money to settin' up the businesses. We don't want no surprises down the line."

"I don't know because I can't be sure of all that I will have to do to get everything done as you've requested. Why don't I bill you as we go along and you can see what I'm charging you for?"

Big Ed spoke. "We ain't gon' be here. We gon' give New York City a little rest. We figure long as we here, there's gon' be gunplay."

"How will I get in touch with you?" Ira asked, looking back and forth at King and Big Ed.

"You won't. We'll get in touch," King answered.

"If that's the way you want it to be, but you're not getting any of the benefit of having money. I don't know how much money you're traveling with, but it's my guess if you get stopped by the authorities, you'll have a hard time explaining where your money came from."

"What you proposin' that's different?" King asked.

"If you contact me, I can have a certificate of credit issued by a bank in your name in any major city of your choosing. You don't have to carry a lot of money and you can account for it if you run into problems with the law. Of course, you'll have to trust me with the knowledge of your whereabouts."

King stood up and walked over to the window and stared down at the street below. It always came down to the same thing: you had to trust somebody. King, despite his suspicions, had a good feeling from Ira. "Alright!" King agreed and pulled a money belt from beneath his overalls and placed it on top of the trunk. "There's ten thousand dollars in there. I'll call you and tell you where to send it." Big Ed followed suit and placed his money belt on top of King's. "Let's shake on it," King suggested. Ira got up, stepped around his desk, and stretched out his good hand.

SATURDAY, MAY 24, 1919

The boxcar rattled and clanked in a familiar rhythm as the train hurtled down the track. The big, sliding door was cracked open a few feet and allowed the occasional streetlight to shoot narrow bands of passing light into the darkness of the boxcar. Whenever bands of light did penetrate, they swept across the straw-covered floor. King sat alone on a bale of hay in the corner of the boxcar, shrouded in shadows.

He sat in the shifting dimness and listened to the rhythmic metal sounds of the train rolling along in the early morning darkness and recalled that this was the first time he had traveled alone since he left New Orleans in 1916. He exhaled slowly and allowed the rocking monotony of the train's movement sweep over him. The train was passing through the outskirts of a small town in Pennsylvania. Most of the township buildings were dark, but here and there were house lights glowing along lonely dirt roads. The clouds that had caused an overcast sky earlier in the day were being pushed eastward by a west wind. The constellations were beginning to appear on the dark, blue satin of the night sky as the openings increased in the shifting clouds. King stared at the darkened countryside that was rattling past, and he felt a gnawing loneliness.

Splitting up with Big Ed had been one of the most difficult decisions he had ever made and he still puzzled over the intelligence of it. It was the result of an impulse that occurred at four o'clock in the morning, a week prior to his catching the midnight freight train. They all had been sitting on stools in the kitchen of the Biloxi after closing time. Butterball was busily clanking pots and mixing spoons while cooking up omelettes and smoked sausages on one of the big six-burner stoves. Leah and Mamie were talking and laughing with Smitty's wife, Cassandra, at one end of the long prep table while King, Smitty, and Big Ed sat at the other end, close to the stove, downing shots of rye with Butterball.

"Me and Cassandra, we goin' out to Frisco," Smitty said. "She got a brother out there who say they's plenty of work in them shipyards and plenty of land to be bought by anybody that's got the money."

"I heard good things about Frisco," Big Ed said. "They say that a colored man ain't ridden so hard out there."

"I heard the very same thing," Smitty nodded his head in agreement. "Say, I got an idea! Why don't you all come on out to California with us? There's bound to be somethin' we can set our hands to."

"I don't know," Big Ed said, glancing at King for direction. "I don't think we's made up our minds as to which way we gon' go."

"Ain't it just like men to pick up and leave once you get used to them," Mamie said in a loud voice. Only her smile made the abruptness of her words acceptable. "And generally, we're happy to see them go too."

Smitty would not be deterred from his line of questioning. "How come you boys won't come to California with us? Ain't you interested in seein' the country we fought for? I hear there ain't no other state prettier'n California."

"I guess I am," Big Ed said. "The first time I left Nebraska was when I joined the army and I know I ain't really seen that much of the world even though we was all over France. It's just you can't see that much from a trench or out the back of a truck that's barreling down a road. Still, I don't know if there's a prettier place than Nebraska when the sun first breaks through after a thunderstorm in the spring. The whole sky's a gray purple with dark clouds tumblin' across it and below it is miles and miles of green corn and wheat, just a bendin' before the wind all at the same time, like people in church. The sun shoots through them clouds in different spots and makes the fields glow green like phosphorous." Big Ed shook his head and took a deep breath. "You could smell the damp richness of the soil and the greenness of growing things. It's in the air."

"You'd never know he was just talking about the smell of mud," King said with a chuckle.

"In the army I seen all the mud I ever wanted to see," Smitty declared.

Leah looked directly at Big Ed. "I know what you mean. My family had a small farm in Missouri. I remember standing out on the porch after a strong rain, smelling the dampness of the earth and waiting for a rainbow."

"I didn't even mention rainbows," Big Ed said, smiling at Leah. "In Nebraska we got a big sky. It goes as far as you can see. See, you ain't got no sky here in New York. The buildings block it all out, but in Nebraska you can see both ends of the rainbow even if it's thirty miles away."

"I remember on some nights," Leah said as she looked into Big Ed's eyes, "that the loudest sounds you could hear would be the bullfrogs and crickets. And how the birthing of a calf or a colt was the biggest thing to happen in a season."

"My father used to say, 'You got to take joy in simple things, if you want to make your life bein' a farmer.' When I first joined the army, I used to dream about returnin' to the farm, but I sort of got away from all that," Big Ed laughed with a shrug. "I even got used to walkin' on pavement."

"Now you have money to do whatever you want," Cassandra said before putting a forkful of omelette in her mouth. Butterball slid two more plates down the prep table. Smitty took one and offered the other to Leah. She declined with a shake of her head. King picked up the plate and handed it to Big Ed.

"Big Ed, I've never heard you talk so much before," Mamie said with a teasing grin. "You must really love that farm in Nebraska."

"Truth is, I ain't ever wanted to do much but farmin'. I ain't ever thought about what I'd really like to do. Now we got money, I can't think of a better way to spend it exceptin' on a farm or a garage." Big Ed looked at King and said, "But, we ain't really made any plans. I guess me and King needs to sit down and parley a piece on what we gon' do."

Leah interjected. "Ed, there's nothing wrong with a farming life if you don't owe your crop to the bank. It's hard work but it can be a good life, a life where you get to watch your children grow." There was a disjointed moment of silence as all eyes turned on her because of the quiet intensity in her words. It was clear to all present that she was offering herself to Big Ed.

Smitty stood up and raised his glass. "Here's to the Professor. The only educated man I ever met who made sense." It took several seconds before the others followed the sharp change in the conversation, but King stood and raised his glass immediately. Big Ed and Butterball raised their glasses, followed somewhat reluctantly by the women.

"To Professor!" King called out, remembering the pallor of his friend's face in the hospital ward shortly before his death. It was strange that out of all the experiences they shared together, the images lodged closest to the surface were of Professor's dying moments, memories that left a terrible taste in King's mouth. The rye went down his throat with a burning sensation but did nothing to alter the taste on his tongue. He realized that it was time for Big Ed to go back to his farm.

King had seen the way Leah and Big Ed looked at each other, with eyes filled with longing. He didn't know if what they felt for each other really was love, but it appeared to be stronger than anything he had ever felt. Life was a gamble any way you tried to live it; might as well gamble on love, he thought as he remembered all the colored men who died in the war without ever knowing why they were dying, men no older than himself fighting and dying in frozen trenches merely because they were there. King saw Big Ed lumber over to say something into Leah's ear. She nodded her head and smiled briefly in response to Big Ed's whispered message. When King left later that evening, the primary image that he remembered was the expression of need in Leah's eyes when she looked at Big Ed. It had to be love.

The train rattled and clanked along in the early morning darkness. A cold wind whipped through the partially opened door and whisked through the car's darkened interior, rustling the hay. The wind brought a frosty chill with it. There were no longer any lights flickering past. The train appeared to be traveling through open country.

King stood looking out the door as the force of the wind flapped his clothes about his body. The wind carried the smell of freshly plowed earth. To King it was a rich smell, fraught with the memories of his childhood. The landscape was shaped by shadows and the gleaming light of faraway stars. There was no moon and there were only a few electric lights twinkling in the distance. The Milky Way overhead seemed unusually bright. King saw that the train was ascending to a ridge where the terrain dropped away sharply.

He sat down in the open doorway of the car, with his legs dangling out, and despite the wind lit a cheroot. As he took a deep puff of the tobacco, he thought about Mamie. It was she who had introduced him to Cuban cheroots. She had also tutored him in the ways and dress of the city. In many ways, he was grateful to Mamie, but he did not love her. Their relationship was one of mutual convenience and it had been what he wanted for a while. Now he was happy to be leaving. He had begun to feel the growing need to escape Mamie. She had begun to expect things of him that were not part of their original bargain. It was not that she expected expensive gifts, although she liked gifts, but more that she expected him to feel things he didn't feel and to spend more time with her than he wanted. She always seemed to be asking questions with her eyes that he had neither the words nor the inclination to answer. Staring out into the darkened landscape, King breathed a sigh of relief. He had escaped more than one danger. He wondered whether he would ever fall in love. The train's whistle blared out again, sounding a little bit like a scream.

FRIDAY, JUNE 18, 1920 ♛

Journer Braithwaite ran swiftly down Rue de Charlemagne and turned into a small alley leading into Market Square. She was gasping and out of breath. She peeked around the corner to see if she was still being followed. The street was crowded with hawkers' carts and other morning traffic. Horse- and ox-drawn carts were lurching slowly along in both directions. There were very few cars because Rue de Charlemagne was informally re-served for the slower, unmotorized traffic. Journer saw both men clearly for the first time since she discovered that they were following her. One man was tall, dark skinned, and wiry, while the other was of squat build and was light skinned with a gleaming, bald pate. They were obviously looking for her. The tall man had a long neck and a head that seemed al-most too small for his body. He and his partner nosed their way through the slow-moving traffic like ferrets seeking prey.

She frantically looked for a place to hide. The alley had doorways lead-ing off of it, but they were to people's homes. If they didn't know her, they wouldn't let her in their doors without some long-winded explanation. She needed something immediately. She rapidly walked down the alley and into the maze of stalls known as Market Square. She hunched down and continued quickly between the rows and rows of stalls, hoping to lose her pursuers. Journer got caught behind a slow-moving donkey cart that she couldn't get around. Finally, at a large intersection, which consisted of a convergence of rows, she was able to turn into an aisle going in her di-rection. She stopped for a moment in the shade under the canvas awning of Old Mrs. Whitaker's fish stall. The smell of shrimp, crawfish, and catfish was strong in the early morning sun despite the ice Mrs. Whitaker had placed on it to keep it fresh. Sweat dripped down Journer's dark brown face as she peered around the canvas searching for the two men.

Market Square was teeming with sellers and buyers moving between the canvas-covered stalls. At first she did not see the men. Then she saw one of them walking slowly down one of the outer rows of stalls, the thick-set, light brown–skinned man. Journer noticed that he had a pronounced eyebrow ridge with a receding forehead, which made him look like the caveman pictures she had seen on the sides of carnival wagons. The man was searching carefully. He stopped and signaled to someone on the other side of the square. She couldn't see the tall man with the long neck, but she knew he was nearby. She stepped farther behind the canvas. Her heart was fluttering and she was breathing hard.

Mrs. Whitaker, an old woman in her late sixties, watched Journer standing near the rear of her stall and followed her glance to the searching man. "You got to go, child," Mrs. Whitaker urged. "You wait and they's just gon' come through and search each stall." Mrs. Whitaker looked out on the square, her face lined and wrinkled with the years. "You got a chance if you wait 'til they's abreast of us and then you head back the way you come."

"I got to go the other way, Missus Whitaker," Journer said with desperation. "I got to get to the bank. If I don't pay on our loan today, they gon' close our diner down."

"Honey, I advise you to just give them the money if they catch you. Don't fight with 'em and make 'em mad. You 'member what they did to poor Fannie Bouvier? She still walk with a limp and her face is all scarred up."

"Missus Whitaker, I appreciates yo' advice, but I got to go contrary. My family ain't got nothin' else but the diner—and my dad, he's too old to start over."

"Duck down, honey, they gettin' close," Mrs. Whitaker warned as she watched the caveman draw nearer. "Maybe yo' pappy ought to rethink about payin' them DuMonts. Since y'all ain't set up to challenge them, it seem like it's part of the price of doin' business."

"We tryin' to pay our way out of debt! We ain't got no extra money fo' thugs!" Journer declared from her kneeling position. "One mo' year and we'll own our place free and clear! Otherwise, every dollar we earn, we eats or puts in the diner."

"A year's a long time. It's yo' health that's most valuable, honey. You remember that. These men ain't playin' no game. They gon' hurt you when they catch you, even if they don't catch you now. You gon' have to be on your toes every time you sticks yo' head out the door. Anyway, what kind of mens leaves a woman to do a man's job alone?"

"I was supposed to meet Phillip in the causeway, but I saw them mens following me and I just took off," Journer explained.

"Phillip who?" Mrs. Whitaker demanded.

"Duryea."

Mrs. Whitaker frowned down at her and dropped her voice. "You talkin' about young Phillip Duryea of the Duryeas that run them Teamsters between here and Fayetteville?" Journer nodded. The old lady could hardly contain herself. "Phillip Duryea can't stand up to these men. If he beats the ones that's followin' you, they'll send ten more just like 'em. Now, his father was a different story. He was a man of force. He built his business despite the Klan and everythin'. He was a tough old rooster in his day. But his son can't even get out of his shadow."

"Missus Whitaker, I hears you but I can't give up this money. Just help me, please. Just tell me when them mens is past."

"Of course, child. I's sorry to sermonize. Wait for a few minutes, then crawl out under that apron that runs between this'n and the LeBlancs' stall."

Journer did not say anything more. She did not want to engage in further conversation with old Mrs. Whitaker. But the old lady's words had hit home. She had only spoken what Journer had begun to admit to herself. Phillip was not a fighter, even though he did not lack courage. He could not protect her against the DuMonts. What she and her family needed now was a miracle or a man of force, as Mrs. Whitaker had said.

"Go now, honey, and God be with you," Mrs. Whitaker whispered.

Journer crawled into the darkness under a table and out into the back of the LeBlancs' stall. She saw the LeBlanc family members looking back at her casually as she continued crawling on her hands and knees. They did not want to draw attention to her so every glance was brief. She started to pull back the canvas, but Mr. LeBlanc—a short, balding, brown-skinned man with a thick black mutton-chop mustache that completely covered his top lip—hissed at her and waved her to halt. She stayed on her knees ready to spring up for several minutes before Mr. LeBlanc gave her the all-clear sign. She pushed through the canvas and stood up slowly. She walked purposely back in the direction opposite of that which she had seen her pursuers follow. She turned down a narrow passageway between two of the larger stalls. She stopped and caught her breath. She waited several seconds, then looked back in the direction from which she had come. No sign of the men. She gathered herself and readied herself for the long walk, passing under the arch that marked the entrance to Market Square. She was nearly to the arch when she saw the tall, long-necked man. He stepped out into the aisle just in front of her. Fortunately for Journer, he was looking the other way. She ducked behind a bare-chested man carrying a large bundle of kindling on his shoulder. She kept the bundle of kindling between her and the tall man as she made her way to the arch. She was about to enter the shadows under the arch when she heard a male voice calling her name.

"Journer! Hold on, Journer, it's me!"

She turned quickly and saw it was Phillip, his face smiling broadly. Out of the corner of her eye she saw the tall, dark man's head swivel on its long neck and look toward Phillip running to meet her. Before the tall man could pivot back and see who Phillip was calling to, Journer turned and ran under the arch. She was furious. Phillip had downplayed the possibility of the DuMonts robbing her in broad daylight. Now, stupidly, he was putting her life in danger.

She ran into the crowd. The street outside Market Square was jammed with people, Journer's heart pounding so loudly that all else was merely rumbling in the background. She didn't see people, she saw parts of them: a dirty white, half-unbuttoned shirt, a brown leather shoulder, an indignant curl of the lips, a bare, sweating back. The images merged into each other like a nightmare. She ran blindly into a stocky young woman and fell to the ground. When she stood up she heard Phillip call again, this time from just outside the arch. She turned to look and saw the caveman knock Phillip backward into a nearby stall. As he slipped from view she turned and ran.

She was now panicked, and no longer thinking clearly. Her only focus was to escape. She knew that if the men caught her, no one would intervene. She had seen numerous people, both men and women, beaten savagely on the street, and no one had ever stepped in on their behalf. The white police did not care what happened in Niggertown. Colored people were often killed and their murderers almost always went uncharged. She ran out of an alley into a street with motorized traffic. A car swerved to miss her. Journer barely heard the beeping of its horn. She waited for a break in the traffic and ran across the street into another alley. Instinctively, she was heading back home toward the riverfront.

The tall man with the long neck stepped out into the alley in front of her. Journer was momentarily paralyzed by his sudden appearance. He was perhaps thirty feet away. He put his fingers to his mouth and let out a high, piercing whistle, which was answered by another whistle nearby. His head turned on his long neck with the darting movement of a hunting bird or a snake. The eyes in his small head stared at her without blinking.

A grin was creeping across his dark-skinned face. He walked slowly toward her. "You done took us through quite a chase, little girl! We ain't much for runnin'. That's gon' cost you somethin' extry."

Over the tall man's shoulder, Journer saw a rider on a large chestnut horse pass briefly through the intersection behind him. She screamed out as loud as she could, "Please, Mister. Please help me!" The rider was already out of sight by the time she screamed. The tall man's head pivoted and looked. No one was in sight. He looked back at Journer and smiled broadly. "Ain't nobody comin' to help you!"

"Better say 'joe,' 'cause you sho' don't know!" advised King Tremain as he entered the alley, riding his horse toward them. He had drawn one of his pistols and hidden it under the cover of his folded hands. He studied the surrounding buildings for possible snipers or other such backup. He saw nothing suspicious. The man in front of him was fidgeting nervously with his waistband as if he couldn't make up his mind whether to pull his weapon or not. From the distance, King assumed it was a handgun. He continued to walk his horse toward the man without speaking. He had been in New Orleans for nearly five months, working quietly to open bank accounts and establish himself as a businessman. He hadn't made his presence known to anyone in his family except his Uncle Jake's wife. Nor had he taken any steps toward dealing with the DuMonts. This was an opportunity to begin his assault against the DuMonts.

"Maybe you don't know what you breakin' in on," the tall man suggested carefully, turning to face King.

"Maybe it don't matter to me," King answered, waiting for the man to pull his gun. He wasn't worried. King studied his antagonist. The man's hands had now dropped to his sides. King figured that the man was probably working freelance with his partner. King had seen them chasing the woman through crowds. He had followed along out of boredom. He knew who the two men were because a passerby had told him. King's horse's ears flicked back and he started to boggle. King took a firm grip on the reins and kept control. The horse was high-spirited and decidedly suspicious. It had smelled the presence of someone standing in a walkway between the two buildings on his left. King smiled broadly. It was the man's partner, hoping to ambush him.

"Why don't you let the girl go as a favor to me, seein' as we's just beginnin' our relationship and all?" King suggested affably.

"Nigger, you must be crazy! You must be drinkin' some bad homebrew and it done drove you clear out of yo' mind! Let her go? Shit, that would happen over my dead body!" The tall man moved his hands toward the edge of his jacket and quivered with anticipation.

"That ain't hard to arrange," King answered with a smile as he urged his nervous horse forward. The skittish animal's ears were now laid back flat on its head. "Why don't you have your friend come out in the open? He's scaring my horse."

As if he was only waiting for King to acknowledge his presence, the man burst from hiding and charged straight toward King. The instant the man came into view, the chestnut reared up, forcing King to lean forward and grab the reins to maintain his balance. The man's charge had such speed that he was nearly to the horse before it shied. The movement of the horse caused the man to miss his aim and he clawed frantically at King's clothes for a grip.

King had intended to shoot the man the moment he appeared, but it occurred to him that the discharge of a gun so close to the horse's head might cause it to bolt into a dead run. A panicked horse running full tilt on cobblestone streets would probably spell death for both the animal and its rider. He swung the butt of his pistol savagely down on the skull of his attacker. The blow landed soundly with a crack and momentarily trans-fixed the man midmotion. Before the man could recover, King struck him forcefully on the head again and the man collapsed on the cobblestones. The horse was prancing, ready to break into a run. King pulled the reins firmly and spoke soothingly in the animal's ear. After a few moments, the chestnut became more responsive to the touch of the reins. King walked the horse toward the remaining man.

There was no fear on the man's face, but there was a change in his de-meanor. The quick and savage vanquishing of his partner was unnerving. Sweat dripped down his dark face. The man backed away slowly with his knife at the ready, his head swaying back and forth on its long neck. He glanced away down the street as if insuring that he still had an avenue of escape. "I ain't a-feared of you!" he said unconvincingly.

King ignored the man and said to the woman who was standing wide-eyed in the middle of the street, "Why don't you come over here, and I'll give you a ride at least part ways to where you's going?"

Journer hesitated a moment, looking at her remaining pursuer, who glowered at her threateningly. She started toward the young stranger who had come to her rescue. She didn't know him, but she did know that if she refused his offer, the snake-necked man would probably still come after her. There was no choice; it was better to risk her fate with the unknown than stay and face definite assault and robbery. As she walked around her pursuer, Snake-neck started forward as if to intercept her, but the horse-man reined his horse forward swiftly. Her attacker immediately backed against the wall. Once she was beside the horse, her rescuer lifted her easily behind him. She was impressed with the stranger's physical strength and bearing.

King pointed his pistol at the face of his opponent. "Tell the DuMonts that King Tremain is back!" He turned the chestnut back toward the intersection and trotted away, the hoofbeats of his horse echoing in the suddenly quiet streets.

When Journer got back to the Fleur-de-Lys, everyone was already talking about her daring escape and the stranger on the big chestnut horse. Her aunt, Willa, whose plump body was wrapped in a starched white apron, was serving tables. Willa motioned with her eyes toward the residence in back of the restaurant. Journer complied. The restaurant was filled with people drinking, eating, and laughing, but when she entered, everyone fell silent. People stopped what they were doing to stare at her. As she continued on toward the back of the restaurant, murmuring began, and by the time she entered the residential quarters behind the kitchen, the conversation level had risen to its original volume. In the dimness of the residence's main room, Journer saw her mother and sister bending over her father's prone figure. "What happened? Is Pappy alright?" Journer gasped as she rushed to his side.

Her father lay on the bed and smiled weakly. There was a gash on his forehead and his lip had been split. She saw also that there were a number of bruises on his face. "What happened?" she demanded.

"Your father had to go and act the fool!" her mother said with both concern and anger.

"Ain't nothin', Journer, just a few cuts and scrapes. I'll be perky in the mornin'," her father chuckled. He took Journer's hand in his and said, "The important thing is, you is alright."

Despite his attempt at joviality, Journer could see that her father was hurting. "What happened?" she asked.

Her mother answered. "He went to decoy the DuMonts off you and then did too good a job of it. He got caught and then got stubborn and wouldn't tell them he didn't have the money on him. From what I hear they kicked and beat him for a good half hour before we got some folks out to get them off of him. Them dogs even broke your father's wooden leg!"

"It ain't nothin!" he proclaimed, trying to push himself up to a seated position. "But we gon' have to stay on the alert. We have to arrange to have somebody always sittin' shotgun, whether we's opened or we's closed."

"Slow down, ol' timer," her mother urged with affection. "You don't want to make no sudden moves and leave that gray fur on the bed."

"Don't be talkin' about my wig now, woman," her father warned as he wincingly put his hand on top of his head to ensure that everything was in order.

"Ajax, honey, it's up there, lookin' like a beat-up rug," her mother confirmed as she helped him lay back. As she was adjusting his pillows and blankets she said, "You best not be worryin' about the goin's on in the restaurant. You just get better, that's yo' job!"

"It ain't no time to be sick, Mary! There's things to do and arrangements to be made. We got to protect ourselves from what's got to be comin'," her father protested. "We got to call a meetin' of the Colored Merchants and Caterers Association. We gon' need help! Just think if we prove that somebody can stand up to these hoodlums, then maybe others'll try. Hot damn!"

"Ain't no need for profanity or any more shenanigans, Ajax Matthew Braithwaite," her mother chided, wiping his face with a towel. "You got to rest, honey. You's beginnin' to sweat again. Let's leave him rest for a while." Her mother stood up to usher her two daughters out of the room.

Journer worked side by side with her sister, Sarah, and Aunt Willa until closing time. She was asked over twenty times by different customers to recount the events leading up to her escape, but she declined. She wisely did not want to add to the DuMonts' level of indignation. After the day's-end cleanup had been completed and the receipts had been totaled, the storm shutters were closed and locked. Journer joined her mother and sister at the kitchen counter to drink the last of the pot liquor left from a cauldron of collards and ham hocks.

"Tell us what happened," her mother said, looking at her over the rim of her cup.

"Two of DuMont's men followed me as soon as I left the riverfront. I tried to lose them in Market Square and I would have gotten away, but then Phillip called to me and kept calling me until DuMont's men found me."

"How did you meet up with the stranger?" Sarah asked, poised on the edge of her stool with anticipation. Sarah had been a plain girl and had grown into a plain woman, not ugly, but plain. She had married the first man who asked her to marry him right out of school and now, ten years and three children later, she was unhappy with married life.

"He came out of nowhere. I think he was just passing in the street and I called to him. I didn't think he'd come to help me but he—"

"What did he look like?" Sarah interjected. "I heard he was young." Sarah spent her days and nights dreaming about the romantic interlude that she deserved to experience but would never have. She saw romance and mystery everywhere but in her marriage.

"He was young, somewhere between twenty and twenty-five," Journer said with a trace of a smile at her sister's predictability. "But his age wasn't the most interestin' thing about him."

"What else did you find so interestin' about this young man?" asked her mother.

"He gave me a ride on his horse and took me right to the bank, sayin' he had business there too. When we got there, we went around to the back door where Mr. Rambo runs the colored bank. I stood in line 'cause there was about three people in front of me. I think Reverend James was there and that nose-in-the-air, high yeller daughter of the undertaker was ahead of me, actin' all prissy."

"Not Lela Archambeaux?" Sarah asked, shaking her head. "I thought she was going up north to some colored college?"

"I heard she was pregnant by Billy Bigelow," Mary added.

"I don't know nothin' about that, but this man, he walked up to Jethro Pugh, you know that big, senseless fool Old Man Hollister hired to guard the colored side of the bank? Well, he walks right up to him and tells him that he's got business with young Mr. Hollister. Well, Jethro tells him to get in line. He don't believe a colored man's got any business with young Mr. Hollister."

"I ain't ever heard of one who had," confirmed Mary.

"Well, big stars fallin', it won't be long before day!" Journer said with a smile. "Mr. Hollister came out of the bank and greeted this colored man like they was old friends. They even moved Mr. Rambo out of his office to have a meetin'."

"What you say?" Mary exclaimed with a slow, surprised smile. "This young man must got some money or somethin'! But puttin' Old Big-head Rambo out of his office, ain't that somethin'? I'll bet Old Big-head liked that! What you say!"

Journer laughed. "You's right, Mama. The look on Mr. Rambo's face said everthin'. He was actin' all indignant, shakin' his head like an old gobbler, but young Mr. Hollister just shooed him out of the office. Old Rambo's so full of himself that he's probably still huffin' and puffin' around." Journer had both her mother and sister laughing at her imitation of Mr. Rambo's neck movement.

"So, what's his name?" Sarah asked, with her hands on her hips.

"King Tremain," answered Mary Braithwaite. "If you listened a little bit more, Sarah, you would have heard his name said several times tonight. It seems like a lot of people know him. He got quite a reputation in the French Quarter as a gambler and cardplayer. This here boy could be a bundle of dynamite, if what they say is true."

"I tell you one thing," Journer added, "he ain't no boy except in age.

There's a hardness about him. There weren't no question in my mind that he would have killed both those men right there and they knew it too. He got some real ice in his veins."

"I think we've had enough talkin' tonight," Mary said to her daughters. "We got to be up early tomorrow. Remember first thing in the mornin', somebody's got to go over and get Doc McKenna. We don't know how bad your pappy's hurt. We need him and his spirit if we gon' beat the DuMonts out of takin' our money. So, everybody to bed. I'll check the locks and turn off the lights." Her daughters gave her hugs and climbed the steep staircase to the loft, which served as their bedroom.

Mary Braithwaite heaved her considerable figure erect and went around the restaurant, checking the doors. She had been a winsome lass in her youth, light of limb and step, but the pressures of bearing five children, of which two were born dead, and the years of hard labor had taken their toll. Over the changing seasons she had swollen into a stout woman with huge, rolling buttocks and sagging breasts. Her arms were flabby and she shuffled when she walked, yet her mind was still keen and there was sufficient muscle beneath the fat to work hard fifteen hours a day, seven days a week. Mary blew out the remaining oil lamp, switched off the electric light over the kitchen counter, and took a last look around. In the darkness, it was not hard for her to visualize the years past when she and her husband had worked out of a stall in Market Square or the countless times they had gone hungry to feed the children. It had taken years but they finally owned a building with electricity. It was true, the mortgage was heavy, but it was bearable without the DuMonts. Mary and her husband had big plans for the restaurant. They were even looking into the cost of putting in a flush toilet. But those were fantasies. She lowered herself down to her knees and bent her head in prayer. The family had much to be thankful for, even though they still needed considerable divine intervention.

As always, when Mary prayed in the darkness of the restaurant, she looked up at the huge electric chandelier that hung overhead. She and her husband had purchased the cut-glass fixture from an old aunt for whom it was the sole retirement reward for forty years work in the kitchens of an antebellum mansion. At the time, the aunt lived in an old shack without electricity. The white family that gave her the fixture must have had many nights of laughter over the irony of their gift. Mary and Ajax paid the old woman twice what she asked and would have paid her more except that was all they could afford, and it still took them nearly a year to pay it off. Of all the things in the restaurant, the chandelier represented the future most to Mary and her husband. It was the example of the direction in which they wanted to take their establishment.

As Mary got up from her knees, the idea that had been gnawing at the back of her mind all night sprang full-grown into her consciousness. Journer's rescuer seemed to be the key. Since he appeared to be ready to fight the DuMonts on his own, why not allow it to appear that the Fleur-de-Lys was also under his wing. Mary knew she could create a connection. After all, she had two healthy daughters. Journer was a big-boned woman with a nice figure and a wonderful smile that drew men like honey drew flies. Sarah was more slender of build and gentler of spirit and had her own following among the young swains, until she had married.

Mary had never asked her daughters to be with someone in an intimate way, but if the family business depended upon it, she expected them to do their duty without complaint. It was no less than she had done in the early years of her marriage. "When yo' children are hungry, you find ways to feed them," she often said in memory of those times. Mary Braithwaite was a God-fearing woman, but she averred that a poor man's path to God was far different than that of a rich man. She saw no immorality in any act that was done for the purpose of helping the family survive.

MONDAY, JUNE 21, 1920

The rain fell in sputtering rhythms, beating against the window pane with the sound of a snare drum playing in free meter. Outside the overcast sky did not define itself into dark roiling clouds, but instead presented an even, slate gray ceiling extending without break to the horizon. Only the wind, pushing the rain and bending the trees, gave evidence of the vast power that lay within the monotony of gray. Every once in a while a gust would rush along the eaves of the roof, pressing itself through the cracks along the tops of the walls and then whistle over the heads of the men sitting around a stained, felt card table.

Lester DuMont was speaking. "So let me hear yo' report, Roscoe. I ain't got time for a lot of shit! The whole damn business looks like it gon' fall apart while I listen to yo' stutterin' ass!"

Roscoe, a plump, dark-skinned man who had been trying his best to relay his information, was now rendered totally incapable of speaking. He was stuck on the first syllable of his sentence, "The-the-the-the—"

Lester cut off Roscoe with a wave of his hand. "Can't one of you other idiots tell me what the hell happened at the Merchants Association meeting?"

Dexter Benny, a short wiry man, answered. "I can tell you, Boss. They's organizin'. Them people think they can stand up to you. There must of been forty people from Market Square. Me and Roscoe left when we saw the deacons from the Light of Zion Church."

"Ain't nobody got any brains?" Lester protested. "How come you just didn't break up the meetin' right then and there? They ain't no merchants, they's just street hawkers. These people ain't got no guts unless you let them think they do. They is sheep. You supposed to be the wolf!"

"They had them more than a few carbines with 'em. It wasn't nothin' the two of us could've did against forty people," Dexter said calmly, fingering the hilt of his knife.

Lester didn't like Dexter. He had an inordinate suspicion of little men. He felt that they were always compensating for their size. But Dexter was extremely good with a knife and could throw it with either hand. Dexter's skill with the blade made his casual fingering of the knife while he was answering Lester all the more unpalatable. Lester planned to deal with him in due time, but first he had bigger fish to fry. He needed time to come up with a strategy for dealing with the Merchants Association.

"How about that nigger on the horse? You got the info on who this wild-assed nigger is?" Lester DuMont asked.

Cody Petway bobbed his head on his long neck up and down several times. "Yes, suh, we found out where he's stayin' and everythin'. His name is Tremain. He call hisself King Tremain, but his family knows him as LeRoi."

"Where the hell did this one come from?" demanded Lester. "I thought we had taken care of those Tremains a couple of years ago. Do I have to go out there and wipe out all of them?"

Old Damon Shackleford pulled the tip of his lush white mustache. "It seems to me that was the name of the boy who run off to the army after killin' them deputies in the bayou three, four years ago." Old Man Shackleford was a local historian. He knew most of the colored families of any consequence in and around New Orleans. "As I reckon it, the Tremains been due for a reincarnation of some of their bad blood. You know every thirty, forty years they have a child that terrorizes the Territory. If they got one now, he's the one." There were gasps from men around the table. These were not men who feared other ordinary men, but they were well acquainted with the concept of bad blood and they feared meeting a man who had it running in his veins.

"What you talkin' about, old man?" Lester asked, letting impatience seep into his tone. "I keep you's around to advise me, not to scare my mens with stories of haints and such!"

"I was just tellin' about what everybody knows," the old man said in his quiet voice. "Names like Bordeaux, St. Clare, and Black Jacques is part of local legend and they's all Tremains. I'm thinkin' this boy is—"

"I ain't got time for no fairy tales, Shackleford!" Lester interrupted. He looked around the table at the five men seated there. Other than Shackleford, the rest of the men were young. A couple of them were craving for an opportunity to show what they could do. Lester directed his gaze to Cody. He had always intuitively disliked Cody and his long neck. He reminded Lester of an ostrich that he had seen in a traveling carnival. "Cody, why don't you tell us again why you didn't just shoot this fool down when he first butt in our business?"

"Uh, Mr. DuMont, uh, I said I didn't have no gun. I ain't no kind of shot no way. I just only brought my knife 'cause we was just chasin' a girl. I wasn't ready to deal with no gunslinger."

"How come you didn't give him the bull rush the same time as Davis did? You could've probably taken him! Where the hell is that Davis anyway?"

A lean, muscular man sitting next to Old Man Shackleford snickered. "He's still outside sittin' in the rain like you told him and it look like he gon' sit there all night."

"Thanks, Oren," Lester acknowledged with a humorless laugh. "This here Tremain feller has already done made the gall rise up in my throat and I ain't even seen the man. He knocks one of my best mens senseless as a turkey in a hailstorm and then helps my money get to the bank in somebody else's account. I think I'm gon' send a couple you boys to visit him and make him see that ain't the way we do things around here."

"What you gon' do about Davis?" Shackleford asked. "I think he needs to see a doctor."

"I don't give a damn what happens to him! If he ain't got the sense to come in out of the rain, he ain't no good to me and I ain't payin' no doctor bills for him! Leave him out there or drive him off, I don't give a shit! He's goddamned useless! Two men against one should always come out on top!

"Cody, I want you and Ralph to take care of this Tremain and don't come back without his heart!"

Lester DuMont ran a small organization based primarily on extortion and crooked gambling. He had risen to recent prominence after the DuMont family won an extended gangland war with a rival organization.

In the series of shoot-outs between the two gangs both his older brothers were killed, which was devastating to everyone but Lester, for the two oldest brothers had served as the real brains of the organization. Although Lester did not lack in courage, he did not have the vision necessary for his organization to grow and compete with larger and stronger families. Nor was he a leader who instilled loyalty in his men. It was sheer good fortune that Lester's last spontaneous assault had caught the entire leadership of his enemies in one building, which he subsequently put to flame. Lester and his men sniped their rivals from cover as they ran from the burning building. It was a duck shoot and, as Lester would say, "Nary a duck got off the ground."

As Lester stepped out into the rain to go to one of his women's residences, he had no idea that King was hunting him. All he noticed was that Davis was no longer sitting on the steps. He nodded his approval as he got into the car. He liked to see that his orders were followed. He stared through the window at the passing rain-soaked streets and dreamed that one day all that he drove through would be his. Lester put a cigar in his mouth and Oren, his driver, leaned over to light it. There was no doubt in Lester's mind that he was becoming a big man. His business was generating enough money that he now had to pay off the sheriff—small-time hoods didn't have to make payoffs.

High above the street, on a roof overlooking the building from which Lester had exited, lay King. The rain dripped off his oil slicker. He picked up his rifle, which he had wrapped in an oil-treated cloth, and descended the stairs. In another week, he would be ready to make his move. He had spent three days scouting the DuMonts' various businesses and following Lester on his rounds. King had a pretty good assessment of the DuMont family holdings and of Lester's activities in particular. According to the news on the street, the DuMonts had recently won a territorial war with a rival family and had expanded into new areas.

As King climbed over the edge of the building's parapet and dropped down to the roof of an adjacent building, he would have smiled at the progress he had made in his reconnaissance, if it were not for the image of the man sitting on the steps in the rain. King had watched him sitting there for more than two hours without benefit of a coat or hat. It was a thing that made King despise Lester all the more. King had heard all about the man he had hit with the butt of his pistol and how the man had appeared to have lost his senses. Even though King was the person who had caused the man's incapacitation and was the person who would have killed him without hesitation, he still thought the man was being treated unconscionably. To King, the man was a soldier and as such deserved to be taken care of when injured in battle. Anyone who would abandon a man who had fought on his behalf was a man without honor and someone who could not under any circumstances be trusted.

King opened a door and entered a darkened hallway. Halfway down the hall, King stopped at a door and unlocked it. He had rented a small apartment in a grimy tenement to provide himself a nearby staging area for both reconnaissance and armed sorties against the DuMonts. He quickly doffed his wet army-surplus fatigues and military slicker and put on civies and a fashionable great coat. After carefully locking away his rifle in a metal cabinet, which he had bolted to the floor beneath the bed, King left the apartment and descended the stairs to his car. The rain was still falling as he drove away.

SUNDAY, JUNE 27, 1920

"How long you think you can stay in business without payin' me, huh?" Lester DuMont demanded. He was leaning against the counter that separated the kitchen from the dining area in the Fleur-de-Lys. He pushed away from the counter and sauntered across the floor to where the four women stood. "Hell, if I was a vengeful man, I'd burn this place down with y'all in it! Hell, if I was greedy, I'd take a hundred percent of yo' profits! But I ain't greedy. I'm willin' to take a measely fifty-five percent, 'specially if I can get payment some kind of other way."

Mary could no longer help herself, as the tears started to run down her face. Everything she and her husband had worked for over the years was on the brink of destruction. She looked down at the floor and saw a feeble movement from Ajax as he struggled back to consciousness. He had been hit with a cudgel and kicked until he lost his senses. She was at once thankful that he was waking and yet she wanted him to remain unconscious a bit longer. She knew he would not agree to any concessions to the DuMonts, especially a percentage of the business. His pride was a big thing to him and it was always the source of problems in any negotiation. If there was any possibility of finding a compromise short of losing the business, she wanted to find it quickly. "I'm listening, Mr. DuMont."

Journer, Sarah, and Willa were silent. Mary could hear her heart pounding again in her breast like voodoo drums before the sacrifice. She looked at each of the three men with Lester DuMont, hoping to find a face with compassion, but all she saw were smiles of anticipation.

"Well, I knows you ain't got no money around now, 'cause I had Oren and Luke check the place out, but I knows by the end of the week you gon' have some money and I wants fifty-five percent of it. I don't care about no bills you got to pay or nothin'. I wants inconvenience money." Lester smiled, revealing several golden teeth. He patted his heavily greased hair back into place. "Then after you pays that, we'll talk about yo' bills and such. There's one thing. Since you ain't been exactly straightforward with me, I'm gon' take me a hostage to make sure you do what we agreed. Of course, I'm gon' expect this hostage to respect me and do what I say. If the hostage cooperates real good, the fifty-five percent rate stays. If she don't cooperate, the rate goes up. You got it?"

The implication was quite clear to Mary. The price of staying in business was one of her daughters for a week. She pretended like she didn't understand. "I'll get my things. I'll be ready to go with you in a minute."

Her words were received with a chorus of derisive laughter from the men around the room. "Ain't nobody want to take you anywhere, you fat old bat!" Lester sneered and pointed at Journer. "I wants me that dark brown girl with the big smile."

Mary swallowed hard. The price was high, but it was worth it, if it would buy sufficient time for the family to devise an alternate plan. She nodded, assenting to Lester's proposal.

Journer was staring at her mother with a look of disbelief. "Whatchoo sayin', Mama? You gon' give me up to him to save the restaurant? Ain't no way I'm goin' with him without a fight! This ain't the way Papa would do it. He wouldn't sell me for this place!"

"If it's a fight you want, it's a fight you'll get. I likes to oblige," Lester said with a nasty smile. "Of course, I might have to pass you around to my boys if they gots to fight you. If you come along peaceable like, I'll keep you to myself."

"You low-down dog! I'll die first!" Journer shouted.

"Please, Mr. DuMont," Mary begged. "Let me talk to her alone for a minute?"

Lester nodded, but Journer stared at her mother with anger. "Whatchoo got to say to me? I don't care what it is, I don't want to hear it!"

Mary grabbed her daughter's arm and dragged her toward an unoccupied corner of the restaurant. "Listen here, you little fool; that's yo' father lying bleeding on the floor and these mens is set to kill the rest of us. All you got to do is go with him and they'll leave us alive!"

"What about me, Mama. Ain't I worth nothin'? You just gon' give me away like you do a sack lunch? I guess this restaurant is worth more to you than me, huh? All my dreams about a nice wedding is done, huh?"

"This ain't the end of the world. You ain't doin' nothin' other women ain't done. You can still get married after this."

"Who gon' want me after all of them done finished with me?"

"If you give it up without fighting, you'll come out without a scar. Ain't no reason for nobody else to know."

"I'm gon' know, Mama. I'm gon' know from the inside out!"

"Yo' family is near to gettin' killed! Whatchoo savin' it for? Don't try to tell me that you still a virgin, 'cause I knows you got familiar with that boy who was shot by the Klan. You done already give it up, so what difference do four more men make, 'specially if it buys the life of yo' family?"

"I ain't been with but one man and we'd have got married if'en he hadn't been killed. I ain't lookin' to live the life of no sinnin' harlot!"

"Whatchoo got between yo' legs ain't as important as the lives of yo' family! I done worse to feed you and yo' sister!"

Journer stared at her mother with disgust. "So? That don't make it right! What about what Papa says about doin' things what makes you feel good about yourself and stayin' from things that make you think you ain't worth nothin'?"

"Look where all that pride and philosophizin' got yo' pappy. He lyin' on the floor bleedin'. His life is in the hands of his daughter."

"But look at him, Mama. He still got his dignity. Ain't nobody doubt he's a man."

"When you's dead dignity is just a word," Mary sighed, weary of the discussion. "You decide whether we live or die. It's on you." Mary turned and walked away, but her heart felt crushed. The terrible look on Journer's face when Mary had admitted to doin' worse to feed her and her sister was still with her.

"Y'all work out somethin'?" Lester asked, checking his suit for stains. Mary was silent. He looked at Journer, who was still standing in the corner. "How you want it, little lady?"

"I'll come, but I'll come on my own. I'll be at your building on Front Street at nine o'clock tonight."

"How you think you gon' bargain with me?" Lester demanded. "You ain't got nothin' but yo' life. You some kind of crazy, if you think I'm gon' let you tell me when you comin'?"

"Then come get me!" Journer challenged as she pulled a large cleaver and butcher knife from beneath her skirts. "I been workin' preparin' food all my life and I've learned to throw a cleaver or two," she declared with a grim set to her jaw. "And the first one I'm gon' throw at is you!" Journer cocked her arm until the cleaver was just behind her ear.

Lester's men moved away from him as they sought to take positions around Journer. Lester was standing within fifteen feet of the girl and he didn't think that she would miss him from that distance. Lester laughed. He didn't want to show his fear to his men, so he said with a magnanimous gesture, "I'll tell you what, little lady, I'm gon' do you a favor and accept yo' offer. If'en you don't show you know what I'll do to this restaurant, don'tcha?"

"Don't worry yourself, I'll come as I promised, but if you don't get out of here now with your scum, I'm liable to have an accident with this cleaver!"

"It's 'cause our business is over that I'm leavin'! I ain't a-feared of you and yo' little knife! I'm lookin' forward to seein' you at nine tonight, sweetheart!" Lester patted his hair once again to assure that the waves were even and signaled his men to head out the door. "Evenin', Mama Braithwaite. Give my best to yo' husband if he wakes up." Lester laughed, enjoying his joke, and his men joined in with him.

As soon as they were gone, Mary knelt beside her husband and ordered for someone to bring her water. Journer spent a moment staring down at her father before she turned and went back into the living quarters. She quickly braided her hair into a long pigtail and wound it into a bun, which she fastened at the back of her head with a sharpened wooden dowel. She was not trying to pretty herself. She wanted to get her long hair out of the way. She didn't want to give her enemies anything additional to hang on to, plus she knew that she looked more matronly with her hair in a bun.

Within ten minutes, Journer had a bundle together and was ready to leave. She reentered the dining area and watched as Willa and Sarah helped her mother carry her father to a chair. Blood was flowing down the side of his head and he seemed addled and confused. Journer waited until they had situated him comfortably before she spoke. "I'm leaving now," she said.

Her mother looked up and asked quietly without rancor, "You leavin' us to stand it alone or can we count on you?"

"Don't worry about yo' restaurant! I know what's important to you! I'll keep my appointment! You got yo' restaurant! You don't need me! I ain't ever gon' set foot in this place again! And I swear to God, I never want to see you or talk to you as long as I live!"

Mary wailed, "Don't say that, Journer!"

Journer waved to her sister and aunt and walked back through the living quarters to leave by a seldom-used door that let out onto a small pathway that ran between several small buildings. She waited for several minutes, allowing her eyes to adjust to the darkness before she set out into the shadows of the night.

• • •

Ajax Braithwaite sat up with an effort. His head was pounding like a giant church bell and there was an attendant ringing in his ears. It hurt every time he took an intake of breath. His side felt as if there was a knife penetrating his rib cage and his vision was blurry. The pain caused him to have a sense of disassociation as his thoughts tumbled over themselves, like children rushing out of the confines of a classroom.

"Lay back, Ajax. You got to rest," admonished his wife. "You gon' kill yourself if'en you don't let your body heal."

"Is they gone?" he asked through the red haze that seemed to come to rest just above his eyebrows.

"Yes, thank God. They left about an hour ago."

"What did they take?" he asked, fighting to stay focused.

"They . . . uh . . . uh—"

"What did they leave with!" Ajax demanded. His voice was louder and more insistent. "What did they leave with?" He started calling. "Sarah? Journer? Willa?" Sarah and Willa came to the doorway of the bedroom.

"Can I get somethin' for you, Papa?" Sarah asked with a husky voice. Even though he couldn't see her, Ajax could tell that she had been crying. It was her voice that gave her away. "Where is Journer? Where is Willa?" He asked, forcing himself to speak clearly.

"I'm here, Brother Ajax," Willa answered from the door.

Ajax looked in Willa's direction. He could barely make out her shape in the doorway. She seemed to be part of the blurred darkness of the room. "Where is Journer?" He demanded. "Mary, what have you done?"

"I'm just tryin' to help the family survive, Ajax."

"What price have we paid for this?" Ajax asked, his voice suddenly soft.

Mary stuttered as she answered. "Journer is gon' stay with Lester as a hostage until we give him the money for this week's business."

"Willa, Sarah, I need to talk with my wife in private," said Ajax. He heard the shifting and shuffling of feet and then there was quiet. His wife was still sitting at the foot of the bed. He could hear her breathing. He took several breaths and asked in a trembling tone, "What did we get for Journer?"

Mary was infused with a growing sense of dread. With each question Ajax asked, she saw her plans falling apart at the seams. The very thing she had sought to avoid was going to occur. "This weren't my idea, Ajax," she explained. "It was Lester that brought it up. I offered myself first, but he wanted her. He was gon' burn down the whole place with us in it. We had to give in."

"Might as well have burned the damned place down. Every time I look at it from now on, I'm gon' think, 'Was it worth a daughter?' "

"You got to listen to me, Ajax," Mary pleaded. "They was gon' kill us! Not just me and you, but Sarah and Willa too."

"What kind of lives they gon' have now, under Lester's foot? If he want 'em, he just gon' take 'em. You think I can live with that? A man's got to be a king somewhere in his life. Otherwise he got a pack of trouble keepin' his dignity."

"You and Journer always talkin' about this here dignity. You just putting crazy notions in her head and mixing her up, makin' her think she's gon' be more than just another hard-workin' colored woman."

"A notion is a powerful thing, Mary. 'Specially if you mix it with blood. It's 'cause of notions and blood, this here country was born; 'cause of notions and blood, we's free from slavery. Colored people need mo' notions. And dignity is a mighty fine notion to have in yo' chest. Anyway, ain't much I can give my daughters but notions."

"Them notions gon' cost Journer somethin' terrible," Mary said.

"Not more'n she gon' pay now!" Ajax rejoined as he pushed himself erect and stood, swaying stiffly. "Did he take her with him?"

"No, she told him that she'd be at his house by nine o'clock."

"Ain't got much time," Ajax said. "Where are my clothes?"

"Whatchoo gon' do, Ajax? Lester's got a whole army. You's just one man. You just gon' end bein' killed or hurt somethin' terrible! Why can't we try to get some members of the Merchants Association to help?"

"Ain't time for all that jabberin' before actin'. I got to go save my daughter now! Where is my clothes, Mary?"

"It ain't the end of the world, Ajax. If'en you remember, I sold myself to a lot more than four men and we still had a life after it."

"We was starvin'. I couldn't get no work. Our chil'ren was gon' die. We didn't have no choice then, but we don't want that life for our daughter!"

"She too good to do what I did for the family?"

"That ain't it, 'cause ain't nobody too good to sacrifice for the family, but this kind of sacrifice is one we wants to leave in the past. We don't want that for our chil'ren. We wants things to be better for them than it was for us. Otherwise, why is we workin' so hard day after day?"

Mary burst out, "Don't go! Please don't go, Ajax!"

"Ain't no way I could hold my head up if I didn't go after her," he said as he pulled up his pants and strapped his best wooden leg onto the stump of his thigh. "Mary, you notice how people respect me, not treatin' me like they treats other amputees? That's 'cause I works at it. I works hard at pulling my share and I works on my spirit too. I knows no good can come from bitterness, but I can't live with knowing that, while I drew breath, that DuMont dog had my daughter. What do I got that's mo' important than my chil'ren? Ain't nothin' I can think of; not even my life! I got no choice here. I got to go!" Ajax stood up and pulled a broadcloth tunic over his head. It was a homemade garment with two huge side pockets. Ajax turned back to his wife and said softly, "I couldn't live with myself, Mary, if I let things lie. It's the price of a backbone."

"What good is that, if'en you's dead? What good is it to me?" Mary asked, the tears trickling down her face.

"What good am I alive, if I ain't got no insides? I wouldn't be nobody you know or want to know! I lost my leg in the Battle of San Juan Hill. So I know the color of my own blood and I know seein' it ain't a bad thing if that's the cost of doin' right." Ajax stumped over to the closet. He opened the door and pulled a twelve-gauge shotgun from a recess. He opened the breech and checked the action. He took a box of shotgun shells and emptied them into his tunic pockets. "I got to go now. If the Lord wills, I'll return."

At approximately the same time as Ajax was leaving the restaurant, Journer found King. She hadn't really given thought as to what she would say or even what she might ask. As she was stewing over this problem, standing in a small waiting room on the first floor of the Beau Geste, King passed through the curtains that served as the door and entered the room. There was no recognition in his eyes when he looked at her, and his expression was not inviting. Journer stammered out an explanation. "Uh, sorry to trouble you, Mr. Tremain, but uh, I'm, I'm . . . I need help real bad. The DuMonts have my family in a squeeze."

"So why are you telling me?" King asked.

Journer was speechless. King acted like he didn't know her. A friend had told her that King was one of the high-rolling gamblers playing that evening in a big card game somewhere on the edge of Algiers. She had gone frantically to four different gambling establishments before finding the card game and she never once considered that King would not help her. "I came to you because you helped me before and because it's the DuMonts that I got troubles with. They beat up my papa and they gon' take me hostage 'til we pays protection money."

"Okay, I helped you once," King shrugged. "I still don't see what makes this my business now." He recognized her, but did not feel that there was any bond between them. Yet in one sense he was grateful to Journer for interrupting his card game. The cards had not been going his way and he had lost three hundred dollars. He thought perhaps the break in play would be sufficient to change the direction of the cards. Now he was staring into Journer's beautiful face, listening to her tale of woe.

"You one of the few colored mens in this parish that ain't afraid of them. I didn't know where else to go."

"Look, I'm in a card game. There's a two-thousand-dollar pot on the table and four hundred of it is my money. We took a five-minute break so that I could come out here. If I ain't back in five, I lose my money."

"Please," Journer begged. "I don't know what else to do, Mr. Tremain. Do I just give myself to them so they can use me until my family gets their money collected? What happens to me after I go to them, Mr. Tremain?" She dropped to her knees on the floor and sobbed.

The Braithwaites were one of the few families that stood up to Lester DuMont. King admired their courage. It was only right that he should come to their aid. "Let me finish this hand and I'll see what I can do."

"I'll give you anything you want." She started lifting her skirt slowly to insure he understood what she meant. "I'll give you anything!"

"Drop your skirt, gal," King said with a wave of his hand. "I's helpin' yo' family! Ain't no use in you humiliatin' yo'self. I'm gon' finish the hand and I'll be back."

"Thank God," Journer gasped.

From outside the curtains, a voice called out, "Journer? Journer, where are you? Journer?"

Journer looked toward the door with anticipation. Phillip Duryea's head pushed through the curtains and he saw her sitting on the floor. He stepped into the room with his fists balled. "What's going on here? Journer, are you alright?" he demanded as he rushed to kneel at her side. The man wore his kinky hair close-cropped and appeared to be in his midthirties, about average height and build. He looked at King with an angry gaze. "Did you hurt her? The DuMonts pay you to hurt women?"

King looked at the man and said, "I ain't the enemy!"

Journer grabbed Phillip's shirt collar and explained. "This is King Tremain! He's the one that saved me from Cody and Sampson."

Phillip's frown vanished and was replaced by a smile. He stepped forward with his right hand extended. "My name is Phillip Duryea. I'm happy to make your acquaintance, Mr. Tremain. I'm beholden to you for what you did for Journer. Please pardon my mistake."

"Everybody makes a mistake sometime," King acknowledged with a nod of his head. He looked into Phillip's eyes. "I told her that I would come back after I finish the hand I's playin' in the other room."

"You'll help us, Mr. Tremain?" Phillip asked.

"I'm gon' try, but I got fish to fry now!" King answered. He returned to the room where the game was being held. There were five men sitting at the table. King sat down in his seat.

The owner of the Beau Geste, a Creole named Claude Bichet, was watching the cards, as was his wont during high-stakes games. He was a light-skinned man with thick wavy hair and, as usual, he was dressed to the nines in a double-breasted dark blue suit, with spats over polished patent leather shoes. Bichet was not particularly physically commanding; he was of medium height and build, but he had the air of a man who meant business. He had built the Beau Geste up from a nondescript roadhouse to one of the top sporting houses in Algiers, and it was still his although more than a few had tried to take it away. "Everyone is back, yes? The game begins," Bichet declared.

The final two cards of a seven-card-draw hand were dealt out. A Cajun named Faison Baptiste led the betting with two queens showing. When the seventh card was dealt only King, Faison, and Jimmy One-Eye remained. Faison raised two hundred dollars. King had two pair, but they were low cards. He threw his cards in and stood up. "This ain't my night and this ain't my game! I think eight hundred dollars is all I'm gon' donate tonight!"

"If you lose eight hundred dollars for three nights straight, I still wouldn't get back all I lost to you last week," Faison declared as he was called to show his cards by Jimmy One-Eye. Faison turned over three queens and took the pot.

"Gentlemen, I'll see you next week," King said as he walked out of the card room. Phillip Duryea was waiting for him at the bar. There was a brass band playing loud music on the other side by the dance floor. "Where's Journer?" King asked.

"I sent her to wait at my father's warehouse. I thought perhaps you could help us devise a plan."

"Let's go outside where it's quieter," King suggested. Phillip nodded his assent.

Outside the Beau Geste, the night sky twinkled overhead as King and Phillip stood talking in the shadows by the parked cars. King was suggesting that Phillip delay in making any move against the DuMonts until they had worked out a feasible plan when Faison walked out of the Beau Geste. He was a short, thick man with long brown hair. He called out to King. "Maybe next time you stay longer, eh Tremain? I think luck is smiling on—"

Two rifle shots rang out. A car window next to where King and Phillip were standing shattered and the bullet from the second shot splintered the wood above their heads. King and Phillip both dropped to the ground. Two more shots were fired, then silence.

King had a pistol in his hand and was crawling away from the cars when a voice called out. "He gone! He gone now! He run away!"

"Who's gone?" King demanded. He looked cautiously over the fender of a car and saw the old man who sold spicy fish stew from a cart outside the Beau Geste waving a spoon.

"Chess DuMont!" the old man replied. "He try ambush then run away. He ride his horse toward the old bridge! Another one was with him!" The old man waved his serving spoon in the direction of New Orleans.

"Goddamn DuMonts!" Faison said, picking himself up off the ground. "I just bought these pants! I'll kill the bastards myself!"

"How was Journer getting back to New Orleans?" King asked Phillip.

"Across the old bridge," Phillip replied. "You don't think that Chess might catch her, do you?"

"If he and one of his brothers are on horseback, it seems likely. She couldn't make it across the bridge befo' they closed on her. You best go check on her! I'll meet you at the Hotel Toussant."

Phillip shook his head. "If he's taken her, I'll just have to take some men to Lester DuMont's house on Front Street and we'll force our way in! He won't be expecting us to come to his front door. Hopefully, his men will be spread out all over the city. Maybe he'll be taken by surprise!"

"What about the snipers he got set up on the roofs next to his building?" King asked. "If'en you don't attack with the right plan, you gon' be the one surprised. They gon' shoot you down without you gettin' to the door, much less through the door."

Phillip looked at King with respect. "I didn't know he had snipers set up. But what can I do? If he has her, I've got to go after her!"

"Even if it means yo' death?" King inquired. "He got himself a small army and he live in a fort!"

"Even if it means that!" Phillip answered. "I love her! I got no choice! I've got to go now!" Phillip cranked his car until it turned over. Once it was chugging, he climbed in and drove away.

Faison walked over to King and asked, "You will help him, eh?"

"This is the second time these DuMont fools have tried to bushwack me!" King explained. "I'm gon' have to finish all these DuMonts! I was only thinkin' about Lester, but I see I'm gon' have to do Chess and Eddy too!"

"Just don't get yo'self killed, *mon ami*! You still have three thousand dollars of my money I must still win back! And by the way, my friends are very interested in yo' bootleggin' idea. We should meet soon. Maybe you come out to the house and we eat, eh?"

King and Faison talked a few more minutes, then parted company. The shadows of the night became more clearly defined as a pale moon waxed across the midnight sky. King looked up and chuckled at the unchanging stars, for fate and circumstance had forced him to take actions that he would have rather delayed. But he was not sad. A waiting game would merely give Lester more confidence. King gave the old man who sold fish stew a few dollars in gratitude and left his car parked in front of the Beau Geste to throw off any potential pursuers. He kept to the shadows and the less traveled streets and soon disappeared into the night.

King rode his horse through the quiet streets. The night had deepened since his meeting with Phillip. The moon was nearly gone, but stars overhead glistened as if they had been newly polished. It was nearly ten o'clock and there were a few small-time merchants and hawkers trudging alongside their tired animals, moving their carts and wagons to their nightly storage. King had an unsheathed rifle across his saddle and the barrel gleamed in the dim light. When people saw him coming, they moved wordlessly to the side and let him pass.

He turned down a small street to avoid crossing through Market Square and heard a group of men laughing and taunting someone. King started to take another route, but decided against it because he didn't want to travel on any of the larger streets. The sound of his horse's hooves preceded him. By the time he drew close to the men, he saw they were beating and taunting a man who was huddled on the ground. A couple of the men had long wooden staves and they swung these two-handed, bringing them down on the back of their fallen victim with bone-crushing thuds. As King drew abreast, they stopped to watch. No one missed the fact that he had a rifle across his saddle.

As they stood back to watch him pass, King recognized the man on the ground as the one he had hit on the head when he first met Journer. Suddenly, he was furious. The men standing around the body reminded him of coyotes surrounding an injured wolf. They would never have had the courage to attack a healthy animal, but once their foe was incapacitated they were very daring. He reined his horse. "What's going on here?"

"Ain't nothin'. We just takin' care of somebody that done caused us a lot of grief in his time," a man ventured carefully.

"Yeah. Now it's our turn to give him some back," another cried as he turned and gave the inert body another whack.

"Don't hit that man again!" King ordered, barely able to contain himself.

A tall, big-boned man stepped forward. "You's one man. You got the gall to give orders to eight of us?"

King pulled a pistol from his holster and hissed. "There's eight of you now, but there won't be one left standin' when I'm finished shootin' and I'm gon' kill you first!"

The first man who spoke stammered, "That's him! That's Tremain!"

Suddenly, there was a different mood among the men. Several backed away immediately. One dropped his staff. The big-boned man looked around and found that he was standing alone. He pushed the brim of his homemade hat back on his head so that he could get a good look at King. "You Tremain?" he asked.

"Yeah, you ready to die?" King retorted.

"I ain't got no truck with you. I's just repayin' an old debt. I ain't lookin' to get killed."

"Then back away or commence to fightin'."

"We ain't got no guns," explained a man from the back of the group.

"Ain't nobody said you gon' have an even chance," King answered. "If you come up against me, come ready for death 'cause I don't care what you got!"

"You gon' kill innocent men for beatin' a DuMont man?" the big-boned man asked with disbelief. "The DuMonts done worse to us!"

"I don't like cowards! You didn't have guts to fight that man on the ground when he could stand up, but now he's harmless, you boys got all the guts in the world. You all make me sick! You's all cowards and dogs!"

"We ain't fightin' men, Mr. Tremain. We's farmers and workin' men. Ain't a man among us ever done killed anyone. We was just gettin' an old enemy back for what he done to us."

Without turning, King shot out the street lamp that was on the edge of his vision. "Anybody that don't want to fight and risk bein' killed better skin on out of here, 'cause I'm gon' kill every man jack one of you that's standin' close when my feet hit the ground."

There was no grumbling from the men as they hurried away along the darkened street. King slid off his horse and stooped to inspect the fallen man. The man's right arm was obviously broken and there were bruises and blood covering his face. His breathing was labored. King felt his chest carefully and discovered what appeared to be several broken ribs. He realized that if he left the man lying in the street, more ill would befall him, but broken ribs could not be slung across the back of a horse. Up the street by a street lamp, King saw a man hurriedly trying to turn his pony and cart around and return the way he came. King called out to the man, who stopped and turned immediately to face him. He offered the man twenty dollars to cart the injured man to a doctor.

The owner of the cart agreed. Twenty dollars was worth two weeks of hard work. He assisted King in lifting the man's heavy, inert body onto the cart. King mounted his horse and led the way to a colored doctor's clinic, but he was out making his rounds. King then went to a white doctor named McKenna that he had heard treated colored patients. After diagnosing the patient, the doctor informed King that there was a pretty good chance the man would die unless he operated. King pulled a hundred dollars from his pocket and asked the doctor to do whatever was necessary.

King rode out of the courtyard and headed for Front Street. He stabled his horse down the street from his small apartment and climbed the rickety stairs leading to his rental. He moved the bed, unlocked the metal cabinet that lay under it, and removed two rifles with scopes. He picked up several bandoliers of bullets and, after locking the cabinet, returned everything to its original position. It was a short climb to the roof. Once he situated himself behind a parapet on the roof, he scoped out the positions where he had initially seen DuMont's snipers. Two were exactly where he had last seen them; the third seemed to have disappeared. King felt comfortable with his position. He would be firing from the shadows behind the parapet and he had a flash protector on the barrels of his rifles.

Half an hour passed before King heard the loud sound of a large body of men coming down the street. King shook his head at the noise they were making. They were making no secret that they were coming, which King thought extremely foolish. He always attempted to have the element of surprise on his side. The band of men appeared, turning the corner of the block, and spilled out into the street like a liquid mass. King shook his head disapprovingly. There was no military precision about this attack and they had given their enemy ample warning as to their coming. As if to confirm his assessment, a shot rang out. King saw the flash of the gun's discharge emanating from the shadows of a rooftop adjacent to the DuMont house. When he looked down onto the street, he saw the band of men running every which way. He saw Phillip shouting and gesturing, trying to keep the men focused on their purpose.

Another shot rang out. King saw the man next to Phillip fall. They were trying to kill Phillip. He hefted his rifle to his shoulder and fired three quick shots in succession into the shadows where he had seen the flash of gunfire. Without waiting to see if he had a hit, he began firing at the second sniper and saw the dark silhouette of a man fall backward out of sight. He dropped behind the parapet and grabbed his bandoliers and crawled to his second position on the other side of the building. He was still in shadow when he rose up to assess the situation.

The band of men on the street below were running pell-mell through the streets like cockroaches when a light has been turned on. He saw that Phillip was able to maintain a core of ten men out of the rest and they charged the front door. King saw the flash of a rifle from the spire of the church at the end of the street, which only seemed to increase the panic of the men below. This rifleman had been blocked from his view in his initial position on the other side of the building. King trained his scope on the spire and waited. He saw the man stand up and aim his weapon at the street. King squeezed off two shots and saw the man's body jerk backward and bounce off the wall behind him, then tumble out of sight.

The second-floor shutters of the DuMont house were flung open and Lester looked out through the curtains at the street below. King raised his rifle to shoot, but his intended target turned back into the room before King could put his sight on him.

Journer thought she heard the sounds of gunfire and men shouting in the street from where she lay on the floor. Time passed. As sensation returned, she discovered her face was sore and her lips were bleeding. There was also pain and wetness between her legs. She was lying on her back on a pallet of blankets. She had been beaten nearly unconscious, then held down and raped. She pushed herself to a sitting position and saw Lester looking out the window. She groaned inadvertently from the pain and Lester turned around to look at her. His hair was unkempt and there was a strange smile on his face.

"You ready for some mo'?" His gold teeth gleamed. He was wearing only a pair of pants held up by suspenders. He looked in the mirror and said, "Damn, you done made me mess up my hair. Now, I hurt people for that!" Lester tried to pat his thickly greased hair smooth. "Oh, shit, now I got to put on a stockin' cap! You got to pay for this!" There was more noise from the street and Lester returned to the window.

Journer reached up into her hair and pulled out the wooden dowel that still held her bun loosely in place. Her pigtail fell between her breasts. She held the sharpened dowel daggerlike underneath her skirt. She realized she had to be patient.

Lester turned to face her and smirked. "You think yo' father's comin' to save you? You think yo' friends gon' break in here and save yo' black ass? Huh! Yo' daddy ain't gon' do shit, 'cause Oren done already sent him to hell! Yo' daddy's lyin' back there in the alley, feedin' the rats! And we got some big ones," Lester laughed. "I guess it's cause we feeds 'em. Watch and see, the rest of yo' buddies gon' join 'em! And if you don't straighten up and fly right, that's gon' be yo' future too!"

Journer watched Lester walk around the room and hate clouded her vision. There had been a time when all she wanted to do was escape, to run away in her tattered clothes, to take her shredded dignity to some quiet hole and curl up, but that moment had passed. Now she wanted to kill him more than she wanted to live. This decision was the culmination of the terrible memory of him on top of her, thrusting and sweating and panting, all while he kept a stranglehold on her throat. She was so fixed on her desire to kill Lester that it did not sink in emotionally that her father was dead. Her conscious mind clicked and whirred like an adding machine closing out an account as she waited wordlessly for Lester to come closer. She was surprised at the stillness of her heart.

Lester walked slowly over to her. "Do I got to put a couple mo' fists up-side yo' head, or is you gon' follow the program? 'Cause all the trouble yo' family's done caused me, I's ready to let Oren have you. I understand he rides a woman hard. He ain't nice like I is."

Journer smiled even though it made her lips hurt. "You don't have to hit me no mo'," she said softly.

"What you say? Speak up!"

"You don't have to hit me no mo'!" Journer said, forcing herself to speak louder.

"I didn't hear you!" Lester said, pressing home his newfound victory. "Did you say that you learned yo' lesson? I didn't hear you. You got to speak louder."

"You ain't got to hit me! I learned I can't stand up to you." The words caused bile to rise up in her throat.

"That's better. Now, lay back down there and open yo' legs. All this shootin' and goin's on done made me feel like gettin' a little mo'." Lester knelt down between her legs and stuck a knife into the floor by her head. "If you try to get smart with me, I'll cut yo' throat." He was slipping the suspenders off his shoulders when the knock came at the door.

"Who the hell is that?" Lester muttered, pulling his knife from the floor and rising swiftly to his feet. "This better be goddamned impo'tant! I ain't got no time fo' no bullshit!"

The breeze brought a chill and Journer shivered. She had not been able to react quickly enough. She felt an overwhelming disappointment as she pushed herself to a kneeling position. She now had a firm grip on the dowel. She was concentrating on Lester's back when she heard Phillip's voice.

"Journer? Journer, are you in there?" Phillip yelled. He was standing at the top of the stairs in a darkened hallway lit by a sputtering gas lamp. There were four doors opening off the hall and Phillip didn't know which one to choose. He was panting with exertion. There was blood on his torn shirt from a cut on his forehead. He held a long-barreled revolver loosely at his side. He had used all his bullets and he was searching in his pockets for more. He found three bullets lying in the crease of his pants pocket. He called out. "Journer? Journer, where are you?"

Journer strained to call out but her voice failed her. She wanted to scream, but her throat was strangely constricted. All she could manage was a hoarse whisper. Her desire to scream increased when she saw Lester unlatch the door and sneak behind the drapes that covered a small closet.

"Journer!" Phillip yelled as he popped out the cylinder of his gun and began shucking expended shells on the floor. He was loading the third bullet into the gun when one of the doors in the hallway swung open. Without stopping to think, Phillip rushed through the door, barely snapping the gun's cylinder back in place.

Unbeknown to Phillip, Derrick had followed him upstairs, carrying a knife in his hand. It was not a big, fancy weapon; it had only a six-inch blade, but it was perfectly balanced for throwing. Derrick had been ready to send it into Phillip's back until he saw the door to Lester's bedroom swing open. Derrick did not know what caused him to hesitate: perhaps he wanted to see if Lester could defend himself, or maybe he wanted to enter at the right moment and show his value by saving Lester from Journer's rescuer. Whatever the reason, Derrick kept the knife in his hand as he crept toward the opened door.

From the doorway, Derrick saw everything. He saw Lester rush up behind Phillip. He saw the flash of metal as Lester's knife traveled its arc and imbedded itself in Phillip's back. The penetration of the knife propelled Phillip forward into a headlong fall and the revolver skidded across the floor as it slipped from his grasp. Lester watched Phillip writhing on the floor in pain and laughed. "You some kind of fool! You think you just gon' barge right on into my room. Yo' ass is mine now!"

Phillip rolled over onto his back with an effort and looked at Lester through eyes hazy with pain. "I'll see you in hell!"

Lester chuckled and started toward Phillip, but the sound of the revolver being cocked stopped him dead. Lester turned and saw Journer pointing the long-barreled gun at him with a two-handed grip. His smile disappeared as if it had been erased. "You best be careful with that hog-leg, gal. Hell, it might go off. We don't want that, do we?" Lester took a step in Journer's direction. "You best give me the gun now and things'll go easier for you."

It was Journer's turn to laugh. She opened her mouth wide and a strange high-pitched sound issued from her throat.

"Ahh, shit, you ain't gon' do nothin'!" Lester walked toward her briskly, intending to take the gun out of her hands, but the discharge of the weapon halted his advance. The bullet creased the side of his neck and spun him around. When he turned back to face her, there was a snarl on his lips. He raised his arm to throw his knife at her when the second bullet caught him in the stomach. He staggered backward against the wall, then started walking stiff-legged toward her. Journer pointed the gun at him and pulled the trigger. The gun kicked as the shot went wide. She continued pulling the trigger, but there were no more bullets. The hammer fell on empty chambers. Lester continued moving jerkily toward her like a marionette in the hands of an inexpert puppeteer. When he was almost close enough to touch, she picked up her dowel again. She would not miss her second opportunity. Journer tensed, ready to lunge at Lester even though it exposed her to his knife.

A shiny, flying object hit Lester in the back, causing him to turn around in slow motion. Lester never got to see the person who killed him. He fell facedown on the floor with a knife hilt sticking out of his back, just under his shoulder blades. Journer saw Derrick enter the room and lock the door. His eyes when he looked at her said everything.

Derrick took a moment to survey the scene. Journer's friend looked like he was seriously injured. He had lost a lot of blood and was lying on the floor shivering. The woman looked as if she had put up a fight and was ready for some more. He frowned. He didn't like uppity women. He figured he might have to put her in her place before too much happened. First, he wanted to explore the possibilities of a deal. The DuMonts had nobody left to lead. A man with the right connections might assume control of the organization. Lester had tried to squeeze too much out of the people. They would probably respond to a gentler hand. Without waiting for an introduction, Derrick outlined the general elements of his plan and put the question to his prospective partners.

"And what if we don't take yo' offer?" Journer asked in a hoarse whisper.

"I'll kill the both of you and take credit for it for the DuMont organization. I got my bread buttered no matter which side hit the flo'."

Phillip raised his head. His breathing was labored. "Go to hell! I don't make deals with scum!"

"Then you's a dead fool!" Derrick commented, shaking his head. "I'm gon' have to kill you 'cause I can't have no enemies gettin' well." Derrick picked up Lester's knife and walked over to Phillip. The gusts started up again and the curtains opened and flapped with the power of the wind. When the 3.08 lead slug hit Derrick in the chest, it lifted him off the floor and flung him backward toward the door. His body crashed to the floor and jerked momentarily, then there was quiet. There was only the sound of the curtains flapping in the breeze.

After a few stunned minutes of silence, Journer crawled over to see how Phillip was doing. The room was strong with the odors of the river and the smell of death. Phillip's eyes were closed, but he opened them when he felt her touch. He gave her a weak smile. He whispered something. She had to hold her ear to his lips to hear what he was saying. His breathing had become more labored, but she understood him to say that he was sleepy. She raised his head and placed it upon her lap as she knelt beside him. Journer allowed her thoughts to drift. In one night it seemed that everything she valued had been ruined. She did not understand how or why she had been spared when death was the only answer she sought. Journer caressed Phillip's sweating brow absentmindedly. She was in shock. She did not even respond to the pounding on the door.

Book II

THE SAGA
OF SERENA
AND
KING TREMAIN

Serena Baddeaux first met LeRoi Tremain when she was seventeen at a Negro carnival on Independence Day in the summer of 1920. The carnival was sponsored by several of the Uptown Black Baptist churches, and thus it was an acceptable place to be seen. Her father, a local farmer and an elder in the growing parish, would have banned her attendance had the carnival not been supported by the Baptist church. Her father was a stern, upright man who made sure that his adolescent son and his three teenage daughters did nothing to disgrace the Baddeaux family name.

On the day of the carnival, Serena rose an hour before the rooster crowed to make sure her chores were done and her dress was ready. She and her mother had been working on the dress every evening for a week. As the eldest, her dress had been the last to be completed. Her two sisters had their dresses weeks before because Serena and her mother had spent many late nights with needle and thread. Sometimes she begrudged her role as the eldest, especially when she saw the pampering her baby brother received, but that was the life of a woman on a farm.

It was still dark when she came down the stairs, and there was a chill in the air. She lit the kerosene lamp that hung over the dinner table and started fires in the hearth and in the old potbellied stove. By the time her father arose, she had milked the cow and had started a breakfast of griddle cakes and thick slabs of bacon. Her father gave her a grunt of approval as he walked out the door to the outhouse. Dawn was peaking through the windows when her younger sisters and baby brother came down to breakfast. They were full of chatter about the carnival. She had to remind them that if their chores were not done, they wouldn't be able to go at all, but she felt their excitement. As far as she was concerned, any break from the constant drudgery of farm work was reason for excitement.

Her mother came down shortly after sunrise, when Serena was clearing away the breakfast dishes. She was dying of consumption and she had weakened to a point that she could not walk long distances unaided. Serena pulled a chair out from the table and offered it to her mother, who coughed and gave her a weak smile of thanks. Once she was seated, her mother reached over and picked up Serena's dress and began to examine the stitching around the ruffles on the bodice. Serena turned the flame higher in the kerosene lamp for more light and pointed to the ruffles. "That's as far as I was able to get last night, Mama. Do you feel up to something to eat?"

Serena's father entered the kitchen in stocking feet. He had come from watering and feeding the mules and had left his muddy boots by the door. "I need me some different socks. These is all wore out. Did you finish mending my other ones?" Serena walked over to a basket beside the window and took out a pair of thick wool socks and handed them to her father. As he sat down at the table, he turned down the lamp. "The good Lord done brought us daylight, ain't no reason to waste kerosene." He nodded to his wife and asked Serena, "Did you finish fixing that harness like I asked?" His voice was not gruff, but there was no warmth in it.

Serena gave her father a steady look. "It's hanging in the barn, but I don't think it will hold long. I think you need to buy some leather straps because—"

"You think?" her father interrupted her. "Why is it buy, buy, buy all the time around here? Can't you women make nothin'? Other people seem to make do without running into town all the time to get store-bought."

"If we don't have it, how we going to make it, Charles? All we got here is deerskin! For reins, you need real leather. You ain't bought hide in near three years." She had said words like these many times, in many previous arguments. She understood her husband was not a bad man, but one who was reluctant to spend a dollar if he could avoid it. She looked up and watched for his response.

"You ain't got to defend the girl, Rebecca. All I was saying is, we ain't got to buy something that we can make."

Serena's mother coughed and said nothing more to her husband. She busied herself with Serena's dress. Serena also turned away and finished cleaning the kitchen. It was clear that the women had withdrawn their attention from him. After several minutes of silence, he stood up and left the house.

Serena waited until her father had left and then turned the lamp flame higher. Her mother gave her a brief smile. Serena studied her mother and saw in the lines on her face the sacrifice and hard labor that came with life on a small farm: the endless hours of sweat, the days of blistering sun and the nights of aching muscles, the weeks of tedium and the years of hopeless toil, all to reap the elusive harvest of the dark, brooding earth. If there was one thing that Serena knew, it was that she did not want to be a farmer's wife.

With two mules pulling their wagon, it took nearly three hours for the Baddeaux family to reach the carnival. Her mother was stiff with pain as

Serena helped her get down. Her father had found a space where he could park his wagon down near a small creek so that there was water for the mules. Serena was helping her mother with her shawl when she heard her eight-year-old brother, Amos, calling her name excitedly.

She left her mother's side and went up the embankment to see what had gotten his attention. When she reached him, her brother was speechless. He merely pointed. There in the distance, standing beside some horses, was a tall, light-skinned man in a brown military uniform. Everything about the man was spit and polish; his uniform had been ironed and the creases were still sharp; his shoes were shiny and the brass clasps and buttons of his uniform reflected light. It was an unusual thing to see a colored man in the uniform of the American military service, but this man seemed to personify the warrior. He was big, broad-shouldered, and well muscled. Serena couldn't see his face, but she was curious about him. She had heard rumors about colored men who had fought for America in the big war in faraway places and that some of these men had returned home now that the war was over. She wondered what he had seen. Had he been to Paris or England? She had often dreamed about living in a big city where everything was run with electricity.

"All the colored men from this parish that were in the service during World War One are lined up on the other side of them prayer tents!" Amos shouted. "There was almost a hundred of 'em and they are decked out with medals and everythin'!"

Serena felt her younger brother's excitement. She was about to ask him to take her to see the soldiers when her father said coldly, "Simmer down, Amos. We here to learn the word of God. The soldiers ain't got nothin' we want." The big smile on Amos's face evaporated like water on a hot cast-iron stove. Serena shook her head but said nothing. Her father seemed to take pleasure in taking the joy out of everything. She hurried to assist her mother up the embankment, but her mind was still embroiled with the vision of the man in the uniform. Serena Baddeaux had her first glimpse of King Tremain.

The day was warm and beautifully clear. The carnival was located on one of the few flat and dry grassy areas northwest of New Orleans. There was a slight breeze blowing off the ocean that carried away the regular smell of the damp and rotting swamp. On the outskirts of the tents, there were clowns, wrestling contests, pie-eating competitions, and all sorts of colorful crafts and food booths. The carnival was obviously a success. There were booths set up by the local merchants and crafts people that sold everything from farm implements to possum pie. There were tents filled with people watching jugglers, acrobats, magicians, singers, and musicians, and there was even a traveling theatrical company that was presenting one-act plays. It was so crowded that it seemed like every colored person between New Orleans and the Mississippi border was there.

The cream of Negro society sported their best threads, promenading through the central lane between the tents, while the tongue waggers had a field day discussing who was present and what they were wearing.

Serena's father ushered his family into one of the larger tents in which there was an all-day revival meeting. There they remained until the three o'clock supper break. Serena and her mother had prepared a meal of sliced ham, apples, homemade bread, and blackberry pie. They sat on blankets beside the wagon. When they were nearly finished eating, one of the reverends who had been leading the revival stopped by to chat.

The reverend was a fire-and-brimstone preacher and he always had the frown of hellfire on his face. There were sinners around every corner as far as he was concerned. However, on this visit the reverend sought to be pleasant for he had brought his eldest son along for the sole purpose of seeking permission for him to court Serena. He attempted to smile, which after years of frowning was a difficult act, and produced the expression of a man swallowing an extremely large and bitter pill. There were exchanges as to weather, soil conditions, crop failure, upcoming revivals; the Reverend Broadfoot was known to be wordy. Finally, Serena's father yawned rather expressively and the reverend got the idea. "Young Fred here has come to me to get permission to court your daughter, Serena. I've seen them exchanging looks in the church and they're both from good, God-fearing families. Fred ain't going to be a man of the cloth. He's taking over the farm. He's a good, hardworking boy and he'll make a good life for your daughter."

"I don't rightly see as if there is any problem with what Fred wants, so I'll say—"

"Pardon me, Pa, shouldn't we talk first? I have something to say about this!" Serena interrupted. She had no interest in Fred, who looked almost as sour as his old man, and she didn't want to waste time pretending that she did.

"You . . . you . . ." Her father was flabbergasted. "You challengin' my decision?"

Her mother defended Serena's right to choose. "A girl has a right to say both yes and no, Charles."

Her father turned to the reverend. "I think we can work things out. Let me get back to you."

The reverend and his son took their leave. When they were out of earshot, her father commenced to fuming. "What kind of stuck-up little fool are you? You have to go a long way to do better than Broadfoot. They got a good farm and they're God-fearing Christians. What more do you want?"

No one said anything. It was clear he didn't want their real opinion. He stomped around a bit more. "It's time to return to the revival tent."

"Papa, can't I please just take a look around the carnival for a little bit?" her little brother begged. It had been torture for Amos to sit still during the revival meeting and greater torture to remain with his family while they ate, but it was unbearable that he should not even see the inside of any tent other than the one in which the revival was given. His father was not sympathetic. Serena's mother chose to stay with the wagon and asked that Serena remain with her. Her father agreed with obvious reluctance and ushered the three remaining children toward the revival tent.

"Sometimes I hate him!" Serena said vehemently.

"You shouldn't say bad things about your father, child," her mother said, rubbing Serena's arm soothingly. "He just wants to make a good match for you."

"I'm not going to marry someone just because he thinks it's a good match! I want to travel. I want to see the big city lights. You realize, Mama, that we live only twenty-five miles from New Orleans but I've only been there about four times in my whole life. I don't want to spend my life breaking my back on a farm. I want something better."

Her mother's body was shaken by a terrible fit of coughing. "You work the earth, you're doing God's work. You produce food for hungry mouths. Farming is hard, but it's honest."

"Didn't you ever want something glamorous or flashy? Like sometimes you hear on the radio the stories about people in fancy cars going to shows on Broadway and big-time parties?"

"You got to be realistic about your dreams, honey. You a colored girl living in Louisiana. How you goin' to get to them big cities? How you gon' live when you get there? The devil lays out plenty of temptations in them cities."

"I don't know, Mama. All I know for sure is if he tries to make me marry someone I don't want, I'll run away and never come back!"

"Don't say such things, child. You give me shivers in my heart. Don't ever say that you'll never come back." Her mother started to cough again, but it soon ceased.

"I'm sorry, Mama. I didn't mean to cause you pain."

"I know you didn't, honey." Her mother gave her a hug. "If your father tries to force you to get married, I'll help you run away, but you must swear to come back and see me."

Serena acknowledged her mother's words with a nod of her head and returned her hug.

Her mother pushed herself erect with her walking stick. "Let's go back to the revival."

"I need to think, Mama. Plus, I heard that someone is going around stealing things out of people's wagons. I'll stay here and watch. Why don't you send someone for me in an hour?"

"Alright, dear. I'll tell your father you're watching the wagon."

Serena sat down on a blanket in the shade of the wagon, for the afternoon sun was now burning fiercely. She had been sitting no more than half an hour when she heard the sound of boots treading through the grass.

She was not overly concerned; there were other wagons in hailing distance through the trees. After all, it was a carnival put on by the Associated Baptist Churches, and most families had come for prayer, to barter homemade goods for needed stores, and to socialize. It wasn't until the boots stopped near her wagon that she stood up. On the other side of the wagon she saw three of the DuMont brothers and wished she hadn't stood up. The oldest brother, Chess, had been sweet on Serena for years until she had been forced to reject his advances publicly at a church picnic. She had attempted to discourage him politely, but since sensitivity was not his strong suit, he had ignored her protestations until she spoke her mind in front of other people. After that he turned sour, accusing her and her family of trying to humiliate him. At best, the DuMonts were a shady family living on the edge of the great swamp. They were "cut and shoot" people, known for brewing cheap corn whiskey, gambling, brawling, and trafficking in stolen goods.

"Well, if it ain't Miss High and Mighty!" Chess said, putting a sliver of wood in his mouth and using it like a toothpick. Serena said nothing. She wasn't afraid but she realized that she was in a dangerous situation. She could hear gospel singing—hundreds of voices strong—coming from the revival tent. She could not be sure that she would be heard if she screamed.

"All dressed up in Sunday-go-to-meeting clothes and ain't in the revival," Chess said as he rounded the wagon, followed by his brothers. "Looks to me like she's waiting for somethin' good to happen and she don't believe it's in church."

Serena stooped, picked up the buggy whip her father used to keep the mules' attention, and stood facing the three men. She didn't know what was going to happen, but she planned on fighting.

Chess looked in the wagon. "You just wanna whip me with that whip,

Miss High and Mighty, or do you wanna whip me as you ride me?" His brothers laughed raucously. Chess took a step toward Serena, still pretending to be looking in the wagon. She unfurled the buggy whip and stood waiting for his next move. With a nod of his head, Chess gestured to Pug, the youngest of his brothers, to go around the wagon.

As Pug obeyed his older brother, Serena backed away from the wagon. Now the creek was at her back. The voices from the church got suddenly louder as the singers fell into a rhythmic chorus and response. Chess leaned against the wagon. "What you gon' do, little lady? Can't nobody hear you." He took a step toward her. "It can be easy or it can be hard. It's up to you."

Into this tableau stumbled her little brother, Amos. He came out of the bushes on the opposite side of the creek, breathless, as if he had been running. The DuMonts froze on seeing the boy. Amos looked questioningly to Serena. He could feel that there was something wrong. "Get out of here, Amos," Serena said calmly. "Go get Pa!"

"Get that kid!" Chess shouted to Pug.

Pug started around the wagon, but Serena cracked the whip, narrowly missing his face. Pug staggered backward out of range. Chess growled with frustration and sent his other brother, Eddy, after Amos. Much to Serena's consternation, Amos remained on the opposite bank, watching the action.

"Get Pa, now!" Serena screamed at her brother. By the time Amos turned to run, Eddy was slogging across the creek. Amos had not made it into the bushes when he ran smack into the man in the brown military uniform. Amos was so surprised and scared by the apparition that appeared out of nowhere, he was briefly stricken immobile.

"Go on your way, soldier," Eddy warned as he came out of the creek. "Leave the boy to me. You just mind your own business!"

The soldier laughed. "You Little Eddy DuMont, ain't you? Eddy, Eddy, I do believe you have mistook who you talkin' to." There was no humor in the laugh and there was an evil smile on the man's face.

"Amos, go get help!" Serena screamed at her brother.

Amos, still confused, looked up at the man in the uniform. The man patted him on the shoulder and said, "Go on, Eddy won't bother you. Will you, Eddy?" Amos took off through the bush. Eddy ran to intercept, but King cut him off. "Eddy, you don't want to make a liar out of me, do you?"

"This here soldier boy is a Tremain," Chess declared. "It looks like we gon' get easy pickin's all the way around! This is mo' like it! You done picked a bad day to stick yo' nose into our business, Tremain!" Eddy pulled a long knife blade from his sheath and waved it in front of King.

"Do as they say, mister," Serena warned. "You can go now. My folks'll be here any minute. They won't hurt me now."

King laughed and touched his hand to his hat to acknowledge Serena's offer. "You got spunk, woman. I like that!"

"Do you like this?" Eddy made a sudden lunge at King, blade first.

The soldier easily dodged the knife thrust and grabbed Eddy's arm, which he twisted then broke with a loud snap. Eddy screamed and the knife fell from his grasp. Still holding Eddy's broken arm, the man stepped in close and savagely punched him several times on the side of the head above his ear. Chess was halfway across the creek when the soldier snapped Eddy's neck and let his lifeless body slump to the ground. Then the soldier picked up the knife and waited for Chess to come out of the creek.

"An Arkansas toothpick, I do believe," the soldier commented lightly, referring to the knife. "Come on out of the creek, Chess, and show me how you use this!"

Chess had seen how easily the man had beaten and killed his brother and he was chilled. The man killed like a professional. Chess was ready to quit and run, but Serena was standing on the bank watching everything. Family pride caused him to move forward, despite his fear. His knife was out as he cautiously moved across the creek. He tried to call upon his rage to carry him through. "You's the dog that helped kill Lester!"

King walked to the edge of the creek, waiting for Chess. "I'm King Tremain! You missed me the night you shot at me outside the Beau Geste. Try yo' luck now."

"You's a dead man, Tremain!" Chess shouted as he rushed his opponent, but King Tremain met Chess with a shoulder and knocked him sprawling back into the creek.

King started to laugh. "You better say joe, 'cause you sho' don't know. I'm gon' kill you without stainin' my uniform."

Chess stood up, water streaming down his face. "I know about you, how you's supposed to be so tough! Yo' name's LeRoi Tremain. You ain't no king! I heard all about how you been tryin' to take credit for killin' my older brother, Lester. Shoot, he'd eat you for lunch without breakin' from his regular chores. I's sorry I missed you at the Beau Geste! You ain't no king!"

"I may not be a king to you, but I'm gon' decide whether you live or die, won't I?" King said, moving along the edge of the creek. "I'll be a king for the short time you got left! There ain't no mercy for back-shooters!"

Chess called out to his brother. "Pug, come on down here and help me get this big nigger!"

"So that's Pug. All grown up?" King laughed. "Come on down here, Pug, and die with your brother. If I have to come in that creek after you, Chess, and get my uniform wet, you gon' to die slowly."

Pug started around the wagon, but there was fear in his eyes. Serena cracked the whip in front of him. "Don't do it, Pug! Don't go down there!" she warned. "My people will be here in a minute. You don't have to get in any more trouble." Serena had gone to school with Pug. He was a bit of a bully, but he wasn't mean like Chess.

"Don't listen to her!" Chess shouted. "You better get over here right now. You don't want me dealing with you when we get home!"

King started down the bank of the creek. "You ain't gon' see home again, Chess. You can't threaten him with what's gon' happen ten minutes from now, 'cause you'll be dead."

Chess backed out of the creek, protesting. "Whachoo talkin' about? A whole crowd of people gon' be here soon." He gestured with his knife to King. "I'll settle up with you later." He turned to leave, but King was across the creek in two strides.

King brought Chess to bay near the wagon. For the first time, Chess exhibited some fear. "You must be crazy! Whatchoo so riled about?"

"Let's just say I don't like back-shooters!" King feinted a thrust with his knife and closed in on Chess. Chess slashed back, but his arm was blocked and King was grappling with him.

Pug ran to assist his brother, but King was too quick for him. King head-butted Chess hard across the bridge of his nose. When Chess reeled backward against the wagon, King kicked at his knee and Chess crumpled to the ground with a yelp of pain. King turned just in time to meet Pug's charge. He ducked Pug's knife thrust and slashed the boy across the face. Pug fell to the ground, blood spurting out of his cheek. He scrambled back to his feet and took off running.

King turned to Chess. "Looks like it's just you and me." Using the wagon, Chess had pulled himself erect. King attacked without warning. He parried Chess's defense and got a grip on Chess's knife arm. It was over within seconds. King simply overpowered his opponent and drove Eddy's knife deep into Chess's stomach, twisting the blade slowly in the process. When King stepped back, Chess fell, rolled down the bank, and lay bleeding on the edge of the creek. He tried to sit up, failed, and slumped back into the mud. He coughed a couple of times and then lay silent.

King threw the knife on the ground beside Chess. He touched his hand to his hat again as he nodded to Serena. There was no expression on his face. He started to walk away, but Serena's words made him pause.

"That was cold-blooded murder! That was the coldest thing I've ever seen."

"If I was really cold-blooded, I'd go get that young Pug who ran off," King commented easily, as he adjusted his uniform.

"He's just a boy—"

King interjected. "When you's killin' varmints, you wants to make sure to get all of them!"

Serena protested. "The DuMonts are scum, but they aren't animals. They are still human beings."

"If you was a virgin, you still one now, ain't you? Maybe I even saved your life. I wouldn't complain if I was you."

"You didn't do that for me. You was planning to kill some DuMonts before you ever saw me."

"But this way it's legal, ain't it? Unless, you gon' press charges against me."

"What if I was, would you kill me, too?"

"You's way too fine to kill and got too much spunk to mess with," King saluted her again and began walking away. "I'll see you again," he called over his shoulder.

As Serena watched him leave, she heard people running through the trees toward her. King did not hurry his stride in the least. He disappeared behind some wagons and was lost from sight. She heard Chess moan and looked down at him. He had lost a lot of blood. She had never seen a man injured so seriously before. Yet her indignation did not let her feel sympathy for Chess. She thought if anybody deserved to be killed, it was Chess.

Her father and six or seven other men appeared in the clearing around the wagon. He rushed to her side and began babbling questions at her. One of the other men saw Chess lying by the creek and called everyone's attention to him. Her father left her and followed some of the men down to Chess's sprawled form. Someone asked her if she was alright. She nodded that she was fine.

Suddenly, she was watching everything from a distance. People spoke to her in muffled voices and seemed to be moving in slow motion. She felt slightly delirious. Her heart pounded in her chest and blood rushed in her ears. Hands assisted her to a seat. She could not identify faces. She could not concentrate on anything except whether she would see King Tremain again. He was so different from anyone she had ever known. There was something intriguing about him that she couldn't identify, but there was one thing that was certain: he wasn't a man who was destined to live on a farm.

The day Sampson Davis was brought into the Toussant Hotel on a stretcher, it caused quite a stir among the patrons and the staff. He was borne by two large muscular men but when they got to the stairs, which had a sharp right angle leading to the second story, the semiconscious Sampson almost slid off the stretcher. King, who had been directing the patient transport, rushed to assist the two bearers. For several seconds, the three men struggled for control of both the patient and the stretcher. It was obvious another pair of hands was needed to navigate the turn. King looked around and saw the bell captain leaning against his counter. He called to the man. The bell captain responded with a negative shake of his head and turned to attend some paperwork chores.

King roared, "You better get yo' lazy ass over here and help or I swear you'll regret this day!"

The bell captain looked over at the registration desk where the manager was standing. The manager would not get involved. He put his head down and concentrated on his account books. Finding no support from his boss, the bell captain made his way reluctantly to the three men, but he took his time and his attitude was clearly surly. When he was close enough, King grabbed the man by the neck. He shook the bell captain in an iron grip and whispered something angrily in his ear. The bell captain moved with more alacrity after King's words of encouragement. The stretcher was jostled and lifted around the obstacles and carried upstairs.

Once Sampson was installed in his room, King returned to his own room and sat pondering his next move at a table by the window overlooking the street. The street outside the hotel was busy with both pedestrian and vehicular traffic. Vendors and street hawkers were calling out their wares in competing melodic bursts. Eggs and dairy, fruits and vegetables were all being called out below. King was only distantly aware of the commerce that was being conducted. He was primarily immersed in the problem of what to do about his new ward. King had not intended to assume responsibility for Sampson, but there appeared to be no other alternative. Dr. McKenna had informed him that he could no longer keep Sampson in his clinic, since he was out of immediate danger and there were other cases that were more needy. Sampson had no one else, and King didn't see the point in turning him out into the street after paying for his care. Up and down Colored Town, King had searched but he was unable to find anyplace better than a brothel. So, he brought Sampson to the Toussant.

Perhaps it was because King saw himself as responsible for the man's injuries, or perhaps he had seen too many men stripped of their dignity by the wounds of war. He did not feel guilt. It had more to do with an unwritten code he obeyed. It was not something he had verbalized or fully examined. It just seemed like the right thing. So, hell or high water, he was going to follow it through. The doctor had given him the names of several women who made home visits to care for recovering patients. Sampson was still recovering from two broken arms, several broken ribs, and severe contusions on his head and legs. He would need assistance with his toilet and personal affairs for at least a month. After making arrangements for someone to attend to Sampson's care, King stopped letting the matter trouble his thoughts.

He was preoccupied with finding an out-of-the-way building to serve as his headquarters. Although he wanted to keep his official residence at the Hotel Toussant, he needed a place in which to store equipment and stable his horse, a place off the beaten track. He had been looking for the right property in and around New Orleans for several months. He had considerably more time since the deaths of Lester and Chess DuMont. Their whole family was paralyzed by the turmoil and confusion caused by all the jockeying for power by the remaining family members. King spent days on his horse, looking at different lots.

After one particularly long day's ride, King reentered Algiers along a narrow, overgrown channel leading to an old, little-used wharf. There on the edge of the channel was a dilapidated old villa with rusted wrought-iron gates. It was a large, tiled-roof, two-story stucco affair with numerous windows. He easily climbed the fence and took a look around. Despite its size, it was perfect for his needs. It was built like a fort with an interior courtyard and its own back dock on the river, and, as important, it was located on the edge of a commercial shipping district, which meant the streets were always full of traffic. Its location in the run-down section of the wharf was of particular benefit in that King was less likely to be stopped and challenged by law enforcement. He was excited as he returned to his horse. He hurried to a nearby wire service to send Goldbaum a telegram and set up a phone call at the Beau Geste. There was only one telephone in the hotel and it was in a very public place next to the registration desk.

King's focus on the villa was diverted by the news that Sampson still had not spoken a word, and nearly two weeks had passed. So King began to visit him early in the morning and on more than one occasion attempted to initiate a discussion with him, but Sampson merely nodded his head in response. There appeared no rancor in Sampson's attitude toward King; in fact, King got the distinct impression that the man looked forward to his visits.

During the next few weeks, after finding the villa, King contacted a lawyer and had a meeting with Ross Hollister, the son of Taylor Ross Hollister, the president and principal owner of Hollister Savings Bank. In all these meetings with the white lawyers and bank officials, King portrayed himself as an employee of his own firm. His corporation purchased the villa, not he. A major lesson that the war had taught him was that a colored man could not expect to be treated with any kind of dignity by white America unless he worked for a powerful white man. Several times during the war he had carried orders through German-controlled territory for his regimental commander. He had seen how the slovenly attitude and disrespect had dropped from the white American soldiers' faces when they understood for whom he was carrying orders. Therefore, King had Ira Goldbaum write to the bank and the attorney and convey to them that he was an employee of a powerful business corporation. As such, he enjoyed greater freedom of movement and grudging respect than he would have if it were known that he owned the company.

By the third week, Sampson was able to sit up and, other than his inability or unwillingness to speak, his health seem to be progressing on all fronts. King asked Dr. McKenna to come to the hotel to diagnose Sampson's condition. After a thorough examination, McKenna stated that there was no outward reason for Sampson to have lost his power of speech, unless the beating he had received had caused brain damage. From these discussions King realized that whatever ailed Sampson was beyond the scope of medicine to resolve. But his experiences in the army had shown him that even a mentally healthy soldier, after a certain period of confinement to a bed, could go stir-crazy and act very inappropriately. He set out to provide some outlet for Sampson. King was not motivated out of love or concern, but a sense of responsibility. It was Sampson's absolute vulnerability that had awakened this feeling in King.

One morning King brought in the paper along with a cup of steaming hot coffee. As the woman he had hired straightened Sampson's bed, King opened and read the paper while he drank his coffee. At one point, he noticed Sampson staring hungrily at his coffee mug. King asked him if he wanted coffee and Sampson nodded his head vigorously. King sent for a pot of coffee and, when it arrived, watched Sampson hold his mug in two hands while he loudly sipped the hot liquid. What began as a whim became routine. Every morning near the end of Sampson's ablutions, King would enter with a pot of black coffee and a couple of mugs and the two men would drink their coffee in silence. Occasionally, King would read the paper out loud while they were drinking their coffee. Sometimes Sampson would rap on his bed and wave his hand, indicating that he wanted King to read something over. A relationship was developing without the will or intent of either man.

Often at the back of King's mind was the possibility that Sampson was merely waiting for the right opportunity, that one day he would break out of his malaise and strike a blow in revenge for all that he had lost. That possibility stayed King's hand not one bit; he could no more change his course than a salmon could fight the call of the open sea. It felt right. He was going to do what felt right and he had no great fear of death.

King hired carpenters and master builders to refurbish the villa. Whenever possible, he hired colored people. Both the bank and the attorney's office tried to put pressure on him to hire prominent white businesses, but King did not relent. He had a mistrust of southern whites that he could not put aside. He spent several months having the inside of the villa redone to his specifications. The stucco exterior was patched and repaired but left unpainted. There was no desire to make the building look too out of place with its surroundings. He now owned a safe house where he could hide or from which he could depart covertly by either land or sea.

King had made a regular practice of riding through the areas around New Orleans, and as Sampson grew stronger, he took him along. They were often seen leaving the city limits early on horseback. The war had taught King the value of knowing the surrounding terrain. Within weeks of his arrival in New Orleans, King had purchased two excellent horses: a large chestnut gelding with a deep chest and long legs and an eight-year-old bay stallion with sound Arab breeding. Often he and Sampson spent hours on their horses riding the surrounding hills and trails. King searched out and bought a thirty-foot flat-bottomed river steamer used to carry small cargoes between the port and various ships and barges that plied the local waters. Several times a week he and Sampson took the steamer, which he named the *Mamie Lou*, out into the swamp looking for old landmarks and waterways leading into the bayous.

A friendship was slowly developing between King and Sampson. Initially, they communicated mostly by hand signals and facial expressions, but King discovered that a deaf woman worked in the hotel's kitchen and she taught them both sign language. It was a necessity because once Sampson was strong enough to leave the hotel, he wanted to go everywhere with King. King was forced to buy him a horse and then had to teach him how to drive a car. Sampson was excellent around horses and he took their care and maintenance as his responsibility, but the car was different. He crashed several times before he got fully familiar with the demands of driving. King also started taking him along when he went shooting. Sampson loved going out in the swamp steamer along the bayous and channels of the delta river country. They made several trips before Sampson evinced any interest in firearms. The first time he had gestured to try shooting the guns himself, King wondered if the time had come, but King handed him the weapon without hesitation and showed him how to use it. Sampson had such a good time that when they went back to town, King bought him his own rifle and a bowie knife.

THURSDAY, JULY 22, 1920

The heat of the sun was causing steam to rise from the dampened earth when Serena brought a grain-laden wagon drawn by the family's two mules into Nellum's Crossing. As the sun beat down on her shawl-covered shoulders, she could tell it was going to get hotter. It was only eleven o'clock in the morning. She adjusted her straw hat as the large, faded red structure of the mill came into view through the trees. There were only seven buildings in all of Nellum's Crossing, and five of the buildings were not even in sight of each other. Bellow's General Store and Mack & Peabo's Grist Mill were located fifty yards from each other on opposite sides of the country road, which loosely connected all the buildings to Lake Pontchatrain Road.

Serena slapped the reins again against the backs of the mules and guided them off the road toward the mill's grain chute. The old wagon creaked loudly with its weight of grain sacks. Serena had been concerned more than once during her trip into Nellum's Crossing that the wagon would disintegrate before she arrived. It was obvious to everyone but her father that the old wagon could no longer bear such weight over rough and gutted country roads. "Gee! Gee! Jethro, Gee," she commanded the left-hand mule as the wagon scraped up against the milling dock.

A tall, scrawny white man with a beaklike nose and large Adam's apple stood on the dock and watched Serena Baddeaux. He pushed back his battered straw hat and his eyes widened appreciatively as he watched her jump from the wagon to the dock. "Yes siree, it sure do look like Little Serena done growed up! How do, honey?" he asked as his Adam's apple bobbed up and down.

Serena knew all about Mr. Samuel Mack: the ways he used to cheat on the weight milled and how he always tried to get between the legs of every colored woman he saw. She had been bringing in wagons of grain to be milled at Mack & Peabo's Grist Mill since she was fifteen. She was ready for him. "My father's doing fine, Mr. Mack. How's Mrs. Mack?"

A frown immediately flashed across his face and he swallowed angrily. "Why you askin'?" he demanded. Obviously, the thought of his wife was not conducive with the other thoughts in his head.

"Last time I was by, you told me your wife was doing poorly, Mr. Mack. I was just hoping that her health had returned," Serena explained with a tone of innocence. She thought he was extremely ugly even for a white man. The movement of his Adam's apple reminded her of a garter snake's body after it swallowed a frog. "I have ten jute bags of corn weighing one hundred fifty pounds apiece," she announced. "I know you haven't seen this much grain in a while. I heard this mill hasn't been used in a week. I should get a better percentage than you have posted."

"I can always squeeze out a lower percentage, if'en you wants to come into my office and do a bit of business." He winked at her lewdly.

"You have a sign outside that says there's a twenty-dollar milling fee, plus the mill takes five percent for loads under five hundred pounds and three percent for loads over a thousand."

"That ain't fo' coloreds! That's fo' whites only. Coloreds ain't generally got the same quality as they betters. 'Course, as I said, I could maybe give you a lower percentage."

"How much lower, Mr. Mack? Lower than the sign?" she asked while looking him directly in the eye. She watched him lick his lips and look her up and down.

"You ain't gon' get better but you might get close. It depends on what you got. Can't make no deal unless I see the merchandise, can I?"

Serena was tired of Mr. Mack. She was tired of all the roles she was forced to play in the face of racism. She wanted to blurt out what she really thought. Instead, she contained herself. "Mr. Mack, you stand to make twenty dollars' cash plus forty-five pounds of cornmeal, if you gave me what the sign says. Since you don't want to give me a fair price, I'm going to drive all the way to Swanson's to get the grain milled. Swanson will give me a better price."

The frown reappeared on Mack's face. "You gon' sell to a foreigner?" Mack demanded. The Swansons had only lived in the parish for two generations. He smacked his leg in anger. "Jes', what did we go and fight a war fo', huh?" he questioned the world around him. "Certainly weren't to give foreigners an upper hand over American-born!" Mack's face was mottled with anger and his big nose pulsed red like a beacon.

"I have family, Mr. Mack. Are you going to give me a fair price?" Serena was calm. She was in no danger from Mack as long as she did nothing to aggravate him. Mack was a low-down, Jim Crow cheat, but he was not the kind of man who would take pleasure in smacking a woman around, even if she was a colored woman.

Mack stood for a moment considering his decision. "What you mean, 'a fair price'?"

"I want what the sign says, Mr. Mack."

A voice called out behind her. "Yeah, Cap'n Mack, give her what you's advertizin'." King Tremain rode up with a big smile. He was riding a big gray stallion and leading another horse.

"As I live and breathe, look what the cat done brung in! I heard you was back from Mississippi, Bordeaux," Mack answered with a big grin. He walked over to the edge of the loading dock. "Boy, if'en you don't look mo' jes' like yo' father every day that pass. You gon' have to come by the house and see the wife! She wouldn't let me hear the end of it, if she found out you was by here and didn't come and see her!" Mack jumped down from the loading dock.

"I'll do that later, if you don't mind, Cap'n. I jes' came by to drop off the horse I told you about. I knows you got two races comin' up and I seen this little filly run. With the right rider she might make a little money for you." King tipped his hat to Serena as he slid off his horse. He handed the reins of the filly to Mack.

"She sho' is a trim little number," said Mack admiringly as he patted the horse's neck. "She got real nice lines." He turned to King and said, "They both do, if you know what I mean." Mack ogled both Serena and the filly to make his point.

"This here lady is a friend of mine, Cap'n Mack," King said easily. "I sho' would appreciate it if you would give her yo' best service."

"Oh, she yo' friend, well maybe I can take my thumb off the scale for her."

King said with a broad smile, "Beg pardon, Cap'n, but it's yo' foot she worried 'bout."

Mack guffawed. "Not in front of the payin' customers, boy, not in front of the payin' customers. I'm gon' put this little horse in the back." Mack turned and asked King, "You sho' you can't stop in and see Martha?"

"I'll tell you what, Cap'n, I'll come back by when the lady here picks up her meal."

"We gon' engage the stone tomorrow, her shipment should be ready by Saturday. I'll tell the missus you's comin'." Mack led the filly around the back of the mill building.

As Mack walked the horse away, King leaped up on the dock. "I hopes you don't mind if I said we was friends," he said to Serena.

Serena did not say anything at first. She merely looked him up and down. She wanted to make sure she had his image in her mind. He was a tall handsome man and he was light-skinned enough to be able to travel in the best company. She noted that all his clothes were store-bought.

"You talkin'?" King asked.

"We haven't met. I'm Serena Baddeaux." She held out her hand in the manner she imagined of a great grand dame.

King started to laugh. "Why you gettin' so puffed up? I know who you is and I think you know me. Do we got to pretend?"

Serena frowned at him a moment. "How do you know who I am?"

"I asked."

"Oh, that's good." She nodded her head and smiled at him. "How do you know Mr. Mack?"

"Him and his brother and my daddy and my uncle was all very close. They didn't have no regular colored-white relationship. They had somethin' special. I don't trust too many white folks, but Cap'n Mack is one."

"You mean your father and uncle were friends with Corlis Mack, the sheriff of New Orleans Parish?"

"That be the one, but it was a long time ago. He ain't like his brother, Cap'n Mack. He done forgot he ever was friends with coloreds."

"I thought your name was King. Why does he call you Bordeaux?"

"Bordeaux is my middle name. King is a name I got in the war. He's been callin' me Bordeaux since I was a baby. I ain't gon' try and change him."

"Where do you live?" Serena asked.

"In New Orleans at the Hotel Toussant."

"What do you do for a living?"

"You's full of questions, ain't you?"

"Not really. I just wondered what kind of career could a man who killed so easily have?"

"If you's stuck on that, ma'am, I takes my leave of you." King tipped his hat and whistled softly for his horse, who answered the call and came alongside the dock.

Serena saw with surprise that King wasn't going to argue with her; he was simply going to leave. "I'm sorry. I meant no offense."

King paused before mounting his horse. "Sho' sounded like it to me." He put his foot in the stirrup and stepped into the saddle.

He was leaving. It was not the result Serena had intended. Aside from the possibility that he might be the instrument she could use to escape the farm, she was intensely interested in seeing him again. "Will I see you when it's time to pick up the grain?" she asked in a small voice.

King studied her for a moment. "That depends on you."

"How?"

"Do you want me to come while you're here?"

If she said no, Serena knew that King would ride away without a backward glance and another one of her possible escape routes would be closed. "Yes," she blurted out and then was immediately ashamed by the blatancy of her statement.

"Then I'll come at three o'clock on Saturday, how's that?"

Serena merely nodded her head in response. King touched his hat to her again and trotted off through the trees.

Mack reappeared with a couple of his assistants. "Bordeaux gone?" he asked, as his helpers began unloading the grain from the wagon.

"Yes, Mr. Mack. He says that you've known him for quite a while."

Mack laughed. "Sho' 'nough. I was there the day he was borned. I bailed his daddy out'n jail and brought him to where Bordeaux's mother was laborin'. That boy came out hollerin', ready to do battle with the world. I's the one that said he should be called Bordeaux after his grandfather. How you know 'em?" Mack beckoned for her to walk back with him toward the scales.

"Oh, I met him at an evangelical meeting earlier this month," Serena said simply, showing the usual reluctance to share any information with whites.

"Evangelical meetin', huh? Don't sound much like Bordeaux to me. That weren't when he did the DuMont boys, was it?"

"I don't know anything about that," Serena lied, not wanting to incriminate King.

"That be another story," Mack said as they walked up to the half-ton scale. "You know, you can go on and I'll get my boys to take it into the shed and we'll weigh what's milled."

Serena knew better than to accept that offer. If she was slow enough to fall for that ploy, Mack might skim off forty or fifty more pounds of meal.

"Thank you, Mr. Mack, but I'll wait while it's weighed." Serena turned back to the wagon and took out a one-pound weight and a five-pound weight, which she showed him. "Just to check the scales," she said with a small smile. She was within her rights. It was local custom that a farmer, even colored, had the right to check scales before the selling or milling of grain.

Serena planned to make a quick stop at the general store to pick up supplies and then head to the blacksmith's shop to see if the new issue of *The Crisis* had come in. Serena always looked forward to visiting the general store and Old Mrs. Bellow. The store was a treasure trove of wonderful and exotic smells. When she stepped in the door she was immediately aware of the scent of dried and cured meats, spices, the barrels of pickles and pickled cabbage, and, if she came in the morning, the welcoming aroma of newly baked bread. All this was interwoven with the heavy, sweet smell of fresh-cut leather emanating from the stock of new straps, harnesses, saddles, and machine-made boots. It was a place where she fantasized about having money. Everywhere she looked there were always so many things on the neatly stacked shelves that her family needed, yet did not have the means to purchase. Sometimes she even dreamed of leaving home and asking Mrs. Bellow for a position in the store just to be in an environment of plenty.

As she was totaling up, Mrs. Bellow, the old white woman who owned the store, confided to her that the Right Reverend Pendergast had come up to the Church of the Cross to get assistance for the colored families who had been burned out by the Klan. Mrs. Bellow whispered when she spoke of the Klan. Serena knew Mrs. Bellow had no love for the night riders because she was Jewish and her only son had disappeared without a trace after he had a run-in with a man who was known to be a high Klan official. His disappearance was never fully investigated and no one was ever arrested, but it was common knowledge as to who was responsible.

After she left the store, Serena reconsidered going on to the blacksmith because it was located in sight of the Church of the Cross. It was her family's church and she knew that in any meeting of the church elders, her father would be in attendance, and she didn't relish the prospect of seeing her father. She did not think of it as her church because she didn't like the six-hour Sunday Bible meeting and prayer service, nor the fire-and-damnation, altar-pounding sermons that were given every Sunday. Despite her reluctance, the possibility that there might be an announcement of who had been selected for the NAACP's Annual Spingarn Award drove her onward to the smithy.

She saw Walter Deveroux and his son Gerard standing around the blacksmith, Jonas Stedman, while his assistant, Dante LeBrie, pumped the bellows on the fire. Jonas Stedman looked like a blacksmith. He had a thick triangular neck, which was connected to a squat muscular body. He had bulging, powerful arms that could swing a heavy hammer all day, and he was as black as the wrought iron he twisted so delicately. His smile was easy and friendly, only marred by the many gaps in his teeth. She noticed that the conversation between the men halted abruptly as she drew near.

"How do, Rena?" Jonas called to her as she pulled along the side where horses were stabled.

"I'm alright, Jonas," she answered as she jumped down to water the mules. "Ma's having a tough time, though."

"She still fightin' that consumption?" Jonas asked, picking up a piece of red-hot iron with a long pair of tongs.

Serena set two buckets of water down for the mules. "Yes, God bless her. She's fighting with everything she's got, but its got a strong hold on her. Did the new *Crisis* come in?"

"Naw, we ain't received mail for almost a week. All this Klan stuff out at Possum Hollow must got the post all messed up," Jonas said before he began pounding the hot metal into shape. Molten splinters flashed and sparked as Jonas's hammer fell with a rhythmic clang on the hot iron.

"You probably stopped by to see who done won the Spingarn, jes' like we did," Walter Deveroux said, using a piece of straw to pick his teeth. He was a tall, powerful, stoop-shouldered man with mahogany, reddish-brown skin.

"Yes, I'm disappointed that there's no word on the Spingarn," Serena answered, moving toward Deveroux and away from the clanging of the hammer. "Mr. Deveroux, do you really think that the Klan could stop the mail from coming to Nellum's Crossing?"

"Naw, too many whites get they mail at the general store too, including Black Jack hi'self. They ain't got nothin' to do with it! Them Klan boys is just cowards, sneakin' up on unsuspectin' colored folk. I hope they never ride on me and mine, but if they do, there's gon' be less of them afterward. I swear to God!" For several seconds, his normally passive expression turned into a terrible snarl. His Choctaw blood had left him with high cheekbones and slanting eyes, which gave him a striking and savage look when angered. People often called him "The Indian" behind his back. He didn't like the label so no one said it to his face. Both he and his nineteen-year-old son were men of great physical strength, and though Walter was not known for his temper, he was known to be tremendously tenacious once he had made a decision. He tipped his hat to Serena. " 'Scuse my swearin', Rena. I got sort of het up!"

"I'm with you, Pa," volunteered his nineteen-year-old son in support. "Somebody got to stand up to these dogs. All colored folks ain't afraid of them, shoo!"

Jonas dunked the hot piece of iron into a vat of cold water and the hiss of steam shot skyward. "That new road is what's causin' all the problems," he said as he inspected his work. "There's plenty big money to be made. Ain't no way they gon' let no coloreds stay on that land! That swampland gon' be some of the most precious land around here when that road gets built. It's like W. E. B. DuBois says, we caught in an economic trap."

"They could make plenty money jes' buyin' the colored out," countered the older Deveroux. "Ain't no reason to kill peoples who just want their fair due. It look like they don't think that the colored got any rights!"

"And they say that colored folks ain't got regular smarts," Jonas said as he swung the doors of the kiln open and extracted another red-hot piece of metal with a pair of even longer tongs. It didn't pass his inspection and he returned it to the fire. "To have a decent, God-fearin' life under Jim Crow, you got to be twice as smart as the average white if you colored." He started pumping the bellows. Jonas opened the kiln, assessed the flame, and turned to call his apprentice, but the young man had anticipated his request and stood behind him with an armful of wood. Jonas nodded his head appreciatively and indicated to his apprentice with a gesture of his hamlike hand. "Now you see, if Dante here was white, he'd be goin' to one of them big-city colleges and learnin' all 'bout engineerin' and such. But he ain't, so he's stuck with me. He gon' have a good life, but he gon' work twice as hard to find pleasure in it. This here work ain't challengin' for the mind. It don't take no highbrow mental doin's."

"Seems to me," Walter Deveroux began as he spat out his piece of straw, "anytime you's workin' fo' yo'self, it take up yo' whole mind just to keep it that way; keepin' the bank from fo'closin', keepin' them grain scalpers from cheatin' on yo' harvest; tryin' to buy decent seed stock. It be true most farmin' don't take much highbrow thinkin', but keepin' it yo' farm takes all yo' mind and yo' heart and everythin' else you can put to it."

Serena wasn't participating in the conversation. She had purposefully walked to the other side of the smithy when Dante LeBrie became the topic. Dante was one of the few realistic options, in terms of marriage, that she had available. He had already indicated his interest in courting her a number of times and, frankly, Serena did not want to reveal her decision until the possibility of escaping to the lights and laughter of city life had been completely squelched. She saw some intricate metalwork on several tall, wrought-iron gates leaning against the side of the smithy. Each of the upright bars in the gate was in the shape of a spear, the shaft topped by a long blade.

"It's beautiful, ain't it?" Dante asked, standing slightly behind her. Serena nodded and said nothing. Dante continued, "It's one of the biggest jobs we've had since Black Jack had a new wrought-iron front fence put in."

"Who's it for?" Serena asked, not really curious but attempting to be polite.

"King Tremain," Jonas answered as he took the piece of iron out of the kiln and pounded it a few times experimentally.

"Now that's the dude that the Klan ought to mess with!" Gerard Deveroux declared, with a small laugh.

"Yes, sir," Dante agreed. "He got himself quite a reputation as a gambler who's good at protectin' his winnin's."

"I heard from John-Boy Basin that this young Tremain fought in the Big War," the older Deveroux scoffed. "Then the fool had the gall to tell me the boy fought with the Three hundred Sixty-ninth."

"Tweren't no fool if he tol' you that," Jonas answered. He pounded the piece of metal around the curve of the anvil. He stopped to take a breath and continued talking. "King Tremain came by here on the mornin' of July Fourth, the day he kilt Chess and Eddy DuMont. He was wearin' his service uniform with sergeant stripes and that white rattler insignia on it. So, I asked him straight out, was he in the Three hundred Sixty-ninth, and he took a picture out of a big envelope. Get this, it showed him standin' in the same line as Henry Armstrong Johnson getting metals pinned on his chest." Jonas beckoned Dante to assist him with the pedal grinder. Once Dante got the stone spinning at a decent speed, Jonas began honing the edge of the long metal blade that he had hammered into shape.

"Then it's true that he fought with the Three hundred Sixty-ninth Battalion?" Walter Deveroux questioned incredulously. "He ain't nothin' but a little more'n a boy."

"That boy is the real thing!" Jonas affirmed. "You heard how he took care of them DuMonts, didn't you? He didn't even break out into a sweat. It was over before anybody could get there to stop it."

Walter shook his head. "And I heard he the same one that did Lester too?"

"Yep, Tremain and DuMont feud been goin' on at least one hundred years."

"I guess them DuMonts is pretty sorry to see him come home, huh?" Walter asked with curiosity. Like most good people, he thought the DuMonts were trash, but the Tremains didn't have a good reputation either. They were known to be wild and dangerous.

"Don't get it twisted. Everybody that messed with him is sorry, even his own family. They scared of him too, almost as much as the DuMonts.

Seems like while he was away his mother died fo' no reason and somebody else done took over his father's farm. By the way, they don't call him King, they call him 'Bordeaux' after his grandfather."

"I knows the one!" Gerard interjected. "My pa used to talk about him. That's the Bordeaux that kilt all them white people and hid out for years in the bayous?"

"Yeah, used to be a lot of talk about that one," Walter answered. "They used to send parties of mens into the swamp after him and only 'bout half would come out."

"He's the one that was eventually catched with the help of a colored man?" Dante asked.

"And that colored man was a DuMont," Jonas confirmed.

Serena was adjusting the bridle on one of the mules when Dante came over to talk to her. It was the moment she feared: he would ask her for her decision and the truth was that she had made no decision.

"How you been doin', Rena?" he asked. Dante continued braiding a hackamore from leather thongs as he awaited her answer.

"I'm doing alright. Just working hard," Serena said as she stooped to pick up the water buckets, but Dante put a hand on her shoulder.

"I'll get them buckets, Rena. You done any thinkin' 'bout what I asked you?"

Serena could not bring herself to look him in the face. She stared at his hands, watching his fingers manipulate the thongs into a linking braid. The fear that Dante was probably the best opportunity for marriage she would ever get caused her to speak softly. "Can't really say that I have, Dante, least ways not to say yes or no."

"Well, I just want to do right. I been kind of talkin' with Antonia Martin and I'm thinkin' of askin' her father if I can come a-courtin'. I thought I'd make sure of yo' answer first."

It was decision time. It was true she didn't love him, but there was no contesting that he was a decent man who was ambitious and was willing to work hard in pursuit of his dreams. Whoever he married would have a good life, but that was not enough for her. She knew she had to let him go. "You're a good man and can offer a woman a good life, Dante, but I want to live in a city. I want to see some things before I settle down and have children. I thank you for asking me. I hope we can stay friends."

"Ain't no problem, Rena. I appreciates yo' honesty and not keepin' me hangin'. Truth is, I just wants to settle down and get my family started. In two years I'll have completed my apprenticeship and I got to be ready to move. Jonas say he'll help me set up my own shop. I's lookin' fo'ward to workin' fo' myself."

With a heavy heart, Serena climbed aboard her wagon. "Good luck, Dante. See you, Jonas," she called as she snapped the reins and headed the mules for home. By the time she was out of sight of Nellum's Crossing, tears were running down her face. She realized that she had irrevocably slammed a door on one of her options of escape. She cried not out of lost love, but because of the terrible odds against her attaining her desires. When the tears had passed, Serena was left thinking about the soldier called King Tremain and wondering whether there would be any future with him.

SATURDAY, JULY 24, 1920

Friday day and Saturday morning passed extremely slowly for Serena. She had trouble containing her sense of expectation. She did not know what the next meeting with King Tremain would produce, but she was anxious nonetheless. She wanted to wear her new white dress that she had worn when she had first met him, but she knew that would arouse too many questions from her family. She decided at last on a clean brown frock with a white collar. It complimented the light brown color of her skin. Her mother, despite her physical discomfort, noticed Serena's excitement. She helped Serena tie her hair up in a colorful bandanna. Her mother asked no questions, but sent her off with a weak hug and a smile. As Serena drove the wagon out of the yard, her father yelled at her to hurry back because he needed one of the mules later that afternoon to pull out a stump.

The drive to Nellum's Crossing was uneventful. When she pulled the wagon up to the loading dock of the mill, King was standing there bare-chested with her sacks of milled grain.

"How do, little lady?" he asked as he shouldered one of the sacks and dropped it in her wagon.

"Fine," she answered, noticing the definition of his muscles in his arms and chest. "Where's Mr. Mack?" she asked, trying to seem nonchalant.

"He and the Missus took off for town. They wasn't expectin' no other pickups today and I told 'em that I would handle yo' load."

"They must really trust you," she commented wonderingly. "How did you get to be so close to a man who would cheat colored people out of their hard-earned grain?"

King laughed. "Cap'n Mack tries to cheat everybody. He don't single out coloreds. He figger, if you ain't up on yo' business, you shouldn't be in it. It be like that old sayin', 'A fool and his money is soon parted.' So, he figger why shouldn't he be the one to get that money." He shouldered another bag of grain.

Serena was incensed. "How could you be friendly to a man who cheats ignorant colored folk out of their honest gain?"

"Anybody who stay ignorant in this world deserve what they get. People don't need book learnin' to know when they's bein' cheated. At some point, people got to stand up. If'en they don't, that's on them. I notice, Mr. Mack don't be cheatin' you."

"He tried!"

"But you caught him, didn't you, and you got yo' fair return. He don't cheat them that knows what they supposed to get." King continued carrying the sacks of grain to the wagon.

"Do you think that's the right way to act?"

"Don't matter what I think. The world is the way it's gon' be. It's ruled by the powerful. The weak and the meek ain't got shit! The Bible must be talkin' about a grave when it say, 'The meek gon' inherit the Earth.' "

Their discussion was interrupted by a distant roll of thunder. One of the mules snorted in fear and tried to rear up despite the restraining braces of the wagon harness. Serena struggled with the reins for a minute to regain control. "Whoa, Jethro. It's alright. It's alright."

"Look like you got a skittish critter," King commented as he loaded the last of the sacks aboard the wagon. "You want me to ride along with you, in case he try to bolt?"

"That would be mighty Christian of you."

King whistled for his horse and the big bay came trotting out of the barn. He loosely tethered his horse to the rear of the wagon and clambered aboard. Serena offered him the reins and he snapped them crisply across the backs of the mules and guided them out onto the road.

As far as Serena was concerned, the ride home to her farm was far too short. She was enraptured with King's tales of New York City and its multistoried buildings and miles of neon lights. When they reached the edge of her property, under a large, spread-limbed sycamore, King got on his horse. Serena had explained to him that her father was extremely old-fashioned and would not take kindly to a strange man riding home with his oldest daughter.

They made arrangements to meet at Stedman's blacksmith shop later that week and King rode off toward town. Serena watched him gallop off before she reined the mules toward home. She was bubbling with excitement. Here was the man she had been seeking, a world traveler, someone who appreciated the big-city life, someone who would carry her away from all the pain and fatigue of farmwork.

MONDAY, AUGUST 30, 1920

"We's lookin' for backin', that's why we come to you. Everybody know you's independent and don't owe nobody nothin' and we know that folks'll think two, three times before they mess with you." The man finished talking and pushed his hat on the back of his head and waited for King's answer. His two companions, who were sitting on either side of him, leaned forward also to hear King's response.

King looked across the green felt table at the three men and did not answer immediately. He was puffing on a Cuban cigar with a long ash, which he flicked into a nearby ashtray. The single light that hung directly above the table in a conical shade did little to create a positive impression of the three men, but positive impressions were not King's concern. He had been investigating the bootleg business because there was big money in it, but he had no contacts outside the United States or with any open-sea shipping lines. Without those connections, he was limited to buying from other bootleggers or pirating their shipments. He had been stymied. Eventually he heard through the grapevine that some small-time bootleggers wanted to expand their operations, but they needed capital and protection.

"Just so I understand what you layin' out," King began in measured tones. "You want to run whiskey and other liquor in from Mexico? You say you got connections in Mexico? You need some up-front investment money to really make it worthwhile? You gon' take all the risks in smugglin' and pay two-to-one on every dollar invested? Then you still want protection from me while you distribute the stock? Is that it?"

"Yes, suh," responded a man called Dirty Red. He moved into the light, revealing patterns of reddish brown freckles on light brown skin. "We 'spect we gon' be competin' with some white folks who's runnin' liquor and we knows they ain't gon' take lightly to it. We gon' need some muscle to stand up to them. Like Pete said, that's why we came to you. Them white boys won't stand fo' no colored independents."

Little did they know that this was the type of reasoning that appealed most to King. The oppressive limits unfairly placed on black people always infuriated him. As far as he was concerned, colored criminals had just as much right to operate as their white counterparts. Running liquor had become a very lucrative business. He saw no reason that only white people should make such money. "I could handle all yo' money worries, but it don't seem like a good deal to me, gentlemen." King tapped his cigar again. "I appreciates you comin' to me and offerin' me a chance to get in on the ground flo', but two-to-one ain't worth it."

There was a moment of silence. Then the man who hadn't spoken pushed back from the table. "Mr. Tremain, how much do you want?" The brim of his hat caused his face to be in shadow.

"I want what's fair," King answered easily. He knew that the men were concerned that a larger fish might steal their idea. "You boys gon' bring the booze back here and sell it for ten, fifteen times what you paid. Then you want protection too? Two-to-one ain't right. I ain't interested in takin' over yo' business. I just wants fair return. I got a line on a coastal steamer that I'll throw in the deal, if you let me come in as a full partner."

The man who had pushed away from table spoke. "How we know you can provide real protection? You ain't got no army! You—"

Pete interrupted. "Cool down, Tyson, we is here askin'. We ain't here demandin'!"

King smiled. "There ain't no proof I can give you, but—just one but: ain't nobody ever took somethin' from me that I didn't want to give up and lived."

"How we know that?" Tyson challenged.

"Do you want to try to take something from me?" King had not raised his voice but the threat was so clear that Tyson's companions stumbled over themselves to diffuse the situation.

Dirty Red held up his hands. "We don't want no trouble."

"Uh, we got a bit of a misunderstandin' here," Pete offered.

"Let yo' friend answer the question," King said in the same quiet tone.

Tyson answered, "Ain't no problem. I don't want nothin' you got. I just wanna do business."

"Then let's do business," King agreed with a smile.

After their meeting at the mill, King came to visit or sent word to Serena once or twice every week. She used Amos as her messenger since the one-room schoolhouse that he attended was located at the edge of Nellum's Crossing on the same pine-forested ridge as the Church of the Cross and Stedman's Blacksmith Works. King and Serena often met on sunny days in a glade of magnolias and sycamores at the north end of her family's property. During these visits generally she was the one who talked and he listened. Every once in a while he would stir to ask her a question, seeking further clarification or expressing his own laconic opinion. Despite her mother's failing condition, this was the happiest period of time that Serena had experienced since she was a child. Every visit seemed ideal.

Serena talked a lot about her interests and the deteriorating relationship she was experiencing with her father. She felt free to talk with King about things she had shared with no one else. He always listened attentively and asked good questions. She had begun to look forward to their meetings.

The first time that King came to the house was because she had left word for him at the blacksmith's to bring laudanum as soon as possible. Her mother needed more of the painkilling medicine and King knew where to get it quickly. His sole purpose in coming to the house was to bring the laudanum and check on Serena. She hadn't responded to any of his messages. When King knocked on the door of her house late one Thursday afternoon, her father answered. King politely asked to see Serena. Her father refused, demanding to know why King had the audacity to call upon his daughter without her father's permission.

"I am asking your permission now to see your daughter," King acquiesced calmly.

"The answer is no!" her father declared. "I want my daughter married to a good, God-fearing Christian man. Not some flashy, street-life do-nothing!"

"Don't put on airs with me," King warned softly. "I know where you sleep! I know all about yo' other life."

Serena walked out the door. "Other life? What do you mean?"

"Get back in the house!" her father ordered.

"I want to hear what King is—"

Her father slapped her. "Get back in the house—" He too was interrupted. King had ascended the stairs in one leap and swung her father forcefully into the wall of the cabin. Her father fell to the floor dazed.

King handed her the bottle of laudanum. "I's sorry about coming like this, but you didn't answer none of my messages."

"I know, my mother has really been ill. I've been sitting with her night and day. I want to know what you meant by 'other life.' "

Her father pushed himself to his knees and staggered to his feet. King offered his hand. "I ain't looking for trouble with you, Mr. Baddeaux. I was just defendin' Serena."

"Get off my property!" her father shouted, clenching his fists as if he was ready to fight.

King observed him with an easy smile. "Hold your horses, Mr. Baddeaux. I ain't looking for trouble with you. I wants to get on the good foot with you. In fact, I wants to make amends fo' what jes' happened, but I intends to finish what I have to say to Serena. If that brings trouble, so be it." There was a clear warning tone in King's voice.

"If you're not off my property by the time I get my shotgun, I'll start pulling the trigger!"

King shook his head resignedly. "What makes you think that you'll make it to yo' shotgun?"

Serena watched her father's face and saw his expression settle into hatred. She sighed: that look meant that King would never be welcome in her parents' house, not that she really ever expected to get her father's blessing.

Her father looked at Serena and the hatred did not fade from his expression. He said to her grimly, "If you expect to continue living in my house, you better get inside now!"

"I'll live here as long as I like!" Serena declared. "I spent many hard years working this place. You can't take away my right to live here!"

"We'll see about that when this gangster leaves!" Her father turned to go into the house, but King punched him hard in the stomach. Her father staggered forward, holding his middle, and fell to the floor gasping for air.

King squatted beside him. "She lives here as long as she wants. Whether you like it or not. And I know you don't want to think about what I'll do to you if I find out that you've laid even a finger on her, do you? I hope I've made my point."

There was no response. Her father just lay on the floor holding his stomach. King patted his arm. "I knew you'd see the light."

Charles Baddeaux grunted. "If you come on my land again, I'll kill you!"

King smiled. "You better get me with the first shot," he suggested softly. " 'Cause if you don't, I'll just wait outside 'til you come out of your house, then I'll stake you, while you're still livin', in your own rice patch to let the crows feed on you."

King stood up and ushered Serena off the porch to speak with her. After several minutes of murmured conversation, King mounted his horse and rode back into town.

The ensuing week was hell for Serena. The primary cause of distress was her mother's failing health and the attendant increasing desire for the comfort of laudanum. The other problem was her father. He no longer spoke to her, and while he didn't dare lift a hand against her, he took every opportunity to show her that she was unwanted. If it had been Serena by herself, she could have withstood his hostility easily, but her two sisters and her brother were caught in the middle.

SATURDAY, SEPTEMBER 4, 1920

"*Kyklos* is a Greek word meaning circle. It is the origin of Ku Klux Klan. You see, the founding fathers of our organization knew that we would have to link hands in an invisible circle in order to keep the niggers and Jews and papists in their place. You got to know your history, Jack!" Major Harley swished his cognac around in his snifter. He was a plump, pale-faced man in his late fifties. Only his eyebrows retained their original dark-brown coloring; the rest of his full head of hair was nearly white. "*Kyklos*, my friend; the White Circle has a job to do."

"I often wondered where a foreign name like that came from," Jack Shannon mused over his own brandy. He was a tall, spare man in his mid-forties with jet-black hair whose skin was tanned from working in the sun.

"Ain't no foreign name! It's American!" defended the third man in the room angrily. He had watery-blue eyes and a ruddy, pockmarked complexion. The pockmarks on his skin caused his face to look as if it had been chipped out of granite. His hair was fine, the color of corn silk, and kept falling into his eyes.

"Now, now, Roy. We don't want to argue with our guest," Major Harley said. "I hope you'll pardon Roy Wilcox. He's one of our zealots." Harley took a sip of his cognac and strode over to the table to pour himself some water, but discovered that the bucket was empty. "Rastus! Rastus, get in here!"

A balding colored man in his late fifties appeared at the door, bowing. "Yes, suh, Major Harley."

"Rastus, we're out of both water and ice. How do you think that happened?" the major demanded.

Rastus looked back and forth between the three white men in the study. "I 'spects you done drunk it up, Major, suh." Sweat dripped down the dark brown skin of his face as he waited patiently for direction.

"No, you fool!" corrected Major Harley. "We're out of ice and water because you didn't fill it! Now, I want both buckets kept filled for the duration of the meeting! Do you understand?"

"Yes, suh." Rastus nodded and shuffled over to the table and removed both buckets. The three white men watched him leave.

"You shoulda smacked him, Major, for sassin' you!" volunteered Roy. "Niggers need remindin' of who owns the store!"

Jack shook his head and went over to the maps tacked to the wall to study them. He turned and looked at the major. "If they choose the coastal route, you still have five properties to acquire. Your maps indicate that you've got the deeds for six lots. You've still got a lot of work to get done. You got until November fifteenth to get possession of that land! That includes transfer of title and possession of legal deeds; that's not very much time. The National Bureau of Transportation Committee is going to announce which route Interstate Twelve will take out of New Orleans that day."

"You know, Jack, that we've been treading a thin line for some time now. If the chairperson on the committee knew I owned that land, he'd use his influence to select an alternate route. He's still upset over that time we quarantined his wheat on the docks for three weeks." Rastus entered, set down the two buckets, and left.

"He lost a harvest. I can see why he bears a grudge," Jack acknowledged. "He better not get wind of you running the coloreds off their land. It might affect his decision. I think you'd do better to avoid fireworks and offer them the current price for the land. You'd still make a pretty penny on the deal."

"I'm opposed to paying anything to niggers when I can take what I want," answered Harley. "From what I understand the white citizenry is so up in arms over the general uppityness of the niggers, the night riders may ride again."

"Yeah," Roy joined in. "We're goin' to make a sweep through tomorrow night and run some mo' niggers out!"

"I don't want to hear your plans! I will not become an accessory to murder!" Jack interjected.

Roy looked at the major with a questioning look. "Who's been murdered?"

"You and your riders are getting out of hand! I heard how they burned a colored woman and her daughter to death on Thursday," Jack Shannon commented, sipping his brandy.

"That is pure folderol! All them niggers was given a chance to remove their possessions before their shacks were burnt and no women or children were hurt! It just plain isn't so!"

"The people who guide the night riders are on par with Plato's philosopher kings," explained Major Harley. "We're interested in the social good, not cruelty. We just want to set the record straight and make sure that the mongrel races know better than to vie with us for what God gave to us!"

"Amen," Roy agreed.

"I'm returning a business favor to you by telling you the deadlines as they are communicated to me, but don't confuse me with one of your partners!" Jack said, setting down his glass and straightening his jacket. "I am grateful for that favor you did for me two years ago, but there is a limit to the gratitude and the repayment. I think you could do this deal legally and still make a lot of money. Personally, I've discovered doing business with more honey than vinegar brings people back to the table to deal a second time."

"I'm sure you're right, Jack," Major Harley said as he escorted him to the door. "I don't want you to think we're on different sides. I'll talk some sense into the boys."

Later, when he and Roy were sitting alone in his study, Major Harley said, "We got to watch that Jack Shannon. He looks like he's getting mighty skittish. We need something to keep him quiet 'til this deal's in the bag."

"You want me and the boys to give him a little talkin' to?"

Major Harley guffawed. "You and the boys might not come back from that talk! We don't want to do anything to get his back up. No, we don't want to wrestle the bull, we only want to corral him." The major thought a moment. "Isn't his wife from Baton Rouge? See if we can't get someone in their local klavern to dig something up on her. Tell them it's for the good of the Order."

"Yes, sir. I got the telephone number of one of the deputies over there. I'll get on to him." Roy rose, ready to leave.

"There is something still outstanding, isn't there, Roy? A little unfinished business?"

"You talkin' 'bout the Caldwell place? I got mens out now lookin' for the kid that got away. What's so impo'tant 'bout a pickaninny. He ain't even a full-growed nigger."

"As long as he can appear, that land can't be sold at public auction. There can't be any living relatives or kin that have rights to that property. That one piece makes all the rest work; without it, it's just a good money-making deal; with it we have the chance to make millions. Let me put it bluntly; if he's found, I don't want him to be alive. Do you understand?"

"Okay, Major." Roy scratched his head. " 'Scuse me, Major, but I don't see how this one piece of property gon' make us all that money."

"You've got to have vision. You've got to think ahead, Roy. What happens when they build one of these newfangled macadam roads?"

Roy pushed the hair out of his eyes and answered hesitantly, as if it was a trick question. "Peoples use it?"

"I don't think you have a big enough candle up there, boy, to light up every part of your head; some part of you is always in the dark." The major gestured to Roy with his snifter, indicating he wanted a refill. Roy complied and then Harley continued. "Yes, people will use the new roads, Roy, lots and lots of people. And where there's lots of people, there's things that they need. Business opportunities, you might say."

After another sip of cognac, he continued. "Look at what happened with that first interstate that they put through here. There was nothing beside that road five years ago. Now there's all sorts of business popping up along that highway. Can you imagine the money a man could make if he owned the land around the first fifteen miles of highway just outside of New Orleans?"

"You doin' this for yo'self? I thought you was doin' this to help raise money for the klavern! We got some poor members who ain't even got decent gowns and hoods and we need to fix up our headquarters. It's gettin' all run-down. It needs paintin' and a new porch!"

"Of course, this will benefit the klavern," the major smiled broadly. "I will just need to get reimbursed for my out-of-pocket expenses, which have been considerable, but that is of no matter at this point. Something we can discuss later, no?" Roy nodded his head. "Good, good," answered the major. "I just want to remind you, Roy, that I've already been generous with the klavern. I've donated the ammunition and dynamite you've used a couple of times and loaned a couple of my trucks and I've shown that was I open to another such arrangement! Isn't that so?"

Roy nodded his head in agreement once again.

The major stood up and stretched. "Well, there's many a fish to fry before this weekend. We'd both better get busy on it. Call me as soon as you have closed out the Caldwell case."

"Sho' 'nough, Major!" Roy said smartly as he saluted and went out the door.

Major William Fulton Harley waited until the steps died away and the outside door slammed closed before allowing himself to relax. He poured himself another cognac and sat down in an easy chair. It pleased him considerably that he was known locally as "the Major." His official military records indicated that he had made the rank of lieutenant before he was dishonorably discharged in Virginia for participating in a drunken duel that resulted in the shooting death of a fellow officer. After his saber was broken, he left Virginia and drifted down to New Orleans. He got a job providing security for one of the big grain speculators. His ability to command men and his knowledge of military strategy served him well and as he learned the ways of the waterfront, he found ways to make money for himself. The passing twenty-five years had been kind and had allowed him to conceal his unfortunate incident, while he assumed the rank and title more commensurate with his assessment of himself.

Rastus shuffled into the room and checked the buckets and turned to walk out, but the major's voice stopped him. "Rastus!"

The man turned and faced the major, but kept his eyes downcast. "Suh?"

"Rastus, do you believe that Negroes should get college educations? Should they be allowed the right to vote?"

Rastus stared down at his hands, which were clasped in front of him. "I don't know nothin' 'bout no college. As to votin', I can't speak for nobody else, but I can't tell no difference in them politicians. If they's all the same, I can't see no use in it."

"You're a thinker, Rastus. That's what I like about you," the major said with a chuckle. "You can clear the glasses and go now." Harley watched Rastus carry out the used glasses and thought it wasn't that difficult to break a man's spirit. Twenty years ago, when Rastus was first hired, he had been called William. The major was incensed to discover that there was a Negro in his employ with the same first name. After administering a serious horse whipping to the man, Harley renamed the man Rastus, which, in his opinion, was a more niggerly name. Rastus ran off a couple of times but he was brought back in shackles each time under the allegation of thievery and was left under the major's custodial care. More beatings ensued and soon there was no more rebellion. Of course, there was always the possibility that William-cum-Rastus would awaken from his slumber and realize that his life had been stolen while his youth was being beaten out of him. Perhaps he would pick up a weapon. But Major Harley felt those years were past.

Major William Harley wished that all his dealings were so cut and dried. His problem now, as always, was how he was going to cheat his allies out of their share of the deal. A considerable amount of money stood to be earned if the interstate went along the route as designated, and the major wanted the lion's share, if not all of it. It was his vision. It was his idea, his plans that caused the whole thing to come to fruition. It was only right. The problem was explaining that to his partners. He was not particularly worried about the klavern. He knew that five hundred dollars and some fixing up of their headquarters would resolve many of their concerns. The parish assessor was a different problem. It was he, on the last day before the announcement, who would process all the deed transferences into Major Harley's name and would assure that all documents were affixed with the official seal. The assessor had already indicated that he wanted in for fifty percent. The major had agreed to it, but he knew some unfortunate accident would befall the assessor before any money or property was exchanged.

It served the major's purposes to keep fueling the resentful indignation of the local klavern against the Negroes. He was amused by the unthinking molten anger that surged beneath the surface of his fellow white Southerners and how it was so easily manipulated. All he had to do was find the nearest available opening and its violent energy would always spew in the same direction. It would follow the path of past eruptions. It was all so easy. If the truth be told, in his perception, there weren't many white people who were much better than niggers and very few deserved to be at the top next to him. He would continue to use the klavern until they could serve no further purpose.

Perhaps, he thought as he finished the last sip of his cognac, they might even be directed to dealing with the assessor if certain information were revealed to them.

King Tremain and Sampson Davis walked their horses slowly up the ridge that led out of the lowlands where his family's farm was nestled in the fold of some low hills. The air was crisp and fresh off the Gulf of Mexico and the early morning sunlight promised a day of sultry heat. The original purpose of the ride was to bring money to the bootleggers, but King had paid a visit to his Aunt Reola's little section before the sun had risen. He had been coming to visit her secretly since his return to Louisiana. Reola Bodeen Tremain was his Uncle Jake's widow and had always treated him kindly. As usual, she had been grateful for the money he left with her that morning. She had been working the farm alone with her thirteen-year-old son since her oldest son was sentenced to ten years on the chain gang.

Once he and Sampson reached the top of the low-lying ridge, they stopped in a grove of trees and looked down on the patchwork of fields that the Tremain clan had reclaimed from the swamp over the generations. They saw a small number of distant figures clad in black, attending a morning burial in the family plot. King knew they were burying Ben Willets, his Aunt Clara's husband. Willets was the man who had taken over the farm section that had belonged to King's father. The man had been found beaten to death on the edge of the swamp. His death had caused the family elders to convene a meeting in the barn. There had been some discussion about the possible culpability of the DuMonts. But, everyone knew that King had killed him, although no one had seen him do it.

Letting his horse pick the trail down the back side of the ridge, Sampson led the way. King watched him and wondered. King was always on guard for any change. His relationship with Sampson was a thing of mystery to him. It was surprising how well they got along. He could neither explain it nor define it. All he knew was that it felt good. By some strange quirk of circumstance he made a connection with the man he had made mute.

Halfway down the ridge, King took the lead and climbed to a knoll rising above the ridge. He and Sampson guided their horses into a stand of trees as the burial ceremony broke up. He watched as the black-clad figures trudged slowly back down the hill to their wagons and carts. He felt nothing: not sadness or regret. When he had first returned to New Orleans and had paid a secret visit to the farm, he had been surprised at how dingy and run-down it was. He knew then that he had no desire to return to his father's farm. As far as he was concerned, Willets could have kept it. If Willets had kept his hands off of Reola and maintained a reasonable silence, he would probably still be alive.

King and Sampson reined their horses toward their meeting with the bootleggers. King had checked with some of his associates about the three men who had come to him with the deal, and Pete and Dirty Red had checked out as solid men at the scratch line. The third man was new on the scene and had neither good nor bad references. The meeting place was a grassy, tree-covered dell lying next to a meandering creek. The creek fed into a little-used waterway that connected to a major river channel. King rode into the meeting alone. Sampson was making his way to a hiding place in the thick undergrowth and brush. Although he did not expect treachery so early in the transaction, caution was always appropriate. He had arrived before the appointed time of the meeting. King got off his horse and walked him along the creek until the boat came into view. King tied his horse to the branch of a tree and made his way silently through the thickets and undergrowth to the boat. It was a swamp steamer like the *Mamie Lou.*

As he drew nearer, voices from the boat carried over the stillness of the swamp. A male voice could be heard. "Tyson, you ought to let this matter lie. We's made a deal."

Tyson's voice stated with emphasis, "I don't see why we need this Tremain! We should just take his money and leave! Hell, he ain't nobody!"

"I don't know 'bout you, man, but once I gives my word, that's it," a third male voice said. "My partners don't have to worry 'bout whether the sun is shinin' on me or not."

"Whatchoo mean by that, Dirty Red?" Tyson demanded. "You sayin' I can't be trusted?"

"No, he ain't!" King heard Pete's voice interject. "He just sayin' when he give his word, that's it. He don't go back on it. Ain't no reason fo' us to be arguin' 'mongst ourselves. We got a good deal here. We shouldn't be tryin' to squeeze too much out of it."

"You boys got to think big," Tyson declared with emphasis. "Everybody is out fo' his self. Tremain don't care about us. He'd turn on us if it was worth his while!"

"You ain't from around here, Tyson. Sho' 'nough there's some colored folks who runs on flashin' and scammin', but most ever'body knows who those people is. Most of the rest of us lives by our word."

"What Pete is sayin' is that, we don't shit where we eats!" the third voice interjected.

There was a moment's pause. Then Tyson began to speak. His voice was unusually conciliatory. "Y'all got it wrong. I was suggestin' a way to mo' better our money situation, but it ain't no big thing."

King smiled at the words as he retraced his steps to his big gelding. He turned the horse around and threaded his way a quarter mile through the underbrush before he headed back toward the boat. He didn't like Tyson and it was clear to him that Tyson was not a man to be trusted, but King was intrigued by the question as to when Tyson would feel strong enough to make his move.

King saw that Sampson had hidden his horse in a thicket of stunted dogwood, but Sampson himself was not visible. King kicked his gelding into a canter just before the boat came into view. He wanted to make a suitable amount of noise on his arrival.

Sheriff Corlis Mack puffed his cigar until rings of smoke circled his head. He looked across his desk at the dark-haired man with the ice-cold blue eyes and thought, You're an ambitious rascal and I wouldn't like you standing behind me. Mack smiled. "I've got an assignment for you and a couple of men, Johan. We haven't been getting our full quota of money out of Niggertown since somebody did them DuMont niggers. Some of those businesses haven't paid in months! We haven't had a hammer on them since Bull Gingrich got himself killed. I need somebody to put their foot down on these shiftless niggers. Because you were once assigned to collections, I want you to crack down on a few of the nigger operators that we know didn't pay and leave the message that we want our cut. We aren't going to let them do business until we get our cut. I don't care how they get it done, I just want the money. I'm giving you this assignment because you know how to talk sense to niggers. Get me, I don't want anybody killed yet. Just a few broken bones should do. We'll save the killing for later, if they act mule-headed."

Kaiser stood up and gave his superior a half-salute. "You got it, Boss. I'll take Williams and Herbert. We'll start tomorrow."

Mack nodded. "Yeah, they're good strong boys. Good choices. Only one difference, I want you to start tonight. It'll take a while for them niggers to work something out. The sooner they start working on it, the better."

"Alright! We'll start tonight. You want me to jam Bichet too?"

"No, no; he's paid up on time. Just hit the niggers who're at least fifty percent nigger." Mack chuckled at his little attempt at humor.

Kaiser smiled politely and withdrew. He was extremely irritated with the assignment he had just received. He was in line for the captain's vacancy when Rodgers retired in the spring. An assignment in Niggertown was like being sent to work in the swamps. All the cherry assignments were in the white areas of town, except for perhaps the old area of Storyville. Plus, unusual, freakish things always happened on any assignment that had to do with niggers.

Kaiser contacted the two men he was going to use and arranged to meet them on the edge of Storyville later that evening. It was Kaiser's intent to work his way uptown. He was resolved that if there was a way to make the assignment a success, he would find it. If a few niggers were found in the river, so what? He knew that Corlis wouldn't complain if he produced results.

The evening found Johan Kaiser and his two subordinates visiting card parlors, speakeasies, brothels, and pit fighting halls where cocks or dogs fought to the death. They left behind them a trail of concussions and broken bones, but were unable to get anyone to identify the name of the new top-nigger.

At ten thirty in the evening they visited the Red Rooster, which was one of the best establishments hosting pit fights in the uptown area. Kaiser didn't care that the Red Rooster was one of the few businesses that had made regular payments. He wanted to leave a message, but the three Moses brothers who owned the place heard he was coming and had sufficient muscle around to deter any rough interrogation techniques. Kaiser was extremely frustrated. All he was able to do was make threats, when he really wanted to smack one of the nigger owners across the head with his baton. But a casual glance around at the surrounding muscle affirmed that such an endeavor would be foolish. Kaiser was about to leave when he saw Bradley O'Malley sitting with a prostitute in a booth at the back of the lounge. Kaiser headed back to talk with him.

Bradley was one his many informants. But Kaiser hadn't seen him in a while, so he thought a few questions were in order. Uninvited, he sat down in the booth next to Bradley and stared across at the woman. She was attired in a relatively severe long dress that buttoned around her neck.

"Who's your whore, Bradley?" Kaiser asked.

"She ain't no whore, suh. She my sister-in-law, come to tell me about my brother's troubles."

"Your brother has troubles? Well, we all got troubles and you're especially going to have problems if I don't get some cooperation and information."

"Whatchoo talkin 'bout, suh?" Bradley protested. "I always cooperates the best I can. Can't see I gots any information you needs no ways."

"It's not what I need, it's what I want that you have to worry about!" Kaiser said, slapping the back of Bradley's head. "I want to know who took over from Lester DuMont. Who's the top monkey in Niggertown?"

"You ain't got to hit me like that, Lieutenant!" Bradley protested, holding his head.

"Maybe I ought to just go on, Brad, since this don't concern me at all." The woman spoke nervously and sidled to the edge of the booth seat. She was a plain-featured woman with widely spaced eyes and a gap between her front teeth.

Kaiser stuck his baton across the table and poked her in her bosom. "No, you stay here until we finish." Immediately, Kaiser heard a commotion behind him. Soon the booth was surrounded by large, hulking men.

One of the owners stepped forward. "We ain't gon' stand around and let you mistreat a colored woman in front of us. You hit her with that stick again and we gon' commence to fight."

Kaiser growled. "I am a representative of the law and I'm determining whether I need to make any arrests in this unlicensed institution. You wouldn't hinder me, would you?"

The same man spoke up again. "You don't scare us, we paid up! And you ain't gon' arrest nobody in here on no okeydoke!"

"You Moses boys talk big," Kaiser said with a slight smile. "I hope you don't ever get arrested. I might have to see what you're really made of."

"You ain't invisible either. What goes around comes around," another man said.

Kaiser shook his head angrily. He couldn't touch them as long as they paid on time. It was frustrating, but he had Bradley. "I guess we'll leave now," he said, looking around at the surrounding men, "but I'm going to remember you boys and I have a long memory. Bradley, you'll walk along with me. We still have many things to talk about."

"The girl goes first!" one of the men standing around the booth suggested. His words received a chorus of support and the young lady was escorted out of the Red Rooster.

One of the owners advised Bradley, "You ain't got to go with him unless you want to."

Bradley took one look at Kaiser's face and said, "I'll go with the lieutenant."

Kaiser took Bradley back to his car and interrogated him in the backseat. He prompted Bradley with hard, crunching blows of the baton on his arms and legs. At one point, Bradley was doubled over in pain. Kaiser waited. "What do you have for me?"

When Bradley sat up he began babbling. "There's a rich nigger stayin' at the Toussant. He don't work at nothin' and he got a fine horse and a new car sedan. All his clothes is sto'-bought. Sometimes he wear two pistols in holsters. Everybody say he the one that killed Lester. Maybe he the one you lookin fo'?"

"How do you know so much about this man?" Williams asked from the front seat.

"Cause I is the bell captain at the Toussant. I gets to know everybody who stay there."

Kaiser hit Bradley across the forearm with a quick, hard stroke and

Bradley cried out and began to moan. "You done broke my arm! I done give you all I got. Ain't nothin' else!"

"If he was the one, you wouldn't doubt who he was," Kaiser said, dismissing Bradley's contribution." Kaiser sighed with resignation. "Put him out, boys. We'll have to keep on looking."

The car did not even stop as Bradley was pushed out of the moving vehicle. His body rolled into an inert heap on the street. Kaiser and his companion swerved around the corner in the police car and were gone.

MONDAY, SEPTEMBER 13, 1920

"They rode again yesterday mo'nin'!" a man in the front row shouted, waving his dark brown fist in the air.

"On Sabbath!" another brown-skinned man shouted from a couple of rows behind.

A light-skinned woman with reddish hair shouted, "These ain't God-fearin' men! Killin' and burnin' folks' homes even on the day peoples is studyin' the Bible! They's the devil's servants!" Her words were greeted with agreement by many of the men and women who had come to participate in the meeting at the Frederick Douglass School. It was a warm, humid evening. There was no cool breeze off the gulf. The air seemed to stand still as a waning moon rose in the night sky. The schoolhouse, which stood alone on a large lot on the edge of the colored section, blazed with electric light. Inside the school, which had all its windows closed for privacy, the atmosphere was hot and muggy as well as tense.

The volume level of general conversation rose as Phillip Duryea stepped up to the podium. His left arm was still in a sling. He was still recovering from the stabbing injury incurred from his fight with the DuMonts. He raised his good arm. "Folks! Folks! We need some order if we're to get anything done here tonight! We're here tonight to talk about what we can do to stop the night riders from running off hardworking colored folks from their legally held land."

"Ain't we gon' try to get justice for them that's been killed?" demanded a woman wearing an orange head-tie. There were some amens and rumblings of support among the audience.

"That's part of it, but we got to take it a piece at a time," Phillip answered. "Just to make sure we all know what's behind all this KKK activity, I've asked Mr. Claude Bichet to tell us about the discussions that he's heard in his gambling establishment."

Claude Bichet stood up and approached the podium. As usual, he was dressed elegantly. He had on a brown pinstriped suit with spats. The audience waited for him to speak in sullen silence. He wasn't one of them and this was an ethnic issue. Everyone knew that Creoles all called themselves white.

"You all know me. My family been here for years. I see many people here I know by name. I see Joe Paul Brunzy back there in the back. He work for me at Beau Geste. If you need, he'll vouch for me. I come here only to tell what I hear. To help."

"I heard you got some family along part of that stretch," a male voice called out.

"I do," Bichet answered. "I have a second cousin who owns a farm out where they been raiding."

The audience began to warm up to Bichet. People nodded to each other. Bichet, unlike most Creoles, was owning up to his colored blood. It was a well-known fact that there were only colored families farming in that area. Possum Hollow was the worst of the lowlands, nearly swamp farming, broad tracts that had to be drained regularly and were the first to flood in the heavy spring rains.

Bichet continued. "A couple of months ago, during a poker game I overheard some men talking about bringing the Interstate through the lowlands out where the colored families are. Then just last week, I heard two different men speak on the same subject. This time it sounded like the whole thing was signed and delivered, except for the public announcement. So, when I heard from my cousin about people being forced from their land, it all begin to fit together."

"How come them highway officials don't contact the legal landowners?" another male voice inquired.

"I don't know." Bichet shrugged his shoulders. "I figure the parish assessor must be in on it too. How else they process the papers so quick?"

"All this talk ain't helpin' us!" a large, dark-skinned woman yelled from her seat as she fanned herself rapidly. "Most of us figured that the Interstate or some other federal project must be comin' through. We need to decide what we gon' do to help our brothers and sisters to hold on to their land!"

"You have a plan, Sister Waters?" Phillip asked as he ascended the podium. He nodded thanks to Bichet, who returned to his seat.

"No, I ain't got no plan!" Sister Waters snapped, fanning herself even more rapidly. "But I do got chil'ren to bed and a poultice to make for my husband's horse! There's still work to be done tonight! So, let's get to fig-urin' what we gon' do, if we gon' do anythin'!"

For the next hour the discussion coursed over and around the issue like a hound in pursuit of a hare. The easiest matters to decide related to what churches would take up a collection for the burned-out families, where the homeless would temporarily be housed, and what jobs were available, if any. The questions that could not be answered were, of course, the most important, such as: what steps were needed to be taken to seek justice for the displaced families and what actions could they initiate to prevent other families from being forced from their homes. There were not many constructive approaches offered and there were fewer volunteers to head action committees. The fear of the Klan was strong.

At one point near the end of the discussion, Phillip came back to where King was sitting and asked, "Should I bring up that idea of yours about setting up a corporation to buy the properties?"

"I think it's about all you got, short of bushwackin' a couple of night riders. That's one sure way to make 'em stop! You could try things legal like, but my guess is you ain't gon' beat these whites at their own game! And any colored lawyer fool enough to take the case wouldn't live through the winter. Sho', go ahead, tell 'em, but I don't know that these folk is ready for it."

Phillip returned to the podium and gaveled for attention. "Folks! Folks! Let me have your attention! King Tremain has an idea that might work for us. The only thing is we have got to get together and trust in each other to make it happen. The plan is, we set up an out-of-state business, using a corporation based out of New York to buy the property."

"You need money for that! What are we going to do for money?" de-manded Old Mr. Rambo, the manager of the colored section of the bank that King used.

King stood up and looked around at the assembled brown faces. "I got two thousand in cash." He held up an envelope. "This here is seed money to buy property. I's puttin' it up to show that this ain't no scam. Everybody who puts money up will get back their investment, maybe even a profit." An immediate wave of exclamation swept the audience. Most of the peo-ple in the room made four hundred to six hundred dollars a year.

"How does this corporation work?" Rambo demanded, affixing his pince-nez on his nose and tilting back his head to stare at King.

King smiled. "My attorney in New York will set up a corporation for us. We'll buy the property in the name of the corporation for a fair price. That gives folks who want to sell the money to start somewhere else. The corporation will own the property we buy and we'll own a percentage of the corporation equal to our investment! Nobody's name will be on the deed! Ain't no way the Klan can trace the owners!"

Rambo snorted like a horse and his pince-nez fell from their perch. "That ain't a bad idea!" He shook his finger at King. "Everyday I see white businessmen hide their assets and this is the way they do it! Only one thing, how we know this Yankee attorney gon' do right with our money?"

"We get a lawyer here to read and approve the incorporation papers!" King replied.

"I'll put a thousand up!" exclaimed Old Mr. Rambo, his bald head shining brightly under the church lights. "We'll get Dante Archambeaux to approve the papers! Folks, this is a way we can help our own! This ain't no fly-by-night scheme. White people do this all the time! I should've thought of it myself!"

"Me too, for a thousand!" Bichet called out.

Rambo went up to the podium and signed for one thousand dollars. "Maybe we can use this method for buying other types of property!" he said, rubbing his chin. All eyes in the room were on him. No one was speaking. Only the creaking of the wooden chairs gave evidence that everyone was alert. He looked around and saw all the expectant faces. "We could buy property outside of Desire!" Rambo returned to his seat with an air of importance and began to polish his pince-nez with his handkerchief.

"Now, Phillip, you write this up and anyone who wants to bring money can bring it to the church tonight!" King said. " 'Cause we payin' cash on the barrelhead, ain't that right, Mr. Rambo?"

"Yes, yes, we must move fast. This process takes time to set up!"

"We're talking about bringing the money to the Mount Zion Hill Church and letting the church keep the money," Phillip announced. "We'll have a rider go out and alert all the colored folks in Possum Hollow that there's a buyer who will pay fair price!"

Phillip's father, Claude, stood. "The folks that want to sell will come to the church and sign over their deeds. That way all business is conducted under the eyes of Reverend Pendergast."

"If we gon' buy the property before the Klan runs people off, we needs to move quickly," Rambo urged. "We got to get deeds transferred and documents approved with the official parish seal. If the church gets the money tonight, we can start paying out the money tomorrow."

"Why don't we deposit the money in a bank?" someone called out.

Rambo answered. "The Klan would trace the money within a week, if we tried to buy the property using a local bank." There were many heads shaking in agreement with his words.

"Now, everyone knows that Reverend Pendergast has already been out organizing, trying to get support for our brothers and sisters in Possum Downs over this issue," Philip stated. "He has already collected some money, but not nearly enough to buy one parcel, so we're just going to add our contribution to the pot."

"Where's Reverend Pendergast tonight? Why ain't he here? I want to hear what he has to say about this!" Rambo demanded.

Claude Duryea answered from a second-row pew. "The Reverend Pendergast is over in Possum Hollow as we speak. He's getting prices and written agreements from the colored folk who are still on their land. He realizes that we need to make sure that we can buy the land. So he is getting bills of sale signed by those that want to sell."

"So, our first job is to get all the money together," King urged. "Once we see the money free and clear, it gets used to buy property. That way nobody has doubts that all the money was spent right."

Later, after it had been decided how the money was to be delivered, King and Sampson were sitting in a local hooch house drinking cheap Mexican whiskey with Phillip and his father. The older Duryea was a heavyset man who, despite his sixty years, still looked strong. Arthritis combined with injuries from his youth caused him to walk with a limp, but his spirit was undaunted. After taking a long sip of whiskey, the old man looked at Sampson. "He doesn't speak a word?"

Sampson looked at Claude Duryea and gave no clue that he understood what was said. Although his eyes were staring directly at the old man, he seemed focused on a space several feet behind Claude.

"He don't talk but he speaks," King answered. "He also understands what is bein' said. He just seems to think that most conversation ain't worth much."

"What do you mean, he speaks?" the old man asked.

"There's a deaf woman workin' in the kitchen of the Toussant. I've been payin' her to teach us both sign language."

"You're learning too, eh? So, you're making plans to be together for a while?"

"I don't see why not," King replied. "I need someone I can trust to watch my back."

"He was a DuMont man," Claude observed. "How do you know that you can trust him?"

"I don't know, but I feel it. He know he don't have to stay with me, but I'm treatin' him straight from the shoulder. I don't think anybody ever done right by him before."

"Well, you're going to need him and all your other friends now that we've started on this path. The whites will not take this lying down." Claude Duryea drained the remains of his liquor with a frown. "This whiskey is absolute bilge! Phillip, ask Joe for some of that Kentucky bourbon he keeps behind the counter." Phillip nodded and rose to comply with his father's request. Claude watched his son walk over to the bar. He turned and looked at King for a long moment. "God blessed me with three strong sons. The oldest is dead, killed in the fighting to set up our hauling business. My second son was crippled in that fighting and he's turned so bitter that he might as well have been killed when he was injured. Phillip is the only one left. I want to thank you for saving my son's life during the attack on the DuMonts' house."

King stared at him with surprise. "How you know I was there?"

The old man leaned forward and grabbed King's arm in a tight grip. His voice dropped to a whisper. "Phillip told me about the shot through the window. And then later, I heard about all of Lester's dead riflemen. One was even found in the spire of the church down the street. Phillip doesn't know anyone who could have done that but you. I know you saved his life and Phillip knows it. I just want you to know that you have a friend in me and if you're ever in need, don't hesitate to come to me for help or shelter."

Phillip returned with a bottle and sat down at the table. "Joe raised his prices again. He wanted ten dollars for this bottle. He said he was getting low on his stock of good stuff."

Claude Duryea ran his hand through his kinky, salt-and-pepper hair. "This Prohibition nonsense is just damn foolishness! People aren't going to stop drinking! Someone is going to make a lot of money running real liquor in from passing ships!"

"Or we'll be drinking a lot more moonshine!" Phillip added as he refilled all their glasses, except for Sampson's, because he declined.

"He knows when to quit, I see," Claude commented with approval.

"Ain't nothin' slow about him, except his talkin'," King answered.

Claude took a slow, savoring taste of the new whiskey and smiled. "That's doing better!"

"This plan we got takes time," King observed. "We may have to kill some Klan people if we gon' stop them from runnin' peoples off they land befo' we's ready to buy."

"You best be careful if you do something, because if they can trace the action to you, your whole family's going to have to leave the state," Claude advised.

"My family can take care of itself," King answered in a matter-of-fact tone. "We was raised with guns in our hands."

The manager of the Toussant Hotel polished the surface of the registration desk with a damp rag soaked with an oil and lemon juice mixture. He stopped to admire his work, then continued on industriously. The wood was shining almost as brightly as the brown pate of his bald head when he finished. As the manager of the Toussant, which was one of the three principal quality residential establishments for colored people in the parish of New Orleans, he was responsible for the upkeep and maintenance of the hotel and he took his job seriously. At eleven o'clock in the morning he had the bell staff and waiters standing in a row while he marched up and down to check their uniforms and their hands for cleanliness. Most of them were young men; however, he had a few who had been with him for more than fifteen years.

The bell captain, who was one of his long-term employees, coughed politely and nodded his head toward something that was taking place across the room. The manager swiveled and was horrified to see a heavyset man walking through the main lobby with the butchered carcass of a pig on his shoulders. "You there," he shouted. "You can't bring that through here! Deliveries are made at the service entrance!" The man turned and the manager saw that it was Sampson Davis, the man King Tremain had brought to the hotel. The manager said nothing more as the man continued on into the kitchen. One did not interfere in King Tremain's business casually.

Later, at the registration desk, the bell captain sidled up to the manager and said out of the side of his mouth, "What you think is behind that man changing sides?"

"What man?"

"The man who brung in the pig through the main lobby! You know he used to work for them DuMonts."

"Oh, really," the manager responded. He was not particularly interested. He had to finish checking the receipts for the daily deliveries, but the bell captain was one of his principal informers on other hotel employees. He had to feign attention or jeopardize a valuable information source.

"Yeah, he worked for them until Tremain clunked him on his head. Knocked the daylights out of 'em, I hear tell. He can't remember his own name and don't speak to this day!"

"You look like you been clunked pretty well yourself," the manager gestured with a nod to the numerous contusions on Bradley's face and head, and the splint on his arm.

"I told you all 'bout that. It was that Lieutenant Kaiser. He done this to me because I wouldn't tell him nothin'! He pushed me out'n a movin' car!"

"You don't say," answered the manager. He was a little annoyed with the continued discussion, but he suppressed it.

"What makes it so dad-blamed crazy is that after clunkin' him, that Tremain saved his life; stopped some street hawkers from beatin' him to death! Then if that ain't strange enough, this fool take to following Tremain around like a puppy. Like he done completely forgot who clunked him in the first place. I know people who say there be some big voodoo doin's in all that!"

"Don't mention that word!" the manager hissed. "In the last black magic scare we had in this hotel, I couldn't get the maids or porters to go near room thirteen for weeks! I had to get a priest in to exorcise that room!"

"Shouldn't have no room with that number no way!" the bell captain asserted with a fearful shake of his head while sticking his hand under his shirt for the reassuring feel of the bag of gris-gris that hung on a thong around his throat. It was his principal protection against the whims of the saints and the curses of his enemies. The bell captain also muttered a few Hail Marys to cover all his bases. "I say there's somethin' crazy goin' on," confided the bell captain. "They was enemies, now all of a sudden, they's as thick as thieves and closer than two weevils out of the same sack. It ain't right, if you ask me."

"I don't think anybody's asking you," the manager answered, starting to enter amounts in his expense ledger. "And I can't say that I care long as they pay their bills promptly," he answered as he finished totaling the figures on the receipts.

The bell captain sneered. "Personally, I'll be happy when somebody runs him out of town. He actin' all uppity when he ain't nothin' but buck-nigger trash from the swamp outside of Algiers. He shouldn't be stayin' in no downtown, high-class hotel like this! He is bringin' down the reputation of the Toussant."

"Watch your mouth. Here's Mr. Tremain now," he advised.

King walked up to the desk with a smile. "Good afternoon, gents. I asked the cook to prepare a pig and some chickens for a big card game I's havin' this evenin'. We expects to play all night. 'Course, I'll pay for the extra service. I had Sampson bring in the pig already and I got some chickens in the car outside. If you can send one of yo' men to bring 'em back to the kitchen, I sho' would appreciate it."

The bell captain may have been feeling especially brave, or perhaps he thought his gris-gris would protect him, for he spit into a spittoon and walked off casually as if he hadn't heard King. It was an act of no consequence but its timing and the manner in which the bell captain performed it made it a borderline insult. The manager shook his head in pained resignation.

King's voice, which caused everyone in the lobby to look, stopped the bell captain in his tracks. "Turn around!" commanded King. "You tryin' to disrespect me?" He walked up to the man and stood face-to-face with him.

The bell captain had a sneer on his face, but he was trembling. "I got mo' important business," the man stuttered.

King poked the man in the chest with his index finger. "You all the time frownin' when you look at me. I'm noticin' you got an attitude! You got a problem?"

"No suh, I's just feelin' poorly," the man explained, shaking noticeably.

"You get yo' ass out there and unload that car!"

"I'll have a couple of my boys do it right now!"

King leaned forward and said, "No, I want you to do it and if you drop any of my packages, I'll see you when you get off work. And if I get anymore attitude from you, you in for some shit!"

The bell captain went into his fawning role. "You ain't got to worry about nothin' from me, suh. I takes cares of everythin' you want." But when he went out to the car, he was seething. He thought he heard snickers and chuckles from other hotel staff behind his back. He wondered what was keeping Lieutenant Kaiser from investigating King. Perhaps Kaiser needed to be reminded. Bradley knew that the lieutenant would pull King down off his high horse. He had a trace of a smile on his face when he reentered the hotel with the chickens.

FRIDAY, SEPTEMBER 24, 1920

When Johan Kaiser arrived at the Toussant, it was nearly dusk. He was accompanied only by Williams. They were met at the rear entrance by Bradley, who led them through the kitchen and up the back stairs to the second floor, where King's suite of rooms was located. Bradley had scheduled this time with Kaiser because he knew that most of the kitchen staff would be attending a dinner planning meeting and only a skeleton staff of the custodial crew remained after five in the afternoon. It was his intent that Kaiser's visit should not be observed, but he failed in his purpose. The deaf woman from the kitchen saw them enter as she was checking whether there was enough shrimp in the ice chest to make an étouffée. The deaf woman did not reveal her presence, but watched quietly as they passed.

They were also seen by Sister Bornais, a fortune-teller who was reputed to be a talented seer and interpreter of the tarot. Sister Bornais was also called Black Magic Woman because she prepared and sold all types of protective gris-gris. Among the believers she had a strong influence, for it was widely held that her curses were even more potent than her gris-gris. She had just finished a reading for an elderly woman who had traveled all the way from Baton Rouge for an appointment with her. Sister Bornais watched from another room, through a slightly cracked doorway, as the bell captain used his keys and let the white men into King's door. From the way the men acted, she could tell they were attempting to take King by surprise. She knew the lieutenant well, for he was the man who collected the payoff off the top from everyone who operated a long-term business in the area, ranging from the French Quarter to the colored section of Uptown.

Sister Bornais closed the door silently and stepped back into the room. She assured her client that nothing was wrong. She indicated that she only desired to sit a minute before making the long walk home. Sister Bornais knew whose room the lieutenant had entered. Everyone who came to the Toussant knew that King Tremain had the suite on the second floor at the end of the hall. The lieutenant had a reputation and King had a reputation. She wondered after this meeting whether either man would walk out the door.

King and Sampson were sitting at the table reading the paper when they first heard the key in the lock. Sampson stood up immediately and got a shotgun out of the closet. King's holsters were hanging on the back of his chair, under his coat. He pulled a pistol and cocked it before Kaiser and Williams rushed in. They had hoped to catch King unawares, but instead came face-to-face with a double-barreled shotgun and a .45 automatic. There was a moment of silence before either Williams or Kaiser regained their composure and spoke.

"We're New Orleans police," Kaiser growled. "You don't want to make things worse for yourself, do you boys? You best put down those guns and maybe we'll go lightly with you."

King smiled, but his pistol did not waver. "How come you don't knock? You got a search warrant?"

Kaiser and Williams looked at each other and began to laugh.

"Where you from, nigger?" Williams demanded with a crooked smile. "Talkin' about search warrants! That don't apply to you! You best get it through yo' nappy head that we can come through yo' place anytime we want!"

The desire to kill the two white men was strong, but King realized someone knew they were in his room, for someone had opened the door for them. The sounds from the street in front of the hotel had not changed; therefore there were no police cars in sight. King backed over to the window and glanced out to confirm his conclusion. There was just the normal street traffic. It appeared to King that the two men in front of him were working without additional police support; if that were true then they were operating on a hunch, or there was an informer who gave them a little information. Otherwise, if they really had something of substance, they would have come with a squadron.

King shoved his pistol in his waistband. "You boys must be lookin' for something. Why don't you grab a chair and let's hear what's got you rushin' into my hotel room."

"Nigger, you better shut yo' mouth and—"

King pulled out his pistol and rounded the table swiftly. "I don't like the word *nigger*, so I don't mind killin' you," he said in a quiet tone as he put the gun to Williams's temple. "All it means is I got to go find the rat that let you in and do him too."

The suddenness of King's action and the softness of his words were unnerving to both Kaiser and Williams. King wasn't the run-of-the-mill street tough they normally encountered. Kaiser sat down in a chair. "No reason to get jumpy. We'll sit down. Sit down, Williams!" There was no doubt in his mind that the two colored men confronting him were cold-blooded killers and there was no likelihood that bluster and bravado would intimidate them. If he was fortunate enough to leave the room with his life, Kaiser knew that he would be back at the Toussant within an hour with reinforcements. His desire was to wipe King and his companion off the face of the earth. There was no place for uppity niggers in his world.

King stood in front of the two whites. "Now, I been expectin' a visit from you white boys, but you done put me in a bad situation when you come stormin' in here," he began conversationally. "If I let you go now, you gon' be back here in minutes with every gun you got. It look to me like I got two choices: to kill you slow or kill you fast. Unless you wants to hear my deal. Otherwise, seems like in a couple of days both you boys gon' be fillin' a pine box."

There was a long silence. Then Williams came out of his chair like a shot and dove at King. With a minimum of movement, King sidestepped the charge and clipped Williams hard on the head with the butt of his pistol. Williams fell headlong on the floor and lay in a heap.

"I knows a lot about you, Johan Kaiser," King said. "You got a nice house over on Toulouse Street and a wife with two nice-lookin' boys. Yo' mother got a little house just outside of Fenner. I wonder what Sheriff Mack would say if he knew you killed his wife's younger brother? Or where he's buried? Mack liked that boy. That's why he was promotin' him so fast. Or what he would say if he knew how much you was skimming off the top of his cut?"

"What do you want?" Kaiser demanded.

"Who let you and yo' buddy in my room?"

"Bradley O'Malley."

King smiled. "The main thing I wants is to be left alone. As payment for that, I lets you live and the information that I have stays with my lawyer unless somethin' happens to me. Of course, if I gets found dead, or disappear, then Sheriff Mack gon' get yo' file and I know he gon' take care of you like you deserve."

"Who else knows?"

"Just me and a Cajun man with some knives and he ain't gon' tell nobody, 'cause that ain't his way."

"You got a deal," Kaiser answered in a grim tone. He needed some time to think. All he wanted to do now was get out into the afternoon air.

"Good, we gon' keep yo' boy, here. I know he got plenty to tell us and he gon' be happy to do it. That Cajun man I was talkin' about, he don't like folks with badges."

Kaiser looked over at the unconscious body of Williams and realized he was helpless. There was nothing he could do to save the man's life. He set his jaw and vowed to himself that he would see King and all his buddies lying in an unmarked grave. He looked up at King and asked, "Can I go now?"

"I told you the main thing that I wanted," King said with a smile, looking into Kaiser's pale blue eyes. "But that ain't the only thing. The other thing is: I want to be called Mister, Mr. Tremain. You get me?"

Kaiser's face turned red with anger, but he held himself in check. He felt the walls of the room closing in on him. He grimaced and said, "I understand you." He stood up woodenly.

"No you don't," corrected King, moving over to block his path to the door. "I want you to say it, so I knows you understand what I mean. Practice sayin' it!"

Kaiser stood still, breathing shallowly. His eyes were clouded with hate. He was weighing whether it was better to die rather than be humiliated by the colored man in front of him, which was strange in that he never thought of risking his life to save Williams.

"Say it!" prodded King, daring Kaiser to take action.

"Mr. Tremain," Kaiser answered through gritted teeth.

King walked over and opened the door. "Thanks for dropping in."

SATURDAY, SEPTEMBER 25, 1920

"Well, I see that the Lord has blessed us with full attendance. I expects that everyone is wantin' to hear the progress that we done made and I is happy to repo't that everythin' is goin' along just peachy." The Right Reverend Aloysious Pendergast hooked his thumbs in the armpits of his vest and tapped his fingers on his chest. Reverend Pendergast had large muttonchop sideburns that were greater in quantity and fullness than the hair on top of his head. He had a rich caramel-colored skin and was portly from a life of good eating and too little exercise. "God be praised," he intoned with his deep baritone. "We have saved some good colored families from the hand of the infidel! God be praised, the land is purchased! God be praised! We—"

"I beg yo' pardon, Reverend," King interjected. He did not wish to give the Reverend Pendergast a chance to build up steam with his preaching. King had noticed in previous meetings how the reverend tended to dominate with his preaching, whether he possessed good ideas or not. "I wants to know what happened after the money was received by yo' church."

The reverend gave him a stern look. "It's all in good hands, my boy. The land is purchased. Eight colored families has got a chance to start over somewheres else."

"I believe you bought the property, but where are the deeds?" King asked. "The lawyer in New York say he ain't received 'em!" This statement caused a commotion. Rambo stood up and made his way to the front of the church so that he could hear better. Others were concerned that something sneaky was afoot, so they leaned forward to hear the reverend's answer. The first four rows of pews were filled with people and the mumbling was getting louder.

"Now see here!" the reverend said imperiously. "I don't see why I has to answer to you alone. All these people know and trust me, that's good enough for me. The only bein' I has to answer to is my God. No one else! Only God! That is—"

King interrupted again. "You wastin' time, Rev. Where are the deeds for the properties that's been bought? The money them properties was bought with didn't belong to the church! The people what put up that money got a right to know where them deeds are!"

Rambo stood. "What you getting at? Why are you asking about the deeds?"

"Well, the plan was that the deeds was gon' be sent to New York to be owned by the corporation we was gon' set up," King answered. "I called New York and they told me they never received no deeds and without them there ain't no collateral to set up a corporation."

Someone snickered from the back of the group. "Oh, God! We's our own worst enemy."

"Wha-what!?" stammered Rambo. "I put up a thousand dollars! Where are those damn deeds!"

Sister Waters bellowed. "They's right! Tell us where them deeds is!"

Reverend Pendergast stood up, alarmed by the general outcry. "Wait a minute, good people, you know me—"

"By what right did you change the plan?" Rambo demanded. "You had no say in this at all! He's right, there was no church money in this deal!"

"I ain't got but fo'ty dollars in it, but I is mad too!" An old gray-haired man smacked his hat against the back of the pew in front of him. "Is this gon' be yo' price, Preacher?"

"Good people, children—"

"This ain't a good time for calling people children, Al. We're too old for it," Claude Duryea advised from the second row.

"Now, Claude, we're never too old to be children of God. We'll—"

"No, we're just too old for you to call us children at a time like this! Just answer the question. My family has five hundred dollars in this too!"

"Please, please hear me out." Reverend Pendergast clasped his hands together to emphasize his request. "The deeds are safe. I ain't used them to fill the coffers of the church or to stuff my own pockets with ill-gotten gain. I was just tryin' to use some common sense. Why do we got to send the deeds to New York? Why can't we file them ourselves under the name of the church? If not this one, some other local church? I know someone high up in parish government who can 'seal' the sale of property."

"So you made a decision on yo' own and you didn't send the deeds to New York?" King's words had a low and dangerous tone.

"Where are the deeds?" demanded Rambo. He was apoplectic, his face was flushed, and his eyes were bugging out. "We made it very clear that the church was just the place that was used to orchestrate the deal. Now you're making decisions with our money?"

"The deeds are in a safe place. I'm the only one who knows where they are. You have no need to worry. I won't misuse yo' trust. If you don't like my idea, we can send it out with the mail packet tomorrow. Believe me, I had only yo' interests at heart. Just remember them deeds are safe. I'm the only one who knows where they are."

"That ain't right!" the old man shouted and smacked his hat against the pew. There was a displeased grumbling sound rising from the group as a whole.

Seeing the displeasure on some of the faces of his flock, Pendergast quickly recanted. "Uh, uh, I might consent to tell a few trusted souls where I've hidden the deeds."

"No," King countered. "The mail packet for New York don't come until Monday. Let the preacher keep the deeds hid until Monday and we can come here at nine o'clock in the morning and walk him to the posting office. That way only one person will know where them deeds is." There was several minutes of animated discussion before a rough consensus was developed. It differed from what King had proposed in that it allowed Claude Duryea to hear where the deeds were hidden.

King and Sampson and Phillip and Claude Duryea were standing outside the Reverend Penderdast's church in the warm air of a mauve dusk. The church was a large, whitewashed, two-story structure that stood on a rocky rise on the outskirts of New Orleans. It was surrounded by a small grove of sycamore and dogwood. The four men were standing in the clearing in front of the church when Pendergast stepped out and turned to lock its doors.

"I got a powerful urge to lay metal upside his head," King admitted.

Sampson nodded vigorously in agreement.

"You can't lay into every fool that crosses your path," Claude said. "You got to choose your battles. Otherwise you'll use your energy up in meaningless fighting."

The reverend saw the group of men in the darkening purple twilight and headed down the steps in their direction, but when he saw King he abruptly changed his course and walked away from the group.

"He's not thinking clearly," Claude explained. "It's sad how most people with a little knowledge and a little authority act like total idiots. That's why whenever you're dealing with people, you got to remember to control yourself first, then keep to your strategy. Laying metal upside their heads is a last resort!"

"I just wonder who he knows so well that he can get the assessor's seal on them deed documents?" King mused as he and his three companions walked slowly down the hill toward their cars. Everyone else had already departed.

Just beyond the trees, lining a descending, deeply rutted dirt road, was a small commercial corridor consisting of a general store, a cooperage, a feed store, a seamstress, and a cobbler's shop. There were no streetlights to light the way in this part of Colored Town. The streetlights didn't begin until the railroad tracks were crossed. The stars had not yet begun to gleam.

Nestled at the bottom of the hill at the junction of the road and the cobbled lane was a mixture of shacks and small houses. It was the farthest reach of Colored Town before the Kenner Road took off through the rice fields. Once King and his companions were among the buildings, the smell of cooking fires and hot food was strong. Some people were sitting on their porches husking peas and corn, cleaning collard greens, or smoking corncob pipes. Just beyond the shacks and houses was a clearing where people generally left their cars and wagons before climbing the small hill to the church. The high-pitched sound of children's voices carried in the warm evening air.

Phillip Duryea cranked his truck up a few times before it sputtered to life. King assisted Claude as he climbed into the truck. Before he could step down, Claude held his hand and said, "Reverend Pendergast may be stupid, but he isn't a traitor to his people. He serves the parishioners of Zion on the Mount Baptist Church with a great deal of love. He just made a stupid decision!"

"I just hope you's right!," King rejoined. The truck's engine revved and then it moved slowly down the road and joined a stream of early evening traffic heading out of New Orleans to Metairie and Kenner. King and Sampson drove off in a different direction, toward Nellum's Crossing. Captain Mack had invited them for dinner. Once they reached the macadam highway, King let down his window and felt the warm night on his face.

Journer Braithwaite rubbed her eyes as the smoke from the burning church billowed past her. People were running back and forth shouting directions. Three deacons had organized most of the volunteers into several lines that led from the well to the church, and buckets of water were being passed hand to hand. The pastor's quarters were in ashes, but the flames for the most part had been defied. The main hall of the church was saved, although there were still plumes of smoke curling up the sides of the walls. Journer did not attempt to join one of the lines. She walked heavily over to where the injured were lying on the ground, squatted down on a low bench, and began tearing a linen sheet into strips. It was not yet ten o'clock in the morning and she was already tired. She was concentrating on tearing cloth dressing strips for bandages. Five people lay on the ground, moaning from burns and injuries. One of them, a teenaged boy, was in serious condition.

Journer realized that there was not much that she could do for the injured, and it pained her to feel so helpless when people were in need. She knelt down by the closest person, a middle-aged woman who had received a deep gash in her thigh, and changed her blood-soaked bandage. Next to her, an old man, the caretaker of the church, moaned and twitched fitfully. Another woman volunteer knelt down beside Journer, took a few bandage strips, and began working on the old church caretaker. The woman murmured a few soft words to him as she attempted to bandage the charred flesh on his back.

The most serious burn victim, the teenaged boy, cried out; tears were streaming down his face. Journer rose and moved her bench closer to him. Even in his delirium, he was shaking in pain. His arm was cooked all the way through; it would have to be amputated. She had heard from several people about him. He was the one who had carried several people out after they had been overcome by smoke and flames. His bravery would end up costing him his arm. As he was rescuing his last person, a burning beam had fallen free, struck him a glancing blow, and pinned his arm underneath its burning mass. The young man's eyes opened wide. He lifted his head with an effort and cried, "What's gon' happen? How come I's bein' punished?" He cried out to no one in particular. His head fell back and his eyes fluttered shut.

"You ain't bein' punished," Journer Braithwaite said soothingly. "Can't nobody explain it, 'ceptin' God. Life is just that way. Sometimes, you thinkin' you's doin' right and the whole world falls on you and just crushes you like a bug. Then it gets up and keeps on goin' without ever lookin' back." She saw that he had passed out once more. "We needs a doctor here!" she shouted. "We needs a doctor!" Journer kept talking to the boy, more for herself than for him. She dabbed at his brow lightly with a piece of linen. "You reconciles yo'self to hard work and the fact that a poor colored person ain't gon' get an even break in the white man's world, but then somethin' else terrible happens and makes you wonder whether the afterlife is gon' be any better. It makes you wonder if God really is color-blind."

She knew there was a good chance that he was going to die. His chest was disfigured by broken blisters and burnt flesh and his breathing was uneven. She knew that he would probably not regain consciousness. She wished him a quick death and momentarily envied his impending departure from the pains and disappointments of the mortal plane. She now thought often of death. Life itself did not seem bearable or worth the discomfort of continuing. She felt tainted and unclean. She could not rid herself of the memory that her own mother had bartered her for the Fleur-de-Lys. She had married Phillip more out of gratitude than love. Marriage was something he had wanted and he had risked his life to obtain it. She could not deny him, but she had no emotion left for him.

"Journer! Journer!"

Journer looked up and saw Phillip waving at her as he and three other men carried another victim toward her on a homemade stretcher. The body of the victim was grossly overweight and looked somehow familiar. A feeling of dread clouded her thoughts. As the men drew nearer, she saw it was the inert body of her mother. She couldn't speak. She tried to rise, but she couldn't stand. She was frozen on her knees. The men set the body gently down beside her. Her mother groaned as her body came to rest.

"She tried to stop the Klan from robbing and burning the church," Phillip explained. "From what I understand, she fought pretty hard before they shot her!"

Mary's eyes were closed and her face was contorted in pain. Although her clothes and hair were singed, she had no serious burns. It was the bullet hole in her chest that was causing her problems. With every breath she took there was a terrible gurgling sound.

Journer felt a sudden and intense rush of guilt. All the hateful thoughts she had directed at her mother flashed across her consciousness. She shook her head; she had not asked for this. This was not her doing. She had not called death down upon her mother. She reached out and took her mother's inert hand in her own.

"Mama! Mama, it's me, Journer!" she said, holding her mother's hand.

Mary Braithwaite was delirious. "Water! Water! Please, I'm so hot and thirsty."

Phillip knelt beside Journer and shook his head. "She shouldn't have anything to drink until the doctor examines her."

"Where is the doctor?" Journer demanded. "She'll die before he gets here!"

"I'll find him!" Phillip said as he stood and looked around. He ran toward the church.

"Journer," Mary whispered, lifting her head feebly, her face grimacing in pain. "Oh, Journer, I's so sorry, honey."

"Just be quiet, Mama. The doctor will be here soon," she answered, holding her mother's hand to her cheek. Journer had cursed her mother after her father's funeral and had refused to see her or speak to her ever since. She had heard that her mother had been volunteering at Mount Zion Hill Church, but she had studiously avoided seeing her. Journer had believed there were only ill feelings in her heart for her mother, but all the anger and the blame were swept away, like vapor before the wind, by the vision of her mother struggling on the edge of death. She begged God to let her mother live.

Mary coughed and winced with the pain. "I tried to stop 'em, Journer! I tried to stop 'em! I pulled the mask off'n one of 'em and scratched his white face good!"

Journer caressed her mother's brow. "You did good, Mama! You did good! Please just lie quiet 'til the doctor gets here. Save yo' strength!"

Mary nodded and lay silently for several minutes, her breathing gurgling irregularly. Suddenly, her back arched and her hand clasped Journer's in a fierce grip. She groaned. "Oh, God, I comes befo' you naked and sinful! Please forgive me bein' stupid and ignorant!"

"Mama! Mama, what are you sayin'?"

Mary turned to face her daughter. "I begs yo' forgiveness! Befo' God, I begs it! I was wrong! I was wrong! A restaurant ain't worth the happiness of yo' chil'ren!"

"Mama! Mama, you don't have to—"

"Let me finish, Journer! I ain't got long! I needs to say, I's proud to have you as my daughter! I don't deserve you, but I's proud! You done picked yo'self up and you's doin' the right thing! You's a good woman. Yo' father was right! You got to protect yo' spirit! You got to have dignity! I was wrong, honey! I was wrong! Please forgive me! Forgive me!"

Journer started to cry. "There's nothing to forgive, Mama! You were makin' the best decision for the family. I should be askin' yo' forgiveness! Forgive me for cursin' you, Mama! Forgive me!"

"Just keep doin' right, girl! You's helpin' colored folks! You and Phillip's got my blessin'! Just remember to treat my grandchil'ren better than I treated you! Teach 'em about dignity!" Mary started coughing, each cough racking her body with spasms. Blood started flowing out of the bullet wound. Pain lanced through her body and she arched her back again. She squeezed Journer's hand tightly, then released it. She had passed out.

"We need a doctor here!" Journer screamed. She clutched her mother's unconscious body to her breast and rocked slowly back and forth.

"How long have these people been lying here in the dust?" a voice demanded. Journer looked up with a start and recognized the young colored doctor from Virginia. "Are you in shock?" he asked Journer as she gazed up at him without comprehension.

"Uh, no suh," Journer answered as she put her cheek against the cold flesh of her mother's face.

"There's nothing more you can do for her," the doctor advised her gently. "Why don't you let her lie in peace and come and give me a hand?"

Journer was stunned. She hadn't realized her mother was dead. She allowed the doctor to take the body out of her arms. The sense of loss was unspeakable. She hadn't finished grieving for her father and now her mother was dead. The sadness by itself would have been bearable, but feelings of guilt made her want to fall down in the dirt and scream for another chance. She decided it was better to occupy her mind with work than dwell on the death of her parents. Journer shook off the trauma, which seemed to bind her limbs with invisible cords. "I'll help you, Doctor," she offered.

The doctor looked around. "We've got to get these people to a clean and sterile area where I can dress these wounds. What's the closest building I can use for an infirmary?" Journer had no answer. The doctor walked away to speak with one of the deacons.

It was nearly two o'clock before Journer and the doctor trudged back up the hill from the seamstress shop toward the church. The doctor was exhausted. He had completed several surgeries, including the amputation of the young man's arm. His medical intervention had saved at least three lives. Thus, despite his fatigue, his mood was good. He was a short, thin, light-skinned man with quick, birdlike movements.

"Now what really caused all this carnage? I've heard night riders mentioned, Ku Klux Klan, and I've also heard it was just some low-down crooks. You know the real story?"

"It was the Klan. Before she died, my mama told me she pulled one of they hoods off. It got to be the Klan; they's the onliest ones sinful enough to burn a House of God."

"Is it because Reverend Pendergast has been speaking out on behalf of the folks in Possum Hollow? Oh, that reminds me, he had quite a gash on his head. Let's see to him." The doctor pulled out his watch. "Look at the time! I have to get back to my practice! Let's hurry." The doctor patted her arm affectionately. "I want you to know I was very impressed with your steadiness during surgery. You learned the tools I needed and in what order they were used. Yes, you were very impressive. I know what I'm talking about. I operated on wounded and dying men on the battlefield in France and I've never had an abler assistant! If you ever decide to work in medicine, come and see me."

Journer had sufficiently recouped her strength to continue up the hill. "You fought in the Big War?" she asked.

"No," he chuckled sadly. "Not hardly. Not many Negro soldiers ever got to shoot a weapon. We worked as stevedores and ambulance and truck drivers. Mostly, I worked behind the lines as a medical attendant, even though I had graduated from medical school and finished my residency. It wasn't until the last year of the war that I got a chance to do some real doctoring, when I was sent to the front to serve in the medical corps with the Three hundred Sixty-ninth. Then I got all the secondhand equipment and crisis doctoring I could stand."

They walked on in silence for a while, until they came to the church. Several men were standing around the front of the church with rifles and they watched Journer and the doctor attempt to pass around them.

A light-skinned colored man with red hair and freckles across his nose stepped in front of them. "Sorry, can't go in there. They's meetin'! Ain't nobody allowed in." The man nodded his head at Journer and the doctor. "No offense, folks, but that means you too."

"I beg your pardon!" the doctor exclaimed with indignation. "I'm Doctor Thadeus Washington and I'm here to see my patient, Reverend Pendergast, and I want to see him now because I have other patients to tend to!"

A voice from a church window said, "Let the man in, Red. Somebody's got to fix Pendergast's head." She saw King framed in the window, but he quickly disappeared in the shadows of the interior.

Journer and Dr. Washington entered the church and heard heated conversation in the main hall. There was a broad foyer across the front of the church, which was used primarily for the donning and doffing of rain gear. Arched doorways on either side of the foyer led into aisles of the main hall. Journer noticed that the church was dark and shadowy without electricity, but she could still see the smoke stains on the ceiling and places where the fire burned through the lathing. The voices came from the front of the church. People were sitting in the first few rows. A couple of men were standing around the altar.

As she and the doctor made their way to the front of the church, Journer heard King demand, "I want to know how the Klan knows so much about our business. They didn't break into this church by accident, and from what people say, they knew where to look! This preacher done told somebody! The deeds are gone and he act likes he got the right to keep secrets! This man needs a serious lesson!"

"But first I'll see he gets some serious medical attention," said the doctor as he made his way to Pendergast's side. Journer didn't follow the doctor. She held back while she looked over the crowd for Phillip.

Pendergast was sitting on the stairs of the apse, holding a bloodstained towel to his head. "I admit I have made a foolish decision. I trusted someone that I should not have trusted," he said with a quiet sadness. "I'm truly sorry for what has happened. Just give me a couple of days and I think I can clear it up! Is that all right?" he asked.

"It's obvious to me you can't clear shit up!" King retorted.

"If a man apologizes sincerely, knowing that's all he can say to God, we have to accept it," the doctor said as he cleaned the gash on Pendergast's forehead with a cotton swab.

King looked at the doctor. "Who the hell are you?"

"Now, let's not lose our tempers with each other," Claude Duryea advised from his second-row pew. Claude turn to the reverend. "Reverend Pendergast, King is right about one thing: we need to know who you told. We don't have a couple of days. We need to know now. We need to take action now."

"Just give me a day," Pendergast pleaded.

"For what?" King demanded. "You think you gon' talk some sense into people who would set fire to a church and shoot women? You got as much a chance of that as fillin' these pews next Sunday, when the word gets around how you been buddy-buddyin' with the Klan and done sold a mess of colored folks down the river."

"That's a lie and a quarter!" Pendergast burst out with dismay. "You think lying about me is just?"

"The 'Rev' is a stuffed shirt, but he isn't a traitor," the doctor stated as he snapped his medical bag shut and got to his feet. He saw two people lying on blankets along the far wall and he went over to check on them.

"Who's to know it's a lie?" King asked, giving the doctor's retreating back another long look. He turned back to Pendergast and continued. "You ain't hurt bad. A couple of people is dead. All we got to ask is, 'How come you ain't dead or injured fightin' to save the church and the people's investment?'" King looked around at the people gathered in the first few pews and pointed at Pendergast. "How come he was saved?"

There was a long silence. Journer was sitting with Phillip at the end of the second row. The conversation faded for her as her eyes filled with the sight of her mother dying.

Journer stood suddenly. She felt a shortness of breath. The anger and tension in the church was stifling. She needed fresh air. Neighboring churches' bells began to toll three o'clock and their pealing made Journer think of the Fleur-de-Lys. She had to get back and help prepare for the evening meal. It didn't matter that she had not been back to the restaurant since the night her father was killed. She had to go and tell her sister that their mother was dead. She headed up the aisle toward the main exit. She was strangely unsteady on her feet. The bells seemed to be reverberating unusually loudly. The far wall in front of her shifted out of focus. She stopped for a moment to gather her wits and a firm hand grabbed her arm. It was the young doctor.

"Are you alright?" he inquired, staring at her closely.

"I's jes' tired," Journer answered, taking a couple of deep breaths. "I'll be alright in a minute. I gots to get back to work."

"Where do you work? My car is at the foot of the hill; maybe I can give you a ride, Mrs. Duryea. I've worked with you all day and I don't even know your first name."

"The name's Journer. My maiden name is Braithwaite. My family owns the Fleur-de-Lys and I would thankee kindly if'en you's disposed to give me a lift somewheres nearer the restaurant."

The doctor smiled broadly and answered, "I'd be happy to, Mrs. Duryea." He turned and signaled to Phillip with a wave of his hand that everything was fine.

Just before they entered New Orleans, the doctor turned his Model A down a broad street that ran parallel to a major levee. They saw colored chain gangs dressed in ankle chains and the characteristic dirty, black-and-white striped prison garb. There were many a sweating, brown, bare-backed man shuffling in shackles under the weight of sandbags. Scattered among them were a few white guards armed with whips and rifles. Flashes of sad work songs blew in the window as they drove past. The doctor shook his head. "I hate seeing them use colored prisoners like this." Journer had no response. She closed her eyes and felt the warm breeze on her face.

Traffic slowed to a crawl as the car turned down a narrow side street clogged with horse-drawn carts. "Is your father, the honorable Ajax Braithwaite of the African Knights' Social Club?" the doctor asked.

Journer answered, "Yes. He was. He passed in June."

"I heard about that. My condolences," the doctor nodded. "Eight years ago, Mr. Ajax Braithwaite sponsored my request for donations for my medical school tuition before his social club. He even went so far as to present me to the Northern Stars as well. I was one of the young scholars in need of tuition mentioned in *The Crisis* that year. Even though I was from a different part of the country and he didn't know me from Adam, he sponsored me. And when I was at my lowest, when money was tight and I was ready to quit, he wrote me and sent me ten dollars! He gave me hope and reminded me of my faith. Mrs. Duryea, it is because of men like your father that I am a doctor today. He's the reason I came to New Orleans. I wanted to repay him by serving his community."

Journer was deeply touched. It reminded her how her father was always squeezing money from somewhere to donate to some cause or charity. Now, here, in front of her, was a manifestation of how the money had been spent. Her father, who for the majority of his life appeared to be nothing but a crippled street hawker, had helped someone become a doctor. And now that doctor was helping many others. She felt stronger, renewed, because she saw a path, a way that her life might have meaning. When she got out of the doctor's car and said good-bye, she still carried the oppressive weight of sadness, but it no longer seemed unbearable.

She entered the Fleur-de-Lys and was immediately immersed in the drama of telling her aunt and sister that her mother was dead. The preparation of food for the early evening meal was delayed for over an hour, but with Journer's urging, the work in the kitchen got back on track. The restaurant would stay open because that's exactly what Ajax and Mary would want.

THURSDAY, OCTOBER 7, 1920

After seeing King nearly twice a week all through the late months of summer, Serena did not see him during the last part of September. In fact, she did not see him again until the day the thirteen-year-old colored boy,

Jimmy Sitwell, was lynched a few miles outside of Algiers. Serena never got the exact details of what caused young Sitwell to be lynched, but what she heard was that a retarded white girl had been molested. Someone reported that a Negro boy had been seen in the area half an hour before she was discovered. A mob of angry white men soon congregated and began roaming the streets looking for Negro suspects. Word quickly spread through the colored community and the men began to hide.

Serena and her parents had scheduled that Thursday to travel into the Vieux Carré, the old French Quarter, in New Orleans to see a doctor for her mother and to buy a new plow blade. By the time they had heard about the lynching, they were three quarters of the way into New Orleans. They were told by a colored man on horseback who was riding to Lake Pontchatrain. Serena's father and mother discussed it for several minutes and decided to continue on into New Orleans. They did not want to miss the doctor's appointment. Serena's father lay down in the back of the wagon underneath the canvas. Serena and her mother sat on the driver's seat and road silently to the northern outskirts of the city, to what was known as Colored Town. They had to replenish their store of basic items, so they stopped there. After a few brief conversations with some local merchants with whom they had business, it was decided that it was safer for Serena's father to stay in a vegetable cellar at his cousin's house than continue on with Serena and her mother. There were now roving bands of whites in New Orleans north of Canal Street who were bent on attacking every colored man they found. It would be dangerous for the women, but Serena's mother needed to see the doctor.

Rebecca Baddeaux knew that she was dying; she merely wanted to prolong what was left of her life and perhaps find more than occasional escape in laudanum. It was the desire for laudanum as well as other medicine that now drove her forward. When the discomfort in her chest grew too great, she developed a tendency to rock back and forth; it didn't matter whether she was standing or sitting, she swayed like kelp in a changing current. And indeed, she was in a current, flowing toward the edge of the earth through the channel of decay. Occasionally, she struggled and fought against the current, but she didn't have the stamina. More often she found herself sitting and watching her life slide slowly over the edge, out of sight.

As Serena pulled the wagon out of an alley behind her cousin's house, she knew her mother was struggling mightily with her illness. Serena snapped the reins across the backs of the mules to speed them up. She was determined to do everything in her power to get her mother to the doctor safely. The streets were deserted and silent. Colored Town had closed its doors. The sound of their wagon and the hoofbeats of the mules echoed loudly in the emptiness. In the faraway distance, there was a discordant roar of many voices.

At the edge of Colored Town New Orleans began, and so did the cobblestone streets. An old, dented Model A turned off a main thoroughfare and chugged toward the wagon. Serena reined the mules over to the side of the street, for they were skittish around motorcars. When the car came abreast of the wagon, the driver, a colored man in his fifties, stopped and shouted over the roar of his engine, "You folks crazy? Don't you know they lynching Negroes?"

"I got to get my mother to her doctor," Serena shouted in response.

The man took a look at Serena's mother, who ignored him as she rocked back and forth. "If you's got an emergency, won't any doctor do? There's a colored doctor named Washington three streets over from here."

Serena looked at her mother questioningly, but saw no response, so she turned back to the man. "No sir, I got to take her to her doctor."

"Well, the way you're going, you gon' run right smack into the Klan 'cause they is marching through up and down Ramparts Street. You ought to stay on the back streets outta their way! They ain't gon' care you is just womens! They willin' to take anybody. They burned that boy to death earlier today and they still hungry for blood!"

"We're going to Front Street near Beauregard Square. What's the best way?" Serena asked.

"Take a right at the next street and stay in Colored Town 'til you hit Bridgewater. Take Bridgewater to Front and take a left. God be with you." The man's car sputtered and clanged as it drove away.

Serena and her mother were left alone in the desolate street. She followed his directions. Whenever she heard noises or other cars coming, she pulled the wagon to the side, tethered the mules, climbed into the back of the wagon with her mother, and pulled the canvas over the both of them. Fortunately, there was not much traffic in Colored Town, but once she had entered New Orleans, Serena had to be more vigilant. She and her mother had to stop and hide under the canvas three times before they reached the doctor's office.

The doctor's house and clinic were enclosed in a large two-story building that had wrought-iron balconies and a large interior courtyard. Serena guided the mules through the courtyard to a stable behind the doctor's building and walked her mother upstairs. The doctor, a tall, thin Scots immigrant with pale, translucent skin and carrot-colored red hair, was surprised to see them. He said in his thick Scottish brogue, "You're a wee bit late. I dinna think you were comin'. But if you braved the madness in the streets, I'll see to you as soon as I finish with me other patients."

Serena took her mother downstairs and waited in the servant's quarters, where the doctor's maid lived. The maid was shocked to hear that they had driven by wagon nearly twenty miles on the day of the lynching. She rushed to make Serena's mother comfortable on her rickety bed and gave them both a steaming hot cup of coffee. After they had been waiting for nearly an hour, there was a commotion in the doctor's office upstairs. The maid was called for and she complied obediently. Serena sat by her mother and watched helplessly as she continued to rock in rhythm to inner forces.

The maid returned after half an hour had elapsed. She informed them that the doctor had been called away because of an emergency. Some white men had been shot outside the Klan headquarters. From what Serena was able to piece together from the disjointed narrative of the maid, six of the men had just disembarked from two cars and had started up the stairs of the building when a man, also dressed in Klan garb, walked out the front door. The man produced two guns and fired without warning. Three of the men were seriously wounded and three were dead. The sheriff had rounded up a posse to search for the killer because two of the men who were killed were sheriff's deputies. Two additional dead men were found inside the headquarters, and the klavern's safe had been robbed. The killer had made his getaway in one of the victim's cars. The sheriff had issued an all-points bulletin on the car and every Klansman in the area was out looking for the killer. A colored man, who may have witnessed the killer's escape, was also wanted in connection with the shooting.

The maid advised Serena that it would probably be safer for both her and her mother to stay off the streets for the rest of the night. The maid, whose name was Patience, said there were rumors in the colored community that it was a colored man who did the killing at the Klan headquarters. But the sheriff, in an effort to protect the Klan's reputation, was saying it was a gang of white men and that they were only looking for a colored man in connection with the crime.

The fear that she had suppressed ever since they had entered New Orleans caused her legs to tremble. It wasn't noticeable to anyone else, but she couldn't stop it. Serena refocused on her own mission, which was now to get her mother home safely after she had been seen by the doctor. The safest alternative was to arrange to stay into the evening. She asked Patience if she could feed and water the mules in the doctor's stable. Patience willingly showed her the stables, the feed bins, and the stalls where she could put the mules. Patience went back to her quarters and left Serena to unharness the animals. Serena watered and fed the mules before placing them in the stalls. She brushed Homer down and checked his hooves to make sure he hadn't cracked them on the hard cobblestone streets. When she went in to brush Jethro down, she spoke coaxingly and moved slowly. Although the mule had known her most of its life, it was suspicious of humans and had to be coaxed before it would allow itself to be touched. Serena did not even attempt to check Jethro's hooves. She would leave that task for her father. While she was grooming Jethro, she felt someone looking at her. Serena turned and saw a red-haired white man in his early twenties staring at her.

"You working for my uncle?" he asked, his eyes appraising her from head to toe.

"No, sir." She met his gaze. The way he was looking at her, she knew he was going to be trouble. She moved up near Jethro's head and grabbed his bridle, so he wouldn't try to bite her.

The man opened the gate and stepped inside the stall. "Maybe we should get to know each other. I'm the doctor's nephew."

Jethro's ears laid back. He didn't like anyone standing behind him; that's where the lash came from.

Serena held on to Jethro's bridal, wondering when he would kick.

The man took a step forward and pulled back immediately, for he had stepped into fresh manure. That act saved his life. Jethro lashed out with both hind legs, thudding against the stall's gate and splintering the wood. The hooves missed the man by six inches. The man did not even open the gate—he vaulted over it. He stood outside the stall, staring at Serena. It was clear from his expression that he blamed her for the mule's action. The man pointed at Serena and started to say something, but the sound of the doctor's horse and buggy entering the courtyard stopped him. He left the stables without another word.

Serena breathed a deep sigh of relief. She resolved to get the butcher knife out of the wagon and keep it with her. Outside the stable, Serena overheard the conversation between the man and his uncle, the doctor.

"It was strange to see, that I'll tell you," the doctor said as he jumped down from his carriage. "Bodies in bloodstained white sheets lying all around the entrance of the building. And two dead inside as well."

"I heard it was a gang of men who did it," the nephew stated.

"It was one lone man," the doctor corrected.

"One man? Uncle Steve, you know one man couldn't kill eight men, especially armed men!"

"It was one man," the doctor reaffirmed. "I heard it from one of the dying victim's lips. He saw the man's face before he donned his hood. He told me and the sheriff just before he died. It was one man. A colored man with two-tone shoes."

Serena's heart leapt at the news that a colored man was bold enough to march into the Klan's headquarters and not only rob them, but kill a few members as well. It could only be one man, she thought, as a sudden pang for King's safety overcame her. Serena felt nothing but resentment toward whites. It was only fair that they got some of what they dished out. What should have been a simple little trip into New Orleans had turned out to be a nightmare all because of the whites' hatred of colored people. Now she had to be careful whenever she went to check on the mules, because she didn't want the doctor's nephew to catch her in the stables alone. There was no doubt in her mind that he meant to rape her. She decided to leave the stables before the doctor went inside.

The doctor saw her as she walked back to the maid's quarters. "Bring your mother up now. I'm sorry for the delay. You've been very patient."

Serena bowed her head respectfully. "Yes sir. I'll do that right now."

Serena was not allowed to stay in the examining room with her mother. The doctor had her wait out in the hall.

After a half hour the doctor opened the door of the examining room and stepped out. "Your mother is dying of tuberculosis. Her lungs are filled with congestion. She doesn't have much longer. There is nothing I can do for her but give her laudanum for the pain. I'm giving you enough laudanum to keep her through the next two months. I don't think you'll need more than that. If so, come back and I'll give you some more. I just want to warn you that laudanum is addictive and if you don't dole it out as I prescribe to you, she could kill herself with it." The doctor looked at her sternly. "Do you understand?"

Of course she understood. She wasn't stupid. It was just that she was suffering from nervous exhaustion. "I understand," she answered softly.

Later in the evening, when she and her mother had both returned to the maid's quarters, Serena heard the mules braying. She got up to go check on them when Patience stopped her.

"That's just Mr. Tom," Patience warned. "He's trying to get you to come out to the stables. If'en I was you, I'd just stay put. He ain't gon' kill your mules."

"Is that the doctor's nephew?"

"Yeah, he's a dog in heat. He tries to get some from all the doctor's colored women patients. He don't care if'en you married or with child. He gon' get what he wants."

Serena was asleep when the knock came at the door. It was an old man with dark brown skin and gray hair. Even his eyebrows and his beard were gray. He worked as the doctor's manservant. Everyone called him Uncle Joe. He spent several minutes at the door, whispering to Patience and looking over her shoulder at Serena and her mother. When he left, Patience came over to Serena's pallet and whispered in her ear. "The sheriff's doing a house-to-house search. They done found the car that was used to get away. Now, they checking every colored person in town. If you don't live here, they gon' take you downtown for questioning and anything might happen to you down there 'cause you a good-lookin' woman."

"What do you think we should do?" Serena asked. She was exhausted by this seemingly never-ending nightmare.

"If'en I was you, I'd harness my mules and get out of here right now. If you stay to the backstreets, you could make it easy. Anyway, that's what Uncle Joe thinks and he's a pretty smart old-timer."

"What about Mr. Tom?"

"I'll help you. If'en we's quiet, he shouldn't hear a thing."

Both women got up immediately and began to pack Serena's traveling bag. It was decided that they wouldn't wake her mother until the mules had been harnessed to the wagon.

There was a thin moon in a starless night sky. The grounds within the courtyard were filled with shadow. The stable was dark when Patience and Serena entered. Patience led Serena to the stalls where her mules were and then she lit a small kerosene lamp. Homer was harnessed first, since he was always easier to handle. Jethro balked and resisted, but finally allowed himself to be placed in the traces. Holding the reins in her hands, Serena led the mules out into the courtyard and hooked them up to the wagon.

Serena and Patience packed the wagon and placed her mother in the back so that she could lie down. Then Patience went back to the stable to put out the kerosene lantern. Serena pulled the wagon to the gate of the courtyard and waited in the darkness for Uncle Joe to come with the key to open the gate. While she was waiting, she heard someone come from the main house and go into the stable. Serena held her hand to her mouth in fear. She could not warn Patience without revealing herself. Within a few minutes, Serena heard the sound of a struggle going on inside the stable. She heard the high-pitched sounds a woman makes when she is being hurt. Uncle Joe came out of the darkness and unlocked the gate and pulled it open for her. She hissed at him. "Don't you hear what's going on in the stable?"

"I hear it and I don't like it, but what can I do about it? Tell Mr. Tom to stop? It ain't my business," he muttered. "She should a known better than go into the stable at this time of night. She knows Mr. Tom. If you foolish, you pay."

Serena was shocked. "You're a damn coward! You're a house nigger!"

"A house nigger ain't so bad," the old man said easily. "You the one going out into the night, risking your life. You don't live this long without protection."

"You're not living!" Serena said as she jumped down from the wagon. "You already dead!"

"It don't matter to me what you say," the old man continued to speak without rancor. "I'm going to close this gate in ten minutes. If you's out, good. If you's still in here, that's yo' problem." He turned and walked away into the darkness.

Serena ran toward the stable. She was determined to save Patience. The maid had treated Serena and her mother as family. She had opened up her one-room home to them and shared her food. Serena could not leave without trying to save her.

Inside the stable, the wavering light of the lantern created shifting shadows. Serena could hear the snorts of the horses and mules moving in their stalls. She saw a pitchfork hanging on the wall and lifted it quietly from its brackets. She moved toward the human sounds; the panting and gasping and the sounds of bodies struggling on a bed of straw. She entered the empty stall next to the one in which Tom and Patience were wrestling. The stall's walls were only as high as the gate, which was four feet. Serena raised the pitchfork and readied herself to strike. It was Serena's intention to kill Tom with the pitchfork. She blocked out all distractions. She was totally focused on the action in the next stall. When she came abreast of the two bodies writhing on the floor, Serena looked over the dividing wall and saw that Tom was holding Patience down while he was entering her. Serena raised up and prepared to thrust the pitchfork into Tom's exposed back. Her thrust would surely have killed Tom, if the blow had not been blocked. A hand came out of the shadows and grabbed her wrist. It was so quick, so sudden, that she hardly had time to react. Her scream was muffled when she saw the face attached to the hand.

It was King Tremain dressed in a tailored, double-breasted pinstriped suit. He shook his head, indicating that Serena shouldn't stab Tom. He lifted a bottle of bourbon and, with a striking motion, suggested using it as a weapon. Serena stood back as if to say that if King had a better idea, go to it. King vaulted over the stall wall and hit Tom with the bottle before he could turn around. Tom collapsed on top of Patience. Serena made her way around to help Patience get out from under Tom's unconscious body.

"I don't know how long he's gon' be out," King said. "We got to get goin' now!"

"Who's we?" Serena asked suspiciously.

"I got to go with you and yo' ma now," King explained. "Ain't no way

I can get back across the bridge to Algiers tonight and I got to get out of here."

"Well, I can't leave you here," Serena said with a sigh. She knew that there was a real danger that they might all be killed if King was found in their wagon. Despite the fear, she forced a smile on her face. "Sometimes the mouse helps the lion. You'll have to ride in the back under the canvas with my mother." King returned her smile with his own, along with a nod of appreciation.

"What am I gon' do?" wailed Patience as she stared down at Tom's unconscious body. "When Mr. Tom wake up, he's gon' beat me and beat me and beat me! What can I do?"

King grabbed a hold of Patience roughly and shook her. "Be quiet! If you go to the doctor and tell him that his nephew was havin' you against your will, that you had to knock him out to escape, he will protect you from his nephew. He's one of the few decent white men around here."

Her face wet with tears, Patience looked up into King's eyes and for a long moment there was direct eye contact. She seemed to take heart from something she saw in his eyes. "You sho' that will work?" Patience asked, slightly more confident in her tone.

"Yeah, he always does the right thing. That's why he gots more patients than he has time. And got more friends than he can count. Too bad more whites don't learn that lesson."

King lifted Serena up to the wagon seat and walked over to the shadows by the gate. "Come out, old man. I see you. Or shall I throw my knife where I think you are?"

Uncle Joe came out of the shadows.

"Do you know me?" King asked.

Uncle Joe nodded. "You one of them outlaw Tremains."

"You got it," King admitted. King put his finger in the old man's chest and said quietly, "I'm leaving you alive because I don't want to hurt an old man unless I have to. But if you talk, I'll see to it that you'll pay. And I know you don't want to be used as alligator bait."

Uncle Joe took a step backward. He knew the reputation of the man in front of him. He also knew that King was the man who had done the killing at the Klan headquarters. "If you folks is out the gate before anybody wake up or see and I can lock up, I never saw or heard a thing. You see, I got to be practical. You don't live long without bein' practical."

"Alright, old man," King agreed as he tied the canvas down on one side of the wagon and climbed into the back of the wagon with Serena's mother. "I hope you speak true and do as you say."

The wagon rumbled quietly out of the courtyard as King found space along the wagon side where he had tied down the tarp and made sure that he was thoroughly covered. The streets of New Orleans echoed with the sounds of vehicle horns and the harsh tones of angry voices, but there was little traffic. Serena returned along the route she had traveled into the city.

She could not be sure when she first heard the drumming sound, but by the time she could distinguish it as the sound of hooves, the wagon was moving through a large, open meadow. There was no place to hide. "Somebody's coming hard after us," she said softly over her shoulder. She snapped the reins to spur the mules into a trot. They responded and hurried their pace, but they were old mules. Within a quarter mile they would gradually slow down again. Serena realized this and was prepared to whip them to maintain the pace. She snapped the whip again at their flanks.

"Let the mules find their own speed," King warned from beneath the tarp. "They ain't gon' outrun horses at their best speed and it gon' look mighty strange you beatin' them into a trot in the middle of the night."

"Maybe you should drop out here and try to find a place to hide," Serena suggested.

"Ain't no place to hide in this meadow and they gon' catch up to us before I could make the trees. No, just keep on as if you on regular business. Let's try to bluff them."

"They will kill all of us if they catch you in this wagon. You're risking our lives as well."

"If I wasn't here and they found you, a bunch of whites ridin' hard, your chances is iffy anyway. But you can be damn sure that if they find me, there'll be so many of them dead, the rest won't remember you're here."

"I hope you don't expect me to feel grateful, because I don't. I know you're the reason they're riding tonight. You're the only man I know who's crazy enough to break into Klan headquarters and come out blazing!" The hoofbeats were now a couple of hundred yards behind. Serena could hear the jingling of metal along with the hoofbeats. She looked behind but there was nothing but darkness. The horsemen had not yet cleared the cover of the trees. Serena took a deep breath. "I hope it was worth it! I hope that you got a lot of money!"

There was a muffled laugh beneath the tarp. "I got some money, but I got something better than money. I got all the papers and deeds from their safe."

The sound of running horses grew louder still. Serena could see over her shoulder the dark silhouettes of riders issuing from the trees behind her. Male voices called out. "Who goes there?" "Lay over to the side and halt yo' wagon!" "Stop in the name of sheriff!"

She obediently reined the mules to the side of the road and slowed the wagon to a halt.

The riders pulled up around her. There appeared to be eight or nine men in the group. Someone turned an electric lantern on her.

"Well, what do we have here?" a faceless voice asked ominously.

"Whatchoo doing out on the road in the middle of the night, girlie?" another voice inquired leeringly.

Serena kept her head down and explained in a soft tone, "I'm just bringing my ailing mother home from the doctor. She wanted to rest in her own bed."

"What's your name and where do you live?" the man with the lantern asked.

"Serena Baddeaux," she answered. Out of the corner of her eye, she saw one of the men dismount and begin stabbing various mounds covered by the tarp with a long knife. She realized that her life depended upon her wits. If she could not deflect their attention, King would be found.

"Don't do that, please, sir," she begged the man with the knife. "Mr. Jack Shannon will be powerful angry when we get home."

"You one of Black Jack Shannon's niggers?" the man with the lantern demanded.

"Yes sir, I'm his cook and I'm just trying to get my mother home in time to start his breakfast." Serena fervently hoped that none of the men present knew Shannon well enough to dispute her claim. Black Jack Shannon was one of the most powerful landowners in Parish County. It was only partially a lie. She had actually worked as second cook for Shannon's household and road crew for two summers and had been offered a permanent position, but she had turned it down.

"She's lying! She ain't got no business on the road at this time of night. I say, let's pull her off the wagon and teach her a lesson. Hell, I feel like changin' my luck."

Serena recognized the voice, even though she couldn't see the face. It was Mr. Tom, the doctor's nephew. She felt the fear rising within her like the mercury in a thermometer on a blazing hot day. She also heard the murmurs of assent among the other riders. She was frightened, but her thoughts were crystal clear. If she was going to be raped, it would not happen without a fight. She casually felt under her seat cushion, underneath her dress, for the handle of the butcher knife. Once she had a grip on it, she waited.

There is a mood that grows and takes shape among a pack of men, similar to that shared by communal predators such as wolves and hunting dogs. The mood is particularly strong when the men are bonded by either singleness of purpose or by weakness. Serena was a nigger woman travel-ing alone with her infirmed mother, an easy victim in their eyes. There was a moment of anxiousness and hesitation while the mood continued to build. The men jostled each other to see which one of them would make the first move.

"Tonight we are doing the sheriff's work! You have been deputized to hunt and search for the men responsible for killing two officers of the sheriff, not to mess with some nigger woman!" The man with the lantern had a commanding voice. "We have to set up a roadblock at Nellum's Crossing by five this morning. That's still a good hour away. Herbert! Tom! Get on your horses! We have to ride!"

The man with the lantern introduced himself to Serena. "I'm Sergeant Cassidy of Orleans Parish. Tell Mr. Shannon that Ned Cassidy helped you get home unharmed." He put out his lantern and led the men into the night.

The last man to leave was Tom, and he leaned out of his saddle to say to Serena, "You'll be seeing me later. I've got plans for you!"

Serena drove on for more than an hour in the darkness before resting the mules. She avoided Nellum's Crossing and followed one of the canals northward. She kept going in the direction of the Shannon estate in case one of the riders from the roadblock discovered her. She planned to turn off just before she reached Shannon's Landing, for her father's farm lay in the lowlands on the edge of the estate.

Just before Pointe Bijou, the road led into a dark grove of trees. Both Jethro and Homer snorted and their ears went up. Serena could tell from their reaction that it was not a big cat or a bear, for the mules were not afraid. She hissed over her shoulder, "Somebody's waiting for us in this grove of trees."

Serena held on to the reins tightly as the wagon entered the grove. The fear was a solid weight in her stomach. She felt exhausted and dis-traught. The nightmare was not yet over. What else can happen? she won-dered.

A man came riding out of the shadows, "Remember me? I said I'd see you again."

It was Tom. Serena could tell by his voice. She took the knife from be-neath her cushion and placed it on her lap under the folds of her shawl.

"Just pull your wagon over here. I got a nice place all laid out for us. If you do what I tell you the first time, then I won't have to get rough. You got it?"

Serena was almost relieved that it was only Tom. She snapped the reins on the mules to keep them moving through the grove.

"Hey, didn't you hear what I said? Now I warned you! You should have listened to me!" Tom rode his horse close to the mules and attempted to grab the reins, but Serena thwarted him. Tom then tried to clamber aboard the wagon from horseback. Serena slashed him across the face with the butcher knife and he fell between his horse and the wagon. The wagon rolled past him without stopping. Tom got to his feet screaming, "You goddamn nigger whore! I'll kill you for cut—" There was a soft thud and Tom was silent. Even in the darkness, Serena could see the knife hilt protruding from his white shirt, surrounded by the growing stain of blood. Tom pulled a revolver from his holster and raised the weapon in Serena's direction, but he never had a chance to take aim. There was another thud. This time another blade entered his neck. He gurgled and then fell over backward.

Serena reined the mules to a halt. King pulled himself to a kneeling position with a grimace and said, "You got some fire in you, girl! You alright by me."

Serena nodded and stared into the darkness where Tom's body was lying and asked in a quiet voice, "Where did you learn to be so good at killing?"

"The army," he answered as he clambered over the wagon's side and dropped to the ground. He almost crumpled to his knees but he straightened up with an effort and made his way over to Tom's body. Serena saw that King walked with a limp and that his pants were discolored by blood.

"You're hurt. You shouldn't be walking. Get back in the wagon," Serena commanded.

"Yeah, one of those good old boys cut me a little taste, but it ain't nothin' vital. Remember what the old man said about being practical?" King asked as he was going through Tom's pockets and possessions.

"You mean Uncle Joe? He's a coward! He had nothing to say to me!"

"Just 'cause you don't understand it, don't mean it ain't sound advice. He said, 'You don't live long if you ain't practical' and he was right. It's time for us to go our separate ways. That's what is practical. I've got a long ride to get home." King pulled Tom's body into the bushes and cleaned his knives on Tom's shirt.

Serena jumped down from the wagon. "No reason to ride all that way bleeding. Let me bandage you up."

"This here wound is on the inside of my upper leg, I don't think you . . ."

"What? I don't think you . . . what?" Serena challenged him. "I live on a farm, mister. I'm not one of your dance hall girls. I know about injuries and basic medical remedies. Now, pull your pants off so I can do a bandage on that leg!"

Without the assistance of light, Serena was able to clean up the wound and stanch the flow of blood. She used torn pieces of rags to make the bandages. "How'd you get so hard?" she asked as she wrapped his thigh with the bandages.

"I owe it all to the American Army."

"You aren't in the army now and the war is over," Serena reminded him.

"You don't think this is war? Damn people hangin' colored children from poplar trees while they party and drink! Forcin' themselves on any colored woman they want. This is war, woman! Like DuBois say, '. . . the problem of the twentieth century gon' be the color line!' I got to get on," said King. "Here's two hundred dollars."

Serena looked at the paper money in her hand. Two hundred dollars was a small fortune. "What's this for?" she asked suspiciously.

"You risked your life to take me along. It's payment. You earned it."

Serena was astounded. She had never seen so much money at one time. The thoughts of all the things she could buy swirled through her head briefly, but she blocked them out and said, "It's too much. I can't take this."

"You say it's too much?" Now it was King's turn to be astounded. "You the first woman I ever offered money to who didn't snatch it out of my hand," King marveled. "You got a backbone, woman, and you's honest. You okay with me." King limped over to Tom's horse and painfully mounted.

"I knew it was you as soon as I heard about the shooting," Serena said to his dark silhouette astride the horse. The words continued as if issuing from her mouth through their own volition. "I was frightened for you. I don't think I ever worried about anyone so much who wasn't a blood relative."

"I'll try and see you in the next couple of weeks. I may have to lay low a spell, 'cause one of them Klan boys saw me when I took off my hood and I don't know if I shot him good enough to kill him."

"He's dead, but he told the doctor and the sheriff you were colored before he died."

King rode out from under the trees. "Damn, it won't take long for Sheriff Mack to make me suspect."

"Where will you stay and how can I get in touch with you?"

"If you ever need anythin', you go talk to Jonas Stedman, the blacksmith. He knows how to get in touch with me."

"What about the money?" Serena inquired.

"Keep it." King answered. "Snap them reins and get yo' wagon goin' and let's get some distance between us and this spot. I'll follow you a ways to make sure you get home."

"Nonsense. I'm already home," Serena protested. "I only live two miles from here."

"Then let's get goin'," King urged. "Me and Sampson got to come back out here sometime tomorrow and bury that body. If he gets found, they gon' check on yo' story. Then we got problems."

Rebecca Baddeaux began to sing "What a Friend I Have in Jesus" as her daughter snapped the reins across the backs of the mules and the cart rolled bumpily forward under the dim light of the night sky.

FRIDAY, OCTOBER 8, 1920

The hot noon sun filtered in through the slats of the window blinds, laying out parallel strips of sunlight on the hardwood floor. A loud whirring fan stood upon the desk, doing little but pushing warm air around. Corlis Mack sat behind his desk pondering the events of the past evening. The remains of his homemade lunch littered the desk in front of him. Unlike his brother, he was a big, beefy man who was balding prematurely. He dabbed the sweat that was running down his brow and took several long drinks of his iced lemonade.

There was a knock on his office door, which was always open unless he was having a private meeting, and a young blond file clerk stuck her head in the door. "Major Harley is here, sir."

"Send him in and then close my door," Sheriff Mack growled and picked up his wastebasket and swept the debris from his lunch into it. He knew that Harley was extremely upset by last night's incident at Klan headquarters. Mack knew it wasn't the loss of life or the violation of Klan headquarters that disturbed Harley. Harley was concerned about one thing only and that was the whereabouts of the deeds.

Harley walked into the office with Roy Wilcox. As soon as the door was closed, Harley began pacing back and forth. "Corlis, if those deeds fall into the wrong hands, all the work I've done on this project is down the drain! Of course, I'm also very concerned about the men who lost their lives and what a terrible blow this is to our local organization."

"I know one thing," Roy said in an abrasive tone. "Ain't nothin' helped with the sheriff goin' 'round sayin' a nigger was in on this robbery. Them kind of words could give the niggers the idea that they can stand up to white men and set back all the work that the Klan done to keep niggers in their place." Roy absentmindedly picked at the scabs on his face where he had been scratched.

Mack looked at Wilcox and made an effort to keep the sneer off his face. He was well aware of Wilcox's position with the local klavern and also knew of his recent promotion to Grand Titan. Mack always had a few deputies join the Klan just so he could stay informed of their activities. He feared them no more than he feared snarling country dogs. They had a bite, but if one kept a cudgel handy they were easily beaten into line. He had little respect for most of the men who joined the Klan. They were generally losers: men with a lot of anger who saw themselves as failures and blamed it on someone else, cowards who could not stand by their ac-tions in the light of day. Roy was different. He really liked killing. It didn't matter to him whether they were women or children. And he didn't care who knew.

"What are we going to do, Corlis?" Harley asked, running his hands through his limp white hair. He was still pacing. His face was even redder than usual. His light blue seersucker suit hung in stiff wrinkles, like tired foil, from the bulges of his body.

"I think we just wait," advised Corlis with a smile. Harley's distress somehow contributed to Corlis's overall feeling of comfort. For the first time since early morning his office did not seem so unbearably hot.

"What is this wait shit? Why wait?" Roy demanded. "The Klan head-quarters has been robbed! Brothers holdin' the line against the mongrels has been shot down without bein' given even a nigger's chance. We got to do somethin' strong! Like round up ten niggers and march them through the streets to Congo Square and hang they asses right there!"

"How is that gon' get back at the whites you say committed this crime?" Corlis asked.

Roy was momentarily befuddled by the question. "Well, er, it would show the niggers that they gon' pay no matter who's responsible."

Corlis gave Roy a wave of dismissal. "Let's cut through the foolishness and save everybody some time. I don't want no race war in this parish! I'm pretty sure I know the man who did this robbery and I think that if we keep a low profile, we'll be able to pick him up within a week, deeds and all."

"This ain't yo' supernigger theory, is it?" Roy asked in a snide tone.

Corlis gave Roy a long look. "You're not from around these parts, are you? You don't know who Bordeaux Tremain was, do you?"

Roy shrugged his shoulders, indicating he really didn't care.

"Well, Bordeaux was a nigger from right outside of New Orleans and he would kill twenty punks like you while suckin' on shrimp and never miss a bite."

"Ain't no nigger born can beat a pure-dee blood white man in a fair fight!" Roy blustered.

"You's pretty stupid if you believe that. I been in police work nearly twenty-some years and the toughest man I ever faced was this nigger, Bordeaux Tremain."

"I remember that name. He was killed about three years after I moved here," Harley interjected. He pointed at Corlis. "You were the head of the posse that killed him, weren't you?"

"Yep," Corlis nodded. "It was my first big arrest. I went out with twenty men and came back with six, and every man was bayou-trained. And we still wouldn't have got him, but we had an informant."

"A swamp is like a jungle and niggers know jungles. That's all it was," Roy explained. "They is closer to the monkeys than we is. They got better animal instincts than whites."

"Are you really sure you know who it is?" Harley asked. "Can we rely on it?"

"Can't be too many folk who can kill eight men and escape without injury. You know somebody white like that, Roy?"

"If you know the man who did this, you as a white man in good standing got to turn that name over to the Klan," Roy shook his finger in Corlis's direction. "The Klan has the first right of vengeance! In any white society, the first and most important law is the law of the Klan!"

"Roy, you gettin' on my nerves. If you don't start speakin' more polite, I'm gon' let you cool down in one of my jail cells."

"What did I do?" Roy asked.

"Everythin' you sayin' is bullshit! I represents and enforces the law in this parish, not the Klan. Ain't nobody gon' be marchin' niggers down the center of Ramparts Street neither. You seem to forget there's a lot of guns in the Vieux Carré and there are plenty niggers in the woodpile down there too, even if a lot of people don't admit it. So, I ain't tellin' the name, I'm just gon' pick him up when it's time."

In a grating voice, Roy threatened, "I'm sho' gon' go back and tell the klavern that you won't release the name of the varmint that done this to us."

Corlis stood up and walked around his desk and stood chest to chest with Roy, looking down at him. They stared at each other for several seconds. "Shut up, Roy. You're talking stupid, like you got nigger blood."

Expressions passed over Roy's face like clouds rushing across the sky before an angry wind, but he said nothing. He stood with gritted teeth in silence.

"Good," said Corlis, returning to his desk. "Why don't you wait outside, Roy, until the major and I finish?"

Roy stalked stiff-legged from the room and slammed the door behind him.

"I don't know how wise that was, Corlis," Harley began. "Roy can be hotheaded and undisciplined."

"Send him back to the whore that scratched him!"

"Nigger woman did that to him when he broke into the church for the deeds."

"You shouldn't bring such fools into my office and if you rely on his advice, you'll get what he deserves."

"I thought it was a pretty good idea to give the Klan the name. Then they could handle the whole thing. You wouldn't have to get involved and they would feel beholden to you for letting them clear this mark from their name."

"Don't talk shit, Harley!" Corlis exclaimed. "Have you forgotten about the deeds? If we pick up this man on our own, we get everythin'. We don't have to share with them or the assessor. If you let the Klan do it, most likely some of the deeds will be lost or get burned up. Then the assessor will want his share too."

"How are we going to get around him? When we go to register the documents, he'll be able to stop us."

"Assessors do have accidents." Corlis observed.

"I must have been out of my mind to think that I could trust that thief Harley!" Frank Loebels exclaimed to his nephew, Johan Kaiser. Loebels straightened his jacket and tugged his shirtsleeves into view. "I was a fool. I shouldn't have told him where the deeds were located. I should have worked out my own arrangements."

"Don't be too hard on yourself, Uncle Frank!" Kaiser advised from his chair by the desk as he dabbed the sweat running down his face. "It was Harley's men who broke in and burned the church for the deeds. It's far-fetched to think that Harley was behind the attack on the Klan headquarters. Look, he has used the Klan almost exclusively to do his dirty work. Would he be prepared to kill eight of his own men? If he's really behind this, he has to have developed a crew that we know nothing about. I don't see Roy Wilcox being in on something like this. He wouldn't stand for the killing of Klan members."

"You're right, Wilcox isn't involved. He's a Klan zealot. But I have a hunch that Harley's behind the scenes in this. I can feel it in my bones." Loebels shuddered, still looking out the window. He was a dapperly dressed, small-framed man with big ears and big gray, bulging eyes. His enemies and sometimes his subordinates called him Popeye behind his back. He ran his hand over his military-cut salt-and-pepper hair and said, "He's been trying to cut me out of this deal since we started. It would be like him to think something up like this."

"Let's suppose you're right, Uncle Frank," Kaiser mused as he adjusted his chair for a more direct view of his uncle. "What does he gain by stealing the deeds? You're the parish assessor. He still requires your official seal to register any change in ownership. You can stop him once he attempts to file the deeds under his name at the Assessor's Office."

"That's true," conceded Loebels. Then he frowned and held up his finger. "But what if something happened to me? If I wasn't on the scene, what then? We're talking about the potential of making hundreds of thousands of dollars here. If Harley is willing to take the lives of the men who have been helping him in his ventures, why not me?"

Kaiser nodded as he followed the reasoning. "It would be a pretty bold stroke," he agreed. "I just don't think Harley is up to being as daring against whites as he is against the niggers."

Loebels continued his thought. "Once I'm out of the picture, we both know that my assistant would kiss whichever ass had enough money to let him bend down and pick up some of the pennies. He'd be happy to see me gone. If I could be sure of the whereabouts of the deeds, I'd reverse this little plan on Harley and put him in the pine box. Only one thing prevents me from having it done and that is Harley is very close friends with Corlis Mack. It wouldn't take Corlis long to whittle down the list of suspects to me."

"I didn't know they were close friends," Kaiser said with surprise. "I've seen Harley in his office a couple times, but always with members of the city council."

"You said you didn't think that Harley wouldn't have this level of boldness. Do you think Corlis has it?"

"If they were partners, I could see a plan developing like you mentioned. Corlis can kill in cold blood. I've seen him do it." Kaiser paused before continuing to speak. "Maybe we ought to get you a bodyguard."

"Do it! Can't take chances at this point. It really irritates me that I sacrificed my relationship with Reverend Pendergast over these deeds and now I don't have them! I spent years building up that trust. As soon as I told Harley that the deeds were at the church, I knew it was the wrong thing to do. If only I could eradicate Harley, that would be the answer."

"Why not both of them, him and Corlis?" Kaiser volunteered. He did not mention that he had his own reasons for seeing Corlis dead. Key among them was to remove the threat of Corlis taking action against him because King had divulged information on him. Kaiser said with an evil laugh, "If Corlis were dead it would certainly improve promotional possibilities at the sheriff's department."

"That might be a bit dangerous," Loebels answered. "We'd have to get a triggerman. We're both too visible to have direct involvement in such action. Still, we have to move fast. If we don't achieve our objective within the next few days, we may be the victims ourselves.

"I know a couple of real hard, Italian boys from up north who are runnin' bootleg up the Mississippi. Corlis has been real hard on them. They would take great pleasure in putting a few holes in the sheriff. If we could work out something to guarantee their escape, I'm sure they'd take a try at it."

"They better be good, because our lives will depend upon it. We'll only get one shot at it. If we miss, Corlis will go to ground and we'll be looking over our shoulders until one side or the other prevails. Hell, I think there have been at least five attempts on his life in the last fifteen years. He's survived every one because he's a tough bird and he has an army of informants. We mustn't underestimate him. He started making his reputation way back when he captured and executed Bordeaux Tremain."

"Tremain?" Kaiser sat up. "I ran across one of them niggers just recently."

"Well, watch out for Bordeaux's grandson. From what I hear, he's a killer just like his grandfather."

"What is all this I hear about this Bordeaux Tremain? I've heard bits and pieces but never the whole story. People talk about him like he had supernatural powers."

"I don't know if he did black magic, but I do know Bordeaux had the devil in him. He was the scariest thing in a black skin that's ever been seen in these parts. Corlis Mack was the one that finally killed him and brought his body out after losing most of his men."

"I heard about that, how he lost three quarters of his men, many of them to booby traps."

"That's all true but what made the story so interesting is that Corlis and his brother, Sam, were the best of friends with Bordeaux's two sons. They were so close, they used to go tomcatting together. It's rumored they even screwed and shared the same women, didn't matter whether they were white or black. Every Mardis Gras for years, the four of them could be found together."

"This the same Corlis that hates niggers now?" Kaiser asked somewhat dumbfounded. "It's hard to believe. I've seen him beat lots of niggers to death without even thinking about it."

"Yep, the same one. Then Corlis went away for a couple of years and returned after creating a scandal up in Virginia. He was different after that, changed for the worse; drinking and carousing and he caused a lot of problems around here. His father finally disinherited him. Then he joined the sheriff's department. Once he was in uniform, Corlis developed a mean streak and drifted away from the Tremain boys, but his brother still liked colored girls and he liked one in particular, Bordeaux's niece. Well, lo and behold if she didn't turn out to be the one who brought vittles out to the swamp for Bordeaux. Corlis caught her and staked her to a stump in one of the bayous. He and his brother, Sam, had a battle out there in the swamps over her and Corlis left him for dead. While they were fighting, Bordeaux came to rescue the girl and would have gotten away if one of the DuMonts hadn't sounded the alarm. Bordeaux and his niece died in a hail of bullets."

With a look of consternation, Kaiser said, "From what I understand, this all happened about thirty years ago. Why do people keep talking about it?"

"Because that Tremain family has bad blood. Every thirty or forty years, one of their brood turns out to be a real nasty piece of work. Before Bordeaux there was Saint Clare and before him there was Black Jack and now it looks like this grandson has got it."

"If we take care of Corlis, I'll take care of the grandson and we'll kill the legend along with him."

"If you go after him, get him. Don't make a mistake! You can't underestimate him either."

"I won't. Let me use your telephone, Uncle Frank. I want to get someone over here to provide security for you."

As his nephew went over and cranked the phone for the operator, Loebels said, "Once I get those deeds in my hands, I'll build Pendergast an even bigger church."

"Why are you so concerned about this Pendergast boy?"

"Don't you see, this is an investment. It's good to have friends among the coloreds. As a policeman, you should know this. I wouldn't have found out about the whereabouts of the deeds if I hadn't helped him build the first church. Plus, coloreds who go to church are a lot easier to control. All you have to deal with is their pastor, and thank God, most of them can be bought."

"I don't worry about making friends with them. I put the fear of God in them! They tremble when they see—Hello? Hello, operator, connect me to the police station. This is Lieutenant Kaiser." After a brief wait, Kaiser spoke in clipped tones to one of his subordinates and then hung up. He turned to his uncle and wiped his sweating brow with his handkerchief.

Loebels, in contrast to his nephew, looked comfortable in the heat. "The question is, who do we use to settle the problem of our friends? We need an answer soon." There was a knock at the door. Loebels responded, "Come in."

A gray-haired and bespectacled woman stuck her head in the door. "Sorry to bother you, Mr. Loebels, but there's someone out here who says it's terribly urgent that he speak with you."

"Who is it, Silvia?"

"A Mr. Roy Wilcox," she answered.

Loebels and Kaiser stared at each other, both of them on the alert. "Let him take a chair and tell him I'll be right with him, Silvia." Loebels took a deep breath. "Could this be it?" he asked his nephew. "Could Roy be coming here to kill me?"

Kaiser shook his head and said, "Not a chance. It would be a suicide mission and Roy isn't up to that. He's the ambush type. Invite him in and let's see what he has to say. If he wants trouble, I can handle it. I've got my gun under my handkerchief."

Roy Wilcox's hat was in his hands when he stepped into the assessor's office. He was obviously impressed by the size of the room and the detail on the wainscotted walls. He brushed his cornsilk blond hair back, revealing a scratched and pockmarked face with watery blue eyes.

"Come on in, Roy, and have a seat." Loebels gestured to a chair by his desk. "It's been a while, hasn't it?" Loebels's big eyes stared at Roy with interest.

"It be on three, four years since I last seen you, Mr. Loebels," Roy agreed. He was very uncomfortable with the fact that Kaiser was positioned behind him, so he stood up and changed the direction that the chair was facing, allowing him to see both Loebels and Kaiser.

"What's on your mind, Roy?" Loebels prompted.

"Well, suh, Mr. Loebels, I got somethin' kind of personal to talk about with you and I don't feel all that good talkin' in front of Lieutenant Kaiser."

"Lieutenant Kaiser is my nephew and my blood. If it can't be said in front of him, it can't be said." Loebels was cautious. He would not send his nephew from the room until he was absolutely sure that Roy was not a threat to his safety.

Roy stood up. "That's too bad, Mr. Loebels, 'cause I got some information I knows you want. It's too bad we couldn't talk and work out a deal." Roy turned and walked toward the door.

"Wait a minute there, Roy," Loebels called out before Wilcox opened the door. The word *deal* had his heart pounding. Perhaps the deeds would still fall into his hands despite all of Harley's machinations. "My nephew is privy to all my private affairs. I can assure you that whatever you say to me will be kept under the strictest confidences. Not even the sheriff will hear of it."

Loebels's reference to the sheriff seemed to change Roy's mind, for he turned to face the two men. He studied them for a few seconds and asked in a doubtful voice, "You's blood kin?"

"He's my sister's son," Loebels confirmed. "What kind of deal are you looking for Roy? Let's talk a spell."

Roy walked over to the chair he vacated and sat down. "Sheriff Mack says he knows the low-down polecats who broke into Klan headquarters and murdered some of our men while they was relaxin'. These dogs murdered good men without givin' 'em a fightin' chance. The sheriff knows who these killers is, but won't give the names to us law-abiding white citizens! He don't care that our headquarters been violated! He ain't interested in servin' the citizens of this parish!" Roy pulled a plug of chewing tobacco from a packet that he took from his pocket and stuck it into his mouth.

"I don't have a place to spit in here," warned Loebels.

Roy grunted in surprise and removed the slimy wad from his mouth and put it back into the packet and continued speaking. "We don't want nothin' but justice. The Bible say, '. . . an eye for an eye.' We wants to avenge this here cowardly act! We got a reputation to uphold here. We can't have nothin' like this happen and do nothin'! We'll be the laughin' stock of the parish!"

"What's your deal, Roy?" Loebels asked.

"You help us, we'll help you! You get us the names, we'll get you the deeds. And you have to help us fix up our headquarters too."

Loebels nodded. "That sounds good, Roy, but what about the sheriff? I don't see how we can carry out any such plan while he's around to break it up."

"Maybe it's time he wasn't around," Roy growled with vehemence.

"What about Harley?" Loebels asked. "You were working pretty close with him for a while, weren't you?"

"He cares more about them deeds than he do the Klan. He sat and watched that fat pig of a sheriff insult me and say that I had nigger blood and didn't do nothin'! If that don't beat all, the sheriff said that to me!"

While Wilcox was talking, Loebels and Kaiser looked at each other. Both men realized they needed to search no further; the instrument was in their hands.

MONDAY, OCTOBER 11, 1920

On the day Serena's mother died, a monstrous thunderstorm came rumbling out of the gulf, opening floodgates of water and slinging bolts of lightning at the darkened landscape. Serena was in the kitchen preparing the afternoon meal when she first heard the grumbling bass of faraway thunder and then the light patter of raindrops as blustery winds swept across the roof. Serena went to the back window to look through the curtains at the sky. Gray and charcoal clouds roiled across the heavens like ink spilled in water.

Out of the corner of her eye, she saw her father and one of her sisters standing on the back porch. Her father was angrily shaking his finger in the girl's face. Every once in a while a gust of wind would bring a trace of her father's rough tones. Serena stepped closer to the window, pulled back the curtain, and saw that it was her younger fourteen-year-old sister, Christine, who was the object of his anger. "Tini," as she was called (pronounced "Teeney") was trembling in front of her father, her big eyes blinking in fear and confusion. Tini didn't know why her father was angry at her. She didn't know she was a pawn, but Serena understood it and it made her hate her father. Serena had seen the look on her father's face earlier that morning when he saw Tini laughing with her during breakfast. She knew it would only be a matter of time before he made Tini pay a penalty for the crime of consorting with the enemy.

Serena allowed the curtain to fall back into place. She felt tired, as if the energy had been drained from her. Resignedly, she took off her apron and prepared herself to go outside and confront her father. When Serena reached the back door, she heard something crash to the floor in her mother's bedroom. She paused for a moment, undecided whether to continue outside or to go upstairs and check on her mother. She decided that her mother needed more immediate attention. She hurried upstairs and found her mother half out of bed. Serena lifted her mother back onto the bed and picked up the bedside table that had been knocked over. The bottle of laudanum was on the floor as well, but its cap was still on securely. Serena picked up the bottle and looked at her mother. It was obvious that she was trying to reach the laudanum and overturned the table in the process.

Her mother had weakened to the point that she could not sit up unassisted. Her eyes were blurry and unfocused and her voice was a congested whisper. She waved her hand at her daughter to come closer then gurgled a word that sounded like laudanum and pointed to her mouth. Serena knew what she wanted. She shook her head. "I can't give you more, Mama. You just had a big sip of it an hour ago."

Silent tears streamed down her mother's face. Again she gurgled a word and pointed to her mouth.

"Please understand, Mama. I'm trying to do what's best. I can't let you kill yourself. Mama, please." Serena began to cry. She saw the discomfort that her mother was in and she was intimately familiar with her physical deterioration, for she had watched it progress day by day. Serena was truly confused because there was a voice within her that kept saying, Let her die quickly with dignity. Let her kill herself with the opium-laden medicine. Yet Serena was not yet ready to consign her mother to a coffin.

The sound of her father's boots climbing the stairs gave Serena a less painful direction in which to focus her energies. Her father walked through the bedroom door and she turned to face him. There was no expression on his face. Father and daughter exchanged stares for nearly ten seconds before he broke eye contact. "I wants to speak private like with my wife."

There was an air of dismissal in her father's tone that infuriated Serena, as if he could sweep her aside like so much dust. She planted her feet and made no effort to leave. Instead she decided to challenge him. "Where's Tini?" she demanded.

Charles Baddeaux gave his daughter a cold look. Then a smile suddenly broke across his face. "I sent her to clean out the stalls in the barn while I take the buggy to the Crossing for my Elders' meeting."

"You're going to the Crossing in a storm like this?" Serena asked, surprised that an Elders' meeting could be so important that it would be attended even in a major storm. Before he could answer, his words sank in and Serena deciphered the true meaning. Everyone knew that Jethro would not allow himself to be harnessed to the two-wheel buggy, so Homer had to be the mule her father was using.

Her father said nothing. His smile lingered.

"You didn't move Jethro out from his stall first, did you?" Serena asked slowly.

Her father's smile only grew broader in response.

"You know that she's afraid of Jethro! You know how he's getting more temperamental all the time! How could you?" Serena started to rush out of the room and realized that she still had the bottle of laudanum in her hand. She sat it down on the bedside table and swept out of the room amidst her father's laughter.

"Ain't nothin' gon' happen. Tini's so afraid of that mule she won't go near him!" he shouted after her.

Serena flew out the back door and across the yard to the barn. She didn't really expect Tini to be harmed, but one could never be sure with Jethro. Tini did not have the confidence necessary to handle the larger farm animals.

Jethro was standing near a bale of hay in the center of the barn when Serena entered. The mule was munching away while keeping an eye on Tini, who was cautiously approaching him from the side. Serena watched the mule sidle away from Tini without ever leaving the bale of hay.

Serena marched over to Jethro and grabbed his bridle firmly. The mule attempted to turn its head and bite her, but Serena smacked the animal across its nose and led it toward its stall. At the gate of the stall Jethro reared up, ready to continue his resistance. Serena grabbed his closest ear and tightened her grip on his bridle. She let the mule feel her weight as he lifted her off the ground. The struggle ended quickly for Jethro understood pain. He entered his stall without further struggle. Serena guided the mule in from an adjacent stall and spoke soothingly to it.

Serena left Tini to sweep out the barn and walked back to the house in the pounding rain to look in on her mother.

As soon as she entered the room, Serena knew something was wrong. It was the silence. There was no sound but the steady beat of the rain. Gone was the rhythmic rasp of her mother's labored breathing. Serena rushed to the bed where her mother lay motionless.

Lying with a slight smile on her face, her mother lay with eyes closed. From her expression it seemed that she had at last found peace. The empty bottle of laudanum was between her arm and her side. Serena picked up the bottle and stood for a moment wondering whether her mother had helped herself or her father had given it to her. There was no immediate sensation of grief, merely relief that the ordeal was over. Serena sat down next to the bed and picked up one of her mother's cold hands and held it next to her cheek. She sat for nearly twenty minutes in this position, until she heard Tini enter the house. Serena kissed the hand and whispered, "Good-bye."

Serena stood up and went out to the head of the stairs. She called down to Tini. "Please come here."

"I'm soaked. Let me get changed first. Those old milk cows are so stupid, they wouldn't come in out of the rain. I had to drive them into the barn."

"Mama's dead, Tini."

"Oh, God!" Tini cried out. "This must really be my day! Everything bad seems to be happening to me today."

"This didn't happen to you, Tini. It happened to Mama," Serena reminded her.

"You know what I mean," Tini answered. "I love Mama. I didn't mean nothin' bad."

"Tini, I need you to dress for wet weather, because I want you to go over to Old Mr. Tillman's and see if he'll let you use one his horses to ride over to where Della's cooking for Mr. Shannon's work crew."

"Can we say a prayer for Mama? I feel we ought send her off with a few words."

Serena nodded. "Sure, that's a good idea."

"Let's go outside and stand on the front porch like Mama used to do when it rained hard like this," Tini suggested.

The two sisters stood out on their front porch and prayed without speaking. The rain fell steadily, creating a continuous drumroll on the corrugated metal of the porch's roof. Serena composed her prayers, but they seemed insubstantial and lacked the love, strength, and lyricism she desired. She was just too distracted to pray in the manner she thought appropriate. She waited until Tini was finished, then sent her on her way. Serena walked across to the barn to saddle Jethro and go tell her father.

When she reached the barn a horseman rode up and little Amos slid off the saddle and ran toward Serena. It was raining so hard that Serena could not make out the other rider, but when he alighted from his horse, she saw that it was King under a broad-brimmed Stetson.

After a brief discussion with King, Serena got Amos into some dry clothes and a rain slicker. She said nothing to her brother about their mother's death. It really wasn't the right time to tell him; there was too much to do to stop and explain to an eight-year-old that a life had passed. She bundled him out the door with the explanation that she was going to help at the church. Amos was so excited to ride on King's horse again, he didn't even ask about his mother. All three of them rode King's horse through the rain to the Tillman place. Tini was just then riding a fat little pony out the gate as they arrived. Serena waved her on and slid off King's horse with Amos in tow. Serena informed the Tillmans of the situation and asked if Amos could stay with them until the following day. Mrs. Tillman, a tall, angular, brown-skinned woman with sunken, cavernous cheeks, nodded her head understandingly and assured Serena that Amos would be fine.

The ride into Nellum's Crossing was extremely wet and cold. Serena rode behind King on his horse and while King's body blocked out the wind, the rain, which fell steadily, trickled down her face and neck underneath the hood of her oilskin coat. It was nearly three and a half miles to the Crossing. Both King and Serena were soaked by the time they reached Stedman's Blacksmith Works. After his horse had been fed and watered, King joined Jonas and Serena, who were standing and talking by the smithy's main anvil.

Jonas nodded his head to King in greeting and said, "Rena told me she got to see her father. I told Rena here that I would send one of my apprentices to get him from his, uh, meeting."

"Don't go through any trouble for me," Serena said in clipped tones. "Just tell me where the Elders are meeting."

"Well, it's a ways from here," Jonas said cautiously.

"Where can it be if it's not at the church?" Serena demanded. "I'll just go over to the church myself and talk to the caretaker."

King stepped forward, his hat in his hand. "All Jonas is trying to do is let you stay in the warmth while he sends one of his boys."

"I want to go! I want to be the one to tell him!" She wanted to confront her father over the empty bottle of laudanum. "Just tell me where he is!"

King paused for a moment. "All we is doing is trying to protect you. You just lost your mother. Ain't nobody want to see you hurt worse."

"What do you mean?" Serena asked suspiciously.

"Your father ain't at no Elders' meeting," King admitted. "He got himself a little thing goin' with the schoolteacher."

"What? How long have you known?"

King thought a moment, then said, "A couple of months, maybe—"

Serena looked at him. Her eyes were grim. She said through gritted teeth, "You've been lying all this time! Take me to my father!"

King squared up in front of her. Now his eyes were glinting with anger. "I'll take you to your father, but first let me straighten you out!" King tapped his chest. "I never lie. Lyin' means you afraid somebody might know the truth. I don't care who knows the truth. I'm from the old school: my word is my bond."

"Just take me to my father!"

King turned without a word, put on his hat, and led Serena out into the rain. They walked half a mile along a heavily forested ridge of cedar toward Duncan Hollow. King did not stop or wait for Serena to catch up until they reached Widow Marshall's house.

Behind Widow Marshall's house there was a barn that had fallen into disrepair. The widow had sold all her animals when she sold her farmland ten years ago, so she had no cause to repair the barn. When Serena reached his side, King pointed to the barn.

Serena squinted unbelievingly. "There behind Widow Marshall's house? That's where he meets her?" She shook her head sadly as tears mixed with rain ran down her face. "Everyone must know about this! We must be the laughingstock of the parish!" She could not tell which hurt more, the shame she felt or the sorrow because her father had been untrue to her mother while she lay on her deathbed. She wiped her eyes and with a grim, determined look, walked over to the barn. When King did not immediately follow, she stopped and waited for him. "Don't you abandon me now!" she said with tears still in her eyes.

King walked up to her and said, "I ain't never gon' abandon you." He pulled Serena to him, put a hand under her chin, and kissed her long and hard.

Serena did not fight him as his lips pressed hers open, and he pulled away just as she was beginning to participate. They stood for a moment in the rain looking at each other. She had never been kissed like this before. Suddenly, it was all too confusing. She grabbed the arm of his oilskin and pulled him toward the barn door.

King swung the heavy door open and they stepped inside. The door creaked loudly when it was opened, giving due warning to those within. The barn was dark except for a lantern that was flickering behind several bales of hay. The lantern's light cast the shadow of two silhouettes on the back barn wall. It was obvious from both the movement of the shadows and the noise generated that the individuals were attempting to separate and get dressed.

"Who's out there?" a male voice asked querulously.

"Come on out with your chippy, Charles Baddeaux," Serena answered. "I've got some news for you."

Her father stuck his head above the bales of hay, peering into the darkness. "Serena, is that you?"

"It's me and I've come to tell you that my mother is dead! She died while you went to lie in the arms of another woman! But you probably knew that, 'cause you probably helped her along. You gave her the laudanum, didn't you?"

"Now, wait a minute!" Charles began sputtering. "You got no call to say nothin' like that! I ain't no murderer!" He stooped to get his pants fastened.

"I figured you already knew about Mama, so I came to tell you something that you didn't know. I didn't only lose my Mama tonight, but my daddy is dead as well."

Charles stood up, then ducked down. "Is King out there with you?" he asked worriedly.

"King doesn't have to kill you, old man," Serena retorted coldly. "You are already dead. You killed your own self! If you are alive now, you're not alive as my father! You're just a Bible-thumping fake who couldn't resist temptation long enough to bury his wife!"

"Now, I won't be talked to like that by one of my own chil'ren!" Charles said as he came out from behind the bales of hay. He gave Serena one of his righteous looks. "You ain't the one to judge me! Only God can do that! Now, you told me about yo' Mama, you can go. And, uh, we'll keep this little incident between us. Ain't no need of anybody else knowin'." He hadn't seen King, who was standing in the shadows behind Serena.

"You didn't hear what I said," Serena corrected. "My father's dead. You can't tell me what to do or dismiss me! And let me be the first to tell you that everyone already knows about you and the schoolteacher! How do you think I found your little nest?"

"You gettin' powerful smart. You better watch yo'self. You just might get a smack like you deserve!"

"If I deserve a smack, what do you deserve, adulterer?"

Charles started toward Serena. "Now, I just about had enough—"

King moved out of the shadows for the first time and Charles nearly had a seizure of fear. "What was you going to do, Mr. Baddeaux?" King asked easily. "Was you gon' smack her good like this?" King feinted as if to hit Charles and Charles fell to the ground, trying to escape the antici-pated blow.

"He's not Mr. Baddeaux," Serena laughed. "He's just Charles the Adul-terer. Ain't that right, Charlie?"

"You shamin' me, Serena," Charles said as he picked himself off the floor.

Serena spat back, "It's what you deserve!"

"You shouldn't be sassin' yo' own father like—"

"When are you going to get through your thick skull, my father's dead. He's as dead as Mama. You just look like him. As a matter of fact, you got things in reverse: your soul is dead but your corpse keeps on living. Should be the other way around." Serena walked around her father and asked, "Where's your girlfriend, Charles?" Serena continued on past the bales of hay. "Oh, there you are. Come on out, schoolteacher. I want to see what makes you so all-fired desirable. Come out or I'll bring you out!"

Eunice Marshall stepped from behind the bales of hay. She was a small-boned, caramel-skinned woman in her midtwenties who wore her thick black hair in a long continuous braid that fell straight down her back. "I'm deeply sorry about your mother," Eunice began.

"Deeply sorry?" challenged Serena. "When exactly did you begin to feel so deeply sorry for my mother?"

"I knew it was wrong from the beginning," Eunice explained. "I was just so lonely and your, your . . . I'm so sorry. Please forgive me."

"Your being sorry doesn't stop the pain you caused," Serena answered as she walked around behind Eunice. "You're going to have to pay just like Charles will have to pay."

"What do you mean?" asked Eunice with obvious concern. "I can't erase what's been done. All I can do is have no further contact with Char . . . uh, Mr. Baddeaux."

Serena pulled a knife from the waistband of her skirt. "You can do more! You can share in the shame that you and this fool have brought on my family!" Upon saying those words, Serena rushed Eunice from behind and grabbed her braid, yanking her to the ground. Serena's knife flashed in the lantern light.

Charles screamed out, "No, don't kill her!"

Eunice screamed as well. "Please. Please, don't hurt me!"

Serena's knife swept down in an arc and severed Eunice's braid at the base of her skull. Serena stood up with the braid in her hand and said, "I'm going to nail this up at the general store with a note! You sure won't be able to show yourself around here for a while."

Serena turned and faced her father. "You're lucky I don't cut off something of yours! Your punishment is that you can't come to the farm until after Mama's buried, so that everyone will know that you were caught in the act. By then, I'll be gone."

"What about my clothes and my tools?" Charles asked.

"You'll have to make do, won't you?" Serena retorted lightly. Then her voice turned cold. "If I see you around the house before I leave I'll shoot to kill. You do recollect that I am a very good shot, don't you?"

Charles Baddeaux swallowed his anger. The reputation he had worked so long to build was to be destroyed with no more thought than that needed to swat a fly. His whole life lay on the brink of ruin and for what? All because of his headstrong daughter and a useless, street-life do-nothing. He wished that he had the skills to do battle with King, but Charles knew that he was no match for him. King's reputation as a man of violence was well known. He stared at the two people who had ripped his world asunder and wondered how he might return the favor.

Sheriff Corlis Mack stood on one of the small private balconies of the Lafayette Social Club and stared out at the rolling gray clouds that churned slowly across the overcast sky. A breeze filled with moisture came off the gulf, promising rain and perhaps even a late-season hurricane. The broad, sloping lawns of the club stretched to groves of acacia and cedar, which hid the high walls of the club. The Lafayette Social Club was exclusive and its walls insured that the members would be undisturbed by unsolicited interruptions. He took out his old briar pipe and tamped down fresh tobacco, which he took out of an oilskin pouch. He turned his back to the wind and lighted his pipe.

"Oh, Corlis, you're not going to smoke that terrible thing here during our lunch?" The high-pitched, plaintive tones of his wife annoyed him. Sometimes he wondered why he had married her. The beauty that he had so treasured in their first years of marriage had fallen victim to gravity. The bearing of three children had contributed to the overall disintegration of her sagging flesh, but she had done nothing to forestall her eroding looks except to complain and retire to her room for long periods, suffering from her own version of hypochondria.

"Corlis, we have guests. That dreadful smell is blowing this way. Isn't it dreadful, Hermina? I just don't know how men can stand the awful smell of tobacco." Hermina was her cousin from Baton Rouge who was visiting to ask a favor for her no-account husband.

Corlis returned to the table and looked at the three women who were sitting there. Hermina had brought her sixteen-year-old daughter with her. "How much do you need this time, Hermina?" Corlis asked bruskly.

"Corlis!" his wife protested. "There's a child at the table! Can't we just finish our lunch and discuss these other matters in private?" Corlis gave his wife a withering look, which caused her to lose her fragile sense of propriety. She began to stutter under the intensity of his gaze and started her usual, nervous pattern of half-completed thoughts, "I, I, I ju-just thought may-may-maybe—The-the-there's a chi-child—Thi-thi-this is adult bu-bu-business." Corlis puffed on his pipe and stared at her until she lapsed into silence.

Corlis instructed his wife in cold tones, "Daisy, take Sue Anne to the powder room."

Daisy looked at Sue Anne and started to protest but thought better of it. She rose and offered her hand to Sue Anne. "Let's go, dear."

Corlis studied Sue Anne's body as she left the table with his wife. It looked like the girl had inherited her mother's voluptuous figure. He nodded appreciatively and then sat next to her mother. He clamped the pipe between his teeth and put his hand high on Hermina's thigh and asked, "Now, what do you want?"

Hermina looked around anxiously to see if anyone was watching. "Please, Corlis," she begged. "We're in a public place. Somebody might—"

"Nobody can see shit!" he interrupted. "That's why I chose this table. Now, what kind of assistance do you need?" His hand slid along her thigh toward her pelvis.

Hermina was unable to concentrate on his question. "What if Daisy and Sue Anne come back?" she asked worriedly.

"Daisy knows better than to bring her back right away," Corlis said with a humorless chuckle. "Now what has your asshole husband done now?"

"He's run up a lot of gambling debts." Hermina put her hand lightly over his and asked, "Please can we talk about this in a more private place? I feel uncomfortable talking about this embarrassment in public."

Corlis removed his hand and sat back. He took the pipe out his mouth and said, "There's a price to be paid, if I decide to help you out of your difficulties. If you don't want to pay the price, then pack your bags and head on back to Baton Rouge."

"Please, Corlis, this is so embarrassing. Isn't there some other way I can repay—"

Corlis stood up. "Best get to packing this evening, Hermina, so you're ready for the morning train," he advised.

She put her hand to her mouth. "Please don't send me home! We'll lose our house. I'll do anything you say."

"Good," he answered with a nod of his head. "Come to my study at ten o'clock tonight. Don't wear anything under your robe." Hermina nodded mutely and stared down into her lap. "Tell my wife that I've returned to my office and I'll be late for dinner."

Corlis left the balcony heading inside, but stopped and saw the silhouette of his reflection against the large glass-paned doors that opened onto the mezzanine. He smiled a little at the memory of when, twenty years ago, he had first stood before these doors with a full head of hair and the muscular physique to sweep women off their feet, and how little success he had achieving his sexual desires. And now that he was balding and getting decidedly pear-shaped, he was able to accomplish his objectives with a much higher percentage of success. His smile broadened. He really enjoyed the exercise of power and all of its attendant trappings.

He walked through the doors and went to the railing, which overlooked the first floor and reception desk. As he stood looking down to see which members were present, his smile vanished. There below him, wearing a suit and tie, was Roy Wilcox. Corlis knew that he was not a member. Corlis watched as Wilcox handed a card to the maître d', who glanced at it and waved him through to the restaurant, which was located in a corner of the mezzanine. Wilcox was looking for someone and it was not a friend. Neither his demeanor nor his facial expressions indicated that he was in pursuit of pleasure. Corlis stepped back from the railing and stood behind one of the decorative screens used to conceal dirty dishes left there for pickup by kitchen staff. He stuck his pipe into his jacket pocket and waited.

While Corlis was standing there, one of the colored waiters brought over some dirty dishes he had collected. He stopped in surprise at seeing Corlis and set his dishes down very gingerly. Corlis gestured him to silence and peered out from behind the screen. Wilcox was walking past the restaurant entrance and ascending the stairs leading up to the billiard room and members' lounge. Roy was very uncomfortable in his suit. He kept pulling at his clothes as if they were restricting his movement.

Corlis directed the waiter to go and find out who Wilcox was looking for, although he felt he already knew. His intuition told him that Wilcox was there to kill him. If Wilcox was not there to meet someone for a late lunch, there was no other reason for him to be on the club grounds. Corlis watched as the waiter hurried up the stairs after Wilcox. The waiter caught him near the top of the staircase. A few brief words were exchanged between the men and then Wilcox, without warning, knocked the waiter to his knees and continued on his way.

When the waiter returned with his lip bleeding, Corlis demanded to know what Wilcox had said. "Well, suh, he didn't like no colored man askin' him 'bout nothin'," the waiter said, dabbing the blood off his lip with a grimy handkerchief.

"He didn't say who he was looking for?" Corlis questioned.

"Naw, suh. Leastways, he didn't say no names to me."

Corlis ordered, "I want you to find Captain Hennesy and Captain LeGrande. Do you know who they are?" The waiter nodded. "Good," continued Corlis. "Find them and tell them to meet me in the director's library right away. Tell them it's police business and they should bring their guns! You got that?"

"Yes, suh."

"Good. What's your name, boy?"

"It be Willis, suh. Willis Markham."

"Okay, Willis, go get them!"

Corlis went down a staff hallway, past the linen closets and pantry to the service stairs, and descended to the floor below. He was waiting in the library when his two captains arrived. LeGrande arrived first. He was a short, muscular man with a swarthy complexion and dark, curly hair.

"What it is?" LeGrande asked in his Cajun accent.

"I think I've spotted someone who is here to try and kill me," Corlis answered.

Hennesy entered as LeGrande asked, "Who is this man?"

A brief recap brought Hennesy up to speed. Then Corlis explained, "I want Wilcox brought here with as little disruption as possible. I don't want anyone to know that he's been brought here either. I want to resolve this with as little fuss as possible. Willis Markham, one of the nigger waiters, can point him out to you, if you think you'll have trouble recognizing him."

A plan had formed in Corlis's mind causing him to smile at how well all the ends would be tied together. He scraped his pipe, filled it with more tobacco, and touched a match to it. Once he had puffed the briar to life, he sat in a wing chair and waited patiently. He had no concerns about his captains accomplishing the task set for them. They were both good policemen and also were extremely loyal to him, for they had been with him on the posse when he killed Bordeaux Tremain.

Twenty minutes passed before the door opened and Wilcox was shoved roughly into the room. Wilcox turned to snarl, but LeGrande swatted him with the butt of his gun and Wilcox fell to his knees.

"Search him," Corlis ordered, and put his pipe away. Wilcox was dragged to his feet and his jacket was torn off. All the items in his pockets were placed on the table next to Corlis, including a large revolver.

"Here's his pass. It's signed by Frank Loebels," Hennesy said as he handed the paper to Corlis. He took the pass and examined it. Corlis knew that Loebels was out of town on a fishing trip. The perfect alibi, but Corlis also knew that Loebels would never return from fishing; he would fall off the boat at the appropriate time. No one would ever know that he had been pushed.

Wilcox had recuperated sufficiently from his smack on the head to threaten, "You better watch how you treat me! The Klan ain't gon' stand fo' you to be beatin' on the Grand Titan!"

Because he was Catholic, LeGrande hated the Klan and he was not intimidated by threats. "You got to remember that the Papists have a heavy hand too, eh?" LeGrande laughed as he hit Wilcox on the back of the head again with the butt of his gun. Wilcox fell heavily to the floor a second time and lay there several minutes before stirring.

"Find that nigger waiter named Willis Markham and bring him here," Corlis directed Hennesy, who nodded and departed. Corlis picked up the revolver and spun the cylinder. The gun was fully loaded. He set the gun back on the table and smiled.

Willis Markham entered the room after Hennesy. "Yes, suh, you want somethin', Sheriff Mack?"

Corlis asked LeGrande and Hennesy, "Would you boys mind stepping out of the room for a minute?" They each gave him a questioning look. "I'll be alright," he assured them and pulled back his jacket to reveal the butt of his own revolver. His two captains walked out and shut the door behind them.

Corlis turned to the waiter and asked, "Do you remember this man, Willis? He's a big man in the Klan. Do you remember him?"

The waiter was uncomfortable, but he answered the question. "Yes, suh. He the one you sent me after."

"Did you like it when he hit you in the face?"

The waiter's discomfort grew noticeably with each passing second. He did not know the correct answer to the question. In his world, in which he was largely helpless to control his level and station in society, important questions asked by the whites rarely had correct answers based upon facts or truth. In the white man's world, the colored man's correct answers had to do with timing and context, not substance.

"Is it that hard a question, boy? I'm getting the distinct impression that maybe you liked being smacked in the face! Do you like it?"

"No, suh. I ain't got no desire for that!" Willis answered in an even voice. He maintained an iron-fisted control over his fear and struggled to keep the nervousness out of his words and actions. He was a colored man in Louisiana in a room alone with the sheriff and a Ku Kluxer man who had been roughed up. Every sense that he had developed in twenty-eight years screamed danger. "I just didn't want to be disrespectful, suh," he attempted to explain. "I didn't want you to think I fo'got my place, suh."

"Willis, you're a good boy. That's why I called you in here. I wanted to give you an opportunity that no other colored man has ever had. This man hit you in the face while you were simply carrying out my directions. You didn't do anything to deserve that treatment, did you?"

The first easy question of the interview. Willis almost smiled. "No, suh. That's the truth, suh. I ain't done nothin' what deserve a beatin'. I was duly respectful all the time."

"That's the reason I'm going to give you a chance to get even with this bully. I want you to know this man killed colored women and children as easily as he killed their men. You'd be doing your people a service if you killed him. Really, it would be a service to the whole community. As a matter of fact, see that gun on the table?"

Willis looked at Corlis, then at the gun, then once more back to Corlis. Fear was now evident on his face. He began to back away. "This ain't no place fo' a colored man. Please, suh, I'll just go back to cleanin' them tables."

"Are you a man? Don't you have any pride? Don't you know you have to earn respect? This is one of the night riders who have been burning and killing in Possum Hollow. Are you willing to let him go on, or will you stop him?" Corlis challenged, "Pick up the gun! Hold it in your hands and feel its weight!"

Willis edged backward, "Please, suh, I ain't done nothin' to deserve this. Please, suh, can I just get back to my job?"

"Pick up the gun, nigger!"

With the introduction of that word, the disguise had been dropped. Nonetheless, Willis was totally unclear as to who was the most evil between Wilcox and the sheriff, but he did realize that he was trapped. There was no way to back out. He could only continue forward. He walked over to the table and picked up the revolver. He held it with the barrel pointing to the floor and explained, "I don't know nothin' 'bout handguns, suh."

"Feel its weight in your hands, the heaviness," Corlis urged. "Break it open and check that it is fully loaded. All you have to do is point it and pull the trigger. It's a double-action revolver. You have an instrument of death in your hands, Willis."

Wilcox groaned and sat up slowly, holding his head. It took him several seconds before he became aware of the other two men in the room. When he saw that Willis had a gun in his hand, he blurted out, "What's the nigger doin' with a gun?"

"He's going to kill you, like you were going to kill me," Corlis chuckled.

Wilcox looked at Corlis. "You know, huh?" Corlis nodded in response. Wilcox paused, then asked another question. "Kaiser told you, huh?" Corlis nodded in response again. Wilcox snarled. "I figgered he might tell, so I set something up fo' him too. So, if you don't let me go, he dies."

"I don't care about your threats," Corlis answered and then turned to Willis. "Kill him, Markham!" he ordered.

"Please, suh," begged Willis. "I don't want to take no white man's life, please, suh!"

"If you don't kill him, I'll have to shoot both of you," Corlis advised him, patting his holstered gun. "I'll kill you for trying to help him to escape. Now, kill him!"

Wilcox slowly got to his feet as Willis watched. "Give me that gun, nigger!" Wilcox commanded.

"Better shoot him now," Corlis said with a grin.

Wilcox staggered unsteadily toward Willis. "Give me the gun, nigger!"

Willis fired two shots into Wilcox, causing his body to jerk and tremble with the impact of the slugs. Wilcox fell backward and hit the floor with a loud thump. At the sound of the shots, Hennesy and LeGrande charged into the room, but Corlis stayed their entrance with a gesture and waved them out. Once they were alone again, Corlis ordered Willis to put another bullet into Wilcox's twitching body.

After the third shot had been fired, Corlis walked over to Willis, who was standing transfixed, staring at the smoking gun in his hand. Corlis took out a handkerchief and told him to place the gun in it. Upon receipt of the weapon, Corlis said, "You can go now, but for one thing. If anyone asks you, you tell them you saw me lying dead on the floor in here. You follow?"

Willis nodded glumly, then stared around the room and finally ended looking at Wilcox's body. "What about all this?" he asked.

"Well," began Corlis with a jovial smile, "you just killed the Grand Titan of the local klavern. Your fingerprints are on the gun that killed him. It seems to me, you better start treating me pretty nice and keeping my little secret, unless you want this information to fall into the wrong hands. If you do as I say, you got a pretty good chance in living a long and useful life."

As if he couldn't believe the level of bad luck which had befallen him, Willis asked, "Did I do somethin' to make you treat me like this, suh?"

"What?" Corlis snapped, not comprehending his question. Then as its reasoning occurred to him, he said with impatience, "Nigger, get out of my face before I decide I don't need you!"

Willis backed out of the room and left without a word.

Hennesy and LeGrande entered and took a look around. "How do you want to handle it?" Hennesy asked.

"We'll call it a double murder, but without suspects. If we get too much pressure, we can always turn the nigger over. I want to be dead for at least a week. That should give me time to find out who was involved and whether my friend Harley was in on it. I want a hearse here in fifteen minutes and I want you to treat this as a formal investigative case. Conduct some public interviews. Give the press as little information as possible. Interview that nigger waiter too, but you better prep him first. Don't allow anyone else in here until you get me out of here. I'll call the mayor when I get home. You need more particulars?"

Neither of his captains needed further direction. The two men hurried out to begin what was to be a very interesting week. Corlis smiled and thought about the fates that had allowed him to discover that Kaiser had known about Wilcox's assassination attempt. Obviously, Kaiser's relationship with his uncle was stronger than Corlis had previously thought. As he took his pipe out and relit it, Corlis hoped that Wilcox's threat against Kaiser would be carried out. If not, he would make his own arrangements. Kaiser would become part of the history and lore of the department in less than a week, long before news of his uncle's demise surfaced. Corlis would make sure of that.

WEDNESDAY, OCTOBER 13, 1920

King was sitting down to an afternoon game of Kotch with a few of his gambling buddies in one of the side rooms at the Hotel Toussant when Sampson came in and signed that there was some news that he should hear. Sampson asked permission to bring someone into the card room. King nodded affirmatively. He hoped the interruption would change his luck for he had already lost several hundred dollars to Jimmy One-Eye and Billy Love. The fourth man at the table, Tank Purvis, had lost even more than King, but he was a professional gambler and took his losses in stride.

Sampson returned with Jack Little, a trumpeter in the Red Rooster's ragtime band. Ordinarily, King would have had little to do with Jack because the man refused to call himself colored, but instead referred to himself as a Creole. King had little respect for light-skinned men who refused to recognize their heritage and thought themselves better than their dark brothers due to the lightness of their skin. The army had taught King convincingly that if you had Negro blood, you were going to be treated like a second-class citizen by the white world, no matter how light your skin.

"I need a drink," Jack said breathlessly. "Storyville is going crazy!"

King gestured to a bottle of Irish whiskey sitting on a side table. Jack went over, quickly poured himself two big shots, and gulped them down.

He looked appreciatively at the label on the bottle and said, "This is the real stuff! It sure beats corn liquor!"

"You got somethin' to tell us?" King urged.

"Yeah, man; it's terrible what's happening! Lieutenant Kaiser is down at the Red Rooster right now, breakin' the place up!"

"Why?" Tank demanded. "Them Moses brothers knows how to run a business. They paid protection, didn't they?"

"I don't know about all that, but Kaiser is down there bustin' heads. I think he killed one of the Moses brothers and damned near killed another one. He's sayin' that Sheriff Mack is dead and that he's the new man in town. He's saying he's going to go around to all the establishments where he's been sassed and teach them a lesson about who's boss."

"How long ago did you leave the Rooster?" asked King. The Red Rooster was one of the businesses that King was bootlegging alcohol to and to whom he had promised protection if they bought his product.

"I came here once Lieutenant Kaiser started smackin' folks. He say he ain't leavin' the Red Rooster until it's completely trashed. He say that they ain't ever gon' open up for business again. He even slapped Sister Bornais who was readin' fortunes in the back."

"He gettin' pretty bold to be slappin' Sister Bornais, or my name ain't Jimmy One-Eye. She gon' put a curse on him that'll follow him to his grave."

If it was true that Corlis Mack was dead, King realized that he no longer held anything over Kaiser. He knew that the Hotel Toussant would be an inevitable stop along Kaiser's path of rampage. King stood up and signed to Sampson to go get the rifles. Sampson left immediately. King said with nonchalance to his gambling partners, "Deal me out, boys. I don't want to be sitting here if Kaiser comes here. I donates this bottle to the winner of the hand," King said, setting the Irish whiskey on the card table. "Good luck, boys." King then left the card room without another word and met Sampson at the back door of the hotel. Sampson had several rifles bundled in blankets and a bag filled with bandoliers.

"Let's hit it!" King said as the weapons were dumped in the backseat of the car and Sampson got in behind the wheel. "We want to get on the roof above the Red Rooster before Kaiser leaves." Sampson pulled the car out of the narrow alley that ran behind the hotel and joined the traffic headed downtown toward Storyville.

Outside the front entrance of the Red Rooster, Sister Bornais squatted down and attempted to stanch the flow of blood that was pouring out of a gash in the side of the head of her assistant, Mooja Turner. "Jes' hold on there, Mooja. I'm gon' make you a poultice. You just keep this to yo' head." She took Mooja's hand and put it on the rag she was using to hinder the flow of blood. Her assistant just nodded dazedly, his eyes wandering without ever fixing upon a stationary object. Sister Bornais got up and went over to her mule cart. She was digging through her belongings, searching for her herb charms and fetishes, when Kaiser walked out of the Red Rooster.

When Sister Bornais saw him, she screamed, "I curse you and all yo' chil'rens. By the power of blood and sacrifice you goin' straight to hell!"

Kaiser smiled. "Nigger woman, you better shut your mouth, or I'll slap you down again!" Two of his subordinates walked out of the Red Rooster behind him. Kaiser asked them, "You put the torch to the place?"

"Yes, sirree-bob, and there'll be more than a few barbecued niggers when it's over!" answered one of the men.

"Go get the car, Fred," Kaiser ordered. "We have more business to take care of before this day's over." Fred nodded and trotted off down the street.

"I curse all of you, devils!" Sister Bornais screamed again. She cast some red dust in the direction of the two white men. "You won't forget this day! You gon' regret this 'til you die!"

"You want me to shut her up, Sergeant?" asked his remaining subordinate.

"No, let her scream, Chad," Kaiser advised. Much of his anger and indignation had been spent breaking heads and bones inside the Red Rooster. "She's just another screaming nigger woman. You know you can't stop niggers from screaming." There was an explosion from inside the Red Rooster and smoke began billowing out of the door. People began running from the burning building. The sounds of pandemonium filled the street.

Sister Bornais walked fearlessly toward the two white men and pointed to Kaiser. "There is one who ain't afraid of you! He be King Tremain and he gon' change yo' step! He gon' make you rope like okra and split open like dead fish left on the dock!"

The mention of King's name reawakened Kaiser's anger. He handed his baton to Chad. "Shut that nigger bitch up with this!"

As the man came toward her, smacking the baton in his hand, Sister Bornais pointed to him and shouted, "He gon' change yo' step too. You best leave the side of this Kaiser man! If you stay, you gon' go straight to hell with him!"

The man looked back at Kaiser with a smile and then took a step forward. Kaiser could not be sure of what happened next. All he saw was that his subordinate took a little hop and fell to the pavement. He twitched a moment and then lay still. Kaiser went cautiously over to the body, but he didn't see the bullet holes until it was too late. When he saw blood oozing out of the prone body, he turned to run, but he heard a soft thud and then he noticed he was being driven sideways by a force he was unable to control. Finally, he was able to get his legs beneath him, but he had no balance or sensation. He looked down and saw with surprise that blood was flowing from a hole in his rib cage. When the second shot hit him and knocked him over backward, he was barely conscious. The last thing he saw was Sister Bornais standing over him throwing more dust.

The first drops of rain began to fall as King removed the silencer from his rifle and wrapped the weapon back in its blanket. He stood and walked to the stairs leading down to the street. Sampson was behind the wheel when King reached the car. As they drove off, all King said was, "Good shot."

SATURDAY, OCTOBER 16, 1920

The burial service was held on Pine Knoll about a half mile from the church just outside of Nellum's Crossing. The family and the well-wishers convened at the church at eleven in the morning and had open-casket until half past one. The clapboard church was small and could not contain all who chose to attend, so people congregated in small groups outside the church, awaiting their turn to view the casket. Brother Jordan was at the piano playing a slow, rocking Baptist hymn as the people filed past the body. The notes and chords of the piano surged and pulsed harmonically with the emotions of the mourners. The music had a hypnotic quality that caused many of the people filing past to move to its swaying beat.

The first three or four center rows of pews were reserved for immediate family and close friends; the side pews were for the elderly or sick. Charles Baddeaux was conspicuously absent and his whereabouts were the subject of many different discussions. Serena and her siblings sat in the first row with two of her aunts on either side. Behind them sat an assortment of other aunts, uncles, and cousins.

Serena, dressed in black, sat stiffly facing the coffin. She did not turn or attempt to make contact with the mourners who passed in front to view the body. Her eyes were focused on the polished wooden coffin in which her mother rested. It had occurred to her that in the time after her mother's passing, she had not had time to really mourn or say good-bye. The church was not the place to let loose her grief. There were too many eyes and jabbering mouths. Serena kept her back stiff and held herself straight in the pew. She had decided when she nailed Eunice's braid to the post that she wouldn't give the people of Nellum's Crossing anything else to talk about. The girl that Serena had been was gone and in her place was a woman hardened by shame.

It was the custom in semitropical Louisiana to bury the dead as soon as possible. Therefore the service for Serena's mother was scheduled five days after her death. This delay allowed all the appropriate family members to convene and gave the local mortician ample time to perform his art. The funeral occurred on a Saturday, the first day of sun after the rainstorm. The ground was still wet and muddy, but that didn't prevent people all around the parish from attending. Rebecca Baddeaux had served for many years as a reliable backup to the parish's main midwife, Old Mayra Bedford, so she was well known and liked. Interest in the event was heightened further when the news spread through the community like wildfire about Serena nailing Eunice's braid to the general store's front porch post. In days the details of the whole affair were common knowledge. And when one added the ominous presence of King to the social mix of events, the funeral became the event to attend.

Serena's two aunts, Ida and Beulah, Beulah being her father's sister, had arrived the day after they received Serena's telegraphed messages. They immediately assumed control of the household and began to see that the younger children ate regularly and were washed and ready for visitors. They were both women in their midforties who had assisted with many funerals, and they knew the track. Death was commonplace in the colored community for there was little medical attention and few people lived past fifty. Without apparent discussion, the two women divided up the tasks and set about doing them.

Serena had her mettle tested two days before the funeral when Charles Baddeaux drove up to the farm in the buggy in an effort to resume residence. It was in the late afternoon, after King had ridden back to Algiers. The sky was overcast with dark gray clouds and the rain fell in sporadic torrents that lasted for twenty minutes, then abated. It was during such a torrential outburst that Charles pulled up to the back of the house. While he was getting down from the buggy, Ida and Beulah stepped out on the back porch.

"Ain't no needin' of you gettin' out yo' buggy. We had enough visitors today," Aunt Ida said gruffly.

"I ain't no visitor. This is my house," Charles said as he tethered the mule to the railing that ran parallel to the porch. "I done come home to take my rightful place."

"Yo' rightful place is where you's going in the hereafter," Ida pointed downward emphatically with a finger. "You ain't got no place here!"

Charles looked up to the porch, rainwater pouring off his hat. "You ain't got no right to judge me! You don't know what I been through! I don't have to answer to you!"

"You have to answer to God!" Beulah declared in a loud, indignant voice. "You've broken his commandments and soiled your home with the taint of temptation!"

"Ah, Beulah, whose side is you on?" Charles said as he mounted the stairs to the porch. "You know how hard I worked to keep this place. Ain't no legal way to keep me from my home!"

The front door swung open and Serena stood there with the lever-action Winchester pointed directly at Charles. She cocked the gun and stood silently.

Charles paused, momentarily disconcerted, then regained his composure. He turned to Beulah and said, "Find Amos and have him put Homer in the barn."

"Have you gotten down on your knees and prayed to God for forgiveness?" Beulah demanded, pointing her finger at him.

"Beulah, I's soaking wet. I just wants to change my clothes and sit by my fire. I ain't got time to spend talkin' with you 'bout my 'lationship with God. Now, excuse me." Charles turned to face Serena, who had not moved. "Put down that gun, girl, and maybe I'll give you 'nother chance. There's still a family here to take care of."

Serena shook her head. "You give me another chance?" she challenged sarcastically. "Like it was me who was found doing it in a barn!"

"You ain't gon' shoot me! And I had just 'bout enough of yo' sass. Put down the gun befo' I gets real mad!" Charles took two steps toward Serena. He never got any further. The blast from the gun boomed deafeningly in the confined space of the house. Charles felt the passage of the bullet as it creased the top of his head and blew his hat out into the middle of the yard. The heated discharge from the gun hit him full in the face, driving him backward off the porch. He fell in the mud at the bottom of the stairs.

"My God, child," was all Beulah could say as she looked at Serena with shock. "That was yo' daddy!" Beulah rushed down the stairs into the rain and stooped beside the sprawled form.

"He's not my father," Serena said in a toneless voice. "My father died a long time ago."

"You didn't intend to shoot him, did you, honey?" Ida asked, her face a furrowed pattern of concern. " 'Cause no matter what he done, he's still yo' blood."

"He isn't hurt, Aunt Ida, unless he broke something when he fell off the porch. I just grazed him."

"Did you see her? Did you see her, Beulah?" Charles raved angrily, rubbing his eyes. "She tried to kill me, her own father! By the grace of God, I was saved!"

"If I had wanted to shoot you, I could have," Serena asserted. "If you believe that God saved you, why don't you try to come up these stairs again."

"Watch yo'self!" Beulah warned Serena. "You don't want to blaspheme against the power of the Lord!"

"Let her talk," Charles countered, wiping the mud from his face. "You'll see, she's got the devil in her and she'll do his bidding."

"If I've got the devil in me and I'm not a liar and an adulterer like you, what have you got inside of you?" Serena demanded.

"I'm gon' to get the law. I'll show you that you can't throw a man off his farm!" Charles turned and went to pick up his hat in the middle of the yard.

Serena cocked the rifle and fired a shot into the hat, which flew several feet further out into the muddy yard. "That's just to show you that my aim is still true," Serena declared. "So don't even try to stand with the family at the funeral!"

Charles threw up his hands and decided not to chase his hat. He untethered Homer and climbed into the buggy. "I'll be back," he called over his shoulder. "I ain't finished yet!"

In accordance with Serena's wishes, Charles did not return to the farm until after the funeral. His threat to get the sheriff was empty because Charles had no desire to have it commonly known that his seventeen-year-old daughter had shot his hat off and driven him from his land.

The planning for the funeral proceeded. Assistance came from many members of the church and all the neighbors around pitched in, as was normal for the community of Nellum's Crossing. Several neighboring white families brought casseroles and participated in the setting up of the canvas tarp between the barn and the house. The tarp was intended to provide cover from the rain for the people who dropped by after the service to offer their condolences. The passing of a midwife, colored or not, was an event mourned by the whole community without regard to race.

As Serena sat in the packed church, all the events of the past few days seemed like something out of a dream. She felt a great distance from everything. The people passing in front of the coffin and those who stood around the edge of the church staring at her and whispering all seemed like paper dolls animated by dust devils, just pieces of debris spinning in circles until the wind released them.

Promptly at one-thirty Aunt Beulah stood up, indicating that it was now time for the family to make its way to the cemetery. She gave a few whispered orders, directing her squad of assistants to their preordained tasks, and began marshaling the family toward the exit.

Most of the mourners walked the half mile from the church to the grave site, but King had arranged for a hearse and a limousine for the immediate family, an unheard-of luxury for country colored folks. Since there were no paved roads in the immediate area, King had to also make sure beforehand that the automobiles could make it from the church to Pine Knoll without getting stuck in the mud. He and Sampson were standing by the limousine talking with the chauffeur about the route when Serena came up to him and took his arm.

The chauffeur, a short, stocky, brown-skinned man, took off his hat and said to Serena, "Mighty fine service, ma'am." Serena nodded in acknowledgment and leaned against King. The chauffeur recognized that his presence was not needed and found that the other side of the car needed polishing. Sampson walked ahead along the designated route, in order to guide the vehicles.

"I want you to stay close to me," Serena said, looking up into King's eyes.

"No problem," King answered easily. "Have you told any of your family that you ain't buryin' your mother in the plot that your daddy bought?"

"No. It was my decision and I made it. I'm sure that she couldn't have rested peacefully in anything that Charles Baddeaux bought."

Their conversation was interrupted by Aunt Beulah, who was herding the children and Aunt Ida to the car. After everyone was seated inside, the limousine drove slowly through the trees to the cemetery. King stayed behind to make sure that the pallbearers had sufficient help to get the coffin into the hearse.

The actual burial service was quite short, but there were two incidents that stayed in Serena's mind. Just before the casket was lowered into the ground, Charles Baddeaux pushed through the surrounding crowd of onlookers and looked directly at Serena. He had a small bouquet of flowers in his hand. There was a tremendous look of sadness and yearning on his face. He looked from Serena to Ida to Beulah and back again. It was obvious to all that he wanted to take his place with the family.

Beulah moved to make room for him to stand beside her, but Serena stepped into the space and shook her head. Serena saw that Charles was not looking at her but staring over her shoulder. She turned and saw that King was standing directly behind her. King merely gave Charles a threatening stare. Charles placed the bouquet on top of the casket and then walked away. A corridor through the mourners opened silently for him and everyone stood still until he was lost among the tombstones.

The second incident occurred when the family returned to the limousine. Everyone boarded but Beulah. She waited until all were seated and then said coldly, "If the whole family is not allowed to stand by the graveside, then I don't want to ride. The New Testament say, '. . . if ye forgive men their trespasses, your heavenly Father will also forgive you: But if ye forgive not men their trespasses, neither will your Father forgive your trespasses.'" Beulah paused, staring at Serena, then said, "'Vengeance is mine,' sayeth the Lord!"

As far as Serena was concerned, the rest of the day passed in a blur of pots and pans and faces offering condolences. Once she returned to the farm, she did not leave the kitchen until the last guest was gone. She felt absolutely spent and had no desire to talk with anyone other than King.

It was just before sunset and there was a golden tint on the green rolling hills that surrounded the dark brown furrows of the tilled fields. There was a large, grassy meadow alongside the tilled fields that seemed to capture the waning sunlight on each blade of grass, creating a moving mosaic of green and yellow. It was a beautiful and peaceful scene and had no relation to the angst that Serena felt. She was standing with King near the fence that ran behind the barn.

"I've got to leave here and say good-bye to everything that I've known," Serena spoke with sadness. "It seems so unfair. I've committed no crime, yet I have to leave."

"What about your brother and your sisters?" King asked.

"Aunt Ida has said that she'd stay if it was alright with Charles."

King put his foot on the lower fence railing. "Is Beulah going to stay too?"

"I don't know. She hasn't really talked to me since I shot her brother's hat off on Thursday."

"You is one stubborn woman. You gon' drive this point off the cliff, ain't you?"

"What do you mean?"

"You made yo' point when you nailed the schoolteacher's hair up at the store. All this stuff about your father being dead is weak. It sounds like the way white people think, like you just gon' imagine someone to death! Long as you got some of Baddeaux's blood and bone, you gon' be his child and he gon' be yo' father. Colored people is gon' know yo' father's alive as long as that man's breathin'."

"His fathering was hard and always came with a heavy, righteous hand. Now that he has truly revealed himself, I'm not giving him that recognition. And I plan to continue on saying he's dead."

King gave her a long look. "Sometimes you gots to weigh your decisions. For example, if you got to walk through a bitin' dog's yard, it's better to throw him a piece of meat or shoot him than beat him off with a stick, 'cause one day you ain't gon' have that stick and he's gon' get past your guard." King lit a cheroot, then continued. "Yo' daddy is the same way. He's like a mean dog. He just wants to sink his teeth into you. He don't care if you in his yard or not."

"I don't ever plan to drop my stick."

"Maybe that'll work, maybe it won't. It sort of depends where you planning to go when you leave here."

Serena sighed. "I can always go work in Black Jack Shannon's house as a cook."

"That what you want to do?" King asked, staring at her.

"No, I don't want to live on a farm and I don't want to be somebody's servant, but I really don't have much choice unless . . ." Serena's voice trailed off and she gave him a wistful and mysterious look.

"Unless what?" he prompted.

"Unless I can come and live with you?"

King was momentarily speechless. Nothing on his countenance reflected his surprise, for he was a man used to covering his feelings. King let his eyes drift to watching a large red-tailed hawk that was circling slowly overhead. For a moment there was absolute silence: there was no sound of bird or cricket and there was no breeze.

Serena, sensing a reluctance on King's part, began to modify her request anxiously. "I'm sure that I can earn my way if you just help me find a room somewhere reasonable. I won't be a burden, I'll—"

"Whoa! Whoa, woman," King interrupted, raising his hands with his palms facing her. "You asked if you could live with me and the answer is yes. Now, all this other stuff ain't necessary. What we need to talk about is how we gon' live together. As man and wife or what?"

Now it was Serena's turn to be speechless. Tears formed at the edges of her eyes. She was overwhelmed. She rushed into his arms and stood clinging to him. She basked in the warmth of his embrace. She looked up into his eyes. "Are you asking me to marry you?"

King paused before speaking. "Yes, but this ain't the way I planned to do it."

"Just how did you plan to do it?" she asked, pushing away from him.

"Well, I wanted us to get all dressed up and go out to Storyville, have a big, fancy dinner, and maybe listen to some of that new jazz music. I mean make a night of it!"

"When were you planning to ask me?"

King paused and looked down at his feet. "I ain't never felt about anybody the way I feel about you and it's sort of got me all discombobulated. It ain't nothin' I planned and it ain't nothin' that I thought about; it just happened. Generally, I see things pretty clear, but with you ain't nothin' clear! Like you ain't even given me an answer."

Serena smiled, flashing her white teeth. "The answer is yes. I will marry you. But I'm telling you right now, King LeRoi Bordeaux Tremain, I want more out of life than my mother got. I want to live in the city and wear expensive clothes. I want to own a big house and I want lots of children. Most of all, I want a man who loves me and treats me with respect. If you have to see other women, I'm not the one to be your wife."

"You need to understand two things about me," King spoke with gravity. "First, ain't nobody care mo' about family than me! I was abandoned by my own family when I was seventeen. For a long time the army was my family. I spent a lot of years thinkin' about what I missed and what I wants in a family. Now, I's ready to start my own. I wants to be the head of a house full of strong sons and daughters, but mostly I wants sons.

"Second thing is, my word is my bond. I'll die before I go back on my word. If I say I'll marry you and be faithful to you, you ain't got to worry about other women. 'Course there're a lot of dead marriages around where everybody's faithful, but there ain't no heart or passion. Seems to me if a woman does her part to do her best and a man does his best, there ain't no need for anybody to roam."

"Since we're having this talk," Serena said as she stared up into his eyes, "let me say one other thing. If we get married there's no divorce. I'm only getting married one time and I'll never get a divorce."

"Suits me. I don't see no use in foggin' things up with a lot of legal complications."

"Is that all marriage is to you, a legal complication?"

"Marriage is just a legal way of recognizing what you're supposed to be feeling in yo' heart." King put his big hands on Serena's shoulders and stared into her eyes. "Just for yo' information, there ain't no doubt in my heart."

"Good, because I don't want a halfway Henry bringing pain into my life. I don't want the pain my mother suffered. I'm looking for happiness."

"What'd you say, halfway Henry?" King laughed as he watched the hawk that had been circling high over the meadow peel off into a steep dive. It had sighted its prey. King continued, "I can't promise you happiness, but I can guarantee you some happy times. Happiness depends on your spirit, can't nobody give you that. As for pain, well it seems to me," King gestured in the direction of the hawk as it stabbed down at the earth with its talons and rose slowly with powerful wing strokes, carrying a squirming rodent, "seems to me like pain and death as much a part of livin' as birthin' and laughin'."

They stood in silence and watched as the hawk became a dwindling silhouette in the growing purple of the evening sky. A breeze, originating in the low hills to the west, caused the grasses of the meadow to bow before it like devout supplicants before the messiah. The breeze also brought the smells of livestock and damp, fermenting fodder. It was a strong, penetrating odor for which there was no relief as long as the wind stayed constant.

"Smells like the Piersons didn't keep their hay covered during the rains," King commented knowingly.

Serena said nothing. For her the smell epitomized everything that was wrong with life on a farm; it was an indication of work that had not been done well, as well as the work yet to be completed. It seemed to her that even in a happy family, the endless demands of farming could suck the juice out of life. More than ever she was committed to leaving despite the sorrow that it would cause her in terms of leaving her siblings and the house in which she was born.

The sky was beginning to darken into a deep navy. Only a few stars were visible. The sound of crickets began to dominate the quiet landscape. Serena said quietly, "King, I can handle the pain that comes from natural causes. I just don't want any pain that comes from deceit."

King stuck out his hand and said, "Then we got a contract."

There was no kiss, only a simple handshake between the two of them. There would be rituals later, but they would be purely for form. King and Serena had already sealed their agreement to be husband and wife and only death would cause the agreement to be broken.

Church bells pealed from spires across the cityscape, tolling the eleventh hour of the morning and signaling the commencement of church services. Major William Fulton Harley unlocked the door to his place of business and climbed the narrow stairs to his second-floor office. He was wheezing a bit when he reached the top of the stairs; he reminded himself to get more exercise. He stopped to catch his breath and thought he smelled a trace of tobacco originating somewhere on the second floor.

Harley called out loudly. "Rastus! Rastus! I told you I'd have you whipped if I found you sitting around smoking your pipe on my time!" He headed to his office with indignation. The door opened just as he reached it and Rastus came out carrying a tray with cups and a coffee urn. The smell of tobacco was even stronger with the door open. Harley could not believe that Rastus would be so audacious as to smoke in his office, but the evidence appeared to remove any doubt. Harley raised his hand to slap Rastus across the face, but saw that there were cups of fine china on the tray for which he had paid dearly, and he restrained himself. He brought his hand down and said through gritted teeth, "Find my riding crop! You need a lesson!"

"Suh, I ain't smoked! It was—"

"Don't you try to lie to me, nigger!" Harley shouted. "And don't you say another word or I'll knock the shit out of you! Bedammed the porcelain!" Harley stared at Rastus and the man looked down at the floor and said nothing. "Now, I've tried to work with you. Lord knows I've tried, but this is too much. I'm going to have to call in one of the boys from the klavern to teach you a lesson that you won't forget!"

Rastus quailed noticeably and began to plead. "Please, suh. It weren't me that smo—"

Harley swung and hit Rastus high on the side of the head with his fist. Rastus fell backward, tipping the tray and its contents. Only the presence of a wooden cabinet stopped him from falling to the floor. "Goddamn it," Harley bellowed, holding his hand, which was stinging from the impact with Rastus's head. Harley looked down at the broken porcelain on the floor and shouted, "Look what you've done! You're going to work a long time to repay the cost of what you've broken and it might need to be on a chain gang!" Harley wanted to hit Rastus again, but the stinging pain in his right hand made him think better of it.

"William Fulton, leave that boy alone and come in here so we can talk!" Corlis Mack laughed as he came to the door of the office. His still-smoking pipe was clasped between his teeth.

Harley dropped his jaw. "You're alive!" he said with surprise. "Captain Hennesy said you were dead. What's going on?"

"Let him clean up and get out and we'll talk."

Rastus stooped and began cleaning up the mess on the floor. Harley stared down at him and indicated some small shards with the toe of his boot. "Get those pieces under the bureau too!" Rastus picked up all the pieces obediently and wiped the floor clean of spilled coffee and cream. He stood up and tried to ease past Harley. There was blood oozing from a small cut above his eyebrow.

"Looks like we had a misunderstanding here, Rastus. You don't have to worry, I won't be calling the klavern. Take care of that eye and bring some fresh coffee up, okay, boy?" Harley patted Rastus on the arm and went on into the office, closing the door after him.

Corlis looked at Harley questioningly. "You're not going to apologize?"

"I don't apologize to niggers. I didn't know that you did."

"When they live in your house and have the opportunity to poison you, you got to treat them differently than regular niggers. Rastus has access to many things that could cause your death."

"Rastus?" Harley laughed, indicating that it was foolish to even consider such a thing. "I broke him long ago! He wouldn't dream of lifting a finger against me. He understands our misunderstandings, but hell, man, I don't want to talk about him! I want to know why you are letting it be known that you had been killed."

"Roy Wilcox tried to do me at the Club!"

"What! Not Roy!"

"Yep, I had to kill him. You know I have a cousin who works in the assessor's office? Well, she told me that she saw Wilcox go into Loebels's office on Friday afternoon."

"That must've been after we met!" Harley exclaimed. "I knew he was angry, but I had no idea—"

"Yep, it appears he went straight there after he left you."

Harley's ruddy complexion paled. "You don't think that I was involved, do you?"

"No. There's no benefit to you if I'm dead. As a matter of fact, your deal is greatly jeopardized without me. You see, I have something on the assistant assessor."

"The assistant? What about Loebels? The assistant can't do anything without Loebels's approval."

"Loebels is dead. I received word this morning." Corlis lighted his pipe and puffed it to life again. "If you saw the paper this morning, you'll notice that his nephew, Lieutenant Kaiser, and a deputy were killed on the edge of Storyville yesterday afternoon. I guess Wilcox arranged it to cover the contingency of being double-crossed. He seems to have contracted professionals to do the job."

"I don't think he arranged any such thing," Harley said. "I was at Klan headquarters last night. Nobody knew where Roy was and the men he would have used were there working all day yesterday."

"Are you sure?" It was Corlis's turn to be surprised.

"Roy isn't my only contact in the klavern. If he had made such arrangements, I would have heard about it."

"If he didn't kill Kaiser, who did?" Corlis mused. "My men estimate that the killer fired a point thirty-oh-six from at least two hundred yards. Fired four shots and hit the designated targets in the chest with each shot. It was expert shooting."

"We know lots of men who shoot that well," Harley countered.

"Not with moving targets," Corlis said. "One hundred fifty yards at a moving target maybe, but two hundred to two hundred fifty yards? Without a miss? Nope, there's only a few that can do that and even fewer with a motive."

"How do you know there were no misses?"

"Because of the amount of time it took. Kaiser didn't have a chance to run after the deputy was killed. He was cut down within seconds after the deputy. I also had my men search the street for spent bullets. There were none."

"At that range, point thirty-oh-six-caliber bullets should have passed through their bodies."

"That's another thing. My ballistics squad sergeant tells me that the killer cut into the nose of his bullets to make them spread."

"You've really done some research into this case." Harley marveled.

"We're treating this as the murder of police officers in the performance of their duty. And it happened on a street populated with colored businesses. In combination with my alleged murder, this case has all the elements of a political bonfire."

"What was the purpose of having yourself declared dead?"

"I remove the target of the attempts from view and then I have the time to check people out."

"How are you going to come back to life?"

"I'll get myself registered in one of the private hospitals and have my doctor contact the mayor. I'll be recuperating from wounds received from the attack. I'll explain that my injuries incapacitated me to such an extent that my loyal captains took it upon themselves to save my life. They'll get medals. It'll be a big event!"

"What about arresting the real murderers?"

"Well, that brings us back to the tricky issue of who killed Kaiser? You see, I just want Roy Wilcox to disappear. I don't want to try and explain to some of that Klan trash why I had to kill one of their leaders. I also don't want the Klan marauding and taking their vengeance out on innocent niggers. It's bad for business! Night riders scare decent white folks too. People don't buy liquor when they're afraid to walk the streets and we have a couple of very big shipments to move. So, I'd like to find a nice fall guy, but I can't do that until we know who all the players are."

"Don't you have some ideas?"

"Yep, I think I know who attacked the Klan headquarters and he could be the one who killed Kaiser as well. But it's just a guess."

"Who are they?"

"It's one man, if my hunch is correct."

"One man? Is this your supernigger theory?"

"Call it what you want, but when we bring this LeRoi Tremain in, you'll see what I mean. He's the grandson of Bordeaux Tremain. If you remember, about four or five years ago we lost a shipment of guns from the pirates and I lost a couple of deputies."

"I remember, but those men were killed by arrows."

"This Tremain is the one who is supposed to have killed those men. Do you remember me telling you about a sniper who killed all of Lester DuMont's sentries?" Corlis lit his pipe as Harley shook his head, indicating that he didn't remember. "It was sometime in June or thereabouts. About a week after Lester DuMont was killed, we received a call from a colored church just uptown from Storyville that there was a body rotting in the belfry. Now, this church is down the block from DuMont's headquarters. When we investigated, we discovered four other men's deteriorating bodies on the roofs surrounding DuMont's building. The smell and the birds helped us find them. We think we also found where the shooter actually situated himself. Some of the shots were over two hundred yards and they were fired in the darkness of the night."

"If you're right and he's killing police officers—" Harley left his thought unfinished.

"It won't be long until he gets to me," Corlis continued. "We can't have that. I've put out the word to have Tremain picked up. We have to do it without killing him, if we want those deeds."

"How can I hel—" Harley's question was interrupted by the tinkle of porcelain.

Corlis was on his feet instantaneously. "What the hell are you doing, sneaking around?" he demanded of Rastus, who stood trembling by the table where he had placed the tray.

"Nothin', suh. I's just bringin' coffee like the major asked," Rastus replied. His whole body was shaking and he kept his eyes down.

"Look at me!" demanded Corlis. He walked over and stood in front of the smaller Rastus. "How much did you hear?"

"Answer him!" Harley jumped to his feet and grabbed a short wooden pole used for opening the upper windows of his office. He advanced on Rastus, smacking the pole in his hand.

Rastus collapsed to the floor and commenced to plead. "Please, suh, I ain't heard nothin'! I was jes' bringin' coffee! Please don't beat me again! Please, suh. I swears on my momma's grave, I was mindin' my business! Please don't hit me!"

The abject fear and total emasculation of the man caused Corlis to take a step backward. It was then he saw a puddle of liquid forming beneath Rastus.

Corlis was disgusted. He turned away.

Harley shouted at Rastus. "Nigger, the sheriff asked you a question! You better answer!"

"Leave him alone," Corlis said shaking his head. "Can't you see, he's pissing on himself out of fear!"

"What?" demanded Harley, who came closer and saw the puddle. "Goddamn it! You're pissing on my floor!" he shouted at Rastus.

"I's clean it! I's clean it! Please don't whip me!" Rastus tried to wipe up the urine with his pants leg.

"Get him out of here!" Corlis demanded. "He's sickening!"

"What about my floor?" Harley asked. "It'll stain."

"Let him clean it up later! I'll buy you a new one when our ship comes in. Just get him out of here now!"

"You heard the sheriff, get out of here!" Rastus got to his feet slowly and shuffled from the room with lowered head.

Harley turned to Corlis with a big smile on his face. "I told you, I broke him a long, long time ago!

Corlis clamped his pipe in his mouth and grunted. "You ought to be real happy about that."

It was seven o'clock in the morning when King and Sampson heard someone banging on the wrought-iron gates that blocked entry to the large wooden side doors of the old villa. King strapped on his holsters and bid Sampson to get Serena from the kitchen. After the killing of Kaiser, King considered the Hotel Toussant too exposed, plus he now had to take extra precautions because of Serena, so although he still kept a suite at the Toussant, he had moved with Sampson and Serena across the river to the villa on the edge of the canal. Since not many people knew about the villa, King was cautious when he looked out through the peephole in the door.

He saw Claude and Phillip Duryea along with Dr. Washington and another older man he did not know. From his vantage point, he could not see a wide view of the street. So he waited for a signal from Sampson. A low hoot from the third-floor balcony gave the all clear. King opened the door and walked out to unlock the gate. "Wasn't expectin' no visitors," he said tersely.

"We've got some news we think you need to hear," Claude said as he entered the gate, leaning on his cane.

"I guess I needs a doctor too?" King asked as Dr. Washington walked passed him.

Washington immediately turned. "If you don't want me to enter your house, I'll wait in my car."

"It's alright, Doc." King waved him inside. "I was just wonderin' why all you boys felt the need to come for an early mornin' visit." Claude turned to answer, but King waved him to continue on inside. After the men entered the villa, King spent several seconds studying the street for unusual activity. The doors of the livery across the street were opened. King could see the three colored grooms working in the stables, saddling horses for waiting white riders. The warehouse several buildings down the canal already had the colored stevedores loading trucks and ox-drawn wagons. He could hear the rhythmic chant of the men as bags were passed hand to hand. The tannery next to the livery was still closed. It didn't open until eight. Everything seemed normal.

King locked the gate and followed his visitors into the villa. Serena took on the hostess role and seated the men at a large wooden table lo-

cated in the center of a large, covered courtyard. She was introducing herself to Claude and Phillip. "You meetin' my betrothed," King said to the
visitors as he joined them.

At first there was a surprised silence, because it was unexpected news.
King had not shared his intention with anyone outside of Sampson and
Serena. Dr. Washington was the first to respond. "Congratulations, Miss
Baddeaux," he said, reaching across the table to shake her hand. Claude
and Phillip also congratulated the betrothed pair with smiles. The other
visitor merely nodded his head and smiled briefly.

Serena smiled. "Thank you. Would any of you like coffee? I have a pot
brewing on the stove." There was a chorus of affirmatives and Serena departed for the kitchen.

King looked at the visitor who didn't speak and said, "I don't believe I
know this man."

"This is Will Lake," Claude said, putting a hand on the man's shoulder.
"He works as a manservant for Major Harley."

"My peoples calls me Willie," Lake said softly and bobbed his head in
acknowledgment of his introduction. He kept his eyes on the floor and
continuously kneaded a homemade leather hat in his hands.

King saw both fear and indecision in the man and he didn't like it. He
turned to Claude and Phillip. "You brought Harley's man to my house?"
he questioned with an edge on his voice.

"He was working on Sunday morning in Harley's office when Sheriff
Mack arrived to have a meeting," Dr. Washington explained.

King turned on the doctor. "Say what? I heard that Corlis Mack had
been killed. Even one of his lieutenants, Kaiser, thought so. You sho' this
man ain't got bats in his head?"

"It was him," Willie confirmed. "The major was surprised hisself. He
thought the sheriff was dead too. He turn almost pale as a ghost when he
seen him, but it was Sheriff Mack true enough. I ought to know, 'cause I
seen him plenty times befo'. Mostly he come to talk 'bout they liquor business, but this time he come to talk to the major 'bout some deeds fo' Possum Hollow."

King looked at Claude. "You believe him?" he asked, suspicion entering his voice. King turned again to Willie and studied him. The old man
was definitely afraid. It bothered King that the man had been brought to
his private villa. "This what you brought him here to tell me?"

"Go ahead and tell him the rest, Mr. Lake," urged the doctor.

Willie Lake ran a hand over his short, kinky, salt-and-pepper colored
hair and began to speak slowly. "The sheriff say he gon' send some men
'round to pick you up. He say he don't want you kilt, until they finds out

'bout the deeds. The sheriff say he think you the one who kilt Lieutenant
Kaiser and had a hand in killin' some of DuMont's men too."

King stood up and signaled to Sampson to take a look out from the top
of the building. Sampson trotted up the stairs and disappeared. "Any of
y'all check to see if you was followed?" he asked.

"We took precautions," Claude answered. "I'm sure that no one knows
we're here."

King looked at Willie, then at Claude and Phillip. "I appreciates this
warning, but I don't see why you want to bring Harley's man to my house.
You could've told me without him."

" 'Cause I wanted to see you, Mr. Tremain," Willie answered. "I wanted
to see the colored man that got Sheriff Mack scared. I done heard 'bout
you, suh. They say you got Bordeaux's blood. But I heard from colored
folks you's a fair man. So I wanted to talk to you direct. Now, I brought
you somethin', some info'mation that could save yo' life and I wants to ask
you two favors in return."

"What is it?" King asked in clipped tones.

"I needs five hundred dollars!"

The doctor jumped to his feet. "This is absurd. I didn't know you were
doing this for money. I would have never brought you here if I had known
your purpose!"

Willie looked at the doctor and tears welled up in his eyes. "I took
plenty risks to come here. I done humbled myself in all kind of ways in
this hellfire some peoples call life. I even done pissed on myself in front of
the major and Sheriff Mack, pretending I was too scared to talk, just so I
could get here this mo'nin'. But I done it and I done it fo' a purpose. I got
one son. He just been released from a chain gang and it seem like it done
made him madder at everythin' and everybody. He my only man child.
The girls is married and moved away. My boy is the youngest. He all I got
left." Willie stopped speaking for a moment and shrugged. "My life is over.
My wife is dead. There ain't nothin' left fo' me, but I could go to my grave
smilin' if'en he was headed up north somewheres. I knows if he stays
'round here, they gon' kill him. He ain't one of those who can smile at
harsh words and bend with the lash. So I is askin' money fo' him. It be a
grubstake fo' him to start a new life somewheres else."

"What's the second favor you askin' fo'?" King asked.

"I said my life was finished and I means it. I been 'shamed of myself fo'
a long time. I think maybe I's already dead, but I just don't know it. If my
son gets taken care of, I's ready to die now. There ain't nothin' here I
wants to stay fo'. Only one thing," Willie paused and took a deep breath.
"I want to take the major with me. Ain't no reason to leave him here after
all the humblin' I done took from him."

Serena entered with the tray of coffee mugs and set it down on the table. She served the men quietly and then sat down. King saw her dabbing at her eyes and knew she had overheard the discussion.

King smiled at her, took a drink of the hot, dark liquid, and nodded his approval. The words the old man spoke had the ring of truth to King and he had learned to rely upon his gut feelings. He turned to Willie. "I'll give you a thousand dollars. How you want the money?"

WEDNESDAY, OCTOBER 20, 1920

At the hour of sunrise there is a low-lying mist that stretches across the marshlands of Louisiana like a thin gossamer blanket. It brings a cool, wet, tingling sensation when it touches the bare skin. There are patches of land, hillocks, and knolls that rise above the reaches of the mist, and it was on one of these that King had situated himself. He rested in a clump of oleander between two magnolia trees. The sun was a pale yellow disk on the eastern horizon that had not yet burned through the cloud cover. King picked up his rifle and sighted down the barrel. The balcony upon which his target sat was still hidden by the mist, but the sun would soon make its presence felt and would burn away the shrouding haze.

King had been in position for nearly an hour. Mosquitoes and gnats buzzed about his face, but he kept still. Perspiration dripped down the side of his face. His body was tired and sore from the activities of the last evening. He wanted to stretch his legs and rub the soreness out of his joints, but he maintained his position. The key to any ambush was stillness.

Neither he nor Sampson had slept since the night before. The night and early morning hours had been spent raiding Harley and Sheriff Mack's liquor storehouses. Yet King realized that his next actions were the most critical of all. He had to kill Sheriff Mack; otherwise he would be hounded by law enforcement until he was brought to ground. He glanced back through the trees behind him and saw the grove in which the horses were tethered. He knew that Sampson was nearby but could not see him.

He found that whenever he was sitting in a blind or waiting for the enemy to appear, it made the time pass faster if he allowed his mind to travel and roam over the people and events that were impacting his life. He smiled at the fate that had brought Willie Lake to the villa the day before. The old man had turned out to be a treasure trove of information. And when King had challenged him as to how he got his information, the old man explained that there was a flue that connected Harley's office and the kitchen. If there was no fire in the office hearth, every word said in the office could be heard if one stood close enough to the kitchen flue. King had questioned him for more than an hour and that is how he had learned that Corlis Mack was going to have an early morning meeting with his closest captains and lieutenants at the Lafayette Social Club.

The mist was thinning. There were now motionless tendrils of fog where the land had previously been blanketed. King curled the strap of the rifle around his wrist and waited. It appeared that the time was drawing near. He allowed the barrel of the gun to rest on a thick oleander branch and sighted through the scope the hazy outline of the balcony. His concentration had to be unbroken.

Corlis Mack called for another urn of coffee and Willis Markham appeared and quickly refreshed the pot on the table from a pitcher. "Don't splash anything on this table," Corlis warned. "We've got important papers laid out."

"Yes, suh. I'll do my best, suh," Willis said, pouring the hot black liquid slowly to the top of the urn.

"Bring some more of those biscuits and some more jam," Captain Hennesy requested. "LeGrande as usual ate more than his share."

"You must be quick as a cat if you want to enjoy more than one biscuit," LeGrande rejoined, and the table rippled with laughter.

"I want some biscuits too," said one of the lieutenants with a chuckle.

Willis went out and returned with a large, covered straw basket filled with biscuits and a small tureen of jam. After he had placed the items on the table, he asked, "You wants anythin' else, suh? 'Cause otherwise I goes back to ironin's the linen fo' this mo'nin's breakfast."

"No you won't," Corlis countermanded. "You'll stand outside that door and ensure that we won't be interrupted. You know that I don't want anybody to know that I'm here or that I've been here. Have I made myself clear?" Willis nodded his head. Corlis continued, "And I know you'll follow my instructions to the letter because you want to please me, don't you?"

Willis nodded meekly and was backing away from the table when he heard a soft plopping noise. Then he saw Captain Hennesy fall across the table and drop the biscuits he had taken out of the basket. Blood and bits of bone were visible in the large hole in his back. Several of other men at the table stood up in surprise. The man directly across from Sheriff Mack jumped to his feet and was spun around simultaneously with another plopping sound. Inadvertently, the man had saved Corlis Mack's life. His body had obstructed the bullet intended for the sheriff.

After the second bullet, Corlis was on his feet and running heavily for the glass-paned door leading to the safety of the hallway. As he neared the door, the glass pane immediately in front of his face exploded as a bullet smashed through it. The shards of glass flew in all directions, stinging him in the face and blinding him in the left eye. Corlis staggered backward in momentary shock, then headed for the door again. Corlis's leg was knocked from underneath him before he reached the door and he fell to the floor, hitting his head forcefully on the ceramic tile. He lay unconscious, out of King's view and the hail of bullets that killed many of his subordinates.

King slipped his rifle into a leather sleeve and searched for spent bullet casings. He was disgusted with himself. He knew that he had not killed the sheriff. He would now have to leave the state of Louisiana. It was a given that Corlis would leave no stone unturned in pursuit of him. King dropped a hood that he had taken from the klavern headquarters. It had someone's initials on it. The sheriff's men would find it in the process of their investigation. King didn't think that it would throw Corlis off for long, but it would confuse things for a while.

He moved swiftly but without haste through the underbrush toward the horses. Sampson was mounted and holding his horse as he emerged from a thicket. King shook his head and shrugged his shoulders in response to Sampson's silent question. The two men rode off through the trees, knowing that they had at most twenty-four hours to be packed and out of the state.

Willie Lake stood by the flue in the kitchen and smiled. He could hear Major Harley in his office ranting to a sheriff's deputy. The looting of his liquor storehouses had the major in a rage, and the news the deputy brought had done nothing to improve his mood. Willie stepped away from the flue and went to the stove to taste the bubbling soup. It was a thick broth of okra, corn, and shrimp. He ladled out a small bowl and tasted the steaming liquid. He nodded his head in approval. It was among the best that he had ever made. He looked at the large clock over the table and saw that it was fifteen minutes to noon. He knew that the major liked his lunch promptly at twelve. Willie began to prepare the luncheon tray.

Before he went down to the storm cellar to get the wine, Willie stopped by the vent. He could hear the voice of the sheriff's deputy informing Harley that Corlis had been shot and that everything possible was being done to investigate the crime. The deputy told Harley that a

Klan hood had been found at the scene and asked whether he knew any-one with the initials LT. Willie smiled broadly. It was too good to be true. He almost whistled as he descended the stairs to select a bottle of wine.

He chose a bottle of Merlot that had been imported from France. It was the special reserve that Harley kept to impress his most prestigious guests. The opening of such a bottle would anger Harley even further. Upon his return to the kitchen, Willie checked the bread that was baking in the oven. It had risen nicely and possessed a golden crust. Willie de-cided to give it a few more minutes to ensure that it was perfect. Every-thing was almost ready. He looked at his apron and saw that it was stained. He went and pulled out the white satin apron that Harley had him wear at important social events. It was important that Willie look his best. After all, it was going to be a celebration.

The stairs creaked as the deputy descended them, and then Willie heard the front door open and close. Above his head, Willie could hear the sounds of the major pacing back and forth across the wooden floor. Willie busied himself with the tasks necessary to preparing the tray. The bread was removed from the oven. The major's special silver service was laid out on his finest linen. Soup was ladled into a large bowl and placed on the tray. The finest of the crystal goblets was chosen. Willie was slicing the bread when the clock struck twelve noon.

He heard the major walk to the head of the stairs and shout, "Where the hell is my lunch, Rastus? You better get your black ass up here with my food!"

The tray was ready except for the last item. Willie went to the sack in which he carried his personal effects and withdrew the object that King had given to him. He placed it on the tray next to the steaming bowl of soup. When he picked up the tray, the hand grenade rolled into the porce-lain bowl with a clank. Willie wrapped the napkin around it, to keep it in place.

"Rastus, do you hear me? Nigger, I'm talking to you! If you don't get your ass up here with my lunch this minute, there'll be hell to pay!"

"I's comin', suh," Willie answered as he exited the kitchen. He would not even pull the pin until he set down the lunch tray. King had explained the workings and operation of the grenade. All Willie had to do was get within a couple feet of the major and it would be all over. Harley was right, there'd be hell to pay, only it was coming for the major sooner than he thought. "I has yo' food, suh. I's coming! I's coming!" Willie said with a broad smile as he mounted the stairs.

• • •

Serena stood on a small wooden box, swathed in a dress of white satin. It was the most beautiful garment that she had ever seen. The shiny material was smooth and cool to the touch. She could hardly believe that she was wearing such a dress. It really looked like Serena's lifelong dreams would come true. She held her breath and pinched herself, half expecting to wake up on her father's farm. Journer Duryea was kneeling beside her, basting the hem and insuring that the material hung evenly. Martha Mack, a short, plump blonde in her late thirties, was trimming the veil with satin.

"This sho' is a beautiful wedding dress," Journer said as she held a needle between her lips. "We was blessed to find a seamstress with a dress ready-made," she mused as she moved around the hem of the dress, tacking the uneven sections.

"From what Mack tells me, Serena, you young folks is more'n blessed. You got folk who care about you and yo' future's in front of you," Martha observed. "We just got to get you out of the state alive. Corlis is turnin' over the countryside lookin' for Bordeaux! That's why Mack didn't want you all to get married at the mill."

Across the warehouse, in a room that served as the office for Duryea Drayage, sat King, Sampson, Captain Mack, Claude, and Phillip. The men were seated around a scuffed wooden table drinking shots of whiskey.

King raised his glass. "Here's to Will Lake. May he rest in peace."

Phillip raised his glass. "And here's to William Harley, may he burn in hellfire!" The men laughed and downed their alcohol.

Mack raised a glass and said, "To me brother's leg, may it pain him all the way up to his ass!" There was another round of laughter.

"Now, why did you pick Bodie Wells?" Claude asked. "That isn't beyond the reach of Corlis Mack."

"I bettin' that he won't find out that I'm there. If you the only ones that know, shouldn't be no problem. You see, Bodie Wells is close enough fo' me to sneak down here every once in a while and check on my bootleggin' business. You Duryeas should come in with me. Money's comin' in hand over fist. You can buy all the trucks you want after just one year."

"I appreciate the offer, but we'll pass. There's too much gunplay for my blood," Claude said, pouring himself another whiskey. "I still don't see why you're going to Bodie Wells. You could hide in Mississippi or Texas and be closer."

"I'm goin' there 'cause it's a colored town, run by colored folks, and lived in by colored folks. I ain't ever lived anywhere where colored people made the rules without fear of the white man. I want to see what that's like and whether it will make any difference in the way I feel when I get up in the mornin'. Plus, they the only colored town I knows of that gots electricity. After the army, I don't much care for the smell of kerosene lamps. Anyways, I's just plannin' to stay there six months or so 'til I get all the kinks out the bootleggin' business. After that we's on to New York or San Francisco, dependin'."

"Watch yourself," Mack advised. "The only difference between colored people and whites is the whites have the power. If colored folks had the power, the world would be the same; there would be just a different colored people on the bottom."

Serena stepped back up on the box and rubbed the material of the dress between her fingers. "I never wore anything that cost thirty dollars before. I bet my whole wardrobe wouldn't sell for half that."

"And we didn't even pay full fare," Journer added. "Manda was probably gon' sell it to that Mrs. Long fo' a hundred dollars, befo' the woman reneged on her. Yes, you was blessed to get this dress in one day, sho' 'nough."

Serena nodded in agreement. She closed her eyes, clasped her hands together, and sent a silent prayer of thanks. She was really leaving behind the unremitting toil of the farm and she was getting married, married to someone who planned to live in San Francisco. The city's name had a magical sound. It seemed to roll off the tongue. It evoked images of tall buildings, long bridges, and electric lights everywhere. She was so excited, she had trouble standing still. If only her brother and sisters could see her. As soon as she thought of her family, a cloud of doubt and guilt began swirling through her mind like mud stirred up by the rushing of clear water. She would not see her little brother and two younger sisters again for many months. Nor would she be there to help them or represent them before their father's tyranny. She wondered, for what seemed the thousandth time, if she was doing the right thing.

Serena took a deep breath and tried to quiet her internal butterflies. A knock on the door interrupted further introspection. A male voice beyond the door said, "How're you doing in there? The truck's nearly loaded. You folks need to get on the road before eight and it's half passed seven now."

"We're comin', Phillip," Journer called out in response. She stood up and flashed a smile of even white teeth at Serena. She held up a mirror for Serena to see herself. "I know this ain't the way you was thinkin' of gettin' married. It may not be a ceremony made in heaven, but you sho' gon' look like an angel."

"You look beautiful," Martha confirmed.

"You ready?" Journer asked. Serena inhaled deeply and nodded her head.

The three women stepped out of the room into a large, high-ceilinged storage area. Crates and boxes were stacked along one side almost to the roof. Reverend Pendergast was standing on a soapbox in front of King's truck. He had a Bible in his hand and he was wearing a red-and-black church robe. King walked over and stood before him as Claude escorted Serena toward the makeshift altar.

For some reason, the ceremony seemed to blur for Serena. Pendergast's voice seemed far away, as if he was talking in another room. Primarily, all she could hear was the beating of her heart and the rustling of her dress. She remembered turning to King and looking in his eyes and saying, "I do," and she heard him say the same words to her, but all other sounds were muffled. When he slipped the ring on her finger and she saw the jewels twinkling in the pale light of the warehouse, her vision blurred with tears. It was the most beautiful moment she had ever experienced.

"I now pronounce you man and wife," Pendergast intoned. "King, you may kiss the bride."

Serena felt King's arms around her and she felt as if she was wrapped in a warm blanket. Then his lips touched hers and she pressed herself against him and felt the hardness of his body against her. Sensations of hope, doubt, and awe twisted together like the strands of a braid, creating substance out of air, and bound her heart and thoughts to her new path into the future.

BODIE WELLS, OKLAHOMA
MONDAY, NOVEMBER 1, 1920

Cordel Witherspoon had not completed his lunch when the Thomas brothers entered Wrangel House looking for Joshua and Mariah Morgan. From the way they burst in, the two brothers were looking to cause trouble. Cordel watched as they pushed their way roughly between the tables of the crowded dining room. The Thomases were from a large family of sharecroppers who scratched out a living from the sullen earth west of town. They had lived on the same parcel for nearly a hundred years and they had farmed the soil until it was listless. As a result, many of the fourteen children worked in Clairborne or, as common theory held, stole whatever they could carry or drag off. For some unknown reason these two

Thomas brothers had taken a particular dislike to Cordel and they were always roughing him up when the opportunity arose. Fortunately for Cordel, they saw the Morgans first. Leon Thomas, who was the burlier of the two brothers, walked over to the table the Morgans were sharing with another couple and said in a threatening tone, "You was warned to get out of town! You sold us some bad feed! It killed two of our horses!"

Mr. Morgan, an older, chocolate brown–skinned man in his late fifties, replied in a calm raspy voice, "All scores are settled. I paid you for the loss of your stock in front of Marshal Bass. We've closed our business and we will be leaving town as soon as we get a fair offer for our property."

"You must be hard of hearin'!" Cyrus Thomas sneered as he joined his brother at the Morgans' table. "He told you to be gone by the next time we was in town. You ain't listening!" Cyrus grinned, showing big gaps in his teeth. He put his hand on the hilt of his knife.

"We don't want no trouble here, Cyrus!" Ma Wrangel said as she waddled into the dining room from the kitchen. She was a big woman, but she moved quickly on her feet. "You got a problem, get Marshal Bass. He'll handle it without bloodshed."

"You shouldn't be havin' no gutter slime like this eatin' in here!" Leon declared to the room in general. "Now, Bass been called away. It look to me like us townsfolk got to take care of this problem."

"You's right, Leon. Maybe we ought to escort them to the edge of town with some tar and feathers."

The dining room was silent. Cordel picked up his bread and sopped the last of his stew out of his bowl and prepared to slip out without being seen. He knew no one in the dining room would stand up to the Thomases without the backing of Marshal Bass. He didn't want to see the Morgans humiliated for they were good people, but he was helpless to stop the Thomas brothers. He was nearly to the door when a woman's voice made him stop and turn around. It was the light-skinned woman who was sitting at the table with the Morgans. She and her husband were new in Bodie Wells, and nobody knew much about them except that they seemed to have money.

"Why don't you leave these people alone? If you have a legitimate problem, do as Mrs. Wrangel said and wait for the town marshal to handle it." The woman spoke as if she had no fear.

"Was I talkin' to you?" Leon demanded. "You better shut yo' mouth, if'en you don't want me to shut it fo' you!"

"I've never been shut up when I wanted to speak and I won't be now!" The woman was bold. The attention of everyone in the dining room was riveted by her next words. "You men are just bullies. Picking on people you know can't stand up to you! You wouldn't dare act this way if some-body was standing up to you!"

Leon looked at his brother in surprise. "Ain't this a bitch! This heifer must think she white!"

"Yeah," nodded Cyrus, leaning on the table. "Let's see if her man can—" Cyrus never finished his remark, for action exploded at the table.

From his vantage point near the door, Cordel could not tell exactly what happened, but when the tumult ended, he saw that the woman's husband had Leon bent over backward across an adjacent table with a gun in his mouth. Cyrus was on the floor, leaning unconscious against the table at which the Morgans were sitting.

"Apologize to my wife!" the man demanded as he jammed the pistol further down Leon's throat. "Otherwise I'm gon' blow yo' brains all over these people's food!" The people sitting at the table jumped up and moved away. Leon was left gurgling on the barrel of the man's gun. "Keep yo' hands up, or I'll let the hammer fall!" Leon nodded and kept his hands in the open. "Now, I'm gon' give you a chance to apologize and I wants the whole place to hear you!" Leon made some muffled sounds and the man demanded, "Louder unless you's ready to die!"

"I's sorry! I's sorry!"

"That's good!" the man acknowledged. "Now's here's somethin' from me to teach you some respect!" In one quick movement, the man picked up a steaming bowl of hot stew and turned it over on Leon's face. Leon screamed in pain and anger and rolled off the table as the man stepped backward.

"My eyes! My eyes!" Leon screamed. "I'm gon' kill you fo' this! I'm gon' kill you! I'm gon' kill you!" Leon was crawling on the floor, rubbing his eyes.

"Then you must be ready to die now!" the man answered and kicked Leon in the head. Leon was knocked under the table by the impact.

The woman saved Leon's life by pleading with her husband, "Don't kill him, King! Please don't kill him!"

The man called King looked at his wife, and even from the door Cordel could see death in his eyes. Cordel shuddered but he couldn't move away; he was immobilized by the drama in front of him. The man exhaled slowly. "Okay, but we gon' have to deal with them later!"

Leon, still blinded, was struggling to regain his footing. He gripped a table for support and was pulling himself up when King struck him again and shattered his arm with a loud crack. Leon screamed like an animal and fell to the floor. It was a horrible sound.

"King, please," the woman shouted over Leon's screams.

"I just wanted to leave him with somethin', Serena!" King explained.

Cordel watched as King walked over to the table at which he had been sitting and pried loose a bowie knife that had been stuck into the table. Once the knife had been removed Cyrus slumped to the floor, and it was only then that Cordel saw that Cyrus's hand had been pinned to the table by the knife. It was too much. Cordel turned and ran out the door. He could hardly wait to tell Lightning Smith that Leon and Cyrus Thomas had been struck down by one man. He ran all the way to the livery on the edge of town, where he worked as a stable hand.

WEDNESDAY, NOVEMBER 3, 1920

"What the hell do you mean they haven't been home yet? They were in town on Monday! You went out to the Thomas farm and the family didn't know where they were, or they wouldn't tell you?" Booker Little tapped his cigar in a chipped clay plate and stared across the table at Deputy Oswald Simpson. The dim light from an overcast sky shed little illumination through the uncurtained window and left the storage room virtually in shadows.

"I went out there, Mr. Little," Deputy Simpson answered, fingering a turquoise amulet that hung around his neck. "Ain't nobody seen them boys since Monday mornin'! Ain't no reason for the family to lie to me. I wasn't there to make no arrests. They was worried too! It's pretty damn cold! A body could easily freeze to death in this weather and it look like it gon' snow some more."

"Why didn't you arrest this stranger at Wrangel House?" demanded Booker Little angrily as he poured himself a shot of scotch. He was a big-boned, light-skinned man with a jutting jaw and heavy eyebrows, and his jaw seemed even more pronounced with his angry expression.

Simpson shook his head and explained. "There was way too many witnesses who seen the Thomases start it all. Ain't no way I could arrest him and make it stick!" He looked down at the bottle of scotch and the two shot glasses and licked his lips.

Booker saw Simpson's look and ignored it. "What damn witnesses?" Booker demanded. "We never had witnesses before!"

"Well, this Negro seem like he done give 'em some backbone or some-thin'," Simpson stated. " 'Cause everybody who was there had somethin' to say, even Ma Wrangel, and you know she ain't ever admitted to seein' anythin' before."

"I don't like the sound of this! I've worked damned hard to get to this point and I don't want to lose it all because of some wandering, high-yellow thug! We're on the verge of running the Morgans out; we've got Mace Edwards isolated and it's three months to the mayoral election and I've got that wrapped up!" Booker banged his fist on the table and the bottle and glasses jiggled precariously but did not fall. "I want this trouble-maker run out of town before this weekend! Do you hear me? I don't care how you do it!"

"But Mr. Little, Elmo Thomas is out of town and Marshal Bass gon' be back tomorrow. How am I s'posed to run 'em out if'en they don't do somethin' else? I don't even know if I can go up against this man alone."

"Ozzy, Bass is retiring in two months. You want to be the next marshal, don't you? Well, the new circuit judge and Sheriff Lynch are going to be influenced by what I have to say, particularly if I'm the next mayor. The railroad's coming through here, there's a lot of money to be made, and the next town marshal stands to make a substantial piece of that. If you don't get this man and his wife out of town soon, you won't be my first choice. You follow? You best get a few men and arrest him tonight."

Simpson nervously rubbed the good-luck amulet around his neck between his fingers and wondered how he would accomplish the task set before him.

FRIDAY, NOVEMBER 5, 1920

"So how long do you plan to stay in town, Mrs. Tremain?" Marshal Bass asked as he took a loud slurp from his coffee mug. The single light over his desk cast clearly defined shadows that did nothing to improve the decor of his sparsely furnished office. The wind whistled through the outside eaves, reminding the occupants that winter had returned.

Serena took her time in answering. She was not fooled by the country ways of the town marshal. She realized intuitively that there was design behind his seemingly innocent questions. "We're just stopping here for a brief rest. We're on our way to San Francisco." She took a sip of coffee and frowned at its brackish taste. "Do you have any milk?"

Bass smoothed the edges of his graying handlebar mustache and chuckled. "The old pot do got a taste to it, but I'm sorry, ma'am, I don't keep such fineries in here." He stood up and went over the potbellied stove and threw a couple more pieces of wood in its interior; the flames roared appreciatively. Bass turned to Serena once more. "I hope you'll pardon me, but most days it's just me and the old kettle. Now, you say you're stopping here for a rest? You folks look mighty young to need a rest."

The wind buffeted the wooden structure of the marshal's office and the wind keened with a high and lonely note, mimicking the call of the wolf. King leaned forward in his chair. "What you aimin' at, Marshal? You got questions goin' every which way, but I don't see no point. Why did you ask us to come here?"

Marshal Bass looked at the hard eyes in the youthful face in front of him and saw a killer. His thirty years in law enforcement had taught him the signs. He smiled. "I've got no point, son. I just like to find out a little about the new folks who come to Bodie Wells, that's all. It ain't official business. If you want, you can get up and leave anytime."

King laughed. "You's a crafty old dude. Let's talk. We ain't got nothin' to hide. But let's shortcut this whole fishin' trip so we can get on with our day. We's from New Orleans, where I had to leave suddenlike 'cause some whites wanted to regulate me. I didn't see no reason to stay around and it didn't have nothin' to do with obeyin' the law. Me and my wife got married legal befo' we left. We gon' leave here as soon as we see our families is gon' make it. I ain't lookin' to start no trouble in yo' town and I ain't lookin' fo' excitement."

Bass smiled despite himself: the youngster was clever. By volunteering so much information, it would make further questions suspicious. "So, you're newlyweds, huh? Well, congratulations," Bass acknowledged with a friendly smile. "I guess you folks are honeymooning here in Bodie Wells, huh?"

"No disrespect meant, Marshal, but this ain't much of a town to honeymoon in. We plans to do our honeymoon in San Francisco. We came here because we wanted to be somewheres where the colored folks was in charge in a town that had electricity. Bodie Wells was the only town we found. That's the reason we chose it."

Bass stared at the two young faces. "Don't expect too much. There ain't a place in this man's United States where whites ain't runnin' the show. Sometimes they're just behind the people you think is in charge, people who look colored, but in their hearts want to be something lighter. Anyways, far as I can tell, colored folks is just white folks without money, education, sunburns, cowlicks, and opry music."

"You's the second person I've heard say that," King said with a laugh. "We ain't got polka either, but I was thinkin' it was things you can't see that made us different, like our fightin' spirit and our singin' and dancin'."

"A man is a man, a woman is a woman; after that seems like it just depends on which end of the hate you's on, son. If you's on the bottom end, you's like us: singin' the blues and findin' the land of milk and honey through religion. If you's at the top, you's like the whites: living good and rewriting other people's history. Like the history of this town is being written eight miles away in Clairborne."

"Clairborne?" Serena asked. "That's the town where they have the signs, 'Nigger don't let the sun set on you here'?"

"Yep, that's it. The people there own a lot of the land in this town and a good many of the colored folks here work in Clairborne. Even my authority comes from the circuit judge who's based in Clairborne."

"The way you sound, Marshal Bass, you haven't been too happy with Clairborne's control over Bodie Wells."

"Ain't nothing perfect," Bass acknowledged. "I've managed the best I could and I did right by my lights. That's all a man can do."

"Speakin' of doin' right," King interjected, "what am I to do if'en them Thomas boys try to brace me while we's in town? I ain't lookin' for trouble, but I ain't interested in takin' no stuff either."

"Well," Bass answered, running his hand over his close-cut graying kinky hair, "if I see them, I'll stop them, because I don't want any gunplay either. 'Course, nobody has seen them since Monday, so there's some question about where them boys are. You don't know anything about that, do you?"

King shook his head. "The last time I saw them, they was down and out. I didn't even see them leave town."

After Serena and King had left his office, Marshal Raymond Bass sat for some time thinking about King Tremain. King's hands were not those of a farmer and he didn't appear to be a businessman, yet he had money, more money than someone his age could earn legally. Bass had learned through unobtrusive investigation that the Tremains had taken a suite of rooms at the Wildhorse Inn and that his substantial account at the town's bank had been created by money wires from New York. What was his business, Bass wondered. There was no doubt that King had other men's blood on his hands. He had the eyes of a man who spilled blood easily. Yet Bass did not get the sense that King killed for money. He concluded, rather, that King placed no value in human life, not even his own.

If he had not planned to retire in two months, Bass would have investigated King Tremain more diligently. The truth was, he was tired of law-enforcement work, tired of risking his life for people who didn't seem to care. He had hoped fervently that the interim period before his retirement would be uneventful, but this was not to be the case. King had been in town less than two weeks and already three men had disappeared. From the types of injuries the Thomas brothers had received, if they hadn't made it home by now, in this weather they were dead.

Everyone knew that the Thomas brothers were Booker Little's henchmen and that they performed his dirty work. And everyone knew that Simpson was also in Booker Little's pocket. That association had caused Simpson to stretch the letter of the law on more than one occasion, but if Bass was present, Simpson always obeyed his direction. More than once, Bass had considered firing Simpson for letting his ambition and greed direct his enforcement of the law. He had held off because in a town of nearly nine hundred people, he needed deputies and there was no one else of character who wanted the job. Simpson had a little shack on the edge of town and generally arrived at the marshal's office around eight in the morning. But today he hadn't been seen at all. Bass opened a drawer of his desk and took out a turquoise amulet that was strung on a leather thong. He had found it in the dirt in front of Ozzy's cabin. It was Simpson's good-luck charm. Bass knew that Simpson would never go anywhere without it, if he was conscious. No, it didn't look like the days prior to his retirement would be calm.

MONDAY, NOVEMBER 22, 1920

Mace Edwards stood at the front window of Wrangel House and looked out on the one paved street of Bodie Wells that ran through the center of town. He was a light-skinned, solid chunk of a man, with a pronounced jaw and thick eyebrows. He had a contemplative look on his face as he stared out at the winter weather. Main Street was covered with snow and the wind was bringing more. Big, fluffy snowflakes were rapidly swirling and falling, pushed by the power of forceful blasts off the plains. Traffic along the street was at a minimum, but occasionally he would see someone, bundled up in coats and furs, scurrying on some important mission. When the temperature hit zero, most folks stayed indoors.

Mace turned away from the window when Ma Wrangel brought in a platter of broiled steak and baked potatoes. The smell of the food wafted through the room and made his mouth water. "Smells like you put your whole leg in it this time, Ma," he said as he walked over to the table where Clara Nesbitt and Cordel Witherspoon were sitting.

"Pshaw, boy, this ain't nothin' that required hard cookin'," Ma Wrangel answered as she set the platter down. "I always been able to broil a piece of meat with my eyes closed."

Reverend Cornelius walked in from the front hall, rubbing his hands together for warmth, and went over and stood by the cast-iron stove that heated the dining room. "How do, folks?" he asked while spreading his hands above the heat of the stove. "The Lord works in mysterious ways. I see that the food is just being served."

"That isn't mysterious," Mace said with a laugh. "You haven't ever missed the opportunity for a cooked meal and even when you're late, you seem to get more than your share."

Reverend Cornelius smiled good-naturedly at the jibe. "I'm going to pray for you, Mace. I see that the seeds of cynicism are becoming embedded in your heart." He walked back to a basin and washed his hands.

"Isn't Marshal Bass coming?" Clara asked as she got up to give Ma Wrangel some assistance in setting the table.

"Oh, I forgot," Cordel said with a worried look. "The marshal went with Octavius Boothe and Lightning Smith to help the McGirts get their wagon out'n the creek that feeds Buffalo Canyon."

"Perhaps we shouldn't have set out the food so soon," Clara suggested as Reverend Cornelius returned and stood behind a chair.

"Pshaw," countered Ma Wrangel, carrying in a large pitcher of water and a covered basket of biscuits. "I knew them boys was gon' be late 'cause Raymond done called me on the telephone." Ma Wrangel was justifiably proud that she had one of the five telephones in Bodie Wells and rarely missed an opportunity to mention it. "Come on, Reverend, bless the food and don't be long-winded. I don't want no grease gettin' cold on my steak."

They gathered hands and Reverend Cornelius said a brief grace. Then they sat down to partake of the redolent food. Ma Wrangel was considered one of the best cooks in the region and her food confirmed that conclusion every time she served it. They ate with only minimal interchanges between them for nearly fifteen minutes, until the meal was interrupted by the entrance of Marshal Bass, Octavius Boothe, and Lightning Smith.

After hanging their coats and wiping their boots in the front hall, the men entered the dining room. Both Bass and Smith went directly to the stove to warm themselves. Octavius went back to wash his hands. There were still remnants of snow on Marshal Bass's handlebar mustache, and Lightning Smith was shivering from the effects of the cold.

"Is everything alright?" Mace asked, curious about the men's silence.

Lightning looked at Bass meaningfully. "It be colder'n hell out there." He was standing so close to the stove that his damp clothes began to steam.

"That's to be expected, Mr. Smith," the reverend chided. "The hell-fires burn with the heat of damnation, but I caution you to remember that there are women present."

"I's sorry. I wasn't thinkin' right." Lightning nodded his head to both of the women.

"Don't mind Lightnin', Reverend," Ma Wrangel said as she hauled herself erect. "We done heard much worse from the drovers that comes through here." She picked up the platter of steak and potatoes and went back to the kitchen.

Octavius returned and sat down at the table next to Mace. "Did they tell you?" he asked Mace.

"Tell us what?" Mace rejoined.

Octavius reached and pulled a biscuit from the covered basket. "We found the Thomas brothers," he said before taking a big bite of his biscuit.

"Where? Are they alive?" Clara asked.

"They's frozen solid down at the bottom of Buffalo Canyon," Lightning answered, sitting down at the table. "Their wagon was all splintered up around 'em."

Mace looked around the table with a smile. "No disrespect to the reverend here, but I think most of us want to get up and cheer at the news that these two have passed on to their reward."

"What if I told you," Marshal Bass mused, "we couldn't find all of Leon's body and it wasn't bitten off by animals?"

"What?" exclaimed Clara. "What do you mean, 'You couldn't find all of his body'?"

Octavius stabbed a steak with his fork. "It look like somebody tried to bury pieces of 'em, but the ground was too hard."

Ma Wrangel came out of the kitchen with a basket of biscuits. "Say what?" she demanded. "You sure it just weren't badgers and coyotes?"

"Weren't no varmints!" said Lightning. "Leon's hand and one leg was cut clean off, like with an axe. Ain't no varmint got a bite like that."

"Why don't you start from the beginning," suggested Mace. "I know plenty people who would've liked to chop those boys up, but I can't think anyone who would desecrate a dead body."

"I'm pretty sure it was done before they died," Bass said.

Mace turned to Octavius, who was digging into his steak. "How'd you find them?"

Octavius finished chewing a big piece of steak and answered. "The horses. The cold drove them to the McGirts. The McGirts, bein' the good folk they are, went out lookin' and found the bodies."

"They is good people," Ma Wrangel affirmed. " 'Cause once I seed the brand, I wouldn't have gone out in this weather."

"I don't understand," Clara said, adjusting her wire-rimmed glasses. "Did someone murder them or was it an accident?"

"Somebody had a hand in it," Marshal Bass said. "Somebody cut the horses loose and pushed the wagon over the bluff above Buffalo Canyon."

"Elmo is gon' know it weren't no accident," Octavius agreed. "He gon' come to town with guns at the ready."

"Do you think that Tremain fella did it?" Ma Wrangel asked. "His wife barely stopped him from killin' them right here in this room."

"Naw, I don't figure it to be him," Bass said, helping himself to the steak and potatoes. "If he'd a'done it, don't think we'd ever find the bodies. He's a cold one, that one is. And now he done bought the Morgans' holdings, he gon' be careful. He ain't one to leave evidence lyin' 'round."

Clara nearly choked. "They bought the Morgans' business?"

"Paid full askin' price too," Ma Wrangel answered, shaking her head. "I just don't figure that."

"These the new people who started attending services at Second Baptist?" Reverend Cornelius asked. "They paid full price too, huh?"

Octavius was also surprised. "I didn't know that. They could have squeezed the Morgans good, 'cause they sho' was in a tight place."

"But they didn't," Mace mused. "Where does anybody that young get that kind of money?"

"And they don't come from rich people," Clara added. "The wife, Serena, has asked me to help her with her diction and grammar. She's even willing to pay me for my time."

"You should do it," Bass asserted. "Not only for the extra money, but we need to know somethin' 'bout these people. I tell you, I think this Tremain is one of the most dangerous men we've seen around here. I believe that whoever crosses him will end up dead or disappeared."

"You're just sayin' that 'cause Ozzy Simpson done run off without tellin' you," Octavius said, reaching for another biscuit. "He probably over in Kernerville right now visitin' his girlfriend."

Marshal Bass threw Simpson's turquoise amulet on the table. "Without that?" Everyone recognized the amulet and all present knew the value that Ozzy had placed on the good-luck piece. There was silence.

Mace pushed back from the table and stood up. "You don't know for certain that Tremain had anything to do with Ozzy's disappearance, do you?"

"If I did, I would have arrested him, or at least tried to."

"You think he would have resisted?" Clara asked.

"Ain't a doubt in my mind someone would get killed," Bass said, and took another bite of his steak.

TUESDAY, NOVEMBER 23, 1920

Big Daddy Bolton threw his napkin down on top of his unfinished food and pointed a thick, stubby finger at his son Frank. "I told you last time that I was through with helping you out of your problems! You're going to have to marry this one!" Big Daddy's granite block of a jaw jutted out defiantly and his thick bushy eyebrows seemed to bristle independently. The overhead light of the dining room gleamed on the pink, bald dome of his head. "I won't buy them off this time! I won't let you squander what has taken a lifetime to build!"

"But Big Daddy," Sarah interceded. "Surely, you want to protect our son's reputation from being the talk of Clairborne. We after all are a family of stature in this community. This girl is white trash! We don't want her in our family! He has other marriage options—"

Big Daddy interrupted with a wave of his beefy hand. "Don't defend him to me! Admit it, he's useless! He's a drunkard and a womanizer! On top of that he's a sucker and a fool when it comes to both business and gambling. All the men his age laugh at him. No decent young girl in this town would marry him! Unless it was for money!"

"That isn't true, Daddy. Sandra Maddox would marry me and she's from a good family!"

Big Daddy shook head as he stared at the big dark eyes of his son's face. The boy had his mother's big doe-eyes and he too looked like prey. "It shows what a fool you are if you don't recognize that it's not she who wants to marry you. It's her father who wants her to marry you." Big Daddy pointed his finger again at his son. "You're nearly thirty years old and you have no business skills! The only reason Maddox wants his daughter to marry you is because he thinks I would help his business."

Frank quailed and a trace of a whine entered his tone. "What am I gon' do, Daddy? Her brothers have threatened me."

The question and the tone infuriated Big Daddy more than the foolish promiscuity and gambling debts, for they presaged a thick vein of weakness running right through the center of his son. It was not a new realization, but like a rasp it always grated and, as always, it struck Big Daddy to his core. Through gritted teeth he said, "You should have thought of that first before you took your pleasure!"

"But Daddy, I'm in line for Grand Titan. It's a position of respect. I'm some—"

"A position of respect?" Big Daddy barked derisively. It really seemed that all that he had accomplished and amassed during his lifetime would be left in the hands of a total idiot. "That really shows what a fool you are! Let me explain it to you, boy! If you're white trash, you join the Klan. If you have money, you join the Elks! If you have money, class, and power, you join the Masons! I'm a third-generation Mason and I've got a son who joins the Klan?"

"We got Masons in the Klan! Colonel Blanc, he—"

"That just proves assholes are everywhere," Big Daddy interrupted. "Only you and your friends call him Colonel. Everyone else calls him T-Bo. Masons use the Klan to do their rough stuff. We don't dirty our hands. Only trash does that kind of work."

Frank looked to his mother and back to his father. "You never sponsored me for the Masons!"

"You never did a damn thing to deserve it!"

Sarah coughed behind her napkin. "I'm sure, Big Daddy, that we do not have to bring vulgarity into the sanctity of our home."

"Be quiet, woman! I believe I've worked long and hard enough to curse at my own table if I choose! Plus, what's worse, vulgarity or the endless stupidity of your son?" Big Daddy pushed away from the table and hauled his barrel-shaped body out of his chair. "Sarah, I've got a meeting with your brother Skip and Booker Little."

"I can help you with dealing with the niggers, Big Daddy," Frank volunteered.

"What are you going to do, scare them? One night you'll ride with the Klan and you'll run across a nigger too tired to run and he'll get out his rifle and kill five or six of you."

"Niggers don't scare us," Frank asserted. "We know how to control them. We're dedicated to preserving the ways of Little Dixie."

"Great," Big Daddy said sarcastically and walked out of the dining room before Frank could say anything more. He passed through a hallway and entered his office. His frustration with the unfortunate ironies of life washed over him like a cold tide of unpleasant memories. Even if Frank was half the man of Big Daddy's nigger sons, it would be some consolation. He was gathering his thoughts when old Uncle Ben knocked at his door.

"Dey some people here," Uncle Ben rattled out in his faint, scratchy voice. "Dey say you 'spectin' 'em." Uncle Ben waited patiently at the door for direction.

Big Daddy smiled; the old Negro was getting more gruff and terse with each passing year. "Send them in, Ben," he said. Sarah had been pressuring him to help Uncle Ben return to Mississippi where he had been born. Big Daddy hadn't said no, but he couldn't imagine his household without Uncle Ben's presence. The man had worked as a manservant for him for more than forty years.

The door opened and in walked Undersheriff Skip Dalton and behind him followed Booker Little. "How do, Skip?" Big Daddy asked, reaching across the desk to shake the undersheriff's hand. Skip Dalton was a dark-haired pale man with a lean and sinewy look. He was instrumental in assisting Big Daddy in some of his more dangerous and sensitive pursuits. He looked nothing like his sister, Sarah, to whom Big Daddy was married.

Booker Little stood at the edge of the desk and waited to be recognized. Big Daddy made no effort to shake his hand, but Booker's face gave no indication that he had noticed the slight.

Big Daddy stared across the desk at a product of his indiscretion. Here was another one of his sons, one who showed more clearly his Bolton lineage than did his all-white brother. He definitely possessed Bolton's cunning and ambition. With a small loan from Big Daddy, he had built up the businesses in Bodie Wells from scratch and he was well on his way to putting a stranglehold on Bodie Wells like Big Daddy had on Clairborne. Like father, like son. "Long time no see, Booker," Big Daddy said without inflection.

"Yes sir, Mr. Bolton," Booker said with polite smile. "I try to run the business in such a way that we don't need to meet often."

Even for a son, he was too confident for a Negro. Big Daddy countered sarcastically, "But you seem to have failed this time, though. Not so? After all, I hear that someone else other than us bought the Morgans' property. I also hear that some of your assistants have been found dead. And lastly, someone seems to be printing a fly-by-night newspaper that does not represent our interests well. We could lose this upcoming mayoral election. What do you have to say about these things?"

"We've discovered how the paper is printed," Booker answered. His face was serious, the smile was gone. "Clara Nesbitt has been getting it printed by the *Colored Chronicle* in Johnsonville."

"Florence Nesbitt's girl? She travels almost fifty miles round trip to get this trash published? What are you doing about it?"

"Well, nothing, sir," Booker explained. "You said to keep things calm while the circuit judge is in town and I followed your orders."

"That's a good idea" Skip affirmed. "The judge is only going to be here through January fifth. After that, Marshal Bass retires and we'll have a freer hand. We do anything before that and Marshal Bass will wire the judge and we'll have him sitting on our shoulders watching everything we do."

"I think we can stop the distribution of the paper without causing much of a stir," Booker offered. "Some of the town folk are whispering and meeting about incorporating Bodie Wells into a township. I don't believe there's much of a chance of success, particularly if the employers in Clairborne make it known that—"

Big Daddy interrupted, "Hell, most people in Clairborne don't know about or don't care what's going on in Bodie Wells. We are the ones who stand to lose the most if the town incorporates. We'll have to go this alone. If you lose the election for mayor and we can't influence the appointment of a new marshal, our control over Bodie Wells will be lost. We need a plan."

"This is the holiday season," Booker offered. "If we let things rest now, maybe they'll think that they've won. Then after Bass retires, we'll pick up in February and we'll catch them unprepared."

"Where is Elmo Thomas?" Big Daddy asked. He had to stop himself from smiling: Booker had recommended the exact same path of action he would have.

Further conversation was preempted when the door opened and Sarah walked in, followed by her son, Frank. She had a big smile on her face. "Why Skip, Big Daddy told me you were going to be here. I just didn't think you'd pass without greeting your sister and nephew." She went over and kissed his cheek in a manner that clearly indicated that she had other things on her mind than greeting her brother. "Why don't you shake hands with your uncle, Frank?" she said with a smile, but her eyes were throwing daggers at Booker.

Frank could hardly complete the pro forma action with his uncle because he too was staring at Booker. "What are you doing here?" he challenged, an angry expression contorting his face.

"We're talking business. My business! So, it's none of your business!" Big Daddy said the words with relish. His only legal son was such a painful disappointment to him that in a perverse manner, he now desired to cause this son some discomfort.

"Surely you don't mean that," Sarah said with a frown. "This is your only son. He's going to be your heir. He should know the ins and outs, especially the orders you're giving the servants." She gave Booker a meaningful look.

"I mean it! He's useless! Booker here has done better—"

"You're not going to compare your only son to a Nigra bastard!" Sarah pronounced "Negro" in such a way as to indicate she meant to say "nigger" but her breeding wouldn't allow her. Sarah began hyperventilating behind a handkerchief that she pressed to her mouth. Her son, Frank, who was used to ignoring these episodes, rushed to her side with pretended concern. Neither Skip, who grew up with her, nor Big Daddy moved a muscle.

"Some bastards are worth something, while others who have all the fortune from birth are not worth manure," Big Daddy said easily.

Big Daddy's words made Sarah drop her pretense and stare at him with hatred. She turned to her brother. "That's your nephew he's insulting. Aren't you going to say something?"

Skip knew on which side his bread was buttered: he put up his hands and backed away. "This is between you all."

Sarah turned and marched from the room. Frank was left standing there in confusion. With an expression and a gesture, he made a silent plea to his father, but his father simply made a fist and gave the thumbs-down sign. Frank Bolton, humiliated in front of his half-white brother, shuffled from the room with head down and fallen shoulders.

"Maybe we could use someone with Mr. Frank's skills," Booker suggested as Frank neared the door. "I have a plan I'd like to discuss with you that could involve him."

Big Daddy looked at Frank's face and saw a look of pure hatred directed at Booker. Instead of being thankful that Booker would want to include him, Frank hated him all the more for having the audacity to show charity. Big Daddy turned to Booker and saw him smiling in response to Frank's look. Big Daddy was beginning to like the situation more and more. Maybe Booker was smarter than he thought. Just what did he have planned for Frank?

"Alright, Frank, you can stay!" Sarah started to reenter the room, but Big Daddy stopped her. "Not you, Sarah. You've accomplished your goal: Frank is part of the meeting. Now close the door!"

Big Daddy turned to face the three men in his office with a big smile. He was planning on enjoying the competition between Booker and Frank.

It seemed that Frank had all the advantages, but Big Daddy wouldn't give even money for his success. It was a terrible thing to say, but he could see his blood more clearly in Booker.

Tuesday, December 28, 1920

Christmas Day had passed without word from King. He had been gone over a month. Serena did not know where he was, nor did she have anyone to contact who could tell her. All he had said before he left Bodie Wells was that he might be gone for some time. Initially she figured his trip had something to do with his bootlegging business. He had made several short weekend trips in the past, returning each time with wads of cash and cases of liquor. Yet this time was different. As the weeks passed, she began to fear the worst. It even entered her mind that he might be dead. It was the darkest and loneliest holiday season that she had ever spent. She had never endured so much time in silence. She missed her sisters and her little brother and felt an aching sense of loss when she thought about her mother. But she cried on no one's shoulder. She gritted her teeth and kept herself busy.

The wind had died down for the first time in a week. Sounds of traffic echoed along the corridor of Main Street as people returned to their homes after the dinner hour. With a fire crackling in the potbellied stove, Serena sat in her rocking chair holding a letter addressed to King Tremain, Bodie Wells, Oklahoma. There was no information about the sender. The handwriting was in a bold, irregular scrawl. Serena picked up the envelope and held it up to the light of the bulb: there appeared to be two sheets of paper within it. She considered the possibility that the letter might contain some clues to King's whereabouts, yet she set the envelope back down on the highboy as she had done a hundred times before. As always her examination led to no conclusion.

Her days were spent working with Sampson in the receiving, inventorying, and placement of shipments of fabric, leather goods, foodstuff, ammunition, hunting weapons, and an assortment of other items for the general store. The stock was coming in rapidly. The store would be ready to open in the middle of January. The carpenters completed their work in the main building, including her dress shop, and had begun to work on repairing the barn and granary outbuildings. There was always work to do. Sometimes she and Sampson worked themselves to the brink of exhaustion. She had chosen to stop going to the beauty parlor, because the talk generally centered around the latest gossip. After two weeks she had heard all the stories twice, plus she had neither time nor the inclination for gossip.

Her nights were spent in the second-story flat above the store in the rocking chair beside the stove. In the beginning, her principal pastime was reading the Bible, but through Clara Nesbitt she discovered a whole new range of fiction and poetry. She now spent evenings reading stories by Chesnutt, J. Weldon Johnson, and Hughes. But there were many evenings when she was incapable of visualizing the concepts and images developed in print. On such nights she was filled with doubt and fear and would return to stare at the letter on the highboy many times.

Outside on the street, there was the sound of boisterous men laughing and talking. The weather had taken an unseasonal temperature swing upward into the low forties and some drovers and farmhands suffering from cabin fever had come to town to drink and carouse at the Black Rose, located a mile outside of Bodie Wells. Serena looked at the tall pendulum clock and saw that it was after eight o'clock in the evening. It was late for a bunch of men to be on the street; during the winter all town businesses closed at six in the evening. It occurred to her that the men might have come from the cockfights that Lightning was rumored to have every fortnight or so. Her perplexity ended when she heard a loud banging on the store's front door.

"Tremain, come out! I hear you's the one responsible fo' killin' my brothers! Come on out here and deal with me like a man! I'm Elmo Thomas and I'm callin' you out!"

Serena stood up and walked over to the window and pulled the curtains back to look down on the street below. She could see two men standing in the street. The loud banging on the store door continued. Shades were pulled up and curtains were opened up and down the street as people peered out their windows to see the cause of the commotion. Serena knew that no one but Marshal Bass would come to her assistance.

"Tremain! Are you yellow? Come out and deal with me face-to-face!" More banging.

Serena donned her shawl and then went to the bureau and took out a revolver that King had given her. With gun hidden under the shawl, she went downstairs to open the door. When she reached the bottom of the stairs Sampson stepped out of the shadows holding a shotgun. He followed her to the door, which she unlocked and opened.

Elmo Thomas stood there swaying with drink. He was a muscular brown-skinned man whose nose had been broken many times, and he had a twisted, evil smile. He leered at her and said, "Where Tremain? He afraid to come down and deal with me? Do I have to come in there searchin' for him?" He pushed open the door roughly, throwing Serena backward. Elmo would have continued on into the store if Sampson had not jammed the barrel of the shotgun into his throat and shoved him up against the wall.

"Don't make any sudden moves, Mr. Thomas. The shotgun has a hair trigger," Serena advised. She straightened her shawl. And don't come back here again, Mr. Thomas. My husband will come looking for you in due time. If I know him, he'll be happy to visit you after I tell him about this."

Despite the shotgun against his neck, Elmo threatened, "If I ain't seen him by New Year's Day, I'm gon' come back here and burn this place down!"

"I wouldn't try that if I were you, Mr. Thomas. That might be the last match you ever light. Your family has already lost two sons. We'd be adding another to the list. Of course, I've heard that you breed like roaches, so the loss of three sons may hardly be noticed. Let him go for now, Sampson."

Sampson backed off the shotgun but kept it pointed directly at Elmo.

Elmo pulled back out of the doorway and rubbed his neck angrily. "I ain't gon' fo'get that! Ain't nobody put a gun on me and lived to the following' season." He pointed a finger at Serena. "I'm gon' remember you too and what you said 'bout my family! You gon' be mine and I'm gon' break you! You high-yellow—"

Serena interrupted. "Kill him, Sampson, if he says another thing!" Sampson moved forward with a smile, ready to pull the trigger. Elmo stepped back with a look of fear on his face. "Good-bye, Mr. Thomas!" Serena said as she slammed the door in his face.

There was a moment of silence, then Elmo could be heard screaming to the street at large: "Tremain is a damn coward! I went to call on him and he sent his woman to the door! He a yellow-bellied back shooter! He can't stand up to nobody who's lookin' him in the eye! I'm gon' come back here on New Year's Day and turn him out and I'm gon' burn his sto' to the ground. I swear this on my brother's grave!"

Serena and Sampson stood looking at each other as they listened to Elmo's voice slowly wane in the distance. Sampson signed that he would sleep downstairs on guard for the night. She gave his arm a grateful squeeze and went back upstairs.

She walked straight over to the highboy and picked up the letter and opened it.

There were two sheets in the letter. The smaller one, perhaps half the size of its partner, was written in the same scrawl as the envelope. It was from Captain Mack and it began,

. . . I don't know if this is one of my brother's tricks or not, but a woman came here named Mamie. She had a little boy with her who she claimed was your son. I didn't tell her nothing, but she gave me a letter to send to you. She told me that you told her I was about the only family that you had. I can't tell you how good that made me and Martha feel, boy. We told her, we didn't know where you was, but if we got a chance we would forward her letter. I hope you and your new wife is doing good. No matter what you thinking, don't come back here! Corlis has people all over the place looking for you. You done shot his leg off and now he's madder than an alligator with eggs.

If you decide to come back, don't come to the mill! Corlis has got people watching us. Go to Poindexter's and he'll contact me. We'll still find a way to help you just like when you was seventeen and needed money and a horse.

You take care of yourself, boy. You all we got.

Serena's hands were trembling when she began to read the second letter:

Hello King,

I can't tell you how much I've missed you since you've been gone. You're one of a kind. I never had a chance to tell you how grateful I was that you appointed me manager of the Rockland Palace. A regular paying job is on the path to happiness. Cap or one of the guys stop by every once in a while to make sure things are running well. The Palace is one of the most popular places in New York City and we regularly take in a profit. Life is so crazy. Now that I don't need the money I get from singing, I have more offers for work than I can handle. I have an offer to be part of a traveling revue. I really want to do it. I want to see where my singing career will go if I invest time in it. But I have a problem and it's not the Palace. Vince knows the ropes better than I do.

I don't know how to tell you this, but six months after you left, our son was born. Yes, I knew I was pregnant before you left, but I didn't want you to stay if that was your only reason for staying. If you stayed, I wanted it to be because you loved me. It was hard for me to accept then, but I realize now that you didn't know how to love.

I came looking for you to find out whether you had learned how to

love in the time that you've been gone. I hoped that there still might be a future for us. Even if we can't get together, I thought you would like to see your wonderful son. He reminds me so much of you. He is not even a year old and he's already walking. He is tough and fearless. Nothing scares him. I was hoping that I could leave him with you while I travel with the revue.

I have been talking with your lawyer friend Goldbaum and he's the one who told me you were in New Orleans. I have been here two weeks and no one knows where you are. Please contact me as soon as you get this. I'm staying at the Tri-Color Hotel on the edge of Storyville. I really love the music that's being played in some of the clubs down here.

Oh, by the way, a friend of yours invited me out to his farm next week. He wants to see your son. The man's name is Alfred DuMont. He says he's known you all your life. I'm really looking forward to some home cooking.

Your loving Mamie

Both letters slipped from Serena's grasp and fell to the floor. She could barely walk back to her rocking chair. She seemed to have lost contact with her legs; they did not respond as they should have and trembled on the verge of collapse. She dropped into the chair like a dead weight. She sought to calm herself by putting her hands in her lap and taking long, regular breaths, timing them with the movement of the rocking chair.

She had seen a worn photograph of this woman in King's belongings when they moved from the Toussant to the villa. She had asked him about the photograph and he had told her that Mamie had been his woman in New York. Serena had studied the woman's photograph a long time. It portrayed a voluptuous and very dark-skinned woman dressed in big city finery in a park setting. The woman was so dark that the features of her face could only be seen in very good light. She remembered remarking in surprise that she was shocked that King would go out with someone so dark. His response had been crushing. She could recall the exact words he said: "Don't get caught up in that color shit! Army taught me if you got the blood of Africa in you, it don't matter what color you are, you ain't white! It's just another way the white got you hatin' yo'self. Until every man jack of us is ready to be proud for what we do, rather'n what we looks like, we gon' kickin' our own selves in the ass! In the army I seen this color shit mess up a squad of men. Don't be bringin' no high yellow shit to me! I hate that!"

It was the first time they had argued. She saw another side of him that day, the side that strangers saw. It was clear that he felt very strongly. She saw it in the flash of his eyes, tone of his voice, his use of vulgarity, and the heavy, ominous presence that seemed to appear out of nowhere. She said nothing more to him about the subject of color, but she did ask him to get rid of the photograph. He refused. She started to make an argument, but he cut her off once more with the intensity of his words. "I ain't arguin' with you! I'm keepin' it! It's important to me! Don't get it twisted! I married you, not her! Worry about today, not a yesterday you can't change!" Without waiting for her response he had stalked out of the room and she knew better than to follow him. Serena picked up the photograph again, trying to see what King had seen in the woman. What Serena saw was a big, black, overdressed country nigger woman with hot-combed hair putting on airs. Serena was not only irritated that King refused to get rid of the photograph, but also that he had gone out with a woman so dark. She had carefully placed the picture back in his papers and left the room. From that moment on, she had felt that the woman's presence had invaded her house, and it did not take long for her resentment of Mamie to grow into hatred. She didn't speak to King about it, but it was never far from her thoughts.

Serena had known this woman was going to be trouble when King refused to get rid of her photograph. The letter was merely confirmation of her premonition. As Serena rocked in the chair, questions began to march past, some answered, some unanswered. What did this child mean? Was it possible that King had met up with this woman and had decided to live with her because of the child? No, that wasn't like King. He would honor his vows to Serena, but he might bring home this child. Serena wondered what this meant for her, for her dreams. For one thing sure, her dream family didn't have some other woman's half-African bastard as her oldest child. That damned Mamie didn't have the courtesy to die a natural death! Maybe the DuMonts might be helpful in this situation. She sat rocking in her chair until the light of day signaled a new sunrise.

THURSDAY, DECEMBER 30, 1920

Serena rose at six-thirty and it was bitter cold. There was frost glistening on the windowpanes as the morning sun broke over the horizon. She put two logs in the embers of the potbellied stove, bathed in cold water, and dressed for the day. When she went downstairs, Sampson had already made coffee and started a pot of beans, but the fire beneath the beans had nearly burned down to embers. Serena was surprised. It was unlike him to fail to tend to his responsibilities. She called out to him but there was no answer. She rebuilt the fire, poured herself some coffee, and sat at the old wooden table by the window in the kitchen, looking down upon Main Street. During the night, the temperature had fallen well below freezing and the wind had returned. Across the street, Serena saw icicles hanging from the eaves and a post-office poster was flapping back and forth in the wind.

She held the cup in both hands as she sipped the hot, dark fluid and felt its heat. Her mind was unable to escape the cloud created by the letters. She wondered whether she was doomed to the life of a single woman in a strange town. The beans began to bubble on the stove and she rose to move the pot to a cooler area. It surprised her that she felt so exhausted so early in the morning. She heard someone running along the wooden planks that served as sidewalks for Main Street. She looked out the window and saw Cordel Witherspoon rush into Wrangel House. Serena watched as Cordel came out with Florence Nesbitt and Mace Edwards. They were in a hurry. All three ran down the street toward the bank and the doctor's office. It was obvious something was up. She shrugged, knowing she would learn about it soon enough. Then she heard a sound that she had not heard in a long time. She heard Sampson laughing behind the store. It was not a little chuckle; it was a full-throated belly laugh. Only one person could get Sampson to laugh like that.

Serena picked up the hem of her dress and ran to the back door so fast that she nearly fell headlong. She stumbled into the hallway leading back to the barn. When she opened the door, she saw King working with Sampson, unloading big crates from a large truck. His back was to her as he and Sampson carried a large crate into the barn. Sampson saw her and nodded in her direction with a big smile on his face. King turned his head and caught her eye just before entering the barn.

Serena looked around to see if King was accompanied by anyone, particularly a child. He appeared to be alone, but she feared jumping to conclusions. After a seemingly endless period of time, King exited the barn and walked toward her. She saw the smokey vapor of his breath as he approached her. There was a smile of genuine appreciation on his face as he looked at her, and the look moved her heart. She fell into his arms and felt the reassuring strength of his body against hers. She closed her eyes and let herself melt against him. The image of Flo Nesbitt and Mace Edwards running down the street faded completely from her mind.

After twenty minutes of furious interrogation, which produced no justifiable explanation for his extended absence, Serena wisely dropped the subject and allowed King to persuade her to come out and watch the unloading of the truck. Serena was wrapped in a heavy shawl as she sat on a bale of hay in the barn watching King and Sampson open crates. King was as happy as a child to show her some of the items that he had brought back with him. There was a new gramophone along with ten fragile playing records, several new dresses that Journer had helped him select, and many large bolts of fabric. King was particularly proud of the ice maker, a huge piece of equipment that he had purchased in Louisiana.

King pointed to the ice maker. "This here machine is what's gon' make Tremain Dry Goods the only place to get ice in the summer outside of Clairborne. It gon' make our business. We'll always have cold beer and sarsaparilla on hand for our customers and we won't be makin' no trips to Clairborne for ice. Everybody in Bodie Wells gon' be buyin' ice from us."

Serena just nodded her head. She was speechless. The merchandise that he had purchased hardly made a dent on her consciousness. She held in her hands a delicate ruby pendant on a golden chain that he had given her, but it did not register. She was thrilled just to sit and look at her husband, who was finally home after a long and probably dangerous trip. There was no doubt in her mind that he was the most handsome man she had ever seen. The feeling of fatigue seemed to drop away from her as she watched him. Even Sampson, who rarely smiled, was laughing as he helped King unload the heavy crates.

"Hold on a minute there, Sampson," King said with a chuckle as Sampson carried a narrow box out of the truck. "That one's for you. Go ahead and open it."

Sampson went over and sat down with the box and opened it very carefully as if it were explosives. Inside the box was a new rifle with a telescopic sight enclosed in a chamois sheath. Sampson took the rifle lovingly out of its sheath and sighted down the barrel. The smile on his face said what his tongue could not. He let his hand run lightly over the tooled surface of the barrel. He was very pleased.

"That ain't all, folks. There's more!" King said cheerfully and climbed back in the truck and brought out three paper-wrapped packages. "There's one for each of us." He handed a package to both Serena and Sampson. Serena and Sampson looked at each other, then began to unwrap the gifts. King was too impatient to wait for them to neatly open the packages. "Go ahead and tear the paper!" he urged them.

"No, save the paper," Serena advised. "This is good-quality butcher paper. We can use this to wrap dry goods." She opened the package and saw a beaver-skin coat. She was silent. It was something that she had longed for ever since seeing Olivia Little's coat. Sampson had received a beaver-skin coat as well. He rubbed the fur against his face. Then he stood and put the coat on and turned around while running his fingers through the rich pelt.

"I knowed we didn't have no winter coats when we came here," King observed happily. "I picked these up at the best furrier I could find in Shreveport. Now we's ready for the cold. Bring on the snow!"

Sampson turned and walked into the store without a word. King looked at Serena questioningly, but she dismissed his concern with a wave. She had seen the tears trickling down Sampson's face before he went inside and knew what he was feeling. It was a feeling that she too shared. No one had ever given her gifts that indicated or demonstrated that she was loved. It brought tears to her eyes as well, but she was under no pressure to hide hers. She ran to King and buried her face in his chest.

"I missed you so and you never called." She sobbed in his arms. "I was beginning to think that maybe you were dead, or—" She thought about the letter from Mamie and fell silent.

"I done explained that it was mo' dangerous to call than let things be," King answered in an understanding tone. "Now I knows if I has to go away again, you wants to hear from me regular like. You gon' have my lawyer's number in New York. You'll be able to check with him, 'cause if I can't talk to you direct, I'll call him."

Their embrace was interrupted by the entrance of Marshal Bass, Flo Nesbitt, and Mace Edwards. Serena wiped away her tears and looked questioningly in their direction.

Flo Nesbitt's eyes were also red. She stuttered as she began to speak. "I ju-just ca-came by to tell you how gr-grateful I am that you saved my daughter's life, Mr. Tremain. She's my only child, the only family I have. I am—" Flo broke down and began to cry in raucous sobs. She would have slumped to the ground if Mace had not come to her assistance.

Serena rushed to Flo's side. "What happened? Did something happen to Clara?"

"Your husband didn't tell you?" Marshal Bass asked. Serena shook her head and looked at King inquiringly.

"He saved Clara's life!" Mace interjected. "Some white men had run Clara's car off the road and were forcing themselves on her when your husband stopped them."

"When was this?" Serena asked.

Mace answered. "She was returning early this morning from getting the Bodie Wells *Clarion* published in Johnsonville when three white men forced her car off the road. They must have been waiting for her."

"She shouldn't be driving alone at that time of the morning," Bass commented.

"I couldn't stop her," Mace said. "You know how headstrong she can be."

"Why didn't you tell me?" Serena asked King.

"There was so much to talk about, I just didn't get around to it," King explained with a shrug. "Serena, why don't you take care of Mrs. Nesbitt and I'll talk to Mace and the marshal?"

Serena acceded with a nod of her head, but it was clear that she didn't like being sent away. She turned and went to minister to Flo.

"Clara said that you killed at least two of the men," Bass said to King. "I need to know exactly where this happened so I can get out to those bodies before someone else finds them. If those bodies get carried into Clairborne, there'll be hell to pay for the folks in Bodie Wells. The man who got away has probably already made it into Clairborne."

King gave Mace a questioning look and then looked at Bass. "I don't know Mace that well, Marshal. You vouchin' for him? I wouldn't like nobody to go runnin' to Clairborne with what I got to say."

"Mace won't ever go runnin' to Clairborne and I vouch for him as a steady man in any situation. Tell me where the bodies are."

King chuckled. "Don't worry about it, the two that's dead, they's already buried where no one will ever find them. And I knicked the third man pretty good. He ain't gon' be goin' nowhere in a hurry for a long time. If I had mo' time I'd found him and done him too!"

"What about their car?" Bass asked.

"Me and Sampson went out and picked it up early this mo'nin' befo' first light. I done dropped it off at Octavius Boothe's shop. I'm sho' he gon' have it disassembled by this evenin'. I didn't leave no evidence but the last man, and me and Sampson looked all over for him, but he must've crawled beneath the underbrush. We couldn't find him nowhere."

"Where did you bury the other two?" Bass asked.

"Dropped 'em down an old mining shaft a mile or so off Old Lubbuck Road with a couple of hand grenades. They won't be findin' them bodies soon."

"What about the third man? How good did you knick him?" Bass couldn't let loose his pursuit until he was assured that Bodie Wells would be safe from reprisals by the whites in Clairborne. "Do you think he made it to the road?"

"He got one point thirty-oh-six bullet in the leg and one in the shoulder," King answered in a matter-of-fact tone. "I don't think he made the road. He didn't turn and fight once while I was huntin' him. He ain't got the grit to make the road with all the pain he's feelin'. He done gone to ground somewhere. Couldn't track his trail of blood in the dark and when we returned the wind had picked up and the trail was gone. Now, I just want the temperature to drop below freezin' and we can leave him where he lays. Let the weather take care of him."

Flo Nesbitt walked over and stood swaying on the edge of the conversation. The men looked at her, then continued their exchange.

"What if some good ol' boys find him," Bass challenged, "before he dies?"

"He didn't never see me. All he saw was my bullets," King answered with a shrug. "His two friends is gone and so is the car. Ain't nothin' left to show what happened, 'cause me and Sampson cleaned up the place good when we went back for the car. What he gon' say? What he gon' tell 'em? This just gon' be another one of them prairie mysteries."

"What about my daughter? What about justice?" Flo screamed. She rubbed her swollen and tear-reddened eyes. She had become nauseated by the men's discussion. They talked as if they were discussing the affairs of a breed mare. They were concerned with distant intellectual concepts such as evidence and blame, but not one word addressed the tragedy and violation done to one of the women of their town. It was intolerable. She turned and walked away without a further word. Serena gave King a questioning look and followed Flo to make sure she was alright.

King looked at Mace. "She got all the justice she gon' get from that particular white man. I bet, if he lives, he don't go on no more night rides with the boys. She push for any more than that and I'll be on the block too."

"You don't have to worry about that," Bass advised. "As soon as she gets a chance to think about it, she'll see the light. I knows she didn't get a chance to say it like she wanted, but she's real grateful to you, King. From now on, you'll always have her in your corner and she's a good friend to have."

Mace stuck out his hand to shake hands with King. "We don't know each other, Mr. Tremain, but your intervention on Clara's behalf has made me also want to become your friend. And you don't need to worry about anything that's said. Everything that we've discussed will be kept close to the chest for as long as I live."

"Speakin' of keepin' things close to the chest," Bass moved closer to the two men and dropped his voice, "we gon' have to say somethin' that gon' end all the questions about this, 'cause you know some Negroes can't keep their mouths shut. Clara told me somethin' that could turn this into a powder keg. She said she recognized the third man and he was Frank Bolton."

"That's Big Daddy Bolton's son?" King asked. Everyone knew Big Daddy. Within his first week in Bodie Wells, King had heard his name mentioned several times.

"Sho' is," Bass confirmed. "Frank is a pretty big turnip in the Klan too. Now, we got to find a way to wrap this thing up so it don't start no race war. We don't want the sheriff in Clairborne ridin' in here with twenty, thirty men roustin' folks."

"Why don't we say that the men done this to her got away? And she didn't recognize them 'cause they was hooded."

Mace nodded. "That's good! I like that! By the time she was found they had escaped. We brought her straight to the doctor back to town. She didn't see any of her attackers clearly. So we don't know who the men are."

"We could even float out some kind of reward for information that leads to the capture of them criminals."

"What do we say they done to her?" Bass prodded, remaining focused on his task. "If it gets out that she was raped, the next white man found dead somewheres will make the people in Clairborne think one of us did it for revenge."

"Let's just say they roughed her up pretty good, which they did," Mace suggested. "I know it won't stop the gossip in the town, but if it's the official word, the fools in Clairborne will accept it. Maybe if Clara and I move up our marriage plans, that might—" Mace left his thought unfinished.

"Don't do nothin' to change yo' plans," Bass countered. "Ain't nothin' you can do. Folks gon' talk. All we can do is make sho' ain't nothin' real they can base it on." Serena returned with a pitcher of water and offered a metal ladle around.

Bass doffed his Stetson to Serena. "No thanks, ma'am. I've got to get over to the doctor's office. Then I'll have to check on Mrs. Nesbitt." He turned to King and said, "We ain't gon' say nothin' 'bout you bringin' her in, King. That way can't no finger point to you. But some of us will know that you did a hero's job this mornin'. Good day to you."

"He speaks for me too," Mace said, extending his hand again.

"I's glad I was there on time," King said as he shook Mace's hand. "But there's a couple questions that's botherin' me. Was they waitin' for her, or was it the luck of the draw they got her? And if they was waitin' for her, how'd they know she was gon' be there?"

"It bears some thought," Bass said, rubbing his mustache. "If you wouldn't mind takin' a ride with me, I'll stop by for you late this afternoon."

"Sho' 'nough, Marshal."

Bass looked at the truck and all the merchandise that had been unloaded. "Looks like you got a small fortune in goods here."

"And I got a bill of sale for every man jack piece of it too," King answered with a smile.

Bass returned his smile. "I'll bet you do. I'll bet you do."

Mace and Marshal Bass walked toward the small alley created by the opening between Dorsett's cabinet shop and the apothecary and subsequently disappeared around the corner.

"Negro, when were you going to tell me?" Serena said with her hands on her hips and a playful smile on her face.

"Tell you what?" King asked with a raised eyebrow.

"You know what I'm talking about!" she said pointing her finger at him. "This morning! All the stuff that you did this morning."

"Did the carpenters finish all the work in the store?"

"Yes, but I don't see what that has—"

"When was you gon' tell me about it? Seems to me that's way more important to us than Clara Nesbitt's business."

Serena moved closer to King until her breasts were touching his chest. She looked up into his eyes. "Oh, so you want to argue with your wife after you have been away for both Thanksgiving and Christmas? You're a hard case, King Tremain."

"Ain't no harder than the woman I married."

Sampson came out of the store with his mouth full and a hunk of bread in his hand. His cheek was bulged with the bread he was chewing.

"Are you hungry, Sampson?" Serena asked.

Sampson stopped and looked at the bread in his hand and then back at Serena. His expression seemed to say, "Sure I'm hungry! Why do you think I have a pound of bread in my hand?" but all he did was gesture that he was hungry.

Serena grabbed King's arm. "Why don't I make us a big breakfast of eggs, grits, and sausage?"

"Sounds like a dream come true," King said, giving Serena a squeeze. "I ain't been eatin' much regular food. Just let me and Sampson lock the truck and the barn and we'll be right in."

"I'll wait here for you," Serena answered as King and Sampson hurried to secure the new shipment. Sampson put the rear gate on the truck and drove it all the way into the barn. After he came out King placed a heavy crossbar on the door and locked it down with a large iron padlock.

As they ascended the stairs to enter the back door of the store, Serena had King and Sampson arm in arm on either side of her. "We'll sit down to the first family meal we've had in a real long time," she announced as they entered the darkness of the store.

"It's almost noon! Where's my damn horse?" Booker demanded. "I told Cordel over an hour ago that I needed my horse immediately!"

Lightning Smith was bent over with a horse's hoof between his legs, nailing on a shoe. He did not look up and, despite a mouthful of nails, he spoke fairly clearly. "You wasn't the first in line. I gots other peoples befo' you. I told Cordel not to saddle yo' horse 'cause she got a shoe that's crackin'. I needs to change it befo' you takes her. Otherwise I can let you use Old Red. He got good shoes."

"I wouldn't ride that nag if it was the last horse on earth! I'll take my own horse! I want Cordel to saddle her now!"

Lightning spit a nail into his hand and seated it with a few light taps of his hammer. He checked the fit all around the horseshoe, then tapped home all the nails with short powerful flicks of his wrist. He let go of the horse's hoof and stood up. "You can take her. That be up to you. I recommends you stay off the pavement and rocky ground 'cause that shoe gon' go soon. You could hurt yo' horse bad. If you stays on dirt and grass, it might last 'til you get back here, dependin' on how far you's goin'."

The mare had a nice ground-gobbling gallop. Booker guided her over rolling hills and through the underbrush of small gullies and ravines. He stayed off the traveled roads. He would rather have set out under cover of night to perform this particular mission instead of broad daylight, but he had no choice. As soon as he heard that Clara Nesbitt had been brought in alive, he knew something had gone wrong with the plan. She was supposed to have been killed. Frank had even boasted that he and his friends would have some fun with her first.

In the distance, the Ouachita Mountains raised their forested shoulders to the sky. The tops of the snow-capped peaks were indistinct in the afternoon haze. Booker was headed overland to the Ouachita Road that connected the towns of Clairborne and Idabel. It was also the road one traveled if the destination was Johnsonville. Booker was headed toward an abandoned mining camp that was about ten miles off the Ouachita Road but only a mile or so off the unpaved road that forked to Johnsonville. The trip would have been faster in a car, but the means of ingress and egress were restricted to the roads. Booker wanted full flexibility in case he had to leave the site in a hurry.

He reined the mare down into a dry riverbed and followed it uphill several miles through rising ridges until he came to Sardis Ridge, which curved fifteen miles southwest toward Pine Creek Lake. He crossed the ridge and traveled the length of Rattlesnake Canyon until he came upon the old mining camp. There were five dilapidated wooden buildings still standing in the camp, the largest of which was an old two-story saloon. Rather than boldly reveal himself, Booker alighted from his horse and led it to a stand of tall pines that overlooked the camp. He studied the five buildings, which consisted of several small houses, a saloon, and a barn-like general store. After that he studied the surrounding ruins and forest. There was no sign of life. He made his way cautiously into the camp, coming up behind the saloon. He stared into the darkness of its interior. This was the place they were supposed to leave Clara's body.

It had been a marvelous plan. Booker had been quite proud of it. It got rid of one of the central figures in the group that was challenging his power, and the *Clarion* would die with her. It would throw his opponents into confusion. Her body would eventually be found, and even though there would be no evidence as to who killed her, it would nonetheless, send a message: don't be foolish enough to mess with Booker Little. But somehow, somewhere the plan had not been carried through to fruition. It was like Big Daddy to change plans without warning, but Booker didn't think Clara's escape was a premeditated action on Big Daddy's part. Something went wrong.

Booker could not afford to sit back and wait. His involvement required that he investigate for his own well-being. He pulled his .38 revolver from its holster and pushed open the back door of the saloon. The door swung open with a loud squeaking sound.

A raspy voice called out, "I ain't dead yet, nigger! I still got my gun!"

Booker ducked immediately and wondered whether he had walked into a trap. The voice sounded like Frank Bolton's. Booker's mind began to click along. If it was a trap, he had too much open space to traverse to get safely to his horse. The other two men must be stationed in the buildings on either side of the saloon. Since Frank already knew he was there, Booker called out, "That you in there, Frank? You sound like you're in a bad mood. What happened to the plan?"

There was a minute of silence, then the voice called out, "Booker? That you? Thank God! Thank God! I need help! I been shot! You got to get me to a doctor!"

"You in there by yourself, Frank? Where's your two pals?"

"They're dead. Some strange nigger killed them and he would've killed me too, but I escaped! He tried to hunt me down like I was an animal! He had some kind of machine gun! He sprayed the bushes with bullets lookin' for me! The bastard got me a couple times too. I lost a lot of blood. I need a doctor. Get in here and help me!"

Booker did not change his position. "How did you know it was a colored man who was hunting you?" he asked in a conversational tone.

"Did you hear me, boy? I said I need a doctor! I need help!"

"You ought to be more polite, Frank. Seeing that no one knows you're here but me. If I was a mean man, I might leave you here. You could die out here." Frank did not answer. Booker checked the sun, then pulled his watch out of his pocket and flicked open the fourteen-carat-gold lid. It was nearly two o'clock and the sun was already dipping behind the western ridges of the Ouachitas. "It's going to be cold tonight, Frank. Probably drop to the teens. Think you can live through another night of that, Frank?"

"I'll give you anything! Please help me! Once I'm home, I'll see that you get a reward!"

"How did you know the man who was hunting you was colored?" Booker holstered his gun and sat down on the steps by the door.

"Are you gon' help me?"

"Of course, Frank. Just answer my question."

There was a moment of silence. Then Frank answered, "He kept tauntin' me, callin' me a little white boy, sayin' that the booga-man was looking for me to send me to hell." Frank stopped to catch his breath. "Alright, I answered your question, now help me. Please."

"Throw your gun out, Frank, and I'll come in for you."

The sound of a heavy metal object skidding across a wooden floor emanated from the darkness of the saloon. "There it is. Please come now and help me."

Booker stood up and pushed the door open slowly. He stepped inside the doorway and closed it behind him. He stood against the wall. The room was in darkness for all the windows were shuttered. He stared into the shadows, waiting for his eyes to adjust to the dimness. "Where are you, Frank?"

"Over here by the staircase."

Staying against the wall, Booker edged around the room to the left toward the stairs. As his eyes accommodated to the lack of light, he saw on the right the dim outline of a long wooden bar and the muted reflections of the cracked mirror behind it. Then he saw movement near the bottom of the stairs. It was Frank trying to sit up.

Booker threaded his way through some tables and chairs and assisted Frank to his feet. Frank groaned and leaned against him. Booker was positioning Frank to help him hobble out the door when Frank pulled the derringer on him.

"You's a dead man if you try to run out on me now, nigger! I got two bullets with yo' name on it. Take that waist gun you carry out slowly. Slowly! No quick moves. I want you to lift it out slowly by its butt and toss it over there."

Booker did as directed and tossed the gun toward the front door of the saloon. He was frightened but he didn't show it. "You wouldn't shoot your own brother, would you, Frank?"

"Nigger, you ain't my brother!" Frank jammed the derringer against the side of Booker's face. "You's just a half-breed, nigger bastard that my father had with yo' nigger bitch mother! Just 'cause you got an education don't change nothin'! You still just a nigger! Now, let's go! If there any tricks, I'll blow yo' black ass away." Frank held the gun in his left hand for he had been shot in his right shoulder. He slung his gun arm around Booker's shoulders but kept the derringer pointed at Booker's head. "Let's get to the door. Then we'll figure things from there."

Dragging his injured left leg while leaning on Booker's shoulder, Frank hopped toward the back door. They had to negotiate a difficult turn around one of the supporting posts. Frank lost his balance while twisting around on one foot, and Booker did not compensate—he allowed himself to be pulled off center. As a result, Frank fell heavily into the post, smacking it with his right shoulder. Frank cried out in pain and involuntarily dropped the small gun. Booker sprang away and left Frank clutching a piece of his lapel. Booker lost no time searching the shadows on the floor for the fallen derringer. He pushed tables and chairs out of his way seeking the weapon. It was now a matter of life and death. Booker had to kill Frank, otherwise Frank would kill him. There was no middle ground now. Booker was becoming distraught when he saw the small gun gleaming faintly under a distant chair. He dove under the table in pursuit of it.

Frank saw what Booker was doing and hopped in the direction in which the other gun had been thrown. Frank made one or two hops unassisted, then fell headlong to the floor. The landing nearly cost him his consciousness. He struggled against the pain to stay in the present. He shook his head to clear the red cobwebs and rolled over and looked for the revolver. He saw it on the other side of the table to his right. He crawled toward it, pushing chairs out of the way as he progressed. Booker's voice stopped him just before he put his hand on the gun.

"Hold it right there, Frank! Don't move a muscle. I don't want to kill you unless I have to."

"What do you want from me?"

"I want some guarantee that you won't come after me with the Klan or the law."

"Okay, you got it! I swear I won't go after you."

"The problem is, Frank, I don't believe you!"

"That's your problem!" Frank reached and grabbed the revolver. As he turned to shoot, Booker fired both barrels of the derringer. One of the shots went wide but the other hit Frank in the stomach. He convulsed from the impact of the bullet, then raised the revolver and began firing into the shadows. "The Klan's gon' come down hard on Bodie for this! I won't forget you neither!" he shouted. "Come on, you bastard, let's finish this. Let's shoot it out! We gon' burn yo' town to the ground! We gon' cook a mess of niggers!" Frank's shouts echoed through the saloon. He did not know he was alone.

Booker had slipped out of the saloon as soon as he saw that he had not killed Frank with either of his shots. He had no other weapon and he saw no reason to challenge Frank when there were at least three bullets left in the .38. Booker hurried up the hill to the stand of trees. Once he mounted his horse, he decided to go to Johnsonville and spend the night. It was only eight miles away and then he could return early in the morning and finish the job, if necessary.

It was two o'clock when King went over to the livery stables to get his big chestnut gelding. Cordel Witherspoon saddled King's horse and tightened down the hackamore. King gave the chestnut a handful of sliced apples and stepped into the saddle. Marshal Bass met him outside the livery and they rode out of town together.

"Where we going?" King asked as they reached the edge of town and headed north toward the Ouachitas.

"I'd like to take a look at the scene where all this happened," Bass answered. "We can't afford to be loosey-goosey. The whole town could be in danger."

"That's about a two-and-a-half-hour ride. Why don't we take a car?"

" 'Cause I knows a back way and I don't want nobody seein' us drive away together. Then on the way back, I thought we'd drop by the Black Rose Saloon. I heard that Elmo Thomas is comin' in with a couple of his buddies and I thought you might want to come along for that."

King smiled. "Yeah, he stopped by for a visit while I was away. I want to see him."

The two men rode through the rolling hills toward the rising foothills for thirty minutes without speaking before Bass asked, "How come you came to pick Bodie Wells?"

"I told you before, Bodie's about the only colored town in Arkansas, Louisiana, Texas, and Oklahoma that got electricity. I didn't want to give up electricity and indoor plumbing."

STANDING AT THE SCRATCH LINE · 341

"Yes, I guess there ain't too many towns of our folks got electricity. We wouldn't have it neither if Big Daddy hadn't corralled a mess of people to vote on the Pine Creek Lake Dam Project. Bodie Wells still wouldn't have got the electricity 'ceptin' we was on the way between Clairborne and Idabel and Big Daddy owns the company that pumps the water into the two cisterns on the edge of town. It be the same water company that sells water to Clairborne. Yesiree, Big Daddy made a killin' on the Pine Creek deal."

"Colored folk around Bodie Wells look like they's doin' pretty good too," King commented. "And they has good farmland. I was surprised to see colored folk with such good-quality bottomland."

"That's 'cause they diverted two rivers to flow past Clairborne into Pine Creek Lake. Them rivers used to flood this whole area every spring. It was sometimey tryin' to plant a crop out here. Some years you could bring it in, others the water would take it."

"I's surprised the whites ain't moved to reclaim this land," King said. " 'Cause once they see colored folk own somethin' valuable, they try to get it."

"They's movin' in alright. That's what Booker Little's all about. He frontin' for Big Daddy, like he think Big Daddy is gon' remember he's his son. I can't stand it. It's what's really makin' me retire: colored folk don't seem to want to work together. Once somebody get a little money, he like to forget where he came from. Like he ain't colored no more, like he ain't got to fight the same battles as the rest of us. I don't understand colored folks. Even the church don't seem to help."

They rode on in silence until they entered the dry riverbed. There were fresh prints of a shod horse in the fine silt. The two men followed the hoofprints when they left the riverbed at Sardis River and crossed down into Rattlesnake Canyon. The prints seemed to be traveling to the same destination, until Bass turned his horse up a steep defile and began to climb out of the canyon. King alighted from his horse and led it up the defile by the reins. When he got to the top, Bass was waiting for him. King looked back at the lone hoofprints continuing through the canyon. "Where does the canyon lead?" he asked.

"To an old abandoned miner's camp," Bass replied and turned his horse toward the road to Johnsonville. King mounted and followed him. They were picking their way through a heavily wooded area. There were stands of pines, sycamores, and cedars providing cover for them as they cautiously approached the site of the attack.

"How come you was travelin' on the Johnson Road?" Bass asked in a low voice.

King dropped his volume as well. "I heard that there was roadblocks to stop whiskey runners on them new highways. I didn't want no whites messin' with my stuff so I come a back way myself."

"You runnin' whiskey?" Bass asked.

"I ain't sayin' yes and I ain't sayin' no, but as long as it ain't in yo' territory, it ain't yo' concern."

Bass gave an understanding nod as he dismounted and led his horse into the shadows of a small glade. King jumped down from the stallion and came over to stand with Bass. Within a few minutes he outlined the circumstances and layout at the time he had come upon the attack. They were about to traverse the site when they noticed the same hoofprints that they had seen in the riverbed.

"Somebody's been here since we was here this mornin'," King observed. "The ground was too hard this mornin' for prints like that, plus me and Sampson brushed down the whole area."

"Somebody from Bodie Wells," Bass acknowledged. "Well, ain't no need to show 'em that we been here too. I seen enough. Let's go by that old miner's camp. It looks like it might be part of the puzzle."

A brief reconnaissance of the area around the miner's camp showed where the horse had been tied before the rider descended into the camp itself. King and Bass followed the footprints to the back of the saloon. They entered and found Frank Bolton's body. He was lying in a puddle of congealing blood in the interior of the dark saloon.

King and Bass agreed that it was not in the interest of Bodie Wells for Frank Bolton to be found dead. They had to dispose of the body. There were several mine shafts nearby, but only one suitable for hiding a body. Bass and King carried the body far into the descending shaft, after which King threw in a couple of hand grenades.

"You always carry such?" Bass asked after the explosions had caused the shaft to collapse.

"A colored man can't always tell what he gon' need," King replied. "I bought a mess of these on the black market after we was demobbed. They come in handy every now and then."

"I'll remember that," Bass said, giving King a strange look. "Let's hit the trail," Bass advised. "Them explosions could echo a long way in this country."

"First, we better check and see if there's anything else in the saloon that might lead to Bodie Wells."

"You's a sly one," admitted Bass. "That's the smart thing to do, but we better hurry."

A search of the saloon produced a torn piece of pinstripe fabric, a two-shot derringer, a .38-caliber revolver and a .44 Colt single-action revolver. Bass packed the evidence in his saddlebags and the two of them headed back toward the Black Rose Saloon. Bass took a totally different path home; picking his way between the trees, he rode his horse up a narrow ravine that opened onto Rattlesnake Canyon. Once more, King dismounted and led his horse up the steep course of the ravine.

"You always do that?" Bass asked when King joined him at the crest of the ridge.

"I weighs considerable more than you," King answered, mounting his horse. "We done rode over twenty-five miles today. I saves my horse, 'ceptin' for emergencies." The trip home took longer because neither man wanted to leave a trail returning to Bodie Wells. They traveled on rocky terrain whenever possible and took periodic detours to throw off any followers. By the time they arrived at the Black Rose it was nearly eight-thirty in the evening and the stars had established themselves in the night sky.

The Black Rose was nestled at the bottom of a furrow of two large, rolling hills. It did not have electricity, but it was, nonetheless, a well-lighted establishment. From the south, its second-story lamps could be seen for miles on a clear night. It was called a honky-tonk by the temperance element, who were always seeking to close the business. But they were never clever enough to outwit its owner, Wichita Kincaid. She ran her establishment with her own particular flair. She had music six nights a week and was only closed on Sabbath. She had a stable of clean girls provided for those with the money to pay for the pleasures of feminine flesh. She ran legitimate card games in the back rooms and served decent bootleg liquor.

Adjacent to the Black Rose was T-Bone Barnett's Corral and Livery. Barnett had one of the largest string of horses in southwest Oklahoma and was known far and wide as an expert in judging horseflesh. T-Bone was a short, dark, powerfully built man with an extraordinarily handsome, smooth baby face that was quick to break into a smile. As King and Bass dismounted, T-Bone came out of the barn and greeted Bass.

"How do, Marshal?"

"It goes, it goes," Bass said, trying to stretch out the stiffness from being in the saddle over five hours during the day. "T-Bone, have you met—"

"I ain't met him, but I know who he is." T-Bone interrupted with an easy smile. "You Tremain, ain't you?"

King nodded. "How do you know?"

"I heard you rode a big chestnut. Soon as I saw this horse, I knew who you were. Ain't another horse like this in this county, I'll bet."

"No there ain't," King concurred. "I puts time into trainin' my horses."

"We'll be in the Rose for a while, T-Bone, long enough for the saddles to come off and the horses to be fed and watered."

"You don't normally have long-winded business at the Black Rose, Marshal. What's up?"

Bass answered with a question. "Is Elmo Thomas there yet?"

"Yep, him and two of his boys came in about an hour or so ago. They was packing plenty steel too. Everybody was wearin' a sidearm. One of the boys had a scattergun."

"Thanks, T-Bone," Bass said and walked with King toward the Black Rose. "Let me tell you right now, King, I ain't lookin' for no gunplay. I'm just comin' to remind him not to get wild in Bodie Wells. I figured if you had a peacemaker, maybe you boys might be adult enough to put this pissin' contest on the back burner until the holiday season is over."

"The way he and his boys is armed, I'm sho' that Elmo got the Christmas season on his mind." King said dryly. "Only thing is, he only want to give little lead presents."

"I don't plan to enter with my gun drawn, so don't be too quick to slap leather. I just want to talk."

"If you keep talkin', you gon' be by yo'self," King observed. "You knows these people is trash and if you thought you really could trust 'em, you wouldn't have asked me to come along. Now we both know that; let's be on our toes."

As they got to the door of the saloon, Bass said, "No offense meant but I didn't want you to come with me. I'd have chosen anybody but you, but there ain't nobody else who got as much sand as you do and can handle a gun as well. Boy, I know you's a man-killer. I like you, boy, but I knows if'en I wasn't retirin', we'd be bangin' heads and I knows I'd be gettin' the worst of it."

"Pops, why don't we put this talk aside and get to gettin'?"

Bass turned to King. "Oh, now you's callin' me Pops, is you?"

King chuckled. "You's callin' me boy!"

Bass pushed open the door. "If'en I know'd you be sassin' me I wouldn't have asked you to come along."

The Rose was jumping for a Thursday night. Little Boy Bones was playing a hard Texas rag on the piano, hitting every key that he thought was relevant. Behind him played a banjo and a clarinet, weaving their counterharmonies in with his body-shaking music. Every table was occupied with early New Year's revelers. The bootleg was flowing and folks were out to have a good time. A couple of men were up shouting bets at a whist game that was going on in the corner. Several couples were dancing in the center of the floor in front of the bar and a number of people stood drinking at the bar.

"I'm gon' follow yo' lead," King said in Bass's ear. Then he walked along the wall toward the end of the bar.

Bass walked right into the center of the room and asked in a loud voice, "Anybody seen Elmo Thomas? I's lookin' for Elmo Thomas. I just wants to have a few words with him."

One of the men standing by the whist game said in a loud voice, "Is that the old toothless marshal? I thought he was dead."

A woman sidled up to the man and said in a high nasal voice, "I heard he used to have a bite, but it's been so long everybody who knew about it is dead." There were guffaws around the room. The crude witticisms appeared to appeal to the humor of the crowd. There was loud laughing and catcalls coming from every corner.

Bass didn't respond, nor did he take a step back. He merely waited with his arms at his side.

"Who say he's lookin' for me?" The voice, brash and arrogant, came from a muscular brown-skinned man who wore his hair greased back. The man stood at the top of the stairs buttoning his shirt. "Who say he's lookin' for me?"

"It's me, Elmo," Bass answered calmly. "I wanted to talk to you before any New Year's celebrations got started. I knows you's got a followin' and they' do pretty near anythin' you say—"

"You ought to know better than to come out here lookin' for me, Marshal!" Elmo said as he slid down the bannister and walked over to confront Bass. "I don't like people who come say they lookin' for me! It gives me bad ideas!"

"I don't want no trouble, Elmo. I just want to work somethin' out for the law-abidin' folks of Bodie Wells."

"You already got trouble, Bass!" Elmo shouted.

A man to King's right was quietly pulling a shotgun from a bedroll. King stole up behind him and waited until he had fully withdrawn the weapon. The man was standing next to a supporting pillar and he could not see King.

Elmo was quite confident. He turned and addressed everyone present. "You may be retirin' earlier than you think, Bass, 'cause we gon' leave you with a little somethin' tonight!"

The man with the shotgun cocked it and started to move around behind Bass. King blindsided him with the butt of his pistol and would have hit him again, but the man collapsed too quickly. King stepped out into the room and said loudly for all to hear, "I'm lookin' for you too, Elmo, but

I don't want to talk. I'm King Tremain and I just want to spill some of your blood!" He opened his jacket and revealed his other gun. "I'm carryin' killin' irons from the hips on down! Come on, let's hear the cold steel sing!"

There was absolute silence in the room. A man who had been playing whist stood up suddenly and King had a pistol trained on him.

"The next man to move quickly dies," King warned. Then suddenly King laughed. It was a deep throaty chuckle. "You folks don't know me, so let me show you somethin' just to prevent a fool from makin' a bad choice. You folks see that red can on the table behind me? I'll shoot it twice and still have time to kill Elmo before he moves!" Without warning, King glanced back quickly and fired two shots. The can sailed off the table and fell to the floor with a clatter. King now had both guns in his hands. "You was bold enough to come by my place when I was out of town. I heard you threatened my wife! I'm standin' in front of you! Now, what you got? Here's death talkin' to you. Make yo' move!"

"Stop it! Stop it!" screamed a woman's voice. "I won't have a killin' in my place this New Year's! Any man that fires a gun or pulls a knife is banned from ever coming here again!" It was Wichita Kincaid, the owner of the Black Rose. She was standing on a balcony adjacent to the staircase.

King ignored her and taunted Elmo. "I hear you like knives, Elmo. How come we don't just go and do it blade to blade down by the corral? I'm sho' all these people gon' want to see when I cut yo' heart out!"

Wichita shouted at King. "I don't know who you are, but if you don't shut up, I'll have my men throw you out!"

"You better say joe, 'cause you sho' don't know!" King replied. Then he urged, "Send 'em! Ain't nobody throwin' me out of nowhere! I'll leave thirteen or fourteen men dead on this floor before I die! Send 'em, sugar! Let them take three steps!"

It was as if everyone in the saloon was caught in a tableau. Nobody moved. There was absolute silence again.

Bass spoke to King. "Perhaps it's time we were on our way, King. I've said my piece and I believe you've said yours."

"I ain't ready to go yet," King countered.

"Why not?" the woman demanded. "You're ruining my business and you've proved that Elmo is afraid of you. What else do you want? Will you please leave now!"

"Anythin' you say, Miss. I don't want to overstay my welcome. You want to come with me, Elmo?"

Elmo Thomas moved for the first time since King challenged him. He raised his open hands to show that he was not palming a weapon and went and sat at a card table. "Go with you? I ain't goin' nowhere with you! I come to town to play cards and have me a woman! I ain't studyin' you!"

King saw that the man on the other side of the table from Elmo adjusted his seat as King moved around the room. He figured the man had a gun under the table, but the man would not have a clear shot until Elmo moved. So when Elmo edged his chair back from the table, King was ready. He fired both pistols, drilling four shots into the man's body, knocking him over backward in his chair. A revolver slipped from the dead man's hands and he lay still. King walked over to the table and hit Elmo on the side of the head with his pistol butt. "You want to play dirty? I love to play dirty!" King stomped on Elmo's hand. Elmo screamed in pain. King threw back his head and roared. He turned and glanced around at the silent observers. "There any more who want a piece of this?" He looked down at Elmo on the floor. "Get up and fight, dog, or I'll kill you where you lay!"

"Not in my joint, you won't!" Wichita said and two of her men appeared next to her with shotguns.

King smiled. The blood was bubbling in his ears. Every fiber of his being was alive and he did not want to leave without killing Elmo. "Looks like you might do some of yo' customers along with me if'en you use them scatterguns. And you can't be sure you'll get me!"

A man at a table stood up slowly with his hands high. "I ain't part of this and I ain't got no gun. I's gon' take my leave now." Two other men stood up as well. One of them stuttered, "I-I-I ain't c-c-come to t-town for no tr-tr-trouble either!"

"If too many people start movin', I'm gon' commence to shootin'!"

"Don't do it, King," warned Bass. "We've completed our business here."

"We ain't finished!" King disputed. "You know sometime down the line this dog's gon' try and bushwack me!"

Wichita descended the steps. "King Tremain, before you run all my customers away, can we palaver?" She was a beautiful brown-skinned woman with big doe eyes and long, curly black hair that fell around her shoulders. "I can't let you kill any more people in here. Let my boys carry Elmo over to Johnsonville where he's wanted for robbin' their bank. They'll try him and send him on to Idabel Prison. If you want to kill him after that, it's your affair." She turned to Elmo. "You leave here with your life. What do you say?"

King looked down at Elmo, who was sitting on the floor holding his crushed hand. "You want that, Elmo? Or would you rather just get on yo' horse and ride on home?"

"You ain't gon' let me go!" Elmo answered.

"I'll give you a twenty-minute head start. In the darkness, you might have a chance. Or, you could end up like yo' brothers! You make the choice."

Elmo looked around the room and saw no support in the eyes of the onlooking crowd. "I takes Johnsonville."

TUESDAY, JANUARY 25, 1921

"This sho' some nice material you got in here, Mrs. Tremain. Bodie Wells done needed a sto' like this for some time," Ida Hoskins said as she examined a bolt of fabric.

"It comes all the way from New York, Mrs. Hoskins," Serena declared with pride. "We expect to carry a different selection of fabric in the summer, so don't buy all the material you'll need for the year on one shopping trip."

"Do y'all barter? I ain't got enough money for what we needs," Ida said quietly, not wishing to share the information with the other customers who were looking at the store's wares. Ida Hoskins was a small, wiry, brown-skinned woman. Although her clothes were worn, they were clean and neat.

Serena nodded. Ida looked dependable. Serena asked, "What are you bartering?"

"I sews good. I sees you got clothes patterns. If'en somebody want some of them things in yo' catalogs, I could make them, or I could work helpin' to make adjustments on them ready-made dresses you got in the window. Or, I could bring you some meat when we butchers in the spring. My husband cures a mighty mean ham."

Serena went behind the counter and got a book and returned to Ida and said quietly, "Mrs. Hoskins, we allow up to twenty-five dollars' credit. Why don't you get things you need and we'll total up and you'll just sign the book for the amount."

"What about interest? Bolton and Little charge interest."

"At Tremain Dry Goods all we care about is that you pay what you owe. We don't have interest on our accounts."

"Well, I'll say!" declared Ida Hoskins with a smile. "I can see you gon' get a lot of business. And I don't mind puttin' the word out myself."

"You do that, Mrs. Hoskins. You do that."

There was the sound of someone running on the wooden planks outside the store. Serena looked up and saw Cordel Witherspoon run by. He turned into the main store. She heard his panicked voice jabbering at King, and then he ran out of the store and down the street.

King put his head in the dress shop. "Clara's mother done shot Booker Little."

"What? When?" Serena exclaimed with surprise.

"Shot him dead in front of Marshal Bass's office," King answered. "Point-blank range." He walked over to the cash drawer and began to count its paper money contents.

Ida Hoskins shook her head. "I declare, that don't sound like Flo Nesbitt."

Serena took off her apron and asked, "Why? Why would she shoot Booker?"

"She must have found out it was him what told those white men when Clara would be travelin' to Johnsonville last month."

Serena took out a brush and hurriedly began to reposition the pins in her hair. "Is it true? Did Booker tell those white men about Clara's going to Johnsonville to get her paper printed?"

"Yeah, it was him," King answered as he continued to separate the bills into different denominations. "We matched them hoofprints we saw with his horse. Lightning even kept the shoe. Then, of course, we had that piece of material from his suit. We knew it was him."

"Why did you wait? Why didn't you do something about it? Clara was attacked almost a month ago."

"I wanted to do him, but Mace and Marshal Bass thought it might cause reprisals from Big Daddy, Booker being Big Daddy's house slave and all. They thought we should wait until just before the election to bring out the information. I guess that's why Bass showed Flo that little snip of cloth today."

"Do you think Bolton will tell the riders to ride on Bodie Wells now that Booker's dead?"

"Can't honestly say, sugar," King said with a shrug. "Depends if he figured out that colored folks killed his white son."

Ida put her hand over her chest. "Frank Bolton is dead? Oh, my God!"

"Yep, Booker done killed him; killed him the evenin' after Clara was attacked," King confirmed. "Now, Big Daddy Bolton don't have no heir but Mace Edwards. Kind a funny, ain't it? He might end up killin' the only child he got left and the only one who was worth a damn!"

Serena countered, "He still has Wichita Kincaid."

"She ain't Big Daddy's daughter. She's his wife, Sarah's daughter!"

Serena turned to Ida with surprise. "What? She had a colored child and she lived to grow up? How come she's alive? To protect her reputation, a white woman would normally kill a child like that or send it to be raised somewhere else! Oh, this can't be true! Flo and Mabel would have told me about this!"

Ida pursed her lips. "As far as I know, only Bass, Wichita, and Octavius Boothe know about it! I wouldn't have known, but I overheard Bass and 'Tavius talkin' about it a few years back."

"How do they know?" Serena asked, her curiosity awakened.

"Well, Romelus Boothe is father to both her and Octavius!"

Serena put her hands on her hips. "I heard that Octavius's father was lynched! So, that's the reason behind it?"

Ida stepped closer to Serena. "Sarah Bolton done favored that particular Negro too much. What with all of Big Daddy's playin' around with colored women, I guess she thought she'd turn the tables on him."

"I tell you in these small towns, folks' lives get all twisted together," King observed.

Serena looked at Ida. "Does Big Daddy know about Wichita?"

"Sho' do. Him and Sarah must have some sort of agreement, 'cause he the one done set Wichita up at the Black Rose. That's why 'that place don't ever get raided and the Klan don't burn no crosses there."

Serena declared, "If I carried a child for nine months, I'd never give it up! It would be my child! I can't imagine anything being more important than my child! I'd never give up a child I carried for nine months! Never!"

The church bells were tolling twelve noon as King and Serena were standing behind the counter in the store, totaling the morning's sales. Because the storm shutters were closed as insulation against the cold, the store was illuminated by bright ceiling lights. Serena was standing next to King, watching him shuffle through the paper money.

King nudged Serena. "If we keep on practicin' like we did last night, we just might get a chance to see how you act with a baby, Mrs. Tremain."

Serena gave him a sly smile in return. "Was that only practice? I thought you were an expert, Mr. Tremain."

King let his hands drift over the small of her back and come to rest on her behind. "Best bottomland in the state of Oklahoma," he declared.

"That better be the only stretch you try to farm," Serena teased warningly.

There was a sharp rapping on the front door. King and Serena looked at each other. "You didn't tell that Hoskins woman to come back so soon, did you?"

"No, I told her she could start work after lunch. She shouldn't be here until one o'clock."

A voice outside yelled, "King Tremain! We need you!"

"Bodie Wells is gettin' busier than dog shit on a New York street corner."

"King! You need to wash your mouth out with soap!" Serena chided.

The rapping continued. Sampson appeared with a shotgun. He asked in sign if he should open the door and King nodded his okay. The voice of Marshal Bass said, "Open up, King! We got problems!"

Sampson unlocked and opened the door. Mace Edwards and Raymond Bass stepped inside. Both men took off their hats upon entering and nodded to Serena.

"What's on yo' mind?" King asked as he walked over to the two men.

"You have a place we can talk?" Mace asked.

King showed the two men into a small sitting room off the foyer. "Must be somethin' hot for both of you to be comin' here." Sampson walked in behind him.

"It's hot," Bass answered. "Zeke Wakefield, he's a truck driver for one of them wheat combines, walked into my office, fresh from Clairborne, and told me there's men in the town square up there wearin' Klan getups! He say they're gettin' ready to ride on Bodie Wells!"

"Why?" King asked. "Did he say why?"

"Nope. He just got out of town as soon as he could and he picked up any colored folk that he saw headin' this way!" Bass answered. "He say everybody colored who in Clairborne is either tryin' to get out of town or is hidin' out. Woe to any colored man found on the street today."

"What you want me to do?" King asked.

"We can't afford to get into a shooting match, but we need you to stand with us. If we can get the whole town to turn out in a show of solidarity, we may be able to dissuade the whites from taking violent action."

"Far as I know, the only thing white folks understand is violence. Talk don't mean nothin' to them. They sho' didn't listen to the Indian and they ain't been listening to us!"

"Mace is right, King. Listen to him," Bass advised. "If we get into a shoot-out with the Klan and we kill too many of them, they'll call in the army and wipe Bodie Wells off the face of the map. They don't want no stories about colored folks fightin' back floatin' around. It might give some other folks ideas."

Mace joined in. "Let me try talking first! Let them take the first shot before we start fighting. I don't plan to roll over for them, but I want a peaceful solution if it's possible. Will you stand with me?"

"Nope! I ain't gon' stand in the street and face the Klan. That be givin' my life away. Tell you what, I'll be on a roof with an army machine gun coverin' you. Don't make sense to me to stand out in the street in front of a bunch of ignorant Klan boys. All they want is to spill some colored blood."

"You have an army machine gun?" Mace asked.

"Sho' do! And if any shootin' starts, I promise you not many of 'em will get to see their mamas again. So, you best speak yo' best words and plan to move if the lead starts flyin'. I'm gon' be sendin' some folk straight to hell!"

"Don't be too quick on the trigger, King," Bass cautioned. "There's people who got their roots here, buried their family and loved ones in this ground. They gon' want to continue livin' here. We got to do right by them. I'm askin' you to stay yo' hand 'til there ain't no other choice."

"Long as it ain't my folks who gon' be sacrificed, I'll do what you say." There was more knocking at the front door. Sampson went out to open it. King stepped to the door of the sitting room and looked out. He saw Serena standing in the doorway leading into the store watching. She looked at him with questions on her face. King beckoned to her to come stand beside him.

Reverend Cornelius, heading a group of people, waited patiently at the front door to be invited in. Sampson gave King a quick glance, seeking direction. King strode to the door and asked, "What I can I do for you, Reverend?"

The reverend nodded at Serena. "Hope we aren't disturbing you folks, but we heard that Mace and Marshal Bass were here."

"They are," Serena said as she came over to stand by King's shoulder. "Why don't you folks come on into the kitchen. We have more room and chairs in there."

"Thank you kindly, Mrs. Tremain," Reverend Cornelius said as he entered the foyer, leading Ma Wrangel, Lightning Smith, Octavius Boothe, Buck Henry, and Dr. Stephens.

King gave Serena a wry smile, surprised that she would invite strangers into her home. She flashed him back the look of a woman who had something to show off and ushered their visitors into the kitchen. King collected Mace and Marshal Bass and they too went into the kitchen.

After everyone was seated and Serena had served coffee to those who wished it, Mace asked Reverend Cornelius, "Were you able to contact the pastors of the other churches? Are they sending out riders to tell folks on the surrounding farms?"

Isaac Cornelius answered. "All, but Reverend Johns. He is out of town.

But we did talk to a few of his church elders and they promised to do whatever they can."

"I think we ought to pack up the women and children and get out of town," Buck Henry declared, his forehead beaded with sweat. "We can't stand up to these ruffians. They'll burn us out!"

Ma Wrangel grunted her displeasure. "Some colored folks is better at runnin' than others. I ain't got no place to run and no place I want to go. I ain't packin' nothin'. Me, my cast-iron stove, and my old, repeatin' Winchester, we stayin'!"

Lightning added his sentiments to Ma Wrangel's. "Ma done spoke for me too. We got peoples buried in this ground and years of sweat and blood spilled to build this here town. Ain't no wheres else to go!"

"I don't think they'll be bloodshed, if the whole town is in the street to meet these fools!" Mace said. "These people are basically cowards! They won't fight unless they feel they have the upper hand."

"What you think! Who gives a damn what you think!" Buck Henry exploded. "It wasn't ten years ago that they burned the original Johnsonville to the ground! All they saved was that damn printin' press! You just tryin' to give folks false hope. A smart man would cut his losses and get the hell out while the gettin' is good!"

"So why don't you be smart?" Ma Wrangel prodded. "Now, yo' partner, Booker, been shot and killed, you pretty well finished here anyway."

"Folks! Folks!" Reverend Cornelius interjected. "The only way we'll survive is through unity! We can't let our differences tear us apart before we have even met our common foe. We're in this together!"

"If you want to be fools and stay, that's up to you," Buck said as he stood up. "I'm gettin' my family out of here!"

King spoke for the first time. "If you leave, don't expect to come back and pick up where you left off. And don't take no money out'n yo' bank. All you and yo' family can leave with is the clothes on yo' back! If you don't stay and fight for the town, yo' buildin's is forfeit and we'll settle the bank business up later."

"Who are you to tell me anything? You haven't been here six months!"

"No, we haven't," Serena answered. "But we're prepared to stay and fight for what is ours!"

"That mortuary is big enough for a school," Octavius said as he looked Buck straight in the eye.

"And we need a new schoolhouse too!" Ma Wrangel agreed.

Buck looked at the faces around the table and kicked his chair over. "I'll burn it myself before I leave you anything!" He started for the door but King intercepted him.

"You in my house. You pick up that chair befo' you leave."

Buck stared at King and then back at the people around the table. He went over and picked up the chair. He straightened his jacket and walked out the door. King followed him out to the foyer.

Before Buck went out the front door, King warned him, "If you set a match to anythin', I'm gon' come after you and set yo' ass on fire! See if I don't! And don't let there be no money missin' from the bank."

When King returned to the kitchen, discussions were under way as to who would meet the Klan and where other people would be stationed. King's military experience was extremely helpful in making contingency plans in the case that violence was unavoidable. There was so much to be done that they did not have time for long discussions. After the assignments had been distributed and the people were leaving, Dr. Stephens stopped in the foyer and handed King a letter.

"Joe Wilkerson asked me to drop this off to you," Dr. Stephens explained. "He's busy sending telegraphs to all the surrounding colored towns."

King thanked the doctor and stuffed the letter into an inside pocket. He didn't have time to read it at the moment. There was too much to do. He still had to unpack the machine gun and assemble it. He followed the doctor out the door and thought no more about the letter.

When Ida Hoskins arrived at one o'clock, she assisted Serena in putting large sheets of pressed wood over the store windows as additional protection from errant bullets. "You and yo' husband done made a big difference in this town, Mrs. Tremain," Ida Hoskins commented as she struggled to lift a warped shutter into place. "There was a time when somebody came to rob the bank or ride on the town, folks just stayed in their businesses and their houses and didn't do nothin' to help. Now, look at the folk go runnin' to help." She gave a big shove and the sheet squeaked into place. "We is becomin' a real town where law-abidin' folk can live!"

The caravan of two cars and a truck followed the road as it swerved through the gullies and across the ravines that drained the foothills of the Ouachitas into the Little River. The weather had slacked from the chill of winter and the temperature had risen once again to the high thirties. There was no sun visible in the sky, only an overcast gray that stretched to the horizon. An inconstant wind swirled and eddied, creating dust devils along the side of the road.

"Don't you worry, Big Daddy," Skip Dalton assured his passenger. "We gon' find out what happened to Little Frank, even if we have to hang that nigger Booker up in front his store!"

Big Daddy looked over at Skip's profile as he steered the car along the tortuous road. "I'm not worried, Skip. And by the way, it's my store. He only operates it for me."

"You know what I mean. We'll get the information out of him one way or another!"

"Did you tell that scum you have back there in the truck that I don't want any shooting until we've had a chance to talk? I don't want to be sitting in the middle of a shoot-out in a colored town."

"I told 'em like you asked, Big Daddy. As for a shoot-out, I'll bet the niggers are so scared that by the time we get there, it'll be a ghost town. They remember what happened in Johnsonville. Most of 'em are probably half the way to Atoka right now."

Big Daddy didn't answer. He was wondering about Skip's level of intelligence. It seemed that he had cleared all the dance halls and speakeasies to assemble his army and it took only one look to see that they were undisciplined rowdies who were just looking for a good time. Big Daddy wondered if it came to a fight how many of them would break and run. It was a question that he did not want answered in his presence.

Big Daddy pushed down his window and let the clean Oklahoma air clear his thoughts. The truth was that he wouldn't have come if Sarah hadn't nagged him ceaselessly. She wanted him to investigate Frank's disappearance, which was the furthest thing from Big Daddy's mind. It sounded cold-hearted but Frank's disappearance was a godsend to his father.

"Bodie Wells is just four miles around this bend," Skip announced as the car turned off the paved road and bumped along on a gravel and dirt lane.

Despite the bumps and occasional ruts, the road was well maintained. Big Daddy could see that it had been graded since the heavy rains of last October. When had they started doing that? he wondered. That wasn't the action of people who pick up and run at the first threat of danger. It was a big effort maintaining a road as long as this one. Big Daddy almost chuckled out loud for he remembered part of an inauguration speech he had given last July at the state capitol when he was reelected for the second time to the House of Representatives. He was halfway through his speech when he decided that he would show his hand in the upcoming floor fight for a controversial highway bond; his words were: ". . . When a group of people get together to maintain more than a couple miles of roads, they begin to have a community identity for they are making an investment for the future in the place they have chosen to live, a place where they have chosen to raise their children. We're talking about

Americans, people who pulled themselves up by their own bootstraps. We're talking about people with grit and determination. They've made a commitment, the government ought to join them! . . ."

If it was true for whites, it was true for the colored; that single fact is what so many whites misunderstood about the racial question. A different skin color and being an ex-slave did not stop a person from wanting the dignity and stability that any normal person would want. Big Daddy was under no illusions about the superiority of skin color. He was a well-read man who knew that history was written by the victors and had little to do with reality. If the road was any indication, the people of Bodie Wells were prepared to stand up and fight.

During his time in the legislature, Big Daddy had heard a lot of stories about hushed-up incidents where the colored towns had wiped out roving bands of night riders and regulators. He shook his head and watched acres of tilled earth pass outside his window as the car followed the road over low, rolling hills. He was irritated with himself. He had allowed himself to be nagged into participating in a foolish act. He felt pretty confident that he could control the whites in his caravan, but what if the coloreds were led by some hothead or someone with revenge on his mind. If shooting started, Big Daddy was not optimistic about his chances. He was a big target, he couldn't run fast, and he would be perceived to be the leader.

"There it is," Skip announced as he pointed a long finger in the direction of the town. Bodie Wells was a jumble of buildings nestled in a valley between two low hills. Its three church spires could be seen standing high above the rest of the structures. They drove past several outbuildings and there was no sign of movement. "What did I tell you?" Skip said smugly. "The niggers have hightailed it!"

Big Daddy noticed that once the town started, the main street was paved in asphalt. There were a lot of white towns the size of Bodie Wells that didn't have a paved main road. The town had done a lot of improvements in the ten years since he had brought electricity to Bodie Wells.

The caravan turned onto Main Street and there were two men standing alone in the street in front of a small barricade. Big Daddy recognized them as Marshal Bass and Mace Edwards. It was almost ironic, but he was extremely happy to see that two of the cooler heads were in charge.

The car came to a stop in front of the men and Skip jumped out. "What the hell is going on here? What are you two niggers trying to do? I have a deputized posse. You better get this damn trash out of the street so we can drive on to where we want to go."

"You know you don't have jurisdiction here, Mr. Dalton," Marshal Bass said without inflection.

Skip answered. "I'm investigatin' a crime and I advise you boys to co-operate and maybe we'll leave some of this town standin'!" Three deputies got out of the second car and came over to stand with Skip.

Mace spoke for the first time. "If you don't have a warrant from Judge O'Brien, undersheriff, you have no authority to conduct an investigation here in Bodie Wells!"

Skip laughed and turned to the men standing on the back of the truck. "He says we have no authority here! That we can't conduct an investiga-tion! What do you think, boys?" There was a chorus of jeers and rebel shouts. Then a shot rang out.

Marshal Bass was spun around and knocked to the ground. Another shot rang out in response and a man fell off the truck, his rifle clattering to the pavement.

"Don't shoot! Don't shoot!" Mace called out as he turned from side to side.

The men in the truck were looking around for where the answering shot originated and got more than they bargained for. People started emerging on roofs and from behind buildings. All along Main Street windows opened and rifle barrels poked out. Within a few minutes there were nearly two hundred people in the street and almost half of them carried firearms.

Big Daddy was out of the car in an instant and called Skip over. After a few minutes of discussion, Skip turned and shouted, "No more firing! No more shooting!"

Someone on the truck shouted, "Look! The niggers is settin' a barri-cade behind us!" After that the street was silent. Where before the men in the truck had been laughing and joking, they were now silent and there was fear on their faces.

Big Daddy walked over to where Mace was assisting Bass to his feet. "You going to be alright?" he asked Bass.

"I'll live," grunted Bass. Dr. Stephens and an assistant rushed to his side and helped him back to the doctor's office.

"We're here to find out what happened to my son Frank," Big Daddy announced. "He disappeared after he had some meeting with Booker Little."

"Two other men also disappeared with him," Skip joined in. "We want to find out about them too."

"Don't know anything about it," Mace answered. "They didn't come to Bodie Wells and meet here. Nobody in Bodie Wells has seen them! Maybe you ought to check in Clairborne."

"Who appointed you to be spokesman?" Skip challenged. "I don't like your sass. A white man has asked you a question, boy!"

"I don't want trouble. Neither do the people of Bodie Wells. But the days of being railroaded are over. I've told you the answer to your question. Whether you accept it or not is not my problem, but you and your regulators won't run through here shooting and burning, unless you want to leave feet first."

"You'll be among the first to die!"

"You're right," Mace answered with a smile. "But I'll die with you and Big Daddy."

"Go sit in the car, Skip!" Big Daddy ordered. Skip stood for a moment, his face reddened with anger. Then he turned on his heel and walked away. After Skip had reluctantly returned to the vehicle, Big Daddy turned to Mace and said, "You're a pretty brave man." Big Daddy looked around at all the people in the streets. If it was possible, it seemed like the crowd was growing in size. "You appear to have the town behind you too."

"We're just law-abiding folk, Mr. Bolton," Mace answered. He nodded toward the truck. "And we worked too hard to build this town to have Klan trash riding through, burning and killing innocent people."

Big Daddy nodded. "None of us are really interested in death, so why don't we find some appropriate solution to this problem? I think we can work this out between us, don't you?"

Mace gave Big Daddy a long look before he responded, "What's to work out?"

"I need to find out what happened to Frank and I think Booker may be able to provide some answers. Where is Booker? Why isn't he out here?"

"He's dead. A woman shot him this morning!"

"He's dead?" Big Daddy asked with incredulity. "Why? How?"

"It seems a mother thought he was one of the men responsible for violating her daughter. It was unfortunate."

"Did he do it?"

"From what little evidence we've been able to gather, it appears so. We haven't had time to conduct a full investigation."

"Who's the girl?"

"Clara Nesbitt, and the doctor has confirmed she was definitely violated."

Big Daddy recognized the name. Something had gone wrong with Booker's plan. The girl was supposed to be killed. Now Booker was dead and Frank and his two companions had disappeared. Big Daddy gave Mace an appraising look and wondered just how clever he really was. "Did the girl say how she escaped from Booker?" he asked in a casual tone.

"She said that four hooded men forced her car off the road early one morning last month. They were having their way with her when they were interrupted by some hunters from Johnsonville who were attempting to flush some quail. When they saw what was happening they fired shots over the heads of the four men, who escaped into the underbrush."

"She wasn't able to identify any of the men?"

"No, she couldn't. The girl was pretty incoherent afterward but we were able to get one thing out of her and that was she didn't see their faces because they wore the hoods. It appears the other three got away scot-free and Booker would have too if he hadn't come back here."

"How did her mother find out Booker was involved?"

"His horse had a notch in one shoe and its hoofprints were found all around the site and the girl tore off a piece of his jacket, which was found near where she had been violated."

Big Daddy shook his head. This was the most disturbing part of Mace's story. Booker was too smart to be on the scene. He wouldn't make a foolish mistake like this, unless Frank forced him to be present. If that was the case, then it was the smartest move Frank ever made. He could not have found a better way to get rid of Booker. "Are you sure that Booker didn't act alone?"

"The girl said there were at least four men in masks who attacked her."

"She couldn't tell whether they were white or colored?"

"It was dark. It happened so suddenly. She couldn't identify their race."

"Alright, Mace. You've answered my questions, but you may have an official visit from the county sheriff's office to settle this case." A gust of wind traveled the narrow corridor of Main Street and nearly blew Big Daddy's Stetson off his head. He clutched at his hat and started to turn back toward his car when Mace's words stopped him.

"If you're saying that someone else is going to come through here later with a mob like that," Mace indicated the truck with a gesture, "we'd rather get it over with now! No reason for us to sit around guessing when the Klan is going to come again."

"You're prepared to die?"

"Yes. If it means that the remainder of my life must be lived in fear, I'm ready to die now. I'm not leaving this town. This is my home and I plan to fight for it!"

Big Daddy looked at Mace and the determined expression on the younger man's face tweaked Big Daddy's memory. It reminded him of something or someone dimly seen through the veil of faded recollection. Despite himself, he admired Mace. The man demonstrated a level of courage and resolve that neither Frank nor Booker had ever shown. And if the townsfolk in the street were any indication, Mace was also a leader of men.

"What kind of guarantee are you looking for?" Big Daddy asked.

"You're a politician, Mr. Bolton. You have a bright political future on the national scene. You have several controversial bills coming up before the legislature. You don't need a race war in your backyard. If you give your word that there will be no more riding on our town, that'll be enough."

"My word? You trust me?"

"I have no other choice. I know you're a decent man. Otherwise you would not have paid for college for me and Booker. I also know that you're a crafty politician. You know there's nothing to be gained by burning us to the ground."

"Are you the next mayor of Bodie Wells?"

"Why? I don't see what—"

"If you're the next mayor of Bodie Wells, you have my word. Is that all?"

"One more thing, sir. There's this watch. I know it belonged to your father. Booker's dead, so I'm returning it." Mace handed the gold watch to Big Daddy.

"I gave this to Booker's mother," Big Daddy said with a sad smile. He handed the watch back to Mace. "I have no other son, so I'm giving this to you now." Big Daddy turned and walked away without a further word.

As the caravan pulled out of town, Skip said, "Don't worry, Big Daddy, we'll come back and burn that nigger warren to the ground!"

"No you won't! You'll leave them be. I don't want the Klan riding on that town again!"

"What about Frank? What about Knute? They shot him in the arm!"

"He was a fool to fire in the first place. He's lucky they didn't kill him! As for Frank, God be with him wherever he is."

Big Daddy watched the countryside as they drove over the road and thought that a well-maintained road was an investment in the future. People maintained roads because they planned to continue living in that locale. Then Big Daddy thought of the watch that his father had given him and he knew suddenly where he had seen the expression on Mace's face. It was the same expression that Big Daddy's father had when he was committed to doing something that others said couldn't be done. Big Daddy almost chuckled. The watch was finally in the right hands.

Book III

THE LOSS
OF FAMILY

As the caravan pulled out of town, King released his grip on the machine gun and sat back. The tension and the anxiety of waiting began to dissipate. Despite the briskness of the weather, sweat dripped down his face. When Bass had been shot, King had been ready to pull the curtains back from the second-story window and release a fusillade of lead upon the caravan. Mace's shouts had just barely caught his attention before he pulled the trigger, and thus the death of the men in the vehicles had been prevented.

Sounds of cheering erupted from the street below. The people of the town were celebrating. Hats were being thrown into the air. Mace's name was being chanted by hundreds of voices. King was happy for Mace, but he did not participate in the revelry. He was disappointed. He had been mentally prepared and psyched up for a fight. It was a long anticlimactic fall for him emotionally. He took a deep breath and remembered the letter Dr. Stephens had given him.

He decided that he would remain where he was and read the letter. The envelope indicated that the contents were from Captain Mack. King tore open the envelope and read the barely legible scrawl.

January 15, 1921
Dear King,

I'm really surprised that I haven't heard from you since I wrote you the first letter in December. I just hope that you and your new wife are alright. I'm sorry to be writing you with this news. The woman from New York, who said she was the mother of your child, was found last week in the swamp. She was out of her head delirious. Her body looked like it had been tortured and abused. It looks like the DuMonts took advantage of her and passed her around. The woman's people are coming to get her in the next few days to carry her home. I hope she regains her senses. There was no sign of the baby.

I have put out feelers, trying to find out if anybody knows about the child, and had no success. Corlis sent me a message to mind my own business. So it looks like once again, he and the DuMonts are working together. If you decide to come back, you best be on your toes. There's a trap waiting to slam shut on you. I'll keep on searching for the child, but

*the baby may be already dead. It would be foolish for you to hope for any-
thing different.*

*I know nothing will stop you from coming now, but it's very danger-
ous. You got be very careful. Remember, Corlis has people watching us.
Go to Pointdexter's hunting cabin or Baptiste's fishing dock. They'll tell
me when you arrive.*

Martha and me, we pray for you, son.

King's hands were trembling when he finished the letter. He had a
child? It was almost too much to comprehend. He was a father and didn't
know it. Mamie had come all the way to New Orleans looking for him.
What happened to the first letter? There was a tightness in his jaw and a
grim expression on his face as he took the machine gun off its tripod. He
stripped the weapon down mechanically, not thinking about anything
but his child lost somewhere in the marshes and bogs surrounding New
Orleans.

After his own father was killed, King had spent many a night wishing
for a father who would take an interest in his affairs and be concerned
about his welfare. Fatherhood was extremely important to him. His Uncle
Jake had tried to fulfill that role for him until his death, but it wasn't the
same. His uncle already had sons and a family. Although there was never
an inhospitable act, King always felt a bit like an outsider in his uncle's
house. The thought of a son renewed King's desire to be the head of his
own house. He wanted to see his blood flowing in the veins of strong and
fearless sons, to see his seed thrive and pick up the gauntlet that he passed
on, to carry it into the future.

On the way back to the store, King stopped and checked with Wilkerson to see if the first letter had ever arrived in Bodie Wells. To his chagrin,
Wilkerson confirmed that the letter was delivered directly to the store. As
King made his way slowly back to the store, the people were still celebrating in the streets. Why hadn't Serena told him about the letter? Several
giggling children ran past him. Without conscious decision, King turned
to watch them. What did his child look like? More important, was the
child still alive?

Serena was standing in the doorway when he got to the store. She
rushed out to hug him, but he pushed her away.

There was a questioning look in his eyes. "Wilkerson said he gave you
a letter for me over a month ago. How come you didn't tell me about it?"

The look on Serena's face said everything. She stammered, "I, uh, I . . ."

"Did you read my letter?" he asked with an edge in his voice. She
nodded mutely, but her eyes were pleading with him. King exhaled and

his lip tightened into a snarl. "I guess I really don't know who you are, do I?"

"What's wrong? What's the matter?" she asked with concern in her eyes.

He did not answer, but simply gave her the letter and walked past her into the store. He went directly to the bedroom and began to pack his clothes.

Serena appeared at the bedroom door a few minutes later. "I didn't know anything like this was going to happen," she started to explain. "I was concerned—"

"I don't have time for bullshit!" King interrupted. "Where's the god-damn first letter?"

"Please, King! Please!"

"You best get the hell out of my face! Just give me my letter!"

Serena sagged visibly and left the room. She returned a few minutes later with the letter folded in her hands. She attempted to explain. "You were gone so long, I thought you had left me! I was so worried—"

"You didn't have nothin' to worry about! I married you, not her!" King stuck out his hand. "I's havin' a real hard time even talkin' to you right now!"

"Oh, please, King! Please! I'm so sorry! Let me go with you, I'll help you. Please, let me show you—"

King held the open palm of his hand in front of her face. "I don't want to hear yo' crap! I don't want to hear yo' words! Hell, I don't even know if I can trust you! Just give me the damn letter!" King stalked over and snatched the letter out of her hand and then returned to his packing. He stopped for a minute to peruse the letter, then he turned to face Serena. "You read this letter, didn't you? You know what lies between me and the DuMonts? They wasn't gon' give my child no gifts! What did you think they was gon' do with him? What was you thinkin'? If'en you'd told me when I first got home, maybe I could've saved them both from hell! How could somethin' you want be more important than a child's life?

"I admit to puttin' many a man in the grave, but they was men or made the decisions of a man. They was growed and took the consequences of losin'. But you a colder killer than me cause yo' silence done put the shadow of death over my firstborn child! And that baby ain't done a thing to you!"

Tears began trickling down Serena's face. "I was wrong!" she wailed. "I was wrong! Please, don't let it end like this! I'll do anything! I'll do anything!"

King threw the letter on the bed. "This letter say I had a son! I had a son! And thanks to you, the DuMonts have him!"

"Please stay with me. I'll bear you another son! I'll give you many children! Just let me make up for this!"

"Yeah, but do you think I'm gon' forget about this one? I ain't ever seen this child's face, but I love him! I don't even know where this feelin' came from, but it spilled out of that letter powerful-like. It was full-growed when it touched air. All of sudden, I is a father and I feels it to the marrow of my bone. You think I can stay here with you while there's a chance I can save this baby?"

"What about you and me?"

"Damned if I know! I can't be thinkin' about no you and me. This child is big on my mind!"

King's words took the starch out of Serena. Her sobs racked her body.

King continued packing and soon he had three cases filled, which he gathered up before he left the room. "I got business in New Orleans and I ain't promisin' to come back to stay. You done tore a big hole in things!"

Sampson was standing on the staircase as King came to the top of the stairs. He saw the bags in King's hands as King descended the stairs. Sampson gave King a questioning look. King did not respond, but continued toward the back door. Sampson thumped his chest and made a gesture, asking if he was going with King. King stopped. He hadn't considered Sampson. Sampson thumped his chest again, repeating the gesture and the question.

King set down his bags. "I'll send for you in a month. You stay with her until she is able to get some help in here. I'm goin' to that warehouse in the swamp that we bought befo' we left."

Sampson shook his head and made a hand signal that meant he and King should go together.

"I want you with me," King explained. "But I got to do the right thing. She gon' need yo' help for at least a month. After that, you can join me."

Sampson dropped his eyes and walked away. His whole body showed the pain he was feeling.

King walked out the back door and did not look back.

"Good night, Mrs. Tremain. If you need anythin', don't hesitate to ask. You been real good to us, so my husband will be happy to help you move any heavy things that you need to get ready for business on Monday. I ain't bein' polite either."

Serena smiled. "Thank you. I appreciate your offer. I'll remember it. Good-night, Mrs. Hoskins. Best to your family."

"Good Sabbath, Mrs. Tremain," Ida said, as she wrapped herself in her coat and hurried down the street.

The wind whistled down the corridor of Main Street like the sound of a cheap harmonica. February was ending with falling temperatures. The thermometer stayed below ten degrees for several weeks at a time. Sometimes the wind would sweep northward off the Red River and bring a momentary warmth, a present from southern climes, but other times the wind would roll down the side of the Ouachitas and hit the foothills like a giant snowball.

Serena locked the front door and went upstairs and stoked her fire with wood that Sampson had brought from the woodshed. She had drawn enough water from the downstairs tap that King had installed to heat water for a bath, but she didn't have the energy to carry the water upstairs. Although she had Ida Hoskins working in the store with her and Sampson weighing out grain and feed sales in the barn, it took a lot of work to deal with customers and keep the store provisioned with staples. The reconciling of receipts and orders alone took more than two hours each evening after closing. Running the store was hard, strenuous work and the paperwork took long hours to complete. She didn't mind the hard work. It was the loneliness that was almost overwhelming. Part of the reason that Serena worked so hard was to escape, through activity, the feelings of isolation.

She spent many evenings thinking about the letter and why she had not given it to King when he first arrived. She did not completely understand it herself, but she rationalized it as an act committed out of an instinctual desire to protect her unborn children. Serena had been the firstborn in her family and she knew that commensurate with the responsibility shouldered by the oldest child came dictatorial power, power to determine the level of justice and pleasure enjoyed by the younger children. She could not willingly give another woman's child such primacy over her own, especially a dark child who would forever remind her of its mother.

Serena walked over to the calendar and saw that King had been gone more than a month. She missed King more than she knew was possible. The space taken up by the lower register of his voice seemed to stretch for miles and she noticed the absence of his sound everywhere she turned. Every morning she awoke with a dull ache in her chest and a coldness between her shoulder blades. Her consuming desire was to just lie back against the warmth of his body and feel it enfold her, protecting her from the chills of the night. She had begun to daydream with increasing frequency about the ways that they had made love. Sometimes late at night she would sit in the rocker by the stove and touch herself under her flannel bedclothes as she thought about him.

Serena finally forced herself to carry two buckets of water upstairs and placed them on the stove. Until the water heated she sat in her rocker and darned King and Sampson's socks. Then she washed up and donned her flannel sleeping gown. She turned down all the lamps and placed the revolver by the headboard. She still had not been able to get the electricity hooked up in the apartment. There was another foul-up in Clairborne. She tried to free her mind of all the worries that seemed to be closing in on her and prepare for sleep. She pulled back the covers of the bed and removed the bed warmer. She climbed into bed and waited for sleep.

Sleep did not come. Despite her desire to keep her mind blank, her memory was stirred by some unseen implement and images of King floated unbidden across her consciousness. Strangely, the memories brought the sensation of touch with them. It was almost as if they had substance. The memory that most often haunted her was the one in which she was sitting astride him and he was deep inside of her. She was controlling the movement, but when he chose he would lift his hips and she would be briefly airborne. Then she would feel him deeper inside of her as his muscles bunched beneath her. Sometimes, his hands would travel up the flatness of her stomach and cup of her breasts. Then she would feel the calluses on his hands. All the time, she would continue to slowly grind on top of him, building, building to a takeoff point that caused her skin to tingle. She felt his hands on her throat and her breasts, moving in rhythm to her hips. Suddenly she felt his rigidity inside her thrusting, pressing upward, penetrating her until she filled completely. In the darkness, she could see the dim outline of the muscles on his chest and the glint of his dark eyes. She threw herself back and forth on top of him, jerking until it seemed that she could contain the explosion no more. The release caused spasms to writhe through her body before she subsided into sleep.

Serena awoke the next morning as a gray light filtered through the shutters on the windows. She was tired as if she had worked all night, yet she had slept the dark, dreamless sleep of the dead.

It took her only an hour to discover that Sampson had packed his bags and was gone.

SATURDAY, MARCH 19, 1921

Captain René LeGrande stood quietly while the sheriff cursed Dr. Boyer. He knew that the doctor was merely providing the best medical advice that he could under the circumstances. It was not really Boyer's fault that Sheriff Mack was an obstinate fool on occasion, but it was foolhardy to make declarative statements that consistently had the effect of irritating the sheriff. Corlis Mack was a powerful man with connections throughout the parish and into the legislature and, most dangerous of all, he was merciless. All of his enemies and many of the people who had pestered him ended up as alligator bait in some lonely bayou. Captain LeGrande had firsthand knowledge of this because he had actually been the man who had left many of the victims tied to stumps at low tide.

"Boyer, get out of my sight, you goddamn asshole!"

Dr. Boyer attempted to explain. "Corlis, you have to have more surgery on that leg. That's all there is to it! If we do it soon, all we have to do is cut out the infected areas. If we wait, you endanger your life!"

"Old Dr. Devereaux doesn't think I need more surgery!"

"Old Dr. Devereaux is just that, old! He can barely see and he has done nothing to stay abreast of the latest advances in medicine. He's stuck in the past! I'm giving you the best advice you're going to get!"

"I'll think about it, Boyer! Get him out of here, LeGrande!"

LeGrande returned after ushering the doctor out of the room. "Maybe you should listen, eh?" he suggested to Mack. "Devereaux is old, you know."

"You too! Damn!"

"Even if you and me weren't friends," LeGrande tapped his chest, "I have a good thing here. Why jeopardize it, eh? Without you, it's a whole new political situation. I don't want you dying from something we could avoid."

"I said I'd think about it! These damn doctors are just barbers with a couple of science courses. The thought of these fools cutting on me again is not enticing. Enough about this!"

"What did you do with that little pickaninny? You've got to remember, we may have to produce it in trade for the deeds."

"I sent it to a colored orphanage in southwestern Texas. Nobody but me knows its name or location and I can get the child anytime. I told the people at the orphanage the boy's parents had been killed by King Tremain and that he wanted to kill the baby too. So, even if he finds where the baby is, they won't release the baby to him."

"Good! Good! How are we doing on finding that nigger Tremain? We know he's around here somewhere. I want all your available men on it! The DuMonts should be willing to help. Tremain just recently burned their tribal home to the ground, didn't he? Is there anything left standing at DuMonts' Landing?"

"Nothing but ashes and bodies. The women and children got out okay, but he got most of the men, all except for Old Man DuMont himself and a couple of others. I saw at least ten, twelve bodies out there and there are probably more."

"Didn't the Old DuMont nigger have anything to tell you?"

"He says he may have a lead to some of Tremain's friends. He will come to my office in a day or two. It is no doubt, the DuMonts are finished as a force to be reckoned with in southwest New Orleans. This is a bad-blood Tremain; he bad business."

"I want to spill his bad blood! He owes me a leg and I'm going to collect! I tell you if he's caught, there'll be a big bonus for the man responsible! One thing! I don't want him hurt! I want to be the one who causes him all the pain and I'm going to take my time! I don't want a mark on his skin before I start! You remember that embezzling bank clerk who wouldn't tell us where the money was hidden?"

"The one you skinned?"

"That will seem like a horse race compared to what I have planned for Tremain! Every time I look at my amputated leg, I see him! Every time the pain makes me grit my teeth, I think about him! I've been confined to this wheelchair since he tried to kill me! I'll make him relive every bit of misery that I have experienced since he destroyed my leg!"

The wind was warm as it swept leaves and debris in fits and starts through the trees that lined the dirt road. Billowing charcoal clouds were rolling across the gray expanse from the southwest as big, fat raindrops fell from the darkening sky and splatted intermittently on the ground. The heavens were in turmoil. It looked like hurricane weather. Charles Baddeaux pulled his hat down more firmly on his head and snapped the reins sharply across Jethro's back. The mule started from the sting of leather and pulled the wagon at a faster pace briefly, but true to form he had returned to his usual plodding gait within a half-mile. Charles Baddeaux snapped the reins repeatedly as he and the mule vied for control over traveling speed.

The wind noticeably grew in force. Gusts were rushing through the surrounding trees and bushes with a loud and constant rustling. Tree limbs were whipping back and forth and small branches were separated from their moorings as the wind swirled and surged. The rain started to fall just as Charles pulled in behind Templeton's Roadhouse. After securing Jethro firmly to a hitching post, Charles made his way to the back door of Templeton's. The rain poured out of the sky and fell to earth with a roar. The wind was not content to let the rain fall straight down; with powerful blasts it drove the rain in slanting sheets. Although Charles was wearing an oilskin, he was soaked before he finished tying the reins to the post.

Templeton's Roadhouse was whites-only and didn't allow coloreds inside the establishment. Colored people could be served only through a window in the back door. They were allowed to sit at the tables in the back. There was no cover over these tables and when it rained there was no protection from the elements for the colored customers, except for the narrow covered porch adjacent to the purchase window.

There were five colored men huddled on the porch drinking Templeton's home-distilled rye whiskey as Charles stepped up to the window. Several of the regulars eyed him with distaste. Charles had been on the side of temperance before he was banished from the farm; as a matter of fact, he had preached against the devil gin many times from the altar of his church, and never failed to speak harshly to any besotted colored man that he met. An anonymous voice intoned, "Look like a backslidin' Bible thumper done come up here to drink in front of us!" A large dark man said, "Mr. Tight-ass done discovered there was wine drunk in the Bible."

The first voice responded, "No, he need a drink! After that schoolmarm done left the parish, the only butt he seein' is that mule's!"

"Ain't a chicken mo' his size?" The men all laughed.

Charles ignored the men and bought a small jar of rye. Their snide comments and chuckling soon subsided into silent drinking. Things were not good at the farm. It was as if Serena had poisoned everyone against him. Whenever he entered a room in which the children were laughing, they fell silent. If Beulah was in the room she would begin muttering prayers to herself and if Ida was present she would roll her big cow eyes disgustedly. He felt like a pariah in his own home. It had never occurred to him that a time would come when he would not be happy to see the inside of his house after a hard day's work. Some days he would leave the house before sun up and work in the fields until well after dark. Then he would find work to do in the barn as an excuse not to go into the house. Generally, he waited until his body was wasted with fatigue before he returned to the house to sleep, so wasted that he would not dream. Exhaustion became his only escape from the nightmare of living. And if he was foolish enough to allow himself to fall into the arms of sleep without the escort of fatigue, he found himself pacing the path of nightmares, dreaming of his waking moments. There seemed to be absolutely no satisfaction in life.

Charles hadn't planned to drink, but thought otherwise when he got to the window. With all the rain and the water trickling under his collar, a little nip would keep him warm. And why shouldn't he celebrate? He was going to get revenge and money, too! It was a good reason to celebrate. He was meeting Alfred DuMont with information that would help in the capture of King Tremain.

Charles had discovered that when he was in a morose mood, a small jar of rye set him free to drift partially submerged in his subconscious. The alcohol seemed to shield him from the uneasy streams of thought that like flitting schools of fish nibbled away at his self-respect. An occasional jar of rye offered protection from these predatory little fish that darted away into the depths every time he reached to examine them more closely. He had barely taken a sip when Alfred DuMont appeared out of the rain-distorted landscape. Alfred said nothing, but came to stand beside Charles. Charles offered him a drink and Alfred declined with a shake of his head.

"You got the money?" Charles asked with a lowered voice.

Alfred also kept his voice low when he responded. "You got the information?"

"Yeah, I got somethin'! I know who is forwardin' the letters to Tremain! I'm pretty sure they know where he is!"

"If you want the money, you got to come with me."

"Come with you where?" Charles asked, immediately suspicious.

"I don't just walk around with that kind of money," Alfred explained. "I got it on my horse. I just don't want to give you nothin' in front of the loose lips on this here porch!"

"That makes sense," Charles agreed. "Where do you want to meet?"

"There's a grove of sycamores off to the right of the road to Lake Ponchatrain about a mile from the Crossing."

"That's a good ways from here!" Charles said reluctantly. "Why you want to go so far? There's plenty of places closer where we won't be bothered."

Albert cleared his throat and said, "The truth is I buried the money in that grove of trees. I didn't know if I could trust you. I didn't want to get robbed! I got to answer for this money!"

Charles nodded understandingly. "I'll see you there. I'm gon' drink some more of this rye, I don't want to waste it all." He took a large gulp out of the jar.

"I'll help you a little bit. I don't want to be waitin' out in the rain by myself." Alfred took the jar after Charles finished and nearly emptied it.

"Whoa! Whoa!" Charles said, looking at the remaining rye with displeasure. "Ain't nobody asked you to guzzle the whole thing!"

"Finish it off and let's go!" Alfred urged.

Charles followed Alfred, who was mounted on a horse, at some distance because he could not whip Jethro into a faster pace. He saw Alfred disappear under cover of some distant trees and made straight for the grove. When he pulled under the trees, he saw that DuMont was not alone. Three white men were waiting with him. Immediately, Charles got a very bad feeling. He looked questioningly at Alfred, who shrugged his shoulders in response.

"Where is LeRoi Tremain?" one of the white men asked.

Charles looked back and forth between the men, then pointed to Alfred. "He know I don't know where Tremain is. I just know of somebody who might know where he is. It ain't guaranteed they know, but they's the best guess I got!"

One of the white men kicked his horse alongside the wagon and swung the butt of his Winchester at Charles's head. Charles ducked, but the wooden stock caught him on the shoulder. He grunted with pain, and before he could recover, the rifle butt slammed into his back. He shouted, "I don't know nothin' but what I told you!" He turned to protect himself with his arms from his assailant, but not quickly enough. He was struck upon the shoulders again, but this time the stock of the rifle clipped his head and he fell off the wagon into the mud. He was allowed to lie there while they waited for him to regain his senses.

Charles looked up at Alfred and said in a shrill voice, "You lied! You lied to me and you's lyin' on me! Tell these mens I don't know nothin'!"

"Your name is Charles Baddeaux?" asked one of the white men, looking down from his horse.

Charles pressed himself out of the mud and attempted to wipe the mud off his face as he answered. "Yes, suh, I's Charles Baddeaux, but I swear I don't know—"

"Don't swear!" ordered the man. "I don't want to hear you blaspheme! I am Captain LeGrande of the New Orleans Parish Sheriff's Department. Now, Charles, this can be easy or hard. It's up to you. I need information, eh? I don't want to beat you to death, but I do need information. My two deputies here, they are prepared to beat you to death. We'll break all your bones first, so it will be extremely painful, eh? So, why don't you tell me everything you know about LeRoi Tremain, eh? And maybe, just maybe, you might make it home this evening."

Charles began babbling the full chronicle of events, as he knew them, since King Tremain had entered his daughter's life. No one else spoke, except for the occasional question by Captain LeGrande. After he finished telling about Journer dropping off letters from Serena to his daughters and how he had overheard that she was a wife of one of the Duryeas, Charles fell silent. Rain mixed with blood trickled down his neck. He wanted to stand up, but he was afraid that he would be struck with the rifle again, so he remained seated in the mud.

Captain LeGrande studied him for several minutes in silence. Then without warning he said, "I believe you, Charles Baddeaux. Your story is too crooked and human to be anything but the truth! You are in luck today, eh? You will live." LeGrande said to one of his deputies, "Pay them, Gitan!" He turned his horse and rode out from under the trees into the rain.

Gitan threw some bills into the mud. "Forty dollars and it is more than the information's worth! Take it and run, niggers!" He and the other deputy reined their horses around and followed the captain.

Alfred was off his horse in an instant and scooped up the money. He remounted as Charles pulled himself painfully to his feet. Charles leaned against his wagon and said accusingly, "You lied to me! You lied to my face and you got the gall to take all the money too! You's a low-down dog, DuMont!"

"Leastways, you got a house! I ain't got nothin'! Tremain burned everythin'! Everythin'! I got women and chil'ren living in canvas lean-tos. This money gon' feed the mouths of my women and chil'rens!"

"I see, I take the beatin', you take the money?"

"You ought to thank God, man! We's both lucky to be alive now. They was gon' kill both of us! You saved us both, but I still needs this money. If better times come, I'll pay this whole amount, but right now things is tight! I got to think of my family." Alfred kicked his horse into a trot and rode away into the rain.

It took Charles nearly ten minutes to climb up into the wagon. Each movement caused sharp, lancing stabs of pain to flash across his back and side. Once he was in the seat, he picked up the reins and flicked them across Jethro's back. The mule started off with a jerk, which caused Charles to wince in pain. The wagon moved out into the sluicing rain. It battered upon his head and shoulders with the percussive sound of an endless drum roll. Charles's hat was still in the mud, but he did not want to get off the wagon to retrieve it. He was happy to remain in the jerking and rocking seat of the wagon as Jethro found his own way home.

SUNDAY, APRIL 3, 1921

Patches of clouds floating across the night sky obscured the full moon as it traveled across the dark blue expanse of twinkling stars. Sometimes the moon could only be seen as a pale circular shape through the opaque clouds, but for brief moments it appeared unfettered and then its pale blue light fell to earth exaggerating the shadows. A truck pulled up next to a large unlit building. Four men got out of the truck and lifted out the stretcher upon which Corlis Mack was sitting.

"Easy boys," Mack advised, flicking the ash off his cigar. "I ain't chopped liver! I just had this damn leg cut on a week ago! Get in step with each other and minimize the jerking!"

Captain LeGrande opened the door with a smile. "Hello, Boss. How're you doin' this fine evening, eh?"

"If you have what you say you have, I'm real happy! You may be the next undersheriff."

"I would not send such information to you so soon after surgery if it was not so." LeGrande stopped to inspect Corlis's leg. "There's a lot of blood in your bandage and it's starting to leak through. Who wrapped this for you? They didn't do well, eh?"

"Fuck the leg! Where's Tremain?" answered Corlis, puffing on his cigar.

"You wait in the conference room. I will bring him to you," offered LeGrande. "He's in the basement and the stairs are too steep to carry you down on the stretcher. Plus, you don't want to aggravate that leg, eh?"

"For a good officer, you're getting to be a pain in the ass about this leg business! I want to go down to the basement! I can't have any fun in the conference room!"

"I don't want to argue with you, eh, Boss? So I have taken the precaution of having Dr. Boyer waiting in the card room. I knew you would get too excited and I won't stand by and watch you endanger your health, eh?"

Corlis clamped down on his cigar. "Maybe you won't be the next undersheriff after all." He waved his hand dismissively. "Alright! Alright, you win. Bring that bastard into the conference room. Bring up both of them! I want to look in their eyes!"

"Maybe you let the doctor rewrap your leg first?"

"Goddamn it, LeGrande! Don't push your luck! Just bring up the niggers!"

Corlis was making himself comfortable, plumping up pillows and trying to find a less painful position for his leg when King and Phillip were brought bare-chested into the conference room. Corlis was still on the stretcher that had been set to rest on a table on one side and a bureau on the other. Both the prisoners had manacles about their hands and feet and there were bruises on their faces and torsos from punches and kicks.

An evil smile spread across Corlis's face as he exhaled a thick cloud of smoke. "I am very happy to see you, nigger!" he said to King Tremain, who returned his look without expression. "I've been waiting for this moment for a long time! You failed in your attempt to kill me and only shattered my leg. I have spent nights thinking of the things I'm going to do to you. The main problem is how to condense the misery I've been living in over the last few months to two weeks. I've got some ideas. I think I'll start on your friend first and let you watch as he comes apart piece by piece. You're a first for me, Tremain. I never killed three generations from the same family before. I killed your grandfather. I gave the DuMonts guns that killed your father. Now I'm going to kill you. What do you think of that, nigger?"

A deputy standing behind King slapped the back of his head. "The sheriff wants an answer, boy!"

King looked Corlis in the eye. "I's sorry I missed yo' fat ass!" A clubbing blow with a baton knocked him to his knees. The deputy raised the baton to hit him again but was stopped by Corlis.

"That's enough!" Corlis warned. "No reason to break his spirit before I get to him. I want to cause all his pain. Hit that other one for me!" Phillip was pummeled to the ground by hard blows of the baton. "Don't kill him! We must remember, I want this to last at least two weeks!" Corlis stared at King, who slowly got to his feet. "What do you think now, nigger?"

King turned and looked at the deputy behind him then he turned and faced Corlis. "That leg done already killed you, you just don't know it! You already dead!" King spit in Corlis's face.

"Don't touch him!" Corlis shouted at the deputy who stepped forward to hit King. He wiped his face with a handkerchief. "I told you that I'm the one who's going to hurt this nigger!" Corlis pulled himself up to a seated position with an effort. His face was blotched red and apoplectic as the blood coursed through the capillaries under his skin. "Bring that nigger here," he growled. With deputies on either side of him, holding his arms, King was brought in front of Corlis.

"You think you're pretty tough, huh, nigger?" Corlis said as he puffed his cigar to a bright red ember. Without warning he pressed the glowing end into King's chest and the skin underneath it sizzled. Corlis laughed as he held the lit cigar against his victim. King writhed in the deputies' arms, but they were strong men and they held his arms fast. However, they did not reckon on his legs. King lifted both feet off the ground and kicked at Corlis. His missed his intended target but he did knock one end of the stretcher off the table and Corlis tumbled to the floor with a scream.

LeGrande leaped into action and knocked the struggling King unconscious with the butt of his service revolver. He then bent to minister to Corlis, who was barely alert. The blood was pulsing out of the bandage. LeGrande sent for the doctor and ordered the prisoners to be returned to the basement. As he looked down into Corlis's pale, sweating face, he saw evidence that King's words may have had some truth. Corlis was murmuring something barely audible. LeGrande leaned down and placed his ear next to Corlis's lips.

"I want him!" Corlis whispered. "I don't want to see another mark on him! I want you to keep him alive and uninjured until I am ready to begin! I want to scar his face! I want to cut off his cock piece by piece!" The pain caused Corlis to gasp, but he fought for control. "You hear me, LeGrande? I will break all of his bones myself!"

"What if you're laid up for a couple of months, eh? I am very accomplished at causing pain and I can make him pay."

"No! No! I want to do it! Save him for me! I want to be an artist. I want to start with a clean canvas!"

The doctor entered the room and exclaimed "Oh my God!" when he saw the extent of the damage done to the stump of Corlis's leg.

As the doctor injected an anesthetic into Corlis's arm, Corlis grabbed a hold on LeGrande with the other hand and uttered in a husky voice, "Save him for me!"

WEDNESDAY, APRIL 20, 1921

The riverboat's steam whistle announced its arrival at the port of Algiers. Bells along the passenger corridor were clanged by colored boat hands to alert any who had missed the bellowing sound of the boat's low-pitched whistle. People hurriedly began to gather their belongings and baggage in preparation of disembarkation. In the steerage section, where the colored passengers were allowed to ride, Serena watched the dock for signs of Journer or Sampson. The commotion on the docks equaled that aboard the *Mississippi Prince* as scores of colored stevedores lined up to unload the heavy bags of grain and dry goods that had been shipped from America's heartland to the gateway of New Orleans.

Serena saw no one that she recognized as she prepared to follow the other colored passengers to their rear exit ramp. She was dressed in an old cotton shirt, heavy denim overalls, and a weather-beaten straw hat. She looked like one of the many rural farm women who had come to town to sell their wares. She had purchased homemade blankets and woven shawls as well as woven straw hats to serve as her goods so that her disguise was complete.

After the cold of Bodie Wells, the damp, humid warmth found at the mouth of the Mississippi gripped her like a hot, wet glove. Even though there was no sun in the gray, overcast sky when she looked across the river at New Orleans, the ripple of heat waves distorted the view. Perspiration dripped down her face as she swung the heavy packs onto her back and followed the trail of black and brown humanity down the ramp. At the base of the ramp, a burly, red-faced white man barked out orders to the disembarking colored passengers. Serena was forced to stand in line on the edge of the pier while she watched white passengers disembark with carefree laughter and go on their way. The white man was a port official who took his time inspecting and checking the wares that the colored passengers were bringing into town. When he found something he particularly liked, he took it without explanation. When he got to Serena, he used his foot to nudge through the open packs of her goods. He saw a straw hat that he liked and took it, then he moved on to the next passenger. One of the colored porters who was assisting him marked her packs with a red crayon and gestured with a nod of his head to the exit, indicating that she could leave.

Serena packed her possessions and walked through the gate after showing the crayon marks to the colored man charged with guarding the exit. She joined a stream of people who were leaving the docks. Her heart was beating as she released her grip on the small revolver that was in her pocket. She was not sure that she would have fired it if she had been prevented from leaving, but she had kept it near to hand just in case. The roadway narrowed as the path funneled between the bright-colored canvas stalls of vendors and hawkers. A man in a broad straw hat that covered his face sidled up against her and lifted one of the packs from her shoulders. Serena was about to turn on him with invective, but she recognized that it was Sampson.

Sampson led her through several narrow alleys and finally out into a broad street where a covered truck was waiting. They piled into the darkness of the back and the driver took off slowly, then gained speed as they left the merchant area around the Algiers waterfront. Serena did not say anything until they reached their destination. The truck pulled to a stop in front of an old, run-down, two-story house with boarded-up windows that was half-hidden by foliage. Bright pink and white oleander blossoms festooned the large bushes growing right next to the structure. No other buildings were in sight because the house was standing in a dense grove of magnolias.

Journer Braithwaite was waiting on the steps when Serena got off the back of the truck. Journer rushed forward and held her a few minutes without speaking. Claude Duryea, his right arm in a sling, limped out and stood on the porch.

"You got here in good time," Claude said as he gave her a hug at the top of the stairs.

"I left as soon as I could," Serena explained. "I had to get somebody to supervise the store first and then I had to hire extra help. Is there any news about King?"

Claude shook his head sadly. "Not a peep! Wherever they have him and Phillip, it's under wraps. Nobody seems to know anything. Come on in and get the travel dust out of your throat."

Serena turned to the truck. "What about my packs?"

A red-haired colored man with freckles across the bridge of his nose walked around the front of the truck and answered her. "I got 'em. I'll bring 'em for you. We ain't met. I'm Dirty Red, one of King's friends." He set down one of her packs to shake her hand, then continued on inside the house.

Serena walked into the house and it was surprisingly bright. She discovered that, unlike the outside, the interior had been freshly whitewashed and the hardwood floors had a shiny gloss. The windows were all covered by thick sheets of metal and the brightness of the interior was created by several large oil lamps situated on the walls around the room "Whose place is this?" she asked.

"Yours," Claude answered. "Once King was captured, we could not be sure if any of his old places were secure. So, Sampson found this and has had the house refitted for our needs."

"What do you mean, secure?"

Claude sighed and said in a cracking voice, "We don't know whether they are torturing them. We really don't know if they are even alive. We don't know anything!" Claude's voice trailed off.

Dirty Red continued for him. "We figures that if they tortured them, they talked!"

"King would never talk!" Serena countered indignantly. "He would never tell them a thing!"

"I appreciates all what you is sayin'," Dirty Red said with a humorless chuckle, "but King was the first to say, 'Anybody can be made to talk!' So he said, 'Always plan like the enemy knows everythin' the captured man knows.' That's what we doin'!"

Serena gave Dirty Red a cold look. "You've made plans, have you? What plans have you made for helping him escape?"

Dirty Red shook his head and said, "I's just here to help. I understands you bein' angry and all, but it shouldn't be comin' to me. I's waitin' to help carry out whatever plan you say!"

"I'm sorry. I was wrong," Serena said, dropping her shoulders. "I'm so nervous. Forgive me please."

"Would you like to lie down and rest?" Journer offered.

"No, I want to get right into this. The longer they have them imprisoned, the more time to cause pain. Can someone tell me what's been done so far?"

"Let's go sit down at the table in the kitchen," Claude suggested.

Over the next hour and a half, Claude and Dirty Red explained the actions that had been taken. Serena listened, asking questions intermittently. No charges had been filed, nor was there a record of King and Phillip's capture and incarceration. It had also been ascertained that neither of the men was being held in the city jail or any of the substation holding cells around the city. It was clear that Corlis had secreted them in some private location and that his actions were not in compliance with normal arrest procedures.

After listening for quite a while, Serena asked, "Has anybody been following the sheriff? If they're important enough to hide away like this, I'm sure he's made a trip out to see his prisoners."

Dirty Red answered. "We been watchin' him. He's up at Presbyterian Hospital gettin' another surgery on the leg that King shot off. The only other place he's been is the Lafayette Social Club and he had some kind of fall while he was there, so he's back at the hospital again."

"Yeah, he's been out of commission off and on since King shot him," Claude affirmed. "We've been trying to keep a tail on the man he appointed to act in his stead, Captain LeGrande, but he hasn't been leading us anywhere but the Lafayette. He's using that as his headquarters."

Dirty Red sucked his teeth. "That LeGrande is a mean piece of work for sho'!"

"He's got to be the key if Mack is laid up," Serena mused. "The sheriff wouldn't let some underling take charge of such important prisoners!"

"That's the second time you said that," Journer observed. "How do you know the sheriff thinks they are important prisoners?"

"Think about it," Serena suggested. "Remember when those two Negroes from up north were accused of robbing the governor's residence of thousands of dollars in gold and silver dishes? Or when those rice farmers were charged with raping three white women? From what I heard when they climbed the gallows, it looked like they had been tortured and beaten. No one knew where they had been hidden and those were important cases."

"Why is Mack keeping them hidden?" Claude asked. "Maybe if we knew that, all the rest would fall into place."

"I think you're right," Serena agreed. "The only thing that stands out in my mind is the time King shot up Klan headquarters for those deeds."

"He was the one that did that?" Journer asked with a surprised expression on her face. "I thought that was done by a white man."

Claude nodded. "I figured it was him, particularly when he paid everybody back for money lost on the investment. That Possum Hollow property hasn't sold yet."

"Hot damn! King Tremain is some kind of Negro!" Dirty Red said, slapping his thigh. "It couldn't be nobody else but him! Shot up Klan headquarters! Hoo boy!"

"He didn't tell you?" Serena asked Claude.

"No, he plays things close to his chest."

"You right," agreed Dirty Red. "He don't tell you nothin' unless you's involved and even then, he ain't wordy."

"Those deeds might be it," Claude mused. "That new highway's route hasn't been finalized yet. If it travels along the path through Possum Hollow and Mack had title to that land, he could attract the type of money to invest in all that coastal property. He could make millions!"

"Maybe we can get those deeds back from New York and bargain for their lives," Journer suggested.

"You can't trust the sheriff!" Dirty Red exclaimed. "You can't bargain with him! He'll turn on you after he gets what he wants!"

"I think Red's right," Claude agreed sadly. "We've got to find Phillip and King before Mack recovers from his surgery. If we don't have them before that, we best prepare the winding sheets."

"What if I got a job at the hospital where the sheriff is recuperating?" Serena suggested. "Maybe I could find out something."

Claude responded. "We have people all over that hospital and they haven't uncovered a thing! I think the country club is a better bet because that's where LeGrande spends a lot of time. It's where Corlis used to conduct his business."

"Perhaps Journer and I could go together tomorrow and apply for work there."

"You best go by yo'self," Journer said. "The chief porter responsible for hiring the colored help don't hire no dark-skinned girls to work there. You got to be light, or high yellow."

"I'll go by myself then," Serena said. "I'm getting tired, but I would like to hear how King was captured. It isn't like him to give up without a fight!"

"He and Phillip broke me out of city jail and wouldn't have been caught if some Uncle Tom Negro hadn't identified them to the police while they was gettin' away through Saint Mary of Magdalen School." Journer asserted. "They didn't dare fight it 'cause they were surrounded by colored children gettin' out of Sunday school."

"We know who that Tom is too! Sampson saw him callin' to the police!" Dirty Red declared. "He the bell captain from the Hotel Toussant! We got people out lookin' for him! He in hidin' now, but he gon' come out soon. Then we'll get him!"

"King was taken without firing a shot?" Serena questioned.

Claude nodded. "He didn't have a choice. The police would have opened fire while the children were all around. Many a child would have died if they had fought it out."

Serena asked, "Why was Journer arrested?"

Journer answered. "They were tryin' to find King and they were pretty sure I knew where he was."

Serena frowned. "How did they figure Journer was a link to King?"

"We don't know the answer to that," Claude said. "All we know is that Journer was picked up in the market on Friday and King and Phillip broke her out of jail on Sunday."

"While I was locked up, they beat me and kept at me about King," Journer explained. "But I didn't tell 'em nothin' 'cause I didn't know nothin'! But I sho' was happy to see them boys Sunday mornin'!"

"How did you get away?" Serena asked Journer.

"They had a good plan! They brought me a change of clothes, so's I'd look like a housemaid and they put me on the back of one them carriages that wait for Mass to end outside Saint Mary's. I rode right past them police."

Dirty Red joined in. "After she was gone, the two of 'em cut back through Saint Mary's grounds, headin' for the river. That's when that bell captain saw 'em and gave a shout! Them kids was let out of school just as the police was closin' in. They didn't have no choice but to throw up their hands."

Serena stood up and swayed unsteadily. She was exhausted, as if she had been toiling for long hours back on her father's farm. Sampson was at her side at once and she leaned heavily on him as he assisted her up the stairs to her room. At the door she asked him if he was hopeful about King's being alive, and Sampson signed in response that now that she was in New Orleans, he knew everything was going to be alright.

Serena turned and buried her face on his shoulder and wept silently. The tears flowed as if they were supplied by the great, meandering Mississippi; they had washed over all her restraining levees and were seeking their own way to the sea.

THURSDAY, APRIL 21, 1921

"I expects you all to be punctual for this here presentin' line," the head porter declared angrily, walking back and forth in front of the men and women standing in line for his inspection. He was a tall, brown-skinned man with ramrod-straight posture who held his head back in such a position that he looked down his nose when he addressed his subordinates. "I requires that every man jack of you be here and dressed in a clean uniform by seven o'clock in the mornin'! Anybody that got a problem with that best be lookin' fo' work somewheres else!" He gave a particular stare at a pretty, light brown–skinned woman standing at the far end of the line. "This here establishment is the Lafayette Social Club! It been here more'n a hundred years, servin' some of the finest families in New Orleans Parish! We expects and demands the very best from the colored help! And I, Clarence Thomas, is in charge of makin' that happen!"

The head porter paced in front of the line of his subordinates, letting his words sink in. Occasionally, he would stop in front of a particular individual and give him or her a stern look. None of the people in the line dared murmur a word or do anything but look straight ahead.

"Alright! Present hands and gloves and head ties!" Thomas ordered. "Thelmina, bring me my rod!" A plump, dark-skinned woman in her mid-fifties came out from behind the counter that separated the kitchen from the prep room and handed Thomas a thirty-inch-long pole, three quarters of an inch in diameter. Thomas then proceeded down the line, inspecting both sides of each pair of hands. Each of the male waiters presented a pair of white gloves after his hands were inspected. Each woman wore a white cotton head-tie tied in the same manner. Thomas took his time examining these articles as well, ensuring that there were no stains or blotches marring the stark whiteness of the material.

"Alright! Get to yo' stations!" Thomas ordered after he had completed his inspection. "I want there to be clean glasses and fresh ice water at each station befo' eight o'clock openin'! Get to gettin'!"

"Thelmina, get started with the mornin' setup!" Thelmina hurried to do his bidding. Thomas walked over to where Serena was waiting. "What do we have here?" the head porter asked, looking Serena up and down. He put his rod under his arm and awaited her response.

Serena stood a little straighter as she answered. "A new employee, I hope, Mr. Thomas. My name's Rena Love, sir."

"Hmmm," Thomas grunted approvingly. "You is well spoke. Do you got some schoolin'?"

"Yes sir. In between my farming chores, I tried to get as much as I could." Serena adopted a solicitous tone as she had been prepped to do. "Due to my mother's illness, I wasn't able to finish." It was a lie, but one she had also been directed to tell.

"Good, good. Too much learnin' can make a Negro foolish and make him act out of his place, but a little learnin' stops him from bein' just any old handkerchief-head field nigger. Let's see yo' hands!" Serena proffered her hands. Thomas inspected them, giving particular attention to her nails. "Hmmm," he grunted. "Let's see yo' teeth." Serena opened her mouth wide. "Good! Good! What you been chewin'?"

"I had a bit of mint, sir. I always try to chew some mint a couple of times a day to keep my breath fresh."

"You's a pretty smart girl," Thomas said with an approving nod. "But the real secret to fresh breath is spearmint." He withdrew a bag from his pocket. "If you keeps a couple of sprigs with you at all times, you can be sho' yo' breath is always gon' be nice. You got references?"

Serena nodded and handed him a folded note. "Reverend Pendergast has written me something."

Thomas's eyebrows raised. "Reverend Pendergast! I do say! You got good folks behind you, girl." He opened the note and nodded his head as he read it. He looked at Serena. "You done kept accountin' books fo' a store? Then you can read and do figgers?"

"Yes, sir."

"You may be just the type of girl we wants here. I's gon' start you off with Thelmina. You gon' be doin' setups. You know about settin' a table?"

"No, sir, but I'm a fast learner."

"I bet you is, girl. I bet you is. Thelmina, go and see if we can find some uniform to fit her. Shouldn't be too hard. She just a bit bigger'n Helen."

Serena's first day went quickly. She learned how to set tables, how to fold napkins, from which side food was served, how to clear dishes without distracting the diners, which ropes to pull to operate the dumbwaiter. She was also given a tour of the facility by Thelmina.

The second day Serena discovered that there were two taskmasters who ruled over the colored workers at the Lafayette Social Club. Clarence Thomas was in charge of the wait staff. Minnie Stokes, a large, purple black-skinned woman, ran the kitchen. She was the head cook and tyrant over all that transpired within the domain of food preparation.

Serena was preparing a tray for the lunch service when she heard a woman at the serving counter scream in pain. She ran to help and discovered one of the maids bending over, holding her arm. "What happened? Are you alright?" Serena inquired.

Thomas arrived just after Serena. "What the devil is goin' on?" he demanded.

"That black bitch burned me! She poured scalding soup on my arm!" the maid accused, pointing her uninjured limb at Minnie.

Minnie stood behind the counter and sucked her teeth. She put her hands on her prodigious hips and declared, "I told that high-yeller nigger bitch to keep her hands out'n my food! I don't let no nigger pick over what I cooks!"

"Minnie, Minnie, you know I is short-staffed," Thomas complained. "Now, you done crippled me! This girl won't be able to work today! Somebody get me some fat for this burn!"

Minnie was unrepentant. "You can find a high-yeller dog like that on any corner! You can't find no cook like me just anywhere! I ain't gon' work no place where a damn chippie think she can just put her hands all in the food!"

"What is going on down here?" the maître d' demanded as he descended the stairs. He was a pale, thin white man with a receding hairline and a long nose. "That caterwauling Negress has upset some of the members!"

"It ain't nothin', suh!" Thomas said meekly. His whole bearing had changed in the presence of the maître d'. "Just a little accident. It ain't nothin'! We takin' care of it now! We sorry about any discombobulation, Mr. Weston, suh!"

"You better make damn sure that it doesn't happen again, Clarence! I'm holding you responsible!" Weston turned on his heel and headed back up the stairs.

"Damn it, Minnie! You done put my ass on the line!" Thomas said bitterly. "Thelmina, take Dietra to the infirmary and get her arm bandaged."

"Keep that tramp out'n my food and yo' life gon' be grits and honey again," Minnie said as she moved some pots around on the stove.

"I was two people short. Now I's three people short. How I'm gon' do service for Captain LeGrande and his men?"

"You got another one of them high-yeller girls right there!" Minnie said, pointing a spoon at Serena.

Thomas shook his head. "She ain't ready. She just started."

"You the only one know that!" Minnie answered. "All LeGrande care about is she got titties and ass."

Serena faced Thomas. This was her opportunity. "I can handle it, Mr. Thomas," she asserted.

Thomas looked at Serena doubtfully. "Can you balance a loaded tray? How many plates can you hold at one time? You got our menu down? What is we servin' today?"

"I don't know the menu and I can't balance a loaded tray yet," Serena admitted. "But I do know how to use the pushcarts I've seen around. I could take the food off the dumbwaiter and use the cart to take food to Captain LeGrande."

"There!" Minnie said with a nod of her head. "That child seems to got more brains than Dietra right off! She might could make LeGrande forget all about today's special!"

"She only been here two days!" Thomas grumbled. "But I ain't got nobody else! Okay, girl, you gon' be responsible for servin' the cap'n until Dietra come back. But let me tell you one thing: the cap'n and his men get the real silver service for their meals. And here at the Lafayette, we count our silver every evenin' just to make sho' none of it don't just get up and walk away. You gon' be responsible for every fork, knife, and spoon you take. You understand that?"

"Yes, sir. I'll account for every piece."

With a loaded luncheon cart, Serena knocked on the door to the second-floor conference room where LeGrande was having a meeting with his men. A muffled voice said Come in and Serena pushed open the door.

Three white men sat around a large circular table. The table was covered with stacks of paper and rolled-up maps. The room smelled of tobacco and sweat. Serena rolled the cart next to the table. One of the men was speaking and she waited silently for him to finish.

"Captain, them Italians is probably runnin' their bootleg through Possum Hollow. There's a lot of small islands and channels right through there, but if we leave a couple men with a small boat I'll bet in less than a week we'll know about their shipments."

One of the other men turned to Serena with a frown. "What are you doing here?"

Serena curtsied. "I didn't know whether you wanted me to serve, sir. I was waiting for a break in the conversation." She shook her head. "Honestly, I didn't hear anything, sir."

The third man laughed. "Don't get too suspicious, Sergeant Beaumont. She's smart enough to know that she shouldn't hear what we're talking about, eh?" He asked Serena. "You must be new. I haven't seen you before."

She curtsied again. "Yes sir, I started yesterday. My name is Rena. I'm only filling in until Dietra returns."

"Captain, she shouldn't be standin' in here while I talk about this!" Beaumont complained. "Why can't she wait outside?"

"She's too pretty to wait outside," LeGrande said with a wave of his hand. "Let's break for lunch now! If you're worried, put away the maps and papers, Sergeant. You can serve us now, Rena."

"Thank you, sir," Serena said almost joyfully. She pushed the cart closer to the table and began unloading the covered tureens and dishes with specific attention to making the least clatter possible.

"What's the special today?" LeGrande asked, watching Serena bending down to lift dishes off the lower shelf of the cart.

"Shrimp étouffée, chicken jambalaya with dirty rice, and corn biscuits."

"Hmmm, smells good," LeGrande said, sniffing the aromas rising from the plates. "You like the jambalaya here, don't you, Sergeant Pointdexter?"

"Sho' do, Cap'n," answered the tall, lanky white man who had limp brown hair and a toothy, horselike smile. "Ain't nobody can make a jambalaya like Minnie."

Soon there was no discussion, only the slurping of working-class men at table. Serena was quick to step forward to refill bowls as needed from the covered tureens. After the men finished eating, she cleared away the dishes and silverware. Before she left the room, she asked, "If Dietra is not here tomorrow, would you like me to just bring in the food and then wait outside?"

LeGrande chuckled. "Don't you worry your pretty little head about what Sergeant Beaumont say. You just come on in here any old time. You're too good-looking to wait outside, eh?"

"Is there anything else, Captain LeGrande?" Serena asked with a curtsy.

"No," he answered with a wink. "What I want ain't on the regular menu."

Serena returned downstairs to the prep service area and was elated. She had made contact and had stirred LeGrande's interest. Her problem was how to use that interest to her benefit.

Later that night, Serena was sitting around the dining-room table with Claude, Dirty Red, Sampson, and Journer. Serena was discussing LeGrande. "He knows where King and Phillip are being held! I'm sure of it! He seems to be in charge of everything else that would normally be handled by the sheriff."

"Okay, so he knows," Dirty Red conceded. "What do it matter? He ain't gon' tell us!"

"What if I can tease him into meeting me some place where we can kidnap him?"

"Kidnap Captain LeGrande?" Claude nearly gagged on his coffee. "We're talking about the parish police! Are you serious? Those fools are looking for us!"

"No, she got somethin'!" Dirty Red countered. "They lookin' fo' us, but they ain't expectin' fo' us to be lookin' for them! We might just get the captain on the sly! It'd be somethin' that King would try."

"You said, 'Anybody could be made to talk'!" Serena declared. "If we kidnap him, we can find out what he knows."

"The question is how do we do it and then how quickly can we put the plan into action?" Claude observed. "It looks like the sheriff may be getting out of the hospital the beginning of next week. Whatever we do has to be done before that."

"I know how," Serena answered with a determined expression. "Find me a place, an apartment where I can bring LeGrande. It can't be too sleazy and it can't be too fancy. It has to be on a dark street with lots of traffic. I need it by the day after tomorrow."

"You're playin' with fire, Serena," Journer cautioned. "Anythin' can happen with LeGrande. He can be mean."

"Fire can be used a lot of different ways and I'm ready to burn my hands and everything else to get my man back. Whatever I have to do, we'll get LeGrande! As King used to say, 'Everything is on the table and the stakes are high!' "

The next morning Serena held her breath, hoping that Dietra would remain home sick for a couple more days. Dietra did not appear by seven. Standing in the presenting line as hands and gloves were inspected, Serena silently rejoiced in Dietra's continued absence. As lunchtime grew near, Clarence Thomas directed her to serve LeGrande's conference room again. Serena hurriedly prepared a pitcher of cold lemonade and took it up to the conference room.

LeGrande was alone when Serena entered. "Oh, it's the pretty girl from yesterday," he said as she put the lemonade on the table.

"I'm just checking if it will be three for lunch again today, sir."

"No, I've two city councilmen coming, eh. So, make it lunch for five. We'll take the special, whatever it is." LeGrande paused and looked her up and down suggestively. "Too bad the menu's not bigger. There's some other things I wouldn't mind sampling, eh?"

Serena curtsied. "At the Lafayette Social Club we aim to please, sir. We want to make sure that the right people are satisfied. We can make changes in the menu to order."

LeGrande turned around and gave Serena his full attention. Then a smile slowly spread across his face. "I'm interested in something sweet and juicy. I don't see it on the menu," he said in a husky tone.

The door swung open and Dietra walked in. "I's back," she said to Serena. "You can go back to the kitchen now."

LeGrande's angry voice cut through the ambience. "Did I ask you to come in?" His words were directed at Dietra and she was momentarily confused.

"Suh?" Dietra asked, shaking her head.

"I didn't give you permission to come in here, did I?"

Dietra did not miss the seriousness of LeGrande's tone, but her desire to reclaim her assignment drove her forward. "I was just comin' to send the new girl back to the kitchen. Servin' the conference room is my job. She new. She don't get no position on the second flo' until she broke in."

"Get out!" LeGrande ordered. "And don't ever come back in here without knocking for permission, eh! Do you understand me?"

"Yes, suh," Dietra answered meekly, but the look she gave Serena out of the corner of her eye was filled with hate. She backed quickly out of the room and closed the door quietly.

"I think I may have a problem there," Serena said, nodding at the door through which Dietra had exited.

"I can smooth that for you. You don't worry, eh? You come see me after lunch."

Serena gave LeGrande her sweetest smile. "All right, sir. I'll tell Dietra she can serve lunch then."

"Do what is best, eh? I'll see you this afternoon."

"Yes, sir. Do you want coffee or beer with your lunch?"

LeGrande nodded in appreciation. "You're a smart girl. Better bring coffee. These council boys are temperance people."

"I'll tell Dietra."

Once outside the conference room, Serena exhaled and momentarily leaned against the wall. In front of LeGrande she had been icy calm. Alone, she was almost trembling. She had set the stage for the first part of the plan. Now she needed a moment to think about how to make her next move. Dietra was waiting for her by the dumbwaiter. Serena did not intend to stop and talk. She continued past Dietra to the service stairway and said in passing, "He's ready for you now."

"Wait a minute, you chisling heifer! You need some straightenin' out!" Dietra grabbed Serena's arm to swing her around, but Serena was prepared and used Dietra's impetus to swivel and stand nose to nose with her assailant.

Serena stared directly into Dietra's eyes. "You don't want a piece of me! I'm not after your job. We're not competing." Serena wadded a towel in her fist and turned to walk away, but Dietra grabbed her arm again.

"I ain't through with you!" Dietra snarled.

"Yes, you are," Serena snapped as she spun and hit Dietra under the eye with the fist that had the towel wadded in it. Dietra fell backward over a cleaning bucket and landed on the floor with a crash. Without waiting a moment further, Serena descended the service stairway to the kitchen. She passed Thomas on the stairs; he was on his way to investigate the commotion. He gave her a questioning look and in reply she shrugged her shoulders, indicating she was in the dark as well. Serena was not fearful that her altercation with Dietra would affect the implementation of her plans. LeGrande would not think it unusual for colored girls to vie for the prestige of serving him. If anything, it would disguise her true intentions more completely.

Three o'clock came far too soon for Serena's comfort. At first it had seemed as if the day was dragging by: each minute was a definable entity, with sixty distinguishable parts, then suddenly it was two-thirty, and then it was three. She went to the conference room unprepared and without a strategy.

LeGrande was alone in the room, standing by a map that was tacked on a large easel. He appeared to be studying a bit of coastline. He turned to her as she entered and asked, "Where have you been, eh? I waited for you to come back."

"I had a little trouble with Dietra, but it's all over now."

"How did it end with her?"

"She fell over a pail."

"I see," LeGrande mused. "And you, of course, had nothing to do with it?"

"Not a thing, but it still worries me a little bit."

"If you had nothing to do with it, why are you worried, eh?"

"I heard she was Sergeant Beaumont's girl. I'm worried she might try to use him to get to me, but I wouldn't be worried if I was under your protection."

LeGrande walked over to her and put his hand beneath her chin. "I don't give my protection to just anyone, eh? Only those who deserve it! How do I know that you deserve it, eh?"

"I guess you have to find out," Serena suggested.

LeGrande grabbed her shoulders and turned her around so that she was facing away from him. His hands rubbed her body through the material of her uniform. His touch was rough and uncaring. He was not concerned about her response to him. He guided her from behind to a table, lifted her skirt, pushed her thick woolen underpants down, and bent her down over the wooden surface. It did not take him long to enter her. He held her so that she couldn't move and thrust his penis into her repeatedly.

As her body was being invaded and violated, Serena concentrated on a red book that she saw on the shelf of a distant wall by the door. It was fire-engine red and lay on its side as if it had been recently thumbed through. Her thighs were pressed hard against the edge of the tabletop as LeGrande jerked back and forth within her. His grip had grown tighter as he reached his peak. Suddenly, he began thrusting harder, grunting heavily with each thrust until she felt the spasm of his ejaculation. Serena was glad that she was faced away from him for she didn't think that she could have made herself smile while he was inside her. She did not want to turn around and face him now. The truth was she never wanted to face him again unless she had a gun in her hand. He withdrew from her and she shuddered with disgust.

Misunderstanding her reaction, LeGrande murmured in her ear from behind, "It was good for you too, eh?"

"I never felt anything like it before," she answered, trying to stay focused on her objective. She wanted to run screaming from the room. Then within seconds she was paralyzed by the prospect of King finding out that she had been had by a white man. She was not sure how King would react to that information, but none of the potential responses that she thought of were positive. In that one moment she knew that she had to kill LeGrande and that she would never tell anyone that he had ever touched her. No one would ever know. The secret would die with him.

She pressed against the table and stood up with an effort. She pulled her pants up slowly. She didn't want them to touch her. Everything she wore felt dirty and slimy. She wanted to rip off all of her clothes and burn them. She pulled her dress down and felt as if her nakedness was still visible. She felt very close to tears. She had to blink them back out of her eyes. She willed herself to think only of her objective. She thought of killing LeGrande and discovered that she could smile. She turned to face him. "Can I see you tomorrow night, Captain?" she asked in a soft voice.

"Evenings are hard, eh?" LeGrande answered while tucking in his shirt. "I am a family man, you know? I must spend some time with my wife, eh? I've got responsibilities and two little ones to look after. Evenings are hard, but we can have plenty of afternoons like this, eh?"

"If we keep doing it here, soon everyone will know, all the staff! I want to have some type of reputation. I'm from a good family. I don't do things like this. With you, it was different, but I don't want to be the butt of jokes like Dietra is."

"Of course, of course," LeGrande said with a nod of his head. "Discretion is always good. You are right! As a matter of fact, we are having a police association meeting here tomorrow evening. That would be ideal! You come here tomorrow night." LeGrande patted her butt and said, "And I will not have to rush like I did this afternoon."

Serena moved away from him. She did not want to feel his hand upon her skin. "I've got to get back to my station, Captain. I'll see you tomorrow night." She gave him a brief smile and headed for the door.

"Come at eight o'clock," LeGrande called after her. "Find the waiter named Willis Markham. He'll let you in here to wait for me."

Serena nodded and opened the door. She saw the title of the red book as she stepped out into the corridor: *Paradise Lost*.

FRIDAY, APRIL 22, 1921 ♛

Willis Markham sighed loudly and looked at the big pendulum clock that stood in the hall. It was nearly seven o'clock in the evening. It was going to be another long day and he was hungry. He wouldn't be allowed to eat until the end of his shift. All he had eaten was a bowl of cornmeal mush and a couple of biscuits since starting work. He had arrived at the Lafayette Social Club at six-thirty in the morning and was scheduled to work until at least midnight. He walked down to the kitchen and Minnie and the new girl that Dietra had tangled with were spooning out big ladles of gumbo into tureens. It made his mouth water.

"I needs two dinners for the change of shift," he announced to Minnie. Within three minutes the new girl had prepared two plates of corn pone, rice, and broiled catfish. Willis had to shake his head. The word among the colored staff seem to be on target, the new girl knew her stuff. Willis put covers over the dishes and put them on his tray. This was the assignment he liked least. He opened the basement door and then descended the flights of stairs to a long, dark hallway that turned and abruptly ended at a large metal door. The smell of the food was driving him crazy, but he knew better than to pick at it before he delivered it. As usual, there were two parish police sitting at the end of the hallway guarding the door. Willis called out before he arrived because he noticed the guards were nervous men. He did not want to get shot serving their dinner.

He didn't know what the police were doing guarding a metal door in the subbasement of the Lafayette and he didn't want to know. One time he had come down unannounced to bring coffee and he had seen two naked colored men in shackles being hosed off with water. One had been beaten severely, his face a swollen mess of scabs and bruises. The other was fairly unmarked, but he had intense red eyes that Willis sometimes saw late at night in his dreams. Willis placed the dishes on a small table. He did not look into the white men's faces, but kept his eyes down. They said nothing to him. Willis picked up the plates from the previous shift and returned to the kitchen.

Willis looked at the clock that hung over the service stairwell and saw that it was nearly eight o'clock. Captain LeGrande had told him to bring the new girl up to the conference room and let her in to wait for him. Willis went over to the counter and caught Serena's attention with a gesture. She had a large mixing bowl of cabbage in her arms when she came over to the counter.

"You Rena Love?" Willis asked.

Serena nodded, "You Willis?"

"Yes'm, I gon' let you in the conference room for Cap'n LeGrande. You ready to come?"

"No, I have some pies coming out of the oven in a few minutes. Why don't you open the room for me and I'll be along?"

"I can't do that. That conference room s'posed be locked all the time. The cap'n keep serious papers in there."

"Well, I can't come now," Serena said as she turned and went back into the kitchen. Willis looked at the clock and wondered if he would get in trouble if the girl was late. He glanced back into the kitchen and saw Minnie whispering in Serena's ear as they watched him. He knew Minnie didn't like him. She was probably slandering him again. He turned away and went back upstairs.

Willis went to the door of the main dining room and looked into the brightness of the room. It was a feature of the room along with its high ceilings that always created awe in him. The main chandelier had over one hundred bulbs and the four smaller ones each had fifty. The best silver and crystal was laid out on damask table linens. Each colored waiter had on a black jacket and a white shirt. Nearly one hundred of the most powerful people in the parish were sitting down to another fabulous dinner at the Lafayette Social Club. Willis straightened his jacket. It made him feel proud to work for the establishment. He would be able to tell his children about class and classiness. He pivoted and headed back toward the kitchen.

Willis met Serena on the stairs and escorted her to the conference room. He pulled out a ring of keys with a flourish and opened the door. Serena stepped inside, but before he could close the door behind her she said, "I forgot, my brother was going to pick me up tonight. He's probably out there now, waiting for me. Would you tell him he doesn't have to wait, I'll be home later?"

"Sho'! What he look like?" Willis wasn't really happy to run an errand for her, but he wouldn't reveal that to her. If she was giving it up to Captain LeGrande and she was anything like Dietra, he didn't want to be her enemy. She described Sampson to him and he nodded, affirming that he understood. After she closed the conference-room door, he went down to the servant's entrance to fulfill her request. He walked outside and saw an old truck sitting under a weeping willow. He called out as he walked toward the vehicle, "You Rena's brother? Hey, you Rena's brother?" Willis walked up to the door.

A squat, powerfully built man leapt out of the vehicle and stuck a knife against Willis's throat. The blade was pressing sharply into his neck. Willis stammered, "Uh, uh, I was just lookin' for Rena's brother! I ain't lookin' for no trouble!"

Another man got out of the truck. "You got trouble if you keep talkin'! You gon' lead us up to the room where you took Rena. If you balks or does anythin' out'n the ordinary, yo' blood gon' be stainin' the carpets." The man grabbed a hold of Willis's collar and shook him. "You with me?" the man demanded.

Willis gave the man a wide-eyed nod of understanding and was released. The two men donned black jackets over their white shirts and then took some long-barreled pistols from a bag and hid them under white towels. "Let's go," the taller man urged and pushed Willis toward the colored entrance.

The three men passed through the kitchen barely raising an eye. The evening's event required the hiring of extra serving staff so there were many colored men that the regulars did not know. At the top of the service stairs, Willis urged them to seek refuge in a linen storage alcove to let the head porter pass. They skirted behind the maître d's station and made it to the conference room without being seen. Willis pulled out his keys and unlocked the door. Once inside the room, the squat, silent man took the key ring from him.

"We done the first part. Now all we got to do is sit and wait," announced the taller man.

"What you want with me?" Willis whined. "I ain't done nothin' to y'all!"

The new girl walked over to him. "You're the sheriff's boy! You do all his errands. You may have information that we want!"

"You folks is crazy! I don't know nothin' 'bout the sheriff's doin's!" Willis exclaimed. "I just waits on him here at the Lafayette! You better get out of here befo' Captain LeGrande finds you!"

The taller man with red hair and freckles came over and knocked Willis to the ground with a blow to the side of the head. "We ain't got time to play with you!" the man snarled. "We's waitin' for LeGrande!"

A red fear flashed through Willis's mind, offsetting the dull ache throbbing above his temple. These Negroes were waiting for the captain and they were ready for violence. "What you want with me then? I tell you I don't know nothin'!"

There was a knock at the door and everyone in the room stopped still. The door handle was turned but did not open for it was still locked. The knocking resumed, louder than before. The new girl straightened her clothes and went to the door. The man who had hit Willis exposed his pistol and pointed it at Willis's head. The squat, powerfully built man went and stood behind the door. The new girl opened the door.

Willis couldn't see, but he heard LeGrande's voice. "How's my little octoroon?" There was the sound of a struggle, which ended suddenly. Willis saw LeGrande's unconscious body being dragged into the middle of the room. He was propped up in a chair, his hands were tied to the arms of the chair, and a glass of water was thrown in his face. The squat man looped a cord around LeGrande's neck and stood behind the chair.

Willis was now truly frightened. They were going to kill LeGrande in front of him and he was going to be involved. No one would believe he wasn't in on it from the beginning. He saw that LeGrande was groggily coming to his senses. The new girl was standing in front of him.

"Where's King Tremain?" she demanded, and then she slapped LeGrande across the face.

LeGrande started to shout. "You bi—" But the man behind him tightened the cord around his neck and his voice dropped to a hissing gurgle. The cord was kept tight until she commanded that it be loosened.

There was a hard edge to her voice as she spoke. "Let me ask you again before we take you and your flunky out for more questioning. Where are King Tremain and Phillip Duryea?"

"You'll never get away with this!" LeGrande growled, his voice husky from the pressure of the cord.

There was another knock at the door, softer but nonetheless insistent. LeGrande snarled, "You see? You niggers are finished! My men—" The man behind LeGrande tightened the cord again and he gurgled into silence.

Willis watched as the woman went over to the door while the freckled man positioned himself behind it.

Sergeant Beaumont pushed open the door and slurred drunkenly, "She ready for me yet, 'cause if she's as good as you say, I'm ready for her!" The man behind the door knocked Beaumont to the ground with the butt of his pistol. "What the hell?" Beaumont exclaimed as he was dragged to his feet. "You niggers in some deep shit now! You must not know who I—" Beaumont's words were cut short as he was knocked to the floor again.

"Say another word and you's a dead man!" the man with the freckles threatened, waving the pistol at Beaumont.

Beaumont growled. "You ain't gon' shoot me, nigger. The whole place gon' come runnin' soon's they hear yo' gun! But I can shoot you!" He fumbled for his revolver and the freckled man shot him several times in the chest. Willis would not have known that Beaumont had been shot except that he heard the soft cough of the gun and saw Beaumont's body shake with the impact of the bullets.

"Roll him up in one of those small carpets before he bleeds all over the place," the woman ordered. "We've got to get LeGrande and Willis ready to go!"

Willis was trembling. He knew he was going to die. "I knows where they is! I think they's the men down in the basement!"

"Shut up, nigger!" LeGrande commanded in his husky voice, but he was choked off again by the man with the cord.

The woman walked over to him. She now had one of the pistols in her hands. "What did you say?" She pointed the pistol at him.

"I think the mens you wants is downstairs in the basement. I saw some colored mens in chains down there last week!"

"Let's go!" the man with the freckles said with a triumphant smile. The squat man began making hand signals rapidly.

The woman read his sign and said, "Sampson's right! We have to clean up here first! The blood has to be cleaned up. We can't leave any evidence that we've been here. Put a gag in LeGrande's mouth and roll him up in the carpet. We still have to take him with us!"

After Beaumont's body had been rolled into a carpet, Willis heard the man with freckles complain, "Serena, I can't get up this blood without soap and water!"

"Go and get a pan of water from the service station!"

The man objected. "I don't know where that is and I can't ask nobody!"

"Red, take Willis. If he does anything stupid, kill him!"

Willis was hauled to his feet. The blood was wiped off the side of his head and he was sent out with the freckled-faced man. Willis walked like he was in a dream. He could hardly hear anything above the sound of his pumping heart. Pain and sensation were subordinate to fear. He prayed that no one would notice them and the gods saw fit to answer his prayer. They made it to the service station and returned with towels and soapy water. When they were once again in the conference room, Willis exhaled, happy to be alive. LeGrande was already rolled in his carpet when Willis was set to cleaning up Beaumont's blood.

Serena went out and brought two service carts into the room and the rolled-up carpets were placed on them. She said, "Dinner is over. The speeches are being given. The waiters are all in the main dining room, waiting to clear the tables. We can use the dumbwaiter to get the carpets downstairs. Nobody should see us."

Willis could hardly remember the next events. He seemed to be watching everything from a distance. He heard his captors whispering something about dynamite, but he didn't catch all of it and he knew better than to ask. They made it to the dumbwaiter safely and loaded the bodies onto it, but as they were descending the service stairs, they saw the head porter coming up the stairs carrying more table linen.

Thomas saw Red and Sampson coming down the steps with Serena and Willis and stepped in front of them, pressing his rod into Sampson's chest. "What the hell you think you doin'?" he demanded. "You Negroes don't work here! Mr. Weston! Mr. West—" Red knocked Thomas down the stairs.

"Clarence, can't you take care of anything by yourself? This better be good!" Weston declared as he came out of the linen closet at the top of the stairs. He stopped when he saw Thomas lying in front of him. "What happened, Clarence?" he asked as he stooped over to check the head porter. As Thomas struggled to his knees, Weston warned, "Watch it, goddamn it, Clarence, you're getting blood on the linen!" Weston turned to Willis and Red, who were coming down the steps toward him, and demanded, "What the hell are you jungle bunnies standing around for? Help him up and pick up that linen carefully! Honestly, you coons are too stupid sometimes."

Both Red and Sampson looked at Serena for direction and got an unobtrusive nod before they went to help Thomas, who was still on his knees in a daze as blood dripped from his mouth. Serena pushed Willis down the stairs in front of her.

"I don't recognize you boys," Weston observed. He had no chance to say anything else. Sampson hit Weston on the point of his chin and knocked him backward, sprawling across the floor.

Willis heard Minnie exclaim, "Oh, Lord, what's happenin' now?" Then he saw her come out from behind the counter with a meat cleaver in her hand.

"Don't do it, Minnie!" Serena warned. "I've come for my husband who's locked down in the basement. I don't want to hurt anybody else if I don't have to, but I'll kill anybody who stands in my way!"

Minnie nodded her head and said, "I knew you was too good to be true. Ain't nobody like you come to work here befo'! Yo' name ain't even Rena, is it?"

"Don't worry about it. Just go behind the counter and stay there," Serena advised. She turned to Sampson. "Get those bodies out of the dumbwaiter and drag them down to the basement!" She put the pistol behind Willis's head and said, "Lead the way to my husband!"

Willis pointed to Thomas. "He got the key. I ain't got the key for nothin' down in the basement!"

Serena pushed Willis toward Thomas. "Help him to his feet!"

"You niggers ain't gon' get away!" Thomas scoffed as he was helped to his feet. "The whole police force is here tonight! They gon' come down on you like white on rice!"

"You won't live to see it!" Serena said as she prodded him with the pistol in the direction of the stairs that led to the basement.

"If you gives yo'selves up, maybe I can talk to Captain LeGrande for you," Thomas offered as he stumbled forward. "I knows him well. Maybe he won't hang all of you."

"All I want from you is to open the door to where they're keeping my husband!" Serena replied, prodding Thomas down the stairs.

"That cut-and-shoot nigger is yo' husband? They don't keep nobody down here 'ceptin' niggers who can't stay out of trouble. I seen lots of 'em in my day and the only ways they leaves here is to the gallows or feet first."

After he dragged Weston's body down the stairs after them, Red demanded angrily, "You mean to tell me you helped these white bastards torture and beat colored men?"

Thomas drew himself up to his full height as he walked down the stairs. "You see it's niggers like you that gives colored folks a bad name. People like you is better off on the gallows. You don't know yo' place and you cause white folks to be suspicious of the rest of us!"

Minnie came to the top of the stairs. "They got guards down there, Rena. You best be quiet."

Willis watched as Red's gun coughed softly and Weston's body shook from the impact of the bullet.

"That's a white man you killin'!" Thomas said in a horrified voice. Red hit Thomas hard on the back with the butt of his pistol and Thomas fell to the ground with a groan. Red bent over Thomas's crumpled form, took the keys out of his pocket, and said, "Only reason I don't kill you now, you Tommin' no-good dog, is you gon' open the door for us." Thomas was hauled roughly to his feet.

Willis was assigned with Sampson to drag the rugs with bodies in them down into the basement corridor. After he completed that task he was shoved to walk down the darkened corridor in front of Serena and Red, shoulder to shoulder with Thomas. It was one of the longest walks Willis ever took. Each step had a separate life. Every movement was accompanied by a sense of slow motion. It seemed to take hours to get to the shadows of the first door. Red handed him the keys and Willis unlocked the door. The door opened with a creak that sounded as if it reverberated down the corridor.

They continued creeping forward until a male voice called out from farther down the corridor, "That somebody comin'?"

Red pressed the barrel of his gun against Thomas's back, but Thomas kept his mouth closed with a determined frown.

Willis, seeing that Thomas was refusing to speak, said, "It's just me and Clarence, boss. Cap'n LeGrande sent us down to check to see if'en there's anythin' you mens want befo' the kitchen closes." The guns behind them prodded him and Thomas to continue forward.

The sound of chuckling greeted them. The guards were still out of view around the corner. "What I tell you, Joe Bob? The cap'n ain't forgettin' 'bout us! Maybe he even gon' send some relief so's we can go upstairs."

Another male voice answered. "Maybe you right, Tillman. Maybe you right!"

Joe Bob said impatiently, "Come on! Hurry up, niggers! We gon' tell you what we want!"

Willis and Thomas rounded the corner and Thomas broke into a run. "Watch out! Watch out!" he cried as he ran toward the two white guards. "There's some bad nig—" A bullet hit him in the shoulder and knocked Thomas off balance. Not hearing the discharge of a gun, the guards were unprepared for the fusillade of bullets that tore into their unsuspecting flesh. They were driven backward against the wall and crumpled to the ground without ever having the chance to return fire.

Red and Serena pushed Willis into a run, keeping him in front of them. They burst through the door that had been guarded and saw two naked colored men shackled to the wall. The stench of human excrement was overpowering. One man was a mass of sores and scabs while the other appeared to be only bruised. But neither man noticed their entrance. They both seemed to be in a stupor. Red went out to check the guard's bodies for keys while Serena knelt by her husband and touched his face lovingly.

Willis watched as Red returned with keys jangling in his hands. "I had to shoot Thomas in the hip," he explained as he tried different keys on King's lock chains. "He was tryin' to escape down the corridor."

Soon both men were released from their chains. Sampson appeared with a container of gasoline and several sticks of dynamite. An older, gray-haired man followed him into the room and ran to the second man, exclaiming, "Oh, my God, Phillip. What have they done to you, my son? My son!" The man started crying as he held his son in his arms.

Red said, "We got to get to gettin'! We's been blessed with luck, but don't let us press it. We need to be gettin' out'a here! I can carry King, but we gon' need a stretcher for Phillip."

Sampson smacked his chest with his hand and pointed to King, indicating he would carry him. He went over and lifted Serena to her feet and then stooped down and lifted King easily in his arms and carried him out the door.

"We'll use one of those rugs to carry out Phillip," Red suggested. "I'll go get one!"

Claude stood up. There were angry sparks in his eyes when he spoke. "We need to leave somebody shackled to the wall, so when this room blows up, there will still be somebody left in the chains. That way, it'll look like King and Phillip were killed in the explosion."

"I got just the man for one pair," Red answered and before he went out the door, he grabbed a hold of Willis and said, "You come with me!"

Willis and Red retrieved the two rugs and dragged them along with their contents into the room. Then Red took him back down the corridor to get Weston. Willis dragged Weston's body back toward the room. On the way back, Red stopped and got Thomas by his feet and dragged him into the room as well. Red immediately set to shackling Thomas to the wall.

"I needs a priest if'en I gon' die," Thomas moaned.

"You ain't gettin' shit!" Red spit out. "My daddy was picked up by the police and nobody ever saw him after that. They probably brung him here and you probably the one who served food to the men who killed him! You's a goddamned traitor to yo' own people! This is too good for you!"

"I ain't studyin' you!" Thomas said weakly. "I'm gon' go to the Pearly Gates. I've lived a good life. I'm an elder in my church!" Thomas stifled a gasp and began to pray, "Our Father who art in heaven—"

"Unroll LeGrande out of that other carpet!" Serena ordered Willis over the sound of Thomas's praying. "He's the other one that should be shackled to the wall."

Willis numbly set to the task assigned as Red and the older man hefted Phillip up in the rug and carried him from the room. Willis wondered if he was to share the same fate as Thomas and LeGrande. He did not want to give the rescue party an excuse to kill him, so he put his shoulder into it and unrolled LeGrande onto the floor.

The captain had regained full consciousness, but his hands were still tied behind him and he had a gag in his mouth. He started kicking and struggling as soon as he was free of the carpet. Serena fired her pistol at the cement floor in front of his face. Chips of cement flew in every direction and LeGrande ceased struggling. Thomas even stopped praying for a moment, but he soon began intoning his prayers again. Sampson returned and Serena directed him and Willis to untie LeGrande and chain him to the wall. Sampson stunned LeGrande with two blows from his fist. The captain was dragged to the shackles and chained against the wall.

Serena then directed Sampson to check and make sure that everything outside was ready. Willis slumped against the wall and waited for further direction. He watched as Serena went over and pulled the gag from LeGrande's mouth.

"You were going to pass me on to Beaumont, were you?" she asked in a flat, emotionless tone.

LeGrande's eyes were wide as he struggled against the chains. "You won't get away. Once my men free me, I'll track you down and I'll hang every last one of you!"

Serena went over and tapped the gasoline can. "When your men find you, they'll think you're my husband because you'll be charred to a crisp."

"Wait a minute! Wait a minute!" LeGrande demanded in a hoarse voice. "We can work something out here, eh? You don't have to kill me! I can help you escape! I have money! You can have it all!"

Serena smiled and shook her head. "There's nothing that you have that I want more than the pleasure of killing you!" Sampson returned and gave Serena the thumbs-up sign. She nodded her head in response and Sampson picked up the gasoline can and began carefully pouring it on LeGrande and Thomas, just enough to soak their clothes.

"Wait a minute!" sputtered LeGrande. "Wait a minute! I know something you want to know!"

Thomas turned to LeGrande. "Why don't you shut up, white man. Ain't nothin' you gon' say gon' stop her! Get ready for kingdom come!" It was the first time that he had ever spoken to a white man without being solicitous. It surprised him. It felt pretty good. He closed his eyes and tried to ready himself to meet his maker.

Serena turned to LeGrande as Sampson left the room. "Uncle Tom's right, white man!"

"Don't kill me! I know where the baby is! I—"

"Shut up!" Serena ordered as Sampson returned with two long fuses and a lit cigar. He set the cigar down on a table and affixed the fuses to a bundle of dynamite sticks. When he was finished, Serena gestured for him to wait outside. After he left the room, Serena turned to LeGrande. "You were saying?"

"Let me loose and I'll tell you where the baby is! I'm the only one who knows where it is! If you kill me, you'll never find it!"

"The baby is alive?" A cold fear lanced Serena's heart, but it was replaced immediately by anger. Mamie had raised her head again.

"Yes! Yes, I didn't hurt it. I put it in a colored orphanage in south Texas near Port Arthur, not too far from the Louisiana border!"

"You're sure that no one else knows where it is?" she asked.

"I'm sure! Just release me and I'll take you right to the—" His words were interrupted by the bullets that Serena fired into his body. She kept shooting her pistol until the slide locked in the open position. The silencer on the gun had caused it to make minimal noise, but the recoil of each discharge and the smell of cordite brought home the fact that she had a killing weapon in her hand. She was trembling. She had given everything to rescue King. She alone had earned the right to bear his children and she would never allow another woman's child to intrude. Serena smiled. With LeGrande's death Mamie's presence was eradicated forever. Old photographs would be all that King would ever have to remind him of her.

Thomas began to hum "Nearer My God to Thee." Serena stared at him and all the anger and resentment and humiliation came rushing back, flooding her consciousness with the desire for more revenge. LeGrande's death was not enough. His death alone could not pay for the violations done to her family and friends. She turned and called to Sampson.

Sampson entered the room puffing on the cigar. At her direction, he lit the fuse. As the fuse began to spark and sizzle, Thomas began to hum louder. Sampson pulled out his pistol and aimed it at Willis, but Serena shook her head and pushed his arm down.

"He's done what we told him. He's cooperated. Let him live. If he talks, he'll jeopardize his own life because they won't believe him." She turned and walked out of the room. She and King would go on as before, as if the baby had never been. As time passed, it would become a dimly remembered casualty of war.

Following Serena down the hall, Willis babbled his thanks and gratitude, but Sampson cut him short with a gesture and all three of them hurried down the corridor to the stairs leading up to the kitchen.

"You better get out of here, Minnie," Serena warned as she and Sampson crossed to the door. "We're going to blow the building apart."

"Damn, girl! You ain't even been here a week yet and you done destroyed the whole damn place! I'm leaving with you!"

Serena nodded and Minnie gathered up her belongings and followed her out the door.

Willis was left standing in the kitchen by himself. It didn't seem real. He was alive. So many times within the last hour and a half it looked like his life would be cut short and yet here he was. He started for the door, then had a second thought. After the explosion, no one would know what was what. His hunger had reawakened within him and compelled him to go into the pantry. He might as well help himself to a few items. When the explosion shook the building, Willis was loaded down with a couple of hams and a container of butter. He still might have escaped if he hadn't stopped to take a brisket of beef. He never saw the beam that fell and crushed him beneath it.

SATURDAY, APRIL 23, 1921

"Get the hell out of my way, Boyer!" Corlis shouted as he sat on the side of his bed, waiting for his clothes to be brought by Sergeant Pointdexter. "I'll have you arrested for obstruction of justice. See if I don't!"

Dr. Boyer, a small chubby man with round, wire-rimmed glasses, was not intimidated. "I would not be serving you well if I did not attempt to prevent you from leaving this hospital prematurely, Corlis. You need to listen to me. You are not completely out of danger yet. It's true that the infection is under control, but the sutures are not completely set yet and your moving around may put stress on them. You don't want the sutures to be pulled open because then you will be subject to new infections."

"I've listened to you too much already, you little butcher! If I had left here last week I could have prevented what happened at the Lafayette last night! Now I'm telling you get out! I don't want to see your face unless I call you!" Corlis's voice had dropped to a gutteral snarl. The set and determined expression on his face, combined with his tone, made the doctor bow out of the room without another word.

Pointdexter reentered the room with Corlis's clothes. He gave Corlis a toothy, apologetic smile. "The doctor cut the right leg off your pants. He say the amputa—"

"Don't say that goddamned word!" Corlis ordered. "And don't mention that doctor to me again! Just go get one of the orderlies to help me get dressed!" Corlis looked over at the crutches he had been practicing with awkwardly for the last week and rage filled him. Everywhere he went he would now need help. He couldn't even take a shit by himself.

During the car ride over to the Lafayette Social Club every bump and rut in the road caused Corlis to grimace, but no exclamation of pain escaped his mouth.

"Tell me again what happened last night, Anthony," Corlis said, pulling out a cigar and fumbling for a match. Pointdexter, in an effort to assist him, pulled some matches from his coat pocket and almost missed a turn in the road. "Keep your hands on the wheel and your eyes on the road!" Corlis ordered, holding on as the vehicle swerved back on the road. "Tell me what happened last night," he said once again.

"We don't know exactly how it happened yet, but the Lafayette was blowed up last night," Pointdexter explained. "We was all in the main dining hall, the one with the chandeliers, and we was listening to that long-winded Councilman Hill's speech about how he done helped us clean up the bootleggin' in New Orleans Parish and—"

"Damn it, man! Tell me if you found out the cause of the explosion!" Corlis interrupted impatiently. "What type of investigation did you conduct?"

"Well, er, I was waitin' for Captain LeGrande to take charge, but he never showed up," Pointdexter said with an apologetic cough. "We don't know where he is. I went by his house this mornin' befo' I came to get you."

"You mean to tell me you didn't conduct any investigation?"

Pointdexter swallowed uncomfortably. "There wasn't much to see last night. The electricity got blown out with the explosion and the fire burned for quite a while and caused a lot of smoke. All we did was try to put the fire out and search for survivors. That's still goin' on this mo'nin'. It looks like a bomb done went off somewheres near the front of the building. Least ways that's what Dietrich say. He saw a lot of bombin' in the Big War."

"What about my prisoners?"

Pointdexter smiled for the first time. "I checked that immediately, knowin' how impo'tant they was to you. They didn't get away, that's for sure! Everybody that was down at that end of the buildin' was killed for sho'!"

"How do you know?" Corlis was getting a bad feeling. Could it be that Negroes were getting so bold that they would attack an honored and distinguished establishment like the Lafayette Social Club, even when it was filled with police?

"I sent some mens down there with flashlights to dig out whoever was down there, but they didn't find nobody alive. They couldn't even find a whole corpse."

"Then how do you know the niggers didn't escape?"

"Cause they found pieces of them still shackled to the wall. I went down myself once the way was cleared. We found the head and arm of one body still chained to the wall. The other body was found across the room with a chunk of the wall chained to its arm."

Corlis smacked the side of the car with his fist. This was the final frustration. He had been turned into a cripple by a nigger who had escaped to his reward without ever having to pay the full price for his act. "Any other bodies?" he asked grimly.

"Lots of 'em! The flo' collapsed and everybody who was in the kitchen was burned to a crisp."

"Did you at least question the colored help?"

"Uh, no. It was just hell and confusion last night. We was just tryin' to save white folks. The staircase to the second flo' collapsed and a supportin' pillar fell into the dining room. Then we had to fight the fire too! We was lucky to escape with only twenty-seven dead, not countin' them guards in the basement, of course. But I'll round up all the colored help and bring 'em in for questioning."

"Damn it, Pointdexter, it's too late now! Hell, they probably stole the place blind before they left! I can see it now. After the explosion they probably disappeared with everything they could carry! Niggers are like that!"

"That sounds like it's true for white folks too, sir," Pointdexter observed.

"I'm not talking about whites, I'm talking about niggers!" Corlis snapped irritatedly. "What about the porters working at the front gate? Did you check to see if anybody strange came through the gate before the explosion? Or left immediately after it?"

"I talked to them. An old colored man by the name of Jacob is in charge of the gate porters and he said the only people who came through last night was white people. He said he didn't know most of them, but he was told by the maître d' John Weston to let them in if they had an invitation. He said some white men came through in a big car who had funny northern accents. He let them in because they had an invitation. Jacob said they were among the first ones to leave after the explosion. He saw them leave as he was headin' for the main buildin' to help the rescue effort."

The wrought-iron fence of the Lafayette Social Club came into view. As they pulled up to the gate, Corlis was happy to see men in parish police uniforms guarding the entrance. They snapped to attention when they saw who was in the car and saluted. Corlis gave them a weary salute in return and the car drove on toward the damaged and still smoldering main building. He was surprised at the amount of destruction the building had experienced. The whole front half had collapsed and a good section of the lower two stories were gutted by fire. Men, both colored and white, were heaving on ropes with block and tackle to lift heavy pieces of construction out of the way. At one corner of the building someone had set up a table and was taking statements from a line of colored workers dressed in bedraggled and dirty uniforms. Corlis could see that someone had taken responsibility for organizing the rescue and salvage effort.

The car pulled to a stop near the front of the building and Pointdexter got out and ran around the front bumper to assist Corlis out of the vehicle. "Get back, goddamn it!" Corlis snarled as he fumbled for his crutches. He got them under his arms and, using the car door, pulled himself erect with an effort. "I'm not an invalid yet! Now, who's in charge around here?"

"Uh, Sergeant Dietrich, I think, sir," Pointdexter looked around, unsure of the correct answer. "I think he's sittin' at yon table, sir."

"I'm going over to the table to talk with Dietrich. In the meantime, I want you to get on top of those damned utility companies and get electricity and phone systems working out here! Don't let them give you any excuse! Tell them they will answer to me if we don't have power and telephones by this evening!" Corlis made his way awkwardly to the table.

Sergeant Felix Dietrich stood up as soon as he saw the sheriff approaching. He pushed his dark hair out of his pale blue eyes and straightened his uniform. "Good morning, sir," he said smartly as Corlis lurched alongside the table. He beckoned for one of his men to bring a chair for Corlis.

"What's going on here, Sergeant?" Corlis asked, looking around at the men sifting through the rubble near the front of the building.

"We've just given up looking for survivors, sir," Dietrich explained in clipped tones. "There may be more, but we can't get at them until we get some big construction equipment in here. I've assigned a work crew to search through the debris, to find out the type of bomb it was. There's no doubt in my mind that it was very sophisticated. It reminds me of when I was in Europe."

The chair was delivered and Corlis sat down heavily. "Do you have any idea as to who might have set it? It couldn't be, for example, a couple of niggers with a few sticks of dynamite?"

Dietrich threw back his head and laughed. "That's a good one, sir! It's really great to see that you can keep your sense of humor. Whoever was responsible for this must have known something about architecture, because they set the explosive next to the supporting columns of the front of the building. It was a professional job, sir. They used a bomb device made up of both gasoline and dynamite and they must've had a timer—far too complex for ignorant Negroes. But that sure was a funny one, sir! Wait until I tell my men. They'll get a howl out of that one!" Dietrich stopped laughing and suddenly became serious. "Sir, if I may, I do have a few ideas, but I don't want to talk in front of the coloreds. You know what they say about the jungle telegraph."

"Get these niggers out of here! I want to hear your ideas!"

Dietrich barked a few orders and the colored workers were directed to return to the salvage effort. "I'll get a statement from each one of them before they leave, sir," he explained to Corlis. He sat down next to the sheriff and said in a lowered voice, "I'm pretty sure it was them Italians." Dietrich pronounced the word "Eye-talians." He moved his chair closer to Corlis and continued speaking. "When we intercepted their big bootleg shipment last week near Possum Hollow, they threatened our men. I know that Captain LeGrande invited them last night to negotiate some kind of agreement. I think he was planning to charge them a small percentage of the shipment for free passage past the port as long as the alcohol wasn't to be sold in New Orleans."

"LeGrande was smart," Corlis said with a nod. "Would have made us a pretty penny too. How did you know he invited the Italians?"

"Because he assigned me to sit at their table and keep them company. They were antsy from the start, claiming they wanted to meet right away. Since the captain was filling in for you, he didn't have time to meet with them earlier, you know, with glad-handing councilmen and such. The captain came to the table just before he left the room and said he had one more brief meeting, then he could meet with them. These Italians were almost rude. To tell the truth, I wanted to get up and slap a few of them myself, but you know Captain LeGrande—he was calm. He said he'd be with them as soon as he could.

"The Italians left a few minutes before the explosion. They were angry as hell, saying they had never been so insulted. They threw their napkins down and one even turned over his chair when he got up and left it lying on the floor. If I had known what they were going to do, I would have killed them then! They must think we're country fools down here!"

Corlis sat for a few minutes and fumed. His anger was growing. These bastards had robbed him of the chance of killing King Tremain slowly, the way he deserved. Revenge had been on Corlis's mind every minute of every day and suddenly the opportunity was gone, taken by some fools who couldn't wait fifteen minutes to have a meeting. If that was the way of it, then let them feel his wrath. He would do everything in his power to kill every one of them he could find. They had made one enemy who would never forget and he would be merciless.

MONDAY, JUNE 13, 1921 ♕

The wind had powerful arms that stretched across the landscape, and it had a thirty-mile piece of Oklahoma in its grip. It gusted northeasterly at fifty miles an hour for fifteen minutes, then rushed at forty miles an hour straight up the sides of the Ouachitas for twenty minutes without any loss of power. Even for those safe in their vegetable cellars, the roar of the wind was the voice of God. It seemed to fall directly from the heavens and it swept down upon the homes of the unsuspecting and shattered their wooden dwellings like a fist. Pieces of lumber and parts of roofs were sent tumbling as if they were child's toys. Then came the tornado.

A wave of nausea washed over Serena. It felt like a hand was squeezing her stomach, forcing half-digested food back up into her throat. For a moment she was sure that she would throw up, but the urgency passed. Serena, Ma Wrangel, and Ida Hoskins were sitting on the floor in the total darkness of the store's cold-storage cellar. Serena was struggling with her body to restrain every gasp and intake of breath that the nausea caused. She did not want the other women to hear her. She could feel the warm trickles of sweat running down the sides of her face.

Outside, the wind howled as it rushed along Main Street, blowing shingles loose and signs from their moorings and causing shutters to clatter as they were banged open and closed.

The nausea was returning, the pressure was building; this time it seemed unstoppable. The waves washed over her. She was caught up in the rhythm of the tide. Despite her efforts to suppress it, it began to rise in her throat.

"You reckon that twister done passed us yet?" Ma Wrangel asked.

"I ain't about to go up and see just yet," Ida replied. "I've seen these dern things jump around like a hoppy-toad; can't predict 'em."

The urge to throw up passed. Serena could lay back and rest once more and await the next onslaught.

"You don't sound too good, Serena, girl," Ma Wrangel observed with concern in her voice. "Sounds like you strugglin' with the devil over there."

"You're right, Ma. I'm not feeling too sprightly. It's probably something I ate."

"Oh, pshaw, she hardly eats at all," Ida Hoskins said. "I ain't seen a body in a long time that needs a big plate of beans and rice as much as she does."

"Rena, you best come on over to Wrangel House and let me put a steak on the griddle for you. Can't have the owner of the best dress shop in southwest Oklahoma feeble 'cause of the want of vittles."

"Saturday we had two families come all the way from Johnsonville," Ida announced proudly. "When we get in those pedal sewing machines, we'll have work for two women full-time."

"Rena, what you say to that steak?"

"Oh, Ma, really, food is the last thought on my mind."

Outside the volume of the wind dropped and the silence was complete for about ten seconds. Then the wind returned more fiercely than ever. It roared as it issued from the giant maw of the west, the output of warm moisture-ridden northerlies meeting the dry cold southerlies on the battlefield of the plains. The tornado touched down in its spinning frenzy and lifted a wooden wagon from behind a shed and threw it over the Wrangel house and across Main Street, slamming it into Dorsett's Cabinet Shop. The tornado rose like a huge vacuum cleaner and lifted the roof off the barbershop and flung it out behind the town. A tremendous shrieking rent the air as the tornado settled down on Lightning Smith's livery stable and sucked it apart, exposing to its uncaring power the luckless animals contained within. In seconds the tornado was gone as if it had never been. There was silence.

Serena was exhausted. All she wanted to do was stick her finger down her throat to relieve the pressure in her stomach. She was willing to stay slumped on the floor if only she could rest in peace. She said nothing, pulled her knees up to her face, and rested her chin on her hands.

Ten minutes passed before Ma Wrangel said, "I think that's it! It sounds like it's gone on to bother somebody else!"

"I'll take my time checkin' on it, if you don't mind," Ida said. "I doesn't mind sittin' here a few minutes more."

"I have to get out of here!" Serena said, overcome by another wave of nausea. She crawled to the stairs and began to climb to the trapdoor.

"Be careful. The twister is a jukey thing," Ma Wrangel warned.

Serena opened up the trapdoor and crawled out on the floor. She lay for a moment, then pulled herself to a standing position. Ma Wrangel was climbing out of the cellar when Serena ran for the back door. Serena was vomiting in a bucket when Ma Wrangel joined her. "I couldn't hold it any longer," she explained as she wiped her mouth with a rag.

"Are you sure you're alright, Rena?"

Serena nodded and stood up. She smiled. "I'm doing much better. It's funny you should call me Rena. Only my family called me that."

"Well, I's part of yo' family, girl. You part of this town now."

Ida came running out of the back door. "That twister done tore up part of Main Street! You got to come see! There's a wagon stuck in the front of the cabinet shop and the whole portico in front of the store is down!"

"Well, let me go check and see if my stove is still sittin' there," Ma Wrangel said as she walked back inside with Serena. "Rena, you be sure to come for that steak this evening, or I'll come and drag you over!"

"Yes, ma'am," Serena answered. Serena walked to the front of the store to survey the damage. The portico in front of the store had collapsed and some of the wooden plank walkway was gone. Main Street was littered with pieces of wood and debris. Many of the businesses fronting on the street had broken windows, splintered shutters, and pieces of their roof missing. The barbershop was destroyed. One wall was completely gone; the others had fallen inward. Bodie Wells had suffered under the heavy hand of the tornado, but that was not the most pressing thing on Serena's mind. She was pregnant and it was not King's baby.

She knew that when she missed her first period something was amiss, but she prayed to God that she was just late. Then she missed the second one and she knew. There was no doubt. She did not have time to devote much of her conscious energy to the problem earlier because she was concentrating on nursing King back to health. Now that he had gone back to New Orleans, the weight of her dilemma settled heavily on her shoulders. She did not know where to turn for help. Bodie Wells was a small town and she had already learned that gossip was a major pastime. Ma Wrangel wouldn't talk, but how could Serena explain it to her. Could it be explained at all? The truth sounded like a fabrication. Serena didn't want to lose Ma Wrangel's respect, but most important, she didn't ever want King to find out. She wanted to get rid of the child growing within her, as if it never existed.

There was no doubt in her mind that she couldn't allow this baby to come to term. She had realized this while she had been busy nursing King out of the stupor into which he had sunk. Whatever he had seen and experienced during his imprisonment in the basement of the Lafayette was buried deep within him and he would not speak of it to her. In fact, he would hardly speak at all. Yet his very silence was expressive. It was a terrible, grim, brooding silence that seemed to issue out of a deep well of anger.

When she had first brought him home, he lay in bed for a full week without speaking. He did not want to sleep in the same bed as she, so she took the adjoining bedroom. Then one morning she came in and he was gone. He did not return home until dusk. Serena was beside herself with worry, but when he came in that evening he offered no explanation, nor did she demand any. Nearly a week passed before she got up in time to see him before he left. It was before first light when she heard his boots on the stairs. She followed, dressed only in her robe, and discovered him in his gun room, cleaning some pistols. The look he gave her when she entered the room nearly broke her heart; it was cold, flat, and lifeless. He left shortly thereafter with his rifles, pistols, and a military can filled with ammunition. All he gave her was a few terse words and a nod before he climbed into his truck and drove off, disappearing in the morning darkness.

It was then that she knew he had not forgiven her and it made her pregnancy all the more unwanted. She wanted to erase everything that separated them. She wanted to return to the mood and the moment that existed when he had come home bearing gifts before New Year's. Strangely, she was almost happy when he received the letter from Claude Duryea and decided to go back to New Orleans. Although she was concerned about his safety, she needed him gone for a while so she could take steps to rid herself of the life inside her.

"Serena! Serena!" Someone was knocking on the front door. She started from her reverie as if awakened from a deep sleep and went to the door. It was Clara Nesbitt.

As soon as Serena opened the door, Clara rushed in and gave her a hug. "I'm so glad to see that you are alright. Ma Wrangel said you weren't feeling well."

"What else did she say?" Serena asked. She knew that neither Ma Wrangel nor Ida had missed the signs of morning sickness.

"Only that I should help her get you over there for a steak dinner tonight. Listen, Dr. Stephens sent me over to see if we could use your sewing room for a temporary hospital. We've got a lot of injured people. He says you have more room than he does and you have the best light in town."

"Tell him to bring them over. Ask Ida to clean off the sewing jobs and put an oilskin on the table."

"I knew you'd do it!" Clara asserted. "You Tremains are such good people. I'll go tell Doc Stephens right now. Oh, by the way, Lightning Smith's livery stable is wiped out. He was found behind it still holding on to one of the supporting timbers. We had to pry him loose. He's in shock. He keeps walking around looking for that old horse of his. Nobody has the heart to tell him that his horse was found spread-eagled on a hill on the other side of town. Doc was wondering if you'd let Lightning take care of the livestock that you have in your barn; that may help to bring him back to reality."

"Sometimes reality is pretty tough to come back to," Serena observed.

Clara stopped and looked at her for a moment and in that instant saw inside of her. She saw through a window that appears only intermittently in relationships and may last only seconds, but through which sometimes a soul may be seen, with all its doubts and fears. Both women saw each other clearly and understood that they shared some of the same fears.

Tears glistened in Clara's eyes as she walked over and put her arms around Serena. "You're right. Sometimes reality tests your faith." The two women held each other for several seconds. Then Clara pushed back and said, "My mother said she heard you had morning sickness but you were trying to hide it." Clara looked her in the eye and said, "By tomorrow, it will be all over town. People will be wondering why you aren't celebrating. What's wrong, Serena?"

"I'm pregnant." Serena turned and walked away into the store. "Tell Doc Stephens he can bring his patients over in fifteen minutes." The window was gone. Clara paused and stared after Serena, then turned and went out the front door.

She had never thought there would be a possibility that she would ever destroy a child, even an unborn one, particularly her own. It was unthinkable and at the same time necessary. King would never look at that child without seeing his torturer and her rapist. She had seen the hate smoldering, never allowed to truly catch fire but never extinguished either, that was burning just beneath his expressionless look. She understood that by King's lights, he had to kill Corlis; otherwise the sheriff would haunt his thoughts for the rest of his life. King didn't like ghosts. That was part of the problem: this child would be part hers and part ghost.

"Miz Rena? Miz Rena?" Serena swam to the surface of her consciousness. She had gotten lost in thought again. Lightning was asking her a question.

"What can I do for you, Lightning?"

"Miz Rena, can I stay out in yo' barn. I ain't got no place else to go. Everythin' I had is gone," Lightning explained in a soft voice. "My can of money done swooshed up in the sky. Everythin' done blowed away. Even ol' Red is dead. I had that horse almost sixteen years, since he was a colt." He stared at the floor sadly. "I just want to stay in yo' barn."

Lightning's humbled state touched Serena. "Lightning, you can have a pallet by the stove downstairs until my menfolk return. Then we'll fix you up a room. I've got work for you now. If you want it, you can earn your keep."

Tears formed in Lightning's eyes and he stuttered. "Clara's right 'bout you folks. You is real good peoples. You don't have to worry 'bout a thing. I'll work for anythin' you folks wants to give. Even though I ain't got nothin', I don't want charity." The tears began to stream down Lightning's purple black face. "You got to pardon me cryin'!" he protested, wiping his face with his crumpled hat. "I ain't no weaklin'! I ain't used to doin' this kind of thing, but I can't seem to stop. I worked my whole life and everythin' is gone!" The tears continued to come. Lightning covered his face with his hat, turned, and walked away. "I'll just go check on thin's in the barn, Miz Rena," he explained as he walked out of the rear of the store.

"Dinner's at six-thirty," she called after him. She had not even planned to prepare dinner and didn't know what she was going to cook, but it seemed the thing to do. The old man had suffered a life-shattering setback. She wanted to ease his pain. It was sure obvious that she wasn't the only one with problems. Serena walked over to the stacks of denim overalls and pulled out a pair for Lightning. She had noticed the ones he was wearing were torn and dirty. She picked up a flannel shirt and wrote both items down in her inventory book.

Serena and Ida were closing the store for the evening. Dr. Stephens had finished with his patients and the sewing room had been returned to its original state. Serena was wondering whether Ida was the source of the gossip about her morning sickness and was about to ask her about the matter when Cordel Witherspoon entered the store. "Mrs. Tremain, Ma Wrangel say she expectin' you for steak tonight."

"Oh, I can't, Cordel. I told Lightning that I would cook dinner for him."

Ida said, "Don't worry 'bout him, Mrs. T. He can eat with me and my husband tonight and tomorrow night too, if he need it. You need to go on and get a good meal into you. Let Ma Wrangel take care of you tonight. We'll take care of Lightnin'."

"Ma Wrangel expects you in half an hour," Cordel said before he went out the door.

In the face of Ida's offer to feed Lightning, Serena felt chagrined for wanting to confront her over the gossip issue. "Good-night, Ida, and thank you so much for inviting Lightning for dinner tonight," she said as Ida went out the door.

Ida stopped and gave her a quick peck on the cheek. "See you in the mornin', Mrs. T. I'll close the shutters before I go."

Serena went upstairs and for some undefined reason went into the bedroom that she and King had once shared. The bed was made and there was nothing on the bureaus or side tables. He had left everything neat and military. She went to the left side-table and opened a drawer. Inside was a neatly folded letter. She picked up the letter and smelled it. It smelled of him. On the day King had received it, he had gone on a long horse ride and he had carried the letter next to his skin. She could not resist opening the letter again and reading its painful message.

Friday June 1, 1921
Dear King,

I can barely think to write this letter. Phillip died in the early hours of this morning. He did not live to see the sun rise again. He died in darkness and in pain. He struggled mightily with death, but his body was too torn and ruptured to live. Mortal flesh is only mortal. I am sorry if my tears have blurred the words I have written. I cry for my son. The only son I had left. I cry for the horrible way he died. These last weeks were hell for him and for me. Sometimes when I saw him striving to hang on to life, to take that next breath, it made me realize how much I loved him and how helpless I was to aid him in his last battle.

We will bury him this Sunday next to his mother and his older brother. This formality brings me no pleasure. It is an empty good-bye. My son should not be lying in the earth, under flowers, so soon. He should be still standing tall, admiring the summer blossoms. He should have been given the chance to grow into one of those pillars that support our community. Now, none of that will happen.

I am left here with nothing but echoes and pale memories. For the first time in my life, I feel hate, sodden, disgusting hate! I have always maintained that hatred is for small men, men who cannot look themselves in the eye and find joy. I now find that I am one of these men. I am not big enough inside to find forgiveness. When they murdered my son, they crushed my soul and crippled me before God. I cannot rise above this! I want to live by the Old Testament! I want an eye for an eye, a life for a life! I must have revenge or go mad!

I know that you too have suffered at the hands of these dogs! I ask you to join with me and let us ride upon them like the Horsemen of the Apocalypse. With you beside me I know we will send these beasts through the Gates of Hell. I cannot and will not rest until I see Corlis Mack's blood spilled out on the floor.

You have been a good friend and we owe you much already. What I propose is dangerous. I want you to feel free to say no. Your courage has already been tested and found to be solid. Our friendship will endure whether you join me or not.

My prayers and best wishes to your wife. She is a brave woman and
without her fearless efforts, you and Phillip might still be imprisoned
under the Lafayette. You and she are both cut from the same cloth.

All my Blessings and prayers,
Claude Duryea

Serena folded the letter and placed it back in the drawer. She thought
of King's last words to her before he and Sampson left for New Orleans: "If
I don't call or come back in two weeks, I'm dead and don't waste time
looking for me!" She was worried and concerned about King's safety, but
Sampson was with him and Corlis Mack was not expecting them. Serena's
intuition told her that King would return. During his absence, she too had
a dangerous journey to make, and she had to make sure hers was completed by his return.

She locked up the store and made sure there was sufficient wood in
both the downstairs and upstairs stoves. She put on a shawl and hurried
across the street to Wrangel House. "I need to speak to you, Ma," Serena
said as she came into the empty restaurant.

"Ain't nobody here but us chickens. Squawk any way you feel like,"
Ma Wrangel shouted from the kitchen.

"I need somebody to help me lose this baby," Serena said as she stood
at the kitchen door and watched her hostess move pans around on the big
cast-iron stove.

Ma Wrangel's big body paused midstride and then continued on moving between the chopping board and the stove. "Ain't no reason to take a
racehorse chance like that if'en you don't have to, honey," Ma Wrangel
observed as she threw some sliced onions in a skillet with oil. "This somethin' you got to do?"

"It's not my husband's child!" Serena answered without inflection.

Ma Wrangel stopped to look at her. "That don't even sound like you,
Rena. Must be somethin' mo' to it than that. You ain't the kind of woman
to play games on yo' man and he ain't the kind to take it lyin' down. Must
be somethin' mo' to it than that!"

"The truth is hard to believe," Serena stated.

"Try me," Ma Wrangel urged.

"I let a white man have me so I could break my husband out of the
prison where they were keeping him, and I killed him after I found out
where my husband was."

"Rena! Rena! You's a colored woman in a white man's world. That
ain't hard to believe. Let me tell you, girl, at least a third of the women in
this town had to lie down for some white man durin' they life to either

save a man or feed their chil'ren. You don't get this many light-skinned Negroes from lyin' naked under a full moon!"

"King won't understand it. He hates most white people!"

"Sounds like a healthy colored man to me." Ma Wrangel slurped some gravy and offered Serena the spoon. "Taste this. Don't that thyme just bring the flavor out?" Serena took a taste and nodded her head in agreement. Ma Wrangel continued, "Honey, if you looks at the way a colored man is treated in these here United States in nineteen twenty-one, it don't seem that he can do anything but hate them whites. Slavery was supposed be over more'n fifty years ago, but look at it! He can't look no white man in the eye and best not even smile at a white woman. You knows a colored man got too much spirit to take that without some kind of doin'!"

"I don't want this child, Ma! Now, are you going to help me find someone, or do I do it on my own?"

"You talk to Clara?"

"About what?"

"She pregnant too. Her and Mace decide they gon' keep the baby anyway, bedamned what people say! You got to gives yo' man a chance to be big! Don't go off thinkin' he gon' be small 'bout this. Trust him, honey! Even yo' man ain't so hard he want to chance losin' you over this here baby."

"I'll think about what you said, Ma, but right now I want to know who can help me with this!"

"The only one around with a lot of experience with this is Wichita Kincaid out at the Black Rose Saloon. She got about six women workin' out there pleasurin' men and I hear she ain't had a pregnancy out there in more'n two years." Ma Wrangel stepped out from behind the stove and put her hands on her hips. "I hears Wichita uses a mess of different potions, but her womens use 'em befo' they with child. It's always mo' dangerous after you's with child. Them potions used to kill a live child is sometimes strong enough to kill the mother. This ain't gon' be no lightweight thing, now. And you sho' don't want nobody stickin' no metal up there and scrapin', hear me!"

"Are you sure that it's safe for you to go alone tonight, Boss?" Sal Fiore asked as Marco Volante was straightening his clothes in front of the mirror. "These southern country fools have killed about twenty of our people so far. What makes you think you can trust them?"

Marco turned and looked at Sal. Fiore was a good man and someone you wanted on your side in a fight, but he was not a thinking man. It was apparent from the way he was dressed. Fiore was wearing a dark wool pinstriped suit with a black shirt and white tie. His shoes were two-tone and he had at least three rings on the fingers of each hand. In New Orleans he looked exactly like what he was: a northern gangster. He made no effort to blend in at all.

"A prolonged war isn't good for business," Marco said, adjusting his tie. "Everybody loses money. We're here to negotiate a deal so that business can continue. The deal is more valuable to them than killing me. As long as I don't step on someone's toes, I don't have a thing to worry about." Marco nodded his head at his image in the mirror. The cream-colored suit looked good on him.

Beppo Lucca walked into the room. "The car's downstairs waiting for you, Boss," he announced. Beppo was a stocky, muscular man with prematurely gray hair. He was there for muscle. He was good for the close in silent work, excellent with the knife and the garrote. "I should ride with the driver, Boss," Beppo urged, his craggy features shaping a plaintive look.

"He said, 'Come alone,' guys. Otherwise, I would keep you by my side. If they intend to do me, I don't think the presence of two soldiers would stop them. I've got to move forward with courage. I can't let these people think that we're afraid of them. Plus, the deal I've been authorized to put on the table will make them rich."

"Why should we give these dogs anything?" Sal protested. "We should rub 'em out! Let them feel the power of the Black Hand."

Marco chuckled. "Your way means loss of business and more loss of life on our side. If we wait a year, let them enjoy the money we give them and let them relax. Then their guard will be down. Then we send somebody down to hit everyone in the top two layers of their organization! Then we'll have what we want and it won't be nearly as costly as a protracted war. It's another version of the Trojan horse."

"Whatever you say, Boss," Sal said, shrugging his shoulders. "I still think at least one of us ought to go with you."

"I have to say no, Sally," Marco said, checking his interior coat pockets for a pen. He found what he was looking for and closed his jacket. "But I really like it that you guys are concerned about my welfare."

"You got heat?" Beppo asked, offering his .38 revolver.

"That's too big. They'd find that. I have my little two-shot derringer for just in case. If you get a chance, try to find Leo Pagnozzi. He's the Don's contact man in New Orleans. We should have heard from him by now. Okay, guys, wish me luck. If things go wrong and we get separated, meet me tomorrow night at that place we agreed upon by those north levees. I'm ready to go." Marco headed out the door for the stairs. Beppo and Sal followed him to the car, which came to pick him up.

Beppo went around to the driver's side and asked the Negro driver, "Where are you taking my boss, in case we need to get in touch with him?"

The driver said, "Sorry, suh, but I ain't allowed to tell nothin'!"

Beppo reached through the window, grabbed the driver by the front of his gray jacket, and pulled him partway out of the car. "I asked you a question, jungle bunny, and I want an answer!"

"I's just the driver," wailed the victim. "I don't know nothin'!"

"Let go of him, Beppo!" Marco ordered. "He's just doing his job. I'll see you boys later tonight."

As the car pulled away from the hotel, the driver tipped his hat to Marco. "I's much obliged, suh, for you pullin' him off'en me. He coulda beat me, but I wasn't gon' tell him nothin'." The driver put his thumb under the lapel of his gray jacket and said proudly, "I's a gray jacket! I works for Sheriff Mack."

Marco's mind was far away, but he found it more comfortable to listen to the driver's babble, it better than staring out at the incomprehensible nightlife of the New Orleans streets, so he asked, "How did you get a job working for the sheriff?"

"Name's Bradley O'Malley, suh, and I is somewhat famous around these parts 'cause I done helped the sheriff catch one of the toughest and meanest Negroes that ever growed up in these here United States. After that, Sheriff Mack, he gave me a job as his driver." Bradley stopped the car to let a parade of musicians and dancers lead a coffin down a side street. Through the car window Marco saw several trombones and trumpets and a tuba among the musicians, while other marchers carried torches. The blaring music played by the band was slow, rocking blues and everyone in the procession kept step with the music.

"What's that?" Marco asked, pointing at the disappearing parade.

"It's a funeral procession with second-liners," Bradley answered as he put the car into gear and continued through the intersection.

"They have funerals at night with music like that?"

"They has them whenever they can get the band that they want. Shoot, some bands work twenty-four hours on the weekend. Peoples in New Orleans wants to die in style. You can't do that without a good band."

"Interesting," Marco commented, sitting back in the seat. "You were telling how you helped catch this mean Negro?" he asked just to keep the conversation going.

"Well, suh, I seed him tryin' to hide behind some school chil'ren and I let out the alarm. The policemens surrounded the school and lo and behold, he gave up quiet as a kitten."

"Doesn't sound so tough and mean to me," Marco said mildly.

"Ohh, he was tough alright, and mean too! He killed both colored and white like he was butcherin' animals! He didn't care. Everybody was scared of King Tremain 'ceptin' me. I stood right up to him every time he brace me, I did!"

Suddenly Marco was very attentive. The name King Tremain reverberated in his mind like the bells of St. Mary's at Sunday noon. He was very careful not to let his interest enter his voice as he asked, "King Tremain? Is that a common name? Is he from around here?"

"Yes, suh, he from right outside of New Orleans. He comes from one them big swamp-nigger families that lives out on the bayous. As far as I know, ain't no other King Tremain."

"What did the sheriff do with him after he was arrested?"

"Oh, the sheriff had somethin' special in mind for him. He disappeared after that." Bradley dropped his voice to a conspiratorial whisper. "I heard from somebody who ought to know that King Tremain got burned up in the Lafayette Social Club fire. Part of his burnt body was found still chained to the wall in the basement by them rescue teams."

Marco Volante sat back in the seat, lost in thought. He felt a little disappointed that he hadn't had a hand in King's demise, but he was also happy to hear that King had met an unpleasant end. If he could be sure it was the same man, he might be able to free himself from the distorted black faces and bloody hands that frequented his dreams. "Why was the sheriff so interested in this man?" he asked.

Bradley dropped his voice again. "From what I hear, he the one that shot the sheriff's leg off. Some people say he did it from near to three hundred yards away. Ain't nobody doubt that King Tremain could shoot!"

Marco sat back in his seat again. Don Vitorio Minetti was killed from about that distance. It was too great a coincidence. It had to be the same man who was in New York. Marco felt a rush of disappointment. He would never vindicate himself. It had been a dream, a fantasy, that one day he would be able to return to New York with Tremain in chains and clear his name.

"We's here, suh," Bradley announced as he steered the car through the gate of a tall stucco fence. A narrow gravel and dirt road led up to an old two-story antebellum mansion that had a broad lighted porch that ran the width of the house.

"Where are we?" Marco asked as he got out. There were people in evening clothes talking and drinking on the porch, and every window of the mansion was lit from the first floor to the gabled rooms of the attic.

"We's at Sheriff Mack's country estate. This place is where he throw his parties and where he come for to play pinochle. Tonight's a pinochle night. Ain't but eight guests total. I hopes you plays pinochle."

"I play," Marco answered, still looking around. He didn't see any guards or men with guns and there were women on the porch. Perhaps Corlis was on the up-and-up. Marco turned to Bradley. "Are you supposed to drive me home?"

Bradley gave him a big smile. "Yes, suh. The sheriff he told me to drive you both ways."

Marco exhaled and said, "I'll see you later then." He walked up the stairs to the house. He felt a bit more comfortable; they wouldn't leave an assassination attempt in Bradley's hands. He presented his invitation card at the door to a colored man dressed in gray livery.

"I's obliged to ask you to wait here, suh." The man turned and went down the hall to a room and knocked on a door.

Marco's heart had begun to sink. The women on the porch were garishly dressed and appeared to be either prostitutes or women who were paid to attend parties to befriend the guests. It was Marco's experience that the presence of wives and ladies of character dramatically reduced the possibility of foul play.

"Mr. Volante?"

Marco turned to stare at a bulky, red-faced, balding man. He stood with the aid of a crutch and had one empty pants leg folded up just above the knee. "Sheriff Mack?" Marco asked as he stepped forward with his hand outstretched.

"You can call me Corlis. Why don't you come on back to my office and we can have some privacy to talk?"

"That's what I'm here for," Marco said with a smile as he followed Corlis's thumping gait back to a small room off the hall. The room was cozy. There was a desk with a large leather chair behind it and two wing chairs in front. The walls were lined with photos of men in police uniforms. Corlis sat down behind the desk and gestured to Marco to take one of the wing chairs.

A colored waiter appeared at the door. He was dressed in the same gray livery as the man guarding the front door. "You wants somethin', suh?" he asked.

"Yes, Theodore, I'll think we'll have a bit of drop." Corlis turned to Marco. "Do you like single-malt bourbons? I have the genuine article and it's a sipping delight."

"I'm open," answered Marco.

"Bring the bottle, Theodore, and two sipping glasses." The waiter bowed and closed the door. "What do you think of New Orleans, Mr. Volante?"

"It's a lot different than either New York or Chicago, but I really haven't been here long enough to see much of it."

"Then how do you know it's so different?"

"I saw a funeral tonight with a band playing ragtime. You'd never see that up north."

Corlis smiled. "We do generate our share of funerals, some by natural causes, some assisted, but everyone wants good music when they die. Do you like music, Mr. Volante?"

"I like some. I've never really given a lot of attention to it."

"Around here, it's important to pick your music before you die. Otherwise someone does it for you."

Marco smiled and said, "Sheriff Mack, I've got such a good deal for you that I don't believe we need to talk about people dying. Let me lay out the details. I'm sure you'll be pleased."

The waiter returned with a tray holding the bottle and two glasses. He set the tray down and departed, closing the door behind him.

"Let's put our cards on the table, Mr. Volante. Why should I trust you? We had a meeting scheduled with your people before your men bombed the Lafayette Social Club. Your men killed some people who were very important to me. I have a hard time overlooking that." Corlis poured the glasses to the rim and offered one to Marco.

Marco set his glass down without drinking. He had listened to the sheriff's slow southern drawl and heard the anger beneath it. Marco said slowly, "Sheriff Mack, our men had nothing to do with that incident. Our men are disciplined. They follow orders. There's a penalty associated with not following orders and it generally means loss of life. They had no authorization to take such actions, so it wouldn't and couldn't have been them."

"So you say," Corlis said with a nod of his head. "Try the bourbon. It's an insult down here to refuse to drink with the man you've come to make a deal with."

Marco picked up his glass and drank half of it. "The reason I am here is to negotiate a deal that is beneficial to both of us."

"You're here because we've cut your shipment line. You're here because I killed every one of your men that I could find. That's why you're here. You're here to make a deal for six months. Then you'll try to kill me. I know all about your tactics, Mr. Volante."

"If you really feel that about my mission, why did you agree to meet me?"

"I didn't agree to meet you! I told your superiors that I would kill the man sent to bring me a deal. Now I want to make it clear to them that there is no negotiating after a betrayal. There is no deal! This is my territory and I run it by myself! I brought you out here because I needed to send your superiors a message," Corlis said, pouring himself another drink.

"What is it? You want me to carry it back?" Marco asked. He drank the rest of his bourbon.

Corlis leaned over and poured him another full glass. "You'll carry it back alright, but it won't matter if you know it or not. Your body will tell the full story."

Marco's pulse began to sound like slow drums in his temples. He wondered whether he should try to shoot Corlis with his derringer and make his escape.

As if in answer to Marco's thought, Corlis lifted a big .44 magnum revolver from his lap and said, "Don't think about trying anything. You're safe tonight. I don't go back on my agreements. You'll have safe passage back to the hotel as I agreed, but after that you're on your own. We'll see how good your men really are, won't we? Another drink?"

"I don't need another one yet," Marco answered in a toneless voice. "Why are you doing this? We could make money together. We could be partners!"

"Don't take me for a fool! You'll try to kill me in six months! Listen, this is your last night on earth. I've got cards, women, and booze. Do you want to spend your last night trying to sell me some bullshit or would you like to taste one of our southern belles and have some real fun?"

"You're a cold bastard," Marco observed. "You say you're going to kill me and then you offer me some cheap-ass prostitutes!"

"I've been called worse," Corlis said lighting a cigar. He offered his cigar box to Marco, who declined with a shake of his head. Once he got his cigar puffing, Corlis said, "If you're talking about those women on the porch, they're just to keep the guards alert. The real, special poontang is upstairs. I've even got some coontang up there. Any one of those nice girls will suck anything you want to expose."

As they left the office a hulking blond-haired man joined them. Corlis turned to Marco. "Meet Albert Cox. You may be seeing him later. Of course, it will be under different circumstances."

"I want to leave now!" Marco said.

"Don't be a spoilsport," Corlis chided. "This is a free evening. The sky's the limit! Don't you want to be caressed by beautiful women before you die? I'm giving you a choice most men can't make on the eve of their death."

"I don't want what you're offering! I don't want—" Albert hit Marco in the kidneys from behind. Marco wilted like a plant left in the sun without water. It took an extreme effort not to fall to the floor. His eyes watered, but he stayed on his feet.

"Are you ready for the tour now?" Corlis asked cheerfully. Marco barely nodded his head. Corlis smiled. "Good! Good! Let's go to the card room. I want to introduce you to some of my business companions. Some of them need to see how I manage my business operations." Corlis led the way up the staircase, clumping with his crutch along the hallway to the last door.

The card room was significantly brighter than the hall or the office. It was a large room with electric lightbulbs in ornate wall sconces. There was a small chandelier directly over the card table, its cut-glass edges gleaming through the cigar smoke that sifted and curled up through it. Four men were sitting at a green felt-covered card table talking loudly about the cards that had been played. Three more men stood around the table adding their perspective to the actions on the felt.

One of the men sitting at the table asked, "Where is the ace of spades? I've been counting. I know it's out there."

"Gentlemen! Gentlemen!" Corlis called out in a loud voice. Once he had their attention, he introduced Marco. "Gentlemen, I want you to meet our messenger, our Diogenes, who will not twist or misinterpret our message, but who will relay it faithfully to our associates in Chicago. Here is Marco Volante, a man who is still wanted in New York City by certain friends of ours." Corlis turned to Marco with a smile and winked, "Surprised you, huh? We're not as country as you think! We know about you. You would never be the one picked to bring us an honest deal."

Corlis turned and faced his guests and said, "I think it's only fair that Mr. Volante see that he's not just dying for a bunch of bindle stiffs. I want to introduce you to him." Corlis turned to Marco and pointed out different men to him. "That's Fred, the mayor of New Orleans; that's Harry, the next governor of Louisiana. The only man that can beat Long's machine.

That's Orwell, the president of Merchant's Insured Bank; here's Barney, the new assessor. I think's that's enough. He's got the idea now. Thank you, gents. Let's go up to the top floor now."

A tremendous explosion went off in front of the house and everyone but Albert, Marco, and Corlis rushed to the window and pulled the curtains all the way back. "Isn't that your car that's burning, Fred?" one of the men asked.

"Goddamn it! What's going on out there, Corlis?" Fred exclaimed. "I can't replace that car!"

Corlis ordered, "Sergeant Dietrich, go out and get me a report!"

Felix stood up and saluted. "Will do, sir. Hold the deal until I return." Felix went and strapped on his holster and went out the door.

"Good thing that car was a campaign donation, isn't it?" Orwell asked.

"How do you know that?" Fred challenged.

"I gave it to you, you fool!" Orwell snapped in return and all the men at the window laughed.

They were milling back toward the table when the second explosion went off, followed shortly by a third.

Everyone was facing the window but Marco and Albert, when King walked in the door dragging Felix's body. He wore a light-colored Stetson with a broad brim and a long oilskin coat. Albert was the first to react. He attempted to pull his gun from its holster, but King's bullets hit him before he cleared leather. King's silencer muffled his shots. Albert's body crashing to floor was what drew everyone's attention from the window.

Harry demanded, "Who the hell are you?"

King smiled and answered. "I'm the ace of spades and I ain't been played!"

Corlis's face turned white as the blood drained from it. The door at the end of the room opened and Claude Duryea walked in carrying a double-barreled shotgun. Outside the window came the sound of strafing fire from a big machine gun.

Orwell asked, "What's going on, Corlis? Who are these men?"

"Tell him, Corlis!" King urged. "Tell him who I am and that tonight all yo' asses is mine! You boys have done yo' deeds on this here earth!"

"You're alive?" Corlis was aghast. His face revealed his shock.

King laughed easily. "You put a kink in my step, but you didn't break my stride."

"How can you be alive?" Corlis choked out, his anger swelling his throat.

"Black magic!" King replied with a smile. "Black magic strong tonight! You feel it, Claude?"

"I feel it," answered the man with the shotgun.

Suddenly, Marco realized who was standing in front of him. The machine-gun fire outside the window brought it all together. The same sounds had predominated during the hits on both Don Vitorio and Don Pascarella. "You're King Tremain!" he exclaimed with surprise.

"Corlis, who the smart white boy in the plantation suit?"

"A greaser from New York who's going to die the same way you are!" Corlis twisted to pull the magnum from the waistband of his trousers. King's first shots were intended for Marco, but Corlis staggered into their path, trying to pull the big gun clear. The bullets hit Corlis in the chest and shoulder, knocking him off balance, and when he hit the floor the big revolver discharged. Corlis screamed as his remaining good leg was shattered. Claude opened fire at the same time, discharging both barrels. Corlis's guests threw themselves on the floor to avoid getting shot. King motioned for Claude to leave and threw two hand grenades into the room, shouting, "You run with the devil, you die with the devil!" He turned and walked out the door. The concussive blasts of the grenades shook the walls and pieces of plaster fell from the ceiling as King walked down the stairs toward the front door.

There was a bunch of women in the foyer cowering on the floor. When they saw King they shrieked and huddled together. One of them kicked a bag toward King and said, "There's the money. Take it!"

"Give him all of it, Mary Jo!" another woman urged.

"Alright! Take it all!" Mary Jo said, pushing a larger bag toward him.

"This from Corlis's safe?" he asked. She nodded. "How much is it?" King asked, pointing at the larger bag with his pistol.

"About twenty-five thousand dollars," the woman answered. "There's ten thousand in the smaller one," she said as he pointed to the smaller bag.

"Open it up!" King directed, pointing at the larger bag. She obeyed and pushed the bag closer to him. He looked inside and assured himself that it was filled with paper money. "I'll take the larger one. You girls can have the ten thousand dollars. But if you wants to stay alive, you best hit the back door now, cause I'm gon' blow this place up! And once you hit the back door keep goin' straight, 'cause if'en you show up around the front of the house, I'm gon' take it that you means to fight!" Then King took the bundle of dynamite out of his coat pocket and lit the fuse. He set the bundle by the interior pillars of the hallway. Bag in hand, he walked out the front door like he owned the place.

When King had first started firing, Marco had thrown himself backward toward the doorway through which he had entered. He landed near the door and scrambled to his feet. He got out of the room just as bullets splintered the doorjamb behind him. A few of the buckshot pellets from the shotgun blasts had embedded themselves in his shoulders and chest. Blood was seeping through his clothes. The only other door in the room opened out onto the hall. There was no other way out. Outside the window there was a young evergreen tree growing close to the house. The explosion of the first grenade made up his mind. He ran through the window with as much power and speed as he could muster. He hit one of the wooden supports with his shoulder and the window shattered, raking his bare skin with slivers of glass. He fell down into the tree, branches snapping beneath his weight. He grasped futilely for solid hold until a branch swung up and smacked him hard in the face. He was able to grab the branch and significantly slow his fall. The branch broke once it had to bear his weight and he fell eight feet to earth. He landed off balance and a warning pain shot up his leg as his ankle twisted.

Marco lay for a minute on his back under the tree, trying to gather his senses. Using branches of the tree, he pulled himself erect. He could not put weight on his right foot. He put his hand to his face and discovered that he was bleeding from several different places. The blood was dripping onto his clothes. He saw big red splotches on his jacket and pants. He had nothing to stanch the blood with so he couldn't give it a great deal of attention. Leaning against the tree he quickly surveyed his surroundings. Four cars were still burning, the flames leaping high above their metal frames. The lights on the front porch were out and he could see no one moving. Further down the drive were several cars that had escaped the explosions. He dropped to his knees and crawled to one of the three cars that had not been destroyed. Fear was heavy upon him. He did not feel the chafing and abrasions on his hands and knees as he pushed himself as fast as he could go. Once he was beyond the burning vehicles the darkness covered him. The first car was locked, so was the second, but the third was open. He saw there was no key in the ignition and pulled himself through the back passenger door into the backseat and lay on the floor. He had his derringer in his hand. As he lay there in the darkness he heard a tremendous deafening explosion. The ground beneath the car shook with its force.

Marco heard a heavy truck drive up from the gate, its brakes squeaking as it pulled to a stop. He heard muffled voices and the sound of heavy equipment being loaded into the truck. Another car arrived shortly thereafter. He listened as the man from the car greeted the men loading the truck.

"Looks like you boys been busy." The voice had a slightly nasal southern drawl.

"We done got rid of somebody who didn't like you! How do, Anthony."

428 · G U Y   J O H N S O N

"I'm doin' alright, LeRoi. So, you heard that, huh? Must've been from Cap'n Mack 'cause he's the one who told me you got hitched."

"Sho' did! Tied the knot and jumped the broom! Listen, Anthony, everybody call me King now. I appreciate you do the same."

"Didn't mean no offense. I guess I was thinkin' about all the huntin' and fishin' we did out on the bayous with our uncles when we was mere boys."

"I hear you made sergeant, huh? So it's Sergeant Pointdexter now?"

"Yep, yo' little war with Corlis done left a lot of vacancies for promotion. I expect to move up even more."

"Cap'n Mack told me you might even be in line for the appointment to sheriff until they organizes the election. That right?"

"Can't count yo' chickens befo' they hatch," Pointdexter answered with a chuckle.

"You's a fair man, Anthony, and a good man. You always was. I hopes you get it. I knows everybody includin' colored folks will get a fair shake from you. Now, 'bout this situation here, I figgers them Italians bootleggers done hit the city of New Orleans hard, killin' the mayor and the sheriff and all. Y'all folks best come down hard on 'em! Meanwhiles you should try to catch that one that Corlis was plannin' to kill. He maybe got some information that will help you."

"I'll use that Italian bootlegger idea, but I ain't arrestin' nobody to be tortured. That's Corlis. That ain't me. Them days is over long as I have any say in it. We gon' try livin' by the letter of the law."

"As I said, you's a good man and a fair man. I wish you luck! We gots to hit it befo' yo' troops arrive."

"Yep, you got about ten minutes befo' the first ones get here, Le—King. You best take the back road past the Duelin' Oak and come around that way."

"Thanks, Anthony, we'll follow yo' advice!" The truck door squeaked open and Marco heard it slam shut as King climbed aboard.

"One more thing, King. I know you got a bootleg business too. I appreciate if you'd stay out of New Orleans with it. You can go around and take it where you want, just don't bring it in the city. That way, I won't have to see you in no official capacity."

King answered, "Fair enough! Fair enough! Best to yo' family!" The truck's engine rumbled to life and, with the growl of gears, chugged down the road.

Marco was shaking his head. So that's how King Tremain was able to breach Corlis's security. A Sergeant Pointdexter had given him the key and that same sergeant was going to give the newspapers a false report.

That report would marshal the forces against the Don's bootleg operations and business would be severely hampered, if not choked off. All Marco's strategies and plans had ended up in ruins. Back in Chicago, his enemies would be saying that Marco had blown another critical assignment. Some might even compare it to New York. Once again, King had been instrumental in the destruction of Marco's dreams, aspirations, and reputation.

Another explosion shook the ground. Marco peeped out of the rear window and saw the side wall of the mansion collapse and the second story cave in on top of it. He heard the sound of running feet. Marco ducked down again and gripped his derringer firmly.

The driver's door was yanked open and a gasping man fumbled with the key. Marco lay on his back ready to shoot the face that looked over the seat. Then the car roared to life and swerved out past the burning cars and accelerated down the gravel road through the gate. The car continued to accelerate despite the ruts and holes in the road. Marco found himself bouncing hard on the floor and was occasionally thrown against the door as the car turned sharply at high speed. Marco thought, This fool is going to kill both of us driving at this speed on this narrow country road.

Marco pulled himself up onto the seat and discovered he was being driven by Corlis's colored driver. "Bradley?" Marco tapped the man's shoulders. Bradley turned his head and saw Marco's bloody face and screamed. The car shot forward as Bradley stamped his foot down on the accelerator pedal. The car now careened off the road as Bradley had difficulty maintaining control of the vehicle. All the while Bradley continued to holler at the top of his lungs.

"Stop this goddamned car!" Marco ordered, pressing the barrel of the derringer against Bradley's face.

"Is you a ghost?" Bradley wailed, his eyes wide. " 'Cause if'en you's a ghost, I's already dead!"

"You fool! I'm no ghost! I'm the man you drove here earlier this evening! Now stop this car!"

"I ain't lettin' no ghost suck up my soul! I ain't stoppin' 'til I get's to a church!" The car hit a large puddle of water and skewed sideways before Bradley could control it. They tipped precariously as their hydroplaning tires hit a few patches of dryness and were briefly snagged by the absence of water. Bradley was loudly intoning a prayer as he wrestled the car back in the correct direction without losing too much speed. "Oh, God, I'll go to church every Sunday and tithe my ten percent. Just don't let this demon get me! Ain't it enough I got King Tremain on my plate and I ain't even begun to ask fo' help with him yet!"

Marco fired one barrel of the derringer through the passenger-side windshield. The glass shattered. Some of it stayed together, spiderwebbed with small fractures, but the pieces from a large hole were blown back into the car, little flying razors cutting and embedding themselves into flesh. Both Bradley and Marco received numerous cuts from the shattered glass.

"Oh God! Oh God! Oh God!" Bradley wailed even louder.

"Stop this car! Stop it or I'll shoot out your window too!"

The shattering of the window seemed to have gained Bradley's attention for he slowed down and pulled off the road. As soon as the car rolled to a stop, Bradley opened his door to get out.

"Where are you going?" Marco demanded, jamming the hot barrel of the derringer against the man's cheek.

"Ooowww!" Bradley cried. "That hurts! I's just givin' you a chance to return to where you's from that's all!" He was rubbing the gris-gris around his neck furiously.

"Look at me, you fool! I'm bleeding but I'm not dead! Look me in the eye, or I'll shoot you myself!"

Bradley quailed. "Folk say you look a demon in the eye, it take yo' mind! Lord knows I don't need that. If'en you's don't mind, Boss, I'll watch my foots for a while."

In frustration, Marco slapped Bradley on the back of the head. "You superstitious fool! If you look at me, you'll see I'm not dead!"

"Ain't necessary to be smackin' on folks who scared of the supernatural, suh!" He raised his eyes warily, ready to flinch and look away.

"I jumped out the goddamned window, you idiot! That's how my face got all cut up!"

"Well," admitted Bradley. "I ain't ever heard of a ghost usin' no gun! Maybe you is what you say you is, but how did you get in here?"

"I hid in the car before you came! I'm losing my patience with these stupid questions. You hear that?" The sound of distant sirens was drawing closer. "Either you drive me back to my hotel, or I leave you on this road to find your own way home."

"I drives you," Bradley agreed. "It ain't gon' be safe for a colored man out here tonight with all these white mens dead."

"What are you going to do about King Tremain? He'll be looking for you. Are you ready to stand up to him now?" Marco asked to distract himself from his own fears.

"You jokin' 'bout somethin' that's serious fo' me. I's gon' have to leave town. He the kind of man who'll kill yo' whole family just to get to you. He one mean and crazy nigger! Ain't nobody standin' up to him! He done blowed up the sheriff's whole house!" Bradley slowed the vehicle as they entered New Orleans again.

"Did you know your boss, Sheriff Mack, was going to kill me?"

"I's just the driver, suh. They don't tell me nothin'! Oh, look, it's another funeral. Whoever this is, they wanted to die in style! They got a big band and even their second-liners are in uniform! Whooeee! That take money!" Bradley stopped the car to let the funeral procession pass.

A brown-skinned woman stepped out of the crowd and came over to the door. Her head was wrapped in a yellow kerchief and she wore big gold bangles in her ears. She leaned down to look into the car window at the driver and asked, "You Bradley O'Malley?"

Bradley was suddenly very humble as he answered in a servile tone, "Yes'm, Sister Bornais. I done bought gris-gris from you befo'. In Congo Square, you remember?"

"Yes, I remember you. You the sheriff's man!" She leaned down closer and said, "I bring you a gift." She opened her palm and blew some red and green powder in Bradley's face. She stood up with a laugh and said loudly for all to hear, "It is a gift from King Tremain and with it, I curse you! I curse you with pain and blindness until you die! And you will die soon, sheriff's man!"

Bradley began to scream immediately. "My eyes! My eyes! I can't see! Oh, Saint Jude, help me!"

"No one can help you!" she cackled. "Call anybody you want, it will not change yo' fate!" She stopped when she saw Marco staring at her. She reached into her bosom and pulled out a pouch and poured more powder into her palm. "Does the white man want to try some of this medicine?" she asked as she came over to the window, but Marco pushed the window up and locked it. She stood outside the car laughing. "The white man is afraid! The white man is afraid!" Bradley was now in a full panic. He was blathering incomprehensibly as he writhed in the front seat.

Marco reached over the seat and grabbed the man by the shoulders, but Bradley twisted easily out of his grip. "Get a hold of yourself!" he shouted. Bradley arched his back violently and screamed. Marco saw his contorted face straight on and was horrified. Bradley was foaming at the mouth and there appeared to be blood running from his eyes.

Bradley began mumbling. "I got to get out! I got to get out! Let me out!" He began kicking the door in a frenzy. Marco reached over and unlatched the door, which swung open, and Bradley pushed himself out of the car onto the street. He began screaming and clutching at himself. A crowd of people now surrounded the car, watching Bradley's frenzied actions. He staggered to his feet and began to run haphazardly through the crowd. People made way for him. No one wanted to touch him. Sister Bornais followed him screaming, "I curse you, sheriff's man! I curse you!"

Marco watched as the crowd slowly followed Bradley's movements down the street. The key was still in the ignition. Marco pulled himself over the front seat and started the car. His ankle bothered him when he applied brakes or changed gears, but he drove the vehicle out of the intersection and headed toward his hotel. He didn't recognize the street names and turned the wrong way and drove into a cul-de-sac. He turned the car around and drove back to Ramparts Street, one of the few streets he knew. There was a crowd of people halfway down the block standing around a horse-drawn beer wagon. A police car arrived and as the crowd backed out of its way, Marco saw the reason for the assembly. A man wearing a gray jacket lay crushed beneath the wagon's front wheel. Marco turned the car abruptly in the opposite direction and drove away as fast as the traffic would permit.

SATURDAY, JUNE 25, 1921

There are clear summer nights in the foothills of the Ouachitas when the blue light of the pale moon causes the jagged-peaked mountains to glisten as if they were made of silver. The sky itself appears to have been brought lower and closer to earth by the weight of the glowing moon. The stars twinkle and the Milky Way beckons. The silver mountains rising out of the inky shadows of countless ridges seem to scrape against the sky itself. It was on such a night that King and Sampson returned to Bodie Wells.

It was nearly twenty minutes past nine when Sampson pulled the truck in behind the store. When King stepped down from the truck he noticed there was a light shining in a small room off the back entrance and there were numerous lights still on the second floor. The back door opened and a man's scratchy voice called out, "Who done pulled they truck behind this sto'?" King could see the barrel of a shotgun sticking out the door.

King stepped in the shadows and called out, "King Tremain. Who are you?" Pistols were in his hands.

The man put down the shotgun and came outside. "It's me, Lightnin' Smith. Yo' Missus say I could stay here after the twister done destroyed my place. You best come on in here quick and see her. She mighty sickly."

King found himself running up the back steps, through the hallway to the staircase leading to the second floor. Three at a time and he was at the head of the stairs, then down the hall to their bedroom. He opened the door and saw Ma Wrangel and Wichita Kincaid sitting by the bed putting cold towels on Serena's forehead. Serena appeared to be sleeping fitfully. Her head kept turning back and forth and her legs twitched sporadically.

"What's goin' on here?" King demanded as he walked toward the bed.

"Lower yo' voice. We got us a sick chile here," Ma Wrangel advised, changing a towel.

"How she get sick?" His voice was lower, but there was still urgency in it.

The two women looked at each other and then Ma Wrangel turned to him and said, "She fell from a stepladder and hit the floor badly."

"Did she hit her head?" King asked as he knelt by the bed and touched her hand. Serena's skin seemed to be on fire. King repeated his question. "I asked you, did she hit her head?" The two women looked at each other again. "What you keepin' secret?" King asked as he looked from Ma Wrangel to Wichita and back.

Ma Wrangel answered slowly. "The fall was hard, but that ain't what's got her lyin' on the edge of death. . . . She uh, . . . uh—"

Wichita interjected in clipped tones. "She took some potions I made and it looks like she took more than I told her to."

"What kind of potions?" King asked, an edge creeping into his voice.

"Potions that help cause a miscarriage," Wichita replied.

"What?" King asked, not comprehending the words being said.

"She wanted to lose the child!" A trace of exasperation entered Wichita's words.

King stood up and turned to face Wichita. "What child?" he growled.

Wichita felt a sudden chill. She shivered. She was in the presence of a dangerous man and she had heard a tone in his voice that made her feel that danger might not be too far away.

"Ain't no use in turnin' yo' anger on us," Ma Wrangel said as she wrung out a towel that had been soaking in a bucket of ice water. "Serena is with chile," Ma Wrangel explained as she continued to dab Serena's face and neck. "She say she want to lose it! She say she got to lose it, 'cause it's a white man's chile. The white man who raped her while she was gettin' you free. She say it's LeGrande's chile. She done killed him dead. Now she want to kill his chile. She don't care if she kill herself. She say she got to do it, 'cause she done seen the hate in yo' eyes. She know you can't love no white man's chile. And she think maybe you gon' hate her for havin' his baby too."

King felt as if he had been clubbed in the stomach with the butt of a rifle. Serena was pregnant by LeGrande. Serena had allowed herself to be violated to save King and she hadn't told him. Now she was prepared to risk her own life in order to get rid of the unwanted baby. He immediately felt guilty for all the angry thoughts he harbored against her.

He turned to the two women who were watching, trying to gauge his reaction. "I thank you for stayin' by her side and tendin' her. Why don't you let me take over this evenin' and you can go home and rest. Me and Sampson'll work on keepin' her fever down. I'd appreciate it if you'd stop by tomorrow mo'nin' and give her a look-see. The doctor ain't prescribed no medicine, has he?"

"Doc Stephens don't know nothin' about women's potions," Wichita replied. "That's why me and Ma Wrangel is tendin' her. If Serena wants to live, she gon' make it. She's young and strong. My worry is that she don't care whether she live or not. She's embarrassed about facin' the town folk. And mostly, she thinks because she been violated and humiliated you won't take her back."

"Then she ain't got nothin' to worry about. She my wife. Ain't nothin' gon' change that. And don't let nobody be foolish enough to say somethin' about this!" King sat down in the chair that Ma Wrangel had vacated and pulled in closer to the bed. He wrung out another cold towel and softly pressed its coolness against Serena's burning skin. He appeared to forget that Wichita and Ma Wrangel were in the room. Ma Wrangel brought him a stack of fresh towels and Wichita left him some system-cleansing herbs for tea, should Serena regain consciousness during the night. Just as they reached the doorway, King turned to them. "Did she say anythin' about a baby, a baby that was nigh on to a year old?" The two women shook their heads and continued down the stairs.

The noise the logs made when King put them into the stove caused Serena to move fitfully as if she was just beneath the surface of consciousness. King moved his chair closer to the bed and took her hand in his. He looked down on her fevered face and watched as droplets of sweat made small shiny trails down the smoothness of her skin. She was twisting and turning on the bed as if she was seeking a way out of the prison of sleep. Ever so slowly her fitful movements ceased and she appeared to sink into a deep slumber.

King lifted her hand to his lips and kissed it. Holding her hand next to his cheek, he closed his eyes and said, "I been wrong. I've been holdin' blame against you. I got to admit, I was deep hurt by the way you handled the letter and I'm still hurtin'! I ain't ever gon' give up lookin' for that boy! If he's alive, I'm gon' find him!"

King exhaled and was silent for a moment before he began to speak. "I was ready to walk away from you, but seein' that you was willin' to sacrifice yo'self to save me, I got to stay. You paid yo' debt in a higher court. Ain't nothin' more I can ask! I can't promise it'll be the same, but we got somethin' worth savin'! Maybe we can get back where we used to be. Let this baby come on! This baby ain't gon' get between you and me! We got some big city lights to see and the money to take us there in style! Don't give up on livin'!"

Serena made no movement to indicate recognition, nor was there any evidence of her attempting to break through the opaque barrier into consciousness. There was only the rise and fall of her chest and the sound of her regular breathing.

King awoke the next morning stiff and aching. He had fallen asleep leaning forward in his chair, resting his head and arms on Serena's bed. The pendulum clock at the foot of the stair clanged out six o'clock. As he sat up, he noticed her hand was lying on his arm. He felt her forehead and it seemed considerably cooler, almost normal. He stood up slowly due to stiffness. There was a slight chill in the room. He dropped a couple of logs in the potbellied stove, stirred the smoldering embers with an iron poker, and then pumped a leather bellows until the logs caught flame. He picked up the bucket in which the ice had melted and carried it downstairs. The smell of coffee greeted him. Sampson and Lightning were already outside unloading the truck. King poured himself a cup of the hot black liquid and sipped it, feeling the heat of it burn the back of his throat.

When he returned upstairs, Serena turned her head and looked at him. He hurried to the bed and knelt beside her. She was still weak, but she gave him a tired smile.

"I was worried about you," King admitted, taking her hand. "I was worried that maybe you wouldn't fight to come back. Last night I did a lot of thinkin' about everythin'! This baby you carryin' ain't gon' get between us. This baby is comin' because you sacrificed yo'self for me! This baby been paid for! Family ain't only about blood. I was thinkin' that I don't like everythin' I do. Ain't no way I can expect to like everythin' you do. I figure if'en you knew what the DuMonts was gon' do, you'd have done different! Anyways, you saved my life, so let's call it water under the bridge and go on. You's my wife. You's my family and that's real important to me! This baby you carryin' is part of that family! We goin' through this here life together! Man and wife!"

Serena said nothing, but she smiled and gave his hand a faint squeeze. Then without warning she slipped back under the translucent cover of unconsciousness. Her breaths were long and even. She appeared to sleep. Her hand relaxed and lay quietly in King's grasp like a half-opened flower.

Ma Wrangel came over at seven o'clock just before her breakfast rush and was delighted to see Serena's improvement. She bathed and tended to Serena, clucking like an old mother hen. Then she rushed back to Wrangel House to check on the status of things in the kitchen.

Serena slept for the next two days with only intermittent moments of wakefulness. But on the third day she awoke and King saw that the spark in her eye had been rekindled. He knelt by her bedside and kissed her softly.

"You want anythin'?" he asked.

"I'm starving! What is there to eat?"

"What do you want?"

"I want some pancakes, grits and bacon, some oatmeal, a slice of ham and—"

King spread his hands. "Whoa! Whoa! Is you sure you can eat all this?"

Serena nodded her head emphatically.

"Alright, I'll go over to Wrangel House and order it. You want it all at the same time, or you want staggered shifts?"

"I want it all now!"

"Okay, I'll be back in a minute."

As King walked out the door, she called out after him. "Bring me up one of those big dill pickles from the barrel downstairs when you come back!"

MONDAY, JULY 4, 1921

The train's whistle blared as it rushed through a small town, warning the inhabitants that the *Chicago Express* was passing through. The train continued hurtling down the track. The regular sound of its metal wheels passing over lengths of rail added a syncopated percussion to the other noises generated by the linked rail cars as their locomotive steamed along at nearly forty miles an hour.

Through the windows of the sleeping car, the sky was overcast with a trace of blue on the western horizon. Marco Volante stared out the windows and his mood matched the sky. The constant movement of the train caused the bandages on the wound in his side to seep with blood. He could not find a comfortable position, one in which his injury was not aggravated by the train's movement. He knew that if he did not see a doctor

STANDING AT THE SCRATCH LINE · 437

soon, his life would be in jeopardy. Over the ten days in which he had been traveling northward from New Orleans, he had lost a lot of blood. The pain of sitting up was making him light-headed.

His journey to Chicago had been a march through hell. He could not count the number of ferries, barges, buses, and trains he had taken in his escape from New Orleans. There was no other word for it but escape and he was lucky to do it with his life. Unwillingly, his thoughts drifted back to the night that King Tremain had killed Corlis Mack. One image rose out of the turmoil and dominated the rest. It was the flicker of a knife blade created by distant streetlights against the shadows of nightfall.

After Volante had driven away from the sight of Bradley's crushed body lying under the wheel of the beer wagon, he finally found his way back to his hotel, a reputable but out-of-the-way establishment. The hotel was located on a narrow street far from the Vieux Carré and its attendant nightlife. Volante parked around the corner from the hotel and studied the street for the signs of the sheriff's men. Despite the lateness of the hour, there was still some pedestrian traffic, and an occasional vehicle would pass every so often. He got out of the car and slipped into the alley that ran behind the hotel. He entered the establishment through its back entrance and climbed the stairs to his room without seeing anyone except a Negro porter who was asleep by the back door.

With trepidation Volante tiptoed down the hall to his room. His hand was on his derringer. The hallway was well lit by electric bulbs shining from regularly spaced sconces. He reached his room without incident, but he noticed that the door was ajar. Immediately he knew something was wrong. Both Sal and Beppo were veterans; neither man would leave a hotel door open in enemy territory. Volante considered leaving without going into the room, but he couldn't get out of New Orleans without money. He also needed to find out what had happened to Beppo and Sal. He pushed in the door and stepped into the darkened room. He closed the door behind him and switched on the overhead light. He crept to the end of the narrow, five-foot hallway and peeked into the room. Tables and chairs were overturned. Lamps lay broken on the floor. It looked as if the room had been used to stage a life-and-death struggle.

Beppo was lying on his back by the couch, with a wire wound tightly around his neck. His eyes were still open in a glassy-eyed stare of surprise. Volante went over to him, knelt down, and closed Beppo's eyes. Then he went to find his other subordinate. He found Sal in the bathroom tub, lying in his own blood. His throat had been slit. Volante's heart began to pound. Both his soldiers had been killed. The sheriff's plan seemed to be moving along despite the fact that its deviser was dead and no longer concerned with the outcome. He forced himself to organize his thoughts. He needed money and he needed guns if he was to get out of New Orleans alive.

The money was still where it had been stashed, under the rug beneath the couch. There was just over twenty thousand dollars, most of it to be used as bribe money for port officials and law enforcement types. Volante quickly stuffed the bills into a money belt, which he slipped around his waist beneath his shirt. When he returned to Chicago, he wanted to return with that money in hand. He wanted to show some small recompense to offset his failure to attain the desired objectives. His whole mission had been disrupted by factors beyond his control, but in his organization, excuses only paved the way to hell.

He realized that it was only a matter of time before whoever killed Beppo and Sal returned to check whether he had gone back to the hotel. He stooped down to check Beppo's body for his .357, but it was gone. He had a hunch that Sal's was taken as well. It was clear that his pursuers planned to kill him with either Sal or Beppo's gun. He went to the drawer and was emptying a box of .45 shells into his pocket when he heard the door squeak open.

The overhead light was on. There was no place to hide. Volante ducked behind the dresser bureau and waited. He heard footsteps walk to the end of the hallway. The sweat began to run down his face. He didn't even pull his derringer. It was useless except at close range. Volante tried to slow down his breathing so as not to give his presence away. A voice called out, "Signore Volante? Signore Volante, it's me, Leo Pagnozzi. Are you here? My Uncle Joe Petino told me to help you!"

Volante breathed a sigh of relief and stood up. "A hell of a good time to show up, Leo. I need some help! It looks like the sheriff's boys hit us hard. I need some help getting out of New Orleans back to Chicago."

"That's what I'm here for," Leo answered with a smile. He was a medium-sized, dark-haired man in his early twenties. His dominant feature was hair. His hairline was close to his eyebrows, which appeared as one long row of hair above his eyes. It did not matter how many times he shaved; he always had a five o'clock shadow on his cheeks.

Volante noticed thick, coarse dark hair on Leo's hands as he leaned casually against the wall. He appeared to show no surprise or sorrow at seeing Beppo's body lying on the floor. Leo's apparent lack of emotion disturbed Volante. "Let me get a few things," Volante said as he began to pack a small travel bag. Behind the top cover of the bag, he discarded the spent shell from his derringer and replaced it with a new one. "I'm ready," he said.

"Let's go then. The cops'll be crawlin' all over this place soon." Leo pushed himself erect and smiled at Volante. "Hey, you got a gun?" he asked, offering Volante one of his.

Volante declined. "No, but I won't need one, will I?"

"Go ahead and take it," Leo urged, offering the revolver butt-first. "You can never tell what's gon' happen. It always helps to have an equalizer with you."

Volante took the gun and looked down at Beppo's body. "It didn't help him," he commented dryly.

"Well, maybe he wasn't lookin' where he should be lookin'!" Leo suggested without sympathy. "We got to get out of here. I got a car waitin' downstairs. Let's go!"

Volante picked up his bag and walked out of the room, followed by Leo. They went down the stairs toward the back door through which Volante had entered earlier. The porter was no longer sleeping by the door. Just before he got to the door, Volante thought he saw the porter's feet sticking out of the half-open pantry. He didn't stop to investigate. The porter was not his responsibility.

Two husky men were waiting by the car. As Volante descended the stairs, Leo shoved him roughly from behind. Volante missed a step and stumbled down the remaining stairs, ending up sprawled on the pavement. "What the hell!" he exclaimed as he picked himself off the ground. When he stood up he saw a pistol aimed at him. "What's going on?" he demanded.

"I'm Leo Minetti Pagnozzi! Does the name Minetti ring any bells, you goddamn Judas?"

Volante suddenly realized that he was the object of a hit. Leo was going to kill him to avenge either Vito or Tony's death, or possibly both. Someone hit him from behind before he could react. He did not lose consciousness, but he was stunned. He was kicked and punched into the backseat of the car. One of the burly men joined him. Volante sat up with an effort. Blood was running down the side of his face. "You got it wrong, Leo," he explained. "I didn't have anything to do with the deaths of Don Vito or his brother!"

"I don't want to hear your goddamn cowardly lies, asshole!" Leo snarled. "If he says another goddamn thing, Tosca, hit him!" The hulk next to Volante grunted and nodded his head.

Volante rode in silence. He was thinking about a way to escape. He figured that the gun that Leo had given him was either empty or malfunctioning. He still had the derringer, but it had only two shots. Nonetheless, if he used it at the right time, he might surprise his assailants. The car turned onto a road that led to some isolated and decaying docks on the edge of the Mississippi. Tosca produced a gun and motioned for Volante to get out of the car. He obeyed.

The moon had long since left the cloudless night sky. The stars overhead were dim against the diffused light of New Orleans. Out on the black waters of the Mississippi, there were many well-lighted boats, barges, and ferries plying up and down the river. The only electric light emanated from a distant lamppost near the entrance of the docks. Volante thought of all the people in the distant boats and ferries who would continue on living and breathing after he was dead. More than anything, Volante wanted to be on one of the lighted vessels traveling on the great river, to be part of the educated conversations over dinner, to be drinking at a long bar with beautiful women.

"You betrayed my grandfather when you arranged the hit on Don Vito Minetti!" Leo declared as he stood on the other side of the car. "My mother was the daughter of Don Vito Minetti. Your boss, my Uncle Joe Petino, is married to my mother's sister. Even though Don Cabresi had given you asylum, we been waitin' for our chance. We never forget! I swore to my mother that I would kill the dog who murdered my grandfather!" Leo began taking off his jacket and rolling up his shirtsleeves. He pulled out a knife with a short, thick blade. "They call me Leo the Knife. Guns are okay, but I prefer to kill with this. It causes more pain. It lets you get up close, so close you can smell the fear. I'm goin' to get real close to you!"

"Did you kill Beppo and Sal?" Volante asked.

"You noticed the knife work, huh?" Leo asked with a smirk. "My Uncle Joe, he likes things done thorough. Uncle Joe thinks Don Cabresi had gotten soft in his old age. He doesn't think the Don has the balls or energy to run the rackets down here. He thinks it's time for him to take over. Your two boys had to pay the price for being on the wrong side, but their deaths were easier than yours is going to be. Since Mack didn't kill you, I get to do it, and I'm going to take my time."

Volante stepped back from the car and pulled out the revolver that Leo had given him and all three of his captors laughed. He flipped open the cylinder. The gun was empty.

Leo walked around the front of the car and came toward Volante. "Do you think I would be stupid enough to give you a loaded weapon?" He started to run at his intended victim, but Volante threw the revolver at him, causing him to duck. The revolver whistled past Leo and hit Tosca's partner on the bridge of his nose. Volante had no time to enjoy the success of his aim. Leo was on him quick as a cat, thrusting and slashing with his flickering blade. Volante barely staggered out of reach of each arc of the knife. Leo laughed as he circled his victim. With each attack, he struck at Volante's torso. He was enjoying himself and was in no particular hurry. He was toying with Volante, trying to wear him down by making him dodge the moving blade.

After a few minutes, Volante began to get winded from evading Leo's quick lunging attacks and he was beginning to breathe heavily. So far he had only been nicked, but he could tell Leo was getting closer with each sally. He fumbled in his right-hand pants pocket for his derringer and Leo chose this moment to attack.

Leo did a quick forward roll, which somehow allowed him to get within striking distance of Volante. He lunged with his blade. Only at the last minute was the thrust blocked by Volante's bare left hand, but he paid a penalty. The keen edge of the knife sliced open his palm. Leo kept up his attack until he drove the blade of the knife into the soft flesh of Volante's side.

Volante squealed and staggered backward. Leo stood for a moment, admiring the blood covering the short blade of his knife. "That was for my grandfather," he announced. "This one's for my mother!" Leo attacked again without warning. Due to his wound Volante no longer had the ability to take evasive measures. Leo feinted and drove his blade hard past Volante's guard, aiming directly for his liver. It was a well-aimed thrust and hit the mark squarely. The blade, however, was stopped by Volante's money belt. The momentary hesitation caused by Leo's surprise was his undoing.

Volante pulled the derringer from his pocket and fired point blank into Leo's chest. Leo stumbled backward but maintained his balance. He looked down at his chest where the bullet had entered and then sank to his knees. "You had a gun?" he gasped before he fell face forward into the dirt.

"I guess you weren't looking where you were supposed to be looking!" Volante gasped, holding his side. He sank down on his knees from the pain of his injury. He heard Tosca bellow and come running. Volante was getting dizzy and light-headed. He watched as Tosca knelt down and cradled Leo in his arms. Tosca moaned and cried over Leo.

Tosca's partner shouted from the hood of the car where he was lying down, "What the hell's goin' on over there?"

"He's killed Leo, Paolo! He's killed Leo," Tosca sobbed.

"Bring that bastard to me!" Paolo ordered. "I'll make him pay for that and my nose!"

Tosca softly laid Leo's body back on the ground and turned to face Volante. "I'm gon' cut yo' tongue out myself, befo' I give you to Paolo." He stood up with Leo's knife and lumbered toward Volante. When he was close enough he reached down and lifted his victim by the collar of his jacket.

Volante waited until the last moment, then fired the last shot of his derringer into Tosca's face. Tosca fell over backward and lay still. Volante pulled himself over Tosca's body and checked underneath his jacket for a gun. He found a .45 revolver in an inside holster. He checked the revolver's cylinder for bullets. It was fully loaded. He snapped the cylinder back in place. He heard Paolo screaming for his two companions.

When Paolo heard no answer from his associates, he stood up and roared, "I'm gon' get you, you bastard!"

Pain was clouding Volante's vision. He wiped his eyes, trying to clear them of the mysterious fog that obscured his sight. He saw the shape of a man coming toward him. He heard the discharge of a gun and the bullet whistled over his head. He took his time and aimed for the man's torso. He fired several bullets in quick succession and the man fell over on his side. Volante fired a couple more bullets into the man's body just for insurance and then he passed out.

He awoke in pain, lying in a pool of blood. He sat up with an effort and felt blood trickle down his side. The night sky was growing lighter. The waters of the Mississippi were not black but a dirty brown. He staggered to his feet and walked over to the car. The keys were still in the ignition. From his suitcase he took a shirt and wadded it over the stab wound, using his money belt to hold it in place.

"Next stop Chicago! Next stop Chicago! End of the line!" There was a knock on the sleeping-car door. "Next stop Chicago, sir."

"Okay! Okay!" Volante acknowledged groggily, awakening from his recurring nightmare about his last terrifying night in New Orleans. When the train at last pulled to a stop, he steeled himself to walk out of the station and catch a taxi. Once in the cab he did not go home, but instead went directly to a doctor who he knew would not report his injury to the police. In a matter of hours he was lying in a convalescent bed recovering from surgery.

The prognosis was that Volante would live, but that did not cause him to rest easy. He had failed in his mission and his boss, Joe Petino, had set him up to be killed. It did not take a clever person to realize that Petino would be even more dedicated to his demise now that his nephew Leo was also dead. He could not go to the Don with this information. It was Volante's word against Petino's. Who would the Don believe: a trusted lieutenant or a man with questionable actions in his past? There appeared to be no easy solution to his problem. He found it ironic that the only reason he was alive today was that King Tremain, the man who had caused him to be driven from New York, had disrupted Corlis Mack's deadly plans.

The next morning Volante had an unexpected visit from Don Cabresi. The Don was a medium-built man with even features and the olive skin of his native Sicily. He was dressed immaculately and his salt-and-pepper hair was coifed neatly in a razor cut. Except for his regal bearing, he could have been a fishmonger like his father in the Old Country. But the Don was a man of the world, aged by conflict and sophisticated intrigue. He was used to commanding men.

Volante tried to sit up, but the Don held out a hand indicating that he should remain supine. Volante was afraid and it left a brackish taste in his mouth. He had seen other men pay with their lives for failure. He did not know what was in store for him.

"So, the warrior returns," Don Cabresi said with a smile. Volante was confused. He did not know what to say. The Don continued. "I have to say, I misjudged you, Marco. You are more man than I thought. We sent you down to do a job and when things did not go as planned, you killed our enemies. I say to you, bravo!" The Don began to clap and he was joined by his two bodyguards as well.

Volante stared uncomprehendingly and attempted to explain, but the Don silenced him with a hand gesture.

"I know all about Petino and his plans. My friends in the police department have been listening in on his phone for some time. Unfortunately, I didn't get the information about his setting you up for a hit until after you left, but it seems you didn't need my assistance anyway. The main members in the group standing against us in New Orleans are dead thanks to you. Petino and his accomplices up here are swimming with the fish. We stand a very good chance of working out a deal to bring bootleg in with the new people in power down there."

The Don stood up. "I'm going to let you rest now. I want you to get well. I have some important assignments for you. You can even be my man in New Orleans if you desire, but more on that when you have recovered." He walked over to the bed and stretched out his hand. Volante took it gratefully and kissed it. The Don bent over him and kissed him on both cheeks. "Get well! I need you!" he said before he left the room.

Volante laid back in his bed and said a prayer of thanks. It was almost too good to believe. He exhaled with a long sigh of relief. Fate was not predictable. What he had expected had not materialized. His thoughts drifted to King Tremain. It appeared that the man who had first jeopardized his life and career in New York had saved his life and career in Chicago. Volante made a silent vow that he would no longer seek King to avenge the deeds done in New York. King had exonerated himself in New Orleans. He and Volante were even on the cosmic scales of justice. He would go on with his life and all thought of King Tremain would fade into the past.

FRIDAY, MARCH 20, 1925

After a long day's work delivering grain orders to a number of farms around Bodie Wells, King Tremain sat at a felt-covered table in his back-room card parlor with Mace Edwards, Octavius Boothe, Tobias Dorsett, and Lightning Smith discussing the news and events of the day. In the years since Mace had been elected mayor and Octavius had been appointed town marshal, King's card parlor had become the informal place where Bodie Wells's leaders met to discuss matters that affected the town. During that time Serena and King had risen to prominence in Bodie Wells's affairs. After the tornado, Tremain's Dry Goods had become the largest business in the township, employing over a dozen people. The general store had been expanded to include a full-service livery stable and a clothing store. Selling quality goods at fair prices, the Tremains had earned reputations as solid businesspeople and citizens.

The men sitting around the table with King were sipping shots of single malt bourbon as Mace relayed some information he had concerning the railroad, which was laying track to pass five miles north of Clairborne. The building of the railroad meant business for Bodie Wells. Most of the people employed in the heavy physical labor at the railhead were either colored or Chinese. It was the only town within twenty-five miles where they could shop for clothing and necessities without fear of racial violence. Mace took a swig of his bourbon and said, "The track boss had a colored man and a Chinaman horsewhipped damn near to death. He had both men's backs laid open to the bone! The colored man and the Chinese man are down at Doc Stephens's lying at death's door. All those men did was complain about the paymaster shortening their weekly pay."

King nodded his head, "I heard that it happens almost every week and if a man complains to the law, they up and fire him."

"I think we got some big problems of our own and we better put our thinkin' on 'em befo' they rise up full-growed," Octavius said with an easy smile.

"What you talkin' about 'Tavius?" Tobias asked. Tobias Dorsett was a man in his early sixties and one of the town elders. His cabinet shop was one of the original businesses around which Bodie Wells was formed.

"Well, I hear that the track manager and the track boss done lost a lot of money gamblin' down in Atoka and the mens they owe down there is putting pressure on them to pay up! For a while they was just willin' to squeeze money out'n the colored payroll." Octavius smiled again, showing his uneven white teeth. "But now it appears the track manager been dippin' into the operatin' money as well and work on the railhead is gon' come to a standstill. So he been out tryin' to sell shares in the company. Of course, the white banks just laugh at him. They knows he ain't got no right to sell nothin'. So, now he tryin' the colored banks. He offerin' to let them hold next month's payroll if'en they buy his paper."

Tobias leaned forward, "Were that the white man I seen meetin' with Buck Henry the other day?"

"I think so," Octavius nodded.

Lightning had gotten up to wash glasses behind the bar. Now he exploded, "Damn it to tarnation! Every cent I done saved in these years since the tornado is in his bank!"

Tobias Dorsett ran his hands through his kinky white hair and shook his head. "You got to figure he gettin' a pretty good kickback on the side to fall for somethin' like this. Buck Henry ain't no fool. He gettin' his!"

"How'd you hear all this, Octavius?" Mace asked. "I thought I was staying on top of things."

"You know I got a cousin who works in the colored section of Atoka Federated Bank," Octavius answered, sipping his drink. "He overheard one of the managers laughin' about the track manager's troubles. He called me a couple of days ago and told me to be on the lookout for him."

"If Buck Henry is doin' business with the track manager, he must be gettin' ready to leave town," Tobias mused. "He know he can't live here after the bank fails."

Mace put his face in his hands and took a deep breath. "If the bank fails, people won't have enough to start over! My God! When you combine this information with the fact that some big-time wheat farmers west of us are fighting for a redistribution of the water from Little River Dam, things look bad for Bodie Wells."

"There are two big rivers between us and them," Tobias observed. "Why should a redistribution of water hurt us?"

"Because they'll divert the watershed above us in the Ouachitas into the canal that passes Clairborne and we won't get spillover either."

Tobias frowned. "That doesn't make sense. Why that will dry up every farm for forty miles around. Even Clairborne farmers will be hit."

Mace shook his head. "This is a war between white men. Big Daddy made some big enemies when he pushed through the Little River Dam Project. He's been fighting them off for better than a decade, but now it looks like they're getting the best of him. They'll dry out every farm that doesn't have a good producing well and then they'll buy the land dirt cheap, change the water distribution agreement, and they'll be growing wheat here fifteen years from now."

There were several minutes of silence as Mace's words reverberated in the room. Then King said, "We can't do nothin' about the water, but we can stop Henry from breakin' the bank."

"How do you plan to do that?" Mace asked.

"Go to the bank and take our money out," King answered with a smile. "I know he ain't gon' leave town befo' tomorrow!"

Sampson pushed through the mesh and stood in the doorway, holding the mesh that hung from the top of the door and was weighted at the bottom by a piece of wood. A light brown–skinned boy, barely twenty months old toddled into the room behind him. The child gurgled when he saw King and waddled as fast as his little legs could carry him to where King was sitting. King picked up the child and sat him on his lap.

"The older boy, LaValle, ain't around?" Octavius asked.

"No, he's with Serena," King answered before he turned his attention to his son. "You looks mighty dirty, Jacques. What you been doin', boy?" King asked. The child gurgled happily in his father's lap and reached for his glass of bourbon. King pushed the glass out of reach and said, "You got plenty of time for that when you's growed." He turned to Lightning. "Ain't we got some lemonade or sarsaparilla for this here child?"

"Sho' do," Lightning answered with a smile. "I made some this afternoon special for him." He took a metal pitcher out of a bucket of ice and poured a small glass of lemonade for Jacques.

"Yo' Missus down to Johnsonville outfittin' folks fo' that big weddin'?" Octavius asked as he watched Jacques gulp down his lemonade.

"Yeah, she travel quite a good deal now with dresses made to order."

Tobias said, "Yo' Missus is a real go-getter! She on about every major town committee there is."

King just nodded and smiled, but he did not voice his opinion. He was intimately aware of his wife's social ambitions and it had become a source of contention between them. She seemed more concerned with social acceptance and image than with charitable purposes of her various committees. What people thought was a principal force in all of her decisions. Nor did she miss an opportunity to deride his continued involvement in his bootleg business. King was impervious to her machinations and her arguments fell on deaf ears. He continued on without the slightest deviation in his activities. As far as he was concerned, she had her priorities and he had his.

"I hear she's making fifteen dresses for that wedding." Mace questioned, "Your older son is with her while she's doing all those fittings?"

"Yep," King answered without elaboration.

Sampson signed some information to King to which he responded with a nod. Sampson then turned to walk out the door and Jacques began to squirm on his father's lap. "Mson!" Jacques called out, pointing to Sampson.

King set his squirming son on the floor. "You don't want to stay with me?" he asked.

Jacques shook his head vigorously and said, "Nell," then toddled to Sampson, who waited for him at the door.

"If that don't beat all," King said with a smile. "He done left me to go play with the dogs!"

Octavius got to his feet. "Let me go on down to Doc Stephens's and see how them two mens is doin'. I'll take a report and send it in to the circuit court judge."

"Don't forget my truck," King said with a chuckle. "You just make sho' you fix that transmission, so's we can make a run to Atoka tonight to pick up our shipment of store merchandise."

Octavius nodded, "I'll go straight to the garage from Doc Stephens's. I'll have it ready by eight." He picked up his hat and waved it around to all present and pushed through the mesh into the darkening purple of the evening sky.

Mace leaned forward and said to Tobias, "Maybe Octavius is wrong about Buck Henry."

Tobias shook his head. "I got to go to the bank tomorrow. I can't gamble that things is gon' be alright. Me and the wife is too old to lose our savings now. Shoot, if we didn't have help from the Tremains, we might not have rebuilt the cabinet shop after the tornado. I'm sorry, Mace. I can't think about the good of the town, I got to take care of me and the missus."

"That go for me too!" Lightning declared. "I done already seen the force of nature take everythin' I had. I sho' ain't gon' give up what I got saved now to no low-down cheat!"

Mace sighed, "Without a bank, Bodie Wells is just a collection of buildings. Everything we fought for and sweated for will be gone!"

"That ain't so, Mace," Tobias countered. "There is plenty of colored towns that don't have no banks and the people in 'em is doin' just fine. Colored folks has kept they money in tin cans, cookie jars, cigar boxes, and under floorboards since slavery and have survived. But if Buck Henry done spent our hard-earned money on a lot of useless paper, this here town is dead; that's the one thing will kill it for sho': stealin' folks savin's."

"I'm gon' pull my money out," King declared. "I ain't trusted Henry since that time them boys in Clairborne wanted to ride on us."

Elijah Wells pushed through the mesh and walked into the room, "How do, everybody?" he called out as he walked over to the small bar. "It be the end of a long week, Lightnin'. I needs a shot of that there whiskey just to wet my throat."

"I best be gettin' home," Tobias said as he stood up. He nodded to King, "I'll see you at the bank tomorrow mo'nin'."

Mace stood up reluctantly as well and said, "I'll walk out with you, Mr. Dorsett. Thanks for the drink, King." Both Tobias and Mace pushed through the mesh and walked out.

"You's here early ain't you, Lige?" Lightning asked as he poured Elijah a drink.

"Yep, I been workin' for the paymaster these last couple of days, movin' boxes and pay records, so I ain't been out sweatin' on the track 'til six and seven in the evening like everybody else." Elijah took a sip of his drink and a smile creased his dark-brown face. He was a likable, young, muscular man with a smooth face and even features. He was one of the few colored men who followed the work of the railroad who had brought his family to Bodie Wells. His wife worked for Serena as a seamstress. Elijah walked over and took the seat vacated by Mace. "There is some crazy stuff goin' at the railroad," he said, shaking his head.

King nodded and asked, "What's this you say about workin' for the paymaster?"

Elijah smiled. "Yep, been havin' an easy job for near three days. It 'pears they expectin' some bigwigs to come out tomorrow with a big shipment of money to stop all the grumblin' by the white workers and the folks in Clairborne.

"Why are they sendin' all this money?" King asked.

"Oh, it's all hush-hush," Elijah answered, dropping his voice. " 'Course, they talk all the time like I ain't there. The track manager, the track boss, and the paymaster been stealin' from the track payroll for over a year. But they is scramblin' now! I overheard that an accountant is comin' on the money train to look at the books they been keepin'."

King asked as he dealt himself a hand of solitaire, "Is they worried about gettin' arrested?"

Elijah scoffed, "They shittin' in they britches! They's tryin' to get money from everywhere! I even saw Buck Henry come sneakin' in to visit them. Course I didn't let him see me. But shoot, they ain't got no time to work nothin' out. The Pinkertons arrive tomorrow and the railroad has got every police department within thirty miles goin' to the railhead tonight to protect that money shipment. I bet there ain't a policeman from between Clairborne and the Oklahoma border that ain't been summoned to the railhead tonight."

"About time them boys paid the piper. They been stealin' from the colored and Chinese for years," King commented as he went through the deck card by card.

There was a knock at the door and Buck Henry pushed through the mesh and was followed by a light-skinned man wearing a brown plaid suit cut in the latest style. Buck Henry was a tall, slender man with a thin mustache just above his lip. He looked more like a mortician than a banker, for he had the oily, ingratiating smile of a coffin-seller. "You playing cards tonight?" Buck asked.

"Sorry, not tonight," King answered, covering his irritation. The fact that Buck had the gall and presumption to act as if no one knew about his dirty dealings made King want to hurt him. But he restrained himself with the knowledge that Buck was the type of man who was most vulnerable through his wallet. All King had to do was wait. Once he and Tobias Dorsett started the run on the bank in the morning, that would deliver the most telling blow.

Buck asked, "Do you mind if we have a drink before we head out to the Black Rose?"

King smiled. He could afford to be generous. "Sho', have one on me. Who's yo' friend?"

"Oh, this is my cousin, Charles Manning from Memphis," Buck replied with one of his oily smiles. "He's just in town to visit for a few days." Buck turned to his cousin. "Charles, this is King Tremain and that's Lightning Smith at the bar. And I believe the other man at the table is Elijah Wells."

Charles Manning nodded to King and Elijah. He had a condescending smirk on his face and possessed a haughty bearing. He removed the riding gloves he wore and tossed them on the table nonchalantly. He turned and waved to Lightning, beckoning him over.

King said in a level voice, "He ain't no servant. If you wants a drink, you get up and go to the bar." He felt an immediate dislike for Manning and he knew his feelings would not improve.

Manning frowned at King but satisfied himself with a smirk and walked over to the bar.

Rafer Brisco and another man pushed through the mesh while Charles was getting his drink. Rafer said, "We's been swingin' iron and sweatin' hard all day. We's as dry as meat cured with salt. Give us doubles of what the house is servin' tonight!"

King announced, "Ain't no cards tonight, but you mens can have a drink or two on the house tonight befo' we close." With words and gestures of thanks everyone got themselves a generous shot.

"The railroad sure been good to Bodie Wells," Buck Henry observed as he sat down at the table with his bourbon. "We got more business now than we had in years. This here town is now one of the largest all-colored towns in eastern Oklahoma and we just seem to keep on growing."

"We's just another boomtown," Lightning countered as he poured a drink for himself at the bar. "When they's finished layin' track and buildin' the depot north of Clairborne, we gon' return to the sleepy li'l town we used to be."

"You wrong there," Buck argued. "From what I hear, there's going to be work for any colored man who don't mind bending his back!"

"You talkin' 'bout that new water project?" Lightning asked. "I heard that they ain't gon' allow no spillover water to run through the farmland around Bodie Wells. They gon' divert it through Clairborne."

"That's just loose lips flapping in the wind. We're in the midst of change. Things aren't ever gon' be the same," Buck answered. "Why, the last time I was in Atoka, I spoke with Lewellen Carwell, the president of Atoka Federated Bank, and he told me about how he's buying stock certificates on the market in New York City and investing his customers' money so he can pay them interest on their deposits. The telephone makes it all possible. You can know within twenty minutes how your stock is doing fifteen hundred miles away. No doubt about it, it's a new day."

"Is you investin' our money like that?" King asked with a stare.

Buck coughed a little awkwardly, "I haven't done anything yet, but I'm considering it. I'm sure you wouldn't mind a little return on your depoisit, would you?"

"I'd rather be sure of my money," King countered.

Charles Manning changed the subject in a jaunty voice, "Anyone interested in playin' a little poker? We're goin' to get up a game out at the Black Rose."

King watched Manning tapping his manicured fingers on the felt and was irritated by his cocky airs. King figured him for a slickster as well as a back-shooter. He knew that he wouldn't trust him to deal straight off the top of the deck.

"Not me," Elijah answered. "I have to go home to the wife."

"I could play some five-dollar limit," Rafer ventured.

Manning scoffed, "Five dollars is small time! We's all men here, ain't we? Let's make the game mo' interestin'!"

"Any limit is too rich for me," Juke volunteered as he leaned against the bar. "I ain't had a full paycheck in a month. I's savin' my money for pussy and some drinks."

The mesh of the back door pushed open and Sampson stepped into the room. He nodded to King and held the mesh open until a large spotted hound padded in, followed by a little Jacques who was holding on to the dog's tail. He fell crossing the threshold. The dog stopped and waited for him to regain his feet, which he did, using the dog's tail as a support. Then he and the dog continued on around to the bar.

Juke exclaimed, "Damn! Is that a blue tick hound?"

"Yep, that's old Nell," answered Lightning. "But you got to hear her sing on a night hunt. She got the voice of an opry star when she got the scent of an elk or a lion in her nose. She run at the head of the pack with Towser, and everybody know he the best huntin' dog in these parts!" He took a couple of big biscuits from behind the bar and tossed one to Nell who caught it and gulped it down and gave the other to Jacques who leaned against the dog as he munched on his biscuit.

Nell started around the table with the boy still holding on to her tail to where King was sitting.

Charles Manning smirked, "She don't look like no huntin' dog to me with a li'l pickaninny holdin' on to her tail. He sho' is a cute li'l nigger though." He reached out to pat the child's head, but Nell instantly pivoted, snarling with teeth bared, and faced him. All semblance of an uncaring, ambling animal was gone. Nell was all hunter now. The man jerked his hand back as if he had touched a hot griddle. It was clear to all present that she could have taken his hand off at the wrist had she wanted to.

Once the intruder had been put in his place, Nell continued on as if the incident hadn't occurred. Jacques, still holding on to the dog's tail, stared at Charles with big eyes as he toddled by. Nell sat down with dignity next to King and little Jacques slid down the side of the dog to the seat of his pants and continued munching on his biscuit.

"Yesiree, Nell loves that Little Jack," Lightning chuckled gleefully. "Can't nobody touch him, if she don't know him! She be a bitin' dog!"

Manning scowled, "You ought to keep that dog to guardin' pickaninnies, otherwise somebody might have to take a stick to her to teach her a lesson."

"You better say joe, 'cause you sho' don't know. It's you who needs a lesson," King said as he laid a pearl-handled Colt pistol on the table. Sampson leaned behind the bar and picked up a shotgun. King hadn't liked the man from the beginning. Now that he had overstepped his bounds, King was ready to take him down. King growled, "My son ain't no pickaninny and he ain't no nigger!"

Manning's face drained of color as the room went silent. Manning sat perfectly still, then said, "Didn't mean nothin'."

"Maybe it's time we call it an evening?" Buck suggested, standing up.

"That's a good idea," King agreed as he stared challengingly into Manning's face.

Both Buck and Manning avoided making eye contact with King as they made their way quickly to the door.

Rafer stood up and said, "Thanks for the drinks and the excitement. I think we's gon' mosey along too." Elijah and Juke added their thanks and followed Rafer through the mesh.

"Time to close up." King said, and stooped to pick up his little son who was already beginning to nod off. As soon as he had the child in his arms, the boy fell asleep and started to snore.

King carried his son upstairs and placed him in his crib. He went to the stove and got some hot water and a wash cloth. He returned to the crib and took off his son's clothes slowly and gently. The boy never wakened while his father washed him down and put a diaper on him. Jacques was potty trained except for a few rare accidents, but he still needed diapers during the night. Once King had a warm nightshirt on Jacques, he stood watching the child sleep. Whenever he looked at Jacques, he felt something in his chest that he could not explain. All he knew was that he would protect and nurture this child no matter the cost or the effort. It was not a conscious decision, but rather something that originated deep within him. Jacques was the first step in the creation of his new family.

King turned and looked at the empty crib across the room and thought of LaValle. He wondered how children of the same mother could be so different. It did not take much to frighten LaValle and he cried easily and often. He ran to his mother with the slightest injury and hid his face in her skirts. He was a weakling and King couldn't stand it. King often wondered whether it was because he was LeGrande's son. Jacques, on the other hand, had fiber and toughness that made his father proud. King recalled an incident in the week preceding in which Jacques had gotten nipped by one of the hounds for being too close to his food bowl. Jacques cried out in pain then picked up a stick and whacked the hound across the nose with it, causing the dog to make a great deal more noise yelping. King knew that if it had been LaValle who had been nipped, he would have run for the protection of his mother's arms.

Even the lack of toughness King could have made allowances for, but the nail in the coffin was that LaValle was always trying to hurt his younger brother. LaValle was jealous of Jacques and he had to be constantly watched. If the boys were left alone together, one could be sure that Jacques was being pummeled by his older brother. It was this bullying, sibling envy more than anything else that caused LaValle to be a continual source of irritation to King, and LaValle, possessing a child's delicate antenna, sensed King's silent anger and quailed in his presence. Aware of

LaValle's fear of King, Serena never left her older son in her husband's care, and no amount of discussion would assuage her concerns. King had argued many times that the situation could be remedied if Serena would turn over the rearing and training of both boys to him. He knew he could make them act as brothers and make them his, but Serena would not allow it, nor would she stop interceding on LaValle's behalf in every confrontation with his father. Frustrated, King relinquished his efforts and had turned his attention to Jacques.

When King returned to the card room, he signed Sampson that he should go get the truck from Octavius's garage. King went into the hall and unlocked his gun cabinet and took out a couple of rifles. He had decided not to go to Atoka. He figured that since the railroad had mobilized all law enforcement in the area to come to the railhead, it was an ideal time to move several large shipments of bootleg that he had stored outside of Johnsonville.

Lightning was in the process of putting the liquor away and locking up for the evening when King said, "I need you to keep an eye on Little Jacques until his mother returns tonight. Sampson and I have few chores to do and we might not get back until tomorrow mo'nin'."

"Ain't no problem" Lightning answered. "I'll tell the missus you gon' be gone."

As he and Sampson drove toward Johnsonville, King mused over the unfortunate relationship between Jacques and LaValle, and, as always, when he thought of his children, he thought of the child who had disappeared in New Orleans. When King had burned DuMonts' Landing he had learned from one of the men he captured that the child had been given to LeGrande. The information he had received from Pointdexter who now served as his man on the scene had revealed nothing new. The whereabouts of the child appeared to have died with LeGrande, but King would not lessen the intensity of his search. Something undefinable told him that the boy was alive and King knew that he would not rest until he found him, even if it took a lifetime.

SATURDAY, MARCH 21, 1925

Serena and King were restocking shelves in the store in the late afternoon when Ida Hoskins came in from the dress shop shaking her head. There was an angry expression on her face as she said, "That fool woman, Yvonne Miller from the beauty parlor, is in sayin' she got to buy some dresses 'cause she movin' to Oklahoma City. I done showed her all the ready-made and she done turned up her nose at 'em. She about on my last nerve! Now she want to look at bolts of material for us to make dresses for her. Should I do that?"

Serena smiled. "Try not to let her get to you. If she's willing to put up three quarters of the total cost, we'll make her dresses. If not, good-bye. How's that?"

"Suits me fine," Ida said with a nod of her head, and returned to the dress shop.

King and Serena worked side by side for nearly twenty minutes before she turned to him and said, "Everybody's talking about the run on the bank this morning and how you pulled a gun on Buck Henry. In front of everybody, King. How could you? Don't you know you're ruining our reputation?"

King replied, "Yo' jaws would really be tight if I let him steal our money."

"Did you hear that Octavius barely stopped him from getting tarred and feathered by a mob?"

"No less than he deserves. He ain't nothin' but a thief."

Seeing that King had no remorse for his actions, Serena changed her tactics. "You smelled like a distillery when you came in this morning. I don't ask where you go, but I'm beginning to wonder when all this cut-and-shoot stuff is going to stop. You are harming other people! I know about your bootlegging trips and I've stayed away from saying anything, but events at the bank force me to speak."

"Speak then. Say everythin' that's on yo' mind."

"We've got a good business here. We don't need money made from criminal activities! We can be respectable! We could be pillars in this community! But how can we when you make no effort to improve yourself and you resort to violence and criminal activity! I mean, look at you; you still speak like a common field hand! Look at the kind of impression you make!"

"That's what important to you, is it?" King asked in a level tone. "Bein' accepted by folks? Let me tell you somethin', the people in this town don't give a shit about you or me! They'd have walked all over you if it wasn't for me! They only respect two things, power and money! Buck Henry talk good, but he wasn't nothin' but slime. You heard how they treated him! Actions speak loud, words is just air! The only time I'd give a damn about what somebody think is when they's payin' my mortgage!"

A child's scream pierced the air. It was Jacques. King looked around. "Where's LaValle?"

"He's in his crib."

King took off running. He went up the stairs three at a time and was down the hall in two leaps. The door to Jacques and LaValle's room was open. From the doorway, King could see LaValle standing outside Jacques's crib, poking a stick through the crib's bars. Jacques screamed out again as the stick jabbed him in the back. King was in the room before LaValle could react. When LaValle saw King he dropped the stick and screamed in fear. King caught him up by the arm in a steel grip and LaValle screamed at the top of his lungs. King lifted the child off the floor and saw LaValle's face, contorted and reddened with fear and pain. For the first time, King saw LeGrande's features in the child's face and his grip involuntarily tightened as he looked in the face of his long-dead enemy.

Serena screamed from the doorway, "What are you doing to that baby?" Her voice was shrill and brought King back to his senses. He set the child down and picked up Jacques, who was still teary-eyed. LaValle ran to his mother and buried his face in her skirts, bawling loudly.

"What kind of beast are you to frighten a child like that?" Serena demanded angrily. King turned to face her and Serena saw a look that chilled her to the bone. There was hatred in his eyes.

"You see that stick on the floor? You see these red marks on Jacques's face and back? That little bastard of yours was stabbing him through the bars, trying to hurt him!"

"LaValle is just a child. He didn't know—"

"Bullshit!" King interrupted. His tone was low and bloodless. "You always come up with excuses for him! Let me tell you one thing straight from the get, Miss Siditty. I ain't gon' let you harm another son of mine 'cause you got different priorities. If I see that bastard lay another hand on Jacques, I'm gon' tear his arms off of him! You better watch him good if'en you want him to grow up!" King took Jacques and walked out the door. "You better find another place for the bastard to sleep too!"

Serena felt like her heart had been pierced by icicles. She sank to the floor and the tears flowed silently down her face. LaValle saw his mother's tears and bawled even louder. She pulled him to her and held him firmly to her breast until he quieted. It was clear that King held an unremitting anger for the disappearance of his firstborn child. It was also clear that he did not trust her with Jacques's welfare. She wondered what type of life was in store. She did not doubt for a minute that King would kill LaValle if he was responsible for any kind of serious injury to Jacques. He had disowned LaValle and called him a bastard.

There were just so many tears in her. Serena stood up wearily. LaValle whimpered to be picked up. Serena's first tendency was to accede to his desire but she fought against it. She thought, You've got to be tough if you're going to survive, if you want to win King's respect. She grabbed him by the hand and led him down the stairs.

Ida Hoskins was waiting for Serena in the store. She had a worried look on her face. "Is everythin' alright, Rena?"

Serena took a deep breath. "Yes, thank you, Ida. Is Yvonne Miller still in the store?"

"Yes, ma'am, but I think you should just let me run her out ands tell her we don't want none of her business!"

"Why?"

"She in there with one of her girlfriends and she ain't been sayin' nice things about you at all!"

"Would you watch LaValle for me?" Serena asked sweetly. LaValle cried in protest but Ida took him and calmed him with loving hands. Serena would not have been able to explain why she looked forward to dealing with Yvonne Miller after an argument with King. Perhaps it was because it was a fight that was finite. It didn't stretch back deep into her past. It wasn't rooted in mistakes of judgment that she had committed and was unable to rescind. The problems with Yvonne Miller could be resolved with simple action. Serena walked into the dress shop with a smile on her face.

Yvonne was standing with Belinda Gordon and looking through bolts of material with a nonchalant air. Serena went up to Yvonne and put her hand on a bolt of cloth that Yvonne was unrolling. Her hand stopped Yvonne from unrolling the bolt further. "May I help you?" Serena asked sweetly.

"Well, if it ain't Miss Uppity," Yvonne said with a smirk to Belinda.

Serena stepped up in front of Yvonne and asked, "Do you want to do business, or is this more of your folderol?"

"You best get out of my face!" Yvonne declared. " 'Cause I'll make you scream like that half-breed child we just heard. You ain't foolin' nobody with yo' airs. The whole town know you tried to get rid of that child and failed. We all know it's some white man's bastard! So don't go actin' all Miss High and Mighty with me!"

Serena smiled and said, "Oh, I see. Wait right here. I think that I have just what you're looking for!" She turned and went behind the counter.

Belinda pulled on Yvonne's sleeve and said nervously, "They don't have what you's lookin' for. Let's go our way!"

Yvonne answered. "You's right, honey. This dump don't got enough class to sell nothin' to me!" The two women walked out the door.

Serena dug through a drawer behind the counter and found a leather bag filled with buckshot. King had once told her that if you had to hit somebody, fill your hand with something first. She picked up the bag and hurried after the two women. Yvonne and Belinda were nearly to the end of the wooden-plank walkway when Serena called out, "Yvonne! Yvonne, you forgot something!"

Yvonne turned and said to her friend, "Don't let this heifer have followed me out'n the store! Tell me she didn't follow me!"

Serena hiked up her skirts and ran to where Yvonne and Belinda waited. "I have a little something for you, something that you can take to Oklahoma City with you!"

"You ain't got nothin' I want! You ain't—" Yvonne never finished her statement.

Serena hit her on the jaw with all the energy and anger that had been produced by her argument with King. Yvonne fell backward off the steps into the street and lay still. Serena turned to Belinda, but she backed away saying, "I ain't in it! This was between you two. My name's Bennet. I ain't in it!"

"Tell your friend if there's a next time, I'll butcher her like a hog. She's lucky she's leaving town. If I see her again, I may go off!" Serena turned and walked regally back toward the store. Belinda began screaming for help for her motionless friend who was still lying in the street.

Ida Hoskins came out of the store armed with a wooden cudgel, ready to come to Serena's aid. She soon saw that Serena needed no assistance and that Yvonne was lying out in the street. "You done knocked her out cold!" Ida said, a little awed.

"No more than she deserved," Serena answered without emotion. Serena entered the dress shop and began putting bolts of material away. Ida came in about ten minutes later and started to help Serena with the straightening, but Serena told her to put up the CLOSED FOR BUSINESS sign and to take the rest of the day off with pay. Ida knew better than to argue. She could see that Serena was distraught and wanted to be alone.

As soon as Ida was gone, Serena began to cry. It was obvious to her in a town the size of Bodie Wells that LaValle would never outgrow or escape the gossip surrounding the circumstances of his birth. However, far more depressing was the hatred she had seen in King's face. What made it all the more tragic was that she had seen how King had in the first couple of years of LaValle's life made a serious effort to make the boy his son, but theirs was doomed to be a star-crossed relationship. Something always went wrong and LaValle would end up running back to hide his face in her skirts. It was apparent even to her that LaValle lacked the toughness of Jacques; that, combined with the fact King detested weakness, condemned the older boy to perpetually face King's disgust. Perhaps King could have tolerated the older boy if LaValle had not taken an extreme dislike for his younger brother. Serena was mystified: how could she reason with a three-year-old and explain that for his own sake, he must leave his younger brother alone.

Serena blamed herself for LaValle's weakness. She felt guilty for attempting to abort him. His birth had been hard, for he was born nearly a month premature. His journey into the world nearly killed him and he was a sickly child for his first year and a half of life. He needed a great deal of attention and mothering, which Serena was happy to give. There was something about the vulnerable helplessness of the child that opened her heart like a key in a lock. They developed a special bond that did not include King and when Jacques was born, LaValle ranted and cried, jealous of the attention his brother was receiving. He could not understand why Jacques could suckle at her breast and he couldn't. He had begun to hate his younger brother.

It appeared her family was destined to be divided. Serena had begun to notice that Jacques was already drifting away from her. There was no defineable breach; the distance was manifested in little things. Whether he was hungry, sleepy, or had an injury, Jacques always went to his father first. She was only a last resort. And when she reprimanded LaValle regarding his jealous behavior, he would go whimpering to a corner and stay there until she went to get him. It broke her heart, for she loved her sons equally; one just needed more help than the other. She had spent many a night on her knees praying to God for guidance, but she received no direction.

She did realize one thing, that she no longer wanted to live in Bodie Wells. If LaValle could not have a life without being haunted by the town's small-minded gossips, she was ready to move. Serena figured that a big city provided the best opportunity for her sons. New York was out because Serena didn't want King to see his old friends who would remind him of Mamie, and she especially didn't want him to meet up with Mamie again. Thus, she considered San Francisco. It was the farthest you could get from New York and remain in continental America. Her major consideration was how she was going to persuade King to make such a move.

The day Sheriff Dalton came to town, Serena received a letter from her Aunt Ida telling her that her youngest sister, Tini, had gotten married. Most of the letter was about the wedding and how beautiful Tini had looked in her white wedding dress, but the last part of the letter was about her little brother, Amos, and the conflicts he was having with his father. It took Serena several readings before she finished the letter, because a blinding anger rose within her, blurring her aunt's looping scrawl. Serena's feelings about Charles Baddeaux were still raw and unresolved. What she felt bordered on hate. From the letter it appeared that her father had returned to his pompous, tyrannical approach in dealing with his children, and Serena read between the lines that her father was in part the reason for Tini's marriage as well.

It was the last two paragraphs that made Serena decide that she had to go and get her fifteen-year-old brother and rescue him from his father.

Rena, girl, you know I don't put a lot time in thinking bad thoughts, but after your father done horsewhipped Amos for going to see Sally Love one evening after he finished his chores, I was wishing evil would befall the man. Everybody know Amos been sweet on Sally for near two years and Amos is a good boy. He do his chores. He don't sass. He respectful and polite and knows more Bible than most boys his age. Wasn't no reason to beat the boy. Nobody in his right mind beat his own family with a whip. I tried to stop him, but your father was too filled with his own self-righteousness to listen. Now Amos done run off and is staying with Reverend Small and his family. He swear he ain't ever going back to the farm while his father is alive. Your father been to Reverend Small's twice to get him, but the reverend say no. The reverend is a good man, but his family can't feed an extra mouth. Even though Amos work hard to help around the Smalls' place, he can't carry his weight. If you could see your way to send the Smalls some money, it sure would help things.

As for me, now that Della and Tini is married and Amos is gone, I'm going back to my little lonely patch of land in Texas. I can't stay in this house no longer. I remember when there was laughter here, but your father's meanness done drove all the good feeling away. If you need me,

*I'll always be there for you. Just send a telegram to Taterville, Texas.
Everybody knows me there and I'll come to you,*

Your loving Aunt Ida

When Serena finally finished the letter, she exhaled slowly. It didn't seem fair that people like her father should live while others with good hearts and kindness like her mother should die.

King entered the sitting room and saw Serena's sad face and the letter in her hands. He sat down opposite her. "Bad news from home?"

"Charles, my father, beat my fifteen-year-old brother with a horse-whip."

"A horse whip? Sounds like we got to send for the boy," King observed. "You want me to go get him?"

Serena looked back at King and realized how lucky she was to have him as her partner. When it came to friends or family, he was always there: steady as a rock. There was no question of whether her brother was welcome in his mind. The only question was how the boy was going to get to Bodie Wells.

Ida Hoskins knocked on the door. "Deputy Witherspoon is in the store askin' for you, King. He say Marshal Boothe need to see you right away."

"Thanks, Ida," King said standing up. "He say what this is about?"

"No, sir, just that the marshal need to see you."

"Tell him I'll be right there," King said as he walked over to Serena. "You sure you alright?"

Serena grabbed his hand and held it to her cheek. Tears of gratitude rolled down her face. "I'm alright," she said. "You're a good man, King Tremain. You're a good man. Go on and find out what the marshal wants."

King nodded and went out the door. When he entered the marshal's office Mace Edwards, Deputy Cordel Witherspoon, and Octavius Boothe were waiting for him. "What's this all about?" King asked.

"I got a call from Skip Dalton, the new sheriff of Clairborne," Octavius said. "He say he got some news for me and the people of Bodie Wells. He say he gon' stop by here on his way from Atoka."

"That doesn't sound good," Mace commented. "Dalton has never had a fondness for colored folk. It's too bad his undersheriff, Larry Dogget, didn't run against him. Dogget is a levelheaded man who believes in fair play. We could deal with Dogget a whole lot better than Dalton."

"Yeah, well life ain't about who colored folk deal with better, is it?" King asked.

"What could Dalton want to talk about?" Cordell wondered out loud.

"You think maybe Big Daddy could've worked somethin' out with Oklahoma Pacific to build a depot in Clairborne after all?" Octavius asked. " 'Cause that decision to bypass Clairborne done doomed them and us into bein' just hick, backwater towns. Without a railroad stop closer'n thirty miles, ain't no way we gon' ever be real cities. All because of them damned embezzlers! I tell you one thing, I didn't feel no pity when them vigilantes broke into the jail and strung Hitchcock up!"

Mace disagreed. "Lynching is wrong no matter who does it or who gets lynched! It certainly isn't justice! It's just mob anger being taken out on some helpless fool who may or may not be guilty. We're lucky they couldn't find a colored man to blame it on!"

"You's right," Octavius affirmed. "It's just that without a railroad stop, it makes it even easier to steal water from us, 'cause we nobodies. We ain't even on most maps! That railroad depot would've at least put Clairborne on the map."

"I thought Big Daddy was at the capitol, tryin' to negotiate somethin' about water rights."

The door opened and Skip Dalton walked into the office, followed by one of his deputies. Dalton was a tall, lean man with cold, gray eyes. His flicked around the room. He turned to Octavius and said in a supercilious tone, "I thought I told you to have the town leaders here. Where are the pastors?"

Octavius smiled and said calmly, "All you told me was that you had some news to tell me. You didn't say nothin' else."

Dalton took off his hat and smacked Cordel on the head with it. "Go get the pastors, boy!"

"Stay seated, Cordel!" Mace said as he stood up. "I'm the mayor of Bodie Wells. Say what you have to say and I'll be sure that your information will get to everyone."

Dalton laughed and brushed back a lock of gray-streaked hair out of his eyes before he put his hat back on. "I was hopin' to see you!" he said with a sneer. "Yo' days of bein' an uppity nigger are over! Big Daddy ain't gon' protect you no mo'! It's gon' be a new day for you, nigger, and this whole nigger town! I ain't forgot that time we came in here with a couple boys just to investigate a crime. My nephew was missin' and you niggers had the gall to pull guns on us! We was the law and you gon' stand up to us like you is equal to us! Ain't a nigger within a hundred miles of Clairborne gon' do that and live while I'm sheriff!"

"Won't Mayor Bolton have something to say about that?" Mace asked.

"There ain't no mo' Mayor Bolton! He was shot and kilt outside of Oklahoma City two days ago!" Dalton waited for the significance of his words to settle in before he continued. "Truth be told, I was sorry at seein' him pass. He was a hard man, but a good man, and he was more'n fair with me. 'Course him and me always saw it different on the nigger question. And since he ain't no longer with us, his opinion don't count for much no mo'! Get what I mean?"

"You have something to say, say it," Mace said without emotion.

"The Klan is gon' be ridin' through here again! If I hear of one white man shot, I'm gon' come down on you like Stonewall Jackson on a line of bluecoats!"

Octavius was smiling even more broadly. "Ain't he one of the generals that lost the war?" Before someone could answer, he continued. "As marshal of an incorporated town I got the duty and responsibility to arrest and apprehend them that violate the laws of this town! Now, I ain't gon' be negligent to my duty and my responsibility! Ain't nobody comin' through this here town to ride roughshod over folks! Night riders beware! We gon' fight back!"

"You niggers been spoilt!" Dalton spat. "Ain't hardly nothin' worse than a spoilt nigger! Y'all don't know yo' place! You gon' have to learn the hard way!"

"I'm tired of this!" King said, standing up. He walked to the window and looked out. Then he turned and snarled, "If we got to learn, why don't you teach us somethin' now? I'd sho' like to know what you crackers can teach!"

The deputy came over to King to backhand him, but he wasn't ready for the quickness of King's reaction. King slammed a fist into the deputy's stomach, causing the man to lose his breath and tilt forward. King grabbed his opponent by his chin and the back of his head and twisted sharply. There was snap and the man fell forward, banging his head loudly on the wooden floor.

Mace called out, "King, what have you done?"

Dalton was aghast. "Nigger, you just killed a white man in front of me!" He reached to unholster his gun, but he stopped when he heard the hammer being pulled back on Octavius's service revolver just behind him.

King walked over and disarmed Dalton. He took his gun and checked him for a second gun or weapon. After he was sure that Dalton didn't have any other weapons, King said, "I really hate that word *nigger* and you used it a lot!"

"Nigger, I'll say nigger whenever I fe—"

King grabbed Dalton's throat in a tight grip with his thumb on Dalton's Adam's apple and squeezed sharply, then let go.

Dalton staggered backward wheezing and squeaking, grabbing at his throat.

"That's mo' like it," King said with a shake of his head. "You sound like the rat you is now!"

Mace shouted angrily, "Goddamn it, King! You've jeopardized the whole town! You've let your blood lust put us all in danger! What the hell are you thinking about, man? You're a goddamn fool!"

"I don't suffer to be called a fool but once," King said with an evil smile. "You just used up yo' one time. You want to come again?"

Mace was astounded. "You're threatening me? For what I said?"

"Ten times double, jackass rubber! You damn straight, I'm threatenin' you! A man's got to mind his tongue!"

"What about his actions?" Mace demanded. "Or doesn't that matter?"

"Maybe you ought to ask me what I'm doin' befo' you let yo' white blood talk!"

"Whoa! Whoa!" Octavius jumped up. "Is we gon' start fightin' 'mongst ourselves? Then the cracker wins no matter what happens!"

The blood had drained from Mace's face as he looked at King. "I'm not afraid of you and I won't be intimidated!"

"A man don't have to be scared to mind his tongue and be careful of what he say," King said easily.

"Let's get back to the problem we got in front of us!" Octavius demanded. "What is we gon' do now?"

"Dalton and his deputy either gon' disappear, or be found in a car wreck, don't really matter which," King answered. "Personally, I'd like to have him disappear, 'cause then I'd take him out to a place I know and find out everythin' he knows befo' I kill him!"

Dalton broke for the door, but King hit him on the side of the head, knocking him to the floor. He followed up his attack with a hard kick to the man's stomach. Dalton gurgled and wheezed on the floor.

"This white man wasn't plannin' on givin' us no chance!" King announced. "Is there somebody in this room who think he was jokin' when he say he gon' let the Klan ride on us?" There was no answer. King turned to Mace. "He was probably gon' kill you and 'Tavius first! Then he'd go down a list! What type of life you think folks in this town gon' have if he lives? We ain't got no choice. We got to take him out!" King turned to Mace. "Didn't you say we could deal with Dogget?"

"We could've negotiated with him," Mace declared. "We don't know who the next mayor was going to be! He could have been a man like Dogget!"

"Who here think that Dalton, as sheriff, wasn't gon' have his way!" King demanded. "Who think this man could be trusted if we negotiated with him?" King turned to Mace again. "You think you could trust this slime?"

"I'm not a killer. Killing isn't my first option! I don't let myself sink to the level of my enemies!" Mace replied.

"Them is pretty words," King said with a smile. "Let me tell you somethin' 'bout real life! Colored folks wouldn't own nothin' if they wasn't ready to fight to hold on to it! The Indian done showed us you got to be sneaky 'bout the way you fight! Can't be nothin' organized, or they'll wipe you out like they did the Indians that stood up to 'em. You got to use their own tricks against 'em! We ain't doin' nothin' that colored folks haven't been doin' since slavery. My grandpappy used talk about kidnappin' overseers and hidin' they bodies in the swamp! This here is the same thing!"

"That's just an excuse to cover your desire to spill blood!" Mace rejoined.

King guffawed. "I don't need no excuse to spill blood! I do it when it's necessary and it's necessary now! Let me ask 'Tavius and Cordel somethin'!" King turned to Octavius and Cordel. "Do you believe y'all could've had any type of life in this here town with this fool alive?" King nudged Dalton's leg with his foot.

"I ain't a killin' man," Octavius answered with a deep breath. "But my common sense tells me this man is better off dead. It be clear to me that he hates colored folk! I know this goes counter to what you's thinkin', Mace, but I got to agree with King. You can't negotiate nothin' with somebody who hate you! Dalton was gon' try to take us back to slavery times. A lot of colored folks was gon' get kilt befo' this was gon' be settled, if'en he lived to carry out his threats. And I believe he was gon' try to do what he said! We got to kill him!"

"No! No!" Dalton gasped from the floor. "Y'all niggers just stay out'n Clairborne less'n you got work there and things will be fine! I was just talkin' through my hat befo'. You ain't got to kill me!"

King kicked Dalton hard in the stomach. "Did I hear you say nigger again?" he asked as Dalton vomited on the floor. "I didn't hear yo' answer!" King growled.

"This is sickening!" Mace said, the disgust showing on his face. "The man is down! Let him be!"

"You'd rather it be a colored face that takes the beatin', ain't that right?" King prodded. "You want colored folks to die for what you believe, while you show what a big man you are negotiatin' meanin'less shit with the white man!"

"You insult me," Mace said in a soft voice. "And if I return the favor I risk death. It's really wonderful having you in charge!" Mace stood up. "You don't need me here! I'll leave now. I won't be a part of this!"

"That's too easy," King replied. "You want to believe him, take him with you! You're the mayor! Make yo' bigwig decision. Nurse him and let him go!"

"You sell me short," Mace answered. "I'm a better man than you make me out to be."

"That's too easy. Let's vote on what we gon' do with him first," King interjected.

Mace answered, "When you killed his deputy, you eliminated our ability to vote objectively. Our vote will be in direct reaction to the action you've already taken."

King nodded his head. "You right. I see that, but that don't change nothin'! I just forced the decision that was gon' have to be made. If we do 'em both here and now, ain't nothin' to link 'em with us and it's good riddance!"

Mace looked at King for a long time in silence. "I may have been wrong to think that we could negotiate with him, but in making that error I was seeking the higher ground. I was trying to let Jesus into my decision making. I am trying to be a Christian. It's hard work and I don't always succeed, but I want that philosophy to enter into every decision I make. I don't want to play God and dispense my own version of justice. I seek only to be a good man, a good strong Afro-American man. I know, rather I believe if we let him go now, it would spell the destruction of Bodie Wells. Still, I will not have a hand in killing him. I cannot, I will not let his barbarism make me less than I strive to be. Perhaps it's best that I take my leave now."

"The words you said are good," King admitted. "It ain't my thinkin', but I respect you for the stand you's takin' and I apologize for insultin' you. You's a good man. You think differently than me, but you's a man." King stuck out his hand. "What you said reminded me of a friend of mine, a man we used to call Professor. He was a good man too."

"I accept your apology," Mace said, shaking King's hand. "But I don't think we're traveling in the same direction because you will always have death around you and I want to nurture and encourage living and building."

King smiled. "Death is part of living. It be a cycle."

"But death is on the down side, living is on the up side," Mace countered, donning his hat. "Gentlemen, whatever decision you make, I'll be prepared to live with. Good day." Mace sidestepped Dalton, stepped over the deputy's body, and walked out the door. Cordel got up and locked the door after his departure.

"Let me take him off yo' hands and I'll take care that his body is never found," King suggested. "He'll disappear like Deputy Jessup, won't be a trace of him found."

"You did Jessup?" Octavius asked dumbfounded.

"Let's just say I helped him find his final restin' place," King answered with a smile. "What you say, boys?"

"What about his car?" Cordel asked.

"You disassemble it like you did Frank Bolton's car," King suggested.

"How you gon' get him out of here?" Octavius asked.

"Cordel, go get a rug from my store and we'll wrap him in it," King said with a smile. "But first, drive his car around back and leave it by my barn. Oh, and tell Sampson to come back with you."

Once Cordel left, Octavius said, "In a town this small, you got to watch yo'self, King. Word gets around. Then once it gets around here, it gets to Clairborne. After that, they come for you."

"Yo' words got the ring of truth," King agreed. "I'm thinkin' it's about time to pick up stakes anyway. Bodie Wells gon' have some serious problems to deal with now Big Daddy ain't protectin' it."

"You right about that!" Octavius replied. "The death of Big Daddy means the water is gone, probably soon as next year. We'll still have water pumping through the cistern, but not enough to irrigate everybody. It gon' be tough times ahead for Bodie Wells. Even with Dogget, we still gon' have problems with night riders and other such cowards. Shoot, in ten years this place may be just a ghost town."

"You gon' stick it out?" King asked.

"Ain't no place I want to go," Octavius said with resignation. "Ain't no place else I'd rather fight to stay either. I guess I'm an Oklahoma boy through and through. They gon' have to kill me to get my land. There's a lot colored folks buried in the ground all around here, folks that worked they heart out tillin' and plowin', folks that fought both Indian and white alike to keep this little piece of earth theirs. They blood is flowin' in me and I can't turn my back on 'em. My father was lynched outside of Clairborne and they left his charred body hangin' on a tree about a mile from town. Old Josh Morgan, Tobias Dorsett, and Lightnin' Smith took a wagon one night and cut him down. I was maybe four or five years old at the time, but I helped bury my father. Ain't no way I could leave this place."

"Well, I ain't got that attachment," King said as he stood up. "But I admire it, 'cause that's the kind of toughness that colored folks gon' need to make this country their own." King turned toward Dalton, who was sitting up, leaning against the wall. "Colored folk gon' be part of this here country despite you and yo' kind! Who knows, maybe someday there'll even be a colored president."

Dalton spat on the floor in response.

Cordel and Sampson entered through the back door of the office and

King turned to Dalton. "Yo' time has come and we gon' see what you's made out of! Let's tie him up and gag him, Sampson."

Dalton struggled, but he was easily overpowered. Within minutes he was gagged, rolled in the rug, and carried out to a waiting truck.

Octavius followed King and said, "I got to ask you a favor." King nodded in response and waited. "I takes marshalin' serious," Octavius said as he stuck a toothpick in his mouth. "I ain't never killed nobody, much less tortured 'em. I couldn't rest easy if I knew I delivered somebody over to be tortured. I's askin' you to make it quick for him. I know he wouldn't do the same for us, but I's askin' anyway."

"I'll do what I can," King said with a nod of his head and walked out of the marshal's office.

When King and Sampson returned to the store it was nearly nine o'clock in the evening. They closed and locked up the barn and the garage for the night. Then Sampson went in for dinner while King remained outside, sitting on the back steps of the store. He was lost in thought. After half an hour, Serena came out and joined him. She said nothing, but merely sat on the steps next to him.

There was a sliver of a moon rising in the eastern sky. To the north, the shadowy, looming presence of the Ouachitas reached high into the darkness. Strands of high, dark, gray clouds stretched across the dark blue expanse, pushed by atmospheric western winds. The bright firmament of the Milky Way was only sporadically shrouded by the passing clouds and its distant galaxies seemed to beckon all who could look heavenward and dream.

"What are you thinking about?" Serena asked.

"I'm thinkin' that our time in this here town's comin' to an end," King said chewing on a stalk of rye. "It's gon' change now that Big Daddy Bolton's done been killed."

"He's been killed?" Serena asked with surprise.

"Yep, shot and killed outside the state capitol. You got to figure this fight over water is big business. If they can kill somebody like Big Daddy, who was a big-time politician in this area for years, these people is gon' get what they want and they ain't gon' let no colored town stand in their way. They ain't just divertin' water, they buildin' a canal so's they can barge the wheat they gon' grow here to the nearest railroad depot. They been plannin' this for years. They got politicians lined up, and them that ain't is gettin' snuffed. Bodie Wells is gon' be in for hard times. After harvesttime this year, there's gon' be a Klan meetin' in Clairborne."

"How did you find out all this?" Serena asked.

"Sheriff Dalton told me this befo' he fell down an old mine shaft," King answered.

"You killed him?"

"I had to. He was gon' let the Klan ride on us and said he wasn't gon' let no uppity niggers live within a hundred miles of Clairborne. He was the first line of the comin' storm. He got his marchin' orders after Big Daddy was killed and he came to Bodie Wells to make sho' we knew our place!"

"Aren't you afraid he'll be found and you'll get caught?" Serena asked, alarm in her voice.

"They ain't gon' find him or his deputy, but if they find them they ain't gon' recognize 'em. I dropped a grenade down with 'em. But I am gettin' concerned that maybe we done lived all we can here. Maybe it's time to move on."

Serena's heart was suddenly in her mouth. She was unable to speak. King had mentioned the possibility of leaving Bodie Wells. He had raised the issue himself, something she had been reluctant to do. She didn't want to reveal to him that her principal reason for wanting to move was for LaValle's benefit, to protect him from gossip. She sat silently, praying that King would be motivated to move on his own terms.

"If we stay here," King continued, "we gon' end up fightin' for our business and our lives, and right now it don't look like we can win. So, I'm thinkin' that unless you's determined to stay here, we ought to be settin' sights on somewhere else."

"I want to go to San Francisco!" Serena blurted out and immediately fell silent. She was afraid that she would not be able to control her tongue. Even though it was on her mind consistently for nearly two years, she had been afraid of broaching the subject of relocating. It had been her decision to buy the store and stay in Bodie Wells. If she had brought up the subject of leaving all that they had built up in the last six years King would have wanted to know why, and he would not have been sympathetic once he learned the reason for her request.

"You ready for the big city now, huh?" King asked with a slow smile. "How come you picked San Francisco? New York is where the colored folks is happenin'. Don't you want to go there?"

"I just want to see the Pacific Ocean and I've heard there is a large colored community in Oakland, which is very close to San Francisco. I want to start some place where it's new for both of us."

"Alright, San Francisco it is! I want to be out of here by July," King declared.

"What about our business?" Serena asked.

"Ain't but three thousand dollars tied up in this whole shebang. Ain't nothin' we can't walk away from. Shoot, we could let Ida and her husband run the store and leave the barn and livery stable to Lightnin'. When they get some extra money, they can send us some payment."

"I have to go get Amos, first," Serena announced. "It would be a good opportunity to take the boys down to Louisiana and show them off to my sisters."

"You can take LaValle," King said easily. "But Jacques will go with me out to the West Coast where we'll look for suitable housing so's we'll have a place to stay when you arrive."

The joy that Serena was feeling was dampened, but not extinguished. She did not argue. She knew that King wouldn't concede his position on this matter, but there were other issues to be resolved. She put her hand on his arm. "I need you to promise me something. I need you to promise that you'll never tell LaValle that you're not his father."

King stared at her for a long minute. "Then give him to me for a while and stop protecting him and lettin' him hide behind yo' skirts, 'cause that's the only way I can make him my son."

Serena shook her head. "You're too hard on him! He's not tough like Jacques. He needs a softer hand."

"You ain't preparin' him to be a man! You think this white world gon' treat him with a soft hand? A colored man got to be strong, 'cause if he ain't all this hate out here will make him turn it on himself. You got to give him to me! Don't let him come runnin' to you!"

Serena shook her head again. "I can't do that," she said softly.

King stood up and stretched, then stepped off the steps. "Well, that's that!" he said with finality.

Serena grabbed King's hand and held it in both of hers. "Please, King, I'm begging you! As a personal favor to me! I'm begging you please don't ever tell him you're not his father!"

King looked down into her eyes and said, "I promise, but life will show him somethin' different. Life won't lie! He gon' be on the outside because of what he does and the choices he makes."

Later that night Serena sat by the stove darning socks. In the fire's warm glow she wanted to enjoy what had been accomplished. The biggest hurdle had been passed: they were leaving Bodie Wells. There would be time and space to deal with other matters. The important thing was that everyone, but especially LaValle, was getting a fresh start. Unlike Jacques, he was an unpopular child both with other children and adults. People thought he was a spoiled mama's boy and in a small town that was the kiss of death. It was only due to the fact that King Tremain was his father that he was not the object of overt scorn.

Two weeks passed and the day before Serena was scheduled to leave for

New Orleans, the telephone rang in the store. It was the lawyer's office in New York, calling for King. Serena answered the phone and sent Ida to get King. She was still packing. Serena did not hear very much of King's conversation except when she went down to the store to get a few items for the trip. While rummaging through the shelves, looking for gifts for her sisters, she overheard King's side of the exchange.

"No, I don't put no store in buyin' paper, so I ain't much interested in buyin' no stocks. You's tellin' me that all I gon' have to show for the money I's invested is some paper, right? I done seen what buyin' paper done to our bank here in Bodie Wells. I'd rather gamble it away than just give it away like that. If you feels we got to invest in somethin', buy land! At least they ain't gon' make no more of that! Hell, they print mo' paper all the time."

King listened for a time. "Did the bank receive that last shipment of cash I sent from Atoka? Good! That lawyer you hired down there is workin' out fine. He goes with me to the bank to make sho' there ain't no shenanigans with my money. Okay, you gon' set up an account for me out in Frisco? Good. Oh, another thing. I needs to know is the account in New Orleans still open. I needs to get my wife on it, in case she need money while she's there. So, she got to see the same lawyer I used befo'; that'll work. How she gon' identify herself? Yeah, yeah, that's good; she can use Jacques's birthday.

"Alright, Ira, I'll probably talk to you when I get to Frisco next month. The best to yo' family. No, no; ain't no way I'm gon' change my mind 'bout buyin' stocks. Maybe in a couple of years after we get situated out on the West Coast. Talk to ya'."

King hung up the phone and turned to Serena. "You's set up for the trip home. Red'll pick you up when you get off the ferry and he'll take you to the Hotel Toussant. I had two hundred dollars sent to Reverend Small, along with the date you's arrivin'. He'll be expectin' you."

Serena finished packing and her heart was racing with expectation. Her dreams of leaving Louisiana and going to a big city were finally being realized. And she was ready for it. She had come to Bodie Wells as a country girl, and after seven years she was leaving as a woman. She had learned how to comport herself, speak properly, and run a business. She was ready for the challenges and pressures of living in a metropolitan area.

Serena got down on her knees and prayed. She was thankful and grateful to God for the blessings she had received and much of her prayer was directed to the acknowledgment of her good fortune, but she also prayed for an end to the enmity between her sons and that LaValle would find his place in their new home.

Serena arose from her prayer, walked to the window, and looked out. There were several cars parked in front of Wrangel House and there were a number of pedestrians on their way to the various businesses that lined Main Street. Several children between the ages of five and twelve played tag on the wooden walkway between Wrangel House and the beauty parlor. If all went as planned, this was the last time Serena would see Bodie Wells in the late afternoon. Both Serena and King would depart without fanfare. Only a few people knew that they were leaving. King had insisted upon secrecy. It was his opinion that the less people knew, the better.

THURSDAY, MAY 19, 1927

Amos Baddeaux was standing out front on the steps of a three-room, tar-paper shack when Reverend Small reined his one-horse gig into the front yard. Amos immediately went to assist with the horse as Reverend Small climbed down.

Reverend John Small was a plump, brown-skinned man with close-cropped kinky hair and thick, mobile eyebrows that made his face extremely expressive when he chose to. He walked around the front of the horse and placed his hand on Amos's shoulder. "Don't worry about un-hookin' Old Beauregard, just water him. We gon' need him to go into Nellum's Crossing after I had a bit of a rest."

"Did my father give you any of my clothes?" Amos asked.

"No, son, he didn't," the reverend answered sadly. "He wouldn't let me have nothin'."

"Why? What did he say?"

Reverend Small wiped his perspiring brow and replied with a shake of his head. "Amos, you don't want to know. It 'pears yo' father got a lot a growin' to do befo' he get through the pearly gates. Matter fact, I got some growin' to do too 'cause he got me mad as a stuck pig. I got to get down on my knees and remember 'bout humility."

Fifteen-year-old Amos couldn't let it go. "But Reverend Small, he wouldn't let you have the banjo or the boots I bought with my own money? I worked hard for that banjo!"

"You best forget about them, son," Reverend Small suggested. "We'll go into the general store at Nellum's Crossing and we'll buy you some new clothes and boots with the money yo' sister done sent."

"That ain't right, Reverend," Amos argued. "She sent that money to you for the food and board you been givin' me these last few months. That money was sent to repay you for yo' kindness to me."

"Listen, Amos," Reverend Small said. "It's been a blessin' to me and my family to have a good, God-fearin', hardworkin' young feller like you around. You helped me fix the roof. You helped put the barn door back on and you built me a chicken coop with nothin' but wood leavin's. You does chores every day. You done pulled yo' share, boy. I couldn't spend none of this here money on my family if'en I didn't take steps to make sho' you was ready to travel with yo' sister first. Anyways, she sent mo'n enough money to take care of what little we done put out for you. I expects to return some of this money to her. Now, put a smile on yo' face, boy, 'cause we's all blessed and yo' sister's comin' tomorrow."

"You's right, suh, but gosh, I worked a whole summer's evenin's at the general store to buy that banjo. It just ain't right that he should keep it. He knows how much that banjo means to me."

"Son, you got to let go and let Jesus," Reverend Small said as he climbed the steps of the shack.

"You's right, suh," Amos said as he led Beauregard around to the water trough under the shade of a large magnolia.

It was warm and muggy when Reverend Small and Amos rode into New Orleans the next day. The sun made sporadic appearances between thick, gray clouds laden with moisture, and the wind coming off the gulf brought the warm smells of the bayou and salt water. Automobiles, motoring to and fro, clanked and clattered past the slow but steady gait of old Beauregard, who clip-clopped along, impervious to the loud mechanical noises of the passing cars and trucks.

Amos was wearing a stiff pair of new overalls over a starched white shirt, and his new boots felt unforgiving on his feet. He felt a nervous excitement that manifested itself through a queasiness in his stomach and a dull sense of fear. He did not know what to expect. He hadn't seen his older sister for nearly seven years. Generally, his memories of her were faded and unclear, but what he did remember was her smile. All he could do was hope that she had not changed too much.

When the gig stopped in front of the Hotel Toussant, Amos was awestruck. He had never been to a hotel before, nor ever been in a building that looked so ornate and regal. A colored man in a red hat and a red jacket with gold buttons came out of the hotel and asked in a snide manner what they were doing blocking the hotel's entrance. Reverend Small replied that they had come to see Mrs. Serena Tremain, and the man in the red jacket's demeanor changed suddenly to one of cooperation. He asked the reverend to pull the gig behind the hotel and he would assist with any unloading of baggage. Amos was impressed that the mention of his sister's name should have such an effect on the man.

After tying Beauregard to a railing behind the hotel, they were ushered into a lushly carpeted room that was furnished with overstuffed chairs and carved wooden tables and told to wait. There was an immense cut-glass chandelier hanging in the center of the room, and polished brass lamps sat on many different tables. Amos felt as if he was in a palace like the ones he read about in his schoolbooks.

A woman dressed in an expensive, shiny dress called out, "Amos! Amos!" as she swept into the room.

Amos was startled and for a moment didn't recognize his sister. "Serena?" he asked questioningly.

"Who else fixed you grits and bacon for breakfast? Who made the best and lightest biscuits you ever ate?" she said with a smile and came up and hugged him tightly.

"Gosh," was all that Amos could muster. It was hard for him to believe that this regal woman was his sister.

"My, what a handsome young man you've turned out to be!" she declared as she held him at arm's length so that she could see him. Then she turned to the reverend and said, "You must be Reverend Small." She held out a gloved hand.

"At yo' service, ma'am," the reverend replied as he shook her hand.

"I can't tell you how grateful my family is for the generosity you've shown my little brother. Obviously, you're a man of God who applies those principles to his own life."

Reverend Small nodded his head in a small bow. "That be a big compliment, ma'am. I don't rightly knows I can live up to it, but I'm gon' try."

"I don't know you, but I feel that you are already firmly on the right path, Reverend Small, if only for what you've done for my brother."

"T'weren't nothin', ma'am," Reverend Small said, clapping Amos on the shoulder. "My family was right pleased to have him stay with us."

"Reverend, will you stay and lunch with us?" Serena asked.

"No, thankee kindly," the reverend answered. "Whilest I's in town, there's some chores I got to take care of for my church. We's thinkin' maybe we's ready for a piano to back up our choir. I thought I'd take some time and look about for somethin' we can afford. But first, I would like to return some of the money you was kind enough to send. It was way too much. Didn't need near that amount." Reverend Small extended an envelope to Serena.

"I can't accept it," Serena said with a shake of her head. "That money is yours to do with as you see fit. In fact, I was going to give you a couple hundred dollars more." She produced her own envelope.

"In good faith, I can't accept that," the reverend answered. "Amos here worked hard around my place. He's a good boy. He pull his own weight. If'en we wasn't poor folk, I wouldn't accept no money. It was a blessin' to have him stay with us. It wouldn't be right to take yo' money."

"Then let me donate it to your church. Let it help you find the right piano and maybe have some money left over to help some of the less fortunate members of your church with clothing and food." Serena stuffed the envelope into Reverend Small's hand. "Please accept this. We can afford it."

Reverend Small grasped Serena's hand. "Sometime you do somethin' you think is right. You don't know the cost or the reward, but you do it anyway and then heaven open up and pour its largesse on you. There'll be many a family that'll be clothed and eatin' who might've had to do without, but for you. Our folk will say many a prayer in yo' name. Thank you for yo' generous gift!"

"It is I who feel blessed, Reverend," Serena answered.

"I must take my leave take now," Reverend Small said. "Amos, will you step out with me? I want to show you somethin'."

"Course, suh." Amos walked with the reverend to where the bellhop had left Amos's bundles of belongings.

The reverend stooped down and unwrapped a long narrow bundle and exposed an old but still highly polished banjo. Amos's jaw dropped wide open. "Used to belong to my pappy," Reverend Small explained. "It been hangin' over the fireplace all these years since he passed. The missus and me wanted to find a way to repay you for yo' hard work and good spirit. We stayed up last night and cleaned it up for you. I wants you to have it, to make music with it, to put some joy in people's hearts, to make folks tap they feets."

Amos's eyes filled with tears. He was without words.

The reverend stepped forward and hugged him. "Just remember what I told you, boy. Let go and let Jesus." He turned and walked swiftly toward the exit.

As far as Amos was concerned lunch was like something out of a dream. He had never eaten in a restaurant before, much less a high-class place like the Hotel Toussant. He was awed by his surroundings as well by the fact that his sister had become such a lady. She had the bearing of someone who was used to being served and seemed to direct the efforts of the hotel staff with a flawless gentility. Then on top of everything else, the food was fantastic. Amos had two servings of the corn griddle cakes as well as a thick center cut steak and two big glasses of milk. When he got up from the table, he could barely stand, for he had eaten without holding back, as he would not have done had he been eating at Reverend Small's table.

On the way upstairs, Serena informed him that they would remain at the hotel until the following Tuesday, when they were scheduled to catch a train west through Texas to California.

"Hey, I'm an uncle now!" Amos declared. "Where are my nephews?"

"Only the oldest came with me and he caught a bit of a cough on the trip down here. He's sleeping now, but later on this evening you'll have a chance to meet him." Serena escorted Amos to his room and he was amazed anew at its luxury and fine furnishings. "We'll go through your clothes tomorrow and see what you need to travel to San Francisco. Why don't you take the afternoon to rest and we'll go out to dinner tonight. I'm in the adjoining suite. If you need anything, just knock." Serena kissed him on the cheek and went through the connecting door.

Amos sat down on the bed and admired it softness. It had a real mattress, not just straw filler, and it had real cotton sheets as well as blankets. Amos laid back on the bed but was afraid to close his eyes because he thought he might be dreaming, and he feared that he would suddenly awake to his father's shouts and kicks. There was no reason to be afraid. His excitement was too great for an afternoon nap. He got up and went over to his new banjo and unwrapped it. The Smalls had put new strings on it and it needed tuning. He spent the next several hours acquainting himself with his new instrument.

Amos wasn't sure when he became aware that the door between the two suites was open, but he looked up and saw a five-year-old boy staring at him from the doorway. The boy had light beige skin and curly light brown hair. Amos smiled and beckoned for the boy to come over, but the child ignored his gesture and remained in the doorway. Amos got up and started toward his little visitor, but the boy disappeared with a wail into the other suite. Amos, confused, sat back down with his banjo and played a little blues tune.

Serena came to the door with the boy in tow. "This is your nephew LaValle," she said as she brought him into the room. "We heard the lovely music you've been playing and LaValle wanted to find out who was playing it. I hope we're not interrupting."

"No, ma'am," Amos answered with a smile. "I was just playin' around." He knelt down to get a better look at LaValle, who was hiding behind his mother's skirts. "He named LaValle after Mama's father?"

"Yes, but I call him Val," Serena answered with a mother's smile. "He's one of my little darlings. Val, come on and meet your Uncle Amos." She tried to tug him forward, but LaValle resisted by hugging her leg.

"I can see he's a tetch shy," Amos said with a laugh. "I'm sho' with a little time, he and me gon' be fine. Ain't that right, Val?"

LaValle did not look at Amos, but pointed to the banjo and said, "I want! I want!" Amos laughed. "Don't blame you a bit, Val. It sho' is a pretty instrument ain't it? Got a sweet tone too. You can probably get one like it if'en you shows interest, but this one here is mines. It be a gift to me from some special people. Don't mind showin' it to you though. Come on, feel that wood and the stretched skin on its face."

LaValle looked up at his mother and she smiled encouragingly. LaValle came out from behind his mother and grabbed a hold of the banjo and tried to yank it out of Amos's hands.

"Hey, not so rough!" Amos cautioned.

LaValle tried to shift his grip to the strings so that he would have a better purchase on the instrument, but Amos grabbed his hand. Immediately, LaValle tried to bite the hand that held him.

Amos stood up and held the banjo out of reach. LaValle began to bawl loudly. "What's wrong with him?" Amos asked, confused by the child's reaction.

"Maybe you ought to be gentler and more understanding," Serena suggested. "All he wanted to do was look at the banjo."

"This ain't no toy, Rena! Didn't you see the way he grabbed at it? He was gon' break it!"

"So?" Serena challenged. "I'll buy you another one!"

"This be a special gift to me, Rena! I don't want no new one! Ain't I got a right to keep somethin' special what's been give to me? The family who gave this to me did things for me that ain't been done for me since Mama died. This here banjo is special to me and I wants to keep it!"

LaValle now started to cough raucously even as he continued to wail.

Serena heard the logic of his argument. She nodded reluctantly. "Of course you have a right to keep something that's meaningful to you. LaValle is probably still feeling the effects of this fever he's caught. After a good night's sleep, it'll probably be all forgotten by tomorrow."

Dinner that night was taken at the hotel because of Serena's concerns regarding LaValle. A doctor was called in, but he could not prescribe anything but a sleeping potion since in his estimation LaValle was suffering from a common cold, which he would recover from within a few days. The next day, in accordance with the doctor's direction, LaValle was given another sleeping potion. Serena hired one of the hotel staff to watch over her son who was sleeping soundly and took her brother out to shop for new clothes.

Amos and Serena were standing on the front steps of the Hotel Toussant at ten in the hot and muggy morning air. There was not a cloud in the sky and the unobstructed rising sun was already beginning to steam the moisture-laden earth. The doorman tipped his red hat and said, "It gon' be extry hot today, ma'am." A large, late-model black sedan pulled up in front of the Hotel Toussant and Journer Duryea and Dirty Red got out of the vehicle. Serena and Journer greeted each other warmly and Dirty Red gave Serena a brotherly hug. When Amos was introduced, both Journer and Red were effusive and complimentary of him.

The day passed like a whirlwind for Amos. He had never ridden in such a late-model car. He had never seen the side of New Orleans that was revealed to him that day. He saw debonair colored people wearing the latest fashions; colored people who owned and operated high-priced shops that even catered to white people. He went to a restaurant run by Journer's family where the food was hot and spicy. Shrimp was a delicacy that he had only a few times in his life, and for the first time he was able to eat his fill. The day seemed like a page out of a fairy tale: rich sister swoops down and rescues brother from poverty and a cruel father. It was hard for Amos to believe that his sister had spent nearly fifty dollars at various stores on his new clothes and shoes. He was on the edge of suffering sensory overload. Fifty dollars was an astounding amount of money. The most expensive shopping that had ever been done on his behalf was the previous summer when he needed a winter jacket, overalls, and boots, and the bill came to just over five dollars at the general store. But on this day his sister had taken him to stores that sold only clothing. Secretly, he wondered how such enterprises could stay in business; they didn't sell farm tools, ammunition, or feed—all they had was clothing. It didn't seem possible that a clothing store could be a viable business, but the city appeared to be filled with such mysteries.

It was nearly three-thirty in the afternoon when they returned from the shopping spree. Amos was floating on a cloud. He could not believe his incredible good fortune. Serena directed two of the bellhops to assist him in carrying his new clothes to his room. When Amos unlocked his door he was surprised by what he saw. His room was a mess. The covers had been pulled off the bed. The bundles he had brought with him from the Smalls had been torn open and items were flung around the room. Then he heard the strings of his banjo being struck repeatedly with some kind of object and he saw LaValle in the closet bending over and whacking the skin of the banjo with a shoe. Amos shouted, "Hey!" and rushed to rescue his instrument.

LaValle saw him and an expression of pure fright covered his face. He took off, running for the door and bawling at the top of his lungs. His mother, hearing his screams, knocked open the door adjoining the rooms as she rushed to come to the assistance of her child. LaValle ran right into door as it swung open and it cracked against his head. With a real injury he began to caterwaul even more loudly as he fell to the floor. Serena was instantly by his side. She examined his head for injuries while LaValle gave vent to his sorrows at full blast. LaValle raised his arms to be picked up and she picked up the big five-year-old and hefted him in her arms.

"What did you do to him?" Serena demanded.

"Do to him?" Amos questioned. "I didn't do nothin' to him! He set off screaming when he saw me come in and ran right into the door you came through."

Serena challenged. "Don't lie! He wouldn't start screaming like that for nothing. What did you do?"

Amos looked at the two bellhops and shrugged his shoulders. The shorter of the two nodded his head confirming Amos's statement. "He right, ma'am. He didn't do nothin' to the child at all."

"What started it then?" Serena demanded.

"Look at what he did to my room!" Amos said angrily. "He just tore through my stuff. He broke a string on my banjo by banging on it with a shoe! What's wrong with him?" The two bellhops made a discreet exit before Serena responded.

Serena saw a look flash cross Amos's face as he stared at LaValle and it reminded her of the way King sometimes looked at LaValle. It was a look that combined distaste and revulsion. Suddenly she was angry. "There's nothing wrong with him! How dare you say that? I wonder at what's wrong with you, scaring a little boy like that!"

"Nobody scared him! He's just a little sneak who was scared of gettin' caught is all! He messed up my room! Went through my stuff. He broke my banjo, then ran like a crybaby for you! Ain't ever seen a child spoilt like him!"

Serena was livid. "How dare you! How dare you call him names after all I've done for you?"

"All you've done for me?" Amos asked, his anger rising as well. " 'Cause you done bought me some clothes? If that don't beat all! I'm s'posed to let that little sneak run through my things 'cause you done bought me clothes! Maybe this ain't for me, Rena. I had mo' respect and mo' privacy in Reverend Small's three-room house than I got here!"

"Maybe that's where you belong," Serena agreed.

"Fine, I got the clothes I came in," Amos said. "I'll pack my stuff now and don't worry. I ain't takin' nothin' you bought."

LaValle was squirming to get down. Serena finally set him down on the floor. Her head was throbbing with pain. Things were not going right. She wanted to say something to Amos to make him change his mind, but the words eluded her. She was distracted by LaValle tugging on her skirt. "What?" she asked as she turned to him.

He pointed to the banjo on the floor and said, "Mine? Mine?"

"Sho' give it to him to break up!" Amos said sourly. "Take it as payment for all you done for me! It don't matter what nobody else's feelin's is! I'd rather go back and live with Daddy than go with you!"

Sensing victory, LaValle yanked on her skirt more forcefully. "Mine? Mine?" He continued to point at the banjo.

Her frustration mounting, Serena pivoted without thinking and smacked LaValle's hand smartly. "No, it is not yours! That banjo belongs to Amos! Now you get out of Amos's room!" LaValle stumbled backward in shock. She followed him and smacked his hand again. LaValle toddled through the door bawling louder than ever. Serena turned back to Amos, who was kneeling on the floor quietly gathering his belongings into bundles. "Stop! Stop! This isn't what I wanted and it isn't what I came here for! I came to get you and have you live with us! That's what King and I both want!"

Amos looked up and there was anger and disappointment on his face when he replied, "Yeah, but what we want ain't real! I knew from the get this was too good to be true. I kept tellin' myself I was gon' wake up, that it all was a dream. And dog-gone, if I ain't awake now!"

"This is no dream what I'm offering," Serena protested. "Come with me to San Francisco! I'll put you in the best schools. You'll have a future far away from the hard work and poverty of farming! All this was just a misunderstanding! LaValle's just a little boy! He can't harm you!"

"But you can," Amos answered. "And you ridin' shotgun for him all the time, don't take no genius to see that! You embarrassed me in front of them mens who helped me bring up them clothes you bought, accusin' me of lyin'! I done promised myself when I left Daddy's farm, I weren't gon' put up with no mo' stuff! It be too hard a row for me to hoe. It be better all around if'en I stay here. I done learned one thing from the Smalls: hard work ain't bad if'en the folk you live with is good to you. I done mo' laughin' with them than I have since Mama died and I busted my butt every day to pull my weight."

An image flashed across Serena's consciousness of her arriving in San Francisco without Amos and having to explain to King that he didn't come because of LaValle. Tears started running down her cheeks. "Please, Amos! Please, don't do this! It'll never happen again, I swear to God!"

With a vision that seemed beyond his years Amos said, "What we want ain't real, Rena! Like what Daddy want ain't real. He want me to stand shoulder to shoulder with him in church singin' hymns on Sunday and he want to beat me for no good reason on Monday with a horsewhip and then expect me to be back in church with him the followin' Sunday. It just ain't real." Amos stood up and said, "I's ready to go now, Rena. Do I got to walk back or can I get a ride?"

"Amos, I'm begging you to wait until tomorrow morning," Serena pleaded. "If you still want to go then, I'll have you driven back to Reverend Small's farm. Please do this for me."

"Okay, Rena, if that's what you want, but I don't see what's gon' change by tomorrow."

"Thank you. Thank you, Amos," Serena rushed forward and hugged her brother. "I'm so sorry, Amos. Please forgive me!"

The sincerity of his sister's words and the pain in her voice caused Amos to break down and put his arms around her. She sobbed on his shoulders and Amos, feeling awkward, patted her on her back as he had seen mothers do to crying children. "It gon' be alright, Sis," he said encouragingly.

From the adjoining suite came the sound of LaValle's heavy coughing. Serena pushed back from Amos. "You've always been such a help to me. You're the best brother I could have. I love you and I promise to treat you right." She turned and walked through the connecting door. Shortly thereafter, the door closed and Amos was left with his own thoughts.

It was a difficult night for Serena. LaValle had a fever and his coughing had grown more frantic and grating. Several times during the night, she sent down for hot tea and cold compresses. Around one in the morning there was a soft knock on her door. She was tired and irritated. LaValle had finally fallen into a fitful and restless sleep. Wearily, she got up and answered the door. In the hallway stood one of the maids on the hotel staff along with another woman. The second woman wore a bright yellow bandana tied around her head and had numerous gold bangles hanging from her ears. She was brown skinned and had deep-set, penetrating black eyes.

"This here is Sister Bornais," introduced the maid. "She got potions and poultices and herbs that can cure yo' boy. I thought maybe you might want to let her see yo chile."

Even as a child, Serena had heard of Sister Bornais. Serena's mother had often called on her to assist with difficult childbirths. Serena stepped back and opened the door wide. She was not going stand in the way of anyone who could help her son.

Sister Bornais gestured to the maid. "You best come on in with me, Mattie. I maybe gon' need yo' help!"

Serena led the two women to LaValle's bed. Sister Bornais knelt down by the boy's sleeping form and sniffed the air above him. Then she placed a hand on his sweating forehead and within minutes his fitfulness stopped and he sank into a deep sleep. Serena watched from an overstuffed chair. Her mother had once told her that Sister Bornais was no run-of-the-mill voodoo woman. She had special powers. Watching Sister Bornais at work, Serena believed what she had been told. Her son was sleeping deeply for the first time in days.

Sister Bornais sent Mattie down to brew some tea with some herbs that she gave her. After the maid left, Sister Bornais took out a mortar and pestle and began grinding up small batches of herbs and other materials. She wrapped each batch up in cheesecloth and tied it in a tight little packet. Mattie returned with a mug of hot tea. Sister Bornais dropped one of the packets she had prepared into the mug and waited for it to cool. Once it was cool enough, she awakened LaValle, who started to whimper, but Sister Bornais quieted him with a gentle caress and guided the cup to his lips. He gulped down the potion as if he possessed an unremitting thirst. He was asleep and snoring before she laid him back down on his bed.

Sister Bornais turned to Serena and said, "This chile's just got a tetch of the ague. He'll be over it by tomorrow eve."

"Thank God!" Serena said gratefully.

"The ague ain't really his problem," Sister Bornais continued. "It's just the way the real problem show itself. This here boy is troubled, troubled by spirits, and I can't get no clear picture from him. Let me hold yo' hand."

Serena got up and went over to Sister Bornais. She extended her hand. Sister Bornais took it in her leathery grip for a few minutes and then jerked as if she had been shocked.

"You King Tremain's woman!" Sister Bornais stated.

Serena looked at Mattie before she answered. "Yes, I'm married to King Tremain."

"She didn't tell me nothin', girl! I knows all about you! Yo' mama was Rebecca Baddeaux. I see it all in yo' hand!" She turned to the maid and said, "You can go now, Mattie. You been a big help." After the maid left, Sister Bornais turned back to Serena and said, "You's King's wife, but this ain't his son. I see from yo' hand that King got two sons, but this chile here sho' ain't one of them."

"I don't know what you're talking about!" Fear gripped Serena's throat. Would LaValle ever escape the nature of his birth? She declared indignantly, "You must be listening to idle gossip!"

"The sign don't lie," Sister Bornais said with a frown. "I see three boys, two related through their father and two related through their mother. The sign say that you and King only had one chile together."

Serena was having difficulty breathing. She didn't want to talk anymore. "I don't see that my children are any business of yours! Perhaps it's time you leave!"

"Perhaps," Sister Bornais mused, not making any effort to move. "What I don't see is why you's actin' so hincty about this. It be clear to me that you knows what I'm talkin' about. I just can't see why you's denyin' it! Let me see yo' hand again."

Serena pulled back. "I don't think that's necessary. You've told me all I need to know."

Sister Bornais sucked her teeth and then said in an angry tone, "If that was so, I'd have got up and left. There's plenty people who'd pay good money for what I's tellin' you for free. But I owe it to King Tremain to try to right the wrong I see hangin' over his boys' heads. I didn't ask for this, it come to me. I just see things, kinda 'round the corner; sometime it be days, sometime it be years; sometime it's a vision, sometime it's a feelin and sometime I just know, like I been there and witnessed it. And with you, I is witnessing. I is tellin' the buck-naked truth! There ain't no mistake!"

"Please sell your powers somewhere else," Serena said, standing up. "I'm really tired. I haven't slept in—"

"Sit down and shut up, girl, 'less'n you wants me to leave a curse on yo' head!"

Aghast, Serena sat down.

"What I see is this. If'en you want to help this here chile, you got to help his older brother. The problem with this here chile is there is a spirit that be hangin' over him like a dark cloud. Only way to get rid of that spirit is to do right by the oldest. I's beginnin' to see it now. You got the power to change it all for the better, but for some reason you won't." Sister Bornais took Serena's hand and studied it carefully.

"But I got a clear vision of what's gon' happen if'en you don't do right. This chile gon' be a mama's boy all his life, which ain't gon' be that long really, and mo' than that, he gon' be the cause of the death of his youngest brother. You don't follow what I say, you gon' be left with no sons at all! King's oldest boy gon' be alright no matter what you do, he just won't ever know his daddy. If'en you keeps to the path you's travelin', you ain't gon' have no chil'ren and the only decent grandchile you gon' have is gon' hate you. You done messed with a powerful and vengeful spirit! You done stuck yo' finger in destiny's business and 'less'n you right it, you's got an unhappy life ahead! If you don't take care of it right, I see it spreadin' to yo' family members, to yo' sisters and yo' brother, stopping yo' kin's seed from flourishing, makin' you the only chile from yo' family that bears chil'ren. You best take heed and pay the price to make that spirit move on! I can't say it no clearer and what will be will be."

The color had drained from Serena's face. She sat as if she had been turned to stone. Her eyes were sightless as she stared out into an invisible distance. She made no motion as Sister Bornais got slowly to her feet. Serena remained frozen in her position. Only Sister Bornais saw the connecting door to the adjoining room close quietly, but she said nothing as she gathered her belongings and left the room.

Amos had been ready to sneak out and make his own way back to the Smalls' ranch when he opened his door and saw Sister Bornais with one of the maids standing in the hall at Serena's door. The mention of Sister Bornais's name had him filled with curiosity. She was a legend throughout the parish as an expert in voodoo and black magic. People traveled hundreds of miles to buy her gris-gris. He couldn't leave without hearing at least one of her spells. He had cracked the door as quietly as he could and listened intently. He heard everything and it stunned him. After closing the door, Amos went and sat on the edge of his bed.

What did it mean, " '. . . if Serena didn't do right by the oldest?' " Who was this other son and why did Serena have to do right by him? And could Sister Bornais really predict that LaValle would always be a mama's boy, or that he would be the cause of his younger brother's death? Amos wasn't quite sure what Sister Bornais meant when she said that Serena would be the only one in her family to bear children. Della was already pregnant and due in three months. It was confusing, but he knew one thing was for sure: Serena was in trouble and she needed help.

Amos put his bundles against the wall and began to undress. He couldn't leave his older sister while she was in such distress. She might need him to help her do the things she had to do to chase away the evil spirit. As he went to sleep he envisioned dangerous journeys and foreign cities.

Sunday morning was overcast, and a cool breeze came off the gulf, smelling of salt sea and foretelling of rain. The gray, rain-laden clouds lay in the south far out to sea, but they were marching inexorably northward across the sky like a dark army ready to envelop all in its billowing grasp. Against the pale gray of the sheathing clouds, the sun had barely made its presence known. Only a fading rust-colored tinge low on the eastern horizon gave evidence that the sun had indeed risen.

When Serena knocked on the connecting door between their rooms,

Amos was dressed and staring out the window at the continuous parade of vendors on the street below. "Good morning. May I come in?" she asked.

Amos gave her smile and said, "Sho', don't see why not."

"I've come to apologize," Serena began. "I want you to know that wherever we are, you will have a right to privacy and LaValle will not be allowed to interfere or trespass against you. You don't have to worry about anyone bothering your banjo again! Oh, here is something that I think you need." Serena handed Amos a package of banjo strings.

"Gosh, thanks. These are top quality! When did you get these?"

"I sent out for them yesterday," Serena replied as she turned and walked over to the bags of new clothing. She pointed to them. "These are yours. You owe me nothing. Accept them like your family has bought you clothing. You don't need to feel obligation. We have volunteered to assume the responsibility of helping you get to manhood: clothing, food, and education are all part of that. I want you to know the reason you're with us is that we're family and we love you."

"Gosh, thanks, Sis. I mean, uh, really, uh—I ain't got no words. I just want us to be family too."

"We are family!" Serena affirmed. "I'd just like to explain about LaValle. I've never said this before, but it's taken me a while to reach this conclusion. LaValle's got some special problems, but I'm working to resolve them. I hope I can count on your assistance with him. He's still a little boy. I hope you can find it in your heart to give him a few more chances."

"No problem, Sis. We's family!"

"Good! Good! The last big question, will you come with us to California?"

"Wouldn't miss it, Sis. Wouldn't miss it!"

Serena smiled with relief and gave him a hug. "When we get out there, I'll find you the best banjo teacher around. What do you say?"

"Sounds good to me, sounds real good!"

The day passed quickly. LaValle, Serena, and Amos attended church with Della and her husband's family. Afterward, there was a barbecue at Della's father-in-law's house. People were playing cards, especially whist and pinochle, and there were a couple of horseshoe games going on as well. Children were playing tag and kick the can, while the adolescents stood on the fringes and talked in soft murmurs. It turned out to be a wonderful day. Although the sky had threatened a heavy storm, there were only a couple of showers and then the sun escaped from its gray prison and turned its brilliant smile upon the earth.

Amos was pleased to see Della. She was six months pregnant and

looked so happy and beautiful. She was filled with laughter and her husband seemed to have a good spirit as well. There were many jokes and sig-
nifying remarks directed at Charles Baddeaux, but on the whole their
exchanges rose above his banal existence. Finally, when the mosquitoes
came out to take charge of the evening air, it was called a day. LaValle was
asleep on Serena's lap as they were driven back to the hotel. Amos was
exhausted himself, but on the edge of sleep he heard Serena ask the driver,
a man from southeast Texas, about colored orphanages in that region of
Texas. He replied that he knew only of one in a little town outside of Port
Arthur that was run by the Oblate Nuns, the oldest order of colored nuns
in the United States.

On Monday, Serena hired a car. Both LaValle and Amos accompanied
her as she made various stops around the city as she prepared for their departure the next day. One stop was at a colored orphanage for girls. The
orphanage was located on the bottom floor of a run-down cathedral.
LaValle and Amos could hear the high-pitched voices of the girls all the
way out in the car, which was parked off the grounds. The next stop was a
lawyer's office, then the bank, and after that a shipping office near the
wharf. It was a long day, even though Amos and LaValle seemed to have
worked out a truce. LaValle didn't bother Amos and Amos returned the
favor.

It wasn't until Tuesday morning that Amos learned that they weren't
leaving by train after all, but were booked on a French steamer going to
Port Arthur, Texas. Amos had never been on a ship before, so he looked
forward to the trip with anticipation. Unfortunately for all concerned, it
was a terrible voyage. The rains that had threatened on Sunday came on
Tuesday with a vengeance, accompanied by high winds and rough seas.
Serena, LaValle, and Amos all suffered through some terrible bouts of sea-
sickness.

Everyone was grateful when the ship pulled into Port Arthur's harbor
late Wednesday afternoon. The wind and the rain were still raging, but
the feel of firm earth beneath his feet made Amos almost drop to his knees
and thank God. Serena had them whisked off to a nice colored hotel as
soon as they had disembarked and collected their luggage. After a soak
and a wash in a hot bath, the family reconvened in the dining room of the
hotel for dinner.

Amos knew that they were in Port Arthur because of what Sister Bornais had told Serena at the Hotel Toussant. He figured that Serena was on
a mission of trying to do right by the oldest child, who he deduced was in
the orphanage of the Oblate Nuns. All during dinner Amos tried to drop
hints that she could call upon him for help, but his offers were too oblique

and general for her to comprehend. His problem was that he did not want to divulge that he had overheard her conversation with Sister Bornais. Finally, toward the end of the dinner meal he asked, "Why did we come to Port Arthur?"

"I have a bit of business to take care of here," Serena answered. "It shouldn't take too long. I expect that we'll be able to leave by Saturday."

"Is it anythin' that I can help you with?" he offered.

"No, I just need to meet with a few people and make some arrangements."

It looked as if she chose to complete her mission without including him. Concerned that he would be left out, Amos burst out with, "If it means you gon' take a drive somewheres out'n the city, I'd like to come along!" He spoke with such charged enthusiasm that his announcement caused LaValle to jerk around and stare at him. Then, like dried beans sliding off a scoop, the rest of his words tumbled rapidly out without a break for breath. "This-is-my-first-time-in-Texas-and-I-done-heard-about-how-Port-Arthur-sit-in-some-of-the-prettiest-country-folk-ever-did-see! I'd-sho'-want-to-see-some-of-it-for-myself-if'en-we's-here-anyways! I-don't-mind-it's-rainin', might-even-make-it-mo'-pretty-what-with-rainbows-and-all!"

Serena stared at him. "Port Arthur? It means that much to you? I've never heard anything about the land around here."

"Well, maybe, after bein' sick and cooped up on the ship, I just don't want be stuck in no hotel with nothin' to do, 'specially if I can help you."

"Well, I was going to ask you to help me," Serena began.

Amos was excited. She was finally going to confide in him. "Yes! Yes!" he said expectantly.

"But I was going to ask you to watch over the woman I hired to care for LaValle while I'm occupied with business."

"Why can't LaValle and me come along? I know where you's goin' anyway!" Amos hadn't meant to let the last part slip out.

Suddenly the smiles were gone and there was a hard look on Serena's face and a stern tone in her voice when she asked, "Where am I going?"

Amos discovered too late that he had stumbled onto a minefield. He sensed a cold and implacable presence in Serena that startled him and caused him to stutter. "Uh-uh-uh-th-the-O-bl-blate orphanage."

With the same tone and seeming greater intensity, she leaned forward and asked, "Oh, and just how did you know I was going to the Oblate orphanage?" She was like a big cat moving forward in the presence of prey.

Amos sensed that this was such an important subject to Serena that it made the fact that he was her brother meaningless. He had the distinct impression that he would be sent immediately back to Louisiana if he divulged any of what he had heard Sister Bornais say. "I, er, heard you ask the man who drove us home after the picnic about colored orphanages in southeast Texas," he explained. "And I heard him answer, 'the Oblate Nuns.'"

Her eyes seem to cut into Amos as she asked, "Is that all? Or did you hear something else? Were you up Saturday night!?!"

"I don't know what you's talkin' about," he said, looking into his lap, insolently refusing to meet her eyes. Without looking up he said, "Next day, you go visit that girl's orphanage; that's all I know. Didn't take nothin' to figger if'en we's here, where you most likely be goin'."

Serena sat back in her chair and said, "I see." She was quiet for a few moments, then said, "I'm going to take you into my confidence. I don't want you to mention this to anyone and I mean anyone! Not even King! Do you understand me?"

Amos nodded. There was still a very sharp edge in her voice and he saw that she had the same look on her face as the time she fired the Winchester in their father's face. Yes, he would know better than to ever mention this subject again.

"Good! Good!" She allowed some of the tension to ease up before she spoke again. "I'm thinking of adopting. I haven't made my final decision yet. I'm not sure I'm going to go through with it, but I'm considering it. If I decide not to do it, I don't want anyone to know. It's no one else's business!"

"Sho'! Sho' I got that! Mum's the word!" Amos answered with a big smile. "So, I'm gon' have a new little, er, nephew, niece, what?"

Serena looked him directly in the eye. "I'm looking for a little girl. I already have two boys. I thought a little girl would be nice."

It was nearly noon when Serena walked up the front stairs of the Oblate orphanage. She saw there were rows of children watching her from a number of upper-story windows. Their eyes followed her until she stepped under the chipped and peeling portico above the front door.

A nun in a brown habit and white cowl directed her to the mother superior's office. The office was nearly at the back of the building. As she walked down the central hallway of the first floor, Serena saw boys and girls of various ages assigned to dusting, sweeping, and mopping activities throughout the floor. All the children were dressed in brown uniforms made out of a coarse brown material. She knocked on the office door and a low melodic voice said, "Come in."

Serena entered an ascetic, sparsely furnished office with shiny but rippling wainscoting along the lower wall. The furniture consisted of a wooden desk with a large wooden chair behind it, along with two smaller wooden chairs in front of the desk and a large wooden file cabinet. The only picture that adorned the wall was a framed image of what appeared to be a colored nun in a brown habit and white cowl with a halo around her head.

A small, narrow-faced, brown-skinned woman dressed in the similar brown habit and white cowl sat in the wooden chair behind the desk. She rose when Serena entered. "I'm Sister Mary Katherine, the mother superior of this convent and orphanage. And you are, I take it, Mrs. Tremain?"

"Yes," Serena answered. "I've just come from Port Arthur. Since you're aware of my name, you must've received word of my call and why I wished to come."

The mother superior answered, "The telephone is looked upon as a newfangled contraption in this area, Mrs. Tremain. I received a somewhat garbled message from our local postmaster. Since we're not in the practice of receiving messages and he is not in the practice of taking them, perhaps we can clarify your interests over a cup of hot tea."

"Why, that would be appreciated," Serena replied. "May I take off my coat?"

"Of course. Pardon my lack of manners. You'll find a coat tree outside my door in the hall."

When the tea had been brought, the mother superior asked, "Please tell me how I can help you, Mrs. Tremain."

"I am seeking a boy child who was brought here about six years ago. He would've been between one and two years old at the time. He might have been brought here by a member of the Louisiana sheriff's department."

"Why are you seeking him? Are you his mother, or do you know his mother?"

"No, I'm merely trying to track down a rumor that my husband has an illegitimate son here."

The mother superior's tone never varied from its mellow modulation, but her eyes were raking Serena up and down. "I've worked here nearly twenty-five years, Mrs. Tremain, and in that time I've discovered that all children are legitimate in the eyes of God, no matter how they came into being. What good would it do you to possess this knowledge? And of greater importance, how will it benefit the child?"

"Well, uh, I was considering adoption, if indeed it is his son." Serena was flustered. She hadn't anticipated such penetrating questions.

"What factors would weigh heavily in your consideration?"

Serena put her hand to her forehead. The questions were too probing. "I don't know," she faltered.

"I have no desire to expose a child's hopes and aspirations to idle curiosity, Mrs. Tremain. Perhaps it's best that this is a question most appropriately left unanswered for you. Unless, of course, you're committed to adopting the child."

"If you could at least check your records, to determine if the child is here, I'd be happy to donate a hundred dollars to your food fund."

"A hundred dollars? That's a lot of money," mused the mother superior. "And we certainly could use it—" Her voice drifted into silence as her dark eyes appraised Serena.

"Two hundred dollars! I'll donate two hundred dollars!" Serena declared, a tone of desperation entering her voice.

The mother superior leaned forward. "Two hundred dollars is a majestic amount of money! That would almost cover our operational costs for a month." She took a deep breath. "We feed, clothe, and educate one hundred and thirty-two children here, and every week we turn more away. Our facilities can only reasonably handle around a hundred and twenty children. We try to stay near that range because we don't want our services to the children to diminish to the point that we can no longer serve them effectively. A gift of two hundred dollars would mean more meat and fresh vegetables, and maybe better schoolbooks. A gift that benefits so many must be weighed against the price that one child has to pay. I would like to ask you a few more questions, Mrs. Tremain."

"Three hundred dollars and no more questions!"

A questioning look crossed the nun's face as she asked, "You have that kind of money?"

"Right here, in cash," Serena tapped her purse. She stood up and said, "If you want the money, let's get on with it!"

For the first time, the mother superior frowned and there was a bit of an edge in her voice. "I would not accept a gift of a thousand dollars without asking questions."

"If I don't get what I want, I'll walk out of here with my money!"

"That's up to you, but it will also show that your visit here was a mere dalliance, that your heart was not firm in doing right!"

Her words deflated Serena and took the bluster out of her bearing. Serena sat back down.

The mother superior waited a few minutes before she asked, "What is your husband's name, Mrs. Tremain?"

"King Tremain."

"Are you sure that he is the father of this child that you're seeking?" The mother superior's eyes squinted as she watched for Serena's reaction.

"Well, I'm not sure," Serena answered. "I'm just trying to check out a rumor."

"Do you know how the child ended up here, at this orphanage?"

Serena paused before she answered. She did not want to reveal everything, but she decided that she had no choice. The mother superior was too clever to be taken in by half-truths. "His mother, a woman King knew before he met me, brought him to New Orleans to give him to his father, but she was abducted by a family that was feuding with King's family. The child was taken and given to a corrupt sheriff's captain named LeGrande. Rumor has it that the child was brought here or another colored orphanage in this area."

"This is the only colored orphanage in southeast Texas," the mother superior answered as she pulled a file out of her drawer. "The child you're seeking is here. The deputy didn't know his name and the child was in shock and barely speaking. He is now a healthy seven and a half years old and we have named him Elroy Fontenot. Coincidentally, Elroy means 'the king' in Spanish."

A cold, clammy feeling began crawling up Serena's back. "How did he get that name?" she asked.

"Most children we get already have names. For those that don't, we cycle through a list of about two hundred last names and about a thousand first names. It was mere happenstance that we arrived at Elroy."

Serena had to control herself to speak without stammering. "May I see him?"

"That depends on whether you're serious about adopting, Mrs. Tremain. You see, every child in this institution dreams about the day that some loving family will come and take him or her away from this motherless, fatherless place. When a child knows that he or she is being considered for adoption and for some reason it doesn't happen, the child not only feels the pain of rejection, but feels that the rejection is due to some defect in his or her person. It is for this reason that we do not parade children out for potential adoptive parents. We only allow the child to be viewed in a group, while at play or during classroom work."

"That would be fine," Serena conceded. The clammy feeling was turning to dread. It was an amorphous, undefined fear and it seemed to be taking up residence in the pit of her stomach.

"Good, the under-ten boys have a recess break now." The mother superior stood up. She gave Serena a warm smile. "They'll be playing baseball in the yard. We can see them best from the floor proctor's office on the second floor. Shall we?"

Serena followed the nun up the stairs and down the hall to another office. When they entered, there was a nun standing at an open window looking out into the yard. She was shouting several boys' names and pointing. She turned and bowed when she saw the mother superior.

"Continue on, Sister Theresa," the mother superior said with a smile. "We have a guest who is interested in seeing the boys at play."

Serena walked to another window and stared down at the makeshift baseball diamond below. Her eyes were searching, but she could tell nothing from the distance she was viewing from. Then suddenly an argument broke out among the boys and a bigger boy pushed one of the smaller ones. Another boy, midway in size between the two adversaries, stepped between them. It was clear even from the second floor that the third boy was defending the smaller one. The bigger boy had been all bluster before, but with the entrance of his adversary's protector he became hesitant; even though he was bigger, he was reluctant to take things further with the third boy.

"That boy in-between is Elroy," the mother superior announced. "He's full of mischief, but still a good boy."

The fear now rose up out of Serena's stomach and squeezed her heart in its cold grasp. She swallowed and asked, "May I see him at closer range."

The mother superior gave Serena a long look before she turned to the nun and asked, "When is the under-ten boys' recess over, Sister Theresa?"

"They have five more minutes, Mother Katherine," the nun replied.

The mother superior turned to Serena and said, "Why don't we return to my office? The boys will have to pass it to return to their classroom." Serena nodded and followed the mother superior downstairs and back to the office. They stood at the door awaiting the boys' passage.

Serena was aware that the mother superior's dark eyes were scrutinizing her, but she did not return her piercing looks. Serena stared down at the floor and waited. The sound of boys' voices flooded the hall as a door opened from the yard and thirty or so young boys walked in, two abreast. Their voices fell silent as soon as they saw that the mother superior was standing outside her office with a strange lady. As soon as Serena saw Elroy, fear gripped her. She felt as if she were being choked to death from the inside. Elroy looked like an older and darker version of Jacques. He was definitely King's son.

Serena stumbled backward into the office and collapsed onto one of the small wooden chairs. If she took Elroy home with her, LaValle would lose his primacy as the oldest. An orphanage-toughened boy would hold sway over him. Elroy and Jacques would be King's favorites and LaValle would be the forgotten child. LaValle did not have the fiber to compete with either Elroy or Jacques. If Elroy was introduced, every advantage that LaValle now had would be eradicated. Serena couldn't do it to him. He was her baby. She could not make a decision that would hurt him for the benefit of someone else's child, particularly when that someone was Mamie. Serena just couldn't do it.

"I see you recognized you husband's son," the mother superior said in an even tone. She had followed Serena into the office and had watched her for several minutes before speaking.

"I saw no such thing!" Serena replied irritably. "This has just been a tiring day."

"I see," observed the nun. "Well, what do you wish to do now?"

"Here is the three hundred dollars I promised," Serena said, counting out the money. "But just in case that child really is my husband's illegitimate son," Serena emphasized the word *illegitimate*, "I will send two hundred dollars a year for his upkeep and education. Perhaps, I'll send extra money during the Christmas season for presents for him." Serena closed her purse and prepared to go.

"I cannot accept that," the mother superior answered calmly, but her smile indicated that she saw through Serena's veil of lies.

"Why not?" Serena asked, vaguely alarmed that she might not be able to comply at all with Sister Bornais's directives.

"We cannot accept gifts for one child that cause them to be treated differently than the other children who are also wards here. If you donate money, it must be for the benefit of all the children."

"Fine! I'll send three hundred a year!"

"Wouldn't it be better to give this boy a home? It is apparent that you see his father's features in his face. Why are you trying to buy with money that which is better purchased with love?"

Serena stood up. "I don't see that my private affairs are any of your business!"

"You're right. Only the children are my business. Perhaps you'll reconsider and let your husband come back and see?"

"My husband's too busy for chicanery! Thank you for your time!" Serena walked out of the office, down the hall, and out the front door before she took a deep breath. The rain had begun to fall again and there was a rumble of thunder in the dark gray skies. The car was waiting for her and Serena tumbled in to the backseat as big drops of rain trickled down her face and neck. Since she had left Amos and LaValle at the hotel, it was a long, quiet ride back to Port Arthur. The car was entering the city when she discovered that she had forgotten her coat at the orphanage.

It was three years after Tini had been killed that Serena received the letter from New Orleans informing her of Della's fourth and final miscarriage. The scrawled letter was blotched by the stain of tears, and the lines of Della's normally neat penmanship were uneven and ragged, looping across the page like uncoiled springs. But the thoughts communicated by the words were themselves tightly wound spirals of steel that leaped off the page and then slowly corkscrewed themselves into Serena's heart. The last miscarriage was the hardest and had nearly taken Della's life. Now she would never be able to have children.

The letter fell from Serena's hand. She could not bear to finish it. It was too painful. She sat down in a maroon wing chair in the parlor of her West Oakland home. In the distance she could hear the wailing sound of the Southern Pacific as it pulled into the train station. Through the lace curtains a shaft of sunlight left a geometric pattern on the floor. Outside the parlor window she could hear the sounds of men laughing as the Pullman car porters stomped down the steps of the rooming house next door and headed for the depot. The sunshine and the laughter were discordant with the shadows and sadness that she felt.

Sister Bornais's words regarding the curse were never far from her mind: ". . . *It might even spread to yo' family members, to yo' sisters and yo' brother, stopping yo' kin's seed from flourishing, makin' you the only chile from yo' family that bears chil'ren. You best take heed and pay the price to make that spirit move on!*" It had been difficult at first for her to believe that Sister Bornais's words had substance and power. She had assumed them to be merely syllables mouthed by a crone, but as years passed she discovered the words had all the force of an invisible wind that was capable of ripping apart everything that humans could construct.

Each time Serena received word of one of Della's miscarriages, she would increase the amount of money that she annually sent to the Oblate orphanage. Each miscarriage was a lance thrust into her soul. She felt personally guilty for her sister's misfortune, yet she did not change her course. She could not abandon LaValle. Despite the firmness of her decision, sometimes Serena felt that she could not face another day with a smile and an easy heart. The joy seemed to be seeping out of her life. She let herself be bound tightly by the responsibilities of her daily life and moved from duty to duty with the lifelessness of an automaton.

In 1929, when news of Tini's death had reached her, at first she had thought it was unrelated to the curse, that it was an accident. But when she arrived in New Orleans and the details were revealed to her, she realized that the curse was still manifesting itself. Tini was buried in a closed coffin and the funeral was a drab, depressing affair. Tini's husband, a young man from Baton Rouge, was completely distraught. Her father, who had been ostracized by his children, stood off to the side, a defeated man, smelling of cheap alcohol. Della, dressed in black, stood silently at the graveside with dry eyes; her tears had been expended on her two previous miscarriages. During the funeral only Amos looked at her, and there was an unspoken accusation in his eyes. It was a turning point in their relationship. Even after they returned to California, he rarely spoke to her unless circumstances required it.

Tini had been killed by Jethro. After the service, Serena's Aunt Ida told how it had happened. After Tini's baby had been stillborn, she had fallen into an incommunicative and listless stupor that lasted weeks. One day while her husband was at work, she had ridden a horse over to visit her father's farm. Her father was out plowing the lower field with Homer at the time. Tini went into the barn and had tried to get Jethro out of his stall with a whip. When she entered his stall, the mule kicked her in the head and chest. She was already dead when her father returned from plowing. As soon as Aunt Ida said that Tini had entered Jethro's stall, Serena knew that her youngest sister had committed suicide. Tini would never have had anything to do with Jethro if she was in her right mind.

The last thing Serena did before she left New Orleans was take a buggy out to her father's farm. When she pulled into the yard behind the house, he came out and stood on the porch. She could tell that he was yearning for a kind word or smile from her, anything to knock down the wall that separated them. He was a broken man who had discovered that all he had worked for was meaningless without the love of his family. As far as she was concerned, it was a lesson learned too late. She picked up the carbine that she had wrapped in a blanket and got down from the wagon. Her father looked down at the gun and back at her face. He did not turn away. He thought he was looking at death. He smiled as if he wanted her to shoot him, to free him from the weight of living. Understanding him, she smirked; she was not going to help him escape the pain. She went into the barn and shot Jethro, slowly emptying the carbine's magazine into the mule's body and taking pleasure in the animal's brays of distress. She threw a hundred dollars on the straw and returned to her buggy. She drove away without a word to her father. It surprised her how much she still hated him.

Sitting in the wingback chair, Serena watched as the pattern of sunlight moved slowly across the floor. It did not seem possible that there could still be a sun in the sky given all the shadows and darkness in her life. Daylight itself seemed like a memory. The world had become a pattern of variations in gray and the sunlight could not illuminate her vision. She picked the letter up off the floor, and crumpled the pages in her fist, sitting silently, staring at visions of what might have been: her nieces and nephews at a family picnic; the high-pitched laughter of Tini tinkling across the top octaves of the happy exchanges; the warmth of a large and loving family. She sat for several hours without moving.

At four-thirty Serena heard the front door being unlatched and then footsteps running up the stairs. She knew it wasn't LaValle or Jack (as he preferred to be called) because the boys always worked at their father's pool hall after school, until five-thirty. The step was too light to be King, so she deduced that it was Amos. She exhaled and waited for him to come down so that she could tell him the news from New Orleans. When he did come downstairs, she heard him dragging something heavy down the steps. She called to him. "Amos! Amos, please come here!"

He walked into the parlor and stood in front of her. The boy was gone and in his place was a handsome young man. As he stood before her, she saw both her mother and her father in him. His build and the shape of his head came from his father, but he had his mother's laughing eyes and delicate, full lips.

"Why didn't you stop in to say hello?" she asked.

"I didn't know you were here," he answered in a preoccupied fashion. He shifted his weight from foot to foot as if he was anxious to be on his way.

"I have some sad news from Della," Serena said with an exhalation of breath.

"I know already. I talked to Della yesterday."

"You spoke with her?"

"Yeah, I talked to her before she went into the hospital on Monday."

For some reason it surprised Serena that Amos would communicate more regularly with Della than she did. As she was mulling this fact over she said, "This is a grim and terrible day for our family."

Amos shook his head and grunted disbelievingly. "Like you're really concerned! The only one you care about is LaValle!"

Serena sat for several seconds in silence, shocked by her brother's words. "I beg your pardon?" she demanded.

"You heard me," he retorted impudently. "Like you really care about Della's miscarriage!"

"How dare you!" she shouted, for his words had driven something sharp into her chest. "As long as you live under my roof, don't you ever talk like that to me again!"

"I thought it would come to that! I knew you'd play that card! So I'm moving out today. My trunk is packed and in the front hall!"

More shocking news. Serena was momentarily confused. This was something that Amos had planned. This wasn't a spur-of-the-moment decision. Why wasn't she told that he was considering such a move? "Does King know about this?" she asked, wondering if she was the last to know.

"Yeah, we talked about it."

"Where is he now?" An edge had entered her voice. She was indignant that King would keep information about her brother from her.

"He and Sampson went out early this morning. I guess they're bringing in another shipment."

Serena grimaced. King was bringing in more bootleg alcohol. This was a source of continuing irritation to her. The Tremains as a family had the opportunity to become part of colored society in West Oakland, to be respectable and legitimate. In the five years that they had lived in Oakland, they had purchased numerous pieces of property and had started a number of thriving, legitimate businesses. If King would only drop his cut-and-shoot friends along with his underworld activities, she was sure that they would be welcomed into polite colored society. Despite her best arguments, King had consistently spurned this opportunity for social advancement and risked their reputation for money that they did not need. Serena shook her head and said in a voice filled with acid, "Another fool throws away his family's future!"

Amos had appeared content to leave without arguing further with Serena, but her last comment infuriated him. "How dare you!" he snarled, pointing a finger at her. "You're the one that threw away this family's future! And you've done it over and over again!"

"What do you mean?" she asked icily.

Amos returned her hard look and said, "You think nobody knows what you're doing or what you've done, but you're wrong!"

"What are you talking about?"

Amos waved a hand dismissively in her direction. "Even if I told you now, it would be too late. You had your chance to stay out of the game, but you wanted to roll the dice and you got snake eyes! Now the dice have been passed on and you can't change your throw, because this game is for keeps!"

"You're talking in riddles! If you have something to say, come out and say it! Don't hide behind words!"

For the first time Amos laughed. "Like it's me who's been hiding behind words all this time!" He shook his head and said, "I don't have time to argue with you. Good-bye!" He turned and walked out into the front hall.

For the first time she wondered whether Amos knew about Sister Bornais's curse. Then she discounted the possibility. How could he? He had never said anything in the last five years to indicate that he was aware of Sister Bornais's words. But he must know something. Otherwise why did he blame her for Della's problems? Why did he walk out the door with such anger? What did he know? In between these questions, the aching in her chest swelled with each breath; a rasp was being drawn across her lungs. She knew by evidence of things unseen that she would never laugh and talk with her brother again. There was a finality about his good-bye that crashed and ricocheted against walls of the empty house like the peal of a bell.

The front doorbell rang. Serena made no effort to answer it. The bell rang several more times, then the door was unlocked. A woman's voice called out. "It's me, Mrs. Whitlow!" There was a pause then, "Anybody to home?"

Serena answered tiredly, "I'm here, Mrs. Whitlow. I'm here."

Mrs. Whitlow stuck her head around the doorjamb and asked with concern, "Is you alright, Mrs. T.? You needs me to fix you somethin'?"

"I'm fine, Mrs. Whitlow. I just need to sit and think for a while."

"Okay then, if'en it's alright with you, I'll just go ahead and fix dinner. Is the mister playing cards tonight? Do I got to put on somethin' extry?"

Serena exhaled slowly. "I think he is, so I guess you better put on a pot of chile or chicken and dumplings. The menu for tonight's dinner is on the stove."

"I's on it, Mrs. T." Mrs. Whitlow replied as she went into the kitchen.

In the darkening parlor Serena wondered for perhaps the millionth time if she could have made a different decision at the orphanage outside of Port Arthur. Even if she knew beforehand the problems her family would suffer, did she really have a choice? With her knowledge of LaValle's physical limitations and personality defects, common sense and logic led her once more to the conclusion that he could not have survived the pressures of being the only boy who was not King's son. He was not physically or mentally tough enough to withstand the ostracism that would have naturally developed. One of the driving forces in her life was a need to protect and nurture LaValle. She did not love him more than

Jacques; it was just that LaValle needed more attention. It stemmed from the illnesses of his infancy. What Serena told no one was that she blamed herself for his physical weakness and illness. She blamed herself for trying to abort him. In her heart she was sure that was the principal cause of all of his problems. Serena felt compelled to take any action that would off-set her mistaken attempt to murder her firstborn child.

It was too late to change courses now. Amos had been right about one thing: the die was cast. Even if she thought LaValle stood a chance as a ten-year-old with the introduction of Elroy (which she didn't), how could she go to King and explain to him what she had done? Too many years had passed and too much heartache. All the sacrifices that she had made to ensure LaValle had a healthy life would be in vain.

Serena had not forgotten the rest of Sister Bornais's curse, that LaValle *"gon' be a mama's boy all his life, which ain't gon be that long really and mo' than that, he gon' be the cause of the death of his youngest brother. You don't fol-low what I say, you gon' be left with no sons at all!"* The words uttered by the voodoo woman climbed out of the depths of her memory and slowly criss-crossed her consciousness like a heavily burdened mule train ascending a steep incline. She decided that she would send the Oblate orphanage an-other check. Perhaps she could defer or mitigate the impact of the curse with the expenditure of more money. Perhaps when LaValle was six-teen . . . perhaps that would be time enough to bring Elroy into the fold to avoid this last ominous aspect of the curse. Serena had no desire to lose both her sons, yet she was willing to risk it, if the only alternative was to welcome another child into her house to supercede LaValle's position as the oldest. Serena could not admit it, but it was a primal jealousy that but-tressed her reluctance to include Elroy in her family. It was the fact that he was Mamie's son.

She heard the sound of her sons running up the front porch stairs. Lavalle's voice was loud as he taunted his younger brother. She heard the brash bravado of LaValle's tone and knew that he was trying to bully Jack. The sounds of a scuffle broke out on the porch and then she heard LaValle wail in pain. She pushed herself to her feet and went to the front door. When she opened the door she saw LaValle's angry, tear-stained face. Im-mediately he sought her support and pointed at Jack.

"He hit me with that stick!" LaValle wailed. "I think he broke my finger!"

Jack, who was smaller than his brother, said nothing. He stood quietly and gripped a short wooden pole. He did not try to persuade or manipu-late his mother. He simply stared at his brother.

The look on Jack's face sent a shaft of pain through Serena. She had seen the same look many times on King's face and she realized even without Elroy, LaValle was not destined to hold the top position long. He did not possess his younger brother's toughness. It was simply a question of time. His descent would only be hastened by the introduction of Elroy. After checking LaValle's finger, Serena took possession of the pole and sent the boys to wash up for dinner. It had been a tremendously long and arduous day and she was happy that it was finally over. It's best that I double the money that I send to the orphanage and maybe buy some turkeys for Christmas, she thought as she set the pole by the door. When she turned back into the house, she hoped that nightfall would bring some respite from the harshness of daylight.

TUESDAY, JUNE 15, 1937

When King walked out on the platform of the San Francisco train station to wait for the arrival of the six-fifteen from Los Angeles he was already tired, but he was in no way sleepy. The events of the day were roaring around his mind like high-octane race cars on a small oval track. As a group, the thoughts were whirring around too fast for him to examine closely, but every once in a while one of them would pull up for a pit stop and he would have the chance to mull it over before it too roared away, gaining speed until it lost definition. A long-term mystery had been solved, but its resolution brought only anger and no peace of mind.

His day had begun at one-thirty in the morning in dense fog. He had nosed his fifty-five-foot cutter out of its slip in the Alameda Estuary and cleared the mouth of the Golden Gate in less than an hour despite the thickness of the vapor. He had one man standing at the prow with a signal lamp. The rest of his crew was at the railings keeping an eye and an ear out for other vessels. King had confidence that his powerful twin Chrysler 700 engines would give him all the speed and mobility he would need to avoid a collision. He had a schedule to keep: a rendezvous with a freighter called the *Baja Queen*. The ship was part of a fleet of smuggling ships that King and and his partners had amassed over the last years of Prohibition. Although the ships had been originally intended to smuggle bootleg alcohol, they now carried everything from guns and mercenaries to migrant workers and cigarettes. He stared out into the obscuring grayness of the fog and felt at peace. It was the best part of the trip as far as he was concerned: being alone on the bridge with the movement of the sea beneath him.

The train whistled its arrival. The sun had disappeared behind Twin Peaks and the sky overhead was a pale blue fading to gold, with only a few yellowish clouds floating in the distance. There was no evidence of the morning's fog. A brisk wind swept along the platform, not quite strong enough to blow hats off, but King kept a firm grip on his flat-brimmed Stetson. He pulled his hat more firmly on his head and turned up the collar of his greatcoat, then started to walk down to where the colored car was destined to stop. A redcap walked up to him and asked, "Mr. Tremain, is you waitin' to pick up somebody? Does you need help with luggage?"

"How do, Tommy Lee?" King asked with a trace of a smile. He pulled a ten-dollar bill from his money clip and handed it to Tommy Lee. "My wife is comin' in from LA with baggage," he explained. Tommy Lee nodded gratefully and hurried away to secure a cart. The train chugged into the station shooting steam out of its vents and shrieked to a stop. King gritted his teeth and waited for Serena to disembark. This was not going to be a pleasant meeting, but he was ready for it.

The news that King had received reminded him of the summer in Bodie Wells when he had entered the bull-riding competition in the county rodeo. He had never ridden a Brahman bull before and he had the luck of drawing one called Red Smoke. Once out the gate he discovered the animal was pure muscle. It flung itself skyward, leaving the ground with all four feet, then it took turns throwing its hindquarters to the left and the right. King did not last the required eight seconds. He was thrown off before the bell sounded, but his grip hand was caught in the ropes. He was dragged and tossed around like a rag doll until he freed his hand, then he was thrown against a barricade. He barely got out of the arena before the animal charged him. The news he had heard today made him feel that he was once more astride the Brahman, being pitched to and fro, riding on countless ribbons of muscle.

The colored passengers had only one exit at the back of the car and therefore they trickled out in ones and twos. King watched while men in trench coats and fedoras and women in furs and thick high-heeled shoes walked past him into the station. King turned away from the wind and lighted a cheroot. Then Serena appeared. She was wearing a rust-brown coat trimmed with red fox. Her matching hat was also trimmed in red fox and she had a red fox stole casually draped across her shoulder. Their eyes met and there was no love or warmth exchanged in their looks. King gestured to the porter, indicating that Serena was the one for whom he was waiting. The porter hurried to his task.

King stared at his wife and wondered whether it was possible to hate someone as much as you loved them. He had married a girl who had grown into a cold but beautiful woman. He still loved her as he would never love anyone else, but their marital partnership was over. He had never been able to truly forgive her for not telling him about the letter received in Bodie Wells, and over the years their relationship had turned into an undeclared war. It was not the type of conflict that produced glorious moments or one in which courage was valued. It was a war of attrition, of nerves and manipulation, and perseverance.

After her bags were piled on the cart, Serena walked up to King and said in an icy tone, "I specifically asked that you not be the one to pick me up! Where is Ethel?"

"I told her to go home," King answered evenly. "I specifically wanted to pick you up!"

"You have nothing to say to me!" Serena answered, impatiently straightening the fingers of her gloves. "My brother is lying in the hospital on the edge of death because of you and your criminal activities! Don't say a damn thing to me. Just drive me home!"

King did not respond, but directed the porter toward the parking lot. Serena walked on ahead, her high heels clicking on the cement. When they reached his Cadillac, King assisted the porter in putting the bags in the trunk. The western sky was turning to purple and rust as the dark blue of night rose from the east. The darker colors reminded King of the dried blood from old wounds. The wind intensified as its gusts gained force. King's coattails were flapping around his legs as he slammed the trunk shut. He got into the car and sat facing Serena. A humorless smile played across his lips. He said nothing. He let the silence speak for him, but inside the Brahman was throwing him against the barricades.

Serena turned toward him. "Do I have to take a cab?"

King started the car and pulled it out of the lot into the evening traffic. He smiled his death's-head smile. "Seems to me like you got some questions to answer."

Serena recognized that there was something unusual in King's demeanor. There was no evidence of contrition on his part and there was a dangerous quiet about him. She did not let that affect her indignation or rage. She had learned over the years that a cold, haughty exterior covered a multitude of sins. "What can you possibly have to ask me? It's you who are the problem, you and your cut-and-shoot friends! You'll never be anything but a low-life thug! It's my brother who's paying for your stupidity! Amos never did anything to deserve this!"

"That's just what he said," King agreed. "Only he blames you!" King had to contain himself. He did not want to let the bull loose just yet. He wanted to make sure Serena's hand was firmly coiled in the rope first.

Serena turned toward him and there was rage on her face. "I can't believe you had the gall to say that to me!" Serena declared. "I'm not the one involved in criminal activity! I don't have people gunning for me! I'm the one trying to drag this family out of the gutter! I'm the one trying to make us legitimate and I would have succeeded if it hadn't been for you and your classless friends!"

"Don't get it twisted, woman! It was me and my classless friends that helped you escape the farm and it's my classless money that lets you run around sellin' property for yo' rooty-poot, high yellow, seditty friends!"

Serena noticed there was a hostility in King's tone that he didn't generally use with her. She pulled off her gloves. "I don't have time to argue with you. I want to get to the hospital and see Amos!"

"He don't want to see you and that's for sure! He told me to tell you specifically not to come!"

Serena was momentarily at a loss for words. "Did he say why?" she asked, somewhat deflated.

"Yep! He talked to me about twenty minutes before he went into surgery. It appears that the boy had to get somethin' off his chest that he been keepin' mum about for nigh on ten years."

Now King had her full attention. He had no facility for light conversation, so she knew it had to be serious.

King stopped the car for a stop signal and glanced across at Serena and said in a casual tone. "Now, you know I've been lookin' for my firstborn son for nigh on seventeen years."

Serena forced herself to be nonchalant. "Why are you bringing this up now? Is this to distract me from what's happened to my brother?"

"It's about yo' brother too! You see, by the time I got to the hospital, he couldn't feel his legs or nothin' down below his waist. All the doctors knew was that he had one bullet in the kidney and another in the spine. They was sayin' he had a fifty-fifty chance, but Amos thought he was gon' die for sure. I'm sho' that's the only reason he told me about the night at the Hotel Toussant when Sister Bornais told you to do right by my oldest son. He said that Sister Bornais told you that if you didn't do right, neither yo' sisters nor yo' brother was gon' have kids! He told me about goin' to Port Arthur with you when you said you was gon' adopt a little girl. He said he wasn't worried when you came back empty-handed. He thought you was still plannin' to do right." King was wrapping the Brahman's rope firmly around her hand and knotting it tight.

"He was obviously delirious out of his mind with pain when he told you this hogwash! This is some story that he has made up! You can't be seriously bringing this up!" Although her voice was firm, her protest seemed hollow even to her.

King continued as if he was just carrying on a casual conversation. "I called the Oblate orphanage outside of Port Arthur this afternoon. They have a new mother superior there now. When I told her my name she mistook me for the anonymous donor who been sending the orphanage money every year for the last ten years. You see, the nun who was there before her wrote down yo' name in a journal and you left yo' coat there too. The coat had a monogram in it: S-B-T." King reached over and pulled her coat open. "Just like the one you got in this one. They figured the donor was you 'cause each year they received five hundred dollars in the name of Elroy Fontenot and you was the only one who ever inquired about him. What do you think about that?" Serena was firmly aboard the bull now and ready to ride.

Serena said nothing. The world was spinning. She felt as if she was in a big whirlpool being sucked down to drain at an unknown destination. The atmosphere was growing denser than water. It was hard to get a full breath. Her stomach was rising up in her chest like she was falling from a great height. Strangely, despite all her anxiety, she felt relieved. All the pretense could be dropped. The heavy yoke of the sixteen-year lie could be laid down. She was free of its chafing harness. Yet she had no sense of lightness or release. She had carried its weight until she was exhausted. She was too tired even for fear. She waited to see how King would react.

King stomped on the brake and the big car skidded to an abrupt halt. Serena's body flew off the seat and slammed into the dashboard. Her head banged against the windshield. "What do you think about that, huh?" he snarled. "Ain't you got nothin' to say?" He stared at her for a minute, then put the car in gear and drove on.

For the first time, Serena considered the possibility that King would kill her. She was not frightened by the prospect, although it surprised her. In all the years that they had been together he had never raised his hand to her, but she realized that she had done something that made the fact she was his wife and a woman insignificant. And yet, she had done it precisely because she was his wife and a woman. She was a mother who wanted to protect her firstborn from the undertow and rugged surf of her husband's life. At great personal cost she had done what she thought was best.

King drove the Cadillac through the darkening streets of San Francisco in silence. There was an accident at Dubose and Market streets that caused traffic to inch along. King kept his eyes straight ahead as if he couldn't bear to look at her. His jaw moved slowly back and forth as if he was chewing on his next move. Serena straightened her coat, arranged her stole across her shoulders, and composed herself.

When he spoke, his voice was low and husky like he was out of breath from some heavy exertion. "You know what I feel about family. You knew the whereabouts of this boy was important to me, and for more than fifteen years you've kept this from me! What kind of woman are you? Leavin' my boy to be raised in an orphanage? Is this what you call bein' classy? A life based on lies?"

Serena lit a cigarette, exhaled slowly, then said, "I'm not proud of it, but I did what was best for LaValle. I'd do it again if the circumstances were the same."

King rolled his window down to get some fresh air and nodded. "So, Amos was right about you after all. You care about LaValle mo' than anybody, mo'n yo' sisters and brother, mo'n me and mo'n Jacques. I guess it's too bad you couldn't have spent yo' life bein' LeGrande's whore; you'd a been less pain to yo' family and those that cared for you."

"How dare you! I sacrificed myself for you! That man violated me! LaValle was the result of my trying to save you!"

"Bullshit! You sacrificed yo'self to make up for not givin' me the first damn letter! It's yo' jealousy and fearfulness that done caused all this to happen in the first place! Then you follow it up with years of sneakiness and lyin'! Then you got the audacity to go round talkin' about class with yo' nose stuck up in the air. Amos got you pegged spot on. He say you wants to pretend you's caviar, but all you is is cold fish and you's beginnin' to smell!"

"Amos wouldn't dare say that!"

King laughed. It was not a pleasant laugh. "You'd be surprised at what Amos would say, real surprised." There was the clang and clatter of electric streetcars as King steered the big car across Market Street, bouncing over the metal tracks. When King continued speaking his voice was neutral and without emotion, as if he were reporting the news. "Whatever love Amos had for you is dead now. It died with them babies that was miscarried and stillborn. He said you doomed them children never to breathe when you did nothin' to lift the curse that Sister Bornais said was on LaValle. How many miscarriages did Della have . . . three? Four? I remember back in 1929 we went back to New Orleans for Tini's funeral. Everybody was sayin' she died by accident, but Amos told me this mornin' at the hospital that she killed herself after her baby was stillborn. He said it weren't no accident. He said she was real afraid of Jethro, that she knew better than to go and kneel in the back of that mule's stall with a whip.

That's why she had a closed coffin. The mortician couldn't put her head back together."

Despite her resolve, tears were beginning to trickle down Serena's cheeks. She did not try to wipe them away. She was concentrating on keeping her bearings. If she made any sudden moves, she was afraid that she would break down uncontrollably. Her resolve was eroding slowly like a mud levee before the pressure of the flooding Mississippi River. Serena had spent years developing an internal system of interconnected levees all to protect one lowland area in her life from water. Leaving Elroy in the orphanage was the first levee that she had constructed, a bulwark to prevent the rushing waters of fate from washing over her firstborn, and over the years she had to build many more to bolster the first. Unfortunately for Serena, fate could not be dominated by mortal stamina. The time of floods had finally come and soon all that she could not carry would be submerged and sundered by forces that began long before she built her first levee. She had to take a tissue from her purse; the tears simply would not stop.

"Them alligator tears don't fool nobody," King observed. "You did what you meant to do, you said as much! You robbed me of my son's childhood and you robbed him of the chance to grow up in the bosom of his own family!"

"You know where he is now. You can send for him," Serena said as she dabbed at her eyes with the tissue. "I can't go back and undo what's been done."

"Don't play no pretend shit with me!" King growled. "You know he left the orphanage two months ago! When I asked to speak with him, the mother superior told me he left the orphanage when he turned seventeen. They only keeps the girls until they're eighteen. She don't know where he is. Some of the boys think he jumped a freight to Chicago, but nobody knows for sho'!"

Serena shook her head. "I didn't know that."

King waved a dismissive hand in her direction. "Like somebody gon' believe you!"

"You said that Amos went into surgery. Do you know if it was successful?"

"He gon' live, but he gon' be paralyzed from the waist down. He ain't ever gon' walk again or ever have any kids. That's all three of the other children in yo' family! You and LaValle is battin' a thousand! And by the way, Amos got shot because of LaValle, not because of anythin' to do with my business. It 'pears LaValle talked Jacques into sneakin' down to hear Amos and his new band playin' at the California Hotel. LaValle got himself a bottle of hooch from somewhere and got tore up at the hotel. He started a fight with some tough customers and the bouncer stepped in and stopped him from gettin' his ass kicked. Those boys waited for LaValle after the show. Amos was just tryin' to help him when he got shot. When the shootin' started yo' white boy took off runnin' and left Amos lyin' in the street. And on top of that he didn't tell nobody nothin' when he got home. Jacques went to the hospital with Amos. The hotel called me and told me that Amos had been gunned down."

King slapped the steering wheel for emphasis. "Woman, you done thrown away yo' whole family for that one boy. I hope to hell it was worth it, 'cause he about the only family you got now! While they was waitin' for surgery, Amos told Jacques all about Sister Bornais. Amos asked me to call Della and tell her about the curse too. I didn't feel too good about it, but Amos begged me to do it. He thought he was dyin' and he wanted to clear his craw about Sister Bornais before he met his maker. I couldn't finish the phone call with Della. I had to hang up, 'cause the girl dropped the phone and started screamin'. So, it's just you and yo' white boy now! After seventeen years that's all you got!"

Serena's eyes were red and inflamed from her tears. She wiped them with a handkerchief. "You promised me that you would never tell him that you were not his father," she sniffed.

"You got some gall, if you tryin' to hold somebody to a promise! Seems to me all bets is off and all agreements is canceled. You done thrown our contract in the toilet! It ain't nothin' but shit and paper now!"

"I'm not getting a divorce! I told you that before we got married!"

King chuckled bitterly. "You can't give me what I want! You ain't got a big enough frame to hold a decent-sized heart! I don't care about no damn divorce, but one thing is got to be real clear: this here marriage is finished! I loved you once, but that ain't close to what I feel now! You done pretty well squeezed the joy out of this here house."

They drove in silence until King pulled up in front of a large, three-story Victorian on Fulton Street. King turned off the engine and got out. He took Serena's bags up the front steps and then into the house. When he walked back out to the car, Serena was still sitting in it. King got back into the car. "I'm gon' move out with Jacques whenever he is ready. I figure he still needs you for another year, then we gone! You can go on and live here with yo' boy!"

Serena took a deep breath and turned to face King. She watched his dark profile and said, "I want you to understand something: I was only trying to protect LaValle. I wasn't trying to hurt you."

King smiled. She was riding the bull as he had ridden it, getting banged and scraped against the barricades and being dragged unwillingly from point to point. "It don't matter what you say, yo' actions shows clear what you's about. All that stuff you preach about religion and faith is just a pack of lies! You didn't have no faith in LaValle, that he was strong enough to stand up and learn from what I had to teach, and you didn't have no faith in me that I would reach out to that boy! I told you a thousand times, 'Give him to me!' Sho' I was gon' be tough on him! I'm tough on Jacques. A colored man's got to be tough! I would have made the boy my son through time and sweat! Through time and sweat! And when I called him my son, he'd be proud and I'd be proud! But you didn't trust him and you didn't trust me! You let him run to you and hide behind yo' skirts until he couldn't face nothin' and wasn't worth nothin'. You done turned him into somethin' that hangs on to apron strings in a world that needs men! You's the problem!"

A car further up the hill on the opposite side of the streets flashed its lights twice. King flashed his lights once in return. The car pulled out of its parking space and drove past. King nodded to the men in the car. He turned back to Serena. "You see, you's a small person inside and because of that you think everybody got to be small like you! He wasn't my son, but I took him into my house. I promised you I would never tell him he's not my son. I'm a man of my word. I kept my bond. But you couldn't do the same for me. You kept quiet about my son and his mother bein' in the DuMonts' hands! Since you knew what they feel about the Tremains and me in particular, you knew that boy and his mother was in for some pain! Then when you found he was alive, you wouldn't even try to reach out to my son. You let him get raised in an orphanage! That's so cold-blooded there ain't even a word for it! I ain't clear whether you's a weasel or a snake, but one thing's for sho': I don't want you in my bed!"

Serena opened the door slowly and got out of the car. She walked up the stairs as if she were exhausted, closing the door without looking back.

As King drove away, he was certain that Serena wouldn't untangle her hand from the rope for many years. She was going to continue being dragged and tossed by the bull until she was bruised and battered beyond recognition. Unfortunately for King, her pain was no consolation for the agony and disappointment that he was feeling. His desire for a large family of sons and daughters had irrevocably been crushed like an empty carton under his wife's uncaring foot.

FRIDAY, JUNE 14, 1946

Serena Tremain was having tea with Rosetta Hughes and Wydenia Witherspoon when the phone rang in the hall. Rosetta was in the middle of a story about a local pastor's peccadillo with a prominent colored widow and Serena did not want to interrupt the story. She let it ring several times before she rose to pick it up. "Pardon me, Rosetta, I guess the people I pay to work here don't feel that answering the phone is part of their duties."

"I know what you mean, Rena," Wydenia agreed with a nod of her head. "I have to stay on top of mine all the time!"

"Isn't that the truth!" Rosetta said while sipping her tea. "It's so hard finding good help! Sometimes I just have to get niggerish myself to whip them into line! I tell them, 'Act your age, not your color!' " With the exception of her hair, Rosetta was just another drab, plain-looking, light-skinned woman, but her hair was a lustrous, wavy chestnut that fell to the middle of her back. It was her best feature and she knew it; over the years it had become part of her raison d'être for living.

"Some Negroes," Wydenia confided, setting down her cup, "just because they're working for their own, don't want to do their best. And you know if these same folk were working for whites, they'd be on their p's and q's!"

"You know it, honey!" Rosetta confirmed. "Sometimes, you just got to give them both barrels!"

Serena walked into the hall, picked up the phone, and said, "Good morning!"

A strange voice with a thick southern accent issued from the receiver. "Is this Miz Tremain?"

"Yes. Who is this?"

"I got somebody that wants to talk to you!"

"Who is this?" Serena demanded.

There was silence, then LaValle's voice. "Mama? Mama, I'm in a bit of trouble!"

Serena looked back toward the parlor to make sure neither of her guests had followed her into the hall. She lowered her voice and asked, "What kind of trouble are you in, Val?"

"I owe some men some money, Mama."

Serena took a deep breath. She sought to contain herself, but there was steel in her tone and its edge was sharp. "I thought I gave you the money to take care of that!"

"It's a long story, Mama. I don't have time to go into it right now."

"Do you think I'm made out of money? That I have a pot of gold, that I can continue to pay for your foolishness?"

"Scold me later, Mama; these men want their money! As you often say, I can't undo what's already been done!"

"How much is it this time?"

"Two thousand dollars!"

Serena gasped; that amount of money would buy a very large house in an upper-middle-class white area. Still mindful of her guests she kept her voice low. "I just gave you five hundred dollars! How can you owe two thousand dollars now?"

"I'll explain everything later, Mama! I need the money now!"

"Tell those men you'll pay them later. I want to see your face as you explain this!"

"They won't let me go, Mama, until they get their money!"

"Don't they know who your father is?"

"Yes, but they say he don't care about me. They say I ain't even his son!"

It was the first time that LaValle had ever brought the subject up with Serena. His words had knocked over the container that held her fear and its icy contents had come spilling out, chilling her insides. "Let me talk to the one in charge!" she demanded.

There was a pause and the same strange voice issued from the phone. "You need to talk to who?"

"Who's in charge? Who's the boss? That's who I want to talk with!"

"I's the boss as far as this fool is concerned. He don't get let go until we gets the money! If we don't get the money by tomorrow, then we gon' commence to hurt him!"

"You wouldn't dare! Do you know who his father is?"

"King Tremain, but we ain't talkin' about Jack Tremain. Jack wouldn't be caught dead doin' the stupid things Val be doin'! We talkin' about LaValle the chump who don't look nothin' like King! And you don't never see him with King neither!"

"Well, I assure you King is very interested in the health of both of his sons! I warn you not to hurt LaValle!"

"You can warn all you want, but if we don't get the money by tomorrow he gon' have some broken legs and stuff befo' this is over!"

Serena saw Rosetta Hughes step out into the hall. She put a smile on her face and waved at her guest. She spoke into the phone with her best business voice. "Where can my husband contact you, mister, uh? What is your name again?"

"Roosevelt Tisdale, but everybody know me as Rocky the Rock! We gon' be behind the stables at the polo grounds! In the handler's barn!"

"Fine, Mr. Tisdale, my husband will be contacting you soon!" Serena hung up without further word. She turned to Rosetta, in the hopes that the smile on her face did not seem contrived, and asked, "Did you need something, Rosetta?"

Rosetta walked down the hall toward Serena and fluffed out her long, wavy red hair. "Was somebody calling about your husband's business?" She waited expectantly for an answer.

"Oh, it's just some business meeting."

"I don't believe either Wydenia or I know exactly what type of business your husband's in." Rosetta continued to play with and primp her hair.

"Real estate. He buys a lot of property for development," Serena answered with a casual shrug, but underneath her smiling exterior, she was irritated. She did not like having to answer Rosetta's impudent questions. Nonetheless, Serena could not afford to alienate her guest. Rosetta, the wife of a prominent mortician, was a mover and shaker in colored society. She was on all the right committees and a member of all the right women's clubs.

"Oh," Rosetta said with a disbelieving shake of her head. Then a disingenuous smile appeared on her face. "Wydenia and I have several other things to do today. You know, so much to do and so little time, but we wanted to tell you the committee's decision regarding your wish to be a judge in this year's Colored Cotillion Ball."

Serena thought for a minute: an hour one way or the other wouldn't make too much difference to LaValle as long as he was freed before the deadline. "Why don't we go back into the parlor?" Serena suggested. She suppressed her excitement. So much effort had been invested in the pursuit and attainment of this judgeship. If she was selected to judge the debutantes, it would be a real mark of acceptance by the social mavens of colored society. There was only one shadow over the brightness of her future and that shadow was cast by the recent actions of her husband, King Tremain.

Once they were seated in the parlor, Wydenia and Rosetta looked at each other doubtfully, expecting the other to begin first. King's shadow passed over Serena's heart and with it her elation faded. She knew that she had been rejected because of his actions last Saturday night at the Colored USO Dance.

Wydenia Witherspoon cleared her throat. "First, we'd like to convey the committee's appreciation for the five-hundred-dollar donation that you gave during our Links Quadrille fund-raising campaign for the cotillion."

"Yes, that was very impressive," chimed in Rosetta, fluffing her hair. She owed her social position to her husband's prominence—it was not something she had earned—but that fact did not prevent her from staring snobbishly down at others who were less fortunate.

"Our background investigation revealed that we were not the only socially active organization that you donated money to in our community," Wydenia continued as she gave Serena a smile of encouragement. Wydenia was a caramel-colored woman and unlike her associate, Rosetta, had earned her position by dint of her will, wit, and ability to forge useful partnerships with lighter colored women who looked down on her because of the darkness of her skin. "We saw that you had volunteered and donated money for the Negro Sisters of Mercy, the Colored Children's Baptist Fund, and the Young Negro Scholars College Scholarship Council. Your community work is very laudable."

"Very laudable," echoed Rosetta.

Wydenia continued as if Rosetta had not spoken. "The committee was impressed with your business acumen as well. In short, you were a truly well qualified candidate and you were a shoo-in, but—"

"A shoo-in," interjected Rosetta. "But your husband!"

Wydenia coughed politely to get Rosetta's attention, then said, "But the committee felt that all three judges had to be people of breeding and above reproach, people who the community knew because of their long-time involvement."

Serena interrupted smoothly. "You are suggesting I am deficient in one or more of the categories that you have just mentioned?"

Wydenia stopped, speechless, then collected herself. "No! Of course not! Just that there were a few on the committee who had some reservations and there were many other competitive candidates as well."

"Stop beating around the bush, Wydenia!" protested Rosetta. "The woman wants to know why she wasn't selected!" Rosetta turned to Serena. "It was your husband! What he did the other night at the USO dance threw a wrench into your appointment and we can't do anything about it!"

"What do you mean?" Serena asked in as neutral a voice as she could muster, but Serena knew exactly what Rosetta was talking about. Serena had hosted a dance for the colored soldiers who were being demobilized at the Presidio. King had returned unexpectedly from one of his south-of-the-border jaunts and caught the young doctor William Braxton making amorous overtures toward her. As she understood it, he later confronted Braxton in the men's room and when Braxton attempted to laugh him off,

King knocked him out cold, breaking his jaw in the process. Some friends had to carry Braxton to the colored hospital in their car. All that and more was the rumor, but since Braxton hadn't attempted to press charges against King, no one knew for sure exactly what had happened. "You were saying?" Serena prodded.

"Well, he, uh—" Rosetta looked to Wydenia for help, but none was forthcoming. Finally, she blurted out, "Everybody knows he knocked out Dr. Braxton and broke his jaw."

Serena leaned forward and asked, "How do you know my husband was the one who hit him? How do you know Dr. Braxton didn't fall?"

"That's a laugh!" declared Rosetta. "Everybody knows King saw him with you and everybody knows how street he can be!"

Serena stared at Rosetta for a moment. "Unless you are in possession of specific facts that substantiate your allegation, what you've said is slander! And you can be sued!"

Rosetta set down her cup and stood up. "I think it's time that we be going, Wydenia!"

"Already?" Serena asked with a smile. "I was just getting to know you."

Wydenia stood up with an apologetic expression. "Perhaps next year—"

"Perhaps," Serena replied as she stood up to show them out.

Once the two women had stepped out the door, Rosetta turned and declared, "Just as it was in the old days, there's a difference between house niggers and field niggers. Your husband is a field nigger! And you're not too far from that yourself! We don't invite field niggers to our house! It'll be over my dead body if you ever sit as a judge at our cotillion!"

"That can be arranged right now, you snotty-nosed heifer! For a start I'll rip that rug right off your head!" Serena had no opportunity to implement her threats because Rosetta ran down the stairs with a look of panic on her face. Serena belligerently turned to face Wydenia to see if she had anything to say.

"I didn't say it and it's not my opinion. I was sincere when I said I hope you're interested in the judgeship next year."

Serena's anger prevented her from responding. She nodded her head curtly in acknowledgment of Wydenia's words, then walked into her house and slammed the front door. She was seething. She had fawned and kissed a lot of behind in order to be selected as a judge for the cotillion, and once again King Tremain had totally disrupted her best-laid plans. But she could not let her anger consume her. She still had to deal with the problem of LaValle.

It took Serena two hours to decide that she needed King's assistance to deal with LaValle's predicament. The money was not the problem—she had considerably more in her savings account. The main reason she felt that she needed King was that she wanted LaValle placed under his protection. It was clear that LaValle could not be trusted to make intelligent decisions, and without King's aegis he would soon be just another statistic found dead on the streets of the Fillmore. She picked up the phone and dialed a number. She knew where King was: he was at the Benjamin Bannaker Hotel planning the christening party for Jack's son.

After talking with several different hotel employees, Serena finally got through to King. His voice issued from the phone without greeting or warmth. "I hope that this is important 'cause I'm meeting with the caterer right now!"

"I need your help! Some people have kidnapped LaValle!"

There was a pause. Then King replied, "So what's that to me?"

"This is your son we're talking about!"

"Don't even try to play that card with me, 'cause I got it trumped ten ways from Sunday!"

"Aren't you concerned about your reputation? A member of your family is in danger!"

"Let's be clear! LaValle may be yo' son, but he ain't a member of my family! I don't care what happens to him! They could kill him as far as I am concerned! So, don't try to manipulate me with some foolish shit!"

"I can't believe this! You mean you'll stand by while they hurt him? They may even kill him! You really don't care? Or is this really about us? Are you using him to get back at me?"

"There you go," King said with a chuckle, "into outer space. You can't provoke me. This is about LaValle. If you don't see that he's a stupid, useless, cowardly fool, then it's 'cause you his mother. 'Course you coddled him and helped him be what he is today. The proud hen, worried about her chick. Good-bye, Serena."

"Wait! Don't hang up! I'm asking you for a favor!" There was a pleading sound in Serena's voice.

There were several moments of silence before King started to speak. "Now, this take some gall! Ain't you the woman who read me up and down on Sunday 'cause I done knocked out her rooty-poot lover-boy! Tellin' me that I done destroyed her social standin'! Callin' me a low-life thug! Sayin' she don't ever want to speak to me, or have nothin' to do with me no more! You that woman? You that same woman?"

"Yes! Yes! Yes! And you did cost me the judge appointment at the cotillion!"

"Like that means somethin'! Anythin' you buy and kiss ass for ain't worth shit! In all these years you don't seem to have learned nothin' about bein' human and the ways humans act."

"You're one to talk! You still talk like a field hand!"

"But I'm one damned rich, field hand–talkin' man, ain't I? And I don't kowtow to no white man neither! Good-bye, Serena."

"Please, King! I'm begging you! Please!"

"You beggin' me? This is somethin' I have to see in person!"

"You'd make me beg for this?"

"You said it and it was the only thing that kept me on the line. 'Cause if I decide to help you, I want you to know the cost of it personally! And it gon' cost you big time! And beggin' gon' be part of it!"

"You hate me that much? You want to humiliate me?"

"I don't hate you. I hardly think about you. But let me be clear about this! You gon' have to beg befo' I do anythin' for LaValle!"

"Alright, come over here and I'll beg." She had the pained voice of surrender.

"No, you come over here! I ain't interruptin' my organizin' for this. If you want this, come here! I got a suite on the second floor."

"In a public place? Why?"

"I ain't negotiatin', woman! If you want help for LaValle, you come here and beg!"

It was nearly five o'clock before Serena knocked on the door to King's suite at the Benjamin Bannaker Hotel. He opened the door and stepped out of the way so that she could pass inside. She walked into his spacious suite of rooms, her high heels sinking into the thick carpet. She took off her overcoat and threw it on a couch, then turned to face him as he came toward her. "How do you want it?" she asked.

"Why don't you show me what you got," King said with a nod at the floor.

Serena gave him a long look, then pulled up her calf-length wool skirt and got down on her knees. "This what you want?" she asked with a facetious tone.

"That's the position!" King confirmed with a smile. "But there got to be some words with it!"

"On my knees I beg you to bring LaValle safely back home and make his enemies afraid to take him ever again! I also ask that you give him the full protection of your name!"

"What's gon' be involved in this first request, bringin' him back home? Am I gon' have to kill somebody, or is it just payin' his debts?"

"I don't care what you do. Just bring him home safe!"

"Even if I have to kill to do it?"

"I told you I don't care what you have to do to bring him home safe!" Serena declared as she started to get to her feet.

"Stay down there!" King ordered. "I want to hear you say, 'Even if you have to kill to do it!'"

Serena complied and repeated mechanically, "Even if you have to kill to do it!"

"I just want to get on record what you beggin' for."

"Will you do it?" A trace of impatience entered her voice.

"On four conditions," King answered, lighting up a cheroot. "You got to accept all four conditions or it's no deal. You got that?"

"What are the conditions?"

"First, you gon' be the hostess of the christenin'!"

"What?" protested Serena. "I hadn't even planned to attend!"

"That just shows how the years have twisted you, Serena! You won't go to yo' own grandson's christening, 'cause you hate his mother 'cause she dark skinned!"

"She's not dark skinned! She's black! And I wouldn't hate her if she had married someone else to try to better herself!"

"Shit! You sound white, like you can take credit for the color of yo' skin! That ain't nothin' you earned and it don't mean a damn thing! Skin color is the white man's problem! It's some jive okey-doke to make you shamed of what you is and to confuse yo' loyalty! You ain't even talked to Jack's wife! You don't know what kind of girl she is!"

"She's a burlesque dancer, trying to cover herself by calling it modern dance!"

"That ain't true, but so what if it was? At least she wasn't no party girl! LaValle's wife was layin' down for all the boys in her set before that fool LaValle came along and married her. You accepted Lisette with open arms and she's about as useful as a blind mule with a horsefly up its ass!

"This really shows how messed up you is! You gon' humiliate yo'self and get down on yo' knees and beg me to help LaValle! But you don't love Jack enough to give his wife a chance! Gon' spurn the christenin' of yo' own grandson 'cause the color of his mother's skin is too dark! White blood mean that much to you? Is this what yo' social standin' is all about? Is that why you love LaValle more than Jack, 'cause LaValle's half white?"

Tears suddenly appeared at the corners of Serena's eyes. "That's not true! LaValle just needs more help than Jack!"

"Well you made sure of that, didn't you? 'Cause you never let him risk fallin'. I guess you didn't love him enough to trust that he had the strength to get up from a fall and keep on movin'. Like you shouldn't have bought him a deferment. You should have let him go into the army like Jack did. It probably would have been the best thing for him! But no, you couldn't let him go! You had to protect him!"

"I gave all that I knew to give!"

"It's too bad you only had enough for one person, huh?" King commented with bitterness. "And it was too much for him. He got smothered under it!"

Serena screamed, "I did the best I knew how! What do you want from me?"

"I'll tell you what I want! You gon' be the hostess at the christenin' and you gon' do it with cheerfulness and a smile! I expect you to organize the caterers, the servers, the layout, and the decorations! Now, I'm just gon' list out these other conditions and I don't want to hear no argument! If you don't want to agree, just get up and go on out the door! When you get up off yo' knees, the deal's off!"

King stared at Serena, awaiting her response. She nodded curtly. He continued, "Two: from now on, you'll treat Jack's wife, Eartha, with the respect she deserves. You'll speak to her and you'll answer polite-like when she talks to you! Three: you gon' set a place for Jack and his family at Sunday dinner from now on, 'cause they gon' come! Might as well hire another cook. Every Sunday dinner from now on, the whole family is gon' be gettin' together! Me included! I'll take over my basement pool room and office while I's in the house! Four. This here condition is the most important of all! I want you make sure that my grandson, Jackson Saint Clare Tremain, is always well provided for and if, God forbid, he should ever get orphaned, you personally will assume the responsibility for raising him. He will always be welcomed in your house and if necessary, be welcomed to live with you. You will take his interests to heart and be generous with him in all things!"

There was no immediate answer. Serena was staring at the floor. King relit his cheroot and paced back and forth, waiting for Serena' answer. He turned to face her and saw her crying. "The conditions too tough for you?" he prodded. Serena wiped her eyes and when she looked at him, King could see grit in her look and determination in the set of her jaw.

"If I agree, LaValle will forever be under the protection of your name?"

"As long as I have the strength to provide it!"

"Then I accept all the conditions!" She got to her feet. "May I get up now?" she asked after the fact.

"Only one thing bothers me," King mused. "How do I know you'll keep your word? I wouldn't like another one of my line raised in an orphanage because of you!"

"No grandchild of mine will ever be raised in an orphanage, but if you don't believe me, what do you want me to do to prove I'll keep my word?" Serena asked with a shrug. "Shall I sign it in blood?"

"I'm glad you said that!" King replied. "Blood is exactly what I want! I want you to sign it in blood!

"Are you serious?"

"Dead serious! Why should I believe you? Yo' past record ain't too good. Signin' in yo' own blood is a good way to remember an oath."

"What do you want to do, cut me?" Serena held out her hand.

"No. I want you to cut yo'self! Deep enough to get enough blood to sign two copies of these contracts." King handed her his bowie and waved some papers in his other hand.

Serena stared at him for a moment, then asked, "You have documents drawn up?"

"Yep, I had 'em drafted right after I got off the phone with you! My attorney is out here from New York for the christenin'! You want to read 'em?" King handed her the papers.

Serena sat down at a writing table and laid the bowie on its shiny wooden surface. She read through the papers quickly.

King asked, "Ain't that what we's agreein' to do?"

Serena nodded and picked up the knife in her right hand. She turned her left palm up. She drew the sharp blade of the knife across her open left hand. The blood spurted from the cut and spilled over the edge of her hand. She asked, "Is that deep enough, or do you want more?"

"That'll do for signin'," King answered without inflection.

"Where do I sign?"

"Right here," King indicated the spot with his finger. "Use this quill. It'll pick up the blood just fine!" After Serena finished signing the papers, King handed her a handkerchief to stem the flow of blood from her hand. He then nicked one of his fingers and pressed blood out for the quill. He signed the papers alongside Serena's name.

"You didn't cut yourself very deeply!" Serena observed.

"I ain't got no need for penance or to prove a point. All I said was enough blood to sign these documents so's we got a contract. You the one that took it out!"

There was a loud knocking on the hallway door. King went over to the door and asked, "Who is it?" He heard the muffled tones of Jack's voice and opened the door.

Jack rushed into the room and looked from King to Serena and back again. He was breathing heavily as if he had been running some distance. "Have you heard?" he gasped. "LaValle is being held by Rocky Tisdale for outstanding debts and he's threatening to hurt LaValle if they don't get the money by this evening!"

"Don't worry about it," King said easily. "I'll take care of it."

"What happened to your hand, Mama?"

"Nothing to worry about. Just let your father handle this problem with Tisdale."

"Sorry, Mama," Jack answered, shaking his head. He turned to his father. "I want to go with you. This Tisdale is getting pretty bold! He's operating on the edge of our territory right now! He needs to be taught a lesson! No one holds a Tremain hostage without paying for it!"

King repeated, "I said I'd take care of it!"

"I heard you, Pa, but I'm a man now." Jack looked his father in the eye. There was no challenge in it. He was merely trying to communicate a point. "You either include me in your plans or I go without you." His four years as an officer in the military service had changed him substantially. He had filled out and had come back with the bearing of a man. He was used to being listened to and commanding men. More important to King, Jack had been in combat and come back alive and uninjured.

"I was hoping that you'd stay with me," Serena suggested to her son. "This whole thing has sort of frightened me. I'd feel better if you were by my side."

"I'll leave you a guard, Mama. I'm going after LaValle. I've already got some of my squad outside the hotel waiting. We're locked and loaded!"

"May I speak to your father alone for a minute," Serena interjected. "Perhaps we can work something out that won't require your participation."

Before leaving the room Jack declared, "I'm going, Mama. No matter what you work out!" Jack had the nose and dark eyes of his father and the likeness was even more obvious when his face had no expression. It was only when he smiled that all traces of King disappeared. Jack had a smile that transformed his face into a friendly and welcoming visage.

Serena waited until the door closed and then turned to King, "I want Jack to stay with me! I don't want him to go! You talk him out of it!"

"Why?" King asked.

"Do I have to explain everything? Why risk both our sons? Let one stay here."

"Are you tellin' me everythin' behind this request? I want you to come clean and tell me everything you know! Why do you think Jack is at risk?"

"I don't know what you're talking about!"

"So this has nothing to do with Sister Bornais's words?"

Serena paused and gave King a long, piercing look. "You went to see her, didn't you?"

King smiled. " 'Course! I couldn't trust you to tell me, could I? You just seem to keep on lyin', just like it's got to be a habit. Sure, I went back to

New Orleans to see her after Amos was paralyzed. Sister Bornais spent the whole evenin' with me and told me everythin'! She told me all about how LaValle gon' be the cause of Jack's death and how LaValle ain't gon' live too long neither."

"Then you know why I don't want Jack to go!"

"Sho' do, but I ain't gon' stop him! He's right, he's a man! He makes his own decisions! He was blooded in the Big War. He knows what he's doin'!"

"You'll let him risk his life without intervening?"

"Seems to me that you the one that done put him at risk! And did it for years! Sister Bornais said you sealed both boys' fate when you didn't do right! Now, there ain't nothin' can change what's been read. It's in motion even as we speak. Anyway, you can't stop death from happenin'. You couldn't stop what happened to yo' sisters. You can't stop the rest of the evil you done set in motion! If it's his time, it's his time!"

"Sometimes you can be so cold!"

"Look who's talkin'! I accepted yo' son into my house. You let mine be raised in an orphanage! You the one who started this whole thing! Look what you've done to your own family! You the one that's cold!"

"I'm asking for another favor! I'm begging for another favor! Please don't let Jack go with you!"

"You out of favors!" King answered with a cynical chuckle. "You can't beg me for nothin' 'cause you ain't got nothin' else to trade!" King walked over to the signed documents on the table and took out a small vial of reddish powder and sprinkled it over the signatures.

"What's that?" Serena asked.

"Just somethin' Sister Bornais gave me," King answered with his first real smile of the evening. "She say put a little of this here dust on a signature signed in blood and the one that reneges on the words of the contract will suffer a thousand times the pain they cause! When I told her it was for you, she put some extra special stuff in it too! I thought it might help you to keep yo' feet on the straight and narrow."

There was more knocking at the door. Jack pushed the door open. "Time is pressing, Pa. Are we together?"

"Comin', son," King answered. He slid a copy of the contract over to Serena. "That's for you. Sister Bornais say this contract will stand until the conditions are met, even if the paper record is destroyed." King turned and walked out of the room without saying good-bye.

Serena sat staring at the contract for several minutes without moving as she pondered the agreement she had made on behalf of LaValle. The pain in her left hand where she had cut herself throbbed with a dull ache, but it did not distract her. Oddly, King seemed already resigned to the prospect that neither Jack nor his brother would live their full limit of years. It was uncharacteristic of him to accept such things. Perhaps that's why King had extended the curse with the signature in blood. Until his action, everything was finite. With the death of LaValle and Jack, the curse would also die, except that King had extended it into the future by binding her to a grandchild that she would rather not recognize.

She realized that for most of her life she had lived in a haunted prison constructed of intoned words and chants: words pirouetting in sonorous circles, weaving around her legs and arms, entering her ears and exiting her mouth, combining into sentences and wrapping themselves tightly around her and immobilizing her with their meaning. Just as the words in the contract were now reaching for her, to bind themselves around her—

Serena stood up suddenly. She had to get out of the suite. She was feeling strangely claustrophobic. She needed fresh air. She was halfway to the door when she remembered the contract. She went back to the table and grabbed the papers roughly in her right hand as if to ball them up and felt a sharp twinge on the tip of her index finger. Blood began to flow out of it, quite a lot of blood given the small size of the cut. It dripped down onto the papers, covering both pages with splotches of red. She saw that the powder that King had poured out had ground glass mixed in it. She looked down and saw that her blood had completely covered the powder on her signature. And still the cut would not stop bleeding. It continued to seep from her finger, obliterating words in the contract. It took several minutes before she was able to stanch the flow of blood.

Bare-chested and wearing only boxing shoes and fighting tights, Rocky Tisdale sat quietly on his stool in the chief groom's small office and tried to focus his mind on the upcoming match. He had just finished a vigorous warm-up session and the sweat was still dripping off of him. His normal plan of action was to think about how he would attack his opponent, the strategy he would use, the different combinations of punches available, and most important, he tried to concentrate on the preparation of his mind for the fight. This evening, however, he was having greater difficulty than usual. It wasn't only that he didn't expect a real challenge from the man he was scheduled to fight, but he felt a gnawing excitement because he was on the verge of accomplishing a major coup. It looked like his days as the chief groom for the polo grounds stables might soon be over. He looked around his small shabby office with its garish overhead light, the frayed posters and tarnished mirror on its walls and the worn-out desk and chairs. He would not be sorry to leave it. He knew he was destined for bigger things. It had only been three days since Nino Molinari, one of the North Beach mob bosses, had taken him aside behind the stables and offered him the opportunity to collect on LaValle Tremain's gambling debts. Rocky had done some collection work for Molinari before, but this was his first major assignment.

There was a knock at his door and he heard the voice of one of his grooms announce through the door, "Five minutes to fight time, Rocky! You need anythin'?"

"I'm good, Billy! I'll be out in a few minutes!" Rocky stood up and admired the reflection of his sweaty, muscular brown body in the mirror. He was almost six feet tall and two hundred pounds. He ran his hand over the smooth skin of his shaved head and nodded his approval. Although he had almost forty fights, he still looked good and didn't yet have the scars and injuries characteristic of a bare-knuckle fighter. He owed his looks to the fact that he was good with his fists.

Rocky donned a fancy, blue silk robe that he had purchased with the winnings from a previous fight purse. As he looked at himself in the mirror again, he had to admit he had done pretty well for himself as chief groom. It was a good position for a colored man. It wasn't the money so much as the fact that he had the run of the stables, for his real money came from the Friday night bare-knuckle fights that he organized once a month in the barn behind the stables. The hostler, Old Man Cochran, left him to the daily management of the stables and only appeared if there was a sick horse, or if some society folk were coming out to ride.

Rocky took a deep breath. So much was riding on this evening. Molinari had told him that if he was successful in collecting from the Tremains, he would be offered the chance to run the Fillmore District operations for the North Beach mob. With that plum of an assignment he would become one of the most important colored men in San Francisco. Rocky didn't see how it could fail. The Tremains had a reputation for paying their legitimate debts and it was no secret on the streets that LaValle was not a valued member of King's family. The way Rocky had it figured, King wouldn't intervene on LaValle's behalf and, as a result, Rocky would be free to deal with LaValle's mother. She had been paying all of his previous debts. She would pay this one. No mother would stand by and see her child hurt if she had it in her power to save him. And in the event Rocky did have to go up against King at some later time, he would have the backing of Molinari's organization.

There was another knock on the door. "It's time, Rocky!"

After tying his robe around his waist, Rocky opened the door and walked alongside Billy Childs to the handlers' barn. Thick fingers of fog were drifting inland through the trees and shrubbery of Golden Gate Park and giving the surrounding landscape a surrealistic cast of undulating gray shadows. "What's the crowd like, Billy?"

"We got a full house! More'n regular! Frankly, I's sort of surprised. You ain't fightin' no contender or nothin'!"

"What kind of odds we gettin'?"

"We got to give three to one to get anybody to bet on Cornelius Lester against you! Most bettin' men know he ain't got nothin' but a real long shot at winnin'."

"I want to stop off and say a few words to our prisoner before I go into the barn."

"You sure you want to do that before the fight?" Billy questioned. "I knows you can beat Lester, but this ain't a good idea. You's warmed out now. It's pretty chilly out here. You best stay focused on the fight!"

"I said I want to say a few words to our prisoner!" Rocky repeated, letting an edge enter his voice. He didn't like being questioned.

"You's the boss, Rocky!" Billy answered as he led the way to a sheltered door on the back side of the barn. He knocked out a signal on its surface, consisting of three short taps repeated twice. The door swung open and Jim Tree's scowling, dark brown face stared out challengingly. Rocky noted that Jim's expression changed appropriately when he recognized who was waiting at the door.

Rocky and Billy were ushered into a long, rectangular room that had a row of narrow cabinets lining one wall. It was the colored jockeys' changing room. At one end of the room there was a scarred wooden table surrounded by rickety wooden benches and a bare lightbulb hanging above it. LaValle was sitting at the table with a forlorn expression. He had a swollen and bloody lip, the result of aggravating Rocky with his mouth. His overall appearance was disheveled. His normally wavy, pomaded hair was sticking up in disarray. His shirt was torn and his face was dirty.

The three men he had guarding LaValle all crowded around Rocky wishing him luck for the fight. The two Tree brothers, who had done some bare-knuckle fights themselves, told him what they knew about his opponent. He listened with half an ear. They hadn't fought at the level of competition that he had, so he took their advice with a grain of salt. Ezzard Williams shook Rocky's hand and returned to his seat by the back door leading into the main hall of the handlers' barn. He picked up a double-barreled shotgun and laid it across his lap. Ezzard was Rocky's insurance should King Tremain come with guns.

Rocky pointed his finger at LaValle. "Yo' peoples best have the money here tonight, else we begin to whup on you hard, boy! Might even start tonight, if I ain't too tired."

LaValle looked up at Rocky with fear. "You told my mother that she had until tomorrow to get the money to you!" he protested. "You can't just change the rules like that!"

For some reason, the whining nature of LaValle's words infuriated Rocky. It reminded him of a long-suppressed memory, of the spoiled colored teenagers who attended the private school where his mother worked as a washerwoman and how those same kids used to tease him about his raggedy clothes and how they squealed and whined in pain when he took his vengeance out on them. Even then he had a fearful punch. Without warning Rocky walked over to LaValle and slapped him hard across the face. LaValle wailed as he fell out of his chair and hit the wooden floor. Rocky stood over him. "When you speak to me, you'll say Mr. Tisdale!" He looked down at LaValle's prostrate form and knew that he wouldn't be too tired after the fight. He was going to enjoy hurting LaValle.

When Rocky walked into the main hall of the handlers' barn, a rousing cheer went through the waiting crowd. Billy walked a little ahead of him, clearing a path through the onlookers, all of whom appeared to want to greet Rocky and pat him on the back. Billy led the way to a high stool that was in the corner of a large square taped on the wooden floor. Consistent with traditional bare-knuckle matches, there were no ring ropes. The square only served as a guideline as to where the fighting should take place. More than one observer had been punched accidentally when one fighter had pressed his advantage over his antagonist into the surrounding crowd. Bales of hay had been set against the walls in rising steps and people were beginning to congregate on them, trying to find seats that offered good views of the square.

There were perhaps two hundred men in the room, the vast majority of whom were colored. But a special section was set aside for important white guests. This section was the only area with chairs and it had a long brass rail protecting it from the square. Mateo Molinari was in attendance with several of his men. Rocky exchanged nods with Mateo and smiled. The next twenty-four hours were going to change his life.

Diagonally across the square from Rocky, on a similar stool, sat his opponent, Cornelius "Hurricane" Lester. Rocky was pleased to see that Lester looked like he was fit and in shape. Rocky wanted to give the onlookers the appearance of a competitive match. Lester was a light brown–skinned man and he was taller and leaner than Rocky. He had long, gangly arms but was reputed to have a good punch. Rocky focused his attention on Lester's torso and visualized his fists punching the wiry body. The bell clanged and both fighters were led to the scratch line. After the obligatory announcements, everyone vacated the square except the fighters. Then the bell clanged again and the fight began.

Rocky could not be sure when he heard the first discharge of the shotgun. He had been too focused on the task at hand. Perhaps they were twenty minutes into the fight. He was just beginning to connect solidly to his opponent's body and head. Rocky hadn't shaken Lester seriously yet, but his clubbing punches were beginning to leave their impact on the man's face and rib cage. Lester had already sustained a cut over his left eye and things were only going to get worse. He did not have the punch to keep Rocky off. The second shotgun blast was heard clearly by all present. Lester had just missed a wild overhand right and had staggered off balance. The booming sound of the twelve-gauge distracted Lester and caused him to turn and stare in the direction of the sound. Unfortunately for him, Rocky was under no compunction to divert his attention from the fight. Rocky hit Lester high on the temple with a powerful right cross and stunned him. He closed with Lester and turned out the lights with a savage left hook uppercut combination. Lester crumpled like steamed spinach.

Instead of the cheering that normally punctuated a knockout, there was silence throughout the hall. Most of the crowd was looking in the direction of the door that led into the colored jockeys' changing room, but on one of the top bales Rocky saw two men open their coats and pull out machine guns. He also noticed that Molinari's three men had gathered closely around their boss in a protective ring. Rocky looked toward the door and saw King Tremain enter with his younger son, Jack, followed by three or four other men. They marched through the crowd with a quiet confidence. He waited quietly for them to reach the square.

Rocky realized that Molinari was only waiting to see how he would handle this situation. He knew that if he was found wanting, all offers would be retracted. Rocky steeled himself to confront King with fearlessness. As King neared the square, Rocky called out challengingly, "You come breakin' in here like gangbusters! You need an army to come and pay the debt you owe? All these men is with you 'cause you's afraid of me?"

King answered in an equally loud voice. "I don't owe you shit! I just came to collect somethin' you thought I didn't care about! You done let yo' ambition push you to take what yo' ass can't pay for!"

Rocky prodded Lester's still-unconscious form with the toe of his shoe. "I got a fool lyin' here at my feet who said the same thing! But he ain't woke up yet! Best watch what you say. You could end up like him!" Rocky glanced in Molinari's direction and saw that his men had their hands in their jackets. They were ready for any trouble that might erupt. He felt emboldened by their presence. "Everybody's tough when they got a gun in their hand!" he announced to the crowd at large. "I wonders if'en you man enough to meet me hand to hand in the square? Then we'll see how tough you really is!"

Rocky's challenge was interrupted by action around Molinari. A man with shoulder-length straight black hair stepped out of the throng of spectators and smacked one of Molinari's men with the barrel of a shotgun. Molinari's other bodyguards didn't stand a chance. Two more men came out of the crowd and in moments Molinari and his men were all lying face down on the wooden floor with guns pressed into their backs. Once Molinari had been disarmed, he was the only one who was permitted to resume his seat.

Rocky was a little shocked about the quickness with which Molinari and his men had been rendered powerless, but he knew that he could still save the situation if he could get King to fight him in the square. "Ain't you gon' answer my challenge? Or is you gon' hide behind yo' guns? I thought you was a man!"

King smiled and started to move toward Rocky, but Jack stepped in front of him and whispered something in his ear.

Rocky taunted, saying, "Come on, Tremain! Why don't you show me what you got! You ain't gon' let yo' whelp talk you out of it, are you?"

Jack stepped forward and demanded, "Are you the one that slapped my brother around?"

"He needed some house breakin'!" Rocky asserted. "I had to give the dog a seein' to! You should have heard him yelp, and if you don't watch it, I'll whup you too!"

Jack set down his machine gun and took off his jacket and his holstered pistol. "I'm going to give you a chance to put your words into action. You see, I want everybody to know that when you lay a hand on a Tremain, it leads to pain!"

Rocky smiled and said, "I ain't got no weapons! You ready to meet me bare-handed at the scratch line usin' standard rules?" It was too good a chance for him to pass up. It was almost as good as getting King. Rocky planned to beat Jack until he dropped. He would prove to everyone that there was a new force in Colored Town.

Jack listened to what his father whispered in his ear. "I don't want to use standard rules! I'm not a professional fighter, but I was a soldier. I'll fight by the rules that I know best, which are no rules at all! A man only gets one chance to come to the scratch line. After that it goes until somebody's dead!"

Rocky smiled even more broadly. Whenever somebody said that they didn't want any rules, it was an admission that not only could they not box, but that they thought that strength alone would win the fight. Rocky had learned a long time ago that strength was just one of many factors that a consistent victor possessed. He stepped into the square. "That's fine with me, boy! Come on to the scratch line!"

When both men reached the scratch line, the fight started. Rocky swung first, throwing three quick jabs at Jack's head. Jack eluded the attack easily, but that didn't trouble Rocky. He was tracking the movement of Jack's head, trying to figure out his defensive pattern. Rocky threw several combinations that just grazed Jack's head. Jack appeared to have just enough quickness to elude the big shot, but he could not mount an attack that could force Rocky into the defensive. It was Rocky who was dictating the pace of the fight. Even though his combinations were being blocked or eluded, Rocky was driving Jack backward with every sally of punches.

Rocky's confidence caused him to misjudge an opening. He threw a left hook, hoping to drive Jack into position for a straight right hand when Jack suddenly dove under his guard and rammed him in the chest with his shoulder. The impact of Jack's shoulder knocked Rocky off-stride. It was only the quickness of Rocky's double left hook that kept Jack from pressing his attack further. However, when he began again to circle Jack looking for an opening, Rocky felt a pain in his abdomen and upper thighs, the pain originating in his groin. It was then he realized that Jack had tried to grab his testicles when he rammed him. It infuriated Rocky that Jack should try to fight dirty and anger put springs in his legs. He charged forward throwing punches. The suddenness of his attack took Jack by surprise because in an effort to dodge a combination, Jack's head lined up for Rocky's straight right hand. Rocky did not miss the opportunity. He threw the punch and it landed flush on the side of Jack's head. Jack fell heavily to the wooden floor.

Rocky raised clenched fists over his head and shouted at King, "You sent a boy to do a man's work!"

King looked down at his son and replied, "You better say joe, 'cause you sho' don't know! The fight ain't over yet!"

Rocky walked around the crumpled form of his opponent who was moving slowly as he was regaining his senses. He threw a savage kick at Jack's head, but at the last minute Jack eluded it while at the same time kicking Rocky's knee. The kick took Rocky by surprise. His leg buckled and he fell awkwardly to the floor. By the time he got to his feet Jack was standing and facing him.

King's voice shouted out, "Fifteen thousand dollars on Jack Tremain! Any takers? You want a piece of this, Molinari? You want to bet LaValle's two thousand against my fifteen?" King took out an envelope from his jacket and waved it for all to see. "Fifteen thousand dollars in cash!"

Rocky could not believe it, but Molinari made no effort to agree to the bet. In fact, he kept silent. It wasn't understandable. It was a foregone conclusion that Rocky was going to win this fight! It was like money in the bank. Rocky wondered what would cause Mateo Molinari to withhold his support. He must be looking at a different fight, Rocky concluded. He turned and walked to the scratch line. He intended to kill Jack and make an example of him. He would show them who was worth betting on. He took a deep breath and waited for the fight to start again.

Rocky watched as Jack trotted toward him, then threw himself into a forward roll, tumbling in Rocky's direction. It confused Rocky and he tried to move out of the tumbling path. But he was not quick enough. He was totally surprised when Jack came out of his roll and sprang from the floor. Jack's first punch clipped the top of his head and a forearm quickly followed, smashing into the side of his throat. Rocky staggered backward, trying to defend himself, but Jack whipped his body forward and head-butted him, breaking his nose.

The pain exploded across Rocky's face, a searing pain that burned up through his skull and made bells clang in the background. Blood was now pouring from his nose. He fought to keep his balance and concentrate on his opponent, but he only vaguely saw Jack flying toward him feet first. Jack's dropkick caught him in the chest, lifted him off the floor, and sent him airborne to land on his shoulders, but it was the way that his head banged into the hard wooden floor that caused him to pass out.

Jack turned and said to the surrounding crowd, "My name is Jack Tremain! LaValle is my brother! Anyone who messes with him, messes with me!" Jack walked over to his father, who offered him a towel.

"Why didn't you kill him?" King inquired, referring to Rocky. "He ain't the kind of man to forget a public beating! Plus, he's a front man for the Molinaris! He gon' want to prove this fight was a fluke!"

"We're not at war here, Papa! We're here to teach a lesson! Things have to be kept in proportion!"

"Then we got one more lesson to teach!" King turned and shouted, "Come here, LaValle!"

Jack moved closer to his father and asked in a low voice, "What are you going to do, Papa?"

"LaValle needs a lesson too!" King responded in the same low tone, but he smiled when he saw the look of concern on Jack's face. He assured his son, "Ain't nobody tryin' to kill him! He ain't gon' get no worse than an ass-whippin'! Seems to me this here boy been needin' an AW to be administered for years!"

"That's harsh!"

King warned, "Watch out who you protectin' now! A fool can be the death of you! Yo' soldierin' should have taught you that!"

"He's not just a guy in my squad!" Jack answered, looking directly into his father's eyes. "He's my brother! I'll go to the mat for him!"

"Then you gon' have many chances to do that, but right now step away. This fool has risked lives tonight! We was lucky they didn't slap leather quicker! We was lucky to kill their dogs! Any one of us could have paid with his life tonight! It got to be a public lesson!"

"Do you have to humiliate him?"

King put his hand on Jack's shoulder. "It's got to be a public lesson, son. Anyway he done already humiliated himself and don't know it! He got to know it! Look at him!" King gestured with a nod of his head at the door. LaValle walked through the doorway with a swagger. A cigarette, held at a jaunty angle, was in his lips. He knew he was under King's protection! He glared at anyone who dared to meet his eyes. King muttered to Jack, "That fool needs a lesson bad!"

King stepped out into the square and addressed the onlookers. "My name is King Tremain and I want to make sure you all understand exactly what we sayin'! If you got a problem with a Tremain, come to me! Don't take no physical action against one that bears the name Tremain! We's fair people. We pays our debts and we take care of our own problems!"

King walked over to LaValle and took him by the arm and turned once again to the crowd. "Now, LaValle here done somethin' wrong. He gambled money he didn't have! He run up a big debt and caused quite a few folk to get their jaws tight! It be understandable that someone should want to hurt him bad! It ain't good business to let a gamblin' debt go outstandin'. We understand that, so the family gon' pay this time! But hear me well, this here be the last time! And to show we don't take this kind of behavior light—" King swiveled on LaValle and hit him hard on the side of the jaw. LaValle was knocked off his feet and stumbled to the floor. "We don't encourage no stupid plays in this family!" King announced as he waited for LaValle to stagger to his feet. He waited until LaValle was all the way erect and knocked him down again. King watched as LaValle rolled to his knees and continued addressing the surrounding throng. "Some people got so much rope they couldn't even hang themselves! So what happens when you done used up everybody's patience? At some point you got to pay! Get up, LaValle!"

LaValle refused to get up off his knees. He begged, "Please, Papa, don't hit me no more! I'll pay the money back! Just don't hit me again!"

King was outraged that LaValle had so little personal dignity that he dared to beg for mercy in front of everyone. He was ashamed to be associated with LaValle. "Ain't nobody tryin' to kill you! Get to your feet and take yo' punishment like a man!"

LaValle still refused to get to his feet. He felt safer pleading on his knees. "Please, Papa! It won't ever happen again! I swear! Please, Papa!"

King was livid. "Someone get this slime off the floor!" People stepped out of the crowd and pulled LaValle to his feet. As King walked up to LaValle, the people who had helped him to his feet melted back into the surrounding background of faces. There was panic on LaValle's face as he watched his father move nearer. He recoiled and held a hand fearfully in front of his face as a protection from more blows. King was absolutely disgusted. For the first time in many years, King thought seriously of killing LaValle. He drew back to hit him again but Jack stepped in between them.

"The lesson ain't over," King advised his son.

"Maybe not, Papa, but you got all there is to get out of this student! If you press on, you'll just expose him to further ridicule! I don't see that as helpful to anyone!"

King stared at Jack's face and saw quiet determination in it. He saw no reason to drive a wedge between himself and Jack, so he turned away from LaValle. King addressed the crowd. "From this moment on, know that LaValle's future gambling debts will not be honored by this family! You should only take bets from him when he has the cash on hand! If you play cards with him, check his money first! If you take his marker, you're a fool! He has no way to pay back his debts! Don't let him run up a big bill, 'cause if you hurt him we'll have to come after you!"

"And we will come after you!" Jack stated loudly.

From a stool on the edge of the square, Rocky bellowed, "You're a dirty fighter, Tremain, and I'll kill you for this! I swear I'm gon' kill you for this!" He pulled out of Billy Childs's grip, who was trying to hold an ice pack to the back of his head. "You better keep a sharp lookout, 'cause I'm gon' be comin'!"

Jack put his shoulder under his brother's arm and assisted him to the exit. As they neared the door, Rocky shouted, "You're a dead man, Jack Tremain! You're a dead man!"

Jack called over his shoulder, "Maybe I'll see you sometime!"

King walked over to Rocky Tisdale's stool and slammed the butt of his shotgun hard into the side of Rocky's head. As the man's body slumped to the floor, King said, "And maybe you won't!" One of King's men walked over and crouched beside Rocky's body to check vital signs. When he shook his head, indicating there was no evidence of life, King nodded grimly and said, "We'll take him with us! Get Rico to take Molinari and his people out to the van."

In the car on the way home, Jack drove while LaValle sat quietly beside him. King sat in the backseat and smoked a cheroot. As they passed out of Golden Gate Park, Jack asked, "How do you plan for us to get rid of Tisdale's body?"

"We got to take him out the Gate tonight and let the ocean have him!"

"If we're going to have to take the cutter out tonight, I need to go home and change."

"Ain't no need. This is almost the day of yo' son's christenin'. Me and the boys'll take care of it. Why don't you go on home?"

"In for a penny, in for a pound, Papa, and you don't have anyone who can pilot the boat as well as me. It'll just take a few minutes to change."

"You ain't got to do this! I got me plenty old friends in town for this here christenin', and they more'n happy to help."

"In for a penny, in for a pound, Papa."

"Whatever you want to do, son," King conceded. He leaned forward and asked, "But tell me this. Why didn't you just go ahead and kill that Tisdale when you first had the chance? He was frontin' for Nino Molinari! After you beat him, he got to kill you or lose face with Molinari! It ain't a good idea to walk away from an unfinished fight!"

"I was hoping it wouldn't have to go that far. I saw enough death for a lifetime while I was with the Seven hundred Sixty-first in Europe! Our tank battalion spearheaded a number of the attacks for Patton's Third Army. If I can avoid killing, I'd like to do so. Anyway, if what you say is true, why did you let Mateo Molinari go? They certainly won't sit quietly for long. You could have killed him, but you didn't!"

"I was lettin' him live for a purpose. If you walk away from an unfinished fight, there got to be a purpose behind it that benefits you more'n yo' enemy! I didn't want to worry about no fightin' tomorrow durin' the christenin' and celebration! Plus, I sent him home with a message that the next time they try to move in on me, it's war!"

"How do you know they won't just send out a hit man for you tonight?"

"Because now they know they got you to worry about too! They'll chew on things for a few days before they do anythin'! By then, we'll know everythin' Mateo's men know. My friend El Indio is very good at finding out what people know!"

"How does one get so good at torture?" Jack asked.

"The Mexican police and the federales taught him. Them Indians from Chiapas been fightin' the Mexican government for years and the police types down there don't play! Nino's boys are pretty good at it too!"

"I guess this was the best move," Jack mused, "attacking Tisdale before he began to consolidate his strength."

"Don't get yo' hopes up! We didn't get nothin' major accomplished tonight. All we did tonight is remove the first colored puppet they picked. If we wait a little while they'll choose another one! We didn't get nothin' major accomplished tonight. This fight is a long way from bein' over!"

"You saved me, Papa. Isn't that a major accomplishment?" LaValle asked as he turned to face King. His face was swollen and discolored from the trauma it had suffered. "Isn't that why you came, to save me because I'm your son too?" The anxiety and the desire for acceptance was too apparent in his voice. LaValle's fears and concerns were so obvious that he seemed stripped naked and vulnerable before his brother and father. "I'm your son too, aren't I, Papa?"

Jack stared at his father's face in the rearview mirror, an unspoken request in his pained expression. He didn't want his brother hurt anymore. The glint of his father's eyes were intermittently reflected in the glow of passing streetlights and they gave no evidence of the thoughts behind them. Jack tightened his grip on the steering wheel and drove on into the night.

There was a long silence before King spoke. "Hear me," he declared. His voice seemed to be coming out of the depths of his soul. "Everything that's worth a damn got to be earned! Ain't nothin' free! The stuff you think is free, you just payin' for it somewhere else! Everythin' valuable takes work and sacrifice! I want you to understand that! You see, family's real important to me, but I'd disown any son who brought shame on the family's name! No son that I recognize begs for mercy! Or shows cowardice! Or gambles with money he ain't got! Anyone that I call a son got to be a man and I don't mean an adult male! I mean a man! If you want me to call you my son, you got to earn it! And you got to earn it by bein' strong! The respect that the name Tremain commands was earned with blood and hard work! And we've kept that respect with determination, courage, and grit! So, if you want me to call you my son, you know the path to travel!"

Jack exhaled slowly and steered the car through the obscuring fog. There was little traffic as they passed the private college of USF and headed down Fulton Street toward the Fillmore District. It was nearly midnight, but the neon lights of the city glowed in a luminous aura above the skyline due to the refraction and reflection of light by the moisture in the fog. It was like a multicolored halo that, due to the hills, sat upon the city at a jaunty angle, the conferred divinity of the salt sea and warm inland air. The vapor outside the car appeared to wrap each of the three men in the car in their own world of low visibility and darkness. No further words were spoken and no one sought to break the stifling silence.

It was two-thirty in the afternoon and the main ballroom of the Benjamin Bannaker Hotel was filled with guests celebrating the christening of Jackson St. Clare Tremain. The ballroom sat two hundred people around a moderately sized parquet dance floor and was elegantly lit with three large forty-bulb chandeliers and numerous wall sconces around the room. There were four lavishly set buffet tables, each staffed with willing servers, placed equidistant around the room, that offered endless portions of steamed clams, shrimp, and Dungeness crab, along with barbecued oysters and assorted fried fish. For those seeking meat, there were barons of beef and smoked turkeys. For second dishes, there were trays of scalloped potatoes and pans of seasonal sautéed vegetables. From the bar flowed champagne, beer, and hard liquor. It was obvious to everyone that money had not been spared in the provision of food and drink.

The party also had a certain elegance because all the invited guests and immediate family had been requested to wear off-white or ivory-colored clothes. The invitation had clearly stated that entrance would only be permitted with appropriate dress. It was King's idea to require the dress code. It was the product of a childhood memory, a boat trip into New Orleans with his Uncle Jake when he was eleven. As they were leaving a tree-shaded bayou and turning into a commercial canal they passed a large stone dock beyond which lay a long sward of green grass. And frolicking on this field of green behind a large mansion were white people all dressed in cream-colored clothes surrounded by tables piled high with food. That image was etched into his mind, for it seemed to the eleven-year-old King to be the picture of the carefree life that white people could purchase with wealth. In all of his years, King had never yielded to the force of that image, but when he thought of making his grandson's christening special, he thought of dressing in shades of white. From then on it was a done deal.

Serena straightened her cream-colored silk skirt, adjusted her blouse, and checked her makeup in the bathroom mirror. After she made sure that all was in order, she prepared herself to return downstairs to the party. She shook her head. Party didn't do it justice; it was a gala affair. King had really surprised her. If she had not come herself, she would not have believed who was in attendance. Just before coming up to King's suite, she had been introduced to Captain Seamus Garrity and his wife. Garrity was in charge of all police operations for the Western Addition, an area that included the Fillmore and Divisadero business corridors. Before that she met Reverend Darcy Goodlett and his wife. Goodlett's church, Westlake Baptist, had one of the largest, most influential congregations in the city. Someone told her that Superior Court Judge Brendan Sullivan and Josh Gibson, the baseball player, were sitting over by the steamed shrimp at a buffet table telling each other stories. She smiled into the mirror. She was a hostess at an event that would be talked about for some time in the highest of colored social circles.

Serena went down the stairs and into the kitchen. As soon as she entered, she heard Butterball Brown's gravelly voice yelling at the preparers and second cooks. She waited until he was finished. She had respect for the way he had organized both food and people. Since yesterday, when King had assigned her the responsibility of coordinating the event, she had worked very closely with Butterball and had been impressed with his grasp of the logistics of catering a large affair.

"Cut the fish so that most of the pieces is the same size. That way it take about the same amount of time to cook! And don't you ever walk away from food cookin' in hot oil again!" Butterball could have gone on haranguing his staff, but he saw Serena and he stopped. He left the food prep crew with, "You have forty minutes until we do dessert! Be ready to shift in that direction!" He walked over to Serena and ushered her out of the kitchen. "How's things goin'?" he asked.

"Everything is wonderful. The food is particularly good! I just came in here to tell you that people are asking for you. Um, I believe Ed Harrison and his wife, Leah, and King's attorney, Ira Goldbaum, were all asking about you!"

"So, Big Ed finally got here, huh?" Butterball said with a smile, his fat jowls dimpling with the effort. "I guess they didn't tell you, but I don't normally leave the kitchen until the stove gets turned off. You see, if'en I gots any home fires burnin', I tends 'em. Never can tell when it might need a log stuck in it!" He gave her a wink and suggestive shake of his round body before he went back into the kitchen.

Serena smiled as she returned to the banquet hall. She stood in the entrance and saw the head of the sleeping-car porters union from Oakland hold plates for his wife at the buffet table. She couldn't remember his name, but she used to see him and his wife regularly when she and King still lived in West Oakland. Then Serena saw Wydenia Witherspoon and her husband. She was momentarily shocked. Wydenia was the last person she expected to see. Their eyes met and Wydenia waved a greeting. Serena forced a smile on her face and waved back. She watched as Wydenia led her husband toward her. Serena had not made up her mind how she was going to act. She decided to let Wydenia dictate the course of the conversation.

"Serena, it's so good to see you!" Wydenia effused. "I'd like you to meet my husband, Fred. I had no idea that we'd be seeing each other so soon."

I'll bet you didn't, Serena thought as she shook hands with Fred Witherspoon.

"You folks put on quite an event, Mrs. Tremain," Fred remarked as he looked around the hall. "There are more movers and shakers in this room than you can believe. Your husband sure knows how to get people together! I met Henry Armstrong, the boxer—surprised me how small he was! Met Josh Gibson too and he surprised me at how big he was! Yes siree, I'm seriously thinking about going into business with your husband on a couple of apartment projects. He seems to know where to find the money to let a colored contractor build a big development project. Hey, isn't that the saxophone player, Louis Jordan? He played 'Five Guys Named Moe' and 'Choo Choo Ch'Boogie!' You'll excuse me ladies, I want to talk with him." Before Fred walked away he said, "You're going to be seeing a lot more of us in the future, Mrs. Tremain."

Serena and Wydenia watched Fred make his way through the crowd before they turned and faced each other. Serena looked Wydenia in the eye. "There's no reason to pretend. I know you're only here because Fred sees a business opportunity in working with my husband. We can be polite without being friends."

"You have it all wrong, Serena. I'm not on the opposing side. You're a strong woman with a powerful husband. There are going to be a lot of people jealous of you, but I'm not one of them! We can be allies you and me. We think alike."

"What evidence is there of that?"

Wydenia leaned forward and whispered, "What if I told you that Wanda Goodlett, Tina Patterson, and I persuaded the committee to use a third judge in this year's cotillion? And that I've been empowered by the committee to offer it to you?"

Serena was stunned. The peach she had painfully climbed the tree for that had remained out of reach now fell neatly into her lap. "Wanda Goodlett and Tina Patterson supported me?"

"You can ask them yourself, if you want. They're sitting over there by the bar with Rosetta Hughes and her husband!"

"Rosetta is here?"

"Yes. She claims that her husband forced her to come. And knowing the level of avarice that Maurice possesses, she might be telling the truth. But I think she's happy that she's here. This celebration will be written up in the both the *Bay Reporter* and the *Sun Gazette* tomorrow." Wydenia chuckled humorlessly. "Unfortunately, what she is most interested in is being seen and acknowledged in the social calendar. Nothing else seems to matter. There's so much work we could be doing to help our people. It's a shame to get absorbed in the shallowness and posturing involved with social climbing."

Serena searched Wydenia's brown face for a hint of sarcasm or irony, for her words had sent a cold shaft into Serena's gut. The manner in which Wydenia had made her statement made Serena see it as a total castigation of Rosetta and one that was warranted due to her obvious lack of substance. What Wydenia didn't know was that Serena's thinking and standards of success were closer to Rosetta's than hers. So Serena had been pierced by a dart meant for someone else, a dart that unerringly revealed the shallowness of her own motivation. It made Serena feel uncomfortable. She mumbled, "Look, I've got some hostess duties to attend to. Will you excuse me?"

"Sure, I understand," Wydenia replied with a smile. "You have a lot going on today. Perhaps I can call you for your answer tomorrow after church?"

Serena nodded. "I look forward to hearing from you." She gave Wydenia a polite smile and turned away into the crowd. Social stature and acceptance: two of the most important things that she had ever wanted were within her grasp and yet the prospect of attaining them seemed tainted. On the far side of the room, Serena saw LaValle and Lisette sitting at a table talking animatedly. From the gestures and the expressions on their faces, it appeared that they were arguing. LaValle had been drinking since he had arrived at one o'clock and it was now nearly three. Serena hurried to intervene. She did not want LaValle to do something that would bring further dishonor on the family. As she made her way through the throng of guests with a smile on her face, she actually felt, for some unknown reason, that she was standing before the shadowy door of a long-unopened basement, a basement in which she had sealed many painful thoughts and images. And what was stranger still was that she knew the door was destined to be opened whether she chose it or not. As she passed through the crowd, she marveled at how quickly the joy could be squeezed out of the attainment of a goal.

Captain Seamus Garrity and King Tremain were standing by the bar. The captain was downing his third double-shot of scotch when King said, "I'm glad you and the missus could make it."

"Wouldn't have missed this spread for the world, Tremain," Garrity answered, brushing his graying hair back from his florid face. "You've really gone all out! My wife loves those barbecued oysters. You knew we were coming when you told me you were going to have real Irish whiskey."

"I know you like a taste every now and then," King replied.

"Yes, I do occasionally," Garrity concurred, setting his glass down on the bar for another refill. After his glass was filled again, he turned to King and said in a confidential tone, "Hear you and your boys were out at the polo grounds last night. There's a rumor going around that you killed Rocky Tisdale and some Molinari thugs while you were out there."

"You know rumors is like assholes. Everybody got one."

"Well, there some guys down at the station who feel they have some pretty reliable witnesses. Do you have an alibi?"

"Don't need one. The last I saw of Tisdale he was going out for some fresh air and a swim with a couple of Molinari's boys. Why don't you ask Molinari?"

"It won't be me doing the asking. Because of the Molinaris involvement, it'll probably be someone from downtown. They'll probably assign that fool Hastings to assist in the investigation."

"An investigation?" King frowned. "I didn't know they investigated the death of colored folks! I guess they found Tisdale's body, huh?"

"No! They're not investigating that! They don't care about him. The Molinaris are using their political muscle to put some pressure on you."

"Well, I've got plenty witnesses who will testify that I went to a card game afterward."

Garrity laughed and because he was a stout man, his whole body seemed to shake with each paroxysm. He drank half his drink and advised, "You better watch your back. Molinari is not going to take kindly to you disrupting his plans! They are going to come at you from all angles. They know how to use the legal system well. They have a lot of people paid off."

"That's why Judge Sullivan is here," King explained. "I got lots of people workin' on improvin' my situation and unlike Molinari, my taxes is in good shape! I took yo' advice and got all that cleaned up!"

"If a war breaks out between you and the Molinaris, you know the department will only be interested in arresting your people. You'll have to be extra careful!"

"Which side will you be on?"

"I'd be on your side. I owe you, but I probably won't be here. I'm planning on retiring to that horse ranch you helped me buy during Prohibition. In November of this year, I'll have thirty years in the department and I get a full pension when I retire. I'm gone the day that happens and

Maureen can't wait. She wants to move out there now. Hastings will probably be promoted to take my place. He's been kissing enough ass to get it! And you know what he feels about Negroes," Garrity said, his blue eyes squinting at King.

"I know all I need to know about Hastings! Anyway, he might not be around too long. I hear he's a high-strung type, the type that might eat his gun late at night."

"Just don't let them find your fingerprints on the gun."

"Don't worry, they won't."

"Good. You can't be too careful." Garrity nodded. He turned and pointed to someone behind King in the middle of the ballroom. "Hey, isn't that Big Ed Harrison? I haven't seen him since Prohibition!"

King smiled. "Yeah, that's him. You see those two men with him, big as houses? They're his sons. Come on over! Let me introduce you."

Garrity grabbed King's arm. "Listen, before we rejoin the table, I wanted to give you an update on a matter you asked me to check on." Garrity stepped closer to King and dropped his voice. "What we established last year was that there was an Elroy Fontenot inducted into the army in Chicago in the spring of 1938. Well, now I got more news and it was damned difficult to get!" Garrity pulled a pad from his pocket and flipped through it until he found the page he desired. He squinted at what was written and read slowly, "Fontenot spent two years in the infantry before being transferred into the Nine hundred Sixty-ninth Field Artillery Battalion. His battalion fought in Normandy on D-day and was one of the Negro units to receive a presidential citation."

"Tell me, goddamn it, Seamus, is he alive? You's actin' like a bull that don't want to leave the chute! Is the boy alive?"

"He was demobilized at Fort Bragg, North Carolina, in February of this year and that's where the trail goes cold. I've sent two men back there to see if there is anyone still around from his artillery battalion or anybody who knows where he might have gone. I even called and told the orphanage that we were looking for him. So they'll contact us if he checks in."

"Keep lookin'," King urged. "I'll pay whatever's necessary." There was no outward evidence, but inside King was jubilant. He felt as if a heavy weight had been lifted from his shoulders. His oldest son was alive and there was still a chance that he would be brought back into the family. King clapped Garrity on the shoulder. "Seamus, the department don't know who they losin'! You's a damn good detective!"

"After thirty years in the profession, you develop connections all over the country and if you stay in contact, they can be valuable!"

King nodded but he really didn't hear what was being said. He was a hundred feet off the ground. The only way the news could have been better was if Elroy had been located. But he had made it home alive. For now that was enough. King took a deep breath and lit a cheroot. He felt expansive. He asked Garrity, "Have you met the seven-month-old star of this occasion, my grandson?" Garrity shook his head, indicating that he hadn't. "Come over to the table," King urged. "Let me introduce you!"

Outside the ballroom Serena and LaValle walked up the wide curving staircase to the mezzanine and sat in a couple of wingback chairs next to the balustrade overlooking the main lobby.

As Serena checked her makeup in her powder-case mirror, she stared past the mirror at LaValle's bruised and swollen face. She had intervened between Lisette and LaValle just before he was about to explode. He lit a cigarette. "Why are you so angry, Val?" she asked as she put her powder case away.

"Come on, Mama! You know! Look at my face! It's like I have my own conversation piece! I have to explain where I got these bruises to everyone! Nobody believes me when I say it was a car accident. What do I say? My father beat me up? He shouldn't have made me come! He just wants to humiliate me!"

"I don't think that's the reason he wanted you here, Val. I think he wanted the whole family here in support of this event."

"How can you say that?" LaValle scoffed. He paused and looked at his mother. "Why are you here? You won't even talk to that black girl Jack's married to and I know for a fact that you don't like their baby. Why are you here?"

Serena said nothing. It was true, she didn't like Jack's wife, Eartha. Her darkness reminded Serena of Mamie. It seemed to Serena that she had spent the better part of her life dealing with the problems caused by that one black-skinned nigger woman and she didn't look forward to having another one in her life. Nor did she feel any parental love for Eartha's dark-skinned whelp. It was solely her agreement with King that caused her to be in attendance, but Serena wouldn't tell LaValle that.

Failing to elicit a response from his mother, LaValle said, "He wants to humiliate me. He just wants to rub my face in what he didn't give me! There was no party like this when my son was born two years ago! Why does everything go to Jack?"

"I think your actions have some bearing—"

"Okay! Okay, that may be true now, but I remember he treated us differently from the time we were children! I was just thinking about it last night. He and Jack used to go hunting and fishing all the time, but I was never invited! Jack was allowed to play with the hunting dogs, but I wasn't! Jack was the only one ever invited to go down to Mexico! Jack used to go with him everywhere, but I had to stay with you! Why is that? Why did he treat us differently? Why, Mama?"

Serena did not respond. What could she say? What good would it do now to tell LaValle that it had been her decision that he stay by her side, not King's. King had asked to take LaValle with him and Jack countless times, but always she had refused, fearing that LaValle would be subject to pressures and demands that he could not meet. She never trusted King to treat LaValle with fairness. So eventually, over the years, King had stopped asking and LaValle had been left solely in her charge.

She looked across at her son. Even with the discoloration and swelling, anyone could see that he was a handsome specimen of a man, even-featured, smooth light-brown skin and a dazzling smile when he chose to show it. She saw his lip tremble and realized that he was on the verge of crying. "Pull yourself together, LaValle! You don't want to break down here!"

"Look at me, Mama! I'm living in hell! I'm a member of one of the most powerful colored families in San Francisco, yet everywhere I go I'm the laughingstock!" Tears started to collect in the corners of LaValle's eyes. "Maybe I'm not much of a man now, maybe I'm weak, but I was born with everything that Jack has! If Papa had taken me under his wing like he did Jack, he could've taught me to be strong! He could've helped me be more than I am! It was like that time he took us to that boxing gym; when I came home with a black eye, I couldn't go back! Jack came home with a lot worse than that, but he was allowed to stay in the program and he learned to box! It's a story that's repeated over and over throughout my life! Why didn't he have faith in me? Why didn't he take the time with me like he did with Jack, Mama?"

Serena sat still as if she had been impaled to her chair. LaValle was complaining about her decisions, not King's. An overwhelming sadness settled upon her. She felt the tears welling up from deep within, but with an iron will she forced the tears back down. She was emotionally drained and exhausted, yet she would not give in to self-pity. She straightened her back and tilted her head up so that her jaw was high. She was strong enough to handle whatever life dealt out.

Serena saw that the tears were now streaming down LaValle's face and he made no effort to wipe them away. "Stop that!" she ordered with an edge in her voice. She was impatient with his lack of control. "You're in a public place! Act like a man!"

"Act like a man!" LaValle chuckled humorlessly. "That's the biggest problem in my life! Act like a man! You don't know how hard that is for me! That's the battle I fight every day! You need to be taught how to be a man, Mama! It doesn't just come to you automatically! There's more to it than that! I don't know what it is, but I know that Jack learned it and I didn't!"

"That's absurd!" Serena protested. "You know everything that Jack knows! You're both sons of King Tremain! What more do you need?"

"Okay, Mama," LaValle answered with a dismissive wave of his hand, as if making her understand what he was truly saying was beyond her ability. There were several seconds of silence and then LaValle began to speak again. "You know, Mama, I asked Papa if I was his son on the way home last night. You know what he told me? Everything has to be earned! I have to change my actions if I want him to call me his son! In all that talk, he never answered my question directly! I wonder if Jack ever had to earn it?" LaValle shuddered as the tears took over.

Serena stood up. She couldn't take anymore. The weight was too much. "Of course, you're his son! Now, stop crying! Stop it!" she hissed. "Do whatever you have to do, but stop it! Remember that this is Jack's day! Think of somebody other than yourself!"

LaValle gave her a look filled with resentment and stood up. "It's always Jack's day!" he muttered before he turned away and ran down the stairs.

Serena watched as LaValle descended the staircase and walked out the ornate front door of the hotel. She took a deep breath and then checked her makeup in her powder-case mirror. Everything was still in order. She turned and went down the stairs slowly, as if she were royalty, but inside she felt as if a bomb had been detonated in her soul and everything of value had been destroyed.

Serena saw several reporters from the colored papers standing in the lobby by the entrance to the ballroom. Though she was intent on returning to the party, she felt she still needed a few moments to gather herself. She didn't feel up to talking with any reporters, so she went through a service entrance into the catering hall, which lay between the kitchen and the various dining areas. She saw a group of men standing around King. She recognized Fred Witherspoon, Reverend Goodlett, the union man from West Oakland, and Rosetta Hughes's husband, Maurice. There was a fifth man she didn't recognize. Before she could turn around and leave, Fred saw her and beckoned her over. As she walked toward the group, she heard guffaws of laughter.

Fred raised his glass in Serena's direction and said, "To the hostess with the mostest! This is one hell of a party!" There was a chorus of voices in support.

Maurice nodded his head in agreement. "You'll have to tell my wife where you got this caterer. The food was just fabulous!"

Serena answered, "You have to ask my husband. It's a friend of his. He brought him in from New York!"

"You brought a caterer in from New York?" Reverend Goodlett exclaimed. "You Tremains go all out when you throw a party!"

King said, "He may be movin' his business out to the Bannaker and if he does, he'll take over the kitchen and buy out one of my partners in the hotel!"

"I didn't know you owned part of this hotel!" Fred Witherspoon said with surprise.

"Forty percent. I paid for the renovation of the place!"

"You've got all sorts of business deals going," Maurice observed, rubbing his jaw thoughtfully.

"Gentlemen! Gentlemen! We forget ourselves," Reverend Goodlett declared. "Mrs. Tremain obviously came in here to talk with her husband. We should be sensitive to their needs!"

"No! No!" protested Serena. "You don't have to go!"

"That's alright, Mrs. Tremain," the man from West Oakland said. "I think we've talked enough business and probably should get back to our wives."

"Wydenia's probably looking for me right now!" Fred declared.

"Emmm," grunted Maurice. "Rosetta is going to accuse me of abandoning her! You know she didn't want to come, but I know tomorrow she'll be happy to tell her friends she was here! This was a fine party! And what a great idea it was to have everyone dress in white. It made everything extra classy!"

"Best christening party I've ever been to," Reverend Goodlett said with a nod as he led the way out.

"No doubt about it!" Fred agreed. "Did you see those reporters out in the lobby? This will certainly be a major article in the colored papers tomorrow!" Fred waved to Serena as he followed the reverend.

"My wife will be talking about this party for weeks!" Maurice declared as he slipped a business card in King's hand. "I'll call you next week about that idea!" King nodded in response.

The men began to file out until the fifth man, the one she did not know, stopped in front of Serena. He was a short, well-built man in his early thirties dressed in very dapper white clothes. His skin was a rich, luminescent caramel and there was considerable vitality in his smile. He turned to King. "You haven't introduced me to the missus yet, King. I know I ain't no businessman, but I's still respectable."

"I'm sorry, Henry! I thought you had met my wife, Serena Tremain!

Serena, this is Henry Armstrong, one of the greatest boxers in the world pound for pound! He's a champion in three different weight classes!"

"How do you do, Mr. Armstrong," Serena said, shaking his hand.

"Seems pretty clear, it ain't as good as King's doin' if'en he got a pretty wife like you! You'll pardon me, ma'am, but King must've married you right out of the cradle, if'en you got a big old hardhead boy like Jack."

"Thank you for the compliment, Mr. Armstrong. You know our youngest son?"

"Jack and me is like fingers in a fist. I was best man at his wedding. We started hangin' around together at the hunting parties King gives twice a year. I think we got to be real good friends the year that Big Ed Harrison organized the trip to Alaska and Jack came home on leave from the service to join us. That was back in 1940 maybe."

"I had no idea you knew Jack that well," Serena said with a polite smile.

"And I'm proud to know him too! Anyway, I think I best get back to my girl. I been in here shootin' the breeze with the men too long! It was nice meetin' you, Mrs. Tremain. You sure do know how to throw a party!" He clapped King on the arm and went out into the main ballroom. Serena and King were alone in the catering hall.

Serena exhaled and leaned back against a heavy wooden table. During the celebration she had noticed the warm familiarity with which King's older friends interacted with Jack and how well the sons of all the men got along with each other. She had wondered about it, but with all the pressures of coordinating an event her mind was occupied with other things. Armstrong's words had given her a brief glimpse of the world LaValle had never known and she realized that he had missed something valuable.

"You gave a great party," King declared, lighting a cheroot.

Serena looked at him. He seemed to be the picture of the ideal happy and proud grandfather. In fact, he looked like a man riding the wave of success. King's well-being caused a surge of resentment within her, but she suppressed her feelings of ill will and answered tonelessly, "That was the contract. I fulfilled my responsibility."

King studied her a moment before he spoke. He flicked the ash off his cheroot into an ashtray. "You ain't fulfilled the whole contract yet. You still obliged to carry out the rest of yo' bargain! This party is just another shindig in a line of shindigs. In two weeks it won't be remembered by anyone but them social butterflies. But my grandson, if he should ever need yo' help in any way, you best be johnny-on-the-spot! And if the worst should happen, you'll take him to home and raise him in yo' house! That's the most important part of the contract. That's the reason I had you sign in blood! That's the only reason LaValle is walkin' around now!"

The smile of superiority on King's face infuriated Serena. Her world was in shambles while he acted as if he was on top of the world, like the birth of this child meant something. She had seen the baby. It looked just like she imagined Elroy must've looked like when he was a baby. It looked like King. Whatever genetic contribution Eartha made was not visible. The boy was a Tremain. He had King's stamp on him. It looked like Jack had just been a conduit for his father. Serena could see nothing of herself in the baby's brown body. Somewhere Mamie was laughing, laughing, laughing. King interrupted her reverie with his own, coarse chuckle.

"Looks like you steamin' 'bout to pop," he said, the smile spreading across his face.

Serena couldn't take it anymore. "Sometimes I hate you almost as much as I hated my father!"

"If you still hate yo' father, then you must hate yo'self!"

"What are you talking about?"

"You done become Charles Baddeaux! He's alive in you! You got the same size heart he had. His blood run pure in you!"

"How dare you! I'm nothing like my father! We are worlds apart!"

"Oh yeah? You used to say you hated him because he would lie 'bout important things. That's you to a tee! You lie about important things, don't you?" King began to pace as he spoke. "You used to say you hated him 'cause he was small, mean, and stingy; he wasn't generous! That's you! You didn't think there was enough for LaValle if you let Elroy in. It didn't matter that he was my son. You made a small, mean, and stingy decision when you left him in that orphanage!" King turned and pointed to her. "You said you hated yo' father 'cause he was ignorant! That's you! Like a piece of discount furniture, you got the veneer of learning, but underneath you's cheap pine! You's still an ignorant farm girl! You's still runnin' the same high-yellow bullshit game you was when you was eighteen, like color should mean somethin'! You ain't learned that color is only important to fools who done bought into the race game, people who think yo' color should determine yo' privilege. The white man is laughin' 'cause he got us fightin' amongst ourselves."

"I'm no ignorant farm girl!" Serena protested. "I run a real estate development firm! I move in the very best of social—"

"Usin' my money!" King exhaled the smoke of his cheroot. "Still, I'll admit you's pretty good when it comes to buyin' and sellin' property, but that ain't important in the long term! The problem is you ain't learned nothin' 'bout investin' in people! You ain't learned nothin' 'bout earnin' respect and loyalty. You ain't about givin'! You into takin' just like yo' father!"

"That's not true! That's not true! I donate time and money to a lot of charitable organizations!"

" 'Cause you into social climbin'!" King scoffed. "The only time you's generous is when there's a purpose behind it."

Serena said nothing. She merely shook her head. She didn't have the strength to continue. The events of the last few hours had robbed her of her zeal to argue further.

King walked over and stood in front of her. "The surest sign that you done turned into yo' father is the mood in yo' house. It's dark and cold, just like the way he used to keep it. Ain't no laughter or joy in yo' house!"

Jack walked through the swinging door. "Mama! Papa! The baby's awake now. We'd like to introduce him to the guests. Aunt Leah, Uncle Rico, and Captain Garrity have all asked to see him!"

King put out his cheroot in the ashtray and said, "That sounds good to me! I been wantin' to hold the little feller anyway!"

Jack asked, "You coming, Mama?"

"In a minute, Jack. I've got to check on the kitchen. You start without me."

Jack gave his mother a brief questioning look, then turned and walked back into the main banquet hall.

King looked at Serena and shook his head.

"It wasn't in the contract that I had to be standing with Jack and his wife while they showed off the baby!"

"Don't explain to me! I ain't in it no mo'! I ain't the one gon' enforce the contract. That's between you and the angels! You just go ahead and be small!" He didn't wait for her answer, but followed his son out the swinging door.

King's arguments were damning and she felt in her heart that his assessment was true. She had turned into her father. Serena had thought she had buried Charles Baddeaux long before he died, yet like Mamie he too refused to go away. The world that she had longed for in her youth was a far cry from what she possessed. She was living in a ghost world filled with dreams that had no possibility of becoming reality. She pushed through the door and walked listlessly out of the room.

When King arrived at the table, there was a chair for him between Eartha and Jack. There was only one chair. It was obvious that they did not expect Serena to join them. King sat down and Eartha placed the baby, wrapped in blankets, in his arms. King pulled back the blanket and there was a smiling brown baby with dark brown, glinting eyes staring up at him. As usual, whenever King looked at his grandson, it reminded him of when Jacques was an infant. It reminded King of how filled with hope he had been that his son would be the beginning of many more sons.

Big Ed Harrison walked up to the table and asked, "So this is the little one, huh? He sure look plum like his daddy!"

"Yep," King answered with a proud smile. "This here be Jackson Saint Clare Tremain."

Captain Garrity ambled over with his wife, Maureen. As she cooed over the baby he asked, "How'd he get the moniker Jackson Saint Clare?"

King answered, "Jackson was Eartha's father's name and Saint Clare is a Tremain family name. Saint Clare was his great-great-great-grandfather."

"That's a big name for a little tyke," Garrity observed.

King smiled and said, "He gon' grow into it."

A line of guests formed and passed by the table. Except for his close friends, the faces began to blur for King. He found himself getting caught up in just playing with the baby. At one point little Jackson grabbed King's index finger in his tiny fist and would not let go. King waved his finger back and forth and Jackson starting giggling. The baby's laughter brought such a glow of warmth to King that he held the baby to his chest for a few moments. As long as King lived, young Jackson would be a priority in his life. This child represented the future of King's branch of the Tremain line.

Without intending it, King sank into a reverie that led him back down the chain of memory to his last meeting with Sister Bornais in New Orleans. It had been a hot, humid day in the spring of 1940. Sister Bornais had moved her abode down near the docks. The smells of raw sewage, Brazilian coffee, grain shipments, imported spices, and Cajun cooking permeated the air. She had invited him into a dark room lighted only with candles. Pungent incense burned in holders around the room. She waved him to sit on a pile of pillows since there were no chairs in the room, sitting across from him at a low table.

Several minutes passed in silence as Sister Bornais lighted and puffed on a long-stemmed clay pipe. King quietly studied the woman whose words had had such a profound effect on his family. Sister Bornais wore a bright yellow head tie and did not look as if she had aged at all in the years since King had left New Orleans. Her eyes were still bright and equaled the shine of the numerous gold bangles, bracelets, and necklaces that she wore on her neck and wrists. Her face was smooth and unwrinkled and her movement had none of the stiffness of age.

King cleared his throat to speak but she waved him to silence. She took several more puffs on her pipe and said in a low, husky voice, "I know why you's here. You's seeking a way to break the curse that ties yo' second son's life to the chile of LeGrande." She puffed her pipe several more times before putting it down. "I tol' you befo' there ain't nothin' you can do to change what's already been writ."

"What if I kill LaValle?" King asked.

"That won't do nothin' but hurt yo' grandson! Understand me! Ain't nothin' can save yo' second son from the fate that his mother cursed him to! She the only one could've put a stop to things, but she had to do it years ago. Ain't nobody can do nothin' now!"

"I ain't got no grandson! What grandson are you talkin' about?" King inquired.

"Yo' second son is gon' give you the only grandson you gon' have," Sister Bornais answered as she rang a small bell on the table. "If you have a hand in LeGrande's son's death, the curse passes on to yo' grandson. But if you do right and leave him to the fate that's destined for him, yo' grandson won't be touched and he'll grow up to lead yo' family."

A woman quietly entered the room, bearing a teapot and two mugs. She set down the tray and disappeared. Sister Bornais poured the steaming liquid into the two cups and offered King one. He sipped the hot liquid, which had an initially sweet flavor but a burning aftertaste. "What's this?" he asked with a frown.

"Just somethin' I make up to help me connect. Drink it down! I wants you to hear me good! You's a good man and I wants to help you. When you finishes the tea, give me yo' hand!"

King gulped down the liquid, which other than its taste appeared to have no ill effects, and stretched out his hand. Sister Bornais took his hand in a surprisingly firm grip and held it for several minutes with her eyes closed.

"Yo' grandson's mother is gon' be dead befo' his daddy! Her death is gon' be caused by LeGrande's chile too. Yo' grandson gon' be an orphan befo' he's ten years old!"

"Ain't there nothin' I can do?" protested King. "I ain't used to sittin' around and acceptin' stuff I don't like! It don't make sense that I can't kill LaValle. He's the cause of all of this!"

"Fate don't have to make sense to mortals. You know why the sun rises? Why the sea is blue? Why you was born? What we know is a pinch in a bushel of facts! Anyway, LaValle ain't the cause of this! He a victim too! It's yo' wife who done caused all this, but killin' her ain't gon' stop nothin' neither! There ain't nothin' you can do but help yo' grandson grow to manhood!" Sister Bornais released his hand and seemingly fell into a stupor. Her head dropped down on her chest and she remained motionless.

King waited five minutes before he stood up. His movement seemed to waken her from sleep.

Sister Bornais raised her head. "One mo' thing. The sooner LeGrande's chile dies, the sooner yo' second son dies."

"Does that mean the longer I keep LaValle alive, the longer my son'll live?"

"No!" she answered with a shake of her head. "Ain't nothin' you can do to keep LeGrande's son alive. When fate calls, fate calls! Just don't hurry his death none!"

King pulled out a wad of money and handed it to Sister Bornais, but she shook her head. "You done paid for this years ago!"

"Well, let this pay for my son's visit. He needs to hear—"

"Don't send yo' son to me!" Sister Bornais interrupted. "It ain't good for folk to know how or when they gon' die! It changes their actions but not the result! All it does is give them years of worry! Heed me on this. Don't tell yo' son nothin'!"

King exhaled slowly. "You makes it tough on a man! Can't tell my son nothing?"

Sister Bornais smiled for the first time. "You's tough enough to handle it. Yo' dream of family gon' be realized in yo' grandson and if you do right, you gon' live to see him come to manhood! That should make you happy! That's more than most men know!"

Little Jackson St. Clare Tremain wriggled in his grandfather's arms and cried out. His little voice brought King out of his reverie. He held up his grandson and gave him a playful shake. The baby giggled again. It was a soft, buttery sound, like cream pouring into a cup. King put his cheek against the baby's smooth face and whispered, "It's been said that yo' mama and daddy gon' die. I don' know about all that, but you ain't never gon' be an orphan! You my blood and I swear on all that I care about, I'll see you to manhood! Yo' way is gon' be tough and harder than most, but you got the fiber and the blood to meet the challenge! You gon' be the head of the Tremain family!" King held the baby a few inches from his face and stared into the child's dark brown eyes. There was a moment in which they shared an eternity of ignorance. Then the baby reached out and squeezed his nose.

Eartha laughed and said, "Papa Tremain, let me hold Little Jackson before he tears your nose off. You're lucky you don't wear glasses! He really likes to rip those off!"

King handed her the baby and stood up. He was filled with tremendous emotion. For a moment he thought tears would come. He took a deep breath and remembered that the last time he had cried was over thirty years ago, when his Uncle Jake had passed. A tear squeezed out of the corner of his eye, but it was not a product of sadness. It was the essence of joy.

His grandson had been christened and in time would be his heir. The dynasty that King had desired to establish for so long would eventually be realized. What more could a family man ask? He walked to the bar to drink with Dirty Red, Smitty, and Big Ed. Despite the pain the future would bring, King Tremain was happy. His life had purpose. It mattered not there were still many battles to fight. The war would eventually be won. His seed would take his place at the scratch line.

ABOUT THE AUTHOR

GUY JOHNSON has traveled widely in Europe, Africa, and the Middle East. He graduated from high school in Egypt and completed college in Ghana. Several years after college he managed a bar on Spain's Costa del Sol during the summers and ran a photo-safari service from London through Morocco and Algeria to the Spanish Sahara during the off-season. He has worked on the oil rigs in Kuwait and driven overland from Bulgaria to Afghanistan. He played guitar in a band for several years before starting work as a manager in local government. After working more than twenty years for the city of Oakland, California, he has recently taken a medical retirement.

He has been writing poetry and prose since he was eighteen years old. His first collection of poetry was published in 1982 in a book entitled *In the Wild Shadows*. He has also been included in the anthology of black male poets called *My Brother's Keeper*. His poetry has been published in *Essence* magazine and in various poetry quarterlies. It is his desire to follow in the literary footsteps of his mother, Dr. Maya Angelou.

ABOUT THE TYPE

This book was set in Goudy, a typeface designed by Frederic William Goudy (1865–1947). Goudy began his career as a bookkeeper, but devoted the rest of his life to the pursuit of "recognized quality" in a printing type.

Goudy was produced in 1914 and was an instant bestseller for the foundry. It has generous curves and smooth, even color. It is regarded as one of Goudy's finest achievements.

ALPHA, BETA, GAMMA . . . DEAD

ALPHA, BETA, GAMMA . . . DEAD

Betty Rowlands

FIC
Row

This first world edition published in Great Britain 2007 by
SEVERN HOUSE PUBLISHERS LTD of
9–15 High Street, Sutton, Surrey SM1 1DF.
This first world edition published in the USA 2007 by
SEVERN HOUSE PUBLISHERS INC of
595 Madison Avenue, New York, N.Y. 10022.

British Library Cataloguing in Publication Data

Rowlands, Betty
    Alpha, beta, gamma, dead
    1.   Reynolds, Sukey (Fictitious character) - Fiction
    2.   Women private investigators - Fiction
    3.   Christian antiquities - Fiction
    4.   Detective and mystery stories
    I.   Title
    823.9'14 [F]

    ISBN-13: 978-0-7278-6467-3

All Severn House titles are printed on acid-free paper.

Typeset by Palimpsest Book Production Ltd.,
Grangemouth, Stirlingshire, Scotland.
Printed and bound in Great Britain by
MPG Books Ltd., Bodmin, Cornwall.

A12004703112

One

A man strode through the swing door of the Mariners Hotel and up to the reception desk. Anyone observing him would have noticed a hint of impatience in the way he struck the bell with a closed fist. An olive-skinned, clean-shaven young man with smooth dark hair, who had just handed a key to a new arrival, moved across in response to the summons.

'May I help you, sir?' he said politely.

'Yes,' said the newcomer. He spoke a shade breathlessly, as if he had been hurrying. 'My name's Stephen Lamont and I've arranged to meet Doctor Whistler here. I understand he's a guest in this hotel?'

'Ah yes, Professor Lamont. Doctor Whistler expects you. Room 106 on first floor. Please be so kind as to go straight up. You find lift over there.' He gestured with a smooth, slightly feminine hand.

Lamont nodded. 'Thank you, I'll walk.'

On reaching room 106 he gave a double knock, lightly at first and then again, more strongly, when there was no reply. He waited a few moments before knocking a third time, even harder. He put an ear close to the door and listened, then turned and dashed downstairs to the reception desk. It was momentarily deserted and he pounded on the bell. A young woman appeared; before she had a chance to speak he said urgently, 'I think Doctor Whistler in room 106 may have been taken ill. He's expecting me, but he's not answering my knock and I thought I heard a faint groan.'

'I'll ring his room.' She picked up the phone and keyed in the number. After a few moments she put it down and said, 'He's not answering; I'll get the manager.'

She vanished, reappearing a few seconds later accompanied by a man of about thirty-five, formally dressed in a dark suit.

'We'll go and check on him,' he said and led the way up to the first floor.

When they reached Whistler's room he knocked and waited a few seconds before opening the door with a master key. The three of them took a few steps into the room before stopping short and gazing in mute horror at the crumpled figure lying on the floor in a pool of blood. Then the woman screamed, clapped a hand to her mouth and rushed into the bathroom, while Lamont moved forward and knelt beside the victim and the manager, his face the colour of clay, stepped gingerly round him and picked up the bedside telephone.

In the canteen at the central police station, DC Vicky Armstrong led the way to a vacant table, sat down and raised her mug of coffee in salute. 'Congratulations on becoming a fully fledged member of the team!' she said.

'Thanks!' DC Sukey Reynolds raised her own mug and swallowed a couple of mouthfuls before adding, 'Particularly for your support and encouragement.'

'It's been a pleasure working with you.' Vicky's smile transformed her homely features. 'I must admit,' she went on, 'my heart sank when I heard we had another trainee joining the team and I'd drawn the short straw again. The last one was a dyed-in-the-wool sexist who found it hard to accept that a mere woman could teach him anything.'

'I know – experience counts for nothing when weighed against testosterone,' said Sukey. 'What happened to him, by the way?'

'Praise be, he was transferred to headquarters. Last I heard of him, he was putting people's backs up there like he did when he was based here. A pity about that,' Vicky added with a touch of regret, 'he's got the makings of a really good detective, but he does tend to rub people up the wrong way. That's why it came as a relief to know that you were female.'

'I felt the same about you,' Sukey admitted. 'I'd had more than enough of bossy men.'

'Women can be bossy too, and bitchy sometimes,' Vicky pointed out.

'True, and I have to admit Jim did change his tune after I told him I'd been accepted for fast-track into the CID.'

'Is Jim your partner?'

It was the first time Sukey had mentioned him, although she had volunteered a certain amount of information about her background, including the fact that she was a divorcee with a son at university. It was also the first time that Vicky had asked a direct question about her personal life. 'Not exactly,' she replied after a moment's hesitation. 'He's a DI I first met years ago, when we were both PCs on the beat. We had a kind of a thing going – and then I fell for someone else, got married and left the police to have Fergus. After the divorce I went back to work for them as a SOCO and found Jim had got married and divorced as well and was still based in Gloucester. So we got together again, but I haven't seen him for a couple of months. Not since I moved, in fact. He helped me get settled in the flat and did a few jobs for me, but—'

She lapsed into silence, recalling the sense of desolation she had felt as he drove away, leaving her alone for the first time in her new and still unfamiliar environment. For the past six months the intensive training involved in obtaining the necessary qualifications for a career in the CID had absorbed most of her time and energy, leaving little opportunity for a social life. Just the same, so long as she was still living in Gloucester, they had managed to spend the odd weekend together. During that period there had been the process of selling the house where she had lived with Fergus ever since his father walked out on them ten years ago, and finding somewhere to live in Bristol. She remembered with gratitude what a tower of strength he had been during that stressful time, but the move had not only marked a turning point in her career, it had had a similar affect on their relationship. Since then he had telephoned a couple of times to ask how she was getting on, but there had been no mention of any future meetings.

It was typical of Vicky that she asked no further questions, merely saying, 'Well, it's Friday tomorrow, thank goodness. You doing anything special at the weekend?'

'Gus is coming on Saturday and staying a couple of nights. I've been invited to some neighbours for supper this evening. How about you?'

'Chris said something about a movie on Saturday.' From odd comments Vicky had made during the six weeks they had been working together, Sukey had formed the impression that she and Chris had a long-standing relationship with no firm commitment on either side. It was typical that she was as reticent about her own private life as she was incurious about that of other people.

Sukey finished her coffee and picked up her shoulder bag. 'Well, back to the grind,' she said.

'So what job have they put you on for your sins?' asked Vicky.

'Checking witness statements from the Bryony Close break-ins. Four in a single night, and in each case the residents were on holiday. The same package holiday,' she added.

Vicky gave a knowing grin. 'A mole in the travel agency?'

'That's one possibility we're working on, although there's another we have to consider.'

'Which is?'

'The bookings weren't made individually, but through a member of the group.'

'Well, that's not unusual.'

'No. Just the same, the organizer wasn't one of the victims.'

'Ah, well, keep digging!' Vicky said cheerfully.

It was a little after twelve and Sukey was beginning to think about lunch when DS Greg Rathbone tapped her on the shoulder. 'Drop that for now, we've got something a bit more interesting for you to bite on,' he said.

Sukey closed the file, pushed it into a drawer and stood up. 'What's that, Sarge?'

'GBH at the Mariners Hotel. Gentleman attacked in his room, apparently while waiting for a visitor.'

'Well, there's something to brighten a dull morning,' she said. 'Is he badly hurt?'

'Sounds like it. He was found unconscious and bleeding heavily but we don't know yet what his injuries are. The manager called an ambulance and they carted him off to the hospital before uniformed arrived. They're protecting the scene, but there's bound to have been some contamination before they took charge.'

'We know the victim has to be the first consideration, but it can be a headache for the CSIs,' Sukey remarked as they hurried down to the yard where the cars were parked. 'Where is this hotel, by the way?'

'On the A38, not far from the airport. That's our car; you

drive.' He tossed a key at her and settled into the passenger seat of a silver-grey Astra.

'Right, Sarge.' She got in and started the engine while Greg settled down beside her and closed his eyes. Sukey gave him a sideways glance as she pulled out of the yard. She had taken to him on their first meeting; he gave the impression of being what her late mother would have described as 'a nice dependable sort', with his clean-cut features, keen blue-grey eyes and firm handclasp. In the short time she had been at the station she had learned that he had a reputation – which she suspected had been carefully cultivated – for never missing an opportunity to relax. During the fifteen-minute drive he remained silent, apparently asleep, but the minute she slowed down and signalled before turning into the hotel car park he opened his eyes and sat upright.

'Park round the back,' he ordered. 'The manager has asked us to be as inconspicuous as possible to avoid unnecessary upset to the guests.'

'That's understandable,' Sukey said as she pulled in alongside the police cars discreetly parked out of sight of the road. 'This kind of thing can't be very good for business.'

'Not much fun for the victim either,' he remarked dryly.

Two white vans belonging to Crime Scene Investigators were already there and Sukey experienced a sudden buzz of anticipation. This time last year her remit would, like theirs, have been the collection of evidence for passing on to the investigating officer. There had of course been other cases during the past few weeks in which she had played an active role, but always under Vicky's tutelage. Now she was a fully fledged member of the team.

A woman constable was standing guard outside a door labelled 'Staff Only'. As they approached she punched a code into the keypad on the wall and held it open for them. 'The manager's waiting for you in his office, Sarge. The name's Maurice Ashford. Go along that passage, turn right and it's the second door on the left.'

The manager had thick brown hair that looked to Sukey as if agitated fingers had recently passed through it and the hand he offered felt cold and clammy.

'This is a dreadful business,' he said nervously. 'Nothing like it has ever happened in this hotel before – in any hotels in the group, come to that.' He made a sweeping gesture that encompassed the entire room, with its heavy, slightly old-fashioned furniture, crimson velvet curtains and dark green, deep-piled carpet, before coming briefly to rest on a pier table on which stood a handsome silver trophy. 'That's the annual award for the Hotel of the Year,' he informed them. 'We've won it two years running.'

'Well, congratulations to you and your staff,' said Rathbone. 'Now perhaps you'd be kind enough to tell us how you came to find the injured gentleman, whose name, I understand is – ' he glanced at his notebook – 'Doctor Whistler?'

'That's right: Doctor Edwin Whistler. An archaeologist, I understand. The gentleman who actually found him – at least, who alerted me that something was amiss – is a Professor Stephen Lamont. I have a master key in my desk and we immediately went up to Room 106 to investigate.'

'Just the two of you?'

'No. Erika, my assistant, came with us. They're both waiting for you in her office. I imagine you'll want to see them as well?'

'Thank you, all in good time. Do I take it Professor Lamont came to your office to tell you of his concern?'

'No, he told Erika. She happened to be at the reception desk, and she came running in to tell me.'

'I see. Right, sir, before we go any further, DC Reynolds and I would like to have a look at the room where this unfortunate incident took place. If you would be so kind—?'

'Certainly,' said Ashford. 'Your people are up there already, of course. I'll get a porter to . . .' He reached for the telephone on his desk, but Rathbone leaned forward and put a hand on the instrument.

'If you could spare the time to take us there yourself, sir?' he said quietly.

Two

The uniformed officer guarding room 106 stood aside and pushed open the door to admit Ashford and the detectives. Inside were two CSIs in white overalls; one was checking for fingerprints on the safe, which was set in the wall behind a desk on the far side of the room, and the other was down on one knee focusing his camera on the ugly stain on the carpet. He looked up as the newcomers entered and put up a hand.

'Just wait there a moment, Sarge,' he said and the three obediently halted in the doorway while he clicked away for a few seconds. Then he stood up and nodded.

'You can come in now. We've checked that side of the room, so if you wouldn't mind waiting there for a bit while we finish this side.'

'I see you've dusted the door for prints,' Rathbone remarked. 'Was that there when you arrived?' He indicated a 'Do Not Disturb' sign hanging from a small hook below the room number.

'Yes, Sarge.'

'You noticed it too, sir?' Rathbone turned to Ashford, who was staring in fascinated horror at the patch of blood. He jumped as the detective addressed him.

'Oh, er, yes, Sergeant,' he said. 'Yes, I'm sure it was there.'

'Right. Now, sir, I'd like you to go over your exact movements after you entered the room. As you had the key, I imagine you were the first to go in?'

'Yes, I suppose I must have been.' With an apparent effort, Ashford switched his gaze to the detective. He closed his eyes and said, his voice unsteady, 'The minute I saw him I stopped and . . . I think for a split second I just stared . . . it was like a nightmare, I couldn't believe it . . . and then Erika screamed and made a dash for the bathroom and I heard her gagging . . . I felt sick myself, but I knew I had to get help so I went to the phone—'

'Which is on the table on the other side of the bed,' Rathbone interrupted. 'Did you walk round, or reach across the bed?'

'I walked round the body . . . I mean the man on the floor . . . I kept as far away from him as I could—' Ashford put a hand over his eyes and swallowed. 'There was all that blood . . . I'd never seen so much blood.'

'I appreciate that this is difficult for you, Mr Ashford,' said Rathbone patiently, 'but I'll ask you to try and picture the scene and tell me exactly how the man was lying and where the blood was coming from.'

Ashford swallowed and put a handkerchief over his mouth.

'Try taking a few deep breaths,' said Sukey, recalling that this was how she had learned long ago to deal with similar situations. Ashford flashed her a weak but grateful smile and inhaled deeply several times.

'That's better,' said Rathbone. 'Just take your time.'

'Thank you.' Ashford put away the handkerchief. 'He was lying face down near the end of the bed, at a bit of an angle,' he said slowly. 'I couldn't see where the blood was coming from . . . but I'm afraid I didn't look very closely.'

'You couldn't see any wound?'

Ashford shuddered. 'No.'

'"Near the end of the bed" is a bit vague. Can you be more exact? For example, could you see his entire body, or was it partly behind the bed?'

Ashford swallowed hard. 'I think – yes, you could see all of him except the lower part of his legs and his feet.'

'Good.' Rathbone gave a nod of approval. 'Did he make any sound or movement while you were there?'

'I don't think so. No, I'm sure he didn't.'

'So you rang reception and told them to send for an ambulance. Did you also tell them to call the police?'

'No, not straight away, not until after the paramedics had taken the man to the hospital.'

'I see. And did all three of you wait in here for the ambulance?'

'No, I sent Erika downstairs to look out for it and direct the driver to the staff entrance. I wanted to avoid alarming any of the other guests . . . and in any case, that was the shortest route to this room.'

'And what did you do while you were waiting?'

'I stayed by the phone.'

'And Professor Lamont?'

'He . . . I think he bent down beside Doctor Whistler . . . and then he came and stood beside me.'

'Did he say anything?'

'I think he said something like, "I think he's still alive, but only just" – I can't remember his exact words.'

'Perhaps he felt for a pulse?'

'I suppose he might have done. I'm afraid I wasn't looking, I—'

'So the two of you just waited by the phone until the paramedics arrived?'

'I went to the window after a few minutes to look out for the ambulance. When I saw it arrive I went over to the door to be ready to let them in.'

'And Professor Lamont? What did he do?'

'I suppose he stayed where he was. I don't know. I was in such a state of shock—'

'Yes, quite.' Rathbone's jaw tightened and Sukey had the impression that he was becoming a little irritated by the man's repeated reference to his sensitivity, but he kept his voice level as he continued. 'Did you touch anything else, other than the phone?'

'No.'

'You're sure about that?'

Ashford nodded. 'Oh, yes, quite sure.'

'And the safe was open, like it is now?'

'I suppose so . . . I didn't notice.'

One of the CSIs looked up from his task and said, 'That's how it was when we arrived, Sarge. It's empty,' he added.

'Thanks, Joe.'

Rathbone glanced at Sukey and raised an eyebrow, inviting her to join in the questioning. She gave a slight nod and said, 'Mr Ashford, had Doctor Whistler stayed in this hotel before?'

The manager appeared taken aback by the question, although he answered readily enough. 'I don't know; he may have done. I can't remember every guest who stays here.'

'So to your knowledge, you had never met him before today?'

'That's right, but I don't see—'

'But you did know he was an archaeologist,' Sukey persisted.

This time Ashford was clearly disconcerted by the question. He nibbled his lower lip and frowned. 'I think . . . yes, I'm sure Professor Lamont mentioned it. He said something about him working on a dig somewhere in Greece, I think.'

'This was while you were waiting for the ambulance?'

'Yes, I suppose so.'

'Did he say anything else about him?'

'I don't think so.'

Sukey glanced back at Rathbone, who said briskly, 'Right, I think that's all we can do here at the moment. Let us have your results ASAP, boys.' He turned and led the way out of the room.

Back in Ashford's office he said, 'Thank you, sir, you've been a great help. We'll prepare a statement for you to sign later on, if you'd be so kind. One more thing: please instruct your staff not to speak to the press. It's important that Doctor Whistler's name is withheld until we've traced his next of kin.'

Ashford nodded. 'I'll get Erika to deal with that right away.' He pressed a button on his telephone and gave the instruction.

'And now perhaps we should have a word with Professor Lamont,' said Rathbone.

'Yes, of course.' Ashford appeared to relax, as if relieved that the interview was over. 'You can see him in here, if you like. I'll go and—'

'We'll need to question some of your staff as well, so it would be helpful if you could put a separate room at our disposal,' Rathbone broke in.

'Oh . . . yes, that won't be a problem. I'll check what's available, if you'll bear with me a moment.' He consulted his computer and said, 'You can have 107 for the time being; that's directly opposite 106. I'll get the key; I won't be a moment.'

As the door closed behind him, Rathbone turned to Sukey and said, 'What do you make of him?'

'On the face of it, he wouldn't appear to have any motive for attacking Whistler. He denies ever having met the man before, although he knew he was an archaeologist and he seemed a bit thrown by the question. And he referred to the victim the first time as "the body" and then corrected himself.'

'Yes, I noticed that. Anything else?'

She hesitated. 'He did make a great thing about not being able to stand the sight of blood. I suppose it was genuine – he certainly looked pale and he was obviously badly shaken.'

He nodded. 'Yes, I thought it was a bit OTT, but—' He broke off as Ashford returned, accompanied by a tall man with aquiline features and a mop of grey curly hair.

'Professor Lamont, these officers are conducting the enquiry into the attack on Doctor Whistler – Detective Sergeant Rathbone and Detective Constable Reynolds.' Ashford rattled off the introductions as if he was in a hurry to be rid of them. 'Here's the key to room 107,' he went on. 'I've ordered some coffee to be sent up for you.'

'That's very thoughtful of you, sir. Thank you,' said Rathbone. 'I don't suppose you could manage a sandwich as well? DC Reynolds and I haven't had time for lunch.'

'Certainly. I'll send up a selection. Perhaps you would also care for something to eat, Professor?' he added with an ingratiating smile.

Lamont nodded, but did not return the smile. 'Thank you,' he said curtly.

The manager vanished once again and the detectives and Lamont made their way in silence up to room 107. The moment the door closed behind them Lamont crossed the room, sank into a chair, adjusted the lapels of his safari jacket and stretched out a pair of long legs clad in immaculately creased linen trousers.

'How on earth does a wimp like that get to run a hotel?' he exclaimed. 'His PA showed a bit more backbone – once she'd got over the initial shock she more or less took charge.'

'I gather the sight of blood doesn't affect you in quite the same way then?' said Rathbone. He settled in the second chair in the room, leaving Sukey to perch on the edge of the bed.

'It wasn't exactly a pretty sight, but I did feel his reaction was a bit excessive,' agreed Lamont. 'You want an account of my movements, I take it?'

'If you'd be so kind, sir.'

'Well, I had an appointment to meet Doctor Whistler here at twelve o'clock. I was late – by nearly fifteen minutes, I think, on account of some heavy traffic. I gave my name to the chap on the desk and he sent me up to Whistler's room. I knocked several times, but got no answer. At first I thought he must have given me up and gone out, but then I thought that was unlikely so I knocked again and put an ear to the door and I thought I heard a sound like a sigh or a faint moan. It occurred to me that he might have been taken ill, so I hurried downstairs and got the manager. He and his assistant came up with a key and we found Doctor Whistler lying on the floor in a pool of blood.'

'Can you remember what position he was in?'

'Face down with his head diagonally towards the door.'

'Could you see any wound?'

'No. The blood seemed to be coming from beneath his body, but I was afraid to move him in case I did any further damage. I knelt down beside him and spoke to him; I could tell he was alive because he seemed to be trying to say something although I couldn't catch the words, so I told Ashford to get an ambulance and say it was an emergency. He called reception and gave the instruction, and then spent the next I don't know how long telling me how sick he got at the sight of blood.'

'And what about Erika – his assistant?'

'I think she threw up in the bathroom, but she very soon pulled herself together and went downstairs saying she'd direct the ambulance to the staff entrance and Ashford said, "Good idea."'

'You're certain that was her initiative – to bring the ambulance to the staff entrance?'

'Oh, yes. As soon as he'd made the call, Ashford collapsed on the edge of the bed like a lump of jelly.' Lamont's cultured, slightly high-pitched voice, registered undisguised contempt. '"As a sick girl," as Cassius said when speaking of Caesar. That's a quotation from—'

'Yes, sir, I am familiar with the play,' said Rathbone evenly. 'While you were waiting for the ambulance, did the two of you speak to each other?'

'He kept wittering on about how awful it was and how he'd never been able to stand the sight of blood. I couldn't be bothered to answer and after a while he shut up and went over to the window. When the ambulance arrived he mumbled something about letting them in and sort of tiptoed past Whistler with his face averted to open the door. Like a woman drawing aside her skirts,' he added with a sneer.

Once again, Rathbone gave Sukey a sign that she was to take over the questioning.

'What happened after the paramedics had taken Doctor Whistler to the hospital?' she asked.

As if mildly affronted at being addressed by an inferior officer, Lamont raised an eyebrow before saying, 'We just stood there and after a minute or two the girl came back and said we should inform the police and we weren't to touch anything. Ashford told her to go ahead and we all waited until some officers arrived and took charge.'

'And did you notice any signs of disturbance in the room?'

Lamont closed his eyes for a moment as if trying to recall the scene. Then he said, 'The only thing I remember is the empty safe with the door open.'

'No suitcase with its contents spilling out, or other signs that the room had been searched?'

'No.'

Rathbone took up the questioning again. 'Professor Lamont, will you please tell us the purpose of your proposed meeting with Doctor Whistler?'

'Yes, of course. He'd been working on a dig on Rhodes – that's a Greek island in the Mediterranean – at a place called Lindos, and he'd come across an ancient document buried on the site of an early Christian basilica that he believed to be a letter from Saint Paul. He wrote to Professor Thornton, the Head of the Faculty of Hellenic Studies at the university here, inviting him to visit the site and examine the document. Archie Thornton wrote back and said he'd be happy to look at it, but was unable to travel to Rhodes in the foreseeable future and suggested Whistler bring it to England, which he eventually agreed to do.' Lamont broke off to drink some of the coffee that a waiter had brought to the room and then reached for a sandwich, which he examined minutely before biting into it.

'And Professor Thornton asked you to meet him to collect this document on his behalf?' Rathbone prompted.

'He asked me to handle the whole matter. It so happens I'm currently preparing a paper on the subject of the letters of Saint Paul and I also have a specialized knowledge of classical Greek – which happens to be the language in which the apostle wrote his letters,' he added with an air that struck Sukey as unashamedly condescending.

'You would seem to be the ideal person to entrust with the mission,' Rathbone observed.

'Precisely.' Lamont showed no sign of having recognized the dry note in the detective's voice.

'So when Professor Thornton handed the enquiry over to you,' Sukey began, in response to the by now familiar nod from Rathbone, 'presumably you contacted Doctor Whistler to arrange this meeting?'

'That's right,' Lamont said stiffly.

'Would you mind telling us how the meeting was set up?'

'It was done mostly by an exchange of emails, although we did have one or two telephone conversations.'

'How many people besides yourself and Professor Thornton knew about it?'

Lamont made an impatient sound at what he appeared to consider an irrelevant question. 'One or two people in the department, I suppose. Archie's secretary, of course, and someone may have seen the messages on my desk – for example, while I was out of my office, but if you're suggesting that anyone there—'

His colour had risen and he showed signs of becoming aggressive. Rathbone quickly stepped in and said quietly, 'No one is suggesting anything at this stage, Professor Lamont. DC Reynolds and I are simply trying to build up a complete picture of the events leading up to this attack. Would you kindly let us have a note of the people who have access to your office?'

'Very well,' Lamont said grumpily.

'Meanwhile, we'll prepare a statement for you to sign. And one other thing,' Rathbone continued without waiting for a response, 'I imagine that if this document is genuine it will be of considerable value to scholars?'

'Yes, of course.'

'So did Doctor Whistler at any time give you the impression that he feared having it stolen?'

Lamont shot Rathbone a keen look from his steel-blue eyes and hesitated for a moment before replying. 'Not exactly, but the last time I spoke to him he said something like, "I hope you haven't mentioned this to too many people" and then he said rather hastily, "I have to go. I'll see you at twelve", and hung up.'

'And that conversation took place this morning?'

'Yes, at about nine thirty. I called him from my office to check that he had reached the hotel and to confirm our arrangement.'

'I see. Thank you, Professor Lamont, you've been very helpful.'

Three

The minute the door closed behind Lamont, Rathbone exploded. 'Of all the self-important, pompous prats, that one leaves the rest of the field standing! Giving us lessons in geography and Shakespeare as if we were fourth formers! Now if someone clobbered *him* you'd feel like applauding.'

Sukey grinned. 'You deserve a medal for being civil to him,' she said. 'Ashford was a bit pathetic, but by the time the learned Prof had finished sneering I began to feel sorry for him. I'm a bit bothered about the timing,' she went on. 'Did the attacker know that Whistler was expecting Lamont at midday and make a point of arriving well before then? And how did he know which room to go to without asking at reception?'

'You've got a point there,' said Rathbone. 'If someone had called earlier claiming to be Professor Lamont, the receptionist would hardly have sent the real one up a short time later.'

'Unless he spoke to a different receptionist,' Sukey pointed out.

'Unlikely, but you'd better make a note to check. By the way, I thought it was interesting how their two accounts differed.'

'You mean Ashford making out he'd taken charge of the situation and Lamont giving the credit to "the girl", as he so patronisingly called her?'

'Exactly. What do you reckon?'

'My guess is that Lamont's version is the more accurate, although he might have exaggerated a little. Ashford was probably feeling pretty embarrassed at his performance and was trying to save face.'

'That's how I read it too.' Rathbone finished his coffee and swallowed the remains of the last sandwich. 'Before we see anyone else, let's try and figure out the chain of events. We know Whistler was all right at nine thirty when Lamont called from his office, although he expressed concern about the number of people who might know about the business and then hung up rather hastily. I wonder why?'

'Someone at the door?' Sukey suggested.

'Could be. Of course, at that time in the morning it would probably have been the chambermaid.'

'She wouldn't have knocked if the Do Not Disturb sign was on the door.'

'So perhaps he told her to come back later and then put the sign up.'

'That's probably what happened – but if the bed hadn't been made, we'd have noticed.'

'Just the same, you'd better go and check.'

Sukey crossed the corridor, examined the bed in room 106 and returned to report that the bedding had been roughly pulled together and the cover drawn over, and that the bathroom hadn't been tidied. 'Which means the chambermaid never went in,' she said.

'Suggesting he was so jumpy that he didn't want anyone in there until Lamont had been and gone,' said Rathbone.

'So between nine thirty and around twelve o'clock, someone, who presumably persuaded Whistler that he was Lamont, entered the room, attacked him and made off with the document leaving him lying bleeding on the floor.'

'But Whistler wasn't expecting Lamont until midday, so if the attacker arrived much before then he'd surely have been suspicious,' Rathbone pointed out. 'Well, there's no point in speculating any further for the moment. Incidentally, we still don't know the nature of his injuries, but my guess is he was knifed. PC Hackett is at the hospital; I'll give him a call.' Rathbone took out his mobile and keyed in a number. After a brief exchange with the officer at the other end he switched off and said, 'He's been taken to the theatre but Hackett doesn't have any details. OK, we'll see Erika next and listen to her version.'

Erika Henderson was a tall, slim brunette of about thirty. She was conventionally dressed in a well-cut navy blue skirt and jacket over a plain white shirt, with gold stud earrings and a gold choker. She showed no sign of her earlier distress, although her smile as she acknowledged Rathbone's greeting failed to mask the anxiety in her eyes. She sat down in the chair vacated by Lamont with her hands in her lap and her ankles neatly crossed.

'I won't keep you for long, Ms Henderson,' Rathbone began. 'We just want to check a few details. You must have found all this very upsetting.'

'Yes, very,' she replied gravely. 'I've experienced a few crises in my time, but never anything as bad as this. Tell me, Sergeant, what news is there of Doctor Whistler? I asked Mr Ashford, but he hasn't heard anything.'

'We understand he's undergoing emergency surgery; we have an officer at the hospital waiting for news and we're trying to locate his next of kin. That's all I can tell you at the moment, but you will of course be kept informed.'

'Thank you.'

'Now, perhaps you wouldn't mind answering a few questions. How did you first learn that something was wrong with Doctor Whistler?'

'Professor Lamont came to reception to tell us of his concern and I happened to be there at the time. I'd been with Mr Ashford in his office and I'd popped out to check something. I ran back and alerted him straight away and we all went up to Doctor Whistler's room together.'

'I see. How long had you been with Mr Ashford in his office?'

'I suppose . . . for about an hour or so. We were working on our Christmas and New Year programme.'

'You say you "popped out" at one point to check something – how long were you out of the office?'

'Only a few seconds. Professor Lamont was already at the desk.'

'Was anyone else on the desk at the time?'

She frowned and thought for a moment. 'Now you come to mention it, I don't think there was, but Boris – the member of staff who was on duty at the time – was there when I returned with Mr Ashford a minute or so later.'

'You and Mr Ashford had no other interruptions?' She shook her head. 'And neither of you left the room until this happened?'

'No, of course not.' Her expression became wary, as if she suspected some ulterior motive behind the question.

'That would be about what time?'

'About a quarter past twelve . . . or maybe a little after. I can't say exactly.'

'Thank you. Please tell us what happened next.'

Listening to her while making notes, Sukey had the impression that she had used the time spent waiting to be questioned to organize her thoughts. Her account, which agreed in all essentials with that of Lamont, was given in a brisk, business-like voice with a trace of a West Country accent.

At the end of his questions, Rathbone said, 'Thank you very much, Ms Henderson, I think you've covered pretty well everything we wanted to know.' He glanced at Sukey and she shook her head. 'Right, that's all for now – oh, yes, there is one other thing. The member of staff who directed Professor Lamont to Doctor Whistler's room – I think you said his name was Boris – is he still on duty?'

'Boris Gasspar – yes, he's on until five.'

'How long has he worked here?'

'He came to us about six months ago. I take it you'll want to see him?'

'If you would kindly ask him to come up here in five minutes?'

'Certainly.' She stood up and impulsively put a hand on Rathbone's arm. 'I do so hope you find whoever was responsible for this horrible attack,' she said. 'It's been very upsetting for us all.'

'We'll do our best,' Rathbone promised and she thanked him and left, closing the door quietly behind her.

'Well, that would seem to put Ashford in the clear, although I never seriously thought of him as a suspect,' said Rathbone.

'Neither did I,' Sukey agreed. 'It's nice that someone showed concern for the victim, isn't it?' she added. She was tempted to stress the fact that the concerned party was a woman, as she would have done had it been DI Jim Castle sitting opposite her, but resisted. She liked what she had seen of Greg Rathbone so far, but she had yet to get his measure.

'Anyway, it seems Lamont's account was the more accurate, although it doesn't really—' Rathbone broke off as his mobile phone rang. He answered, gave his name, said, 'Yes, Den. What news?' and then listened in silence for a minute. Sukey watched him closely, but his face gave nothing away.

Then he said, 'Right, thanks. Report back to the station and tell them to inform the coroner. There'll have to be a PM, of course. And find out whether we've been able to locate the next of kin.' He switched off and said, 'I take it you got that?'

She nodded. 'Whistler's dead and we've got a murder on our hands.'

'Right.' He got up and went over to the window. 'It seems that document was worth a great deal to someone. What did Lamont say about it?'

'He said Whistler thought it might be a letter from Saint Paul.'

'I thought all the saint's correspondence was already in the public domain, as the saying goes,' said Rathbone with an attempt at levity.

'Researchers are always coming across ancient documents relating to various religions,' Sukey pointed out. 'I imagine that to scholars they can be as valuable as a work of art. Remember the Dead Sea Scrolls?'

'That's true. Well, we'd better have another word with Lamont and see if he can give us some idea of—' He broke off as someone knocked on the door. 'That'll be Boris. We'll talk about this later. And not a word about Whistler's death,' he warned before calling, 'Come in!'

A slightly built young man with dark hair smoothed back from his forehead entered, closed the door behind him and took a couple of tentative steps into the room. 'You want see me, sir?' he said.

'You're Boris Gasspar?' The man nodded. 'Come and sit down.' Rathbone indicated the chair vacated by Lamont and after a moment's hesitation he complied, perched on the edge of the seat and waited.

It seemed to Sukey that Rathbone made a point of consulting his notebook for several seconds before saying, 'Your full name is Boris Gasspar, I believe?' The man nodded again. 'How do you spell that, please?'

'G-a-s-s-p-a-r,' he replied.

'Where are you from, Boris?'

The man licked his lips. 'I am from Vlora. That spell V-l-o-r-a,' he added.

Rathbone glanced at Sukey, who gave him a blank look

and shook her head. He turned back to Boris. 'Where exactly is Vlora?' he asked.

'In Albania. I have passport, work permit, everything in order.' There was a look of apprehension in the man's coal-black eyes and his hands were shaking.

'That's all right, we aren't checking up on your status,' said Rathbone reassuringly. 'As you've no doubt heard, a guest at this hotel – a Doctor Whistler – has been attacked and seriously hurt in his room. My colleague and I are police officers and we're trying to find out who did it.'

'I know nothing. I hurt no one,' said Boris. He shot a desperate glance at Sukey as if pleading for help.

'Boris, no one's saying it was you who attacked Doctor Whistler,' she said gently, 'but we think you may be able to help us find the person who did. We just want to ask you a few questions.'

Boris moistened his lips a second time. 'I try,' he said.

'Good man,' said Rathbone. 'Now, we understand that Professor Lamont came to the desk at about a quarter past twelve and asked for Doctor Whistler. Was it you he spoke to?'

'Of course. I am on duty.'

'And you directed him to Doctor Whistler's room?'

'Yes. Doctor Whistler say me he expect Professor Lamont and I have to send him to room.'

'What time did he say he expected Professor Lamont?' Sukey asked.

Boris glanced down at his hands for a moment before replying, 'He say twelve o'clock.'

'So he was fifteen minutes late?'

'Yes. That is, no. He come earlier, but not to desk. I see him when he go out to car park by back door. In great hurry, and carry bag,' he added as an afterthought.

'You mean the staff entrance?' Boris nodded. 'How did you come to see him use that door if you were on duty at the desk?'

'Please?'

'The staff entrance is invisible . . . that is, you can't see it from the desk,' Sukey explained patiently. 'Where were you when you saw Professor Lamont the first time?'

Boris shifted uneasily, avoiding her eyes. 'Outside door. I go for smoke.'

'Leaving the desk unattended?' He gazed blankly back at her and she tried again. 'Was there another person on the desk?'

'Oh yes. Millie from office stay there for me.'

'And while you were having your smoke just outside the staff entrance,' Sukey went on, 'you saw Professor Lamont go out into the car park.'

'That right, but I not know then that it was the professor.'

'But you're sure it was the same man?'

'Oh, yes, quite sure.'

'In a hurry and carrying a bag?'

Boris nodded and passed his tongue over his lips before saying, 'Yes.'

'What sort of bag?'

'Small bag, with handles. Dark colour.'

'Let's get this straight,' said Rathbone, speaking slowly and deliberately, 'Doctor Whistler told you he was expecting Professor Lamont at twelve o'clock and said you were to send him straight to his room. Why did you leave the desk around the time he was expected?'

Boris fidgeted with his hands and his eyes darted to and fro between the detectives. 'I need smoke, and I tell Millie the message in case he come early. When I go back just after twelve, she say Professor not come yet. Please – ' the man's eyes were wide with fear – 'you not tell Mr Ashford? I not allowed smoke while on duty. I lose job, my family need money—'

'Boris, what you have told us may be very important,' Rathbone said gravely. 'I can't promise to keep it from Mr Ashford, but if he has to know I'll be sure to put in a word for you . . . tell him what a help you have been to us. I'm sure it won't mean losing your job.'

Boris appeared far from reassured, but he gave a faint, hesitant smile. 'Please, I go back to my work?'

'Yes, Boris,' said Rathbone, 'that will be all for now.'

The man fairly scuttled out of the room as if fearing that a moment's delay might lead to more questions.

As the door closed behind him, Rathbone said, 'Well, that alters the picture more than somewhat. We must have another chat with Lamont. I'll set that up for tomorrow; meanwhile I'd like you to check with any hotel staff and guests who might have been around at the crucial time and ask them if they saw anyone near Whistler's room. And track down the paramedics who collected Whistler and find out whether they found him in the position described by Ashford and Lamont. And do statements for everyone we've seen so far, OK?'

'Right, Sarge.' Sukey made a note of the instructions. She forbore to ask Rathbone what action he proposed to take, apart from setting up the interview with Lamont. 'Just one thing,' she added, 'should we perhaps have a word with Millie to see if she can add anything useful?'

'Good point.' He called reception to make the request. 'She's gone to lunch,' he said as he put the phone down. 'You can see her when you come back after dropping me off at the station.'

'Well, thanks a bunch,' Sukey muttered under her breath as she followed him downstairs and out of the hotel.

Four

By the time Sukey returned to the station it was gone four o'clock. She went straight to her desk in the CID office and began work on statements for signature by Ashford, Lamont, Gasspar and Erika Henderson. The shorthand she had learned years ago while working on her degree in media studies made the task fairly straightforward. It was with a sigh of relief that she finished the last one and began on the results of her afternoon's work.

With any luck, she thought, she could get away by five thirty and be home in time to wind down and have a shower before getting ready for what was described in the invitation as an informal supper. It was the first time she had been invited to a social event in a neighbour's home, although she already knew several of them by sight through encounters in the street or in one of the local shops. One in particular, who introduced herself the day after Sukey moved into her new home just off Whiteladies Road as Priscilla Gadden, had gone out of her way to offer information and advice on local amenities and services, and it was from Priscilla and her architect husband Tom, who lived in what the residents in Sherman Lane referred to as 'the big house', that Sukey had received this evening's invitation.

At five o'clock Greg Rathbone entered the office, rested his posterior on the edge of her desk, picked up the completed statements and glanced at them briefly before saying, 'I've had a preliminary chat with Doc Hanley, the forensic pathologist. He says Whistler was stopped in his tracks by a single stab wound from a thin-bladed knife that penetrated the heart. It didn't do enough damage to cause immediate death so it carried on pumping out blood. So much had leaked into the chest cavity that by the time they got him to the theatre it was too late to save him.'

Sukey shuddered and swallowed hard. 'Poor man, how awful,' she said.

'Did you get a word with the paramedics, by the way?'

'Yes, I managed to catch them and they confirmed the position they found Whistler in. They also said that when they got him into the ambulance he seemed to regain partial consciousness for a few moments and was trying to say something, but the only words they could make out sounded like "No" or "not" and then "Greek".'

'Presumably he was talking about the document,' said Rathbone, 'because Lamont implied that it's written in Greek, but on its own it doesn't help us much. The CSIs found traces of blood on the side of the bed away from the door, suggesting that the wound was delivered there and Whistler staggered forward a few steps before he fell.' He tossed the statements aside. 'Anything else to report? I suppose it's too much to hope for that you happened to find someone who saw a tall man with a bag near Whistler's room at the relevant time?'

Sukey shook her head. 'Most of the rooms on that floor were occupied by business people who went out soon after breakfast. The ones I did catch weren't much help and the chambermaids had all gone home so I'll have to speak to them tomorrow. But I did have a word with Millie, the girl who stood in for Boris while he went outside for his smoke. She confirms the time he went out, but she didn't actually see him come back because she was busy with a hotel guest at the time. All she can say is that when she turned round after finishing with the guest, Boris was there. She told him Lamont hadn't yet arrived and went back into the office.'

'It's a busy hotel,' Rathbone remarked. 'I'm surprised they have only one person on reception.'

'I asked about that,' Sukey said. 'Normally there are two, but the second one who should have been there this morning was off sick.'

'You'd think that in the circumstances Boris could have done without his smoke,' Rathbone observed.

'That occurred to me; in fact, I asked Millie if he was a heavy smoker and she didn't know, but I suppose there's no reason why she should. She spends most of her time in the admin office, which leads off the reception.'

'So I suppose she didn't actually see Lamont arrive?'

'She did, as it happens. The door was ajar and she confirms the time as just before twelve fifteen. She added that he seemed breathless and a little agitated, but he didn't wait for the lift; he ran up the stairs in a great hurry.'

'*Did* he?' said Rathbone with meaningful emphasis.

'And Boris mentioned that he seemed in a great hurry when he went out through the staff entrance,' Sukey pointed out.

'So he did.'

'I wonder—' she began, then broke off, afraid he might think she was trying to be clever at his expense.

'Yes?' prompted Rathbone.

'If Lamont did stab Whistler,' she said hesitantly, 'you'd expect him to have blood on his clothes.'

'Well done for spotting that.' Rathbone gave a nod of approval. 'I thought the same, but Doc Hanley said blood doesn't spurt from that type of wound the way it does when a vein or artery is cut. It was only because Whistler fell on his face that there was all that blood on the carpet. It'll be interesting to have Lamont's reaction to the latest developments. He's coming in at nine thirty tomorrow and I want you there.'

'Very good, Sarge. I'll just finish writing up the notes about my chat with Millie and then if it's all right with you I'll go home.'

At seven thirty that evening Sukey, freshly showered, put on a flowered skirt with a loose white top, brushed her short chocolate-brown curls into their most becoming shape and paused briefly to study her reflection in the full-length mirror in her bedroom. The image that stared back at her was bright-eyed, the cheeks slightly flushed under a light make-up, the expression eager and full of anticipation. Today, she decided, would go down as having a double significance: for the first time as a fully fledged detective constable she had been at the sharp end of a murder enquiry and she was about to fulfil her first social engagement since moving to Bristol. With a nod of satisfaction she slipped on a pair of sandals and a loose cotton jacket, picked up a handbag and the bunch of roses purchased on her way home, and set off.

A couple of centuries ago, the estate agent had informed her, the area surrounding Sherman Lane had formed part of a gentleman's estate, and relics of those far-off days remained in the nostalgic names given to the conversions of the out-buildings into modern dwellings, such as the Coach House and the Lodge. As her own flat abutted on to the Stables, the home of a retired army major called Matthews, Sukey had been tempted to commission a sign reading the Hayloft to hang above her own front door, but when she tentatively mentioned it to Matthews he showed little enthusiasm for the suggestion. 'He seemed to think it suggested naughty goings-on between the stable lads and the housemaids and so lower the tone of the neighbourhood,' she told Fergus, who had guffawed and called the man a silly old fart, but advised her not to do anything to antagonize him.

Sherman House, which stood behind wrought-iron gates at the end of the cul-de-sac, was a Georgian building with a plain but elegant and well-proportioned facade of Bath stone that reflected the warm glow of the setting sun. When Sukey pressed the button on the keypad set into the gatepost, the voice of Priscilla Gadden greeted her by name; then a buzzer sounded and the personal gate swung open. A short gravelled drive led to the house; as she approached she spotted a CCTV camera and several discreetly positioned lights. Before she had time to press the brass bell push, the heavy oak front door was opened by a slim girl with spiky blond hair clad in a body-hugging black top and a magenta frill – hardly long enough to be described as a skirt – above sheer black tights and enormous platform shoes. Her pale face and her voice were equally expressionless as she beckoned Sukey into the hall with a hand tipped with fingernails that matched her skirt and said, 'Come in. We're in the drawing room.' She led the way across a flagged stone floor and up a stone staircase with a wooden handrail, both of which looked as old as the house. There was a window on the half-landing with a deep sill on which stood a huge bowl of roses, making Sukey conscious of the modesty of her own offering. The window frame was obviously new; what was also obvious was that it had been custom-made to be an exact copy of the original.

They reached the first floor; a door on the right stood open and a buzz of conversation and laughter flowed out on to the landing. As her young guide led her into the room Sukey caught her breath at the scale and beauty and at the same time the sheer opulence of it all: the waxed wooden floor under a scattering of richly coloured oriental rugs: the high ceiling with its ornamental plaster moulding: the Adam fireplace with its marble surround: the sparkling chandelier: the huge windows that gave a panoramic view over the city. 'What a superb room!' she exclaimed almost reverently and the girl shrugged and said, 'If you say so. Mum's over there,' before melting away.

A little diffidently, Sukey made her way towards the far corner where Priscilla Gadden, clad in a loose-fitting aquamarine jacket over a calf-length matching skirt with diamonds at her throat and ears, was talking animatedly to a stout, balding man in shirtsleeves. She held a glass of champagne in one hand and with the other, also bedecked with jewels that flashed in the light of the chandelier, she pointed in various directions while the man swivelled his gaze this way and that and gave appreciative nods between taking sips from his own glass.

Watching them, Sukey had a disconcerting sensation of being a visitor to a National Trust property rather than an invited guest, but at that moment Priscilla caught sight of her, said something to her companion and came forward with her right hand outstretched.

'Sukey, how lovely to see you! I'm so glad you could come!' she exclaimed, and the illusion of a moment ago was immediately dispelled by the warmth and sincerity of the welcome and the obvious pleasure with which she accepted the bouquet Sukey offered. 'Patsy!' she called, glancing round the room, and the girl detached herself from a small group of young people by the window and wandered towards them. 'Ah, there you are. Aren't these lovely – put them in water for me, there's a love.' As the girl took the flowers without a word and walked away, her young shoulders seemed to register a simmering resentment. Her mother turned to Sukey and sighed. 'I do so wish today's young wouldn't turn themselves into freaks – but I suppose she'll grow out of it. And she hardly ever smiles at me or her father these days, although she seems happy enough with that lot over there. Do you have this problem with your Fergus?'

'He does wear some pretty way-out gear,' Sukey admitted, 'and he gels his hair into some weird shapes – but at least he's quite amenable most of the time – and he showers regularly as well, which is more than you can say for some of them.'

'Indeed. Ah, Tom,' Priscilla turned to her husband who had materialized at her side, 'will you get Sukey a drink? I simply must go and talk to the Shearers.' She glided across the room to greet a couple who had just entered while Tom Gadden, whom Sukey had met only briefly before, brought her a glass of champagne.

'Your house is beautiful!' Sukey exclaimed and his normally grave face lit up with pleasure. 'It must have been a real labour of love – restoring it, I mean.'

'When it wasn't giving us nightmares,' he replied. 'It's a listed building, of course, so making it comfortable by twenty-first century standards while preserving all the original features was something of a juggling act. Heating was a major headache – double-glazing was out of the question of course, but I think we managed to get it right in the end. Oh, I think I hear the phone – would you excuse me a moment?'

'Of course.' He hurried away, leaving her sipping her champagne and admiring the view. He reappeared a few moments later with a phone, which he handed to his wife with a few murmured words before returning to Sukey's side.

Priscilla took the phone out of the room; when she returned she came over to her husband and said, 'Hester was practically hysterical – she kept saying a friend of Stephen's has been attacked and robbed. Then Stephen took the phone from her and explained that she's upset because a man he was supposed to meet has been mugged and taken to hospital. It seems a rather important document has been stolen. Anyway, he says they won't be coming.' She turned to Sukey looking slightly apologetic and said, 'Some friends of ours who live the other side of the Downs have had a rather distressing experience. He's very clever, he lectures in Greek and biblical studies at the university, but she's, well, she's had rather a lot of illness and gets upset easily.'

'She's a raving neurotic,' said Tom. 'Leads poor old Stephen a hell of a dance.'

'Tom, that's unkind,' his wife scolded gently. 'She's been loads better lately. I wonder if that's the document she was prattling on about when I met her in the library the other day,' she added.

'Oh – what document was that?' said Tom.

'An archaeologist has found what he thinks might be a letter from Saint Paul. Hester was very excited because Stephen has been asked to say if he thinks it's genuine or not. She seemed to think it was a feather in his cap to be chosen for the honour.'

Tom shrugged. 'Well, we all know she thinks he's the greatest genius in the world since Einstein,' he said with a wry smile.

'That's true,' she agreed. 'Tom, please introduce Sukey to some of our other guests and show her where the food is. I must circulate.'

As she disappeared among the chattering crowd Tom remarked, 'Shouldn't say this I know, but when he gets on to one of his hobby horses that chap could bore for England. Hester's his sister, by the way. She won't accept any invitations without him and Pris feels sorry for her because she doesn't have much social life so we have to invite the pair of them.'

Adrenalin had been pumping through Sukey's veins for the past couple of minutes but she managed to keep her voice casual as she enquired, 'What are his hobby horses?'

'Biblical texts, especially the epistles, and ancient Greek,' said Tom. 'I can't say either of them turns me on, but some people seem to find them fascinating. Come to think of it . . .' His tone altered and he looked at Sukey with a sudden show of interest. 'I was forgetting – you're in the police, aren't you? I suppose your people will be involved if the chap's badly hurt. Or maybe they're involved already?'

He fixed her with an enquiring expression as if hoping for inside information, but at that moment Major Matthews bore down on them, glass in hand. 'Ah, Gadden, I've been looking forward to the chance of a word!' he barked. 'Please excuse us if we talk a bit of shop,' he said to Sukey. 'Local politics and all that. I'm afraid you'd find it rather boring stuff really but—' He treated Sukey to a patronizing smile as if a mere woman could not be expected to take an intelligent interest in such matters. Relieved rather than offended, she smiled politely, took the hint and headed for the buffet table on the other side of the room.

Five

By eleven o'clock the guests began to leave. Only a few had come by car; the majority lived in Sherman Lane and headed for home in a cheerful, chattering group, exchanging remarks about the mildness of the September night and making admiring comments on the spectacle of the brilliantly lit city spread out beneath them under a clear moonlit sky. One by one they called out 'Good night' and went into their respective homes until only Sukey and Major Matthews were left. With exaggerated gallantry he insisted on accompanying her right up to her front door, solemnly taking her key, opening it for her and waiting until she had stepped inside before handing back her key, giving a smart salute and saying a hearty 'Splendid evening, what! Cheerio!' before marching back to the Stables.

Sukey went straight to her study and made notes of the information she had gleaned about the absent guests, Hester and Stephen. Although the name of Lamont had not been mentioned there was no doubt in her mind that Stephen was the man whose appointment with Doctor Whistler had in some way led to that unfortunate man's violent death and whom she and DS Rathbone had interviewed that day. She had earlier been relieved to find, on reading the evening edition of the local paper, that the front page had been devoted to a story about a local teacher claiming compensation for alleged sexual harassment in the staff room, while the report on the incident in the hotel had been reduced to a short paragraph on an inside page. News of Doctor Whistler's death had not of course as yet been released and to her relief the few references to local news she had heard at the party were mostly concerned with the former story; no one referred to the latter. If it hadn't been for that telephone call, she reflected as she got ready for bed, no one would have been any the wiser, although fortunately it had not occurred to anyone apart from Tom Gadden that she might have some inside information, and Major Matthews had inadvertently rescued her from the necessity of responding to his question.

The following morning she set off early to avoid the rush hour traffic and had been at her desk for fifteen minutes when Rathbone strolled over with a mug of coffee in one hand and a folder in the other.

'Ashford has given us a room in his conference suite to use as an incident room,' he announced, adding with a mischievous grin, 'You should have seen his look of horror when I suggested bringing one of our vans into the hotel car park! By the way, I've booked an interview room here for our chat with Lamont for nine thirty. He thinks it's mainly a matter of checking and signing his statement, by the way; I didn't tell him what Gasspar has been saying and he doesn't know Whistler's dead.' His eye fell on her notebook; it was open at her jottings of the previous evening and she had been in the act of adding a further comment as he entered. 'Any new ideas?' he asked between swigs of coffee.

'As it happens, yes,' she said. 'Something rather interesting happened at the party yesterday.'

She relayed the scraps of information she had picked up at the Gaddens' and his slightly languid expression became alert. 'You didn't reveal your involvement?' he said sharply.

'No, and I didn't let on that Whistler had died. To be honest, I think they were more concerned about the neurotic sister than either the mugging or the theft of the document.'

'Just as well Lamont didn't show at the party or I'd have had to take you off the case, which would have been unfortunate – just as I'm getting used to having you around.' He looked at her as if he was expecting some expression of gratification at what he evidently considered a compliment, but she merely stared blandly back at him. 'So whatever you do,' he went on, 'make sure you don't have any contact with him outside the investigation.'

'Right, Sarge.'

'Let's run over the evidence – or lack of it – and discuss the line we're going to take. I've asked him to bring in the clothes he was wearing, by the way. He didn't sound too happy about that, which might or might not be significant.'

*   *   *

At a little before half past nine, Stephen Lamont sat in the reception area in New Bridewell Police Station, trying to appear relaxed. The call from DS Rathbone asking him to visit the station to sign his statement and 'help to clear up one or two other points' had been disturbing enough; Hester's uncontrollable distress on learning that his story about Whistler having been taken ill and was having to postpone their appointment was untrue had been the last straw and made it impossible for the two of them to turn up at the Gaddens' party as if nothing had happened. If only he hadn't been out of the room when the police rang; if only Hester hadn't taken the call; if only she hadn't called the Gaddens and blurted out the story before he had a chance to stop her. He just hoped it wouldn't go any further; he'd warned her not to go spreading it around, but she was inclined to be unpredictable and to act on impulse without considering the possible consequences. Which, had he but known it, was what was happening at that very moment.

A bespectacled young woman with a dark ponytail arrived to escort him to the interview. Stephen entered with his head held high; he was damned if he was going to be intimidated by this smooth-talking policeman or his sharp-featured female sidekick. He acknowledged Rathbone's polite greeting with a curt nod, sat down at the table in the drab, featureless room and stared defiantly back at his two interlocutors.

'I hope this isn't going to take long,' he said. 'I have a meeting at eleven.'

In response, Rathbone handed him a sheet of A4 paper and said, 'This is a record of the statement you made to DC Reynolds and myself yesterday. If you agree that it's correct, perhaps you would kindly sign it.'

Nothing would have given Stephen Lamont greater pleasure than to find a glaring mistake in the brief printed account, but on reading it through and finding it scrupulously accurate he merely grunted, pulled out a fountain pen, signed it and handed it back without a word.

'Thank you, sir.' Rathbone slipped it into a folder and sat back in his chair. 'I want to make it clear that you are here voluntarily and are free to leave at any time, you are not under caution and this interview is not being tape-recorded, although DC Reynolds may make a few notes. Is that clear?'

Lamont permitted himself a slightly disdainful smile. 'Perfectly,' he said.

'Good. Now, as I mentioned on the telephone, it is possible that when you bent over Doctor Whistler as he lay on the floor you picked up certain evidence on your clothing. I believe I asked you to be good enough to bring it in for examination.'

'You did, but I'm afraid you were too late. My sister looks after my clothes and it transpired that she had already put them all in the washing machine.'

The woman detective looked up from her notebook. 'Just the same we'd like to examine them,' she said briskly. 'By the way, what about the shoes you were wearing?' she added.

'You wanted those as well? I'm afraid I haven't brought them either.'

'That's no problem, sir. We can send an officer to pick them up, with the clothes, from your home.' He had a feeling as she spoke that she expected him to protest, but he maintained a dignified silence.

'Now, sir,' said Rathbone. 'I have to inform you that since you made your statement yesterday we have found a witness who claims to have seen you leave the hotel by the rear entrance almost half an hour before you came to the front desk and informed the clerk on duty that you were there to keep your appointment with Doctor Whistler. Have you any comment about that?'

Lamont managed to meet the detective's searching gaze without flinching. 'There must be some mistake,' he said. 'I arrived a few minutes late, parked my car, entered the hotel by the main door and went straight to the desk.'

'I see.' Rathbone looked down at his notes before saying, 'The witness also states that Doctor Whistler had told him to expect you at twelve, but that it was nearly twelve fifteen when you arrived. He also states,' he said before Lamont had a chance to say anything, 'that when he saw you leave by the side door you appeared to be in a great hurry and you were carrying a small, dark-coloured bag such as a holdall.'

'How many times do I have to tell you, I didn't arrive early and I didn't go out by the side way. The man obviously confused me with someone else.'

'All right, we'll leave that for the moment. But you admit you were late for your appointment. Why was that?'

'I was a few minutes late leaving my Greek class, and then I was delayed by traffic.' He saw the detective's eyebrows go up and added hastily, 'I teach classical Greek in an extra-mural class three mornings a week.'

'No doubt your students will confirm this.'

'Unfortunately not as they had all left a few minutes earlier.'

'So what was the reason for your delay?'

'I was sorting through some exercises they had handed in.'

'Couldn't that have waited, considering you had an appoint-ment at midday?'

'I suppose I . . . well, I must have forgotten the time for the moment. I do have a lot of other things on my mind.'

'Ah, yes,' said Rathbone, 'the paper about the letters of Saint Paul. I'm surprised that in view of your other commit-ments you find time to take on additional teaching at such an elementary level.' His tone was casual, but his gaze was keen. Lamont stiffened. Archie Thornton, his head of faculty, had also expressed some surprise on learning that he had applied for the part-time post and he had been forced to admit that he needed the money because of having to meet the cost of his sister's treatment. But he was damned if he was going to reveal his personal problems to this blighter. So he maintained a dignified silence and awaited the next question.

'Well, sir, as you insist that the witness I mentioned earlier made a mistake, no doubt you'll be willing to take part in an identity parade so that we can eliminate you from our enquiries?'

The suggestion took Lamont completely by surprise. He felt his face burn and it flashed across his mind that perhaps he should have brought his solicitor.

While he was desperately thinking how to respond, Rathbone said, 'I should make it clear that you are entitled to refuse.'

'Then I do refuse. I find the suggestion extremely distasteful.'

'We understand your feelings and there is an alternative, sir.' It was the woman speaking again. 'One of our photog-raphers can take a shot of you and we can insert it into a picture of a group of people of about your age and build. We can then show the montage to our witness and ask if he

can identify you as the man he saw. If he fails to do so, then
of course—'

Lamont pushed his chair back and leapt to his feet. 'I'm
not staying here a moment longer!' he said furiously. 'I'm a
highly qualified academic of impeccable character and I find
this line of questioning extremely insulting!' He marched to
the door and wrenched it open. 'Good day to you!'

'Before you leave,' said Rathbone, 'there is something you
should know.'

'And that is?'

'Doctor Whistler has died from his injuries. That means we
are conducting a murder enquiry.'

Lamont was halfway through the door, but he immediately
stopped short and rounded on the detectives. 'Why the hell
didn't you say so at the outset?' he demanded. He found himself
back in his chair without being quite sure how he got there.

'We've been waiting for you to enquire about his condition,' said Rathbone in the smooth, bland voice that made
Lamont feel uncomfortable. 'And there is also the question
of the missing document—'

'I . . . yes . . . of course I should have . . . it's terrible news
about poor Whistler. I imagine that when you find the villain
who attacked him you'll recover the document as well.'

'Naturally that is what we're hoping for. This document –
can you give us a rough idea of what it might be worth?'

Lamont made a vague gesture with his hands. 'In cash
terms, I've really no idea. If it's genuine, then it should be
entrusted to a museum or other collection of rare biblical writings for safe keeping.'

'What about a private collector?'

'In that case, its value would depend on what he is willing
to pay for it.'

'Or what lengths he would go to in order to get his hands
on it?' suggested Rathbone. The sub-text of the question was
unmistakable and for the second time Lamont sought refuge
in a dignified silence. 'Do you happen to know of such a
person?' the detective persisted.

There was something disconcerting at the unwavering gaze
of the two detectives, but Lamont did his best not to appear
intimidated. 'Certainly not!' he declared. 'What kind of people
do you think I associate with?'

Rathbone ignored the question. 'Perhaps in the circumstances you might like to reconsider your refusal to co-operate
over the matter of identification,' he suggested.

Something in his manner indicated that a change of heart
was a foregone conclusion. Making a mental note to contact
his solicitor at the earliest opportunity, Lamont replied with
as much dignity as he could muster, 'I see no reason to.'

'In that case it is my duty to inform you that we are free
to take any legal means available to us to obtain whatever
evidence we consider essential to our investigation,' Rathbone
said.

Lamont was conscious of only one thing and that was a
desperate need to get out of the place and seek advice. 'Do
what you damned well please!' he said.

'Your response is noted,' said Rathbone. 'That's all for now,
thank you, sir. We'll keep you informed . . . we'll send an
officer to your home to pick up the clothes and shoes.'

Lamont muttered something inaudible under his breath and
left the room. The moment the door closed behind him,
Rathbone and Sukey exchanged glances. 'Well, that cut him
down to size,' she remarked. 'And that outburst – outraged
dignity or guilty conscience?'

'My guess is the latter,' Rathbone replied. 'He looked
distinctly jumpy when he first came in, as I'm sure you noticed.
We'll have to get a covert shot of the bugger; get the techies
on to it, will you?'

'Sure.' Sukey made a note before saying, 'So, you reckon
he's our man?'

'Who's most likely to be interested in a letter supposed to
be from Saint Paul than someone who's currently working on
a paper on that very subject? My guess is that from the moment
he heard about it he's been slavering at the thought of getting
his hands on it.'

'But Whistler was planning to pass it over to him anyway,'
Sukey pointed out, 'so why on earth should he go to such
desperate lengths to steal it? And besides, Whistler did give
the impression when he spoke to Lamont that morning that
he thought someone else might be after it.'

'We only have Lamont's word for that,' Rathbone reminded
her. 'Besides, he implied that it's valuable and we know he's
had to shell out a small fortune for his sister's treatment.'

'That's true,' she agreed. 'It'll be interesting to see whether Boris picks him out when we show him the mock-up. Incidentally, I thought he seemed a bit jumpy as well; would it be a good idea to run a check on him to make sure he's not an illegal?'

'Some people are often uncomfortable with the police, even when they have no reason to be,' said Rathbone. 'He was very anxious to impress on us that his papers were in order and I imagine the hotel would have made sure before taking him on, but you're right, it wouldn't do any harm to check. I'll leave that with you. Meanwhile, I'll update DCI Leach and ask him what he wants us to tell the press.'

Six

'DCI Leach and I will be meeting the press at midday,' Rathbone informed Sukey half an hour later. 'We're not planning to add much to what they already know – just tell them that the man who was attacked at the Mariners Hotel was the victim of a stabbing, that he died later of his injuries and that we're still looking for the weapon. We haven't traced Whistler's next of kin yet so we can't release his name. We'll say we're following one or two leads and end with the usual appeal for members of the public to report anything suspicious.'

'What about the theft of the ancient document he's supposed to have brought with him?' she enquired.

'We're not saying a word about that or the jackals will sniff out his identity in no time and that will lead them straight to Lamont, or at least to his department. Incidentally, I had a word with Lamont's head of faculty – Professor Thorne – and asked him not to talk to the press either. If he is our man, any publicity at this stage could kybosh our case before it got to court.'

'I take it I shan't be appearing?' said Sukey in a sudden panic. 'I've never had to face the press.'

'Don't worry – it'll just be the two of us plus DS Bob Douglas who's in charge of the incident room. In any case, we want you to keep out of the limelight. We know that your hostess and the sister are buddies and we also know the sister is inclined to be unstable. If she found out that one of the officers on the case was a guest at the party she might take it into her head to try and contact you "off the record", so to speak. We don't want her rushing off to her friend and trying to worm your address out of her, do we?'

'Perish the thought,' Sukey said fervently. 'I hope Priscilla would have the sense not to give it to her. Perhaps I should have a word to make sure she doesn't?'

'Definitely not. That would inevitably mean letting her know that you're involved in the investigation. Say nothing and keep your head down. Have you spoken to the hotel about Boris, by the way?'

'Yes, I've just been having a word with Erika Henderson and she assured me that he was thoroughly vetted before they took him on. She did say that he was in a bit of a state after we'd interviewed him and she'd had to reassure him that he wasn't under suspicion.'

'Well, anyone who's grown up under a communist regime is likely to be wary of the police,' Rathbone observed. 'We must remember to treat him gently next time we talk to him. When are you going back to interview the chambermaids?'

'This morning, if that's OK with you; I arranged it with Erika at the same time. The two who service the first floor rooms are on duty again this morning and she says I can use the linen room to interview them. I gather they're both foreign so language might be a problem.'

'I'm sure you'll cope,' said Rathbone confidently. 'If by any chance they did see anyone at the crucial time we can show the mugshot of Lamont to them as well as Boris.'

'That's in hand, Sarge. The techies know it's a murder case so they'll give it priority.'

'Good. Well, you might as well go to the hotel now and talk to the chambermaids. Be sure and let Bob Douglas know the result – and ask Ashford to repeat the instruction to his staff not under any circumstances to talk to the press. They'll get on to it eventually,' he added resignedly, 'but we'll make it as difficult for the buggers as we can.'

'Will do, Sarge.'

Verena was a thin, pale girl with mousy hair tied in a pony-tail. When Erika Henderson accompanied Sukey to the first floor they found her in the linen room, loading her trolley with clean sheets and towels together with the usual assort-ment of minuscule tablets of soap, sachets of shampoo, body lotion and other luxuries with which hotels the world over provide their guests. Erika had forewarned her of the reason for the visit and although she had raised no objection to being questioned she was evidently ill at ease and maintained a defensive position behind her trolley throughout the brief interview. Her English, however, was reasonable and she appeared to have no difficulty in understanding the questions although her replies consisted as far as possible of monosyllables. Yes, she was responsible for servicing seven of the fourteen rooms on this floor; yes, she was on duty the previous day; yes, she remembered tapping on the door of room 106 and being asked to come back later; no, she couldn't be sure of the time but yes, it might have been around half past nine; yes, the gentleman put the 'Do Not Disturb' notice on the door at the same time; yes, several people had passed along the corridor while she was doing the rooms; no, she hadn't noticed anyone in particular.

In complete contrast, Nina was plump, rosy-faced and cheerful with a mop of bushy black hair. She was much more forthcoming than her colleague, who had made it clear as much by her wooden expression as by the brevity of her answers that she considered her responsibility was to service the rooms and not to concern herself with their occupants. Before Sukey could stop her, Nina offered several titbits about the guests for whose rooms she was responsible: the lady in number 109 was American and left a generous tip every morning; the gentleman in number 110 had slipped – rather furtively, judging from Nina's antics as she attempted to mime his movements – out of number 112 a little before eight o'clock; the couple in number 115 had left the 'Do Not disturb' notice on the door until lunchtime and 'seem very happy' – this information confided in a stage whisper with much eye-rolling and little puffs of laughter.

It was only after several minutes of this performance that Sukey managed to get a word in. In response to her patient probing Nina finally produced an item of significance: a tall gentleman with 'much grey hair' had come up the stairs while she was in the corridor. 'He look first here, then there. Then he go that way,' she explained, energetically waving her chubby arms. 'No, I not see what room he go. No, I not notice time.'

'Was he carrying anything? A bag, for example.'

'I not notice,' the girl repeated. 'I talk to Manuel. He porter,' she added, anticipating the next question.

'Did this gentleman speak to you or Manuel?'

'No.'

'Did you see him again?'

'No.' Nina gave an impatient shake of her bushy head. 'That all? You finish questions?'

'Yes, thank you, Nina. You've been very helpful.' Sukey saw the girl's large brown eyes travel hopefully towards her shoulder bag and she hastily rummaged for some loose change and handed it over. She retraced her steps along the corridor with the intention of giving Verena a similar reward, but there was no sign of her so she began making her way downstairs. Halfway down she met a swarthy young man in hotel livery coming up; on an impulse she stopped him and said, 'Excuse me, is your name Manuel?'

'Yes, madam,' he said. She showed him her warrant card and he nodded. 'You are here about the attack on the gentleman in room 106?' he said, speaking impeccable English but with a strong Spanish accent.

'That's right. You heard about it?'

'Of course. Everyone has heard. It was a terrible thing to happen in this hotel, was it not? How is the gentleman?'

'I'm afraid I don't have that information,' said Sukey and he gave a sad shake of the head. 'But I would like to ask you one or two questions if you'd be kind enough to spare me a few minutes,' she added.

Manuel's face lit up and she guessed that from the moment she showed him her warrant card he had been itching to be asked. He proved to be a useful witness; he told Sukey that while he was talking to Nina some time before twelve o'clock the previous morning a gentleman matching Stephen Lamont's general description had passed them in the corridor. Questioned a little further he confirmed that the man had come up the stairs rather than using the lift and he had appeared to be in a hurry. He apologized at length for being unable to state the exact time but he thought soon after eleven forty-five and certainly well before midday. He also expressed sorrow that, unfortunately, a bend in the corridor had made it impossible to see where the man went. With one hand placed theatrically somewhere in the region of his heart, he swore in language to match the gesture that had he realized the significance of the occurrence, he would have taken steps to obtain this information, but alas . . .

Sukey thanked him, assured him that he had been very helpful and headed for the incident room. Bob Douglas greeted her with a friendly nod and said, 'Get anything interesting?'

'Could be.' She gave him a brief summary of the three conversations before saying, 'If I can use one of the computers I'll bash out a report right away.'

'No problem. Have that one; Anna's taking an early lunch so she can hold the fort while I'm meeting the press.' He indicated an unoccupied workstation and she sat down and began setting up a new document on the screen. 'Want a coffee?' he added.

'Thanks. White no sugar, please.'

When she had finished she saved her work before printing off a couple of copies and giving one to him. He glanced through it before pinning it up on the board, but made no comment. 'I don't suppose the weapon's turned up?' she said.

'Not a smell so far. The search party's been told to look for a knife with a thin blade, maybe about six inches long. I doubt if they'll find it; my feeling is it's more than likely the killer took it with him. If it was a professional job he's probably keeping it for the next contract.'

Sukey looked at him in surprise. 'Professional? Whatever gave you that idea?'

'Just that academics don't normally carry knives. Just the same, it's pretty obvious that Lamont is Greg Rathbone's prime suspect and no doubt he has his reasons. But why commit murder to get the document when Whistler was going to hand it over?'

'On the face of it, he had a pretty strong motive for making it appear the document had been stolen,' Sukey pointed out. 'We suspect he's got money problems and on his own admission it could be worth a lot in the right quarters.'

Douglas shrugged. 'If you say so. You're the ones who've met the guy. Ah, here's Anna.'

A woman in civilian clothes entered the room and went over to the workstation Sukey had just vacated. 'Anna, this is DC Sukey Reynolds. She's working on the case with DS Rathbone; she's been interviewing some of the staff and I've pinned up her report.'

'Fine,' said Anna. The two women nodded and exchanged smiles. Douglas glanced at his watch. 'It's twenty to – I'd better be going.'

Sukey stayed for a few minutes chatting to Anna, who had worked for the police for several years and been involved in some major crimes. 'So far, there's precious little to go on and Bob and I have been able to cope on our own,' she explained as she ran through the procedure for handling reports and pieces of evidence as they came in. 'Of course, if things start hotting up we may need some extra help.'

'Right, thanks for showing me round,' said Sukey. 'I'll just have a quick word with Ms Henderson and then I'll be on my way.' She went to the reception desk, where Boris Gasspar had just handed a key to a new arrival. As soon as he saw her he stiffened and his eyes narrowed.

'Can I help you?' he said.

His voice was not quite steady but she affected not to notice. 'Good morning, Boris,' she said with a friendly smile. 'I just wanted another word with Ms Henderson; is she in her office?'

He relaxed visibly as he replied, 'Sorry, she has gone to city. You want speak Mr Ashford?'

'Yes, perhaps I should. Will you tell him I'm here?'

'One moment please.' He spoke briefly on the telephone before turning back to Sukey and saying, 'Please go to office.'

Maurice Ashford practically leapt to his feet as Sukey entered. If anything, she remarked later to Greg Rathbone, he seemed almost as jumpy as Boris, although for different reasons.

'How much longer are they going to be here?' he demanded, pointing through the window at the group of uniformed police officers meticulously checking a taped-off section of the car park. On the perimeter of the restricted area a handful of reporters, cameras at the ready, were waiting in groups, doubtless hoping for a chance to record a successful outcome of the search. 'It's most inconvenient, having to direct our guests to park first here and then there,' Ashford continued peevishly. 'It's true most of them have been reasonably co-operative,' he went on without giving her a chance to speak, 'but one or two have made it clear in no uncertain terms that they'll think twice about staying here again. And two families have checked out because their children have been upset. What are they looking for anyway?'

'The weapon used to attack Doctor Whistler or any other piece of evidence that could lead us to his assailant,' she explained patiently.

'What kind of weapon? That other detective who came with you promised you'd keep us informed, but we've heard nothing. We don't even know how the man is. Is he still in hospital? People keep enquiring and we can't give them any satisfactory answers.'

'That information hasn't been officially released yet,' said Sukey, 'but as the Senior Investigating Officer will be making a statement to the press at – ' she glanced at her watch, which stood at two minutes to twelve, and decided to take a chance – 'in fact, within the next couple of minutes. I think I can reveal that Doctor Whistler suffered a fatal stab wound. They're looking for a knife or something similar and it's possible that the attacker discarded it before driving away.'

'You mean he's dead? Stabbed? Oh, how awful! How absolutely shocking!' Ashford shuddered and covered his eyes as if he was reliving the moment when he came on the scene. Remembering the fuss he had made about all the blood, Sukey had a sudden mischievous impulse – hastily repressed – to regale him with the graphic details of Doctor Hanley's provisional findings. 'Now I suppose the press will be pestering us again,' he said gloomily.

'I'm afraid there's nothing we can do to prevent that, but please don't repeat what I have just told you until the news has been officially released – and remind your staff not to give any interviews.'

Ashford nodded. 'Yes, I'll do that right away.'

'Thank you.' She went to the door. 'I'll go now. I just popped in to thank Erika for arranging for me to speak to some of your staff. She's out of the office at the moment so I asked for you. By the way, the people I spoke to were all very helpful,' she added as he made no reply.

'Oh, er, good. Thank you,' said Ashford distractedly.

As she drove slowly towards the exit to the car park the reporters, who moments ago had been hanging listlessly around looking bored, suddenly became a herd that went charging towards the hotel entrance with cameras and microphones at the ready. Evidently the news had reached them via their respective networks, which meant that she no longer needed to feel uneasy about having given it to Maurice Ashford. She drove back to the station in an optimistic mood, little suspecting that before long she would find herself in a potentially far trickier situation.

Seven

B ack at the station, Sukey found the occupants of the CID office clustered round a TV screen. Rathbone beckoned her to join them.

'What's going on?' she asked.

'We're just about to run a recording of our meeting with the press,' he said. 'Locals for the most part; the nationals haven't shown much interest so far, but no doubt they will now they know it's a murder hunt.'

The meeting had been brief; DCI Leach revealed that the victim of the attack had died in hospital from massive internal bleeding as the result of a stab wound to the chest. It was suspected that robbery was the motive, but so far it had not been possible to establish what, if anything, had been taken. The identity of the victim would not be released until the next of kin had been informed. The police were following one or two lines of enquiry but no arrest had so far been made and they were still searching for the weapon. One member of the audience claimed to know that the victim had arranged to meet someone at the hotel that morning. This provoked a barrage of questions: was this true and did the police know who that person was? Did he or she arrive to keep the appointment and was he or she a suspect? These and similar questions were politely but firmly stonewalled, the meeting was declared closed and the reporters hurried away to file their stories.

'So how did you get on?' asked Rathbone as the monitor was switched off and people returned to their desks.

'One possible sighting.' Sukey handed him a copy of her report.

He studied it briefly and then grunted. 'Well, it's something to put to Lamont, I suppose, but it's hardly enough evidence for us to pull him in for a formal interview. We'll show the mugshot to Manuel when we get it, of course. Anything else?'

'Erika Henderson wasn't there, but I had a word with Ashford and reminded him about telling the staff not to talk to the press. In the nick of time, judging from the way the reporters hanging around outside the hotel suddenly came to life and made a beeline for the front entrance.'

Rathbone nodded. 'They probably got texts from their mates at the briefing. I daresay some underlings will step out of line just to get their picture in the paper, but the important thing is to avoid identification of anyone connected with the case. The last thing we want is for Lamont's name to be publicized before we have enough to charge him.'

'You're absolutely sure he's our man?' said Sukey.

'Ninety per cent,' said Rathbone in a matter of fact tone. 'Aren't you?'

She hesitated a moment before saying, 'I still don't understand why, no matter how badly he wanted that document for himself, he had to attack Whistler to get it. I thought the whole point of the meeting was so that he could take it away and study it to see if it was genuine.'

'He must have figured that if he'd collected it as arranged he'd have been obliged to go straight back and show it to his head of faculty, who might even have kept it under lock and key in his own office when Lamont wasn't actually working on it.'

'You're suggesting he set out early with the deliberate intention of sticking a knife into Whistler, making off with the document and then returning at the appointed time to find his body in the presence of witnesses?'

'Something like that. It wouldn't surprise me if we discover he's a closet collector of ancient documents and artefacts that by rights should be in museums, as he so virtuously pointed out.' Rathbone gave a harsh chuckle. 'It must have been a shaker for him to realize when he and the others went back to Whistler's room that the guy was still alive and might be able to give a description of his attacker.'

'But he knew he was still alive – he heard him groaning and that's why he raised the alarm.'

'So he says. No one else heard it.'

'That's true,' Sukey admitted. 'Just the same, you'd have

thought he could have dreamed up something a bit less risky,' she said doubtfully. 'It seems a pretty foolhardy thing for a clever man like Lamont to do.'

Rathbone treated her to a condescending smile that was like a pat on the head.

'My dear girl, when you've been in this job as long as I have you'll know that even hardened villains are capable of doing the most stupid and apparently pointless things. Lamont might be clever at deciphering musty old documents, but I don't think he falls into that category, do you?' He spoke patiently, as if he were speaking to a raw recruit. 'Any more bits of advice to give me?'

Sukey felt her cheeks grow hot under the put-down. She had been about to mention Boris's apparent unease on seeing her that morning, but held her tongue.

After a moment she said, 'What do you want me to do now?'

'It's occurred to me that we've only got Lamont's word for it that the document was the only thing of any value unearthed on Whistler's dig. There might have been other equally valuable stuff that he conveniently forgot to mention. Whistler's luggage has been thoroughly checked, but apart from what appeared to be the latest e-mail from Lamont confirming their appointment we found no reference to anything like that. His wallet with cash and credit cards was in his jacket pocket, together with his passport and airline ticket, but we found nothing else in the way of correspondence. So I've arranged for us to go and see Professor Thorne this afternoon to see if he can recall anything that might be significant.'

The Hellenic Studies Department of the university was located in a leafy square a short distance from the main campus. It occupied two former private houses knocked into one, each doubtless once owned by wealthy merchants who had over several centuries contributed to the city's importance both as a port and a centre of trade and industry.

A sign on a door in the entrance hall read Enquiries; DS Rathbone marched in without knocking and informed the middle-aged blonde behind the desk that he and DC Reynolds had an appointment with Professor Thorne. Her expression was almost disdainful as she scrutinized their warrant cards before picking up a telephone and announcing their arrival in a deferential voice. She put the phone down and said, with another noticeable change of tone, 'Professor Thorne will see you now. His office is on the first floor at the end of the corridor.'

'Quite the little ray of sunshine,' Rathbone remarked to Sukey as they climbed the stone staircase. On reaching the landing he cast an appraising glance around and commented, 'I can't think why they use these old buildings; they must be hellishly inconvenient to work in – and cost a fortune to heat in winter,' he added a trifle waspishly. Sukey made no comment; she sensed that it was frustration at the lack of progress in the enquiry that was making him irritable. Meanwhile, she paused for a few seconds at the top of the stairs, mentally contrasting the sickly green walls lined with notice boards, the cold neon lighting and the grubby, uncurtained windows with the unashamed opulence of the Gaddens' house. Both buildings dated from approximately the same period, but they might almost belong to different worlds.

'Come on, let's not hang around,' Rathbone said impatiently. He led the way along the corridor towards a door on which was painted in gold lettering, Professor Archibald Thorne, Head of Department. This time he knocked, but opened the door and entered without waiting for a response.

The man who rose from behind the desk to receive them presented a striking contrast to Stephen Lamont, being short, on the portly side and almost completely bald. Everything about him seemed colourless, from his grey flannel suit to his pallid features and pale eyes behind the rimless glasses that were perched precariously on his small sharp nose. But his voice when he greeted them was surprisingly resonant, and his manner as he waved them to the chairs placed conveniently in front of his desk was brisk and authoritative.

'This is a terrible, terrible business,' he said after the formalities had been exchanged. 'Everyone in the department was greatly concerned to hear of the attack on Doctor Whistler – and then we heard on the midday news that he has died.' He assumed a mournful expression and gave a sorrowful shake of the head. 'It's difficult to believe that these things can happen in a civilized country. Have you any idea at all who did it, Sergeant?'

'It's early days yet, but we're following one or two leads,' said Rathbone. 'When we find the weapon it will take us a big step forward.'

'Quite so.' Thorne cleared his throat. 'I must say, Lamont was particularly distressed at being interviewed a second time,' he continued with an air of mild reproach. 'I'm sure you find it necessary to question everyone very closely, but after the shock of finding Whistler it was a considerable ordeal for him. And before we go any further,' he said before either Rathbone or Sukey had a chance to speak, 'I have known him for many years and in my opinion he is the last person who would commit an act of violence.'

'Thank you, sir, we'll bear that in mind,' said Rathbone.

'Needless to say,' Thorne added, 'you can rely on my complete co-operation, and that of my staff, in your efforts to bring the perpetrator of this monstrous crime to justice.'

'Thank you, sir, that's much appreciated. If you don't mind, I'd like to run over the details of this case from the beginning.'

Thorne nodded. 'Yes, of course, although I fear I can add little to what Stephen Lamont has already told you.'

'Just checking that nothing significant has been overlooked, sir. I understand that Doctor Whistler's initial approach was to you personally. Were you and he already acquainted?'

'No, not at all.'

'Have you any idea why he should have approached you?'

It seemed to Sukey that a hint of self-importance crept into Thorne's manner as he replied, 'Presumably because he knew me by reputation.'

'But I understand you asked Professor Lamont to handle it rather than deal with it yourself.'

Thorne nodded. 'It seemed the obvious thing to do, given the nature of the enquiry. In addition to his specialized know-ledge of classical Greek, Lamont has a particular interest in the apocryphal epistles of Saint Paul – that is, letters attributed to him by scholars but for various reasons never included with his other writings in the New Testament. In addition, it is generally believed that others exist but have been lying undiscovered for centuries. In his letter, Doctor Whistler stated that he believed he had found one such document and wanted it subjected to expert examination.'

'Did you reply to the letter yourself, or did you hand the whole matter over to Professor Lamont and ask him to deal with it?'

'I acknowledged the letter and informed Doctor Whistler of the action I had taken.'

'And you then handed the letter over to Professor Lamont?'

'I gave him a photocopy, together with a copy of my reply.' Thorne picked up a folder lying on his desk and offered it to Rathbone. 'The originals are here if you would like to see them. Naturally, I asked to be kept fully informed so you will also find in here copies of all the emails and notes of telephone conversations that were exchanged between Lamont and Whistler.'

'Thank you.' Rathbone took the folder but made no attempt to open it. 'Apart from yourself, and presumably your secretary, who else might have seen this correspondence?'

Thorne frowned. 'It's difficult to say. I'm out of my office quite a lot and if any messages arrive in my absence my secretary puts them on my desk.'

'What about callers – for example, colleagues or people from other departments?' Sukey asked. 'Presumably they leave their queries and so on with her if you're not here.'

'Sometimes, but my door is never locked during the day and it's not unusual, for example in the case of a minor or non-urgent query, for a note to be left in my in-tray.'

'So any one of a number of people might have seen some or any of the correspondence relating to Doctor Whistler's visit?'

Thorne shrugged. 'I suppose so, but I can't see . . .'

'It would be helpful if you could ask your secretary to make a list of everyone who has access to this office during the day and fax it through to us,' said Rathbone. 'And if you have no objection we should like to take this – ' he indicated with the folder – 'back to the station so that we can study the contents in detail. We will of course give you a receipt.'

Thorne frowned. 'I am reluctant to allow a file to leave the department,' he said.

'Perhaps your secretary could provide us with photocopies?' Sukey suggested.

'Good idea,' said Rathbone. He handed the folder to Sukey and tilted his head in the direction of a door to the left of Thorne's desk. 'Is that her office?'

Looking slightly displeased at having the initiative taken from him, Thorne said, 'Oh, very well. I'll just—' He pushed back his chair, at the same time holding out his hand to take back the folder.

'No need to disturb yourself, sir,' said Rathbone quietly.

Sukey, who had read his thoughts, was already on her feet. She quickly crossed the room, tapped on the door and opened it. A slim, attractive woman with dark hair falling in glossy waves on either side of her face was standing at an open filing cabinet. On the desk behind her a telephone handset lay beside its cradle; evidently she was in the act of dealing with a query.

She turned as Sukey entered and said, 'Yes? What is it?' in a voice suggesting she resented the intrusion.

'DC Reynolds, Bristol CID.' Sukey held up her warrant card.

The woman picked up the handset and said, 'I'll call you back,' before replacing it. She turned back to Sukey and said sharply, 'What do you want?'

'Detective Sergeant Rathbone and I are enquiring into the murder of Doctor Edwin Whistler,' Sukey explained. 'Professor Thorne has very kindly agreed to our having copies of all the relevant correspondence that passed through this department. Would you be kind enough . . . ?' She held out the folder.

The woman's attitude appeared to soften. 'Oh . . . yes, of course, I'll do them as soon as I've finished dealing with this query. It'll only take a minute. Leave it on my desk and I'll bring them in when they're ready.'

'That's all right, I'll wait,' said Sukey. The woman hesitated, then shrugged, went over to the machine and in a resentful silence ran off a copy of each document as Sukey passed it to her. When she had finished she put them in an envelope and handed it over before returning to the filing cabinet, ignoring Sukey's polite expression of thanks.

As the detectives returned to their car after taking their leave of Thorne, Rathbone said casually, 'I've no reason to suppose he'd have held back anything in that file before getting the copies made, but well done for beating him to the draw.'

'Thanks.' Sukey clipped on her seatbelt and turned on the ignition. 'Do you think we'll find anything interesting?'

'I doubt it, but we have to show that we've covered every possibility. Go through that lot with a toothcomb and make a detailed record of every item. If anything particular strikes you, let me know. And when that fax comes through, have a word with everyone who's on it. Which reminds me, Lamont was supposed to let me have a similar list. I'll give him a nudge when we get back.' With that, he settled back in his seat, closed his eyes and said nothing more until they arrived at the station.

It was with a vague feeling of disappointment that Sukey returned home that evening. Her search through Thorne's file had yielded nothing of any apparent significance, the weapon used to kill Whistler had still not been found and it would be some time before the results of forensic tests on Lamont's clothing became available. The initial excitement of being for the first time at the cutting edge of a murder enquiry had begun to wear off and she recalled a comment Jim Castle had once made about the periods of boredom and frustration that characterized detective work. A little wearily, she pushed open her front door, gathered up the day's post and carried it into the kitchen with the shopping she had done on the way home. She cheered herself up with the thought that it was Saturday tomorrow and Fergus would be arriving in the morning for a two-night stay.

She put the kettle on for a cup of tea, stowed the food items away and sorted through the letters. Among them was a brief handwritten note reading, 'Would you give me a call when you get home? Please treat as urgent. Priscilla.' The last words were underlined in red.

With a sense of apprehension, Sukey tapped out the number scribbled beneath the signature. Her call was answered immediately.

'Oh Sukey, I'm so thankful you're back,' Priscilla almost gasped. 'Can you possibly come round right away? I've got Hester Lamont here, in a terrible state. She keeps saying her brother killed that man in the hotel and it's all her fault.'

Eight

The Gaddens' daughter Patsy opened the door. In contrast to her somewhat bizarre appearance of the previous evening she wore little make-up and wore well-fitting jeans and a T-shirt that flattered her young figure. Instead of greeting Sukey in her earlier offhand, almost hostile manner she smiled a welcome.

'Mum will be so relieved you're here,' she said. 'She's in the television room with Hester. She's completely batty, of course – Hester, I mean,' she added in a breathy whisper. 'My dad reckons she must cost her brother a fortune in visits to the funny farm. They're in here.' She opened a door leading off the hall and ushered Sukey into a cosy room furnished with little more than a few comfortable chairs arranged in a semi-circle in front of a large modern television set. 'Would you like some tea?'

'Thank you.'

'I've made one lot but it'll be stewed by now. I'll make a fresh pot.'

On a low table in the centre of the room was a tray of used tea-things. Patsy picked it up and went out, closing the door softly behind her.

Priscilla was sitting on a low stool in front of one of the chairs, holding the hand of a small figure with bowed shoulders and straight, mouse-brown hair hanging limply on either side of pale, nondescript features. As Sukey approached she gave the hand a gentle tug and said quietly, 'Hester, I want you to meet my neighbour, the one I've been telling you about. I think she may be able to help you.'

'No one can help me,' Hester replied without raising her head. She spoke in a monotone, like someone in a trance. 'I'm wicked. I'm the one who should have died.'

Sukey crouched down beside Priscilla and said quietly, 'Why do you say you're wicked? What have you done?'

There was a long silence. Sukey was about to repeat her question when Hester straightened up and looked directly at her.

'Are you the police?' she said fearfully.

Instinctively, Sukey prevaricated. 'Do you want to talk to the police?'

'Pris said you could help me.'

'I'll try. What's the problem?'

'I know I ought to go to the police, but I daren't. Stephen would never forgive me. He's in enough trouble with them as it is and it's all my fault.'

'Stephen?'

'My brother. He's looked after me since—' Her voice broke and a few slow tears trickled down her colourless cheeks.

'Would you like to tell me about it?'

'I'll try.'

'Just take your time.'

At this point Patsy appeared with a tray. She set it down on the table and began pouring out tea. She served first Sukey, then her mother, and finally offered a cup to Hester, who accepted it with shaking hands and a whispered word of thanks.

Patsy quietly left the room and for a while the three women sipped their tea in silence. There came into Sukey's mind a piece of advice that DC Vicky Armstrong had given her during her probationary period: "Be patient with a genuinely nervous witness; avoid pressurising; build up confidence gradually." So she drank her tea slowly, never taking her gaze from Hester's face and giving a nod and a smile of encouragement every time their eyes met. She was struck by the contrast between brother and sister – the former well built, handsome, confident to the point of arrogance, the latter frail, timid and pathetic looking. The hackneyed phrase 'scared of her own shadow' might have been coined with Hester Lamont in mind.

After what seemed an eternity, Hester finished her tea, placed her empty cup on the tray and spoke again in the same expressionless voice.

'Stephen would never have taken that knife if it wasn't for me. He would never have needed all that money and he wouldn't have killed that man if I hadn't caused him so much trouble.' She hid her face in her hands and began to cry in a series of jerky, heart-rending sobs that threatened to rip her slight body apart. Priscilla stood up and put an arm round her shoulders and Sukey took hold of both her hands, while between them they soothed and persuaded and reassured until at last the paroxysm ceased and she sat quietly weeping into the handkerchief that Priscilla gave her. Eventually she turned to Sukey and said in a small, quavering voice, 'Please tell me, what should I do?'

'Why don't you tell me exactly what happened?' said Sukey.

Hester bit her lip, hesitated for a moment, then slowly and deliberately undid the cuff of her long-sleeved shirt and pushed it up, exposing her arm from wrist to elbow. It bore the scars of several wounds, one clumsily bandaged and still oozing blood. 'This,' she said simply.

Priscilla gave a horrified gasp. 'You mean Ste—' she began, but just in time she caught Sukey's urgent gesture and bit back the words.

'You made those cuts yourself, didn't you?' said Sukey quietly. Hester nodded. 'Because you feel badly about something you've done?' Another nod. 'When did it start?' Silence. 'Just lately?' A shake of the head. 'A long time ago?' Another nod. 'And Stephen caught you with the knife and took it away from you?' This time the only reaction was a gaze of stark misery. 'Do you want to tell us about it?'

It was several seconds before she got a response. Then Hester whispered, 'You won't tell Stephen I told you?'

'Not if you don't want us to.'

It was a sadly familiar tale of a young and impressionable woman carried away by the persuasive charm of a dashing, romantic lover who, despite swearing eternal devotion, had abandoned her on learning that she was to bear his child. Torn between the need to confess her predicament to her brother – her sole relative after the death of their parents in an air disaster some years previously – and having a secret abortion, she had chosen the latter course. Racked with grief and guilt, she had suffered a nervous breakdown and ever since had been in the care of counsellors and psychiatrists.

'Stephen never liked Wayne and all he could say when he left me was that I was better off without him,' she said miserably when the pitiful saga came to an end. 'He had no idea about the baby; he just thought I was being feeble and sorry for myself and he got impatient with me until the doctor convinced him that I was ill and needed help. Poor Stephen; I've been a millstone round his neck for such a long time. All that money he's had to find for treatment . . . and he lost the woman he wanted to marry because he couldn't leave me and she wouldn't have me to live with them. I should have made the cuts deeper . . . maybe then I'd have died and been no more trouble to him.' More tears threatened to engulf her.

Sukey took one of her small, fragile hands in both hers. 'You mustn't think like that,' she said urgently. 'It wouldn't have solved anything. You have more important things to think of now. Tell me, what made you say your brother killed that man?'

'It was when the police came for his clothes.' A noticeable change came over Hester; obviously, speaking of recent, tangible events came more easily than reliving the tragedy of her past. 'I'd already washed them because of the stain on the safari jacket he was wearing that day, but it didn't wash out so it must have been blood.'

'Where do you think the blood came from?'

'From the knife, of course – the one he used to kill the man.'

'Why do you suppose he killed him?'

'For the valuable things he'd brought with him, of course.'

'What valuable things?'

'Holy things like an ancient document and relics from an old church in Rhodes. Stephen's very clever,' Hester continued proudly. 'He knows Classical Greek and he's a famous biblical scholar. He tried to teach me Greek once but I'm too stupid – I could never remember anything after Alpha, Beta, Gamma, Delta.' She gave a shy, nervous giggle. 'Isn't it funny how a brother and sister can be so different?'

'Tell us more about the valuable things,' Sukey said patiently.

'Stephen didn't tell me much except he thought they must be worth a lot of money. At the time he didn't seem all that interested in the ancient relics, although he was very excited about the document. Afterwards he must have decided to steal them so he could sell them to pay for my treatment. I suppose the man caught him in the act and that's why he killed him.' She sat back with an air of weary resignation.

'That knife,' Sukey said gently. 'Are you saying Stephen took it to the meeting with this man with the deliberate intention of killing him?'

Hester shook her head in evident bewilderment. 'All I know is that he put it in his pocket when he took it away from me. Perhaps that's what gave him the idea. He'll go to prison and it's all my fault.' Once again, grief and guilt threatened to overwhelm her and it was some minutes before she was calm enough to speak again.

When at last the storm subsided she said in a pathetic whisper, 'Now you know everything but please, please don't tell him I've told you.'

'Of course we won't,' Priscilla said gently, 'but I expect he'll be worried about you and wondering where you've gone. You look cold. Let me put this round you.' She took a rug from one of the empty chairs and draped it round Hester's shoulders and across her lap. 'Just rest quietly for a little while and then I'll take you home.' She made a sign to Sukey and they both went out of the room. Moving away from the door, she said in a low voice, 'What are you going to do?'

Sukey shrugged. 'I've got no choice. I have to report this.'

'You surely don't believe her brother killed this man?'

'Whether I believe it or not has nothing to do with it. What Hester has told us could be important evidence.'

'But she's unbalanced . . . she obviously has a history of mental instability.'

'That doesn't mean she was making everything up.'

'No, I suppose not, but what if she has to be interviewed? It wouldn't take much to tip her over the edge. Do you know the detectives who are conducting the enquiry?'

Once again Sukey avoided giving a direct answer. 'Don't worry, I'll make sure they understand she'll need very careful handling.'

'What about the abortion and everything? Do they have to know that?'

Sukey hesitated. 'I'll have to mention the self-harm because of the knife. Maybe not the reason for it, for the time being at any rate.'

'I suppose that's something,' said Priscilla. She gave a despairing sigh. 'Oh, dear, I'm beginning to wish I hadn't asked you to come. Nothing personal,' she added hastily, putting an apologetic hand on Sukey's arm, 'and thank you very much anyway. I was at my wits' end wondering what to do with her. First she was going to the police, then said she daren't because her brother would be furious . . . I just thought you—'

'You did the right thing.'

'Do you think they'll want to question me?' said Priscilla.

'I'm afraid so, and if you find out anything else after I've left, will you please be sure to tell them?'

Priscilla sighed. 'All right. What do you think I should say to her brother when I take her home?'

'I suggest you say she was so distressed at the thought he might be a suspect that she turned to you for comfort. And please be sure to keep my name out of it.'

'If you say so.'

'It's important.' Sukey edged towards the front door. 'Look, I must go now,' she said. 'I have to make a note of everything Hester told us. You do realize, don't you, that I won't be able to answer any questions about the investigation from now on?'

The bus from Cheltenham arrived on time the following morning. Fergus flung his bulging holdall into the boot of Sukey's car, settled into the passenger seat, gave his mother a peck on the cheek and said, 'Hi Mum, how's the murder hunt going?'

'What murder hunt?' she asked cautiously.

'The stabbing in the hotel. It was in the late edition of the *Gloucester Gazette* yesterday. Are you involved in it?'

'I am, as it happens, but I'm not sure I ought to tell you about it.'

'Oh, come on, Mum, you know you can trust me. I might even be able to give you some tips on solving it,' he added. 'We had our first lecture on criminal psychology on Thursday.'

'Oh, well, the case is as good as solved,' she said dryly. 'If anything breaks over the weekend I'll refer the SIO to you.'

'Seriously though, you will give me the gory details, won't you?'

She gave a resigned sigh. 'Knowing you, you'll give me no peace until I do.'

When they were back at her flat she prepared coffee and croissants while outlining the details of the case that had not so far been released to the press and the events of the previous evening.

'So far as I know we haven't been able to contact Whistler's next of kin, which is why his name hasn't been released,' she said. 'And Hester Lamont's reference to other treasures confirms what Greg Rathbone already suspects, that he was carrying items of considerably greater value than the Pauline epistle.'

'So you reckon you've got your killer?'

'It certainly looks like it, although there's no evidence so far that would stand up in court.'

'All purely circumstantial, and Hester would hardly make a reliable witness,' Fergus pointed out. 'The thing is, do *you* think he's guilty?'

'I see no reason to doubt it, but—'

'You've got one of your famous hunches?' her son suggested slyly.

'Not exactly, but I can't help thinking it all looks a bit too obvious.'

'I suppose you were hoping to come up with a sensational new lead, solve the crime single-handed and get a commendation from the Chief Constable,' he teased her.

She laughed. 'Hardly. Anyway, I'm sure Greg Rathbone will be delighted when he sees my report. He's been sure from the word go that Lamont's our man.'

'Never mind, Mum.' He gave her a consoling pat on the arm. 'Your chance will come.'

Nine

Having emailed over to the incident room her report on her encounter with Hester Lamont, Sukey was half expecting to receive a call from Greg Rathbone, if for no other reason than to express his triumph at the apparent confirmation of his suspicion that, in addition to the Pauline epistle, Whistler had been carrying items of possibly far greater value. But Saturday ended and Sunday came and went without any word from him.

As Fergus got out of the car at the bus station where she dropped him on Monday morning en route for work, he said, 'So long, Mum, thanks for a great weekend and I hope you get brownie points for having turned up valuable evidence.'

'It would be nice to think so, but what Hester told me is only hearsay – it would never be admitted in court,' she said. 'Still, it could be a useful opening. It'll be interesting to see how Greg Rathbone handles it.' She leaned across the empty passenger seat and they exchanged a brief parting kiss before he shut the door. 'Take care, Gus; see you soon.'

On arrival at the police station she was met at the door by Rathbone who tossed her the keys to one of the pool cars and said, 'We're going straight to the incident room at the hotel. A few interesting bits of information from the public came in over the weekend.'

He did not speak again until they were in the car and heading out of the city centre. Then he said, with obvious satisfaction, 'Told you there'd be more stuff than one grotty old bit of parchment, didn't I?'

'You did indeed, Sarge.'

'And you'll be pleased to know that the team has turned up another nugget, this time from one Mrs Potter, a very chatty widow who lives round the corner from Lamont and acts as a sort of part-time cook-housekeeper for him and his sister.

She happened to answer the door when PC Lucy Jennings called to pick up the clothes and while she was making out a receipt Mrs P made some interesting comments about how upset the sister was at what had happened and how worried he was about the effect on her mental state. Her actual words were, "what she might do to herself", which ties in with what you found out.'

'I take it Hester herself didn't appear?'

'No, and unfortunately at that moment a man turned up to fix the boiler, which meant end of conversation. Anyway, tell me more about your friend – the one who asked you round to talk to Lamont's sister.'

'Her name's Priscilla Gadden. She's not exactly a friend – I mean, I don't know her all that well. She lives just up the road from me and she invited me to the party she and her husband gave last Thursday.'

'Does she know you're a police officer?'

'Oh, yes. I imagine everyone in Sherman Close knew before I moved in. It's the kind of neighbourhood when things get around; I happened to mention it to the woman who sold me the flat and no doubt she passed it on.'

'Did you tell her you're working on the case?'

'No, and I've managed so far to avoid letting anyone else know, but before I left after talking to Hester I made it clear I'd have to report everything that passed between us. Incidentally, Priscilla was concerned that she might be questioned and I told her it couldn't be ruled out. And before you ask, I made a particular point of asking her not to mention my name in connection with the case.'

'You reckon she'll take any notice?'

Sukey shrugged. 'I hope so. She doesn't strike me as a gossip, but I expect she'll tell her husband, and the daughter knows I was there although she wasn't in the room while we were talking.'

'What about Hester Lamont? Does she know you're a copper?'

'Definitely not. At first she thought I might be and hastened to tell me she knew she should talk to the police but was afraid to. It seems she went rushing round to Priscilla in a state of hysteria saying her brother had committed the Mariners Hotel murder. Priscilla couldn't think what to do so she turned to me for advice. She introduced me to Hester as "someone who might be able to help her", that's all.'

'I see.' Rathbone, as was his habit, closed his eyes and remained silent until they were turning into the hotel car park. Then he said, 'I'd like to keep you on the case if possible, but we'll have to tread carefully. I'll show your report to DCI Leach and see what he thinks. D'you reckon Hester will tell her brother about meeting you?'

'I should think it's the last thing she'd do. She begged us not to let him know she'd told us her story. I got the impression she's scared of him.'

Rathbone grunted. 'We already know he's an arrogant bastard,' he commented as he got out of the car and slammed the door, 'and he's quite likely a bully as well. The fact that his sister didn't dare tell him about her pregnancy says a lot.'

'He obviously cares about her, judging by what she says about the trouble he's taken to get treatment for her,' Sukey pointed out.

'Think of the expense he's incurred along the way,' he reminded her. 'The proceeds of a few valuable artefacts could pay for quite a lot of visits to a shrink.'

They were admitted through the staff entrance by the officer on duty and went straight to the incident room, where they found DS Douglas studying the notice board while Anna sat working at her computer.

'Anything fresh?' asked Rathbone.

'Apart from the bits I've already mentioned, nothing significant,' said Douglas. He handed some computer printouts to Rathbone, who studied them for a few minutes without speaking before passing them to Sukey. Three members of the public had reported possible sightings of Stephen Lamont: one a Mr Busbridge who had noticed someone answering to his description hurrying across the car park and getting into a car at around the time Boris claimed to have seen him leave, and two women who had been waiting in reception for a taxi at the crucial time and who believed him to be a man they had seen arrive, go to the desk and then 'go haring up the stairs' as one of them described it. They also saw him come rushing down again a few minutes later, but at that moment their taxi arrived and they left.

'And that's it?' said Rathbone.

'More or less.' Douglas showed him a list. 'These are from people who "thought they saw someone acting suspiciously", but when questioned were obviously so wide of the mark they were hardly worth logging. Oh, and the manager's PA came in a few minutes ago to say that when she went out to her car on Saturday, young Boris what's-his-name was outside the staff entrance having what sounded like a furious argument with someone on his mobile.'

'Any idea what it was about?'

Douglas grinned. 'Not a clue. She said he was talking in a foreign language, which I presume was Albanian.'

Rathbone shrugged. 'It was probably nothing. These types get so excited . . . They were probably talking about a match between their rival football clubs.' He glanced at Sukey. 'Want to raise anything about those statements?' he asked.

What she really wanted to do was challenge him about what he meant by 'these types', but instead she said, 'There's nothing in Mr Busbridge's statement about the kind of car the man he saw was driving. I take it that's because he didn't give any details?'

'I took the call,' said Anna, 'and naturally I asked that question, but he'd just pulled into a space and was getting his stuff out of the boot when the guy appeared. First he thought it might have been dark coloured, then he changed his mind and asked me to scrub that out because he wasn't sure. And he had no idea of the make or the registration number. And he didn't notice whether the man drove off straight away either.'

'Well, it's another presumed sighting, I suppose,' Rathbone commented, a trifle grudgingly, 'but it doesn't take us very far forward.'

'The timing's right,' Douglas said. 'I checked on the desk and Busbridge filled in his registration form a few minutes after Boris saw Lamont leave. We managed to trace the taxi driver and the time he arrived to pick the women up tallies with the time Erika Henderson says Lamont came to the desk to say he thought Whistler was ill.'

'That's good.' Rathbone appeared marginally less gloomy at this piece of information. He took the printouts from Sukey and gave them another cursory glance before handing them back to Douglas. 'Well, we'd better get back to the station.

I've sent someone to pick up Lamont and bring him in for another interview. We'll have this one on tape.'

Stephen Lamont had brought his solicitor, John Goodacre, to the interview. Sukey guessed his age at about forty; he had sleek brown hair, smooth, unlined pink cheeks and a perfect set of white, even teeth, all of which contributed to a slightly ingenuous appearance that was belied by his crisp, business-like manner and the shrewd expression in his light brown eyes.

As soon as the formalities were over and the tape was running, he said, 'I should like to begin by making it clear that my client categorically denies any involvement in the death of Doctor Edwin Whistler, he has told you all he knows about the case and he is at a total loss to understand why he should have been brought here for further questioning.'

'You have made your client's position perfectly clear,' said Rathbone. He switched his gaze to Lamont, who was lolling back in his chair with his legs crossed and his hands clasped round one knee. 'So, Professor Lamont,' he continued, 'we are to conclude that after careful reflection there is nothing you wish to add to your earlier statements?'

'Are you asking me to repeat what Mr Goodacre has just said?' asked Lamont, with more than a hint of insolence.

'Just answer my question please, sir,' said Rathbone.

'All right, you may conclude that I have nothing I wish to add.'

'So you had no idea that in addition to the ancient document Doctor Whistler wanted you to authenticate he was carrying some valuable artefacts also recovered from the dig on Rhodes?'

Rathbone spoke slowly and deliberately, never taking his eyes from Lamont's face. Sukey watched in fascination as the expression of lofty disdain on the classical features gave way to a blend of consternation and disbelief. She saw Goodacre's head turn sharply and saw his mouth open as if he was about to request a word in private with his client, but if that had been his intention he had no chance to say so. Lamont banged a fist on the table and almost shouted, 'Where did you get that idea? Who have you been talking to?'

'Please answer the question, sir,' Rathbone said again.

This time Goodacre intervened before Lamont answered. His request for a brief suspension of the interview was granted and the pair were escorted from the room.

The minute they were gone Rathbone rubbed his hands together in glee. 'That knocked the toffee-nosed bugger off his high horse, didn't it?' he gloated.

'Are you going to tell him it was his sister who told on him, Sarge?' Sukey asked uncomfortably.

'Only if I have to – but it's more than likely he'll guess. Serve him right for boasting about what a clever boy he is.'

'Do you suppose he mentioned these artefacts to Thorne?'

'Shouldn't think so, or Thorne would have said.' A barely detectable hesitation before Rathbone answered made Sukey suspect that it was a point that had not occurred to him, but if that were the case he was not going to admit it. 'I take it you didn't find anything in the file to make you think information was being withheld?' he added.

'Absolutely nothing. Not that there was any reason to think there might be, although I hadn't had that meeting with Hester at the time.'

'It wouldn't do any harm to have another look through it. Ah, here they come.'

It was a somewhat chastened Lamont who took his seat and listened passively as Goodacre said, 'My client has agreed to answer your questions in full, while reaffirming his total lack of responsibility for Doctor Whistler's murder.'

'Thank you.' Rathbone leaned forward and propped his chin on one hand. 'So Doctor Whistler did tell you about these additional valuable items I referred to earlier?'

'He did mention them, yes,' Lamont said tonelessly.

'Did he say what they were?'

'There was a gold crucifix, some ornaments and a small jewelled casket that he thought might be a reliquary. It seems there's a local legend that after the saint's death some fragments of his bones were taken back to Rhodes.'

'I don't know a great deal about antiquities,' said Rathbone, 'but as the site of this dig is on Greek territory, wouldn't the correct procedure have been, in the case of such apparently valuable items, to hand them over to the Greek authorities?'

'I suppose it might. The document was the only item that

directly concerned me and Whistler assured me he had permission to bring it to England for examination.'

'So why do you suppose he brought the other items?'

Lamont shook his head. 'I've no idea – unless it was to have them valued.'

'Right.' Rathbone sat back in his chair and waited for a few moments before saying, 'Why didn't you tell us all this at the outset?' in a tone that reminded Sukey of a kindly schoolmaster encouraging a pupil to own up to some minor misdemeanour.

Lamont looked uncomfortable, almost embarrassed. He glanced at the solicitor, who nodded. 'The fact is, I have had some financial problems lately. I was afraid that if you knew Whistler was carrying a lot of valuable stuff you'd start prying into my affairs and find out—' He broke off and for the first time showed signs of emotional stress. 'Do I have to tell you everything?' he said. 'You have my word that it's got nothing to do with the case and there's nothing shady or underhanded about it. It's just . . . very personal.'

'Unfortunately, when a serious crime has been committed it's not always possible to respect personal feelings.' In a sudden change of manner, Rathbone sat upright and spoke in a hard, measured tone, emphasizing each point by jabbing with a forefinger on the table. 'Professor Lamont, you have informed us that you arrived late for your appointment with Doctor Whistler whereas we have witnesses who saw you leaving the hotel by a side entrance a good fifteen minutes earlier; you attributed your later arrival first to heavy traffic and then to a delayed departure from the college; you declined to take part in an identity parade; you disclaimed knowledge of the items of value that Whistler was carrying whereas we now know that was a lie, and you admit that you are in need of money. You knew those items would be worth a small fortune to a collector and I suggest you saw them as a way out of your financial difficulties. Perhaps you hoped to persuade Whistler to let you take charge of them for valuation purposes and later fake a robbery and sell them to an unscrupulous dealer. So, far from arriving late for your appointment you arrived early, but you didn't go to the desk because you already knew Whistler's room number from your latest conversation with him. No doubt he was ready to hand over the document that started this whole thing going, but not the other items. Maybe he'd already made arrangements to entrust them to someone else – unfortunately he is not in a position to tell us. But you were determined to have them; you were desperate; you happened to have a knife in your pocket and when he refused to hand them over you lashed out with it and fatally stabbed him before grabbing them and making off. You didn't dare leave by the front entrance so you slipped out through the staff door and returned shortly afterwards, announced your arrival to the desk clerk, went up to Whistler's room and came dashing down a few minutes later with that cock and bull story about him being taken ill.'

Throughout this recital Lamont had been sitting with a dazed expression on his face, slowly shaking his head from side to side. When Rathbone mentioned the knife his mouth fell open and he cast a despairing glance at Goodacre, who appeared for the moment equally nonplussed. It was, however, the latter who recovered first.

'This is quite preposterous, Sergeant!' he exclaimed. 'Why on earth would my client "happen" to have a knife in his pocket?'

'It was the knife he'd taken from his sister,' said Rathbone. He turned back to Lamont. 'That's right, isn't it, sir?'

Before Lamont had a chance to speak, Goodacre put a hand on his arm.

'My client has nothing further to say at this stage,' he said.

Ten

'We'll let him stew for a while,' said Rathbone as he and Sukey returned to the CID office, leaving a glum Stephen Lamont closeted with his solicitor. 'We haven't got enough to charge him yet, of course, but he's obviously badly rattled and I don't reckon he'll enjoy his lunch.'

'It seems to me,' said Sukey, 'that one of the weaknesses in our case is that no one's come forward to say they saw him arrive at the hotel the first time.'

Rathbone, who was obviously in an optimistic mood, brushed the objection aside with a gesture. 'My guess is that someone will before long. It's early days yet – you have to learn to be patient in this job,' he added with the now familiar touch of condescension that Sukey was beginning to find irksome. 'What's more significant is that he hasn't been able to produce anyone to confirm his story about leaving late after his Greek class on the morning of the murder. The woman in charge of the office found the register in his pigeonhole but she had no idea what time he put it there.'

'It's a bit like that in colleges,' Sukey commented. 'People are coming and going all the time and no one takes much notice of them. By the way, will the bloodstains on the clothing be any help, do you think?'

'We'll have to wait for the report from forensics.'

'What I mean is, will they yield DNA after washing?'

For the second time that morning, Rathbone took a fraction of a second before replying, 'It probably depends on what temperature the sister washed them at – but he's not to know that, is he?'

'No, I suppose not. When do you suppose we'll get the mugshots?'

'They shouldn't take too long. Ah, what have we here?'

He stopped speaking as a uniformed officer entered and handed him an envelope.

'The montage you asked for, Sarge.'

Rathbone opened the envelope and scanned the contents. 'Great, you managed to get him from several angles. I see they've lined up a load of prize villains to slot him in with,' he added, grinning.

The officer grinned back. 'Cream of the county force, Sarge.'

Rathbone handed the photos and the envelope to Sukey. 'There's your next job. Take these out to the hotel, show them to DS Douglas, and then go with him to see if Boris and the other guy who thought he'd spotted Lamont can pick him out.' He glanced at his watch. 'I'm giving our friend until two; that means you've got comfortable time to get there and back before we see him again. If you get a positive ID out of them we'll be well on the way to getting the case sewn up. Meanwhile, I'm going to have another word with Professor Thorne to see if he's remembered anything else that might be important.'

'Right, Sarge,' said Sukey.

You mean you're going to quiz him on the point you didn't think to raise until I mentioned it, she thought to herself with a little inward glow of satisfaction.

'By the way,' she added, 'is someone taking care of Hester? I notice Lamont hasn't expressed any concern about her, which seems a bit odd.'

'We left a Family Liaison Officer with her when we went to pick him up and he seemed reasonably satisfied with the arrangement. She'll stay until he gets home – unless of course we're in a position to detain him today. In that case we'll have to consult her doctor about arrangements for her welfare, but so far the FLO reports that she seems almost unnaturally calm, even resigned to the fact that her brother's going to be charged with murder. We've stressed the importance of making sure there aren't any knives lying around and explained that if they want anything to eat the helpful Mrs Potter has promised to see to it. OK? On your way, then.'

After checking with Erika Henderson that Boris and Manuel were both on duty, Sukey set out for the Mariners Hotel. It was a bright early autumn day and as she left the city behind her she was struck afresh by the abundance of open country that lay on its doorstep and the patches of richly coloured foliage along the way. After living for so many years with views of the Cotswolds from her back garden, she had had reservations about living in an urban environment; to find so much natural beauty within easy reach had gone some way to make up for what she had left behind.

The car park was less full than on her earlier visit with Rathbone and she was able to park fairly close to the staff entrance. The police guard had been removed, but like all the officers working on the case she had been issued with the key code and was able to go straight in. She went first to the incident room, where DS Douglas and his civilian assistant were seated at their respective computers.

'Back already?' he said. 'How did the interview with Lamont go?'

'It's been suspended until this afternoon. DS Rathbone is convinced we're wearing him down, but he hasn't cracked yet. He was pretty shaken when he realized how much we'd uncovered, though.'

'Greg has a good track record for getting his man,' Douglas remarked. 'So what brings you here this time?'

'We've just received the mock-ups from the techies,' she explained, holding up the envelope. 'I've checked with Ashford's PA and the two potential witnesses are available.'

'Good, we'll see them together. You can hold the fort for a few minutes can't you, Anna?' he added over his shoulder and the woman looked up from her screen and nodded.

'Has any more info come in during the morning?' Sukey asked as they walked along the corridor leading to Erika Henderson's office.

'Two separate sightings of cars, one leaving in a hurry and the other arriving in a hurry, but not enough detail to establish whether it was the same one. The timings are about right, though.'

'You're thinking in terms of Lamont carrying out the attack, making off, driving a short distance and then turning round to come back as if for the first time?'

'Something of the sort,' he said.

'That would have given him an opportunity to get rid of the knife, wouldn't it?'

He nodded. 'Exactly, and that may have been part of the

plan. The search has been widened for a mile in either direction.'

'Plan?' Sukey said in surprise. 'My impression, from what Hester told me, is that the reason he had a knife with him was that he had taken it away from her and that it was only by chance that he had it in his pocket.'

'You're saying you don't think it was premeditated then?' said Douglas.

'Frankly, no,' she said candidly.

'There's no proof that the knife he took from his sister was the same one that killed Whistler,' he pointed out.

'No, I suppose not,' she admitted. 'I wonder what he did with the loot, by the way?'

'The boys have been turning the place over all morning, but they haven't found anything so far. He had plenty of time to stash it somewhere safe – or he may have had a buyer waiting. We've taken the seal off room 106, by the way, which made the manager a fraction happier. He makes no secret of the fact he'll be glad to see the back of us,' he added with a grin.

'He's probably seeing the Hotel of the Year Award slipping away from him,' she commented, grinning back.

'Could be.'

'Boris is not a happy bunny,' Erika Henderson confided while they waited for him to respond to her summons. 'The other staff have noticed it as well, but he insists when asked that there's nothing wrong.'

She waited with the two detectives until the receptionist appeared and then discreetly withdrew. He was obviously nervous; there were small beads of sweat on his forehead and his hands were trembling. Sukey took the photographs from the envelope and spread them out on a table by the window.

'Come over here please, Boris, and look at these pictures,' she said, beckoning him as he appeared reluctant to come forward. 'We want you to look very carefully at them and tell us if there is a person in any of them that you recognize. There's no hurry, just take your time.'

So far from taking his time, Boris seemed anxious to be finished with the task as quickly as possible. There were three separate photographs; in each of them a shot of Stephen Lamont had been placed in a different position and among

different people, but in all three Boris identified him with little
or no hesitation as the man he had seen leaving the hotel by
the staff entrance and a short time later asking at the desk for
Doctor Whistler.

'Well, that seems pretty conclusive,' Douglas remarked as
Boris withdrew and they waited for their next witness to
appear.

'He certainly seemed in no doubt that it was Lamont he
had seen,' Sukey agreed. 'It would be interesting to know
what's on his mind to make him so jumpy, though.'

'A lot of immigrant workers are uneasy with the police,
even when they've nothing to fear from us,' Douglas replied.

'That's what DS Rathbone said,' she acknowledged, 'but
we aren't here all the time, are we?'

'He knew we'd be turning up sooner or later and he's probably been on edge wondering if he'll be able to pick Lamont
out,' said Douglas. There was a tap on the door and the porter
entered. 'Ah, here's Manuel.'

'Good morning, officers,' said the porter, beaming. It was
clear that, so far from being reluctant, he was positively eager
to co-operate. 'Ms Henderson says you want my help.'

'Yes, please, Manuel,' said Sukey. 'Do you remember telling
me about a gentleman you saw come up the stairs to the
first floor while you were talking to Nina, one of the
chambermaids?'

He nodded eagerly. 'Yes, yes, of course I remember. It was
Thursday of last week, was it not?' His eyes travelled to the
pictures. 'You want me to point him out to you?'

'We want you to study these very carefully and tell us if
any of the men in them is the one you saw,' said Douglas.

'Yes, yes, I understand.' He studied each photograph in turn
with an air of great confidence that, to the increasing disappointment of the watching detectives, gradually gave way
to doubt and perplexity. A carefully manicured forefinger
hovered over first one face and then another; the detectives
held their breath as it appeared on the point of descending on
Lamont's image in one of the shots before moving on.

Eventually, he gave a despondent shake of the head. 'I
am sorry, I cannot be sure,' he sighed. 'It might have been
him – ' he indicated a grey-haired man who, Douglas later
informed Sukey, was a sergeant based at a station some

miles outside the city – 'or him.' This time the finger rested
briefly on Lamont before moving to the other two pictures,
where the performance was repeated without Lamont
featuring in either case. 'No, I cannot be sure,' he admitted.
His demeanour left them in no doubt that he was as disappointed as they were.

'He probably had dreams of being feted as the hero who
played a vital role in nailing a desperate criminal,' Douglas
remarked dryly as they returned to the incident room. 'Ah,
well, you can't win 'em all and at least Boris had no difficulty at all picking out Lamont. Of course, he'd had more
than one chance to get a look at him; Manuel saw him only
once and he quite likely had one eye on Nina at the time.'

On her way back to the car with the latest piece of the
jigsaw, Sukey found her thoughts turning once again to Boris.
She could not help wondering whether there was more to
account for the unease that his colleagues had reportedly
noticed during the past few days, not only towards the police
but in his general demeanour. On an impulse she returned to
the hotel; Boris was dealing with a guest, but he caught sight
of her over the man's shoulder and his eyes widened with
alarm. When he was free she took from a stand on the counter
a leaflet about local attractions, unfolded it, approached him
with a smile and said, 'Can you tell me about some of these
places?'

It was clear that he was not deceived by her subterfuge, for
he responded by saying in a frantic whisper, glancing round
fearfully as he spoke, 'I tell you all I know. Please, make no
trouble for me.'

'I have a feeling you're in trouble already,' she said, lowering
her own voice to avoid being overheard, 'and, if so, I may be
able to help you.' She put her bag on the counter and used it
as a shield while sliding one of her cards towards him. 'You'll
find my mobile number on this and you can call me any time
if there's anything you want to tell me.' He stared at the card
as if it were poisonous, but made no move to take it. 'Believe
me, Boris, you have nothing to fear from us if you have done
nothing wrong,' she assured him. 'Go on, take it. I'm not
going to leave until you do,' she added as he still made no
move. At last, he picked it up and put it in his pocket. 'Well
done,' she whispered. She refolded the leaflet, put it in her

bag and said in her normal voice, 'Thank you so much, that's really helpful.'

'I don't need to tell you that you're in a pretty sticky situation.' Goodacre looked across the table at his client, who sat with his head bowed and his breath coming in ragged gasps. Lamont made an effort to steady himself. He raised his head and gazed back at his solicitor. 'I can see that,' he said despairingly, 'and I'm sure you don't need me to tell you it wasn't I who killed that man.'

'I'd like to believe that, of course, but—'

'John! What are you saying? You don't seriously think I'm capable of murder?' He felt as if all hope of establishing his innocence was being torn from him. 'For God's sake, man, you've known me for years. Surely you—'

'In a professional capacity, yes,' Goodacre agreed, 'and I've never had any reason to doubt your integrity until now. But we have to be realistic; the evidence against you isn't conclusive, but it is beginning to stack up and—'

'But it's all circumstantial,' Lamont pleaded.

'So far, yes, but you have withheld vital information and you haven't been able to find anyone to support your account of your movements before you left the college to meet Doctor Whistler. Supposing these witnesses at the hotel do identify you, how will you explain that?'

'What can I say except that they're mistaken? Anyway, I don't see how they can because I declined to take part in an identity parade or to allow my picture to be taken.'

'As you had every right to do,' Goodacre said, 'and in the light of your refusal they in turn had every right to obtain your picture by other means.'

'What other means?'

'Covertly, of course. Weren't you told that?'

Lamont put a hand to his forehead and closed his eyes, trying to recall the moment when he refused for the second time to co-operate in the matter of identity.

'Something was said about "other legal means",' he said after moment's thought. 'I assumed they'd use a photo from the university prospectus or something like that. What do you mean by "covertly"?'

'Someone tracks you with a hidden camera.'

'Good heavens, I had no idea!' He felt the net closing ever more tightly, but to his surprise Goodacre allowed himself a fleeting smile of satisfaction.

'That could be useful,' he said, making a note. 'Right, let's run over one or two other points that are likely to prove tricky. For example, I do happen to know that you've been a little, shall we say, pushed for money these past few months.'

'All right, so I had to raise a loan to meet Hester's expenses,' Lamont admitted. 'The drugs she's on at the moment are costing me more than I bargained for.' He put his hands up to his temples and groaned. 'It's so ironic, isn't it? She's been much better these past few months and now this . . . even she believes I killed Whistler . . . and you've as good as said you've got serious doubts. I don't think I can bear much more.'

'I'd like to believe you Stephen, believe me I would,' Goodacre said quietly, 'but we have to face facts. If these witnesses do identify you, and forensics find Whistler's blood on your clothes, it's more than likely you'll be charged. There's no guarantee the CPS will allow the case to come to court, but we have to prepare for the worst. All I can promise at this stage is to consider who best to brief in your defence.'

Eleven

'It's a pity Manuel didn't come up with the goods, but at least Boris didn't let us down,' Rathbone commented. He put the photographs, together with Sukey's report, into his case file before saying, 'There's been a very interesting development. DCI Leach has been in touch with the man in charge of the dig Whistler was working on, a Doctor Makris of the Greek Ministry of Culture. He confirms that in addition to the document, Whistler was carrying certain items that would not normally have been allowed out of the country. He was granted a special dispensation in this case because he wanted them examined by a senior fellow of the University of Athens, who is in London for medical treatment and unable to travel.'

'Did Doctor Makris have any reason to believe Whistler might be targeted by criminals?' Sukey asked.

'On the contrary, according to Leach he's absolutely astounded that such a thing could happen. He's been given the usual assurances that we're doing everything in our power to find Whistler's killer and recover the stolen property, but apparently he sounded pretty miffed. He didn't go so far as to accuse the police of negligence, but apparently he had some rude things to say about security at the hotel.'

'That was a bit unfair,' said Sukey. 'What does he expect – guards and sniffer dogs all over the place?'

'I suspect he realizes he's dropped a clanger by allowing valuable antiquities out of the country so he's trying to shift the blame for their disappearance on to someone else.'

'Doesn't this rather suggest that Lamont might be telling the truth when he said he thought Whistler sounded jumpy?' Sukey said tentatively. 'He might have felt uncomfortable at being entrusted with such precious items.'

Rathbone shrugged. 'It's possible, I suppose, but it doesn't count for much in the overall picture.'

'What about Whistler's next of kin? Is there any news of them?'

'That's another point Makris was able to help with. According to him, Whistler was a bachelor who lived alone and never mentioned his family. The Greek police found an Australian address in his personal effects of someone called Whistler, presumably a relative, but it turned out the person died some years ago. DCI Leach will be fending off demands for more details at tomorrow's briefing,' he added, 'but to be on the safe side I've warned Professor Thorne that if the media get wind of Whistler's reasons for being in Bristol he and members of his department are likely to be targeted by the paparazzi.'

'Which would mean Lamont might be identified as the person he was at the hotel to meet?'

Rathbone nodded morosely. 'I've asked Thorne to avoid naming names and to ask his staff to do the same, but there's no guarantee someone won't slip up. It certainly wouldn't do our case any good.'

Especially as it's not all that strong anyway, was Sukey's instinctive reaction, but she kept the thought to herself. Instead she asked, making the question sound as casual as she could, 'Did Professor Thorne know about the other things Whistler was supposed to be carrying?'

'He had absolutely no idea, and he sounded pretty shocked when I told him. He admitted he'd been puzzled to think that anyone would commit murder for a document of interest only to scholars, but could see the existence of the other items puts an entirely different slant on the case. I explained that we'd deliberately kept that information under wraps and asked him not to mention them to anyone until it was officially released; for his part he assured me that had he known about them he would have spoken up right away.' Rathbone glanced at the clock. 'Well, we've given our man time to consider his position,' he said. 'Let's hear what he's got to say in response to Boris's testimony. Yes, Fleming, what have you got there?' he added as a uniformed constable entered carrying a green metal box.

'We found this stashed behind some books in a cupboard in the suspect's study, Sarge,' said the officer. 'We haven't been able to open it; we've tried all the keys in the desk but none of them will fit. There's something more in it than papers, by the sound of it.' By way of demonstration he shook the box, causing a metallic rattle.

'Careful!' said Rathbone. 'If this contains what I'm hoping, we have some very precious items in here.' He stood up and took the box from Fleming's hands. 'Come on Sukey, let's see what our friend has to say about this.'

Lamont could almost feel the blood draining from his face as he saw what Rathbone was carrying. The detective placed it on the table, checked the time, switched on the tape, ran through the brief formalities and said, 'Right, Professor Lamont, perhaps we can clear up a few points. I see you recognize this box?'

Lamont attempted to moisten his lips with a tongue that seemed to have turned to cardboard in his mouth. 'I have a box at home that looks very like that one,' he muttered.

'This was found in a cupboard in your study and we have reason to believe it contains items relevant to the present enquiry. It's locked, as I'm sure you're aware, but no doubt you have the key with you so perhaps you'll be kind enough to unlock it.' Rathbone slid the box across the table. In silence, after receiving a nod from his stony-faced solicitor, Lamont took a bunch of keys from his pocket, selected one, unlocked the box and lifted the lid.

'Thank you,' said Rathbone. He drew the box towards him and peered inside 'Well, what do we have here?' His tone was almost jocular as he peered inside. 'Quite a little armoury!' Without touching any of the items, he began a recital of the contents. 'One Swiss army knife, assorted cook's knives, very sharp by the looks of them, one very pretty paper knife with a jewelled handle that looks as if it could do some damage. Tell me, Professor Lamont, which one of these did you take to the meeting with Doctor Whistler?'

He was vaguely aware of Goodacre's warning hand on his arm, but he ignored it. 'The paper knife,' he said in a voice that he barely recognized as his own. 'I think you already know the truth, Sergeant. My sister has a history of self-harming. These are knives I've taken away from her. I keep them locked up for obvious reasons.'

'So when did you catch her using this one?'

'It was the morning I had the appointment with Whistler. I found her with it in her hand . . . one of my students brought it back from a recent trip to Syria and gave it to me, but I never showed it to her because . . . well, you can guess the reason. I kept it in the desk in my study . . . I thought it would be safe as she never has reason to go in there, but for some reason she must have. She cut herself with it that morning – not seriously, it never is. I took it away from her; I should have locked it up with the others immediately, but I was in a hurry so I put it into my pocket and—'

'And used it later to threaten Whistler and then stab him when he refused to hand over the valuables from the dig?' said Rathbone.

'No!' Lamont shouted, thumping the table. 'I didn't kill him – I could never kill anybody! You must believe me!' he implored, but he saw no mercy in the implacable gaze of the detective or that of his woman colleague, who sat there watching and listening, as keen-eyed as a blackbird waiting to pounce on a worm.

'All right, Professor. Let's go over it once more, shall we? Do you still maintain that the first and only time you arrived at the Mariners Hotel last Thursday was at approximately twelve fifteen?'

Temporarily thrown, first by the discovery of the knife and then by the sudden change of tactic, Lamont took a few moments to recover before replying, with a desperate show of defiance, 'Of course I do, because it's the truth.'

'And what if I were to tell you that the hotel employee who directed you to Doctor Whistler's room has now positively identified you as the man he saw leaving by the back door some fifteen minutes previously?'

In an attempt to elicit an admission that the evidence had been obtained covertly, Lamont – briefed by Goodacre – said, 'I fail to see how he could do that without my co-operation.'

'So you persist in your denial?'

'Of course I do. He's completely mistaken. The first man he saw must have been someone who looks like me, that's all I can suggest.'

'Let's leave that for the moment,' said Rathbone, 'and consider the explanation you gave for your supposed late arrival. Or rather, explanations, because you gave two.' Lamont experienced a further sinking sensation as Rathbone remorselessly drove his points home. 'According to reports from our traffic division, there were no unusual delays either in the city centre or on the A38 at the crucial time, which would seem to put paid to the first excuse you offered. As to your second version, we have not been able to find any witnesses to support it. Unless you've managed to find one, I'm afraid we can draw only one conclusion, namely that your story is exactly that – a story. Or, to be more accurate, a string of deliberate lies.'

Lamont glanced at Goodacre, who gave an almost imperceptible shake of the head. 'No comment,' he said sullenly.

'There remains the possibility of bloodstains on your jacket, Professor.' Now the woman took up the questioning. 'In the event that we find any, how would you account for them?'

'But I thought—' he began, but this time Goodacre came to his rescue.

'My client has already admitted that he took a knife from his sister and put it in his pocket,' he said. 'It is of course likely that her blood is on the knife and no doubt you will be subjecting that to tests as well. It is unfortunate that the jacket was washed before being submitted for examination, but my client could hardly have anticipated coming under these totally unjustified suspicions.'

'The fact that the garment in question was washed is not crucial,' said Rathbone and the flicker of hope that Lamont felt at his solicitor's words died away as the detective continued silkily, 'you'd be amazed, Professor, at the sophisticated techniques available to forensic scientists nowadays.' He paused for a moment as if allowing time for the information to sink in before saying, 'Think for a moment. Supposing there is blood from another source than the wound your sister inflicted on herself?' The detective leaned forward wearing the accusatory expression Lamont had come to dread. 'Doctor Whistler's blood, for example? How will you explain that?'

Once again, Goodacre intervened. 'That is a purely hypothetical question, Sergeant, and I advise my client not to answer it,' he said firmly.

'Very well. We'll leave it at that for now. Interview terminated at three fifteen p.m.' Rathbone reached forward and switched off the tape recorder.

'You mean I'm free to go?' said Lamont in bewilderment.

'For the time being, yes.' Rathbone closed the folder that had lain open on his desk throughout the interview and stood up. 'Kindly remain at your present address until we contact you again.' He left the room, followed by the woman, leaving Lamont feeling utterly bemused. He remained seated for several seconds until his solicitor took him by the arm and half-pulled him to his feet. Escorted by a uniformed officer, the two of them went downstairs and out of the building in silence; it was not until they were driving back through the city centre that Goodacre said quietly, 'Stephen, are they likely to find traces of Whistler's blood on any of your clothing.'

'Yes, John,' he said miserably, 'I'm afraid they are.'

Back in the office, Rathbone rubbed his hands together and said, 'Well, we've really got him rattled now. Even his brief doesn't believe him.'

Sukey looked at him in surprise. 'You reckon?'

'Couldn't you tell from the body language? That professional mask conceals a very worried man,' he said confidently. 'It wasn't very bright of Lamont to keep the knife, but it's a very distinctive item and I suppose he figured that if he chucked it away it'd be found sooner or later and traced back to him. I expect you're wondering why I let him go,' he added as if anticipating a question she had not thought of asking. 'Think about it. He's hardly likely to do a runner with his sister in such a precarious mental state, and the longer he sits at home chewing his nails the more likely he is to crack.'

'So what's our next move, Sarge?'

'We wait till we've got all the reports from forensics. I know what Hanley said about bleeding,' he went on, again anticipating her question, 'but there must have been traces of Whistler's blood on the knife after the killing and some of it's sure to have found its way on to Lamont's clothes. The boffins don't need much – even a tiny drop can make a usable sample.' He gave a prodigious yawn and said, 'Anyway, now we have the weapon we're on much stronger ground.'

To her surprise, Fergus rang that evening. 'Hi, Mum, how's it going?' he asked. Then, before she had time to do more than return his greeting, he added, 'No, I didn't leave anything behind this time – I just thought you'd be interested to know we had another lecture in criminal psychology this afternoon, this time from a woman who talked about professional hit men.'

'I'm sure that was fascinating,' said Sukey. 'Tell me about it while I drink my evening snifter.'

'Mum, you shouldn't drink on your own,' he said, a sudden note of anxiety in his young voice. 'It's well known that—'

'I know, lonely women who sit at home and tipple are on the slippery slope into alcoholism,' she interrupted flippantly. 'For goodness' sake, Gus, you know I always relax with a glass of wine when I get home – it gives me an appetite for my dinner.'

'I know, but you're on your own much more these days and—'

Touched by his genuine concern, and guessing what lay behind it, she said gently, 'I know what you're thinking and yes, there are times when I miss having Jim around, but I promise you don't have to worry. Listen, are you going to tell me how to spot a professional hit man? Not that I can see our learned professor falling into that category.'

'No, well, you never know when this might come in handy. We were told that they're not always independent of the people who use them; some of them have had military training and they've learned to regard the victim as an object rather than a person with a life and a family and so on. It's important to get into their minds, try and figure out how they see themselves, which more often than not is simply as a criminal . . . and proud of it.'

'Did the lecturer give you any tips for getting into the criminal mind?'

'Er, not exactly; I guess that's for a later lecture. One thing we were told by another tutor was that the police use the acronym MOPS, which stands for a series of keywords—'

'Motive, Opportunity, Preparatory Action and Subsequent Action,' Sukey chipped in. 'Yes, I learned that during my probationary period.'

'Ah, I thought you might have. This lecturer said motive isn't always a useful line of investigation. Were you taught that?'

'I don't remember hearing that one. What reason did he or she give?'

'Something like there could be any number of possible motives and it wasn't important at the start of an enquiry.'

'It's a point of view, I suppose. There doesn't seem to be much doubt about the motive in this case.'

'Has there been an arrest yet?'

'No, but there have been some important developments – and before you ask, I'm not going to tell you.'

'All right, be mysterious. By the way, I forgot to ask how you're enjoying working with DS Rathbone on this case?'

'No serious problems, although now and again I sense that he misses something that could be important and I have to be very tactful in drawing it to his attention. I think he still looks on me as a rookie and doesn't consider my SOCO experience counts for very much.'

'What about your early years as a beat copper – before you married Dad, I mean?'

'That was too long ago to be worth much – at least, not in his eyes. He pointed out to me during my first week that we don't rely on whistles and truncheons any more.'

'Cheek! I'll bet you're hoping to spot a vital clue that he's missed and so cover yourself with glory?'

'It doesn't look very likely, but I live in hope,' she said with a chuckle. She hesitated for a moment before saying casually, 'Seen Jim around lately?'

'As it happens, I bumped into him an hour or so ago. He said something about giving you a call to see if you were free at the weekend. I take it he hasn't been in touch?'

'Not yet. Did he say anything else?'

'Only that his promotion to DCI has come through at last.'

'Only? But that's great news. I'm so pleased for him.'

'I thought you would be. Shall I mention I've told you if I see him again?'

'Why not? Say I look forward to hearing from him.'

'OK. Talk again soon,' he said and hung up.

Sukey finished her wine, switched on the radio and set about preparing her evening meal. It crossed her mind to call Jim and congratulate him on his promotion, but she decided to wait until he called her. As she peeled vegetables to accompany her super-market chicken joint and took a dessert from the freezer, she found herself mulling over two of the points Fergus had made about hit men: their need for preparatory action and a contingency plan for subsequent action. A sudden thought made her stop in the middle of slicing a carrot while she allowed it to take shape in her mind. 'Just supposing,' she heard herself say aloud, and then, 'no, don't be daft, forget it.' But despite the apparently damaging nature of the day's discovery, the possibility that the whole thrust of the current investigation was heading in the wrong direction refused to go away. She spent the rest of the evening trying to decide whether, at the risk of being told to leave theorizing to the more experienced, to share her thoughts with DS Rathbone.

Twelve

'So, who d'you reckon did it, then? Boris the Albanian Avenger? Professor Thorne, the Hellenic Hijacker?'

Even before he spoke, Sukey knew from the patronizing smile that spread over his features that DS Rathbone was going to react to her theory in the way she had anticipated. Nevertheless, she stood her ground and replied calmly, 'I haven't anyone particular in mind, Sarge. All I can say is I have a gut feeling about Lamont – I know every piece of evidence we've got so far points to him, but somehow I just don't see him as a killer.'

'I do realize your experience of murderers is limited,' he said indulgently, 'but believe me, they come in all shapes and sizes. Take that case a few years ago of a respected family doctor, with an unblemished reputation, topping God knows how many of his trusting patients before someone started asking questions.'

'Yes, I remember the case, but the man was a psychopath who killed because it made him feel godlike,' Sukey countered. 'Surely you aren't suggesting Stephen Lamont—'

'I'm not suggesting he's a potential serial killer, if that's what you mean,' Rathbone interrupted, 'but it's obvious he's been under a lot of stress over a long period and in those circumstances the most unlikely people act out of character. I'm pretty sure traces of Whistler's blood will be found on that knife, which should be conclusive even if forensics can't recover DNA from Lamont's clothing.'

'I think it's more than likely,' Sukey agreed, 'but there could still be an innocent explanation.'

'Such as what?' She could tell by his tone that he was beginning to lose patience with her.

'Supposing his story is true and the first time he saw Whistler was when he went up to Room 106 with the manager. He told us he knelt down beside him and we know there was a lot of blood about; supposing he got some on his hands and clothing without realizing it and then put his hand in his pocket and transferred some on to the knife?'

'Supposing, supposing!' he jeered. 'Remember, Whistler was still alive when he was found, and I can assure you a professional hit man would have done a thorough job so the victim would never have an opportunity to identify him. And did you notice any blood on Lamont's hands when we interviewed him shortly after the killing?'

'No,' she admitted, 'but if it was only a smear we could easily have missed it, or he could have wiped it off with a handkerchief. And I know neither you nor DS Douglas think it's significant, but I still think it would be interesting to know why—'

'Sorry, your next bit of theorizing will have to wait,' he interrupted with a glance at the clock on the canteen wall. 'DCI Leach wants to see me in five minutes and he doesn't like being kept waiting.' He gulped down the remainder of his tea and was gone, leaving her fuming.

'OK if I sit here?' DC Vicky Armstrong appeared from behind her with a mug of tea in one hand and a plate containing two buttered scones in the other.

'Please do. You'll be better company than DS Rathbone,' Sukey said with feeling.

'I thought you were looking a bit miffed,' Vicky said, grinning. 'Has he been telling you how much you have yet to learn about the noble art of detection?'

'That's what it amounted to,' Sukey said ruefully. 'I should have known better, I suppose, but I just have a hunch that our chief suspect – no, our only suspect – is either the victim of an unfortunate chain of coincidences or there's something very sinister going on in the background.'

'Something nasty in the woodshed, eh?' Vicky took a bite from one of her scones and followed it with a mouthful of tea. 'Do you often suffer from hunches?'

'Yes, now and again – and sometimes they turn out to be right.'

'I take it we're talking about the Whistler killing?'

'That's the one.'

'Want to tell me about it?'

'As long as you keep it to yourself. I don't want Rathbone to know I've been talking behind his back.'

'My lips are sealed,' Vicky said solemnly. She swallowed the last morsel of her first scone and started on the second. 'Get on with it then.'

When Sukey had finished she sat deep in thought while gathering the remaining crumbs on her plate with a moistened finger. At last she said, 'You reckon someone at the dig knew there were goodies to be picked up and passed the information to someone over here, and that person wanted them badly enough to commit murder to get hold of them?'

'Why not? There could easily be more than one villain involved, maybe even a gang trading in stolen antiquities. One possibility that occurred to me is that the killer tried to con Whistler into believing he was Lamont so that he'd hand over the stuff without quibbling. He only used the knife when Whistler didn't fall for it.'

Vicky pursed her lips and frowned. 'I know you won't want to hear this,' she said, 'but it seems to me that Lamont has a very strong motive. He's admitted being strapped for cash; couldn't he have been the one who tried to con Whistler into handing over the valuable bits as well as the scroll or whatever the epistle was written on and stabbed him when he refused?'

'In that case, you'd expect him to have shown some signs of stress when making his statement after the crime had been discovered,' Sukey pointed out. 'In fact, he was just the opposite – very composed and sure of himself and quite sniffy about the manager who almost keeled over at the sight of blood. It was only later, when he realized how the evidence was stacking up against him and how much we'd found out about his personal circumstances, that he started to lose his cool.'

'Do you think Boris is part of the plot? From what you say, he had no hesitation in picking Lamont out – how do you reckon your master crook managed to organize that?'

'I have to admit that's one thing I haven't been able to figure out, but I'm convinced there's an explanation for it.'

'Well, even if you are on to something, there doesn't seem to be much you can do about it,' said Vicky. 'If you can't convince Greg Rathbone you can hardly go off and start your own line of enquiry.'

'No, I suppose not,' Sukey sighed. 'Thanks for listening anyway.'

'No problem. You doing anything special tonight?'

'Not that I know of. How about you?'

'It's Chris's birthday so I'm taking him out to dinner.'

'That's nice. Where are you going?'

'Oddly enough, to the Mariners Hotel. The head chef is Chris's best mate and he's planned a special treat for him.'

'The Mariners?' Sukey had a sudden flash of inspiration. 'Could you do something for me while you're there?'

'What's that?'

'Find out what time Boris Gasspar finishes his shift.'

Vicky looked at her in astonishment. 'What on earth for?'

'I'd like to know where he lives and what sort of people he mixes with.'

'I'm not even on the case,' Vicky objected. 'What reason do I give for asking that sort of question?'

'Not you, make some excuse to ask Chris to do it. His mate works there, he could find out, surely.'

Vicky looked dubious. 'I'm not sure I want to get involved,' she said.

'You don't have to. Please, Vicky, I've a feeling it's really important.'

'One of your famous hunches?'

'If you put it like that – yes. I'm sure he's got something on his mind and it's not just that he's uncomfortable talking to the police. The staff at the hotel have noticed it even when we're not around, and at least once he's been heard arguing with someone on his mobile. I'm convinced he's under some kind of pressure.'

'Mmm, I think I see what you're driving at,' said Vicky. 'We know criminals from abroad are running scams over here; in fact the Super has set up a special task force to deal with that very problem.'

'Well there you are then. Boris insists his papers are in order and the hotel confirms it, but they could be forged and he could still be an illegal. In that case it would be easy to coerce him into making a false statement.'

'I take it you've raised this with DS Rathbone?'

'Yes, and he simply brushed it aside, put the nerves down to a mistrust of the police after living in former communist states, and DS Douglas said much the same thing.'

'It seems to me they've got a point.'

'I'd still like to know more about Boris.'

'So that you can do some unofficial surveillance?'

'I suppose you could call it that – but only when I'm off duty. I gave him my mobile number and said he could call me if he had a problem, by the way.'

'*Did* you?' Vicky raised an eyebrow. 'I'm not sure that was wise.'

'I don't see what harm it can do. Anyway, will you do it?'

'I suppose so,' Vicky sighed, 'but please keep me out of it.'

According to Chris's friend the head chef at the Mariners Hotel, receptionists on duty during the day normally finished at six o'clock, but it was Friday before Sukey was able to get away from the station in time to take up a position in the hotel car park that enabled her to keep an eye on the staff entrance. When Boris emerged she had just enough time to recognize him before he put on a helmet, mounted a rather noisy moped and set off in the direction of the city centre followed by a trail of exhaust fumes. She kept him in sight without difficulty; when they reached Bishopston he turned into a side street, dismounted and wheeled the moped into the front garden of a house a few doors along. She noted the number as she drove past, pulled into a space a short distance further on and switched off her engine.

'Right,' she muttered aloud, 'at least I know where you live. What now?' She adjusted her passenger door mirror to give a view of him bending over the moped, presumably securing it. Rather than turn and drive back while he was still outside and might possibly glance up and see her, she waited for him to go indoors, but to her surprise he came out and began walking along the pavement towards her. He had taken off his helmet; for a moment she thought he must have noticed her following him and was about to approach her, but he crossed the road several cars behind and continued along the other side.

About thirty yards further on he climbed into the front passenger seat of a black Mercedes parked by the kerb. He appeared to be having some kind of altercation with a man wearing dark glasses who sat behind the wheel. At one point the man turned his head sharply in a way that suggested he had heard something of particular and disturbing significance and held out a hand with an imperious gesture. Boris appeared to shrink back in his seat and then, as the outstretched hand became more insistent, took something from his pocket and handed it over. Moments later he got out of the car, which moved off and headed back to the main road. Sukey made a note of the registration number and at the same time got a good look at the driver as he passed; she judged him to be in his fifties, of distinguished appearance, with regular features, an olive complexion and black hair flecked with grey at the temples. He gave no sign of having noticed her as he drove by.

Meanwhile, Boris had started walking slowly back towards his house; this time he crossed the road ahead of Sukey. As he drew near she ducked and pretended to be searching for something on the floor, hoping he had not spotted her. To her relief his footsteps did not hesitate as he passed; she waited a few more seconds before straightening up, just in time to see him open his front door and disappear into the house.

Thirteen

When Sukey reached home there was a message from Jim on her telephone answering machine, confirming that he would be with her around eleven the following morning. As Fergus had predicted, he had called earlier in the week and suggested – a little diffidently, she thought – that they might 'do something together' on Saturday to celebrate his promotion. She had been happy to agree; the change of career and the move to a new location had inevitably had an effect on their relationship, which had become increasingly intimate over the past couple of years. It was true there had been areas of conflict, particularly over her tendency to do what Vicky had recently described as 'a little sleuthing on the side', but for the most part they had found contentment and fulfilment in one another's company. Lately she had found herself harking back with more than a little regret to the good times while putting the differences to the back of her mind, and she could not deny, even to herself, that she had been counting the days until Saturday. Just the same, away from his influence she had found a sense of freedom that she would be very loath to forgo.

Before preparing her evening meal she wrote a report of her surveillance of Boris Gasspar. When it was finished she toyed with the idea of talking over with Jim her misgivings about the case against Stephen Lamont, but decided against it, partly because it might lead to an argument and she wanted nothing to spoil their time together. She put aside almost without a second thought the idea of showing him what she had written; he would simply advise her to show it to DS Rathbone, something she had already accepted it was her duty to do although she quailed at the prospect. She sensed that, although so far he had appeared fairly even-tempered, the sergeant was quite capable of giving a tongue-lashing to a presumptuous upstart of a newly qualified detective constable.

Despite her misgivings she slept well that night and when she awoke to bright sunshine she took it as an omen that the day was going to turn out well. When Jim arrived he made no attempt to kiss her – in fact, for the first half hour or so she was conscious of a slight restraint in his manner, as if he feared that any attempt at physical contact would meet with a rebuff. She made coffee and they drank it on her roof terrace, which gave a spectacular view across Bristol as well as a glimpse of the suspension bridge over the River Avon and had been a major factor in her decision to buy the flat. He asked questions about her neighbours and the local amenities, and admired her collection of terracotta containers planted with winter pansies and small shrubs. Little by little they began to relax and exchange news of recent events and activities, both at work and at leisure.

During a lull in the conversation he said, 'This chap Rathbone you're working with – how do you find him?'

On the surface it was a casual, almost a throwaway question, but there was an underlying hint of concern that gave Sukey a twinge of pleasure. Was he, she wondered, a tad jealous? She was careful to make her reply sound similarly off-hand. 'He's OK,' she said, 'although he treats me as if I'm still on probation – which I suppose in some way I am. He's well thought of in the department and he's had years of experience in the job, but he's very single-minded and he doesn't hesitate to shoot me down in flames if I have the cheek to suggest anything that doesn't fit in with his assessment of a case.'

Jim chuckled and said, 'Which I'm sure you have no hesitation in doing!'

'On the contrary, I only do it occasionally, when I feel really strongly about something. Not that it gets me anywhere,' she admitted resignedly.

'So what case are you on at the moment?'

'The stabbing of an archaeologist called Doctor Whistler in a Bristol hotel.'

'Ah, yes, DCI Lord has a particular interest in that. The curator at the museum in Gloucester is a friend of his who had dealings with Whistler a couple of years ago. Nice old boy, according to Philip; he came to examine some Roman relics that turned up during excavations for a building site somewhere in the county. I'm told an arrest is imminent, by the way.'

Sukey looked at him in surprise. 'Who told you that?'

'DCI Richard Leach. He and I go back quite a long way, although our paths haven't crossed much for the past few years.'

She looked at him suspiciously. 'And was it solely interest in the Whistler case that prompted you to get in touch again?'

He looked slightly sheepish as he replied, 'Not entirely. I just wanted to know that someone was keeping an eye on you.' He turned to look at her and she read in his expression all that she had half-feared, half-hoped to see. He put a hand over one of hers and said softly, 'I still care for you, Sook. I care very much.'

'I know,' she said in a low voice. They sat in silence for a few moments with their hands clasped. Then something occurred to Sukey and she pulled her hand away. 'Just what else did you tell DCI Leach about me?' she demanded.

'That you have a sharp brain, a good eye for detail, and – ' he hesitated for a moment before adding mischievously – 'that you have a tendency to be a loose cannon.'

'Well, thanks a bunch,' she said, laughing in spite of herself. 'No doubt he's passed that gem to Greg Rathbone with a suggestion that he keeps me on a tight rein.'

'I don't think so. I did add that Chief Inspector Lord thought highly of you as a SOCO and that he gave strong support to your application to train for the CID.'

'Oh, well, that's all right then,' she said sarcastically. She glanced at her watch. 'It's getting on for lunchtime. I imagine you expect to be fed?'

'Naturally . . . but don't provide too much food because this evening I'm taking you to Bristol's top floating restaurant.'

'That'll be great.' She led the way indoors while he followed with the coffee tray. 'Is there anything you'd like to do this afternoon?' she added while putting bowls of soup in the microwave and taking salad from the refrigerator.

'How about a walk over the Downs? Or maybe,' he added with a subtle change of tone, 'you have a better idea?'

His meaning was unmistakable and for a moment she felt her commonsense resolve to confine their relationship to an affectionate friendship beginning to waver, but she made a determined effort to keep it on course. 'A walk over the Downs would be lovely,' she said firmly.

'What would you like to drink?' he asked as they settled at their table. ' Much as I'd love to order a bottle of bubbly,' he added apologetically, 'I do have to drive back and I don't want to start my career as a DCI with a drink-drive charge.'

'Perish the thought,' she said, realizing as she spoke that his intention of going home that evening was not altogether welcome. 'A white wine spritzer has plenty of bubbles – how about that?'

'Good thinking. I'll have the same.' He gave the order and they sat back and took in their surroundings. Through the window of the converted barge they could see the reflection of streetlights dancing in the water of the Floating Harbour. 'This is nice, isn't it?'

'Very,' she agreed. 'I've walked along here quite a few times since I came to Bristol and thought how attractive this restaurant looked. Thank you,' she added as the waiter brought their drinks. She raised her glass. 'Here's to DCI Jim Castle, the scourge of Gloucestershire villains.'

'Thank you.'

They clinked glasses and drank. Then she said, 'How come you know about this place?'

'Rick Leach recommended it. Now, what do you fancy to eat?' They studied the menu for a few minutes before settling on broccoli and Stilton soup followed by poached salmon in a lemon and tarragon sauce. 'It's remarkable, isn't it, how we so often make the same choice?' he said when they had given their order.

She shrugged and said, untruthfully, 'I hadn't thought about it.'

'In fact, we agree about a lot of things,' he went on. 'Wine, for example.' He was studying the varieties on offer as he spoke. 'What about a glass of Chilean Chardonnay? I don't think that would take me over the limit.'

He held out the wine list and as she reached for it her eyes fell on a couple who had just entered. She gave an involuntary start and hastily lowered her head to make a show of studying the list with close attention while the newcomers followed the waiter past their table. When she looked up she saw that Jim was eyeing the couple with a familiar look of concentration in his keen, greenish eyes.

'Do you know them?' he said in a low voice.

'The woman is PA to Professor Thorne, who's in charge of the Department of Hellenic Studies at the university. I've only seen her once, when Greg Rathbone and I called to interview Thorne in connection with the Whistler killing. She did some photocopying for me – I don't know her name.'

'Do you know the man?'

She avoided his eye as she said, 'I've never met him. What's your interest?'

'I think someone should tell the lady to be a bit more careful in her choice of friends,' he replied.

'Are you saying he's some kind of villain?'

'His name is Oliver Maddox and we have reason to believe he's behind some very nasty goings on, including but not confined to people trafficking, but so far we've never been able to get any evidence against him.'

'What else?'

'Our information is that he'll take on anything for anyone prepared to pay for his services and he—' He broke off to give their order to the wine waiter; when the man had gone he leaned forward and fixed her with a penetrating look in his eyes. 'Sook, I have a feeling from the way you were so careful to avoid being spotted that you're keeping something from me.'

She sighed and nibbled at a bread roll before replying, 'Let's not talk about it now.'

'OK, I'll wait for your confession till we get back to your place.' His tone was light, but she knew he meant business. 'Just tell me one thing: is it in connection with the Whistler case?'

She nodded. 'I'd more or less decided not to say anything to you because I know you'll give me an earful for being a "loose cannon", as you call it. I've written out a report for DS Rathbone and he'll probably hit the roof when he finds out what I've been up to, but I hope when he calms down he'll have the grace to admit I've hit on something worth investigating.'

Jim appeared to be about to say more, but at that moment a waiter brought their soup. True to his promise he did not refer to the subject again and the meal passed pleasantly enough as they chatted over a wide range of topics. He recounted episodes from current investigations, particularly those involving her former colleagues in the SOCOs team in Gloucester, and they chuckled together over her heavily embroidered accounts of her differences with Rathbone. The couple that had sparked their earlier exchanges were forgotten until suddenly a man's voice broke into their conversation.

'Chief Inspector Castle, how nice to see you!' Oliver Maddox had stopped beside their table, his companion at his side. In contrast to the fashionable but plain trouser suit she had worn in the office, she was wearing a midnight blue dress that might have come from the collection of a top designer and diamonds sparkled at her ears and throat. 'Allow me to congratulate you on your recent promotion,' Maddox went on, 'and good evening to you, Constable Reynolds.' He treated Sukey to a flash of white teeth.

Startled at the interruption, she hesitated for a second before recovering her wits and saying, 'I don't think I've had the pleasure.'

'But you have met this lady, I believe? She certainly remembers you.'

'Yes, of course.' Sukey nodded politely at his companion, who responded with a glacial half-smile.

'Hasn't the Chief Inspector told you that he and I are old friends?' Maddox went on, still addressing Sukey. His voice had a velvety undertone that reminded her of a self-satisfied cat; his smile persisted but his dark eyes under a strong brow were as hard as jet. She had the uncomfortable sensation that he was looking straight into her mind. 'His promotion is richly deserved, he's a superb detective,' he purred. 'Nothing escapes his eagle eye. I can't believe he didn't notice me pass your table.'

'Ms Reynolds and I have had plenty of other things to talk about,' Jim said pointedly, 'so if you will excuse us—'

'But, of course. I'm sure we have no wish to intrude. Until our next meeting, then.' He raised a hand in a polite salute and there was a hint of mockery in his smile as he moved with his companion towards the exit.

'I think it's time for us to go as well.' Jim signalled to the waiter and asked for the bill. He did not speak again until he had paid and they were back on the quay. Then he took her by the arm and said quietly, 'I'm afraid, Sook, you've strayed into some very murky waters. The minute we get back you're going to tell me all about it. And I do mean all,' he added in a tone that she knew only too well.

Back in her flat, she gave him a brief résumé of the enquiry into the murder of Doctor Edwin Whistler, the build-up of circumstantial evidence that had already convinced DS Rathbone and DCI Leach of Stephen Lamont's guilt and her own suspicion – pooh-poohed by both Rathbone and DS Douglas – that Boris Gasspar might have been in some way coerced into identifying him as the man who left the hotel by the staff entrance shortly before re-entering and enquiring for Whistler at the desk. 'The more I thought about it, I couldn't see Lamont as a killer and I was convinced that Gasspar was under some kind of pressure,' she said, 'so I decided to do a little . . . unpaid overtime, shall we call it? As a result of which, I wrote this.' She handed him the report. 'I'll make some coffee while you read it.'

When she brought the coffee he put her report on the table and said, 'This man you saw with Gasspar – was it Maddox?'

'Definitely.'

'And you're sure he didn't see you?'

'I doubt if he could have recognized me from the distance between us while he was parked, and he didn't appear to glance in my direction as he drove away.'

'He'd already recognized me and he knew your name so the woman with him must have recognized you from the time you went to her office.' He sipped coffee for a moment before continuing, 'He obviously had no reason to conceal from her how he came to recognize me, which must have prompted her to tell him how she knew you.'

'You're thinking she may have some inkling of his back-ground?' Sukey suggested.

He nodded. 'More than an inkling, I'd say. You said she's Thorne's PA; that would mean she had access to everything that was going on in his department, including Whistler's visit and the stuff he was carrying.'

'Only the epistle. Professor Thorne knew nothing about the other items.'

'So he says.'

'That's a point.'

'Tell me more about these other items.'

'I can't really add to what I've already told you. Doctor Makris has sent us a detailed description of the relics but he admits he's no idea of what they're worth – which of course is why they were sent to England. As to the so-called Pauline epistle, assuming it's genuine he says it would be priceless to biblical scholars but impossible to value in money terms.'

Jim thought for a moment before pulling out his mobile and punching buttons. 'Who are you calling?' she asked uneasily.

He silenced her with a gesture and began to speak in a brisk, urgent voice. 'Rick, sorry to disturb you on a Saturday evening, but something's cropped up and I think you should know about it right away. It's to do with Oliver Maddox . . . that's right . . . and Sukey, that is, DC Reynolds, has strayed across his path and come up with some very interesting information . . . yes, I agree we have to give it top priority . . . of course, I quite understand . . . ten o'clock tomorrow at DC Reynolds' flat, then.' Before she could protest he dictated the address and ended the conversation. 'Sorry, he's got a houseful of relatives with kids so his place is out and this isn't the sort of thing you talk about over a beer in the local, so you have an unexpected guest for the night. At least, I'm assuming it was unexpected, but on the other hand—' With a sudden movement he took her by one hand, pulled her to her feet and into his arms. 'I've missed you and I want you like hell,' he said hoarsely, 'but if you don't feel the same, just say the word and I'll—'

She put her free hand behind his head and drew it down until their faces were almost touching. 'Tell me what the word is and I'll be sure not to say it,' she whispered, a fraction of a second before his mouth closed over hers.

Fourteen

'Cosy little pad you've found here, Sukey,' commented DCI Leach. His gaze took in every detail of her sitting room and the view across the city before homing in on her face and scrutinizing her with an appraising expression. 'I hope you're happy working here in Bristol.'

'Very happy, thank you, sir,' she replied.

'This is an informal meeting and I understand you and Jim are old friends, so let's skip the "sir" shall we? On the strict understanding that the arrangement ceases the moment I walk out of here,' he added. He spoke seriously, but she had a feeling that a smile lurked in the depths of his intensely blue eyes.

'Whatever you say.' Just in time she remembered not to add 'sir'. 'Please sit down; would you like some coffee?'

'No, thanks.' He glanced at his watch before settling into an armchair with his bony-wristed arms draped over the sides and his long legs stretched out in front of him. 'I'm due on the golf course in an hour, so let's get down to business straight away. I've had another chat with Jim this morning and he tells me you've written a report on your observation of Gasspar's movements on Friday so I'll run through that first.' She handed him the printed sheets and sat beside Jim on the couch facing him while he put on a pair of steel-framed glasses and began scanning the text. 'You seem pretty sure Maddox didn't see you,' he said when he had finished.

'As sure as I can be,' she said. 'He appeared to be looking straight ahead and I gave him only a very brief glance before he drew level with me. He's got a big car, the street where Boris lives is quite narrow and there were vehicles parked on either side, so he had to drive carefully.'

'But you managed to get his number without appearing to pay too much attention to him?'

'I'm long-sighted so I was able to read it as he pulled out.'

Leach nodded approvingly. 'Useful, that, when on surveillance – either official or unofficial,' he remarked, and this time
a definite hint of a smile lit up his thin, slightly weather-
beaten features. 'However, Maddox is as cunning as a fox,
which is why he's managed to keep ahead of the game for so
long. My guess is he spotted your car turning into the street
behind Gasspar while he was waiting for him and watched to
see where it went. You say you drove well past before parking?'
Sukey nodded. 'Well, that's a standard ploy and I'll bet he
made a note of the fact that you didn't get out of your car.
He might also have seen you checking your rear view mirror
from time to time, as I presume you did while you were
watching for your target to go into the house?'

'Actually, no; my door mirror gave me a good view.'

'And you were careful to keep out of sight while Gasspar
was on his way back?'

'Yes, and he walked straight past my car without hesitating
so I'm sure he didn't know I was there.'

'Which means that if Maddox did spot you, which I think
is more than likely, he had his own reasons for not sharing
his observation with Gasspar. OK, now tell me what prompted
this little excursion in the first place.'

'Boris was obviously ill at ease when we interviewed him
the day of the attack on Whistler, but I accepted DS Rathbone's
point about how coming from a former communist state would
make him uncomfortable talking to the police,' she began,
nervously at first but with increasing confidence, 'but it was
when he came to Erika Henderson's office and found me there
that he became noticeably agitated. When I showed him the
three mock-ups the techies had given us and asked if he could
identify Lamont he went to him without hesitation every time.
He obviously wanted to get it over with and for me to leave
as soon as possible.'

'So he had no trouble picking out Lamont?'

'None whatever.'

'Did you mention this to DS Rathbone?' Sukey shook her
head and Leach gave another slightly enigmatic smile. 'You
knew what his reaction would be so you thought you'd do a
little further investigation on your own?'

'I gave Boris my card with my mobile number and told

him to call me in confidence if there was anything worrying him. He was very reluctant to accept it, but I insisted and eventually he did, but he hasn't called. Ever since, I've been asking myself, supposing his passport and other papers are forged and he's been brought here illegally by someone who now has some kind of hold over him? Is that what's making him so jumpy and is that why he hasn't been in touch?'

'So, having followed him, presumably with the intention of finding out where he lives, what did you plan to do then?'

'To be honest, I didn't have a detailed plan,' Sukey confessed, feeling slightly foolish as once again she detected a glint of humour in Leach's expression. 'I . . . I suppose I thought I might possibly get a sight of some of the people he mixed with, get a feel for his background away from the hotel, that sort of thing.'

'Something to convince Sergeant Rathbone that you had some grounds for your misgivings?' suggested Leach.

'Yes, I suppose so. When I saw him with Maddox it seemed I'd been right about him acting under pressure, but of course I had no idea then who Maddox was.'

'Well, it seems your bit of moonlighting may have done more than turn up a possible new lead in the Whistler murder,' said Leach. 'It would certainly be interesting to know what lies behind Friday's rendezvous. I see that while you were observing them in the car you thought you saw Gasspar handing something over to Maddox,' he went on, referring to her report.

'Yes, and from the impatient way Maddox held out his hand, he didn't seem willing to part with it.'

'Did you tell DS Rathbone about giving him your card?' She shook her head, expecting a reproof, but he simply continued, 'Greg told me of your misgivings, of course, and I admit I've been inclined to accept his assessment of them, especially in the light of the evidence piling up against Lamont. With Maddox coming on the scene we're likely to be into an entirely different ball game. If he's got a hold over Gasspar—' He broke off and gnawed reflectively at his upper lip for a minute or two before continuing. 'Let's begin with the assumption that Maddox wanted to get his hands on the stuff Whistler was carrying and that he knew about the arrangement with Lamont, almost certainly through his girlfriend in Thorne's office. He sends one of his operators to impersonate Lamont in the hope of getting Whistler to hand over the goodies voluntarily, Whistler smells a rat and refuses to co-operate so the guy knifes him and scarpers via the staff entrance, where Gasspar is conveniently waiting.'

'So you reckon Boris could have been primed with the story implicating Lamont?' said Jim.

Leach nodded. 'Of course, it's all conjecture at this stage, but it seems a possibility. He could even have been instrumental in getting the killer into the hotel, again through the staff entrance.'

There was a short silence during which both senior detectives appeared to be digesting this theory. Sukey opened her mouth to speak and then shut it again in a sudden rush of embarrassment. 'You've thought of something?' Leach said encouragingly. 'Don't be shy, let's have it.'

'I was only thinking that being implicated in a murder, plus the knowledge that if he didn't do as he was told might mean deportation or worse, is enough to make anyone jumpy under police questioning, however gentle.'

'I think we can agree on that,' said Leach. 'So what are you suggesting?'

'Assuming Maddox has got some hold over him,' she began hesitantly, 'it might be because he supplied him with false papers. Suppose we get our experts to carry out a thorough check; if it turns out he is an illegal might we perhaps do a little horse-trading – offer him protection if he's prepared to open up about his dealings with Maddox? Could we perhaps hint at an offer of a legitimate work permit as a bait?'

Jim looked doubtful. 'That sounds dodgy,' he said.

Leach nodded. 'I agree; we'd have to make a pretty strong case before going that far. It would need a decision at a high level.'

'In any case,' Jim went on, 'Maddox may have some other hold on Gasspar to ensure he keeps his mouth shut. We've never managed to get any of his underlings to grass on him either – they're all scared stiff of him. And wouldn't immigration have spotted any irregularities in his documents? They're pretty smart at weeding out the duds nowadays.'

'I've read recently that some forgeries are good enough to stand up to quite close scrutiny, especially when there's no particular reason to be suspicious,' said Sukey.

'And Maddox has got the connections and the wherewithal to make sure he gets the best,' said Leach. 'OK, we'll begin by asking Gasspar's employers for access to his records, saying it's part of a routine check and asking them to make sure he doesn't know about it. Now I must be off.' He unwound his rangy body from the armchair and stood up. 'I'll get Rathbone on to it first thing in the morning. Enjoy the rest of the weekend, folks.'

'I'll see you out,' said Jim before Sukey could speak. 'Maybe we could have that coffee now?' he added over his shoulder as the two of them left the room. She went to the kitchen and switched on the kettle; as she waited for it to boil her brain went suddenly into overdrive and when he returned she said, 'Jim, I've just had an uncomfortable thought.'

'What is it?'

'I'm positive Boris gave something to Maddox and my first guess was protection money, but if DCI Leach is right about his role in the murder plan it would make more sense for Maddox to pay him.'

'True,' he agreed, 'and your next guess?'

She sensed that he too was troubled and her heart was thumping at the possible implications of what she had in mind. 'Do you think Maddox might have found out he had my card and made him hand it over?'

He took her by the arm. 'Come and sit down,' he said gently.

'The coffee's nearly ready,' she protested.

'It can wait.' He led her to the couch and pulled her down beside him. His expression was serious. 'I was one jump ahead of you, and so was Rick Leach,' he said. 'That's why I wanted a word with him in private, but now you've cottoned on by yourself we may as well talk about it.'

'So what do you think?'

'Either Boris told Maddox about the card, which seems unlikely from your observation of what went on between them, or the knowledge must have come from another person. Suppose Boris confided in someone he trusted, maybe showed them your card and asked for advice on what to do, and a third party overheard the conversation and reported it to Maddox. He's got spies everywhere.'

Sukey shuddered. 'You make him sound like a Mafia boss.'

'There are certain similarities,' Jim agreed dryly.

She closed her eyes and leaned against his shoulder. 'I'm scared,' she admitted. 'I've got visions of being knifed in a dark alley.'

Jim put an arm round her and gave her a comforting squeeze. 'Don't be daft, Maddox won't come after you. He's much too canny to set his dogs on a police officer. What worries us is that he may decide that there's a weak link in his organization that needs cutting out. In other words—'

'You mean he might have Boris killed?' Sukey faltered. She put a hand to her mouth. 'Because of what I did?'

'I wasn't thinking of Boris. Assuming Rick's theory is anywhere near the truth, Maddox needs him to support his story. I was thinking rather of the supposed confidant I mentioned a moment ago. Maddox might feel it advisable to have him eliminated. Or her,' he added as an afterthought.

'But it's not unusual, is it, to invite possible witnesses to make direct contact with an individual officer?' pleaded Sukey, horrified at the thought that she might unwittingly have precipitated another murderous attack.

'Of course not, and no one's blaming you.' He gave her a reassuring hug. 'In fact, Leach believes you've done a very useful bit of detective work and he'll be having a word with both you and DS Rathbone tomorrow about the next stage of the investigation. And meanwhile, I suggest you write up your version of our encounter yesterday evening with Maddox and the woman from Professor Thorne's office. I'll be making my own report to my Super first thing in the morning.'

The minute Sukey entered the CID office on Monday morning Vicky buttonholed her and told her to report immediately to DCI Leach. 'DS Rathbone is with him already and it's rumoured in the bazaar that something big is breaking,' she said, adding in a low voice, 'you wouldn't know anything about it, I suppose?'

'Why should I?' said Sukey defensively.

'You aren't the only one who gets hunches, you know.' Vicky cocked her head on one side and raised an enquiring eyebrow.

Sukey ignored the implied question and said, 'Well, I'd better not keep him waiting, had I?'

DCI Leach's office was on the third floor of the building

and Sukey used the few minutes it took her to reach it to organize her thoughts as best she could. Leach was sitting at his desk with his back to the window with DS Rathbone opposite him. The sergeant was scanning a document that Sukey recognized as her initial report; when he had finished he handed it back to Leach before greeting her with a curt nod.

'Good morning Sukey, please sit down.' Leach waved her to the empty chair facing him. 'As you can see, I've put DS Rathbone in the picture regarding your observation of Boris Gasspar on Friday evening and I understand DCI Castle of Gloucestershire advised you to write a supplementary report. Have you done so?'

'Yes, sir, I have it here.' She handed over the single sheet; he scanned it briefly and passed it to Rathbone, who read it, grunted and gave it back.

'Right, you both know the situation so far. It seems we are now part of something far more wide-ranging than a straightforward murder enquiry. We have to tread carefully to make sure we don't foul up an ongoing investigation into which a lot of time and planning has been invested. For the time being I intend to limit our part to a detailed check on Gasspar's background – without alerting his suspicions, of course. I doubt if Maddox has got any other agents at the Mariners Hotel, but we must make sure it's done through someone we can trust. We'll want to know how he came to apply for the job, whether he produced references and if so whether they were followed up – you know the kind of thing. Greg, you've made contact with some of the admin staff there so I leave it to you to decide the best person to approach. Meanwhile, we await further instructions from higher up. That's all for now, thank you.'

As the door to Leach's office closed behind them and they began to walk toward the stairs, Rathbone said, 'I suppose you think you've been very clever?' There was an edge to his voice that she had not heard before.

'Not clever, Sarge, just lucky.'

'Let's hope your luck holds,' he said curtly, 'and from now on forget the undercover stuff and stick to carrying out orders.'

'Yes, Sarge,' she said meekly.

'About Gasspar, I don't think we'll waste time dealing with the hotel manager,' he went on. 'The prat will only panic if we show further interest in the man, thinking we suspect him of harbouring a terrorist or some such bollocks. His PA is probably our best bet – what's her name now?'

'Erika Henderson, Sarge.'

'Right. Go and see her, but impress on her that no one, but no one, not even her boss, is to know what you're after.' They had almost reached the CID office. 'Got that?' he almost growled.

'Yes Sarge.'

'Right. Get on with it.' He entered the room ahead of her without bothering to hold the door open behind him.

Fifteen

'Good morning, the Mariners Hotel.'

'Good morning. May I speak to Ms Henderson, please?'

'Who shall I say is calling?'

'This is the Department of Employment.'

'One moment please.'

Seconds later, a woman's voice said, 'Erika Henderson speaking. Is there a query about one of our employees?'

'This is DC Reynolds, and please don't greet me by name,' said Sukey quickly. 'I apologize for the deception. Are you alone in your office at the moment?'

'Yes, why?'

'I need to speak to you in the strictest confidence and it's important no one sees me with you. Can we meet away from the hotel, say during your lunch break?'

'This is official, I suppose?' said Erika cautiously.

'Absolutely. I realize this cloak and dagger stuff will seem unusual, but there's a very good reason. Just tell me where and when would suit you.'

'Well, as it's Monday I need to restock my fridge after the weekend so I was planning to go to the supermarket down the road,' said Erika after a pause. 'They have a coffee shop where you can get a sandwich or a salad. Shall we say twelve thirty?'

'I'll be there. And please, don't mention this to anyone. I'll explain when I see you.'

Sukey put the phone down and glanced at the clock. It was barely nine fifteen; she had the better part of three hours before the meeting. She became aware of DS Rathbone's steely glance across the table that separated their workstations.

'When and where?' he demanded, having evidently been listening to her end of the conversation. She told him and he said, 'OK, I've arranged to see Professor Thorne at eleven. You might as well come along.'

'Right, Sarge.'

A little over an hour later, as they went downstairs to the yard to pick up the car he had already booked, Rathbone said, 'I still think Thorne may have picked up some hint that Whistler had other stuff with him without even realizing it – possibly through a casual reference in conversation to the proposed visit to London.'

'You reckon his secretary might have done the same and told her boyfriend?' said Sukey.

'It's a long shot, but we might as well check. I've asked him not to mention this meeting to her, by the way. You'd better leave the questioning to me this time,' he added as he settled into the passenger seat and clipped on his seat belt.

You're determined to take every possible opportunity of reminding me that I'm still a rookie, aren't you? Sukey thought to herself with a touch of resentment. At least he hadn't suggested accompanying her to the meeting with Erika Henderson. The short journey passed in silence; when they arrived he left her to park the car and went into the building without her. By the time she had found a space and followed him, he had announced their arrival to the blonde receptionist and the two of them were waiting in the hall. The woman's manner was no more welcoming than it had been on their previous visit as she conducted them to a small room on the ground floor, opened the door and said, 'Professor Thorne will join you in a moment,' in a tone that suggested a great favour was about to be bestowed on them.

Thorne himself, arriving a few moments later, greeted them affably and offered coffee, which Rathbone declined without reference to Sukey. 'Before I tell you the reason for requesting this meeting, sir,' he began, 'I must ask you once again to treat it as confidential.'

Thorne nodded. 'You made that very clear, Sergeant, which is why I instructed the receptionist to show you into this room, to avoid unwelcome interruptions.' As before, he was wearing a grey flannel suit with knife-sharp creases in the trousers, which he carefully hitched up at the knees as he sat down. 'Please tell me, are you anywhere near finding the perpetrator of this dreadful crime?'

'It so happens our enquiries have reached a critical stage,' Rathbone replied, 'but there are a number of questions still to be answered and it is possible you may be able to help us.'

Thorne spread his plump hands and said earnestly, 'I'll do anything I can to help bring the villain to justice.'

Rathbone gave a slightly dismissive nod as if to say this was no more than was to be expected. 'During a recent conversation,' he continued, 'you expressed your conviction that Professor Lamont is incapable of committing murder.'

'That is true, and I have not changed my opinion,' said Thorne, 'and before we go on, Sergeant, I should like to say that the poor chap has been considerably affected by your continued harassment. It has brought him to the verge of a breakdown and he is presently on indefinite sick leave. It has also caused distress to his sister, who as you know suffers from emotional problems.'

'It is never our intention to cause distress to innocent citizens, but in a case of murder we have to explore every possibility,' said Rathbone. 'That is why I am here, Professor; as I have already told you, we now know that in addition to the supposed Pauline letter, Whistler was also bringing with him several religious relics that could be worth a lot of money on the black market. I know I've asked you this question before, but I'm asking you once again: are you absolutely certain you had no idea Whistler was bringing any other items with him? We know there was no reference in the correspondence, but is it possible that some chance remark during a telephone conversation, something you hardly noticed at the time, might with hindsight have suggested there was more than just the letter?'

'I thought about it after you asked me the first time, and I can't recall anything significant,' said Thorne with another shake of his head. 'Unless—' He hesitated for a moment before adding, 'I seem to recall some mention of a trip to London that Whistler was planning before his return to Rhodes.'

'Can you remember who mentioned it?'

'I think . . . yes, now I come to think of it, Lamont said something about Whistler having quite a tight schedule and he might have mentioned London.'

'Do you know the purpose of that visit?'

'I'm afraid not.'

'Did that conversation take place in your office?'

'Yes. As a matter of fact, Lamont had just taken a call from Doctor Whistler and it was when it was over that he mentioned London.'

'You were present during that call?'

'Yes, but Lamont's side of the conversation consisted merely of remarks such as, "I see" or "I understand" and something like "all right, I'll wait to hear from you". After he hung up he told me Whistler was having to alter his schedule to take in a visit to London, but he didn't go into any details.'

'You didn't think to ask?'

'Why should I? If it had been any concern of mine, he would have told me.'

'Can you remember what day this happened?'

'I'm afraid not. Several days before Whistler's visit, I imagine; I can't be more precise than that.'

'Was anyone else present?'

Thorne hesitated for a fraction of a second before saying, 'I suppose my secretary might have been with us. I can't be sure. Is it important?'

'That would be Ms Milligan?' Thorne nodded. Sukey, observing him closely, thought he appeared a little uneasy at the direction Rathbone's questioning had taken. 'How long has she been employed at the university?' the sergeant asked.

'I'm not exactly sure. Eighteen months, two years perhaps. I'd have to check.'

'Has she been your secretary for the whole of that time?'

'No, she worked in the registry for some months before she came to me. My previous secretary left, the post was advertised internally and she applied. The Registrar spoke highly of her and after an interview I appointed her.'

Rathbone cleared his throat and leaned forward in his chair. 'Please don't misunderstand what I'm about to ask you, Professor, but how well do you know Ms Milligan?'

'Well, really!' A dull flush crept into Thorne's pallid cheeks. 'Are you suggesting, Sergeant, that I have been having some kind of inappropriate relationship with a member of my staff?'

'Certainly not,' Rathbone assured him, 'and I apologize if I have given offence. What I am trying to establish is whether she has ever spoken to you about her private or perhaps I should say social life. She is a young and, I understand, an attractive young lady so I imagine she has a wide circle of friends.'

Still looking uncomfortable, Thorne fiddled with some brochures lying on a nearby table. 'Well, yes, I'm sure that's true,' he muttered.

'So has she mentioned anyone she has met recently? Someone in whom she showed, shall we say, a particular interest?'

'No, I can't say she has.'

'In that case, perhaps I should have a word with her.'

'I'm afraid she's not here at the moment. She has a dental appointment but she'll be in at two o'clock.'

'Then we'll come back at two.' Rathbone stood up and held out his hand. 'Thank you very much for your time, Professor – and in the meantime, may I remind you to say nothing about this conversation to her or anyone else.'

Thorne gave the required assurances and shook the proffered hand in evident relief that the interview was at an end. As they walked back to the car, Rathbone said, 'What did you make of that?'

'He did seem to get a bit hot under the collar when you asked how well he knew his secretary,' said Sukey, 'but I can't believe the delectable Ms Milligan would find Thorne particularly attractive when she can land someone like Maddox.'

'All the same, it certainly produced a reaction of sorts. Make sure you get back to the station after your meeting with Erika Henderson in time to pick me up no later than one thirty, ' he added as he settled into the passenger seat and clipped on his seat belt. 'I want to be there well before two so that he doesn't have a chance to talk to her before we do.'

'Right, Sarge.' Sukey was relieved to know that his mind was running on similar lines to her own. She would have hesitated to risk a snub by putting the idea forward herself. In the circumstances, she decided not to point out that Ms Milligan probably carried a mobile phone and there was nothing to stop him using it to warn her of the impending visit from the detectives.

'And a propos of your meeting with Erika Henderson,' Rathbone added, 'I hope I can rely on you to tell her as little as possible. And not a word about Maddox – understood?'

'Of course, Sarge.'

*   *   *

When Sukey reached the recently opened Spend and Save Supermarket, Erika Henderson was already unwrapping a sandwich at a table for two in a corner of the coffee shop. A bulging carrier bag lay on the empty seat. She nodded and smiled as Sukey approached. 'I hope this is all right,' she said, 'I sat here because it's reasonably tucked away.'

'It's absolutely fine,' Sukey assured her. 'I'll go and grab a sarnie and a coffee.'

'I can recommend the tuna mayo,' said Erika.

'Thanks, I'll try it.'

When Sukey returned with her tray Erika had finished her sandwich and was sipping her coffee. 'Just dump my stuff on the floor,' she said, indicating the bag of groceries, 'and tell me what this is all about. I've been burning with curiosity ever since you rang.'

Her eyes sparkled over the rim of her cup and Sukey saw her in a new light. At their earlier meetings, although she had been willing – indeed, anxious – to help the investigation and had more than once volunteered information, she had maintained a certain cool detachment. Today she was more like an excited teenager.

'Before I start,' Sukey said, 'I need your promise that you won't tell anyone about this meeting.'

Erika looked slightly hurt. 'You've already said that,' she said reproachfully. 'Of course I promise,'

'And it's important that nothing we say is overheard, so please remember to speak quietly.'

'Understood. Oh, do get on with it! I'm dying to know what it's about. And I only have half an hour,' she added with a glance at her watch.

'It won't take long,' said Sukey. 'In any case, I haven't got that long either. I take it you have access to all the hotel employees' records?'

Erika nodded. 'They're all on my computer.'

'How many other people have access?'

'Maurice Ashford, naturally. No one else; the database is protected.'

'What about application forms, references and so on?'

'They're kept in a locked filing cabinet.' Erika frowned. 'What's this leading up to?'

'We need to know more about Boris Gasspar,' said Sukey.

'Boris? Why?'

'We think he may know the whereabouts of someone we're anxious to speak to.'

Erika's eyes nearly popped out of her head. 'You mean a criminal?' she said in a squeaky whisper. 'Has this got anything to do with the murder of Doctor Whistler?'

'I'm afraid I can't answer that question,' said Sukey.

'Why can't you ask Boris yourselves?'

'I can't go into that either.'

'So, what do you want me to do?'

'First of all, tell me how he came to apply for the job?'

'We register staff vacancies at an agency specializing in hotel and catering staff. We needed a receptionist and they sent him.'

'Does he have a National Insurance number?'

'Of course. We wouldn't have taken him on without one.'

'Did he give any references?'

'Yes, from another hotel – somewhere in Croatia, I think it was. Or maybe Serbia, I'm not sure offhand. I remember their letter was in rather quaint English.' Erika gave a smile of amusement at the recollection.

'So he'd had some previous experience in the business?'

'Oh, yes, he knew his job. His previous employers spoke highly of him and we've found him a very satisfactory employee.' Her expression became concerned. 'I do hope he isn't in any kind of trouble. He does have an anxious look about him from time to time, but he always insists that he's OK.' Erika glanced at her watch again. 'Is that all you want to know? I really should be going.'

'We'd like to see his paperwork,' said Sukey. 'You probably won't want to part with the originals, but photocopies would be fine.'

'That's no problem. I can do it when Maurice is out of the office. How will I get them to you?'

'Call me when they're ready and I'll arrange to pick them up.'

'I take it you won't want to come to the hotel?'

'No; we could come back here if you like.'

'Why not?' Erika reached down to pick up her shopping. 'Is that all, then?'

'Just one other thing. You told DS Douglas you heard Boris

having what you described as "a furious row" in a foreign language on his mobile. I don't suppose you have any idea what language he was using?'

Erika shook her head. 'All I can say is that it definitely wasn't French or German, and I don't think it was Spanish or Italian either. I don't speak any of those languages but I've heard them all when I've been abroad on holidays.'

'Thanks. That could be helpful.'

'Is this person you're trying to find foreign then?'

'I don't know. In any case, there's nothing to suggest he was the person Boris was talking to.'

Erika gave a knowing look. 'All right, I won't ask any more questions.' She put a finger to her lips and whispered, 'This conversation never took place!' in a melodramatic undertone before heading for the exit.

Sixteen

When Sukey arrived back at the station after her interview with Erika Henderson it was a little after one
fifteen. There was no sign of DS Rathbone by the entrance
so she went up to the CID office, where she found Vicky
standing by her desk with her jacket on and her bag over her
shoulder, apparently on the point of going out.

'If you're looking for DS Rathbone, he's with DCI Leach,
but he'll be back in a minute,' she told Sukey. 'He's just rung
through to tell me to stand by to go with him to the Hellenic
Studies Department at the uni to interview Professor Thorne's
secretary.'

Sukey blinked in surprise. 'I went with him to see Thorne
this morning,' she said, 'but the secretary was at the dentist
so he arranged to go back this afternoon. I assumed I'd be
going with him.'

Vicky shrugged. 'All I know is he told me you've got a car
and I'm to collect the key from you.'

'Any idea why the change of plan?' asked Sukey as she
handed it over.

'Haven't a clue. Did anything come out of the interview
with the prof?'

'Not a lot.' Sukey outlined the exchanges between Rathbone
and Thorne and Vicky chuckled over her description of the
latter's look of dismay when he thought he might be suspected
of a liaison with his secretary. 'He looked really embarrassed,
but I can't imagine she'd be interested in him. If he's there
this afternoon you'll see what I mean.'

'Maybe he fantasises,' Vicky suggested.

'Could be. Anyway, she's coming back at two and Rathbone
wants to make sure of getting in ahead of her, before she can
speak to Thorne.'

Vicky raised an eyebrow. 'Why so?'

'He thinks there might be some sort of collusion between the two of them and as it happens the same thought occurred to me. On the face of it it's difficult to see how it could be relevant to the killing of Whistler – except, of course, that the secretary does have a very dodgy boyfriend and might have passed something on to him without realizing its significance.'

'Her boss is hardly likely to know about that, is he?'

'Who knows? He certainly didn't get it from us – at least, the Sarge never mentioned it this morning. Ah, here he comes.'

Rathbone strode into the room, yanked his dark blue fleece jacket from the back of his chair, slung it over his shoulder and beckoned the two women over. 'DCI Leach has decided it's better if you don't come with me to interview the Milligan woman because she knows you've seen her in the company of Maddox,' he told Sukey as they obeyed the summons. 'We've no idea how much she knows about him; she may of course be completely in the dark about his dirty dealings, but with this big undercover operation going on we can't take any chances. There's to be absolutely no mention of him during this afternoon's meeting,' he said to Vicky. 'We want her to think the purpose is solely to clear up some loose ends about the Whistler case.'

Vicky nodded. 'Understood, Sarge.'

'It's just as well she wasn't there this morning, then,' Sukey commented. 'She could have got curious and wanted to know what we were doing there.'

'Right,' said Rathbone without looking in her direction. 'Got the car key, Vicky? Good, we'll be on our way.' Over his shoulder as they made for the door, he said, 'Sukey, while I'm out you can be writing up your meeting with Ashford's PA.'

'Will do, Sarge.'

During these brief exchanges, DS Bob Douglas had entered the office. The moment Rathbone and Vicky had left he strolled over to Sukey's desk. 'So you've been taken off the Whistler case?' he said.

'So it would seem. How did you know?'

'I was with the DCI while he was talking to Greg Rathbone. I'm more or less off it as well, now that we've shut down the incident room at the hotel – greatly to the manager's relief.'

'Have there been any other developments that I don't know about?'

'Not that I've heard of. Did you get any joy out of Ms Henderson this morning by the way?'

'She's going to let us have photocopies of Boris Gasspar's paperwork. He has a NI number and the hotel followed up a reference he gave them, so it looks as if he might be here legally after all. If that's the case, it rather puts the kybosh on my theory that he was blackmailed into giving false evidence against Stephen Lamont. Assuming the reference was genuine of course.'

Douglas chuckled. 'And you'd just love to find out it's phoney, wouldn't you? I know how you feel; it's great when one of your hunches pays off, especially when everyone else thinks you're barking up the wrong tree.'

Sukey gave him a grateful smile. The contrast between his sympathetic manner and Rathbone's thinly veiled contempt was heart-warming. 'Thanks for saying that. Tell me, do you still think Lamont is guilty?'

'To be honest, yes, but it's going to be difficult to build a case the CPS will allow to go to court. I admit that on the face of it Gasspar's link with Maddox does muddy the waters a bit, but it doesn't necessarily mean it has anything to do with the attack on Whistler. Lamont hasn't been able to produce a single witness to back up his story, whereas in addition to Gasspar more than one independent witness saw a man answering Lamont's description at a time he swears he wasn't there. They can't all have been got at by Maddox.'

'I suppose not,' Sukey admitted with a sigh. 'Well, I'd better get on and write up my report.'

When she had finished she printed off a copy, put it in DS Rathbone's in-tray and then went to the washroom. She was away for only a few minutes, but when she returned there was a general buzz of excitement in the office.

'What's going on?' she asked Anna, the civilian worker whom she had met at the incident room at the Mariners Hotel.

'Someone's reported seeing a body on the banks of the Avon, a mile or so downstream from the suspension bridge,' said Anna. 'The DCI has summoned DS Douglas so I guess he'll be assigned to the case.'

A few minutes later Douglas returned. Catching sight of Sukey, he came over to her and said, 'I guess Anna's put you in the picture. DCI Leach has put me on the case and as you're

at a loose end this afternoon he suggests I take you along for
the experience. I've booked a car.' He picked up his jacket
and headed for the door. 'Come on, let's go.'

They left the city centre and headed along the Portway in
the direction of Avonmouth. A mile or so beyond the famous
Clifton Suspension Bridge the nearside lane had been closed
causing a tailback of cars whose drivers, despite furious
gestures from the police urging them to keep moving, persisted
in slowing to a crawl while craning to see what was going
on. Douglas got out of the car and walked ahead to speak to
the officer directing the traffic; as Sukey at last drew level he
signalled to her to pull in behind a long line of emergency
vehicles, including two fire engines, an ambulance, several
police cars, a police van and two smaller vans that Sukey
recognized from her days working as a Scenes of Crime
Officer. Ahead, the fire crews and a team of police frogmen
were dragging various items of equipment from their vehicles and disappearing with them down the steep side of the
Avon Gorge to the riverside path below.

A middle-aged couple standing on the footpath beside one
of the police cars were talking to another officer, who made
an excuse and broke off the conversation for a moment when
he spotted DS Douglas. Evidently they were old friends, for
he greeted him as "Bob" and Douglas addressed him as
"Snoopy" before introducing Sukey by saying, 'Meet DC
Sukey Reynolds. She's just finished her six months with Vicky
Armstrong. Sukey, Sergeant Brown, Traffic Division.'

'Glad to know you, Sukey,' said the sergeant. 'I got that
disrespectful nickname because my real one's Charlie,' he
explained. 'You can just forget it – and that's an order,' he
added.

'Yes, Sarge,' she said primly.

His manner, which had been only half serious, became grave
as he said, 'You might find this a bit hard to take. A goner
that's been in the water for any length of time isn't a pretty
sight.'

'I know, I've seen one before,' said Sukey. 'During my five
years as a SOCO,' she explained in response to his look of
surprise. 'And that one had its head hacked off,' she added.

The sergeant pulled a face. 'That must have been seriously
stomach churning,' he observed. 'Well, I'd better get back and

finish talking to the Telfords.' He jerked his head in the direction of the man and woman who were still waiting a short
distance away. 'They spotted the body while they were walking
Monty along the riverside path.' Hearing its name, the black
and white cocker spaniel sitting patiently at their feet stood
up and wagged its tail. 'They don't have a mobile,' he went
on, 'so they came up here and managed to flag down a passing
patrol car. I was taking some details when you arrived.'

While they were waiting for him to return, Sukey and
Douglas went to the protective rail that ran along the edge of
the gorge and peered down through a gap in the tangle of
trees and bushes. The tide was low, reducing the river to a
narrow channel and exposing a wide expanse of glistening
mud the colour of milk chocolate. Gulls screeched and
swooped overhead and a heron stood motionless at the water's
edge a little way downstream from where they were standing,
staring intently into the muddy depths and apparently unfazed
by the activity on the opposite bank. They waited while the
sergeant finished dealing with the couple, escorted them to
their car and held up the traffic to enable them to pull out and
drive away before walking back. He indicated a gap in the
railing, where the last of the frogmen was just disappearing
down a flight of steps.

'Down here and mind how you go,' he warned them. 'It's
fairly steep, but there's a handrail of sorts. We haven't been
able to get close enough to the body yet to establish any
details, but it's near enough to the bank for us to see it's
female,' he said as Sukey and DS Douglas cautiously followed
him. 'There's a fire crew down there now, making a walkway
over the mud. They've got to work fast because the tide's
coming in. It's this way.' He set off along a grassy path in the
direction of Sea Mills until, round a bend in the river, they
saw a group of firemen laying a line of aluminium planks
across the mud while teams of frogmen and SOCOs stood by,
awaiting the opportunity to carry out their respective tasks.
Two uniformed officers were shooing away a few curious
would-be onlookers out on an afternoon stroll.

Sukey took a pair of miniature binoculars from the pocket
of her denim jacket and focused them on the corpse, which
lay behind a spit of mud that generations of rising and falling
tides had sculpted into a shape like the head of some strange

sea monster. The contours outlined by the clinging, mud-stained garments and the long hair wound like strands of seaweed over the face and throat confirmed that the victim was female and probably quite young.

'The headless body I mentioned just now had been in the water for some days and it looked pretty horrible,' she said, shuddering at the memory. 'It doesn't look to me as if this one's been in there all that long. What do you think?'

'I think you've got a point,' said Douglas, who had been carrying out a similar assessment. 'Snoopy's right – they'll have to work fast,' he added with a glance at his watch. 'According to my reckoning it was low tide more than three hours ago and it's coming in at quite a rate.'

They watched in silence while the firemen laid the last plank in position. A man in civilian clothes was the first to make his way gingerly along the improvised walkway. When he reached the motionless figure he squatted down and took a stethoscope from his pocket.

'That's Doctor Hanley, our forensic pathologist,' Douglas explained.

The examination was soon over. Hanley returned to the bank and picked up the bag he had left on the ground, spoke briefly to Sergeant Brown and then walked over to where Sukey and DS Douglas stood watching the proceedings.

'Afternoon, Sergeant,' he said. 'Young woman, aged about sixteen at a rough guess. I reckon she's been dead at least a couple of days, but she hasn't been in the water as long as that.'

'So it's not a drowning?' said Douglas.

The pathologist shook his head. 'Almost certainly not. There appear to be some injuries, but there's so much mud plastered around I can't be sure whether they were sustained before or after death. When you get her to terra firma I'll have a closer look, but you'll have to wait till she's been cleaned up before I can do a detailed report.' He strolled over to a wooden bench beside the path and sat down.

Meanwhile a team of frogmen had made their way past the body and were examining the shallows prior to exploring the deeper water. Two SOCOs in white protective clothing who had followed close behind them began their examination, one taking photographs while the other squatted down to scoop up samples of mud and water and put them in sealed and labelled containers. The river was rising rapidly as the tide swept up from the Bristol Channel and by the time they had finished and Sukey and Douglas were able to make their own hasty examination in search of possible evidence it was lapping at the dead girl's feet. Minutes later they were forced to retreat to enable the firemen to bring her ashore.

'She's not much more than a child!' Sukey exclaimed. She felt a lump rising in her throat as she looked down at the slender form on the mortuary slab.

Doctor Hanley nodded. 'Sixteen at the most,' he said. 'Not exactly under-nourished, but not much fat on her either. Typical of kids of her age, of course – they all want to look like bean-poles so she's probably been watching her figure. To please the boyfriend, most likely,' he added. 'And from the state of her she's had quite a few.'

'Can you give us a better idea now of how long she's been dead?' asked Rathbone.

'As I said earlier, she was in the water for only a few hours, but she could have died a couple of days before that. I'll know more when I've examined the stomach contents.'

'Is that all you can tell us for now?' Rathbone asked.

'Yes – except that she's recently been subjected to a bit of rough treatment. Not serious stuff, probably some foreplay that got out of hand. See those bruises on the throat?' Hanley went on, pointing with a long, delicate finger at some livid marks below the girl's jaw. 'Whoever put those there might have intended to kill her, but I think it's more likely he acci-dentally squeezed a bit too hard in the heat of the moment.'

'You can't say which?' asked DS Douglas.

The doctor's grin transformed his thin, beaky features. 'No idea, mate,' he said cheerfully. 'It's your job to find out. All I can say for sure is that she didn't drown, she died of manual strangulation.'

Seventeen

I t was after six o'clock by the time Sukey and DS Douglas got back to the station. They went straight up to DCI Leach's office.

'This is going to be a tough one,' Leach remarked when he had heard their account of the afternoon's events. 'I take it there was no ID on the body, Bob?'

'Not a thing, sir. We'll check the list of local mispers of course, but I'm pretty certain none of them answers to that girl's description.'

'Could she have been brought here from somewhere outside the area?' Sukey suggested.

Both men shook their heads. 'I doubt it,' said Leach. 'From what you two have told me, it's most likely that whoever did it had local knowledge.'

'I'd go along with that,' said Douglas. 'She was almost certainly dumped when the tide was full, or nearly full, probably by someone with a boat. We'll have to consult our river expert; he'll be able to give us some idea of where a body would have to enter the water to reach that particular spot before the tide was low enough to expose it.'

'It must have been there for quite a long time before the Telfords saw it,' Sukey remarked. 'It's surprising it wasn't spotted sooner.'

'Not really,' said Douglas. 'There's no river traffic when the water's low and more often than not you can walk the length of that footpath without meeting a soul. It's different at weekends, of course, but this was a Monday morning.'

'That's true,' she admitted, recalling that only a handful of people had turned up during the afternoon while the body was being retrieved. 'But what about the path on the opposite bank? I suppose most of the girl's body would have been concealed by that long spit of mud, but one of her legs was sticking out beyond the end of it. Anyone with reasonable eyesight could have seen it.'

Leach shook his head a second time, but he gave Sukey an encouraging smile. Her mind went back to the day he had called her for an interview after she had completed her probationary six months with Vicky. She remembered him saying that he wanted her to feel free to offer suggestions or make constructive comments as the occasion demanded. It was, she reflected wryly, an attitude that DS Rathbone had shown little inclination to adopt.

'Theoretically that's feasible,' he agreed, 'but in practice, anyone walking or cycling along there who happened to glance across would be more likely to assume it was a piece of rubbish someone had thrown overboard – if they noticed it at all. Cyclists tend to look ahead rather than around them. On balance, I'd say we were fortunate she didn't lie there until the tide covered her a second time. OK, you know what to do next, Bob. Keep me posted.'

'Yes, sir.'

On their way back to the main office, Douglas remarked, 'You've picked up quite a bit of local knowledge today, Sukey. It'll all come in handy some time or other.'

It had been an eventful day. On reaching home, over an hour later than usual, Sukey went into the kitchen and set one of the prepared meals she kept for such occasions to defrost in the microwave before taking a quick shower and changing into a sweatshirt and jeans. The light on her answering machine indicated that there were messages waiting; she poured out a glass of wine and sat down in an armchair with the phone at her elbow, but it rang before she had time to press the replay button. Jim was on the line.

'Thank goodness you're home!' he exclaimed as soon as she answered. 'I left a message and you didn't call back; I was getting worried.'

'Detectives don't always work regular hours,' she reminded him. 'There have been plenty of times when you didn't show and I imagined you being mown down by a thug with a shooter.'

'I know, I know!' he said. 'Scold me if you must, but you know me – one of the world's champion worriers.'

'All right, you're forgiven.'

'So what sort of a day have you had?'

'Eventful. To start with, I think you'll be interested to know I seem to be off the Whistler case.'

'Seem to be?'

'I was supposed to go with DS Rathbone to interview Professor Thorne's secretary – the one who was with Oliver Maddox in the restaurant the other night, but he took Vicky Armstrong instead. Your friend DCI Leach decided he didn't want her reporting back to her boyfriend that I was still involved in the Whistler investigation, just in case Maddox did spot me that afternoon and it was my card that he took from Boris.'

'It's probably a wise precaution,' said Jim.

'Actually, I wasn't all that sorry,' said Sukey. 'My exercise in unofficial surveillance hasn't made me flavour of the month with DS Rathbone and he's made no attempt to disguise the fact.'

'So what have you been doing today that made you work overtime?'

'Witnessing the body of a teenage girl being recovered from the river – or rather the riverbank. She was left exposed when the tide went out and getting her to dry land was quite a performance on account of the mud.'

'Suicide?' asked Jim.

'Definitely not. The pathologist reckons she could have been dead for a couple of days before she was put in the water. Come to think of it, she might be another victim of the Maddox mafia,' she added wickedly, picturing his change of expression as the thought registered.

'Good heavens, is that what—' He realized she was having him on. 'You just said that to wind me up,' he said reproachfully.

'Guilty – but you must admit I'm rather good at it.'

'You're rather good at other things as well,' he said with another, more subtle change of tone. 'When am I going to see you again?'

It had been a tiring as well as an eventful day. Without warning, she found herself engulfed by a mighty yawn. 'Gosh, I'm sorry,' she said. 'I hadn't realized how tired I am, and I haven't eaten yet either. Can we talk about it some other time? I'm simply not up to making plans this evening.'

'No problem,' he said softly. 'I'll call again soon. Take care.'

After he hung up she finished her wine and then checked her messages. She deleted the one from Jim and then listened to the next. It was from Fergus.

'Nothing special, just rang for a chat,' he said breezily. 'I'll try again later.'

The last message was from Priscilla Gadden. 'Sukey, I'm sorry to bother you, but I've had Hester Lamont here all day. She's found out somehow that you're in the police and involved in her brother's case, and she's desperate to talk to you. Can you possibly find a moment to call me back?'

'Not till I've had some food, I couldn't,' Sukey said aloud as she pressed the delete button.

She put her defrosted supermarket shepherd's pie into the oven, topped up her wine glass, put on a recording of Mozart piano sonatas and relaxed in her favourite armchair until the pie was ready. A little over an hour later, feeling somewhat revived, she sent a text message to Fergus on his mobile, promising to call him later, and then keyed in Priscilla's number. Tom Gadden answered.

'Sorry to call so late,' she began, 'but when I got home I found a message from Priscilla and it sounded urgent. Is she there, please?'

'She is, and so is the Lamont Limpet,' he said with a touch of impatience. 'If you can get this crazy female off my wife's back I'll be very much obliged. Wait a minute, I'll call her.'

When Priscilla came on the line she said, 'Oh, Sukey, it's so good of you to call. Could you possibly have a word with Hester? She's convinced now that Stephen is innocent and that she knows who killed Doctor Whistler.'

'Whatever's happened to make her change her mind? Has she found new evidence?'

'I've no idea. She won't tell me anything; she wants to speak to you.'

'I take it she's discussed this with her brother?'

'It seems she's tried to and he's told her to keep out of it.'

'That's probably good advice in view of her mental state,' said Sukey. 'Look, I honestly don't think I can help. There have been certain developments; I can't give you any details, but—'

'You don't mean the police are going to charge Stephen?' Priscilla interrupted in dismay.

'I'm not saying that, but if Hester has some important new evidence she should come to the station straight away and make a statement.'

'I've already advised her to do that, but she won't hear of it – at least, not without speaking to you first. She says you understand her problems; she keeps going on about how sympathetic you are and you should be a counsellor and so on. Tom's getting really hot under the collar and I'm at my wits' end what to do with her.'

'I take it she's not in the room with you at the moment?'

'No, she's watching the television and Patsy's with her. Please, Sukey, will you at least listen to what she has to say?'

Sukey sighed. 'All right, put her on then.'

There was a brief pause before Priscilla said, 'I know this is asking an awful lot, but do you think you could possibly come here and talk to her? I think . . . I know she'd talk more freely face to face. I wouldn't ask if you lived any distance away,' she hurried on, 'but as you're only just down the road . . . or perhaps I could bring her down to your place?'

'Certainly not, and please, on no account tell her where I live,' said Sukey in alarm. 'I don't want her banging on my door at all hours and besides, it so happens I'm now working on a different case.'

'Oh dear!' Priscilla sounded distraught. 'What am I to tell her then?'

'All right, I'll pop round and see what I can do,' said Sukey resignedly.

'Would you? We'd be so grateful.'

'I'll wait for a bit and then come in the car. If I turn up within the next five minutes she'll twig that I live on your doorstep.'

'That would make sense,' Priscilla agreed. 'I'll make sure the gates are open for you.'

Hester Lamont looked even paler and more fragile than Sukey remembered from their previous meeting. She was sitting with her head bowed and her hands clasped in her lap, but on hearing Priscilla say, 'Hester, here's Sukey come to see you', she raised her head and gave a wan smile.

'Thank you for coming,' she said simply.

'You want to tell me something?' Sukey said.

'Yes, but—' She gave a self-conscious glance at Patsy and her mother. 'If you wouldn't mind—?'

'We'll leave you to it,' said Patsy with evident relief.

As the door closed behind them, Hester clutched Sukey by the hand and said, 'I can't tell you how badly I feel at doubting Stephen. All this time he's been swearing he didn't kill that man, and I wouldn't believe him. I kept saying I understood why he did it and that I was really to blame, and he kept saying I'd got it all wrong and I didn't know what I was talking about and then I tried to cut myself again and he got really angry and said if I did it one more time he'd have me shut up for ever. And now I know he was telling the truth all along and I'll never forgive myself, never!' She burst into loud, wailing sobs that racked her thin frame for several minutes.

When at last she was calmer she drank some water that had been left on the table and said, 'I'm sorry, I didn't mean to break down like that.'

'It's natural; you've been under a lot of strain,' said Sukey. 'And now perhaps you can tell me why you're so sure your brother didn't kill Doctor Whistler.'

'It's very simple,' Hester said earnestly, her soft brown eyes fixed on Sukey's face. 'This morning I saw the man who did it.'

'You what?'

'The man who did it – I saw him,' Hester repeated.

'I don't understand,' Sukey said in bewilderment. 'Where did you see this man and how do you know he's the man who killed Whistler?'

'I was doing some shopping in Clifton Village and as I came out of the deli he was getting into a car parked just outside. He was the image of Stephen, except that his hair was shorter but Stephen does go to the barber sometimes . . . and he was wearing jeans and Stephen hardly ever wears jeans . . . but otherwise he, this man, was exactly like him . . . and for a moment I was so sure it was him that I called out, "Stephen, whatever are you doing here?" because of course I thought he was in his study at home . . . he's on indefinite leave while all this dreadful business is going on . . . and he – this man I mean – looked a bit surprised and shut his car door and drove away in a great hurry. And then I realized that it wasn't Stephen's car at all . . . and all of a sudden it came to me. He must be the murderer and it's all been a, what do you call it, a case of mistaken identity.'

Eighteen

As she listened in astonishment while Hester poured out the string of breathless, disjointed sentences, Sukey found herself seriously doubting the woman's sanity. By the time she reached the climax of her story she was like someone who had seen a vision, hands clasped and eyes shining with expectation as she gazed at the one person she felt able to trust. Momentarily speechless after the verbal onslaught, it took Sukey several seconds to find a suitable response. Hester seemed to read her hesitation as rejection; the brightness slowly died from her expression and her hands fell limply into her lap. 'You think I'm crazy, don't you?' she muttered.

'No, of course not,' Sukey said quickly. 'It's just . . . well, it's certainly a remarkable coincidence and I can understand why you've reacted in the way you have after seeing this man.'

Hope rekindled in the trusting brown eyes. 'Then you think I'm right?'

'There's no doubt that there have been cases of mistaken identity,' Sukey said carefully, 'and I do think this one is worth investigating, but all I can do is pass on what you've told me to the officer in charge of the investigation.'

'But don't you see, this changes everything!'

'It may well do, but it really isn't up to me to decide. What I suggest you do,' Sukey went on before Hester could start another protest, 'is write down very carefully everything you saw this morning, what time it happened, how the man was dressed, what kind of car he was driving and so on. I don't suppose you got the car number, by the way?'

Hester shook her head despondently. 'No, I'm afraid not,' she said. 'It was a big black car, I do remember that, and it had some sort of animal on the back shelf.'

'That's not a lot to go on, but it's something.' Sukey tried her best to sound encouraging. 'Is there anything else you remember about him? Was he wearing any jewellery – a signet ring, for example? Shut your eyes for a moment and try to picture him.'

Hester covered her entire face with her hands, like a child playing hide and seek. 'I seem to recall something gold,' she said vaguely. 'A wristwatch, perhaps . . . no, I remember now!' Her voice rose to a squeak of excitement; she lowered her hands and looked at Sukey in triumph. 'He wore an earring. How stupid of me not to think of it. I should have realized it couldn't possibly be Stephen.'

'Very good.' Sukey took a notebook from her pocket and scribbled a few lines. 'Would that be in his right or his left ear?'

'Right,' said Hester without hesitation. 'He came from my left and got straight into his car, so I didn't see the other side of his face at all.'

'Anything else? Any distinguishing marks like a scar or a tattoo, for example.'

'I didn't notice anything like that, I'm afraid.'

'Well, if you think of anything else, write it down with everything else you've told me and then call the police station and ask to speak to Detective Sergeant Rathbone. I'll tell him about this and if you don't feel up to coming down to the CID office he'll arrange to come and see you.'

'At home?' Hester looked aghast. 'But I don't want Stephen to know I've been talking to you . . . he's always telling me not to meddle with things I don't understand.'

'Then I'm afraid you'll have to come to the station.' Sukey stood up. 'I'm going home now and I think you should do the same or your brother will be worried about you.'

'It's all right; he knows where I am. Perhaps Tom and Priscilla would let me meet the detective here,' Hester said, sounding almost desperate. 'Then Stephen wouldn't know anything about this until it's all cleared up.'

Sukey felt a twinge of sadness. Clearly, Hester was still clinging to a pathetic belief in her theory. Aloud, she said, 'That's a good idea. Why don't you ask them?' Gently brushing aside the woman's earnest thanks, she made her escape.

As she returned to the hall, closing the door behind her, Priscilla appeared from another room. 'How is she now?' she asked anxiously.

'Calmer, but she's in a pretty volatile state of mind. She claims to have seen Stephen's doppelgänger in Clifton this morning and she's convinced that this man and not Stephen committed the murder.'

Priscilla's jaw dropped. 'How extraordinary! Do you think there could be anything in it?'

Sukey had been tired before she set out on this bizarre visit and the interview had taken more out of her emotionally than she realized. She put both hands to her temples in an effort to soothe away the weariness seeping into her brain. 'I honestly don't know,' she said. 'Coming from a more rational person I'd be inclined to take it seriously, but in Hester's case—'

'Yes, I know what you mean.' Priscilla cast an anxious glance over Sukey's shoulder and lowered her voice. 'What have you told her? Tom's insisting on taking her home the minute you've finished with her so that we can all get some rest.'

'That's all right,' said Sukey. 'That's what I advised her to do and I don't think she'll argue. I've also told her to write down what she's told me and then to ring the station and ask to speak to Detective Sergeant Rathbone. That seems to have satisfied her for the moment, but whether it'll be taken seriously is up to the SIO to decide. Senior Investigating Officer,' she explained in response to Priscilla's questioning look.

'I see. Well, thank you so much for coming.'

'No problem, but it's only fair to warn you that she may ask if she can meet the detectives here.'

Priscilla rolled her eyes in despair. 'Tom'll go ballistic!' she groaned.

'Her idea, not mine,' Sukey assured her. 'Anyway, one way or the other I'll keep you posted.'

As soon as she reported for duty the following morning Sukey managed to snatch a brief word with Vicky Armstrong. As she had anticipated, Vicky was sceptical.

'You don't reckon there's anything in it, do you?' she said.

'I don't think Hester was making it up – I mean, I'm sure she did see someone with a close resemblance to her brother and that must have put the idea about mistaken identity into her head. How much of what she told me is accurate and how much is embroidery is anyone's guess, but the fact is she's now beating her breast with guilt at having doubted him.'

Vicky shrugged. 'She's hardly a reliable witness, is she? I'll mention it to DS Rathbone, but I doubt if he'll act on it. Maybe you'd better put in a written report.'

'Yes, I'll do that when I've got a moment,' said Sukey. 'Just now I'm up to my eyes in the Avon river case. DS Douglas has just dumped the file of local mispers on my desk.'

'Lucky old you,' said Vicky cheerfully.

Sukey went to her desk and began work on the daunting task of checking reports of teenage girls missing from homes in Bristol and the surrounding areas. The most recent was dated over a week ago, which suggested that the unidentified girl whose body had been washed up on the muddy banks of the Avon had either disappeared from home so recently that her absence had not yet been reported, or that she came from further afield and had for some unknown reason made her way to Bristol before meeting her violent end.

After a couple of hours of fruitless searching she felt in need of a break, so she pushed the file aside and wrote a brief account of her meeting with Hester Lamont the previous evening. After printing it off she put it in DS Rathbone's in-tray and went down to the canteen for a much needed cup of coffee. When she returned twenty minutes later she found him with her report in one hand and his phone in the other. As she entered he said, 'She's just walked in, sir. We'll come right away.' He cradled the instrument and glared at her.

'Just what do you imagine you're playing at?' he demanded.

'Playing, Sarge? I don't understand. All I did was—'

'Disobey orders,' he barked, brandishing the report under her nose and making no effort to keep his voice down. 'You were told you were off the Lamont case – or are you too thick to understand plain English? DCI Leach wants us both in his office about this load of garbage . . . now!' He turned on his heel and headed for the door. Aware that heads were turning in her direction, Sukey felt her cheeks burn as she followed him out of the room. She braced herself for another verbal onslaught the minute the door closed behind them, but he marched along the corridor in silence, his face grim.

DCI Leach's expression as they entered his office was only marginally less unfriendly. He was seated at his desk and held out his hand for her report on her interview with Hester Lamont without inviting either of them to sit down. He scanned it briefly, put it on the desk in front of him and said, 'Perhaps you'd care to explain why you agreed to see this woman when you were expressly told you were to have nothing more to do with this case.'

It was hardly a fair statement as no such specific order had been given, but Sukey had the sense not to argue.

'I assure you, sir, that I had absolutely no intention of disobeying orders,' she said. 'I went to the Gaddens' house at the urgent request of Mrs Gadden because Hester Lamont had gone to see her in a state of agitation bordering on hysteria, begging to be put in touch with me because she had something important to say concerning her brother.'

'Why you?' said Leach.

'If you recall, sir, I met her once before at the Gaddens' house and I made a detailed report of the conversation.'

Leach pursed his lips and raised an eyebrow in Rathbone's direction. The sergeant cleared his throat and said, 'That's true, sir; the report is on the file. It's chiefly concerned with the unfortunate events in Ms Lamont's life that led to her mental breakdown. She was not aware at the time that she was speaking to a police officer.'

'But she knows now?' This time the eyebrow was directed at Sukey.

'Yes, sir, but I've no idea how she found out. When I spoke to Priscilla – Mrs Gadden – I told her she should advise Hester to get in touch with the CID office and tell them what was on her mind. She said she'd tried that but Hester flatly refused to confide in anyone but me because she said I'd been kind and sympathetic last time. The Gaddens were getting desperate, so in the end I agreed to listen to what she said. Everything that passed between us is contained in that report.'

Leach leaned on one elbow and fiddled with his glasses as he reread the single sheet of A4 paper. After a moment or two he looked up and met her eye. His expression was kindlier than when she and Rathbone first entered the office, although he did not smile. 'I can see that you acted with the best of intentions,' he said, 'but please remember in future that investigations can be put at risk through well-intentioned, but misguided, actions. Your proper course in this case would have been to decline the request and advise Mrs Gadden to contact us herself if Ms Lamont continued to refuse to do so. We could then have sent a trained counsellor to interview her. Is that understood?'

'Yes, sir,' said Sukey meekly.

'Good. Has there been any progress in finding an ID for the Avon River victim?'

'Not so far, sir.'

'Well, keep at it. That's all for now.' He handed the report back to Rathbone and said, 'You'd better follow this up, Greg. There may be nothing in it, but we can't risk a defence counsel getting hold of it . . . assuming the Lamont case ever gets to court.'

'Right, sir.'

Sukey half expected some caustic comment as she and Rathbone made their way back to the CID office, but he had the grace to remain silent – possibly, she suspected, because his failure to refer to her earlier report had caused him a twinge of embarrassment.

Later, when she went down to the canteen for lunch, Vicky came and sat at her table demanding to know what had passed during the interview with Leach. 'The sarge was like a bear with a sore head for the rest of the morning,' she confided gleefully. 'We all felt for you when he started bawling you out so when he came back looking less than pleased with himself we wondered whether he'd been given a flea in his ear.'

'Not exactly, but I think he was disappointed I didn't get more severely reprimanded than I did.'

'Serve him right. He's a really good cop,' Vicky went on, 'but he's on a pretty short fuse at times. He ranted on for about five minutes about having to follow up what he called the ravings of a madwoman, but when he calmed down he told me to set up a meeting with me, Hester and the same FLO we sent last week when we took Lamont in. That should reassure her.'

'You will keep me posted, won't you?' said Sukey. 'I've still got a feeling about that case and in a way I wish I hadn't been taken off it, although – ' she glanced round and dropped her voice – 'I was never actually told as much in so many words, only that it was unwise for me to be at the interview with Thorne's secretary. What happened about that, by the way?'

'Not a lot. The woman was quite definite she'd heard nothing about Whistler planning to go to London and there seemed no reason to think she was lying.'

'I'll bet that pleased DS Rathbone,' said Sukey dryly. 'The last thing he wants is to come across anything that casts doubts on Lamont's guilt.'

Vicky nodded. 'That's true, but what he wants more than anything is one solid piece of evidence that will justify charging Lamont.'

'Have the results of the DNA tests on his clothing come through yet?'

'Yes, and they're inconclusive, so we're a bit bogged down at the moment. We've checked the people Lamont and Thorne told us might have gone into their offices and possibly seen or heard something relevant, but we've had no luck there either. The next step is to renew our appeal for help from the public. That's going out on the news this evening.' Vicky pushed back her empty plate and stood up. 'Well, back to the grind. Any progress on the river victim, by the way?'

Sukey shook her head. 'I'm afraid not. Reports on finding the body got into the late editions yesterday and more details are in today's, but so far we've had no new report of a missing girl. A description has been circulated to the national media, but if we don't get a response soon we'll have to publish a picture.'

The response, when it came, was of a totally unexpected nature.

Nineteen

The following morning Sukey received a call from Erika Henderson to say that she had made photocopies of all the paperwork she had in her file concerning Boris Gasspar.

'Would you like me to put them in the post or would you rather I handed them over to you in person?' she asked and then added in a slightly lower tone, 'Actually, I would prefer to meet you if you can spare the time.'

'Any particular reason?' Sukey asked warily. The thought came immediately into her head that as she was no longer on the Whistler case she should, strictly speaking, refer this call to DS Rathbone and get his approval or otherwise to still attend the meeting.

Before she had a chance to explain her situation Erika said, 'Hold on a minute.' There was a pause, during which she could be heard in conversation with a man, presumably the hotel manager, who was in the room with her. After a few indistinguishable exchanges she said, her voice slightly raised as if he was about to leave, 'Right, Maurice, I'll be with you right away.' Returning to the phone she said hurriedly, 'Sorry, I have to go now. Are you free at lunchtime today?'

'As far as I know, but—'

'If you're pushed for time, I could meet you somewhere closer to the police station than Spend and Save. There's a café called the Rendezvous near the centre that I use sometimes.'

'I know it,' Sukey said hesitantly. During the break in their conversation she had been trying to decide how best to respond to Erika's request. Whatever she had to say, it was clear that she had no intention of revealing it over the phone. She glanced round the office; there was no sign of either Rathbone or Vicky, no one to whom she could turn to for advice. This was ridiculous, she told herself; merely to collect something she had been told to ask for in the first place could hardly be construed as disobeying orders. In any case, Erika's reason for wanting to meet her might have nothing whatever to do with the Whistler case, and if it did she could simply explain the changed circumstances and refer her to DS Rathbone.

Having thus rationalized the situation she said, 'As things are at the moment I can make it. What time do you suggest?'

'Let's say twelve thirty?'

'All right, but if something crops up I may have to cancel. I'd better have your mobile number just in case.' She jotted it down and hung up just as DS Douglas appeared with a box file under one arm.

'Reports of missing girls from our friends in other parts of the country,' he announced as he dumped it on her desk. 'There should be enough in there to keep you out of mischief till lunchtime.'

'Thanks, Sarge,' she said. 'Where will you be if I come across anything interesting?'

'If that's a subtle way of asking what I'll be doing, the answer is I'll be at the morgue with the privileged few observing Doc Hanley dissecting the Lady in the Avon.'

Sukey grimaced. 'Rather you than me, Sarge, but why the delay?'

'Pressure of other work, so he says. I've seen quite a number of PMs in my time but I can't say I'm looking forward to it,' he added with some feeling.

As soon as he left she opened the file and began working through the reports. After a preliminary run through she weeded out those that were obviously irrelevant to the current enquiry and set them aside. Of the remainder, a considerable number were of girls whose families believed for one reason or another might have come to the South West. She was able to eliminate most of these fairly quickly, either because they were the wrong age or colouring or had distinguishing marks not found on the body of the Avon victim and vice versa, but there were some that she put aside for more detailed investigation. She became so absorbed in the task that on glancing up for a moment she was surprised see that it was gone twelve o'clock. She returned the rejected reports to the box, put the rest into a folder and stowed them away in a drawer. She was on the point of leaving to keep her appointment with Erika Henderson when DS Douglas appeared.

'Thank goodness that's over,' he said, dropping into the chair next to hers.

Noticing that he was paler than usual, she said. 'Was it very gruesome?'

'No more than any other, but like I said it's never something I enjoy watching. As Doc Hanley has already told us, the cause of death was manual strangulation, but of course he had to stick to the rules and go through the complete procedure.' He took out a handkerchief and wiped his forehead. 'I was thinking of grabbing some lunch, but I'm not sure I can face food.'

'You ought to eat something,' she said sympathetically. 'Something light – soup and a salad, perhaps?'

'Maybe I could manage that. How about joining me? I promise not to put you off your nosh with a lot of gory details.'

'Actually, I'm supposed to be meeting someone for lunch. I could put it off till another time if you feel in the need of company,' she added, half hoping he would accept her offer and give her an excuse to cancel her meeting with Erika, but he gave a half-hearted smile and shook his head.

'No need for that, thanks all the same. There's sure to be someone in the canteen to chat to. How did you get on with the misper reports?'

'Nothing positive so far, but a few worth a closer look.'

'Good. We'll go over them together after lunch.'

When Sukey reached the Rendezvous café she found Erika already installed at a corner table. 'I've ordered an omelette,' she announced, holding up a menu. 'They do good ones here, particularly the mushroom.'

'Right, I'll take your advice.' Sukey went to the counter and gave her order.

'I said I wanted to see you, but I didn't explain why,' Erika said when she returned to the table. 'But before we go any further, have you found the person who killed Doctor Whistler? There was something on the news a few days ago about a man helping with enquiries and then nothing more. Am I right in thinking it was Professor Lamont?'

'I'm sorry, I can't answer any questions about that,' said Sukey. 'Apart from anything else, I'm not on the case any more, so if you don't mind I'd rather not talk about it.'

'Not on the case?' Erika appeared taken aback and Sukey sensed that she was disappointed. 'But why?'

'I can't tell you that either. Look, on second thoughts I don't think I'll stay for lunch. If you'll just give me the photocopies I'll get back to the station.'

'No, please, you've already ordered, you can't go now. At least listen to what I have to say. I do have a particular reason for asking about Professor Lamont.'

'I'd really rather you changed the subject. If what you have to say concerns the Whistler murder I suggest you call at the station and ask to see Sergeant Rathbone.'

Erika looked faintly embarrassed. 'I'd prefer to tell you first. I'm afraid he'd laugh at me or make me feel a fool by telling me I've been watching too many crime series on TV. I'm sure he's a good detective,' she hurried on, 'but to be honest, I didn't find him a very sympathetic character, if you know what I mean.'

Yes, I know exactly what you mean, Sukey agreed mentally. Aloud, she said, 'All right, you can tell me as long as you understand I can't comment or answer any questions.'

'Yes, I accept that, and I promise I'll come to the station and make a proper statement if you think I should.'

'So what is it then?'

Erika leaned forward and lowered her voice. 'The other day, I saw—' she began and then broke off as a waiter brought their omelettes and cutlery.

'Saw what?' said Sukey a little impatiently when the waiter had left.

'Not a what, a who,' said Erika. 'His double. Professor Lamont's, I mean. No kidding!' she went on as Sukey's fork stopped in mid-air on the way to her mouth. 'It was uncanny. I went into an off licence in Clifton Village and this man was there buying wine and I almost said, "Good morning, Professor Lamont" and then I realized it wasn't him at all. For one thing his hair was much shorter and he had a gold ring in one ear, which doesn't quite fit Lamont's image, but he was the same build and the facial likeness was so striking that I felt quite spooked for a moment. And then it occurred to me,' she went on, 'the man Boris Gasspar saw entering and leaving the hotel by the staff entrance, the one he's so sure was Professor Lamont, could easily have been this man. After all, he only saw him for a few seconds and he wouldn't have been paying particular attention – it was only when Professor Lamont came to the desk that he noticed the likeness. And if he wore a wig – this chap I saw in Clifton, that is – Boris could easily have been confused. I can see you think so as well,' she went on, as if encouraged by what she read in Sukey's expression.

After a few moments' stunned silence, during which she tried to get her chaotic thoughts into some kind of order, Sukey said, 'It could be a coincidence, but I think DS Rathbone should know about it. I suggest you have a word with him as soon as possible.'

'Do I have to? I thought if I told you and you thought it might be important, you could pass it on.'

'I'm sorry, you'll have to speak to him yourself. As I said, I'm not on the case any more, in fact I shall probably get my knuckles rapped for agreeing to talk to you.'

'How petty!' Erika said indignantly. 'I didn't know the police had such silly rules.'

'There are reasons,' said Sukey evasively.

'Well don't worry, I won't let anyone know I've been telling you all this.'

'But you will do as I suggest and go and see Sergeant Rathbone? I can promise you he'll take it seriously.' *He'll jolly well have to after what Hester told me*, Sukey thought with no little sense of satisfaction. 'You could ask for Detective Constable Vicky Armstrong if you'd prefer to talk to a woman,' she added.

'All right, I'll do that,' Erika said with evident relief. 'I'm so glad you think it could be important. There's one more thing. When this man left the shop I watched him through the window. His car was parked just outside and I made a note of the number as he pulled away. I wrote it on the back of this.' She held out one of her business cards. 'It was a black Mercedes with one of those ghastly nodding dogs on the parcel shelf,' she added.

'That was quick thinking,' said Sukey. She glanced at the number on the card before handing it back. 'Give that to Vicky Armstrong when you see her. Let's hope this man didn't notice the interest you were taking in him,' she added in a flash of unease.

Erika was quick to reassure her. 'I'm sure he didn't. He

never so much as glanced in my direction and I memorized the number and wrote it down after he'd gone.' Her earlier hesitant manner had given way to the cool, professional efficiency Sukey had noticed at their first meeting. 'By the way,' she went on, diving into her handbag and taking out an A4 envelope. 'I almost forgot – the Gasspar papers! Sounds like something out of a Len Deighton mystery, doesn't it?' she said as she handed it over.

When Sukey arrived back in the CID office she found DS Rathbone at his desk. She handed him the envelope Erika had given her and said, 'These are the photocopies you wanted, Sarge, the ones relating to Boris Gasspar.'

'Thanks.' He glanced at the envelope, tossed it into his in tray and returned to a study of the file in front of him, then looked up and said sharply, 'How did you come by them? That didn't come through the post.'

'Erika Henderson gave them to me just now. We had lunch together,' she added with a hint of defiance.

'Are you two buddies or something?'

'Not exactly. She said she'd prefer to hand them over personally and as she was coming into town anyway I agreed to meet her. It seemed to make sense; things do go astray in the post from time to time.'

'Did she give any reason for wanting this personal meeting?' Rathbone snapped, his eyes narrow with suspicion.

'She didn't have time to explain over the phone. If she had, I'd have refused the request because what she had to say concerns the Whistler murder. I explained I was off it and she should tell you or Vicky if she had any new information. She promised to do that, but if you don't hear from her I think perhaps—'

She stopped as Rathbone's phone began ringing. He grabbed it and barked, 'Yes, what is it?' He listened for a moment and then said more gently, 'DC Armstrong's out. I'll see her – I'll be with her in a moment.' He put the phone down and stood up. 'She appears to have taken your advice,' he said. 'She's in reception.'

It was almost an hour before he reappeared and came over to Sukey's desk, where she and DS Douglas were working on the reports of missing girls that she had earlier set aside for further examination. She saw immediately that his attitude had undergone a noticeable change; instead of the previous mixture of mockery and irritation, it held a definite, albeit slightly grudging, hint of respect. 'I've just had a word with DCI Leach and he wants to see me right away,' he told her. 'It's possible he may want to speak to you as well, so stick around for a while.'

'Don't worry, Greg, I've got plenty for her to do here,' said DS Douglas, who was standing a few feet away. 'So what's going on?' he asked after Rathbone had left the room.

'Erika Henderson was very keen to tell me something that might or might not have a bearing on the Whistler murder,' she said, 'but as I'm off the case now I referred her to DS Rathbone.'

Douglas grinned. 'Very wise,' he said. 'You got carpeted for crashing in on operation Maddox, didn't you?'

'So you heard about that?'

'Of course. Greg wasn't best pleased with you, I gather.'

'You could say that, but it seems what he's just heard from Erika has made him feel more kindly towards me.'

Ten minutes later, they were both summoned to Leach's office. DS Rathbone was still there, standing with his back to the door. He swung round when Sukey and Douglas entered and all three waited for Leach to speak. He sat looking at them for a couple of seconds over the top of his glasses before saying, 'Well, Sukey, it seems circumstances are conspiring to bring you back on the Whistler case despite our efforts to keep you out of it.'

'Sir?' The monosyllabic response to this cryptic remark was all she could think of on the spur of the moment.

'DS Rathbone has just interviewed Erika Henderson from the Mariners Hotel and she has made the following statement. "On Saturday morning I was in the Clifton Wine Shop where I saw a man who so closely resembled Stephen Lamont that I almost greeted him by name",' he began, reading from a sheet of paper lying in an open folder on his desk. 'She goes on to give some details – you can read the statement for yourselves in a minute. The significance of this, of course, is that it gives some credence to a similar claim made by Hester Lamont – a claim both Sergeant Rathbone and I were disinclined at first to take seriously on account of the woman's volatile mental state. We did, however, manage to persuade her to make a formal statement and I have that here as well.'

He picked up the second sheet, passed them both across the desk and waited while Sukey and Douglas read through them. 'Any questions?' he asked as they handed them back.

'Yes, sir,' said Douglas. 'Do we know yet who the Merc belongs to?'

'Our information is that it's on contract hire to a company that owns a chain of launderettes, which we have reason to believe is part of the Oliver Maddox empire. It so happens the enquiry into the Maddox set-up is code-named Operation Dirty Linen,' he added without a trace of a smile.

'Is that a coincidence or do they suspect a link with money laundering?'

'Good question. They're being pretty tight-lipped about it – understandably so. Needless to say, I'll be consulting their SIO every step of the way, and no one here is to make the slightest move on their own initiative. Understood?' A chorus of 'Sirs' greeted the question, which the three took to be a sign of dismissal and began getting up to leave when Leach added, 'There's a couple of other things the three of you should know.' He referred to a file that lay open on his desk. 'About the body found in the river. Doc Hanley found traces of lorazepam in the dead girl's system. It's a drug commonly used by dentists to calm nervous patients and it was probably given to girls who objected to the demands of some of their customers to make them more compliant.'

'Charming,' muttered Rathbone.

'Quite.' Leach referred to the file again. 'Next, I have here a report from forensics on the clothing the girl was wearing. It was saturated and heavily stained with mud, but on examination it turned out that in the pocket of the skirt was a small scrap of paper. They managed to dry it out and found something written on it, fortunately in indelible ink and quite legible. It appears to be a mobile phone number. Does anyone here recognize it?' He read the number aloud and Sukey gave an involuntary gasp.

'It's my number, sir,' she said, 'but I didn't give it to that girl. I never saw her until the day her body was found. The only person I've given it to recently is Boris Gasspar.'

Twenty

'This is something we feared might happen from the moment Sukey reported seeing Gasspar in the company of Oliver Maddox,' said DCI Leach, 'and I'm sure you all realize what it means.'

'Obviously, Gasspar must know the girl we fished out of the river on Monday,' said DS Douglas.

'Not necessarily,' said Leach, 'although there has to be a connection. Sukey gave Gasspar her number on – ' he rifled through the reports in the folder before locating the one he was looking for – 'Monday of last week. He hasn't made any use of it, but we suspect Maddox somehow found out he had it and demanded he hand the card over, probably while Sukey had him under surveillance last Friday. But in the meantime, he must have confided the number either to the girl herself or – what I think is more likely – to a third party, who subsequently passed it on to her. And the reason she never used it is probably because one of Maddox's thugs silenced her before she had the chance.'

'Without realizing that the scrap of paper she'd written it on was in the pocket of the skirt she was wearing when he killed her,' Rathbone speculated.

'Exactly. And as we're reasonably sure she was killed a couple of days before being dumped in the river, that would mean they didn't waste any time.'

'Why do you suppose they waited all that time before dumping the body?' asked Douglas.

'We consulted our river expert on that. It seems there was an unusually high tide about eight hours before we found her. That's one more reason to believe the killers were local – they probably knew that and dropped her in the water at a crucial moment, calculating that it would be swept out to sea by the falling tide. If that had gone to plan it could have been weeks before it came ashore, maybe at Avonmouth or even further along the coast, but unfortunately for them it got caught up on a mudbank. Her long skirt would have been a factor as well – soaked with water it would have acted as a weight.'

'So what do we do now, sir? We can't pull Gasspar in and insist he tells us all he knows about Maddox, can we?'

'No, Bob, we can't. When I passed on the suggestion that we offer him immunity if he shopped Maddox I was strictly forbidden to do any such thing. I'll have to refer these latest developments to Superintendent Baird – he's the SIO at Operation Dirty Linen – and wait for his instructions. I will of course be sending him the paperwork concerning Gasspar's employment record that the hotel manager's PA got for us. I understand you've impressed on her that it's vital nothing gets out about this, Sukey?'

'I have, sir, and I believe we can rely on her discretion.'

'Let's hope you're right.' Leach glanced at his watch. 'Right, let's wind this up as quickly as possible and then I'll have this lot faxed to the Super with a request for a quick response. As we haven't been able to identify the dead girl, the press will soon be clamouring for a picture.'

'Could I ask, sir, if you have any theory about her connection with Gasspar, and, by extension, with Maddox?' said Douglas.

'From what Doc Hanley said in his report, she's had a pretty active sex life,' said Leach. 'That may have been of her own choosing, but in the light of what we now know, I believe it's more likely she was a victim of people traffickers. We know there are organized gangs bringing young women over from countries in Eastern Europe and the Balkans. They lure them here by promising them glamorous jobs in things like modelling that will bring them lots of money and once they're here they force them into prostitution. It's a filthy trade and it would be entirely in character for Maddox to be involved in it.'

'You think there may be a house on our patch where some of these girls are being held?' said Rathbone.

'It's a possibility. There are plenty of properties in multiple occupation in various parts of the city. Some of them we know are used by drug dealers and the two activities often go hand in hand. It wouldn't be difficult to keep half a dozen girls prisoner in such a house with guards to make sure they didn't escape.'

'Escapes do happen now and then, sir,' Sukey ventured. 'There was a case in Cheltenham last year, just before I left to start my CID training.'

Leach nodded. 'True. As I recall, a member of the public found a girl wandering the streets in a distressed state, became concerned and alerted the police. At the moment we haven't anything like that to go on.'

'So you think the dead girl might have been caught trying to escape?' said Douglas.

'Possibly, or she might have been overheard saying something to suggest that was what she was planning to do. We simply have no idea at the moment.'

'Presumably she wouldn't have access to a phone in the house so to make a call she'd have had to get out somehow,' said Rathbone. 'She'd then have the problem of finding a public call box if she was hoping to ring Sukey's number and she'd have needed money . . . and there might have been a language problem.'

'That's true as well,' said Leach. 'If she did manage to get out of the house it would have made more sense to appeal to a member of the public. So far, no one's come forward to report anything of that nature. This is all speculation, of course; we may be completely wide of the mark, which is why I need to refer to the Super as soon as possible.'

'What about the two sightings of Lamont's double, sir?' asked Rathbone. 'Are we still thinking in terms of a link with Maddox and the Whistler killing?'

'That's a further complication,' admitted Leach, 'and again the short answer is we simply don't know. The fact that a key witness in the Whistler case has a connection with Maddox may be nothing more than a coincidence, but until we have more definite information we have to pursue it. I'd like to know more about the company that's leasing the car the doppelgänger was driving – I'll raise that one with the Super at the same time. There's one thing we can all do in the meantime and that is keep an eye open for this man. Any sightings of him or the car are to be reported to me immediately, but under no circumstances is he to be approached or made aware that he's under observation. It'll be up to the Dirty Linen team to mount their own surveillance in the hope they can establish a link to Maddox. Understood? Yes, Sukey?' he added, having evidently read in her expression that something had occurred to her. 'You have a question?'

'Well, sir,' she began hesitantly, 'it's obvious that Maddox is into some very lucrative scams big time. He probably rakes in millions one way and another. We know the items stolen from Doctor Whistler are valuable, but to a man like Maddox they'd only represent small change. As you say, we've no hard evidence as yet that he was involved in stealing them, but there is some reason to suspect that he was. I'm wondering why he'd bother – it seems a bit out of his league.'

'Good point,' said Leach. 'I'll mention it when I speak to Superintendent Baird. I can't off-hand think of a reason – unless of course he's a closet collector of antiquities. Do you have a theory of your own, Sukey?'

'Only that someone at the dig in Rhodes might have let him know that Whistler was carrying something else we haven't heard about, something even more valuable.'

'Or maybe he was just doing a friend a favour,' said Rathbone. His flippant tone made it clear that in his opinion the idea was not to be taken seriously.

Leach, however, did not smile. 'I'll include both suggestions in my report,' he said. 'Any more questions or comments?' There was a general shaking of heads. 'Right, that's it for now. I'll let all of you know as soon as I hear from him how he wants us to play this from now on; in the meantime we'd better carry on with the routine enquiries or the press will think we're sitting on our backsides while the villains get on with their villainy. And remember, every scrap of relevant information comes directly to me before any action is taken.'

Sukey, Rathbone and Douglas returned to the CID office. Vicky was at her computer, writing up a statement she had just taken from a woman who had reported seeing a girl 'looking like what it says in the paper' entering a car with two men 'a few days ago'. According to the somewhat rambling account the witness gave over the phone, 'the men looked rather nasty bits of work and the girl didn't seem to want to go with them'. As the three approached she looked up and pulled a face.

'Any use?' said Rathbone

'Not a lot, Sarge,' said Vicky. 'This woman – a Mrs Purdie – can't even be sure what day it was except that it was "towards the end of last week". From her description of all three people involved they might have been members of the same family, possibly Asian. The men were young and could have been the girl's brothers, but as Mrs P so charmingly put it, "of course they all look the same".'

'Bit of a racist, eh? What about the car?'

'Again, pretty vague. She says it was black but she couldn't describe it except that it was "big and shiny and new-looking".'

'No nodding dog in the rear window I suppose?'

'She didn't mention it but I have a feeling that if I'd asked her about it, she'd have "suddenly remembered" there was one.'

Rathbone grimaced. 'As you say, not a lot of use.'

'There is one thing she did seem sure of, for what it's worth. This incident took place in Mellor Street, which isn't far from the street where Sukey spotted our star witness from the Mariners Hotel.'

DCI Leach summoned the team again on Friday morning to inform them that Superintendent Baird had given permission to release an artist's impression of the dead girl to the press. 'That's the good news, such as it is,' he told them. 'The bad news is that Inspector Comino of the Greek police has been in touch with him, demanding to know what we've been doing for the past fortnight and why hasn't he been kept informed. Which is a bit rich, considering that no one here had heard of him until yesterday, but it seems he and Doctor Makris of the Ministry of Culture have been comparing notes. If we don't come up with something positive during the next forty-eight hours he's threatening to come here to take charge of the investigation personally.'

'Bloody cheek!' said Rathbone.

'I can understand his vexation,' said Leach. 'There have been reports lately of a serious rise in the theft of art treasures from Greek museums and archaeological sites and they feel their heritage is being stolen from them. They've formed a special division of the police, known as the Art Squad, to try and stamp it out. Just the same, we don't want him coming here and raising a dust. If Maddox is involved in the trade and Comino latches on to him it could seriously jeopardize Operation Dirty Linen. Let's hope the picture will bring about the breakthrough we need.'

By chance the picture was not published until the first edition the following day, being elbowed out by extensive reports, full of salacious details, of a scandal involving a star of a local football team and the young and sexy blonde winner of a recent television game show. And it was this chance that provided yet another tenuous link in the chain.

For several weeks Sukey had been considering replacing some of the furniture she had brought with her from her former home in Gloucester. She had once casually mentioned this to Major Matthews during one of his neighbourly enquiries as to how she was settling in and if she needed any information about local services etc. He had recommended a large furniture retailer, and it was on the Saturday morning, the day after Inspector Comino had issued his ultimatum, that she decided to take his advice. It so happened that the store was in the same part of Bristol as the house she had observed Boris enter just over a week ago, but no such thought was in her mind as she wandered through the various departments, making notes of prices and picking up catalogues, occasionally taking a rest in one of a seemingly limitless range of armchairs on offer. Bewildered by the choice, wishing that either Jim or Fergus was with her, she resisted the blandishments of a helpful sales assistant and retreated to the store's café for a restorative cup of coffee before setting off for home. On the way back to the car she stopped at a small general store to pick up a few groceries; as she entered she pulled up short in front of a stand piled with copies of the morning edition of the local paper. The front page bore a banner headline reading 'Do you know who she is?' and below it was a drawing of the girl whose body she had watched being recovered from the banks of the River Avon.

Taking care not to show any particular reaction, she put a copy in her basket before moving towards the first aisle with her shopping list in her hand. Moments later she heard someone behind her give what sounded like a cry of despair. Turning, she saw a young man staring fixedly at the pile of newspapers with an expression of mingled horror and fear on his face. He clapped a hand over his mouth and then crossed himself while mumbling something incomprehensible under his breath before picking up a copy with a hand that shook so violently that he had difficulty in getting hold of it. His head was half-turned towards her and as she saw him in profile she noticed that he bore a strong resemblance to Boris Gasspar. His brother perhaps, or his cousin?

Sukey's training and instinct told her that it would be unwise for him to see her there. She retreated behind the nearest row of shelves and stood for several seconds examining rows of different brands of tea and coffee while keeping an eye open in case he should suddenly appear in search of whatever he had entered the shop to buy. She was not, however, surprised when through the window she saw him run out of the shop clutching the newspaper in one hand. Perhaps that was all he came in for anyway or possibly the shock of seeing the drawing had driven everything else from his mind. She was in no doubt that he had recognized the girl, but did he know who she was, where she had been living, where she had come from and by what means? Was she, in fact, a victim of people traffickers and if so, were they controlled by Maddox? The questions flooded into her mind with the speed of the rising waters that less than a week ago had flowed up the Avon, swept up the frail, lifeless victim and carried her away, only to abandon her on its muddy shores barely a mile downstream.

Twenty-One

There was a shout and a sudden commotion as a teenager in jeans and T-shirt rushed out of the shop, stopped for a moment looking this way and that and then gave another shout before racing off along the street. A customer was heard to remark, above a round of tutting, 'Chap went off without paying for his paper,' which everyone agreed was undoubtedly the case. A short while later the pursuer returned in triumph, this time at a more leisurely pace and jingling some coins in his cupped hand, which earned him a round of spontaneous applause.

'Nice work, Wayne,' said the woman on the till as he handed her the money.

'He were just going into the caff up the road,' he explained. 'Paid up right away, no worries. "Very sorry, forgot," he says. Didn't have the right money but didn't bother about his change either. In a right state, he were.'

'Did you see his face when he picked up the *Mercury*?' said a woman who was unloading her shopping at the checkout, speaking to no one in particular. 'Looked petrified, he did – you'd have thought he'd seen a ghost.'

'Maybe he knows who the dead girl is,' said the woman behind her in the queue. She held up a copy of the newspaper and waved it around. 'She do look a bit foreign, don't she, and I thought he did too. Were it in Marco's you saw him, Wayne?' she asked the lad, who had returned to his task of stacking shelves with tins of soup.

'Thassright, the caff on the corner,' he replied.

'Ah, that explains it. You do see a lot of foreigners in there,' she said knowingly.

The first woman, evidently anxious not to be left out of the conversation, said, 'I went in for a cup of coffee once and while I was there a whole crowd of them came in, jabbering away in their funny language. That was the last time I went in . . .'

'Marco's Italian,' someone pointed out and received a scornful sniff in reply.

'I buy my sandwiches from Marco and I often see foreign workers in there,' said the woman on the till as she rang up the first woman's purchases. 'He says they like to sit and chat to their mates – treat it like a sort of club, they do and he doesn't seem to mind. They come in here sometimes for their bits of grocery . . . always very polite, never any trouble. That's five pounds and seventy-five pence, please.'

'Never any trouble till now, you mean,' said the woman as she rummaged in her purse with skinny fingers. 'You'd better keep an eye on them from now on – especially that one,' she added with a jerk of her head in the general direction of the door. 'Me, I don't trust people what can't even talk English proper,' she announced to all and sundry as she handed over the money and departed.

Sukey had edged closer to the till to catch the conversation. As one by one the women left she moved away, picked up the items on her list, paid for them and left the shop. Outside, she walked a few paces along the street in the direction Wayne had taken in his pursuit of the fleeing customer; a short distance ahead she saw an advertising board on the pavement bearing the words 'Café Marco' in brightly coloured letters with a list of specialities on offer scrawled below in chalk. Bearing in mind DCI Leach's instructions, she resisted her natural inclination to investigate further; instead, she set off for the car park with the intention of calling the CID office in the hope of being able to contact either Rathbone or Douglas and report what she had seen. To reach it she would have to walk along the side street past Marco's; she figured that if the young man was indeed related to Boris they might both be in there, so rather than risk being spotted she crossed over the road and continued walking for a couple more minutes before crossing back again. Her intention was to approach the corner from the opposite direction and so avoid passing in front of the café; she had almost reached it when a black Mercedes turned ahead of her and pulled up outside.

Her heart thumping with excitement, Sukey stopped short and held her breath. What happened next registered on her brain like a series of snapshots viewed in quick succession: the registration number of the car: the nodding dog on the parcel shelf: the tall man with a gold stud in his right ear who stepped out and without bothering to lock the door headed for Marco's: and finally, but no less striking, his uncanny resemblance to Stephen Lamont.

By chance, she was outside a bank where a small queue had formed at an automatic cash dispenser. It offered an ideal vantage point for keeping watch and she took out her card and joined the line while keeping a sharp lookout in case the man reappeared. Something in his bearing and the purposeful way he strode round the corner and pushed open Marco's door told her that he was not there for refreshment. Whatever his errand, her instinct told her it would not take long and she kept her eyes glued to the door of the café as the queue shuffled forward. She took out her mobile and was about to key in the office number when a woman behind her said plaintively, 'Do you want to use this machine or not?' Still keeping an eye open for her target, she hurriedly inserted her card and entered her PIN.

She was just withdrawing her money as the man emerged. She hastily stuffed card, money and receipt in her shoulder bag with one hand while juggling the mobile with the other and still watching him to see what he would do next. He made straight for his car, which she had already noted was illegally parked on double yellow lines; as he opened the driver's door a traffic warden, who had evidently been waiting out of sight round the corner, crossed the road and approached him with a pad of forms in one hand and a pen in the other. Another bit of luck, she thought to herself as she pressed the 'ring' button and waited for a reply. Wouldn't it be great if, like so many motorists issued with parking tickets, the man were to argue and become aggressive, tear up the ticket and throw it in the warden's face, do anything to delay his departure. But instead of writing out a ticket, tearing it off and giving it to the driver, the warden pulled a loose sheet from the bottom of the pad and handed it over. It was too far away for her to see but on reflection she would have been prepared to bet that there was nothing written on it. In return, he received something that might have been a small brown envelope and walked quickly away.

It had all happened so discreetly and the switch was made

so quickly that for a moment she wondered if her eyes had deceived her. Then she heard someone say, 'I've seen that happen before.' It was the woman who had been behind her in the queue for the cash machine. 'Don't know who the driver is, but I reckon that warden's on to a nice little earner. Now if you or I had parked there—'

'You're saying he takes handouts to let people get away with parking on double yellow lines?' said Sukey, affecting shocked astonishment.

The woman shrugged. 'Never seen him do it with anyone else, but I've noticed that one before. Maybe he belongs to the Mafia or something.' Tittering at what she evidently considered a witticism, she went on her way while the driver of the Mercedes started his engine and drove off with the dog nodding benignly through the rear window.

'CID, Rathbone speaking,' said an impatient voice in her ear. 'Is anyone there?'

'Yes, Sarge, it's me, Sukey.'

'What is it?'

'I've been doing some shopping in Gloucester Road and I was on my way back to my car when I saw—' As concisely as possible she outlined the chain of events that had prompted her to make the call.

'Is the guy who bought the paper still in the café?' he asked.

'As far as I know. I haven't seen him come out, but—'

'You're sure he didn't see you watching him?'

'He never looked my way, but in any case he was so shocked when he saw the girl's picture that I doubt if he'd have noticed anything.'

'Good. I'll call the DCI immediately – he'll probably want to speak to you so you'd better stand by.'

'Do you want me to stay here and keep watch?'

'Better not, in case Gasspar's in there as well. Whether or not your man's related to him, this could be the breakthrough we've all been waiting for. Get back to your car and wait there till I call you.' There was a click as Rathbone ended the call. Feeling slightly deflated, Sukey followed his instructions. She had just settled into her car when her mobile rang. A man's voice with a strong foreign accent said, 'Ees thees the perleese laydee?' The words sounded muffled, as if he had a hand over the mouthpiece.

Sukey experienced another surge of adrenalin as she replied, 'Detective Constable Reynolds speaking. Who's calling, please?'

'My name not matter.' He pronounced each word carefully with a pause after each one. 'Please, I weesh speak you.'

'Yes?'

'Ees very important.'

'All right, I'm listening.'

'Not speak on phone. Must see.'

'All right. Come to the police station in—'

'No, no.' He was beginning to sound agitated. 'We meet somewhere.'

'Where are you?'

'Not matter. You say where I see you.'

Throughout the conversation Sukey's brain had been working furiously. She could not be sure, but it seemed more than likely that her anonymous caller had obtained her number from Boris Gasspar and might even be the young man who had rushed out of the grocery store and into Marco's in apparent distress. On the one hand she had been given strict instructions to sit tight and await further orders; on the other, it was essential to keep this contact going. She had to play for time.

'Please listen carefully,' she said, speaking slowly and distinctly. 'Do you know the Gloucester Road?'

'Yes, I know eet.'

'There's a turning off it leading to a car park and there's a café called Marco's on the corner. Do you know it?'

'No. no. Not meet in Marco's.' She could hear his agitation increasing.

'That's all right, I just want to be sure you know where the car park is.'

'Yes, yes, I know car park.'

'Can you be there in half an hour?' That should give her time to contact Rathbone again and either get clearance for her to meet the man herself or send someone else. 'I or another officer will meet you.'

'No, no other!' he insisted. 'I weesh see you, I speak only weeth you . . . please, very important.'

'All right. I'll be there in half an hour, OK?'

'OK,' he said – a little reluctantly, she thought, as if he was not entirely happy with the arrangement.

She ended the call and immediately rang the office again. An unfamiliar voice told her that DS Rathbone was speaking on another line and she left a message asking him to call her back urgently. She took out her notebook and scribbled a note of the incident and then sat and waited for Rathbone's call, but the minutes ticked by and still there was no word from him. She had been waiting, fuming with impatience, for over fifteen minutes when to her dismay she saw the man who resembled Boris approaching. Much too early, of course, but fortunately she had parked some distance from the entrance and was able to watch him unobserved. He stood on the pavement looking first left and then right along the street, from time to time glancing at his watch and taking a few steps in each direction in turn. Whenever an approaching car signalled its intention to enter the car park he stepped eagerly forward, peering at the driver and then retreating as if satisfied that it was not the one he was seeking.

'Maybe I should have told him what car to look out for,' Sukey muttered and then remembered that in all probability Leach, instructed by Superintendent Baird, would insist on sending someone else anyway.

Five minutes to go and still no call from Rathbone. Then another car approached; this time it slowed down and drew level with the man. The registration number was unfamiliar and Sukey knew immediately that it was not a pool car; this was not the police. Something was wrong; as the man stepped eagerly forward she opened her mouth to call out a warning but her shout was drowned in a roar of gunfire before the car sped away.

As Sukey leapt out of her car and began to run towards the figure lying face down on the ground, her mobile rang. Her hand shook almost uncontrollably as, still running, she pressed the reply button. 'Sorry it took me so long to get back to you,' Rathbone was saying, but for a moment she was unable to respond because of the tightness in her throat. 'Are you there?' he demanded. 'What's going on? I can hear screams. For God's sake Sukey, are you all right?' At first he sounded impatient; when she still did not reply, a note of concern crept into his voice. In some strange way it helped her to find her own. 'Yes, I'm OK, but—' She had to break off and swallow hard to stop herself from gagging. She could hear agitated voices, a child was screaming. Pull yourself together woman, you've got a job to do, she told herself fiercely. She reached the victim, saw the pool of blood forming round him, crouched low to feel for a pulse and spoke again into the phone. 'Sarge, there's been a drive-by shooting outside the Stone Street car park. Young Caucasian male, the one I told you about. Still alive but pulse feeble. I need back up and an ambulance,' she said, and this time her voice was firm and clear.

Twenty-Two

'**M**y God!', 'What happened?', 'Is he dead?', 'Shouldn't someone call an ambulance?'

Questions whirled through the air from all sides as the half-dozen or so people who had heard the shots tore across the car park in Sukey's wake towards the spot where the man lay on the ground. They stood in a circle round her, pressing forward, craning their necks, pointing, speaking to one another in hushed whispers. One woman made the sign of the cross, her lips silently moving. The air seemed to vibrate, as if the echoes from the gunfire were still audible.

'Keep your distance everyone!' she called, waving them back, 'and please put that down at once, sir!' she added, seeing a man stoop to pick something off the ground. He glared at her, his expression truculent.

'Who d'you think you are to give orders?' he demanded.

'I'm an off-duty police officer,' she informed him crisply. 'This is a crime scene and no one is to touch anything.' Shock would no doubt kick in when the crisis was past, but for the moment she felt icily calm. She stood up to face him; he was head and shoulders taller than she was and well built, with a shaven head, two days' growth of stubble on his chin and a flabby mound of flesh that rose like a pallid molehill above the top of his jeans. He took a step towards her, but she stood her ground. 'Kindly put down whatever it is you have just picked up,' she repeated.

'It's only a spent bullet,' he said with a sneer, holding out his hand. 'See?'

'It's evidence,' she retorted.

'And how do I know you're a copper anyway? Where's your ID?'

'For God's sake, do as the lady says, Bill.' A heavily made-up blonde with enormous gold hoops swinging from her ears jabbed him in the back. 'She looks as if she knows what she's doing.' Reluctantly, he dropped the bullet on the ground, but remained where he was, resisting the woman's efforts to pull him away. The other onlookers drew back, their expressions varying between shock and morbid curiosity. Two women held handkerchiefs over their mouths; another was comforting the crying child; the men stood gazing as if mesmerized at the figure on the ground. One of the bullets must have torn through the victim's shoulder, leaving a gash and an ugly red stain on the back of his shirt. Sukey watched with mounting alarm as the edge of the pool of blood crept outwards on the tarmac.

'You can't just leave him lying there bleeding to death,' protested the man addressed as Bill. 'My name's Hassell,' he went on, 'I've got a first aid kit in my car and I could—'

Sukey shook her head. 'Thank you for the offer, Mr Hassell, but it's better not to touch him in case we do further damage. An ambulance should be here any minute; the paramedics will know what to do.' She looked past him at the rest of the onlookers and said, 'I've called for more police and I'd be obliged if those of you who actually saw what happened or feel they can give useful information would wait by their cars until they arrive.'

In response, the crowd withdrew a short distance, stopped and turned round, plainly reluctant to move out of sight of the action. Sukey bent down and once more laid a finger on the victim's neck, relieved to find the feeble pulse still there, praying for help to arrive quickly.

Meanwhile, more shoppers returning to their cars stopped to stare; to her surprise, Hassell took over the task of shooing them away saying, 'Keep back everyone; this lady's a police officer and she's in charge. An ambulance and more officers are coming and they won't want you lot getting in their way.'

Even as he spoke, the sirens began to sound and the crowd hastily retreated still further. The ambulance arrived first, sweeping round the corner with its blue light flashing. It pulled up and a couple of paramedics leaped out and bent over the victim. When they touched him he let out a faint groan and a sigh of relief drifted like a trail of smoke among the onlookers.

'D'you reckon he'll be OK?' Bill called out, but the paramedics either did not hear, or they ignored the question. He
repeated it to Sukey, who responded with a helpless gesture.

'It's hard to tell; all I can say is the pulse is weak but it
seems to be holding up.' As she spoke, the ambulance crew
attached a drip to the semi-conscious man's arm and eased
him on to a stretcher. In a matter of seconds they had him in
the ambulance; the doors closed and it raced away, siren
blaring, blue light flashing, leaving behind a bright scarlet
stain on the tarmac.

Moments later the police arrived and took charge.

'Here Sukey, get this down you,' said Rathbone.

Her hands were shaking and the hot tea almost spilled over
as she lifted it to her lips. Her teeth chattered on the edge of
the mug, but its warmth was comforting to her chilled fingers
and the hot liquid gradually sent a restorative glow through
her body. He waited until she had drunk the last drop and
handed the empty mug back to him. He put it down on the
desk and said, 'Better now?'

'Much better, thank you, Sarge.'

'Feel well enough to talk?'

'Sure'

'First of all, you haven't told me why you wanted to speak
to me so urgently. Did you anticipate the shooting?'

'Sarge, if I'd had the remotest suspicion that anything like
that was going to happen I'd have moved heaven and earth
to get armed back-up without delay.'

'Then what?'

'After I spoke to you I went back to my car as instructed.
I'd just got there when my mobile rang and a man with a
strong foreign accent wanted to know if I was "the police
lady".' Shakily at first, but with increasing confidence, she
described the events of the next half hour. As she spoke she
seemed to see the sickening act of violence she had recently
witnessed being re-enacted in her mind's eye like the re-run
of a film: the approaching car that wasn't a police car slowing
down to draw level with the man waiting by the roadside: her
futile attempt at a warning: the noise of the gunfire: the man's
arms flung in the air and his body spun round by the impact
of the bullets before crashing to the ground: the screech of

rubber as the hit squad's car sped away. She ended by saying simply, 'I took charge until uniformed arrived and an inspector told me that CID were on their way. I went back to my car and waited for you.'

She had no idea how long she had waited; it might have been five minutes or twenty-five. She had only a vague recollection of Rathbone pulling up beside her in a pool car, ordering her into the passenger seat and driving her back to the station. He hadn't spoken a word during the journey except to say that someone would bring her back later to pick up her own car. Now that she had told her story she waited passively for further instructions.

Rathbone had been writing rapidly while she was speaking. He thought for a moment and then said, 'OK, the first thing we have to do is establish where that call came from. Give me your mobile and I'll have it checked.' Without a word she handed it over. 'Stay here; I'll be right back.'

She sat back and closed her eyes, feeling utterly spent. When Rathbone returned, his voice seemed to come at her out of a void. 'I've spoken to DCI Leach; he wants to see you and he's on his way here. I don't suppose you've had any lunch?' She shook her head. Food was the last thing she had been thinking of, but all of a sudden she realized she was empty. 'There isn't time to go to the canteen, but I've brought you an energy bar to keep you going,' he said gruffly and slapped it on the desk in front of her. 'When you've eaten that we'll go up and wait for him in his office. Oh, and I've called in Libby Mayhew, one of our FSOs; she's a trained counsellor.'

'I don't need counselling,' Sukey protested.

'You're still in shock and you might need help in recalling details,' Rathbone said firmly. 'This is big, Sukey; you're a key witness in a major investigation and Operation Dirty Linen needs every scrap of help you can give.' With that somewhat ominous remark he waited while she obediently ate the energy bar and then escorted her out of the room and upstairs to Leach's office.

Libby Mayhew was already there; a few minutes later Leach walked in and sat down behind his desk. 'I've spoken to Superintendent Baird and he's coming as well,' he said. 'While we're waiting, we might as well get a few details of the actual attack on record. Exactly what time, and where, did it take place, Sukey?'

Her stomach gave a lurch as she reached for her notebook, realizing that she had no recollection of writing anything in it about the shooting. Yet surely she must have done; it would have been a mechanical response once she had, under the uniformed inspector's instruction, withdrawn from the scene. And there it was: Date: place: time: observations: action taken. She was dumbfounded to realize she had even recorded the make and number of the car. It must have registered automatically the moment she realized it was not one of the police vehicles.

She had just finished going through her notes when Superintendent Baird arrived. He made a somewhat comical contrast to the tall, gangling Leach, being short and stocky with a mop of sandy hair, a freckled face and steady grey eyes. He was wearing an Argyll patterned pullover, corduroy trousers and golfing shoes. 'I hope we can get through this quickly, I'm supposed to be teeing off at two o'clock,' he observed as he sat down. 'I suppose there's no news of the victim?' he added, almost as an afterthought.

'Not yet, sir. We have two armed officers at the hospital and they're in constant contact.'

'Good. All right Leach, let's have the complete picture.'

'May I suggest we let DC Reynolds give it herself, sir? I'm sure you'll find her a very competent witness. She has recorded the basic details in her notebook and I've jotted them down here.' Leach pushed a pad towards Baird who picked it up and ran his eyes over the top page. 'As yet she's had no opportunity to make a full written report.'

Baird turned to Sukey and despite his brusque manner his expression was not unfriendly. 'Now Reynolds,' he said, 'I understand from DCI Leach that he decided to take you off the Whistler case, but that you subsequently became involved in it on the insistence of certain witnesses. Before we deal with this morning's incident, perhaps you could explain exactly how this came about.'

For the moment Sukey was nonplussed. Then she said slowly, 'Well, sir, it started when Hester Lamont refused to speak to anyone but me about what seemed to all of us a very implausible theory of mistaken identity that she believed could

help her brother. Then Erika Henderson called to say the paperwork we had requested about Boris Gasspar was ready and
during the conversation she indicated she had something to
tell me about the murder of Doctor Whistler. I told her I was
no longer on the case and advised her to speak to DS Rathbone,
but she seemed reluctant to do that and insisted on telling it
to me first.'

'What reason did she give for that? Come on, speak up,'
he added impatiently as she hesitated in embarrassment.

'She thought I was more likely to take her seriously
than . . . well, than any of the male officers, sir.'

Baird raised an eyebrow, but all he said was, 'Go on.'

'I agreed to meet her; she gave me the paperwork and told
me she too had seen a Lamont lookalike in the same place as
Hester. I assured her it would be taken seriously and advised
her very strongly to come in and make a formal statement
without delay. I immediately reported the conversation to DS
Rathbone and while we were speaking Ms Henderson came
to reception and he went down and took her statement.'

'Which is here on the file,' Baird remarked. 'So as far as
you were concerned, that was to be the end of your involvement in the case?'

'Yes, sir.'

'And then along comes yet another lookalike, this time to
a key witness in the Whistler murder. Right, now give a
detailed, step by step account of the events that led up to the
shooting today.'

For the second time within an hour, beginning with the
reaction to the newspaper picture of the dead girl on the part
of a man who resembled Boris Gasspar and ending with the
same man being gunned down before her eyes outside the car
park less than an hour later, Sukey described what had
happened. From time to time Baird interrupted with a question; as the interview went on, weariness began to take its toll
and she began repeating herself and stumbling over her words.
It was then that Libby Mayhew intervened, gently but firmly
reminding Baird that she was still in shock, demanding strong
coffee and insisting that she be allowed some respite before
continuing.

When at last Baird appeared satisfied he sat back and said,
'This man who resembles Lamont whom you saw pay Marco's

a short visit and subsequently pass a discreet backhander to the traffic warden – do you have any theory about the reason for him being there?'

'Well sir, from what the passer-by let drop it appears it wasn't the first time. I gather a lot of Marco's customers are immigrant workers and it did cross my mind that this man might be running some kind of protection racket. I've had the feeling for some time that there's someone with a hold over Gasspar that makes him particularly reluctant to talk to me and I've been wondering whether there's something dodgy about his papers that's made him afraid to come forward.'

'We've asked the Home Office to double check his references, sir,' Leach interposed.

'Good.' Baird turned back to Sukey. 'So you think maybe he asked this man, who you think may be a relative, to contact you on his behalf? It's a bit unlikely, isn't it?'

'Either that, or Boris showed him my card and asked for his advice. Maybe they talked it over and Boris decided not to follow it up, but when this other man recognized the picture of the dead girl he decided to act on his own initiative.'

'And what about the dead girl herself? How do you account for your number being found in her pocket?'

'I can only suppose one of them gave it to her, sir. Maybe she was in some kind of trouble and they suggested I might be able to help.'

'It's pretty obvious she was in trouble,' commented Baird dryly. 'I see from the file you have a theory about that, Leach. People traffickers, girls forced into prostitution, that sort of thing?'

'We know it happens, sir, and according to the pathologist this girl had been sexually active and roughly handled.'

'Assuming someone is running a racket of this kind on our patch, is there any reason to suspect Marco?'

'None that I know of, sir.'

'Rathbone?'

'My first thought was drugs, sir, but I've checked with the Drugs Squad and they've no reason to suppose Marco's a dealer, or that any dealers frequent his place.'

Baird frowned. 'So what takes Lamont Mark Two round there on some sort of regular basis, I wonder?'

There was a silence, interrupted by the telephone on Leach's desk. He picked it up, gave his name, wrote on his pad, grunted 'Thank you' and put it down. 'We may have an answer to your question, sir,' he said. 'The victim of the shooting made his call to Sukey's mobile from the payphone at Marco's café.'

Twenty-Three

There was a protracted silence as everyone digested this new development. Baird looked at his watch, shrugged, took out his mobile and keyed in a number. 'Dave? Something's come up and I'm not going to be able to make it. Many apologies.' He put the phone away, frowned and rested his chin on his left hand while doodling on his pad with the right. The others waited in silence; when Rathbone's mobile rang, heads swivelled in his direction and it seemed to Sukey as if there was a collective holding of breath as he put it to his ear.

'Yes, Murray. Uh-huh . . . uh-huh . . . so far so good . . . well, don't relax for a second, we're dealing with a pretty ruthless bunch . . . if you want reinforcements let me know . . . and not a word to the press, OK? Do we have an ID, by the way?' There was a pause in the conversation, during which Sukey noticed Rathbone's expression change. Then he said, 'OK, thanks. Keep me posted. Cheers.' He snapped off the phone and said, 'Sergeant Murray, sir, in charge of the armed unit at the hospital where they've taken the victim of the shooting.' He was addressing Baird, but the others leaned forward simultaneously as if afraid to miss a word. 'First indications are that by some miracle no vital organ has been damaged. There's been considerable loss of blood, of course, and he's in intensive care while they assess the need for surgery. No idea at this stage as to when he'll be fit to be interviewed. And by the way, the name on a bank card found in his pocket is Mr J. Gasspar.'

'I thought he looked like Boris!' Sukey blurted out and immediately felt her colour rising at her failure to observe protocol. 'Sir,' she added apologetically.

Baird appeared not to notice the gaffe. 'A brother, or possibly a cousin,' he commented, 'and alive, praise the Lord!' He spoke with a fervour that took her by surprise and at the same time made her unexpectedly warm to him. 'It looks as if it was a rush job and their top marksman wasn't available,' he went on. 'Which is fortunate for us, but I wouldn't like to be the chap who carried out the attack if it turns out their intended victim is able to give us vital information. He's to be guarded round the clock like royalty, tell Murray,' he added, speaking directly to Rathbone.

'He understands that, sir.'

'I take it there's no news of the getaway car?'

'Reported stolen from outside a house in Portishead a week ago, sir. From a street round the corner from police headquarters,' the sergeant added with a certain grim relish. The news from the hospital had brought about an immediate lessening of tension and even Baird smiled at this gem.

'Implying we can't keep an eye on our own backyard, eh?' he remarked, one eyebrow lifted. 'The press boys'll go to town on that one if it comes out. Right,' he continued, turning serious again. 'We need to find out a bit more about Marco and his café. Was it just an unlucky chance that one of Maddox's mob overheard this chap making his call to DC Reynolds? Or is there a link between Marco and Maddox via the Lamont lookalike who keeps bobbing up like a jack-in-the-box? I'm inclined to the latter possibility. The payphone in Marco's could easily be monitored in some way. Is Marco under orders to keep his eyes and ears open and alert a member of the mob if one of his customers says or does something of interest to Mister Big? His name hasn't cropped up in our investigations before, but I think we need to know a bit more about him. I'll get one of my team on to that. As for you, Reynolds – ' he turned his gaze on Sukey and she was conscious of the sharp intelligence and the strength of will reflected in the keen grey eyes – 'since the victim of the shooting was so emphatic that he wouldn't speak to anyone but you, I have no option other than to keep you on the case, especially as we now have a link with the Avon river victim. You'd better go and see him as soon as he's fit to be interviewed. And good work getting the car number,' he added.

'Thank you, sir.' The after effects of shock were forgotten; she was gratified by the compliment, but her pleasure was far outweighed by the excitement of being part of a major operation. She found herself praying that she would prove a worthy member of the team.

'And it'll be interesting to see if the other Gasspar shows any reaction either to the shooting or the picture of the girl. I understand you have a reliable contact at the hotel where he works?'

'Yes, sir, the manager's PA. She's very intelligent and has shown a great interest in our enquiries into the Whistler murder. I've naturally refused to answer her questions, but I believe I can rely on her co-operation – and her discretion.'

'Right. Check if she's on duty over the weekend and if not get in touch with her first thing on Monday and find out if she's noticed any change in Boris's behaviour since that picture appeared in the *Mercury*.'

'If she isn't on duty, should I perhaps ask for her home number?'

'Better not. It's unlikely anyone would give it without wanting to know who's calling, and that could lead to someone starting a rumour that something's afoot.'

'Very good, sir.'

'You're in touch with the men at the hospital, Rathbone,' Baird continued. 'I'll leave it to you to keep DCI Leach informed and he'll decide when to send DC Reynolds along to interview the victim. And naturally, I expect to be kept up to date with every development, however small.'

'Sir.'

'And one other thing. You mentioned, Leach, that DC Reynolds had drawn attention to the fact that the proceeds of the Whistler robbery were unlikely to count for much on Maddox's annual balance sheet compared with his more usual sources of revenue.'

Leach looked startled for a moment and then said, 'She did say something to that effect, sir.'

'And I further understand,' Baird's gaze swung in Sukey's direction, 'that one explanation you offered, Reynolds, was that this robbery might, so to speak, represent the tip of the iceberg – in other words, that there may be even more valuable items to be, shall we say, acquired?'

Sukey nodded. 'It seemed a possibility, sir.'

'And now we have the Greek police taking an interest in this case,' Baird went on thoughtfully. 'Perhaps we should take another look at the set-up between Maddox and his lady friend at the university. I don't see a mention of this being raised in any of the interviews with Professor Lamont?' This time his gaze homed in on Rathbone, who stirred a little uneasily.

'That's true, sir,' he admitted, 'but it's only fair to point out that neither the name Maddox, nor the man's reputation, means anything to Lamont.'

'So far as we are aware,' Baird pointed out. 'And there's also the matter of the telephone call that Whistler made to Lamont some time before he was due to come to England. Thorne claimed to have no idea what it was about, other than that there was mention of a trip to London, but I don't see any reference to Lamont's version. Why is that?'

'Lamont hasn't been interviewed since we learned of the conversation, sir.' said Rathbone. 'He'd already admitted knowing about the various items Whistler was bringing with him, so—'

'So you'd better go and see him again and find out exactly how and when he came by the information, what was said during that call and whether there were any further calls either way, apart from the one he made to check that Whistler had reached the hotel safely.' Baird's tone was brusque and Sukey avoided looking in Rathbone's direction. 'And take DC Reynolds with you,' the Superintendent went on. 'On second thoughts, you'd better get him to the station. The sister might be around if you went to the house and we don't want to cause another bout of hysteria.'

'Very good, sir.'

'Right.' Baird closed his file and stood up. 'Thank you everyone. That's all for now.'

Back in the CID office, Rathbone said, 'You'd better go and have a bite to eat before you leave, Sukey.' His tone was almost subdued and she felt a wave of sympathy for him. 'When you come back I'll arrange for someone to take you to pick up your car,' he added.

'Thanks, Sarge, but before I go I'd like to get my full report on the file.'

'Good thinking. Let me know when you're ready and,' he hesitated briefly before continuing, 'first thing Monday we'll fix an appointment to see Lamont.'

It was long after five o'clock when she reached home. It wasn't until she had parked and locked her car that she realized there were several items on her list that, with part of her mind speculating about the incident in the shop, she had forgotten to buy. Unable to face the drive to the nearest supermarket, she walked down the road to pick them up from a corner shop a short distance away.

Because of its original use for the storage of hay and in all probability as living quarters for stable hands, the ground floor of her flat consisted of nothing but a narrow hallway from which a short staircase with a half-landing led to the two upper floors. On the first was a bedroom with a small bathroom, which Fergus occupied during his visits and flippantly referred to as the guest suite, together with a capacious storage area containing the central heating boiler. Sukey's own living quarters were on the floor above. As she closed the front door behind her she suddenly became aware that she was physically as well as mentally exhausted and for the first time since moving in she felt a pang of regret at the unconventional layout, which at the time had seemed, by its very individuality, to be particularly attractive.

Wearily, she plodded up the two flights of stairs and dumped her shopping on the kitchen table. When she had put it away and taken a quick shower she poured out a generous measure of wine and, glass in hand, stepped out on to the roof terrace – another feature that had convinced her that this was exactly the kind of place where she would feel comfortable. It was a fine, mild evening and the setting sun bathed the city in a warm golden light. From her vantage point she could pick out the Cabot tower on Brandon Hill and beyond, on the far side of the Floating Harbour, she caught a glimpse of the flags fluttering from the masts of Brunel's great iron ship, the SS Great Britain, proudly restored to something like her former glory. In another direction altogether and well out of her line of vision lay the area that had been the setting for the scene of hideous violence she had witnessed earlier. The memory of those few nightmarish moments would no doubt haunt her for days to come, yet for the moment, far from a sense of horror, she experienced a feeling of elation. She knew she had responded well to an unexpected and terrifying challenge; she had received a compliment from the Senior Investigating

Officer; even Rathbone, recently so openly hostile, had shown her not only respect but consideration. Drawn in by circumstances, she was now part of a team carrying out a major operation.

That the victim of the shooting had survived without life-threatening injury was little short of a miracle and for the sake of the investigation as well as for his own she found herself praying that he would soon be well enough to be questioned. Meanwhile, she looked forward to a chat with Erika who, she had no doubt, would be delighted to give support. Her spirits renewed, she finished her drink and went indoors to see about dinner. She had just put some potatoes on to boil and was about to prepare a salad to go with her ready-cooked chicken joint when her phone rang. Jim was on the line.

'Sukey? Are you all right?'

'Of course I'm all right. Why shouldn't I be?'

'You must be a bit shaken after that drive-by shooting this morning. I heard it on the news and—'

'The media haven't got hold of my name?' she asked in a sudden panic.

'Relax, I heard it from Rick Leach. He says you kept your head and did a sterling job in managing the scene until uniformed arrived. You even got a bouquet from Superintendent Baird, no less.'

'Hardly a bouquet, more a gentle pat on the back,' she said modestly.

'Well anyway, I'm proud of you. I'm concerned for your safety as well,' he added, his tone more serious. 'I understand you're back on Operation Dirty Linen. You will be careful, won't you, Sook? It's not exactly a tea-party.'

'You think I don't realize that?'

'I'm sure you do, but I can't help worrying about you. By the way, if Fergus rings and asks if you know anything about the incident, I suggest you say as little as possible and above all keep stumm about your part in it. He might be tempted to boast to his mates about his Mum's heroism and as you probably know there's a news blackout until further notice.'

'So I understand. Gus is in London this weekend at a friend's wedding so he may not even have heard about it and I've certainly no intention of mentioning it.'

'That's good. That's really all I wanted to say for now. I'll keep in touch and . . . I still care, you know,' he added almost diffidently.

'I know,' she said.

She went back to the kitchen. By the time her meal had been cooked and eaten and the used crockery and cutlery stacked in the dishwasher it was almost nine o'clock. She read for a while and then switched on the TV news at ten and found herself watching an item about the Stone Street drive-by shooting. She hastily switched off and went to bed.

She lay awake for a while, her brain hyperactive after the excitement of the day. As she waited for sleep to come her thoughts turned to the scene in Baird's office and the thinly disguised reprimand he had handed out to DS Rathbone. There was no doubt he had been guilty of more than one lapse in his conduct of the Whistler enquiry. It was not what one would expect from a man of his experience. Vicky had more than once remarked that he was "a really good cop" . . . but? Did she too have reservations? Was there a reason for these apparent oversights?

Twenty-Four

Sukey had mentally earmarked Sunday morning for a visit to the fitness club she had joined shortly after moving to Bristol. After the stress and excitement of the previous day she was looking forward to a session in the gym followed by a refreshing swim in the pool and – as the weather was exceptionally mild for the time of year – lunch in the poolside bar. It might still be possible, but first she had to call the Mariners Hotel to find out whether Erika Henderson was on duty. She had just finished her breakfast and was reaching for the phone when her mobile rang. Erika herself was calling.

'Sukey? I'm glad I caught you. That man who was shot in Stone Street yesterday morning – do you know anything about him?'

'Erika! I'm glad you called; as a matter of fact I was going to call you.'

'What about?'

'I'd rather not talk about it on the phone. Are you on duty today?'

'Yes, till five o'clock.'

'What about your boss?'

'Maurice? It's his day off; I'm here on my own.'

'Then I'll come and see you this morning, if that's all right. Around ten o'clock?'

'Yes, that'll be fine.'

'And by the way,' Sukey added, 'I don't want to come in through reception. If I call your mobile number from the car park, will you let me in by the staff entrance?'

There was a moment's hesitation before Erika replied, 'All right, if that's what you want.' From her tone it was obvious that she was burning with curiosity, but she made no further comment other than, 'See you later,' before hanging up.

As usual on a Sunday morning, the roads were relatively

quiet and Sukey reached the hotel shortly before ten. There was plenty of space in the car park and she found a slot close to the staff entrance. As she switched off her engine and keyed in Erika's number she noticed Boris's Vespa parked under some trees. Evidently the fact that the victim of the shooting was one of his relatives had not kept him away from his job. She recalled how agitated he had become at the possibility of losing it when he had begged her and Rathbone not to tell the hotel manager that he had left his post for an unauthorized cigarette, implying that his family depended on his support.

She waited until Erika appeared and opened the door before getting out of the car and hurrying into the building. Neither spoke until they were closeted in Erika's office and the door firmly shut. She gestured to Sukey to sit down and said, 'You're being very mysterious. Why were you going to call me?'

'First of all, tell me why you're interested in the Stone Street shooting.'

Erika poured two cups of coffee from a jug on her desk and gave one to Sukey before sitting down beside her. 'It's Boris,' she said. 'A member of staff happened to be in reception when the late edition of the *Mercury* was delivered yesterday. Boris was just leaving and he picked up a copy; of course the story of the shooting was on the front page and Debbie told me that he looked devastated – no, terrified was the word she used – when he saw it. She said he let out something that sounded like a sob and crossed himself before rushing away from the desk without speaking to anyone. A few minutes later they saw him roaring out of the car park on his motor scooter like a bat out of hell. He'd finished his shift anyway and by the time I heard about it he'd long gone, so I had no chance to speak to him. He's in this morning as usual, but he looks absolutely terrible and all he says when asked if there's anything wrong is that he's got a bad headache.'

'Has anyone mentioned the shooting to him, do you know?'

'I don't think so. He's never been one to chat to the other staff and I get the impression they don't like to ask him. He's carrying out his duties as usual, but his mind is obviously elsewhere. I thought of asking him to my office to see if I could get him to confide in me, but on second thoughts I decided it would be better to speak to you first. I know you said you weren't on the Whistler case any more, but I didn't think there'd be any harm in asking your advice. Anyway, I didn't have Sergeant Rathbone's number,' she added defensively.

'You did exactly the right thing,' said Sukey.

'Well, that's a relief,' said Erika with one of her characteristic giggles. 'Does that mean if I notice anything else I can speak to you and not Sergeant Rathbone? Not that he wasn't quite nice to me when I called at the police station, by the way.'

'Oh, DS Rathbone's OK, but he's got a lot on his plate at the moment.' Sukey was vaguely surprised at finding herself defending her unpredictable colleague. 'But in any case,' she added, 'things have moved on and I'm back on the case.'

Erika's eyes lit up. 'How do you mean, moved on? Are you close to making an arrest?'

'So far as I know, they haven't moved on that far,' Sukey replied. 'Information is only given out on a need to know basis and as I'm the most junior member of the team I only see my part of the picture.'

'You haven't told me yet why you were going to call me,' Erika reminded her.

'As it happens, you've already told me what I wanted to know.'

'You mean if Boris had seen the report of the shooting?'

'That, and whether he'd shown any particular reaction.'

'So you already suspected that he knew the victim?' said Erika shrewdly.

'From what you've just told me there doesn't seem to be any doubt of it.'

'Gosh!' Erika put a hand to her mouth. 'Do you know who he is? Is he going to be all right?'

'I'm sorry, I can't tell you anything except that we believe the men who carried out the shooting are members of a gang that's the object of a pretty big undercover operation. I can't stress too strongly how important it is that you don't let anyone know I've been here asking these questions.'

'I won't say a word to anyone,' Erika promised, 'but isn't there anything else I can do?'

'Just keep your eyes and ears open, and let me know at

once if you see or hear anything significant, but don't give
any details over the phone. I'll arrange to see you somewhere
away from the hotel.'

Back in her flat, Sukey wrote an account of the meeting
and sent a text message to Rathbone reading simply, 'Have
seen EH – interesting,' before going to the gym as planned.
After a workout and a swim she ate a leisurely lunch and
then, feeling relaxed and refreshed, she drove home and spent
the afternoon reading. Later, she tuned in to the local news
channel; the Stone Street shooting was, naturally, still the main
item, but apart from giving the registration number of the car
used by the gunmen and repeating their appeal for witnesses,
the police had released no information about either the identity of the wounded man or his medical condition, except that
he was 'fighting for his life' and that armed police were at
his bedside.

An hour later, just as she was sitting down to her evening
meal, her landline phone rang. The caller was DCI Leach.
'Rathbone reported your text,' he said, 'I'd like to hear more,
but from now on we're to use the phone as little as possible.
Is it all right if I call round?'

The request took Sukey by surprise. 'You mean now, sir?'
she said.

'Unless it's seriously inconvenient.' His tone gave nothing
away but it wasn't difficult to guess what lay behind the remark.

'It's no problem,' she assured him. 'I'm just having a bite
to eat, but—'

'Shall we say in half an hour?'

'Yes, sir, that'll be fine.'

When Leach arrived he sat down without waiting to be
asked, declined Sukey's offer of coffee and said, 'The ban on
phones applies to emails as well for the moment. We're pretty
sure these villains have access to all the latest technology,
which accounts for the way they've managed to keep a jump
ahead of us so far. They almost certainly know your mobile
number so you're being issued with a new one, but for the
time being it's for use only in emergencies. Right, let's have
your report.'

'It's here, I've done a printout.' She handed him the single
sheet. 'And no, I haven't emailed it to the incident room,' she
added before he had a chance to ask.

'Good.' He scanned the report and handed it back. 'You'll be interested to know that a man in a state of some distress was at the hospital yesterday evening, pleading for information about the victim of the shooting. He refused to give a name; needless to say he was firmly turned away, but from the description it was almost certainly Boris Gasspar and it's pretty obvious that J. Gasspar is a member of his family. The question is, assuming the shooting was a response to J's attempts to contact you, what does he know that Maddox and his mob are so anxious for him not to pass on to the police? More worrying still, if Boris shares that information, is his life in danger?'

'Probably not, sir. If, as now seems likely, Doctor Whistler was killed by this Stephen Lamont lookalike, his evidence will still be important to whoever's been master-minding this crime. But if he's here illegally and terrified of being exposed and deported, that could be an equally strong motive for him continuing to toe the line.'

'Well, we've had the report on his papers and they all seem to be in order, so Maddox must have some other hold on him. It's vital we find out what it is.'

'My guess is that he confided in J and showed him my card. Maybe he asked for advice; maybe J advised him to contact me and ask for help, but for some reason we don't know about he was too scared. J made a note of the number and at some point decided to act on his own initiative. After what's happened to him, Boris will be even less willing to talk to us.'

Leach nodded. 'So far that seems pretty straightforward, but there's the additional complication of your number turning up in the pocket of the dead girl. Did J give it to her, and what sort of trouble was she in that he believed you should know about? Had Maddox's mob forced her into prostitution and had she somehow managed to escape from wherever she was being held?'

'If that's the case, sir, then J must know where that is, otherwise how could he have been in contact with her?'

Leach nodded. 'Good point. Let's hope J will soon be well enough to be interviewed. I'll bring Mr Baird up to speed with the latest developments; meanwhile, I understand from DS Rathbone that he's planning an early meeting with

Professor Lamont. I think you should be there – I'll mention it to Rathbone.'

'Very good, sir.'

Leach got up to go. At the door, he said, 'I think you're turning out to be a very useful member of the team, Sukey.' She opened her mouth to thank him, but he forestalled her by saying, 'So long as you continue to control your tendency to be a loose cannon.'

When Stephen Lamont arrived at the station on Monday morning Sukey was shocked at the change in his appearance. He seemed to have aged by ten years; he had lost weight and his eyes had a haunted expression.

He slumped into the chair that Rathbone indicated and said, in a voice that had none of its former resonance, 'How much longer is this going to go on, Sergeant? I've heard nothing from you or your superior officers since the last time I was here. I'm living in limbo; I can't work, I can't concentrate.' He ran nervous fingers through his mop of grey hair. 'My sister is suffering as well, although I have to say she's being very supportive – more than I deserve. Poor Hester, I've been very hard on her in the past, but I'm beginning to understand something of what she's gone through, even though in her case I have no idea of the cause.'

'I appreciate that you're in a very difficult situation, sir,' said Rathbone, and Sukey was struck by the gentleness of his tone. 'We too have been having our problems and there have been some recent developments that have thrown a completely new light on the murder of Doctor Whistler.'

Lamont sat bolt upright. 'You've found new evidence? Evidence to support my account of what happened that day?'

'Without revealing any details, sir, I think I can say that certain facts have come to light that have made us reconsider our assessment of the case. We believe you may have information that could help us – I'm not suggesting you have deliberately withheld anything,' Rathbone added hastily, seeing Lamont about to protest, 'but it is possible that you either said, or heard another person say, something that did not strike you as significant at the time.'

'What sort of information?'

'I want you to cast your mind back to the time when you

and Doctor Whistler were making arrangements for his visit. At some point in your discussions, he informed you that in addition to the document in which you had a particular interest, he had also been entrusted with certain other items and told to take them to London for examination by a Greek expert who is currently in this country for medical treatment. He described several of those items and indicated they were of considerable monetary value.'

Lamont nodded. 'That is correct.'

'I take it this was during a telephone conversation?'

'Yes.'

'Can you recall anything else he said about this additional errand?'

Lamont gave a wry smile. 'I certainly can. He wasn't happy about it because having to go to London meant he'd have to cut short the time he'd been planning to spend in Bristol. I'd promised to show him some places of interest in the city.'

'Where did this conversation take place?'

'In Professor Thorne's office.'

'Is that where you normally take your calls?'

'No, I have my own office, but if neither I nor my secretary is there they get switched to Archie's PA.'

'Which is what happened on this occasion?'

Lamont made a vague gesture. 'I suppose it must have. I don't remember exactly.'

'I take it Professor Thorne was present?'

Lamont frowned. 'Yes, of course; I was there to consult him on another matter. After the call ended I said something like "Whistler's got to go to London and he's very put out about it". It was only a throwaway remark because I was feeling a bit irritated – Whistler was making a great fuss about having to alter his arrangements. Archie didn't make any comment – I'm not even sure he heard.'

'We know he heard the reference to London.' Lamont raised an eyebrow but Rathbone did not offer any explanation. 'Now, Professor Lamont,' he went on, 'please think very carefully before you answer my next question. Did your end of the conversation include any reference to those additional items that Doctor Whistler was bringing with him? By that I mean, anything which could have suggested they were particularly valuable?'

Slowly, Lamont shook his head. 'Almost certainly not. To be frank, I wasn't really interested in them and as his change of plan did not affect me in any way I saw no reason to prolong the discussion.'

'Did you at any time tell anyone else about these additional items?'

'I believe I mentioned them to my sister, but only in a general sense – that is, I didn't go into details. She may have mentioned them to one of her friends – I could ask her if you like.'

Sukey half expected Rathbone to say they already had that information from her report on her first meeting with Hester, but all he said was, 'That would be helpful.'

'How is Hester?' asked Sukey. It was the first time she had spoken since the interview began and Lamont looked at her in surprise, as if he had forgotten her presence.

'As a matter of fact she has been a great deal better lately, thank you.' he replied.

'That's good news anyway,' said Rathbone. 'Well, thank you Professor Lamont. If you should think of anything else, please let us know at once.'

'Of course.'

Lamont got up and went through the door that Rathbone held open for him. A few paces along the corridor he stopped short and turned round. 'I don't suppose it's important, but Lottie Milligan was in her office throughout my conversation with Whistler.'

'Was her door open while you were speaking?' asked Rathbone.

'Not that I remember, but I do recall something I only half noticed at the time. The usual procedure when putting a call through is for her to say, "I have so-and-so on the line for you". As soon as I say, "Put them through" she waits for a moment to make sure the connection is there and then puts her own telephone down. You can hear the click.'

Rathbone gave him a keen look. 'And?'

'I can't swear to it, of course, but on that occasion I don't remember hearing the click.'

Twenty-Five

The minute Rathbone and Sukey returned to the CID office after their interview with Lamont they informed DCI Leach of the possible new lead. Leach ordered an immediate written report; meanwhile he would pass the information to Superintendent Baird who would no doubt want to question them in person. In less than an hour they were summoned to Leach's office.

Baird was already there, accompanied by a young man neither Sukey nor Rathbone had met before. Baird introduced him as DC Haskins, a member of the team Operation Dirty Linen. 'Before we consider this latest development, he's going to bring you up to date,' he explained. 'Right, Haskins, go ahead.'

Reading from a prepared statement, Haskins began, 'Since receiving DC Reynolds' account of her observation in Mold Street ten days ago of a meeting between Boris Gasspar and a man answering to the description of our target, we have maintained a surveillance operation on the house Gasspar was seen to enter. We observed several young men coming and going and established that some of them were regular visitors to a café called Marco's in Gloucester Road.

'I went in there one day when I knew two of them were present, ordered a coffee and sat down at the next table. They were speaking in heavily accented English, indicating that it wasn't their native language but that they were using it as a *lingua franca*. After a minute or two one of them, who appeared to be having difficulty in finding an English word, said something in Polish that I immediately understood.' He looked across at Rathbone and Sukey as if half expecting some kind of reaction from them; receiving none, he continued with his narrative.

'It so happens that my wife's family comes from Warsaw

and because her father is elderly and has no English I have made some effort to learn Polish. I struck up a conversation with these two men; the Polish one was called Stefan and he was delighted to have the chance to speak to someone in his own language. I helped him with one or two problems with his English and the three of us went on to have a pleasant conversation for a few minutes. Stefan introduced his friend as Jozsef and said he was from Albania. After a little while they got up to leave, saying they had to go back to work. Out of what I intended to come across as a polite interest I asked them what jobs they had and they answered quite openly; Stefan said he was an electrician and Jozsef described himself as a general handyman.'

Baird glanced round the room. 'Any questions so far?' As everyone shook their heads he said, 'Good. Continue, Haskins.'

'I left it for a couple of days before going back. On Thursday they were there at lunchtime; I spotted them as I walked to the counter to give my order and nodded and smiled at them. I noticed they didn't look exactly overjoyed to see me; in fact, they got up very hastily before I could join them and went out, leaving their drinks unfinished on the table. I came to the conclusion that they'd been warned off talking to me.'

'Did you remark on this to anyone else in the café at the time?' asked Leach when Haskins' recital came to an end.

'Yes, to Marco.'

'What did he say?'

'Nothing much. He grinned and shrugged and said something about foreigners being a bit odd. Which coming from him was a bit of a joke, seeing as his family's Italian, but he's lived here since he was a child and considers himself a true Bristolian.'

'Thank you, Haskins,' said Baird. 'That puts you two in the picture,' he added to Sukey and Rathbone. 'We have three reasons to suspect a link between Marco's and Maddox.' He began counting on his fingers. 'One, the call to DC Reynolds was made from his café and half an hour later the man we believe made the call was the victim of a drive-by shooting as he waited for Reynolds: two, customers are discouraged from fraternizing with the locals: three, the Lamont lookalike appears to be a regular caller there. Any conclusions to be drawn from that?'

'Regarding the regular visit from the phoney Lamont,' said Rathbone, 'it doesn't sound like a protection racket, more a case of handing over payment for services rendered, like passing on useful bits of information.'

Baird nodded. 'That appears the more likely. One thing is clear; Maddox knows we're snapping at his heels and no doubt he's doing his best to plug every possible avenue of enquiry open to us. We've reason to believe he has some kind of hold over Boris Gasspar because of his reluctance to talk to Reynolds and now we have two more men reacting in the same way. Let's assume for the moment that Jozsef is the J. Gasspar who finished up full of lead in the ITU. If so, how did he come by Reynolds' mobile number? Did Boris give it to him because he was too frightened to use it himself? Or did he merely show it to him and J decided to act on his own initiative? How did it find its way into the pocket of the Lady in the Avon?' He fixed a steely gaze on Sukey and she felt goose bumps rising in response. 'Any ideas, Reynolds?'

'Well, sir,' said Sukey, a little hesitantly because of the four pairs of eyes fastened on her, 'if we assume the girl had been forced into prostitution, which seems likely in view of the fact that she'd been drugged, she must have been kept in a house being run as a brothel, presumably by the Maddox mob. It would have to be a secure house, but it's possible some of the women made attempts from time to time to break out.'

'True,' said Baird. 'In that case she was probably one of them, which is why they drugged her. Go on.'

'Maddox seems to have a hold over both Stefan and Jozsef. Maybe the women did some damage and Jozsef was told to fix it. Perhaps the girl, thinking he was an outsider and not a member of the mob, begged him for help and he felt sorry for her and gave her my number.'

Baird's glance swept round the room. 'Has anyone got anything to add to that?'

'One point, sir,' said Rathbone. 'Surely, if they were being held against their will, the girls would have to be under constant guard by people Maddox felt he could rely on. Why couldn't one of them be a resident handyman?'

'Reynolds?'

'Perhaps an extra pair of hands was needed, sir – or maybe the guards were women.'

'That's a point. I suppose there's no reason why they shouldn't be. Maybe Maddox recruits them from ex-prison guards who've been sacked for brutality – it would be right in character. All the indications about him so far suggest that we're dealing with a control freak who enjoys tormenting his victims.' Baird turned back to Haskins. 'I believe you've been able to find out where Jozsef and Stefan work?'

'Yes, sir, they both have regular jobs with small, reputable businesses and their papers are in order. I've been able to establish that Jozsef didn't report for work this morning by ringing the company and speaking with a Polish accent, but it didn't seem to have occurred to the woman who answered the phone that he might have been the victim of the shooting.'

'The news blackout is still in force and the media are co-operating,' said Baird. 'I take it there's been no report of suspicious activity in or near the hospital, Rathbone?'

'No, sir, just Boris turning up every so often begging for news and being told to go away.'

'Poor devil.' For a moment the professional mask slipped, revealing the human being behind it. 'Now let's have your report on this morning's interview with Lamont.'

'Right, sir.' Rathbone read out the statement he and Sukey had prepared together. Everyone listened intently and when Rathbone had finished he handed it to Baird, who put it beside the open file on his desk and sat for a few moments tapping his pen against his top teeth.

'In the light of her known association with Maddox,' he said after several moments' contemplation, 'we've been keeping an eye on the Milligan woman. She's been seen out and about with him a few times since Reynolds and DCI Castle of the Gloucestershire force observed them in the floating restaurant just over two weeks ago, but we've observed no suspicious behaviour on her part. It now appears feasible that it was from her that he came to hear about the goodies Whistler was bringing with him. He must know enough about Greek antiquities to recognize that they were valuable enough to interest him.'

'They must be worth more than a couple of grand to rate the attention of a hit man,' observed Leach. 'I don't suppose the putative Pauline epistle has enough monetary value to interest Maddox, but he could probably find a customer for it.'

Baird nodded. 'Some unscrupulous collector who wouldn't be too concerned about where it came from,' he agreed. 'Of course, it's by no means certain that there was any intention to kill Whistler. Even if he'd been conned into handing over the items, believing that he was giving them to the right person, he would no doubt have done as Gasspar did – identify Lamont as the thief when he realized what had happened. Which brings us to another question: how did Maddox manage to find someone with such a strong resemblance to Lamont? Whatever the explanation, it's just the sort of situation that would appeal to him. Another of his less endearing qualities is his warped sense of humour,' he added grimly.

'Excuse me, sir,' said Sukey hesitantly, 'it might have been Ms Milligan who gave him the idea. Maddox might have introduced her to the hit man at some time. She would almost certainly have commented on the likeness; she could even have shown Maddox a copy of a prospectus with photographs of the senior members of the faculty.'

'Good point, Reynolds,' said Baird. 'Another thing we know about Maddox is that he has a fascination for women, so she'd probably do anything he asked of her. Right, Haskins, we continue to keep Milligan under observation. Report to me if she so much as sneezes without good reason. Otherwise, carry on as before. Rathbone, maintain the guard over J. Gasspar and you, Reynolds, stand by to interview him the minute the medics give permission. Thank you everyone, that's all for now.'

Following its publication in the British press, the artist's impression of the girl found in the river had been circulated through Interpol and very quickly identified as their youngest daughter by an impoverished farming family in Albania. It seemed the girl had gone willingly to England, with her parents' consent, with a man who had promised her a chance to train as a model. Nothing had been heard from her since; the distraught parents had been brought over to make a formal identification and the following day during the lunchtime news bulletin they had made an impassioned plea through an interpreter for help in bringing her killer to justice.

This prompted several calls from the public who confirmed an earlier report of a girl seen getting into a car with two men in their twenties. Neither answered to the description of

Lamont's double and the consensus was that the men were coaxing rather than forcing the girl into the car, but that she appeared 'rather reluctant to go with them' and 'once actually tried to walk away but one of them caught her by the arm and stopped her', as another witness described it. Another said the men were 'a bit foreign looking'.

'Still not much to go on,' DCI Leach observed to the team after studying the reports, 'but it's interesting that she didn't seem to be putting up much of a struggle. In any case, we can't be a hundred per cent certain that this was the girl we fished out of the Avon.'

'If it was, they might have cooked up some story to make her go quietly,' Sukey suggested. 'Maybe they even led her to believe she'd be allowed to go home – anything rather than cause a scene that could prompt a member of the public to call the police.

'Or one of them could have stuck a needle in her with a shot of the drug that was found during the PM,' said Rathbone.

'Or it might just have been a family matter,' said Leach. 'Without something a bit more specific, it doesn't help much, I'm afraid.'

It was not until the following Monday that a message came from the hospital that the injured man had recovered sufficiently to be questioned for a short period. It had already been decided that Sukey should be the first to see him and she was given detailed instructions before setting off for the hospital. As she drove into the huge sprawling site, everything appeared normal. The patient was still in a private room in the Intensive Therapy Unit, but she had been told to use a car park some distance from the one that visitors to the unit would normally use.

She found a vacant space and made for the nearest entrance. Two uniformed police were on guard; they did not appear to be armed, but she had no doubt that armed backup was on immediate call. As she approached, a man was in conversation with the officers; he appeared to be pleading for admission and was being firmly repulsed. As, looking somewhat forlorn, he turned away she realized it was Boris Gasspar. Their eyes met; he appeared first startled, then alarmed. He broke into a run and as if by magic two armed officers appeared and wrestled him to the ground. Sukey hurried over as they were about to handcuff him.

'It's OK, I know him and he's not dangerous,' she assured them, showing her ID. They allowed him to get to his feet, still holding him by the arms. 'Boris, please tell me,' she said, 'the man who was shot – do you know him?'

He nodded, nervously licking his lips. 'He's my cousin,' he said, his voice barely a whisper.

'Then I can give you good news. He's recovering. He will live.'

He gave a great sigh, bowed his head and murmured something with closed eyes. When he opened them again they were overflowing with tears. 'Thank you. Thank you very much. I see him now?' he begged.

'I'm afraid not, but I promise we'll let you know how he's getting on.'

'Thank you,' he said again. 'I go now?'

'What do you think?' asked one of the officers, who were still holding him by both arms.

Sukey thought quickly. She could see no reason why they should hold him, but felt unable to take the responsibility of saying he could go. 'I suggest you take him back to your car and call CID,' she said. 'Ask for DS Rathbone, mention my name and tell him I've identified your detainee as Boris Gasspar. I have to go now.' Leaving them to it, she went back to the entrance where the two officers on guard had been keeping a close eye on developments.

'You know that guy?' one of them asked as she showed her ID and gave the reason for her visit.

'Yes, and we're pretty sure he's related to the shooting victim,' she said. 'All he wanted was to know how he was doing; I don't think he'll give you any more trouble.'

'At least it broke the boredom,' said the other with a grin. 'Here comes another medic, by the looks of him. They keep popping in and out, mostly for a fag. There's no smoking in the hospital.'

Glancing over her shoulder, Sukey saw a young man in a white coat with a stethoscope round his neck and his identity card hanging on a cord. He paused to stub out a cigarette in a disposal unit fixed to the wall before approaching the entrance. She saw the two officers intercept him; they made him wait while they checked his ID against what looked like a register before admitting him. Having some idea of the length of Maddox's reach, Sukey realized that she had been feeling a little apprehensive and it was a relief to know that tight security was still being maintained.

Ahead of her was a long corridor with signs and arrows indicating various departments and further corridors leading off on either side. For the moment there was no one about and the way ahead of her seemed to stretch into infinity. She walked on for a short distance, her footsteps echoing on the bare floor, before realizing that she should have taken a turning to the right. She stopped short, swung round and cannoned into a man in a white coat who had been following her, a man whom she recognized as the one who had entered the building behind her. She hastily apologized; he mumbled something incomprehensible and for a split second she detected what appeared to be a flicker of recognition in his eyes. Then he too turned, hurried back and headed along the corridor she had missed.

Twenty-Six

Sukey's heart was pounding as she tried to decide what to do. The officers guarding the entrance had allowed him in so presumably they were satisfied that he was a bona fide member of the medical team. But supposing the badge he wore was phoney or had been stolen? His sharp, sallow features were sufficiently striking to make her certain she had never set eyes on him before, yet the more she thought about it, the more convinced she felt that he had recognized her but for some reason wanted to conceal the fact. Why? She recalled one occasion in a supermarket when, thinking a complete stranger was a friend, she had called out a greeting before realizing her mistake. Her embarrassed apology had been accepted with a smile, but this man's attitude had been entirely different. Some sixth sense told her he should be challenged and if necessary asked to provide further proof of his identity.

He had turned into the corridor she now realized she should have taken, but by the time she had gathered her wits and hurried after him he was nowhere to be seen. The sign they had both passed by indicated that it led to the Intensive Therapy Unit. Surely, she reasoned, if he genuinely was one of the hospital staff, he would have known the way. And the ITU would certainly be his destination if he was an impostor who had tricked his way into the hospital with the intention of silencing forever the victim of the Stone Street shooting. There was no doubt now in her mind; she must alert the armed officers guarding the patient of a possible threat before heading there herself.

She took out her mobile and keyed in the contact number she had been given in case of an emergency. She heard a man's voice say, 'Sergeant Murray', but before she had a chance to speak a hand was clamped over her mouth and an arm like an iron band encircled her chest, threatening to squeeze the breath from her body. She felt herself being dragged backwards through a door that had opened silently behind her; the mobile fell from her grasp and struck her foot; instinctively she kicked out at it in the desperate hope that it would be picked up by someone who, on hearing an urgent voice on the line, would realize that something was seriously amiss and have the sense to raise the alarm.

Sukey had some training in self-defence. She was wearing shoes with hard soles; raising her right knee she dragged her heel as hard as she could downwards against her assailant's shinbone. She heard him give a gasp of pain; the pressure round her ribs eased a fraction and the hand round her mouth relaxed just enough to enable her to bite hard into his thumb. He uttered a curse; his grip relaxed a little more and she gave a backward jab with both elbows, hoping to wind him, but he was ready for it and all she encountered, before a blow to the head knocked her out, was hard, unyielding muscle.

When she came round she was on the floor and the man was bending over her, winding her body mummy-fashion in a sheet. There was a gag in her mouth and already her arms were pinned to her sides, but her legs were still free. She aimed a kick at his groin, but he grabbed her ankles and bound her legs together. Looking round she saw shelves piled high with bed linen and towels and realized that they were in a laundry store. The man grabbed another sheet, laid it on the floor, rolled her over on it several times and tied the ends firmly behind her back. 'Not ideal, but the best I could do in the circumstances,' he said with a sneer before slipping quietly out of the room and locking the door behind him.

Her head was throbbing painfully. He had left her lying face down, but she managed to roll over on to her back. After a few seconds she became aware of the sound of running feet and confused voices. Surely, she thought in a surge of hope, this meant that the armed guard who had answered her call had become suspicious and raised the alarm. If so, they would all be on red alert, but they would have no idea of the nature of the threat or from what direction it was likely to come. Somehow, she must attract attention so that she could tell them who to look out for. She could neither call out nor stand up, but she could at least bend her knees and dig her heels into the tiled floor. By using them as a lever she managed to pull her body towards the door.

Fortunately the room was little more than a cupboard and the distance was not great; nevertheless a lifetime seemed to pass before she was able to start pounding on the door with her feet. At last she heard a shout of, 'Someone's locked in here!' There was a scraping sound as a key turned in the lock and the door began to open. She managed to roll out of the way and ended up lying face down again, panting with exhaustion. Hands rolled her none too gently on to her back; someone in dark blue trousers was standing over her and she looked up to find herself staring into the muzzle of a gun.

They were taking no chances. Another man appeared and removed the gag before yanking her to her feet and starting to unwind the sheets that imprisoned her while the first one barked, 'Who are you?' She gave her name and rank and began to explain how she came to be there, but not until her hands were free and she was able to produce her ID did they accept that she was genuine and not a diversionary tactic on the part of the enemy. Meanwhile, more precious seconds had ticked away.

'We must get to the ITU before the man who attacked me gets to Gasspar,' she almost sobbed.

'This way,' said one of her rescuers and the two broke into a run as he spoke, with Sukey struggling to keep up. 'Don't panic,' he said over his shoulder, 'only the medics are allowed near him.'

'He is a medic – at least, he's posing as one,' she panted as they raced along. 'He must have faked an ID . . . the guard let him into the building a minute or so behind me . . . I got suspicious when he didn't seem sure which way he was going.'

Without slackening speed the leader spoke into his radio to relay the information. Then he shouted, 'Take him out . . . now!'

'What is it?' Sukey gasped.

'He's in there with Gasspar,' he said grimly. 'Leave us to deal with this.'

They charged on ahead, brushing aside everyone in their path while Sukey, still suffering the effects of the blow to her head, stumbled dazedly after them. When she reached the ITU she heard shouts and the sound of a scuffle coming from one of the private rooms. Outside stood a young nurse; her eyes were wide with terror, the knuckles of one hand were crammed against her mouth and tears were pouring down her face. Sukey went over to her. 'How long was he in there with Gasspar before the police went in?' she asked.

'Only a few seconds,' the nurse whimpered. 'I was a bit doubtful because I hadn't seen him before, but it isn't always the same doctor treating him . . . and he showed his pass . . . he said Jozsef needed some medication . . . the police guards were a bit jumpy as well and they checked the name against the list of doctors and it was there so they said it was all right to let him in . . . and then all of a sudden they rushed in after him with their guns and . . . oh, please God, let Jozsef be safe!'

'Amen to that,' Sukey said fervently. As she spoke, the door was flung open and four burly officers in body armour emerged, half dragging, half carrying the phoney doctor, who was handcuffed but still struggling violently, kicking out at his captors and screaming abuse.

'I don't understand, but I doubt it's the kind of language a gentleman would use before ladies,' remarked one of the four as he threw a blanket over the man's head before he was hustled out of the room. 'There's a syringe on the floor under the bed, but we got to him before he had a chance to use it,' he informed Sukey, almost as an afterthought. 'I'm sure you know what to do with it. And Nurse, it'd be as well to check on your patient. He's had quite a fright.'

The nurse was obviously still badly shaken but she nodded and went into the patient's room while Sukey waited outside, uncertain for the moment what her next move should be. Then she had an idea; when the nurse came out she said, 'I need to go in and retrieve the syringe. Can you give me a pair of surgical gloves and some sort of sterile container?'

'Yes, of course, but if you don't mind I'll come in with you. Jozsef's a bit nervous and if someone he doesn't recognize were to go in now I think he'd get upset.'

'I'll bet he would – and so would I after a scare like that,' Sukey agreed. 'I'm DC Reynolds and I was supposed to interview him today – that's why I'm here. We believe he can help us with our enquiries into some very serious crimes. Do you think he's well enough or should I come back tomorrow?'

The nurse hesitated. 'I knew you were coming, of course,' she said after a moment, 'but after what's happened I don't feel I have the authority to let you see Jozsef without permission from a doctor. And on second thoughts, I think it would be better if I collected the syringe for you. I'll be careful how I handle it; I watch police programmes on the telly so I know all about fingerprints and things,' she added, and for the first time her tense expression relaxed and she gave a conspiratorial smile.

'I suppose it'll be all right,' Sukey replied. She had almost forgotten her own frightening experience, but now the excitement was over the memory of the struggle began to filter back into her mind. As the nurse vanished once more into Jozsef's room she became aware that her head was throbbing more violently and her legs were turning to jelly. The room began to spin around her; she grabbed at a convenient chair, sat down and closed her eyes.

When Sukey came round she was lying on a bed with a nurse on one side and DC Vicky Armstrong on the other. She stared at them in bewilderment, tried to sit up and was gently pushed back on to the pillow by the nurse. 'Just lie still while I check your blood pressure,' she said.

'I don't understand,' said Sukey while the nurse fitted a cuff round her arm and switched on the monitor. 'What happened? What am I doing here?'

'You had a nasty blow to the head and suffered mild concussion, but somehow you managed to keep going and raise the alarm,' explained Vicky.

'Yes, I remember now.' Sukey's thoughts were beginning to clear. 'They arrested the man who attacked me and tried to kill Jozsef. After it was over I wanted to talk to him but the nurse wouldn't let me without a doctor's say-so. I sat down to wait and—'

'And passed out,' said Vicky.

'How long for?' Sukey looked out of the window. 'It's getting dark. What time is it?'

'Just after six. You started to come round after a few minutes but the doctor who checked you over wanted to keep you under observation for a couple of hours, so they gave you a sedative and you've had a nice long sleep. How's the head?'

'Still a bit sore, but I'll live. What about the blood pressure?' she asked as the nurse removed the cuff from her arm.

'It's fine, and so's your pulse.'

'Does that mean I can go?'

'As soon as you're ready.' The nurse packed her monitor away and left the room.

Sukey threw off the blanket that had been covering her and stood up. 'I can't go without seeing Jozsef. Has he been given the all clear?'

'Sukey, I'm sorry to disappoint you,' said Vicky, 'but as you were temporarily *hors de combat* Greg Rathbone said I'd better see him and get his statement ASAP.'

'But he said I was the only person he'd speak to,' Sukey protested.

Vicky gave an apologetic grin. 'If you remember, he only asked to talk to the police lady – he had no idea what you looked like and so—'

'You pretended to be me,' said Sukey indignantly.

'No, I just said I was a police officer and waved my ID under his nose and he was perfectly happy to talk to me. The good news is that he's spilled a whole canful of beans and we know now why Boris has been so cagey. I'll tell you about it on the way. Just a minute.' She broke off to take a call on her mobile. 'Yes, Sarge, she's been discharged from the hospital and I'm taking her home . . . what? . . . Gosh, there's never a dull moment in this job is there? Hold on, Sarge, I'll ask her.' She put a hand over the phone and turned to Sukey. 'Operation Dirty Linen's under way, and DCI Leach would like us all back at the station to interview Thorne's secretary who's just turned up in a state of the jitters saying she wants to make a statement. Do you feel up to it or would you like me to take you home first?'

'Are you kidding?' Sukey's voice rose to an excited squeak. 'I wouldn't miss this for the world.'

Vicky spoke once more into the phone. 'She's fine Sarge; we're on our way.'

Twenty-Seven

Despite Sukey's protests that she was perfectly fit to drive, Vicky insisted that she hand over the keys to the pool car in which she had driven to the hospital.

'Greg Rathbone's orders,' she said as they clipped on their seat belts. 'He's come over all solicitous for you. I wonder why? Is there anything you'd like to tell Auntie Vicky?' she added with a mischievous twinkle in her eyes.

'Don't be daft,' said Sukey, laughing in spite of herself. 'He's probably trying to make up for being so hard on me earlier. You've known him for some time – is he always on a short fuse or just naturally subject to mood swings?'

'Funny you should ask that.' Vicky switched on the ignition and drove slowly towards the exit from the car park. 'We've all noticed lately that he's been more inclined than usual to be tetchy . . . and we've had to cover up for him more than once when he's missed something quite important.'

'Yes, I've noticed that,' said Sukey. 'Have you any idea what's behind it?'

'Strictly *entre nous*, Bob Douglas confided the other day that he's having matrimonial problems. It's not surprising; being married to a copper can't be easy.'

Sukey nodded. 'Jim's marriage went pear-shaped after a couple of years,' she said.

Vicky gave her a sideways glance. 'Do I take it he's not anxious to repeat the experience?'

'We've never discussed it.'

Vicky nodded. 'It's the best way. It's the same with Chris and me. Ours is a strictly NLTC relationship – no long-term commitment on either side. It's worked well for three years so far. Anyway, that's enough of that. Want to hear what Jozsef had to say?'

'I thought you'd never get around to it.'

'It was all they needed to trigger Operation Dirty Linen. You were dead right; Maddox had a hold over Boris, big time.'

'What kind of hold?'

'Outwardly, he's the owner of a legitimate international employment agency with branches in several Eastern European and Balkan countries. He fixes up guys like Boris and Jozsef with jobs in this and other EU countries where they earn wages several times greater than they can get at home. He even finds them places to live – in houses owned by one of his own companies. That's another of his sidelines.'

'I suppose it means he can keep an eye on them?' suggested Sukey.

'Possibly – I hadn't thought of that. Anyway, that's his public face; his private one is rather different. In return for helping them to raise their and their families' standard of living, he requires them from time to time to carry out certain services on his behalf – such as repairing damage in a bordello with no questions asked.'

'Or reporting any of his protégés who make calls to police officers?'

Vicky nodded. 'Exactly. It's almost certain that either Marco or one of the regulars in his café overheard Jozsef's phone call to you and grassed him up to one of the Maddox mob, who promptly summoned a hit squad.'

'We figured it had to be something like that, didn't we?' said Sukey. 'Presumably Boris is so scared of getting similar treatment that he's prepared to give false evidence against Stephen Lamont?'

Vicky was silent for a moment, staring at the road ahead. At length she said, 'It's even nastier than that. The Whistler job was a bit more complicated than fixing a window some poor girl had smashed in an effort to escape a life of enforced prostitution, so Maddox had to figure out a different method of getting him to co-operate. After all, a dead Boris couldn't have given evidence against Lamont.'

'That's true. So what did he do?' Sukey prompted, as Vicky still seemed reluctant to continue.

'I warn you, it's pretty horrid. A few days before the Whistler murder he took Boris to a local house he was running as a brothel and forced him to witness some of the nastier things the clients do to the girls there. Boris has a sister back in

Albania and he was told that if he didn't do exactly what Maddox wanted she'd be abducted and taken to a similar establishment where she'd get the same treatment.'

'The man's a monster!' said Sukey in horror.

'A monster, a psychopath, a megalomaniac, you name it,' said Vicky grimly. 'Plus he gets a sadistic kick out of seeing people squirm. He thinks he's invincible as well – he moves quite freely among his minions without any apparent fear of betrayal. You saw that for yourself the day he picked up Boris in his car.'

'Poor Boris, it's no wonder he wouldn't talk to me,' Sukey said sadly. 'So what made Jozsef risk blowing the whistle?'

'It seems it happened much as we figured – Boris has been really unhappy about the prospect of committing perjury and he asked his cousin's advice and showed him your card. Jozsef advised him to use it to shop Maddox and ask for police protection for himself and his family in Albania, but he didn't dare for fear of what would happen if Maddox's mob got to them first. He wouldn't part with the card either, but Jozsef happens to be good at memorizing numbers so when he was on his own he wrote yours down.'

'And later gave it to the girl who ended up in the Avon?'

'So it seems, although by the time he reached this point in the story he was getting tired and the details are a bit vague.'

'I'm not surprised. His English is pretty shaky and telling you all this must have been quite a struggle.'

'It wasn't as difficult as I expected. He understands a lot, but he needs help in finding the right words to express himself. Anyway, you were right when you suggested he was sent to a house that Maddox was using as a brothel to carry out some repairs, but exactly how he came to give the girl the number isn't very clear as yet. Seeing her picture in the paper was enough to make him decide to contact us, come hell or high water.'

They had reached the station. Vicky parked the car and they got out. 'Right,' she said as they made their way up to the CID offices, 'let's hear what Ms Milligan has got for us.'

They were directed to an interview room where Lottie Milligan was already seated at a table opposite DCI Leach and DS Rathbone. Sukey's impression of her at their two previous meetings was of an extremely attractive, self-possessed woman who could no doubt be charming when she chose but who had treated her on the first occasion with thinly disguised hostility and on the second – on that memorable evening in the restaurant when she was escorted by Oliver Maddox – in a distinctly condescending manner. Today, the change in her was so remarkable that Sukey had to look at her a second time to make sure she was the same person. She sat huddled in her chair with her head sunk between her shoulders; her skin under the make-up had a greyish tinge, the hair that had fallen in flattering waves on either side of her face now clung limply to her temples and her mouth drooped at the corners, giving her a hangdog expression. Most striking of all was the deadness in her eyes, which stared out through her fashionable glasses like pale blue marbles. It was as if her whole personality had changed along with her appearance.

Leach told Sukey and Vicky to sit in the chairs placed on either side of her, introduced them and then said, 'Ms Milligan, will you please confirm that you are here of your own free will?'

She nodded and whispered, 'Yes, that's right.'

'We note that you wish to make a statement and we will be recording this interview, but you are free to leave at any time. Do you understand?'

She nodded again; Rathbone switched on the tape recorder and said, 'Right, Ms Milligan, please begin.'

'It won't take long,' she said, in a voice as dead as her expressionless eyes. 'Oliver Maddox is a corrupt and heartless monster who deserves to be put away for life. He's responsible for the deaths of Doctor Whistler and the girl you found in the river . . . many others as well for all I know. He deals in drugs, he's into money laundering – that's where he makes most of his money. He runs brothels, he deals in stolen art treasures . . . you name it. He owns all kinds of dodgy enterprises . . . I can give you details . . . and for a while he owned me.' Her voice cracked and she stared down at her hands, which were restlessly fiddling with the handbag that lay in her lap. 'I'm sorry,' she whispered brokenly, 'I'll be all right in a moment.'

'Just take your time,' said Leach.

'I didn't care what he did,' she said after a moment, 'I was completely under his spell. I'd have done anything for him.

It was my idea to get Sonny Bright to pretend to be Stephen Lamont and steal those things from Doctor Whistler, because of the resemblance. Oliver thought it was a huge joke and he enjoyed forcing that poor man at the hotel to tell lies for him. I was horrified when it ended in murder, but he just shrugged it off. All he was interested in was getting his hands on the things Doctor Whistler had brought with him.'

'Have you any idea what he did with them?' asked Leach.

She shook her head. 'I'm afraid not. If you search his house you might find something about them on his computer.'

'What happened next?' prompted Rathbone.

'Nothing. That is, things went on as before. We did something most nights – meals in expensive restaurants, theatres and concerts, sometimes just the two of us, sometimes with his friends ... and he came to my flat every night and we made love. I know I should have put an end to it, but I couldn't ... even then, I was afraid of him although at the same time it was all so exciting ... he seemed so all-powerful, like a Mafia boss in a movie.' She gave a sad little laugh that failed to conceal the anguish in her eyes. 'He doesn't make many mistakes; that's why he's got away with his crimes for so long ... but he got careless yesterday evening.'

Another wave of emotion threatened to engulf her, but she fought it back bravely. 'We were going to the theatre,' she went on. 'I arrived a bit early; his housekeeper was just going back into the house after putting out the garbage so I didn't have to ring the bell. She said, "Mr Maddox is in his study – he's on the phone, but I'm sure he won't be long." His study leads off the hall and I heard him talking and for some reason I went and listened outside the door. He was saying something about tickets so I guessed he was planning a trip. Whoever was on the other end must have asked if he was taking me with him because he said, "Take Lottie? You must be joking. She's outlived her usefulness – I don't want to be lumbered with her where I'm going".' She raised her head and stared round at the detectives with a look of incredulity on her face. 'He was going to dump me!' she wailed. 'I couldn't believe it ... the number of times he swore he loved me! How could I have been such a fool?' This time a combination of shock, misery and humiliation got the better of her and she broke into uncontrollable weeping.

Leach switched off the tape and he and Rathbone waited while Sukey and Vicky did their best to comfort the stricken woman. When she was calmer, Leach gave her a glass of water and said, 'Ms Milligan, would you like to take a break before continuing?'

She shook her head. 'No,' she said in a hoarse whisper. 'Please, I'd rather go on.'

'Good.' He signalled to Rathbone, who restarted the tape. 'Before we go any further, do you have any idea when Maddox was planning to leave, or where he intended to go?'

'None at all, I'm afraid.'

'Did you tell him what you'd overheard?'

'No, I didn't dare. I sat down and when he came out of his study he looked at me and said, "Lottie, you look ghastly. Are you all right?" I told him I had a migraine and I didn't really feel well enough to go to the theatre, so he took me home. After he left I got frightened; I thought, maybe he only pretended to believe me about the migraine, maybe he's guessed I overheard what he was saying and thought I might be planning to shop him for cheating on me. I know what he can do, how he can get to people, he's got so much power it's unbelievable. I didn't feel safe any more so I packed a bag and spent the night at a hotel. I still don't feel safe, I'm afraid to go home, the only thing I could think of was to come here and tell you everything. I want him punished for all the evil things he's done.' In a sudden, dramatic change of mood, she leapt to her feet and glared wildly at the four police officers. 'Why are you still sitting there?' she screamed. 'Go out and arrest him! I want him put away for the rest of his life!'

'Please, Ms Milligan, sit down,' said Leach calmly. 'You have nothing to fear from Oliver Maddox any more. He and a number of his associates were arrested a few hours ago.'

Twenty-Eight

The following day an explosion of sensational headlines in the local and national press announced that the police, in a co-ordinated series of raids in and around the city, had rounded up a significant number of people of both sexes and were holding them at various police stations on suspicion of being involved in drug dealing and money laundering. At the same time a number of women who had been forced into prostitution had been released from a house in Mold Street.

Superintendent Baird, while delighted at the success of Operation Dirty Linen, was concerned that as few details as possible of the people detained, and particularly of Oliver Maddox and his lieutenant Sonny Bright, should reach the press.

'The last thing we want is trial by media,' he warned the team. 'Nothing would please this lot better than to give a bunch of dodgy lawyers an excuse to plead that they couldn't expect a fair trial.' At the subsequent press conference he made it clear that further arrests were likely and that much work still remained to be done before any of the detainees could be charged. To everyone's relief, after the initial flurry of excitement, the newspaper editors and radio and TV presenters switched their attention to the next headline-grabbing story.

'Superintendent Baird has asked me to thank you all for your contribution to the success of Operation Dirty Linen,' DCI Leach informed Detective Sergeants Rathbone and Douglas and Detective Constables Reynolds and Armstrong when, some days later, he summoned them to a meeting in his office. 'As I'm sure you all realize there are still hours of detective work ahead and a hundred and one loose ends to tie up. A few of them have already been satisfactorily dealt with and I'm sure you'll be pleased to know we've recovered the stuff that Sonny Bright stole from Whistler.'

'That's great news, sir,' said Rathbone.

'It's certainly good news from our point of view, and Inspector Comino of the Greek police is naturally delighted – although there may be a bit of a problem there. He wants to come and pick up the things right away but we need them as evidence, so there'll probably have to be a bit of top-level diplomacy. That's for someone else to sort out, thank goodness.'

'What about the Pauline epistle, sir?' asked Douglas.

'I understand Comino is happy for Professor Lamont to be allowed to study it as planned, on the understanding that it is returned to Greece once he has finished with it.'

'One thing has puzzled me from the beginning, sir,' said Sukey. 'When I went to talk to the paramedics who took Doctor Whistler to hospital they said he had been trying to say something that sounded like, "Not Greek". Have we any idea what he meant?'

Leach gave a wry smile. 'Oh yes, as a matter of fact we have. Sonny Bright answered that question at a very early stage. It seems he's been nursing a grudge against Maddox for some time – he claims he's not been getting his fair cut of the spoils – so he's being very co-operative, no doubt in the hope that it will be to his advantage when he comes to trial. He says that when he went to Whistler's room, pretending to be Lamont, all went well until the moment when Whistler handed over a small holdall containing the things. He said something completely incomprehensible to Sonny; presumably he was speaking Greek and expecting a response in the same language, which of course the genuine Lamont would have given. Sonny merely looked blank, whereupon Whistler realized he was an impostor and tried to snatch the holdall back. They tussled and Sonny pulled the knife on him; he swears he was only trying to frighten him and didn't intend to kill him, but the old boy very foolishly struggled and the knife went in by accident.'

'I wonder if the jury will buy that?' commented Douglas.

Leach shrugged. 'That remains to be seen.'

'What about Marco, sir?' asked Sukey.

'He was pulled in during the first sweep and questioned in some detail about the people who use his café, but we're pretty sure he's clean and he's been released without charge.'

'And Boris and Jozsef?' added Vicky. 'Are their families all right? Jozsef said Boris was absolutely terrified for his sister.'

'They're all fine,' said Leach. 'As a matter of fact, the boys have both gone home on a short visit, just to reassure themselves. Their employers have been very understanding, I'm pleased to say.' He glanced round at the group. 'Any more questions?'

All four shook their heads. 'Right, back to work all of you. There are still plenty of villains out there.'